MW01173296

The
Stonebound Heir
THE CURSED CYCLES BOOK ONE

L.A. Barnitz

Little Hawk Books
Silver Spring, Maryland

Little Hawk Books, LLC
311 Eldrid Dr.
Silver Spring, MD 20904

Publisher's Note: This is a work of fiction, 100 percent written by a human author. Names, characters, places, and incidents are a product of the author's imagination. Any resemblance to actual people, living or dead, or to businesses, companies, events, institutions, or locales is completely coincidental.

Cover Art: Cristina Bencina • cristinabencina.com
Map Illustrator: Sarah Waites • theillustratedpage.net/design/
Cover Typography/Graphic Design: Loren Jabami •
   https://pharaohsdreammuseum.com/custom-commissions
Interior Design: Ross A. Feldner • newagegraphicsonline.com
Author Website: laurabarnitz.com

The Stonebound Heir/ Little Hawk Books, LLC. — 1st Edition: June 2024

ISBN 979-8-9906420-0-3

For those who seek out wonderous worlds, real and imagined.

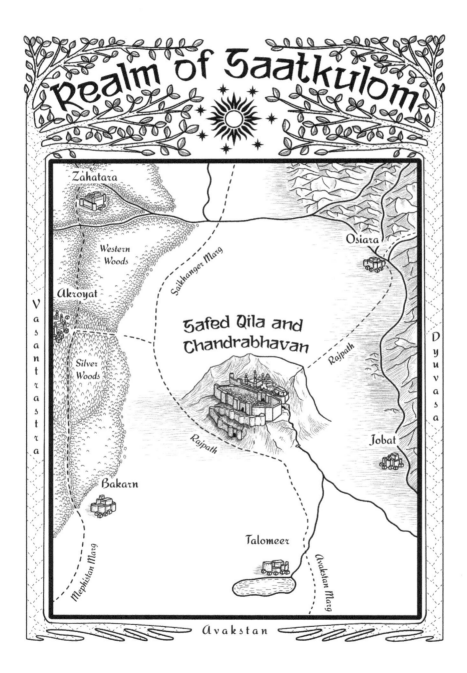

Realm of Saatkulom

Zahatara

Western Woods

Osiara

Akroyat

Sakhanger Marg

Safed Qila and Chandrabhavan

Rajpath

V
a
s
a
n
t
r
a
s
t
r
a

D
y
u
v
a
s
a

Silver Woods

Rajpath

Jobat

Bakarn

Talomeer

Mephistan Marg

Avakstan Marg

Avakstan

The Houses of Saatkulom

 HOUSE OF DURAN: led by Maharani Valena Sandhyatara, Duran's descendants became Saatkulom's ruling house in the thirty-first generation. House members are known for their skills as healers. Their insignia is the upright blade.

 HOUSE OF AVANI: led by Master Jalil Komalratra. House members are renowned as educators, historians and keepers of the shared chronicles. Their insignia is the owl.

 HOUSE OF TILAN: led by Master Ketan Karmika, also known as Crowseye. The house specialties are engineering and mining. Their insignia is the wheel.

 HOUSE OF HANSA: led by Madam Gayatri Prabhugita, the youngest of the Seven leaders. The house is known for music, art, and making textiles. Their insignia is the swan.

 HOUSE OF VAKSANA: led by Master Jordak Dharmavyadha, also known as the wolfmaster. The house is known for hunting and agriculture. Their insignia is the anar tree.

 HOUSE OF DUVANYA: led by Master Darius Palika. The house commands Saatkulom's defenses and their insignia is the bear.

 HOUSE OF SATYA: led by Madam Parama Azumirga. This house originally ruled Saatkulom and is known for its wisdom and spiritual leadership. Their insignia is the chinkara.

Part 1

CHAPTER 1

With each swing of the axe, sweat trickled down Sid's face and back. His own stink disgusted him. Cutting wood had been one of his chores from the time he had been strong enough to hold an axe, and he hated it more than anything in the world. His daydreams were colored by vague plans of slipping into the ale house the next time he and the red giant took game to the village. He had decided he would deliver the proprietor's venison personally and tell him he was looking for work.

"I'm a good worker, yessir," Sid mumbled. He cleared his throat and deepened his voice. "As trustworthy as they come," he said, taking another swing at the last tree he had felled in the forest that morning. "A willing learner." *Thwack.* "Can I handle coin?" *Thwack.* "Of course. I can do sums in my sleep!"

After a couple of tries, his lines improved, but he felt the words weren't sufficient. Putting aside the axe, he picked up a branch and mimed how he would throw the venison down on the bar as if it were nothing. This enactment was in its second rehearsal when he noticed a woman hardly a stone's throw away. His speech died on his lips.

She stood in the forest's shade, just beyond the felled tree he had been breaking down. Sunlight had managed to reach one slender hand pressed to her chest, and the light caught upon her rings. He met her eyes, which glittered as bright as her ornaments. *How long has she been standing there, and how much has she heard?* He dropped the branch and tried to think of what to say. Words were not coming.

Finally, she tilted her head and said, "I hope I am not disturbing you. I did not intend to interrupt your work."

"N-no," he stammered, coming to his senses and giving a small bow. "I mean, you're not disturbing me, Madam."

One of the woman's dark eyebrows arched upward. "Do you know who I am?"

Sid thought, *I know you're rich and beautiful,* but all he did was shake his head.

"I am Valena Sandhyatara of the House of Duran, Maharani of Saatkulom."

Saatkulom, the Seven Houses. Sid had never met a tinker professing to be from that faraway realm, much less its ruler. Why a rani from Saatkulom would be in the Western Woods puzzled him, but whether she spoke truly or not, it was plain she was of far better standing than him. Blood rushed to his cheeks at the thought of the nonsense he had been saying and how badly he smelled. Kneeling with head bowed, he stared at the forest floor. The silence between them stretched out until he could not resist the urge to look up.

Too well-dressed to be a villager, too well-spoken to be a common bandit.

A small smile twitched at the corners of her lips. She ordered him to stand.

What if she is a rani? Trying to make himself as tall as possible, Sid's heels barely touched the insides of his boots.

"Are you lost, Maharani?" he finally spat out, and a stream of words followed. "I could lead you, and your party, I mean, to the village. Help you, I suppose. I know the road that goes to Mephistan and…and even the trails to the north."

She laughed a little, and his heart hiccuped at the clear, silvery sound.

"I am not lost, I can assure you," she said. Blue slippers peeped out from under the hem of her long skirt, and she glided toward him as if she walked on a floor of marble instead of uneven ground covered with brush and splintered pieces of wood. "I am seeking a few recruits who are willing to work hard. Do you know any youth in this area who might be willing to join service in Safed Qila? Have you heard of our capital? You see, I have employed many of our denizens on another project. Quite a magnificent project, though it costs me dearly. I find that we require more people—servants, stewards, artisans, miners, guards—practically every occupation."

"Yes, Maharani. No." Sid shook his head, dizzy with the realization that this might be a great piece of luck, and squandered luck was an insult to the ancestors. "I mean, there are some people in the village, not many, but I, for one, am seeking such employment."

"I see," she said. She stood hardly an arm's length from him. "Are you the kind of young man that the Seven require? Intelligent? Willing to learn the skills necessary to preserve our realm?"

Sid knew the right answer but again words fled from him. He nodded. For cycles he had wished for a life where he had a chance of escaping these woods and proving he could be more than a woodcutter. He knew he could, no matter what others might say.

"All those who serve are duly rewarded, but since the last season of fly fever we have not recruited youth from families who need their members' strength at home. Would your family not miss you?"

The word "rewarded" rang so loudly in his head, Sid almost didn't hear her question. "I, uh, yes, I suppose, but they won't mind me joining your service. It would be an honor."

The woman pressed her lips with one finger as if she were considering a complex equation. "But surely your parents won't want you to leave them?"

"I don't have parents," Sid said, quickly, and he was immediately struck with worry that he might have to explain his circumstances to such a degree that the horrible dullness of his life would end this conversation. "I have a guardian, and he's good to me, but my mother died when I was very small. I never knew my parents."

"How terrible to lose your family so young."

If there was even the tiniest chance that she was telling the truth, he couldn't miss this opportunity.

"Maharani," Sid said, "if you will have me, I know I would serve you well. A lifetime here would not suit me half as well as guarding your realm for a day."

"Of course you want to join our defenses. Every boy does. What is your name?"

"Sid Sol, and I've completed fourteen sun cycles."

"Sid Sol," she said softly.

The air pulsed with heat. The woman pushed back her long dark hair, revealing a brass brooch shaped like an upright blade on her shoulder. She pulled a pouch from her pocket.

"Should you join my service, this is your first cycle's wage," she said. "There is no guarantee you will be invited to become a defender, but you will serve the realm for better or worse for a full cycle. Give this to your guardian. It may ease your leaving."

"Thank you. I will, Maharani," he said brightly. "If I go right now, and collect my things, I can return here before nightfall."

The woman held out the pouch to him but did not let go when he grasped it. She raised her other hand in warning. "It is too late for my party to move on tonight. Go home and think about the choice you are making. If you decide to join us, you will meet me at dawn at the edge of the wood along the road that lies beyond the meadow. If you decide not to join us, you will meet me there just the same to return my coin. Come alone."

That gave Sid pause. *Could she be a slaver planning to kidnap me? But why would a Mephistani offer me gold and give me a choice?*

With a warm smile, the woman released the pouch to him, and he bowed again before starting toward the trail home. Remembering his axe, he returned to retrieve it and bowed to the woman several more times before he finally hurried away.

The weight of the pouch in his hand made him happy. At last, something was happening in his life! Who knew who this woman was, but coin was coin. He would have to do some spying to learn who she was and who was in her party before they met in the morning.

Yes, the woods witch would agree with that.

The witch visited their cabin from time to time when she sold medicines in the nearby village. He was certain she'd be pleased he was "thinking before acting"—a phrase she often repeated—even if his thinking was still a few steps behind his hopes and dreams.

Too bad she isn't around to offer advice today, Sid thought, but he had bigger problems. Much bigger.

His guardian, Red, was a giant almost twice the height of an Ascaryan, and Sid feared that he might not be as excited about the prospect of his leaving as he had told the woman. Not that Red became excited about much of anything, but there had been something in his guardian's grunted response when Sid had recently proposed working in the village ale house that made him suspect he might not support this venture either. And when Red said no to something, it was nearly impossible to get around him.

How am I going to explain this?

Sid tucked the pouch of coins far down into his pants pocket. He had the whole night. He didn't have to blurt everything out at once. *No. I have to find the right way to tell him.*

At the edge of the clearing where their cabin sat, Sid slowed down and made an effort to hide his excitement. By the time he entered the open doorway, he was the picture of weariness.

The red giant, so called by everyone in the Western Woods because he was a giant and because of his wiry reddish-brown hair, was straining the evening's milk through a cloth. Without so much as glancing at Sid, he said in his deep, slow voice, "Was the wood brittle or tender?"

"Mostly tender," Sid said, stashing the axe behind the door. "I didn't cut more than two ranks."

"It is time to move to the northern slope."

Sid pulled out a chair and started to sit.

"The ones that depend on you must be fed first," Red said. "Then we eat."

Sid sighed. He left the cabin and crossed the yard that lay between their home and the barn. Instead of feeding the animals inside, he climbed up into the loft. In the dull light of dusk he sat in the hay near the open window and dug the pouch out of his pocket. One by one, he set the coins on his pant leg. Five gold coins. Each was embossed on one side with a sun and seven stars and on the other with the word "Saatkulom."

By the moons and stars! Three of these will see me set up my own ale house. That leaves one for Red to buy axes and whatever else he fancies, and one to keep Li suited and booted for life. What kind of fool would return these and tell a maharani no?

While he examined his treasure, a familiar voice called out from below, "What are you doing? I'm hungry, and we're waiting for you."

Dropping the coins back into the pouch and shoving it into his pocket, Sid leapt down through the loft door and landed on his feet with a bounce, his hands on his hips.

"What's for supper?"

"Sticks and stones," answered a girl half a head taller than him and thin as a switch.

Lingli's white hair and pale skin and eyes contrasted sharply with the black cloak she wore to protect her and hide the ugly vein in her temple. Was she odd? Yes. Annoying? Yes. But no more so than the giant they lived with, Sid thought, and hardly worthy of the reactions she incited in others.

She believed herself cursed, and maybe she was, but he was done tiptoeing around her. If she had lost her spirit, it wasn't his fault. The best thing he could do was tease and rankle her until she lost her temper like she used to.

"If you cooked that's what it will taste like," he said.

Lingli gave him a shove and ran toward the cabin. "You didn't feed the chickens!"

"You're a thorn!" Sid yelled, but she was already gone.

All evening he kept patting his pocket and wondering how to tell Red and Li about the woman's proposition. The giant served their food without a word. Li hummed her way through supper, repeating a melody over and over with little changes as she composed it.

"Stop it," Sid said. "You're driving me crazy."

"I thought you liked music?"

"Real music and a real singer are fine. You sound like a wounded rabbit."

"Put the words to it. Then you'll like it better," she said, and she started humming the tune again.

"Okay, here it is: *A boney maiden pale as snow, tripped on a rock and stubbed her toe. She was so blasted proud that she never cried aloud, and then she died before the cock could crow.*"

"Is that the best you can do?"

"Boring tune, boring lyrics."

"Boring Sid, boring lyrics."

As the evening stretched on, Sid grew more restless. Each member of the household performed their chores with spirit-numbing predictability. Li cleaned their thalis and cups with ash from the fireplace. The giant twisted long stems of horse grass and reeds into bundles that he would eventually use to mend the roof. Sid sat on his stool near the door, sharpening his small axe and the giant's massive one.

They have no idea of bigger things, no notion of the world. And they're not even curious. They like it this way.

He watched the giant get up from his huge chair, stretch, and step outside the cabin where he spent several long minutes standing perfectly still—giantstill—and staring into the night sky.

Though everyone seemed to know about giants and have a tale to tell, Sid had never seen another and knew very little about the one he lived with. Whenever he and Li had pestered Red with questions about where he came from, the giant had only told them he had lived in a mountain in the east, and there had been a war. A war, Sid recalled, between giants and Ascaryans from Dyuvasa and Saatkulom.

Would raising the name of Saatkulom work against him when he told the giant about the woman's offer? *But that war was so long ago. If her word is true, why shouldn't Red allow me to go? I'm not his child after all. We all must find our way in this world, and when am I going to have a better offer?*

Yet the more Sid pondered how to explain, the more he became convinced that involving Red would doom the entire proposition. That the giant took his role as guardian seriously used to reassure him, but Red's protectiveness and his obtuse answers to questions about the past had become irksome. All Red would say about Sid's arrival at the cabin, for example, was that he and his mother had appeared in the meadow one day. He was barely weaned. She was a young woman called Afsana. Though she was afraid of Red at first, Afsana eventually brought him into the cabin and ate enough food for five men. When Sid asked where Afsana had come from, Red said she never told him.

And then Afsana died. Just a few seasons later, after coming back from the village with supplies, a fever set upon her, and she was gone within days. Red said he could not risk the fever spreading to him or Lingli, so all that remained of his mother—her body, her clothes, even her bedcovers —were burned. The only mark of her presence were her cairn on the edge of the meadow and the tributes Sid made to her before the little shrine he kept next to the hearth.

Having no memory of Afsana, and being unable to extract more from Red, Sid had asked Lingli what his mother was like, but all she would say was that she had a funny accent, pretty hair, and liked to make delicious stuffed parathas. He didn't think Li was trying very hard, being well aware that she knew even less about her own origins and any discussion of parents or ancestors made words catch in her throat like barbed hooks.

Lingli might not want to think about where she came from, but Sid never ceased trying to unravel the mystery of his history. Everyone knew that one's destiny depended on the opinion of one's ancestors, and he had no idea who his were. This bothered him so much he had made a simple shrine from willow limbs, keeping a stone from Afsana's cairn within it as well as a cup of water and a piece of roti. Red said nothing about his construct, but Li rolled her eyes whenever he knelt before it—unsure what to do with his offerings. He tried to never let her see how her dismissals hurt but was greatly relieved when he found an ally.

Though the witch was as likely as Li to find fault with him on any small thing, she was pleased when she saw the shrine. Patiently teaching him how to say the proper words of respect and appreciation, she assured Sid that his ancestors would show favor whether he knew their names or not. Even better, in Sid's opinion, she rebuked Lingli for scoffing at him.

"We are travelers in this world only a brief time, but life in the starlit halls of our ancestors is eternal," she once told him while Li sat mending clothes nearby. "You may choose to make tributes and sustain their spirits just as your descendants' tributes will sustain yours. Or you can ignore the ancestors and wander lost in the otherworld after you die. Try not to be an idiot."

From then on, Sid had made a practice of offering a tribute each night. These venerations both eased his heart and annoyed Li. They also reminded him that she and the giant were not his true family. As the moons passed, this message brought him to a stark conclusion: Red and Li could not guide him, and there were no answers here. When he accepted this, one equally plain thought followed. It was up to him to seek his destiny as soon as he could figure out how. As the witch often said, *The only way forward is forward.*

Sid never looked at this idea head-on. Never planned the how or when or where to, but for the last several moons the thought had become as loud as his own heartbeat. He had to leave this place as soon as possible.

Beyond the open doorway and high above the giant, Sid watched wispy clouds sail across the waning moon and its companion—a smaller, reddish moon that appeared every seventeen cycles and stayed for three before disappearing again. Everyone knew these three bright cycles were ill-starred, and prone to calamities, and some said the gates between this world and the otherworld opened more easily when two moons shone. Ascaryans tread carefully in such times, Sid as much as anyone, and he eyed the sinuous mist that had climbed up from the creek and spilled into their yard with suspicion.

With his arms full of wood, the giant re-entered the cabin and kicked the door closed behind him. Sid sighed, annoyed that he knew exactly how the giant would place the wood in the fireplace and arrange the coals to keep the fire burning until dawn.

He wouldn't care if I left, would he? Surely not when he sees the gold.

"You should go to bed," Li said.

"I'm not tired."

"You say that every night and then you can't get up in the morning."

"Stop nagging me."

A rumbling noise from the giant warned them to stop arguing. In short order, Red would be snoring loud enough to drive off bears, and Li would sew for a while then be off to the garden and her other night chores. As tempted as he was to tell them about meeting a rani just to prove that every day didn't have to be like the one before, the risk seemed too great.

Sid paced around the room a couple of times before sitting by the fire and asking, "If a person was going to join the guard of a realm, what skills would he need?"

One of Red's eyes rolled in his direction. "Hmmm. Strength. Skill with weapons. Loyalty to the lord. A guard must protect the powerful and things the powerful love."

Li paused her sorting through bits and pieces of yarn and asked, "What's the difference between a guard and a soldier?"

"Both are defenders," Red said. "Guards defend the lord's stronghold. Soldiers defend the lord's will in the field, sometimes in other realms."

"I wouldn't let you guard a chicken coop," Li told him.

"Well, I guess that's not a problem for you because you're not a lord, nor even a noble."

The red giant shifted in his chair and frowned at him. "A guard, like a soldier, serves without question. No matter what he is asked to do. No matter if he doesn't agree. No matter if he has to kill."

Such a pronouncement from Red, who could go days without speaking to them at all, made a small knot begin to twist in Sid's stomach.

"But it's a good living, too," Sid insisted. "A guard can earn a good bit of coin every cycle."

"How would you know?" Li asked.

"If I was a guard, we could have good food every season. I could build a fine house and build you one, too. And we could have new clothes."

"Who says we need anything finer than this? Besides, you would likely lose the coin before you could spend it."

"You don't know everything, Li!"

She grabbed her cloak and a vegetable basket. "True, but you don't either." She grinned at him as if she had won the argument and left the cabin.

What's the point of telling her anything? Whatever I do, she'll always treat me like a joke. She wouldn't know good fortune if it slapped her.

He paced around the cabin's main room, knowing the giant watched him.

"You cut two ranks today?" Red asked.

"Yes. The axe went dull halfway through the first one."

"Hmmm. Cutting wood builds strength for wielding weapons. Hunting improves scouting."

Sid gingerly kicked at an ember that had spilled onto the hearth. He feared he was giving his secret away. "I think I'll go to bed."

He left his boots by the door and went to his cot at the back of the cabin, but he didn't sleep. He wished he could find a way to tell them that this was his chance to find his path in the world, but what if Red said no? What if they wanted to go with him to meet the woman? No, he was simply going to make sure she was the rani of Saatkulom, and if she was, he would go. If she wasn't, he wouldn't.

With this tattered piece of a plan in mind, Sid spent hours convincing himself that this was the best course of action before he finally fell asleep.

Soon after, he woke with a start from a dream he couldn't remember. Creeping over to the cabin window and peeking under the edge of the oilcloth, he was alarmed to see that the night was growing pearly around the edges.

As quietly as possible, he pulled a small trunk from under his cot and removed his good kurta, a scarf, and the kufi Li had embroidered for him, all of which he pushed into a sack. He had to go quickly if he meant to avoid her. Because she couldn't abide much sun, nights were Li's days. She'd be finishing her chores and coming back to the cabin to sleep at any moment. Sid collected a pair of logs from the hearth, put them on his cot, and pulled up the blanket, hoping they looked something like a sleeping boy.

Creeping back across the main room, Sid laid the pouch of coins on the mantel, then he put a finger inside the pouch and drew out a coin. He pushed it back. He pulled it out again. Finally, he pushed himself away and left the coins.

If this woman is a slaver from Mephistan, I'll run, but I'll not give her coin back. Let her try to get them from Red.

Covering most of the room's floor, the giant snorted and rolled onto his side. No blanket, no pillow, as still as stone—the giant's breath had become as soft as a summer breeze. Sid knew he should wake him and explain the whole thing. Instead, he pressed his hands together and bowed to Red then slipped his feet into his boots, hitched the sack of clothes on his shoulder, and softly pulled the door closed behind him.

It was hard to tell ground from sky in the morning fog that curled and heaved around the cabin. Sound was dulled as well, and he could barely hear Li in the barn humming the same tune from the night before. When Sid tiptoed away to his mother's cairn on the edge of the meadow, he breathed easier. He bowed to the small mound of stones. Should he feel bad that he was alive when she was not? There was nothing he could do about that. She would want him to do well. Red had always said that much.

Looking back toward the cabin, or where he thought the cabin was, Sid suddenly became unsure of things inside and out. He tightened his grip on his sack and sprinted down the hillside and across the creek.

The fog was still thick when he started up the hill on the other side, and he was grateful for it, planning to slip into the edge of the woods unseen in order to discover more about this rich woman. Unable to see past his own feet and hearing nothing, Sid walked as quickly as he could, but the hill went on and on.

He had begun to question his plan's soundness and worry that the woman and her party might have left already when a man's voice called, "Announce yourself or s-suffer in silence."

Well, so much for stealth. "Sid Sol…of the Western Woods."

There was some muffled noise. *Is he laughing?* Then the voice told him to come forward.

A long-haired nobleman wearing a thick achkan and tall boots held a drawn crossbow aimed at him. He wore a brass brooch shaped like a tree on his shoulder, but Sid hardly noted these details because of the huge wolf crouched at the noble's side. The wolf's gaze shifted from Sid to the noble, as if seeking permission to spring upon him and rip him into pieces.

"The ma-maharani awaits, and she is not patient," the noble said, gesturing uphill toward a dark fringe of woods that Sid could barely make out.

I knew she was telling the truth!

Making a small bow, Sid passed quickly, looking back twice to make sure the wolf didn't follow. A few steps farther, and he saw a light glowing in the fog. Two figures appeared. The torchbearer was a small, dark-skinned man wrapped in white cloth from neck to ankle. And behind him, the rani. She wore a long, fitted coat, and a chain dripping with amethysts circled her head, holding her dupatta in place.

Sid pressed his palms together and bowed deeply.

"Your decision, Sid Sol?"

"I accept Your Majesty's offer. I promise to gladly and faithfully serve you. Saatkulom, I mean."

It seemed that the rani relaxed a little upon hearing this. She reached out to him, and he hesitantly gave her his hand. The noble Sid had just passed emerged from the fog.

"S-someone else approaches," he said.

"You will stop him, brother," the rani said. "But do not fire unless it is on my order."

The noble nodded and disappeared again.

"I assume it is your guardian?"

"I… Yes, probably," Sid mumbled.

"Did he not agree with your decision?"

"I didn't tell him I was leaving."

The rani exhaled slowly. "I see. And the gold?"

"I left it in the cabin."

The rani looked away into the fog but did not release his hand. "Well, this is unfortunate, but I am prepared to ensure that you fulfill your promise to me."

From far away, a pounding sound grew louder and closer, and Sid knew Red was stomping toward them. Ahead, he heard the noble order the giant to stop. The stomping ceased. The rani, Sid, and the torchbearer advanced. At first, Sid saw only the back of the noble, bow drawn, talwar sheathed on his hip. The wolf was on its feet, looking away from them and growling deep in its throat.

Several paces behind the noble, the rani paused, still holding Sid's hand tight. She took the torch from the bearer.

"I am Maharani of Saatkulom, head of the House of Duran. What is your business with my party, giant?"

Sid caught glimpses of the bare-chested red giant in the swirling mist. He towered over them. His arms hung by his sides like young oak trunks, and his hands were curled into fists. There was a deep grating sound coming from him. He was grinding his teeth.

"The boy is my charge."

"*Was* your charge," the rani corrected. "This youth came to me of his free will. He has decided to accept my offer to begin service. And I believe he has left his first cycle's wages to support you while he is gone."

The giant said nothing, but his eyes were fixed on Sid.

The rani said very slowly, "You have fulfilled your obligation as his guardian."

In a croaking voice that was more like a small rockslide, Red said, "Sid?"

Sid heard Lingli, somewhere in the field beyond, calling his name.

"I will tolerate no more delay," the rani said harshly. "Leave this boy and my party at peace. You must know that I have more than one defender here."

The red giant shook his head and moaned so loudly Sid cringed. Leaving Red like this was bad enough. He did not want to see Li.

He shouted, "I'm going, Red. I want to go. You'll be proud, I promise!"

The rani put her arm around his shoulders. "We are leaving now. Trust my word, giant, when I say you are safe from my party if you do not pursue us. You are not safe if you advance another step. The choice is yours."

She handed the torch back to the small man, and Sid let her lead him a few steps uphill toward the forest, but he looked back in time to see Lingli emerge from the mist, running fast. The red giant bellowed at her. The noble raised his bow as the wolf sprang forward.

Pulling away from the rani, Sid yelled, "No! Stop!"

The rani gasped, then boxed his ears so hard his head rattled. When he opened his eyes sharp white lights like swarming bees combined with the mist to obscure everything but the angry woman next to him. He couldn't hear. He looked at the rani in utter surprise, and not a little fear. She roughly dragged him with her up the remainder of the hill and into the forest.

CHAPTER 2

Lingli began breathing hard as she climbed the hill past the creek. She couldn't see him, but Red pounded on ahead of her, and she hoped he knew where to find Sid. If that boy was playing some game, she didn't find it very funny, and she didn't think Red did either, for the giant had burst out of the cabin the moment she had shown him that it was not Sid but two logs under the blankets on his cot.

When Red's thunderous stomping suddenly ceased, she paused, uncertain. She called for Sid, but the fog swallowed her voice, and there was no answer to her cries until the giant moaned mournfully somewhere ahead. Fear blooming in her heart, she ran up the hillside, afraid of what she might find.

Her guardian, hardly more than a looming mass in the fog, ordered her to stop and she meant to, but she skidded past him on the wet grass. Did she hear Sid's voice? She thought so—in the instant before a wet red maw and sharp teeth flashed before her face. A wolf snapped its jaws so close she was choking on its carrion breath as Red pulled her off the ground and set her on his shoulder. Then she saw a noble with a crossbow trained on them. The noble ordered the wolf down.

With its eyes glowing like green coals, the beast growled its intention to murder, and the cost of disobedience appeared to matter little until the noble put a small instrument to his lips. The object made a strangely pitched noise that made both Lingli and the wolf cringe, though it wasn't loud. The wolf retreated to the noble's side.

Looking around from her high perch, Lingli could find no sign of Sid. The field and forest had taken a vague outline but remained colorless and shifting under the fog that only grudgingly began to dissipate. After a few tense seconds, the noble finally lowered his bow and nodded to Red. To her amazement, Red pressed his hands together and bent his head in respect. The noble walked off with the wolf at his side and disappeared into the mist.

"What happened?" she cried. "Did they take him?"

She struck the giant's shoulder with her fist. He said nothing but stood still and listened. She heard nothing.

"We can't let them take Sid!"

Red pulled her down into the crook of his arm and stifled her cries with a heavy hand that covered most of her face. Angry, she tried to escape him but his grip was unshakable, and she became still. Between his fingers she could see him looking toward the woods and sniffing the air. Then she felt his shoulders sag.

"He is unharmed," Red finally said. He removed his hand and rebalanced her on his shoulder, then began walking back down the hillside toward the cabin. Tears left whitish tracks on his stony cheeks.

"Can't we get him back?"

"He is not a prisoner. He rushes to his future."

"What? Who are they?"

"The Seven."

"We must go back! They can't have gone too far." She was confused. Her questions kept stumbling over the notion that Sid *wanted* to leave them.

Out of the mist, a man suddenly appeared in front of them. He was bearded and clothed like the men of the nearest village, and Lingli instantly tensed. The giant stopped and held one hand up as if to promise he would come no closer, but the man put a long pipe to his mouth and blew. A dart hit Red's open palm.

The giant bent over, and she fell to the ground. Clutching his hand, Red roared so loudly the trees shook, and Lingli clamped her hands over her ears. Before he could manage to pull the dart from his hand and hurl it to the ground, the man was gone. Stuck deep in the dirt, the slim dart's polished metal shaft with its red and black fletching was unlike any dart or arrow she had seen in the village.

"Must go now," Red said. He took a few steps toward their cabin.

Getting to her feet, Lingli grabbed his huge hand to look at his palm, but there was nothing more than a pinprick. His reaction seemed exaggerated for such a small hurt.

"But...Sid?"

Red shook his head and started walking.

Looking back toward the forest's edge, she thought, *Why is Red letting Sid go? And how did that villager know he would be here? This is bright cycle madness.*

Knowing that the villagers could be anywhere and too frightened to search for Sid alone, Lingli boiled with arguments to convince Red to go back and follow Sid's trail as soon as he forgot about the insulting dart, but by the time they climbed the rise near their home, the red giant was limping. He hummed deep in his throat in a key that she had rarely heard. Her concern was two-horned now, and she ran ahead to open the cabin door.

Stumbling inside, Red leaned on the arm of his chair. Pain contorted his normally placid expression. Seeing that his wounded hand had turned rough and dark gray, Lingli flew to the shelf where they kept medicines in small jugs, tiny pots, and packets sewn from leaves. The woods witch had given them most of the medicines, including a balm Lingli used for burns, but none of them seemed appropriate for this calamity. She swept all of them into her kurta and carried them over to Red.

"What will help?"

The giant shook his head. "Trunk has…things you need."

Groaning, he pulled his massive chair across the floor with his good arm. He nodded toward an exposed trapdoor in the floor, then fell back into the chair's seat. Lingli set the medicines aside, fell to her knees, and pried up the trapdoor. A trunk bound with bronze seams and clasps sat below. Grabbing the handle on one end, she raised it as high as she could but couldn't bring the bottom of the trunk up to the floor.

"Hmmm."

"Yes, alright then, I'll just open it where it is."

From a hook in the back of the cupboard, Lingli retrieved the red giant's keys. All kinds slid around the ring—long, squat, some square heads, some round heads, some made of iron, and some made of brass. As a young child she had played with this ring with no concern about what the keys might open. She showed each one to the giant. He grunted when she raised a small brass key with a flattened end.

Lying on her belly, Lingli leaned over the hole in the floor, stuck the key into the lock, and released the trunk's clasps. A swarm of moths exploded from a bearskin cover inside, and she dragged it out to uncover coin pouches much like the one she had found on the mantel that morning. Setting them aside, she searched for a potion, a powder, some kind of medicine for Red. Below the pouches lay a scroll, and next to it a metal box whose rusted lid fell off as she lifted it out. Inside was a row of cylindrical objects made of a strange smooth substance that was neither wood nor metal nor parchment nor earth.

"Firesticks," Red said when she held one up. "Gift from the ancestors."

Lingli tossed the scroll out and gently set the firesticks on the cabin floor. Several folded skins—bear, rabbit, and some pelts she didn't recognize—followed. Underneath those were a few stones, one with a cluster of crystals emerging from one end. *Rocks? What things do giants treasure?* Beside the stones was a decorated box. Two pieces of jewelry sat within: a bracelet made of braided grasses and a brooch of polished bone. A hawk diving through the sky was painted upon the brooch.

"Keep those," Red said. "Pin is yours. The other…Sid's. You must give it to Sid."

She looked at him from the corner of her eye and set the jewelry box out, only to uncover a book bound in leather and brass and thick with parchment. After she heaved it out of the trunk, she found two small blankets below. One was blue and held a tiny pair of blue juttis. The other was white, and its folds contained a pair of stained white slippers. Finally, Lingli stared at the floor of the trunk.

"Where is the medicine?!"

The giant shook his head. "No medicine. Get a pack. Give me the map," he nodded toward the scroll.

"What? How can you go anywhere?"

"Listen, Little One," Red said. His words were slurred. She noticed that he was no longer moving any part of his body but his head. His hands and his feet looked more like fieldstone than flesh. "No cure for this. Soon I will not speak. You…must not…stay…here."

"I can't leave you!" Her panic grew. She brought the scroll to the giant.

"Yes. Not safe. Sid…chose his path," the giant said, gulping air between words. "You must go, too. Promise me. Find Sid. Protect him. Make… your life."

She pressed Red's thick arm. "No. I'm not going anywhere! Tell me how to find the witch."

"No time. Open that."

She wanted to argue. Going anywhere without Red was impossible, but she unrolled the scroll across the floor in front of the giant's chair and dragged the pelts over to weigh down the edges. It was a map showing one of the realms of Ascarya Erde.

"The Seven…ride to the Rock," Red said. His face was turning gray. "The fort. Show it!"

Lingli touched her finger to a flat-topped mountain in the very center of the map. Above the mountain was written "Realm of Saatkulom: Safed Qila and Chandrabhavan."

"Stay close to the road. South toward Mephistan…three days." Lingli traced the route with her finger. "Don't go into Akroyat. Don't eat, drink…poisoned. Turn east…new Rajpath. Cross the Silver Woods quickly. Keep watch."

The giant suddenly jerked upright. His eyes rolled upward to show the whites, which weren't white at all, but etched with gray threads. Lingli cried out and put her hands on either side of his face.

"Courage," he managed to say before his mouth ground shut and he closed his eyes. Gray lines etched his face and his skin hardened under her hands.

"No! Wait! Red, please!" she cried. She could scarcely breathe. She tried to move his head, his arms, but he had become still, hard, stone.

The sun was low in the sky by the time her tears were spent. She sat on the floor and leaned against the pillars that were the red giant's legs. In less than a day her family, such as it was, was gone. Had she caused this? Had she made Sid so unhappy with her uselessness and unkind words that all this was the result? Her mind wandered in confusion and grief, but it was time for the evening chores, and she rose to do them.

She fetched water and hay to feed Amul, their horse, who had long since retired from plowing and log skidding and never grazed far from the barn. The touch of his velvety muzzle against her cheek threatened to release a new torrent of tears, but she proceeded to water their cow and feed the hens while she gathered eggs.

How can I possibly go?

The ugly vein in her temple pulsed painfully as it often would when she was frightened. Putting her hand to it, she looked at the barn, the cabin, the well. She could cut enough wood for herself, she reckoned, and even if she couldn't manage large game, she could survive the winter on their potatoes and cabbage and rabbits, or even the occasional groundhog or tender weasel.

She thought she heard something in the distance—footsteps or a low voice. She scanned the clearing around the cabin and the edge of the woods beyond, her gaze resting on the spot where a logging trail passed into the forest. She and Sid and Red often used it as a shortcut to the village. There was nothing. Willing her heartbeat to slow, she thought, *You cannot, will not, fall prey to your fears. No and no.*

She returned to the cabin to fetch the milk pail, but the chill did not leave her. Inside, Red sat in his chair facing the door. She marveled at how every whorl of his hair, every bump and wrinkle on his face, had been captured in stone.

Did one of those who took Sid give the dart to the villagers?

Taking up the pail, she was about to step out the cabin door when, in the dusk-heavy edge of the woods, she spied a flash of light.

Immediately backing inside, she barred the door and tried to swallow her panic. She should have listened to Red and left already. The problem was never whether she could survive on her own. The problem was that she wasn't alone.

If the villagers had found the courage to kill Red, they would show her no mercy. They would do away with the girl-like thing they believed was an otherworld creature in disguise. There were some who had wanted that since last New Cycle Day, if not longer, and now—with no guardian and the bright cycles already begun—they had their chance.

She ran her finger along the oilcloth tacked to the cabin's single window frame. Every nerve in her body screamed *Hide!* but there was nowhere in the cabin they could not find her.

Honor his word. Have courage.

Taking a pack from the peg by the door, she shoved in some apples and roti and nestled in the few eggs she had gathered. The bag of coins

Sid had left behind and their flint and striker went into her pants pocket. Red had filled a waterskin the night before. She set it next to the pack as the voices drew closer.

Someone pounded on the door and called out, "Hello? Anyone home?"

Grabbing up the map, the bracelet, and the brooch from the mess of things on the floor around Red's feet, Lingli shoved them in the pack. She lugged the open book back into the trunk, where it landed with a thwump.

"Someone's home," a voice said, and sniggering laughter followed along with more pounding on the door.

"What if he's not dead?" she heard someone say.

"You heard that noise this morning," another said. "He didn't miss."

Setting aside four firesticks, Lingli swept everything else into the trunk and closed it and the door in the floor. Hands pressed against the oilcloth covering the window.

At her guardian's side she whispered, "I don't know if you can hear me, but I want you to know I love you. Sid loves you, too." She kissed his hard cheek. "From stone, to stone."

One of the tacks holding the oilcloth popped loose. Someone reached in underneath and began tugging at it.

The giant's brass shield in the corner caught her eye, but it was too heavy for her to wield. Instead, she grabbed her iron-tipped fishing spear propped against the wall between the shield and Sid's little shrine. She stabbed the invading appendage. The impaled hand flexed and shook much like a fish, but the accompanying scream shocked her, and she pulled the spear out.

Amid the screams and cursing, someone shouted, "Come out, asura, or we'll burn this place down!"

Not if I burn it down first.

The firesticks were light in her hands. A white cap covered one end of each stick, and a long wick stuck out the other end. In between, the sticks were marked with black symbols that she suspected was writing in a strange language. She remembered once watching Red remove the cap from a stick and strike the end against stone, which had caused it to burn bright for a short time. He had warned them to never light the wicks.

Several hands were trying to rip the oilcloth loose from the window frame. Holding her breath, she took off one of the firestick's caps and swiped the end against the hearth. A flame emerged. She pressed the end to the oilcloth and flames whooshed over it, but the cloth was ripped in so many places it would hardly slow them. She ran to the shelf where they kept the oil jug, brought it to the window, and splashed oil everywhere. Dragging the covers from Sid's cot to the window, she poured oil on them and lit them, too.

Smoke rolled through the cabin. A man had thrown his leg over the sill and was climbing inside. His feet landed on the floorboards, but he could not avoid the burning blanket she threw over him. Falling to the floor, he screamed for help.

Lingli struck the second firestick and left it burning in the remaining bedding before running to the hearth. Jamming her fishing spear into the pack and putting the pack and waterskin on her back, she began scooting her way up the inside of the chimney with two more unlit firesticks in her teeth as the fire spread.

It was a snug fit, and her face and hands were soon as black as her cloak and the soot-covered walls. Scratching and clawing for handholds, the skin on her palms and knees was scraped away and the smoke choked her, but the screaming below pained her the most.

After clambering over the lip of the chimney and falling onto the thatch, she crawled to the roof's edge. Several villagers clustered near the cabin door. She could hear more shouting inside. She struck her third firestick against the side of the chimney and lit a bit of thatch, then touched the wick to the flames and tossed the stick into the thatch above the door. Pushing the last firestick into her pocket, Lingli scrambled to the far end of the roof, where she swung her legs over the edge and hung by her arms for a breath before dropping to the ground. She took three steps before an explosion shook the cabin. Bits of thatch rained down around her as she ran into the woods without looking back.

CHAPTER 3

The rani's anger had so surprised Sid, he hadn't resisted when she pulled him into the woods and marched him past a beautiful, brass-trimmed ratha only to deposit him at the back of a supply wagon loaded with gear, foodstuff, and boys near his age. Releasing him without another word, she strode back to her vehicle and climbed inside, while he met the stares of more than a score of mounted soldiers and archers all around them.

Fear and doubt climbed up his throat. Had the wolf reached Li? *No*, he told himself, *no. Red would never let that happen.*

The wagonmaster, a gnarled old man whose large turban looked as though it would break his neck, gestured with his chin that Sid should get in. When he didn't move fast enough, the man grabbed him above the elbows and threw him into the back. The other boys snickered and grudgingly made space.

For an instant, Sid actually considered calling Red for help, but the boys looked fed and none were bound to the wagon. When he saw a banner bearing Saatkulom's insignia—seven stars encircling the sun—Sid hugged his knees and stayed quiet, trying to recall the reason he thought this was a good idea.

Turning their horses up the road, the soldiers fell into order with some ahead and some behind the rani's ratha. Bringing up the rear but for the last pair of soldiers, the supply wagon had barely begun to roll forward when Red's cry blew over them like a storm front. The boys around him pulled their heads down into their shoulders and covered their ears. Fear flashed in their eyes. Even the soldiers looked at each other uneasily, but another noble riding a heavily muscled war horse ordered everyone to move on as he cantered past, and so they did.

Anguish stabbed Sid in the chest so hard he couldn't catch his breath, but no one noticed his discomfort. He wasn't afraid of the giant but afraid *for* him, having heard Red's pain inside the noise. The raw despair in that blasting sound echoed within him, and with each mile that passed he felt worse.

But Li's there. He'll be alright. Won't he? Yes, he's whole. Definitely fine. I hope.

Pretending an inexplicable interest in forest leaves, Sid hung over the side of the wagon so no one could see his face while he pushed the meaning and memory of that cry down into a small corner of his heart.

Eventually he forced himself to turn his attention to those around him. He counted twenty-two mounted soldiers, four archers, the wagonmaster and the ratha driver, the rani, and the eleven boys in the wagon, including himself. The torchbearer he had seen that morning must have been scouting the way, but he was not among the others. Last in Sid's tally were the two nobles.

The long-haired noble who had held him and Red in his sights had disappeared into the woods with the wolf shortly after they started out, but he reappeared in the afternoon when the party stopped to water the horses. Sid overheard one of the soldiers call him Master Vaksana.

The other noble—the one riding at the head of the party—was called Crowseye. That much he had gathered from the junior soldiers' whispers whenever the man drew near. Considering the noble's black hair and beard and his piercing eyes, he couldn't have been better named, but Sid cautioned himself to practice the house name the noble used to introduce himself. Master Tilan he was, and the insignia on his shoulder was a wheel. He had addressed the boys only briefly, explaining to the newcomers that they were obliged to do the wagonmaster's bidding, but it seemed to Sid that he would be the one to shape their course and therefore the one to please.

By the next day, the recruits were tired of counting trees and riding in the back of the wagon like infirm elders. Holding a nettle to the back of someone's neck without being detected or pushing a boy out of the back were popular pastimes, but they left Sid alone. They had seen the rani press him into the wagonmaster's hands, and no one wanted her displeasure aimed at themselves. He couldn't blame them, and still preferred their rude jokes and capering laughter to silence. Silence made space for memories of that echoing cry and Lingli calling his name in the fog.

That evening, as the party climbed a long hill, someone in the line whistled sharply, and the wagonmaster drove them right behind the ratha into a clearing ringed with huge stones that emerged from the ground like a mouth of old teeth. As soon as they stopped, the old man jumped into the back of the wagon and rummaged around in a trunk until he pulled out a long metal bar with a cloven head on the end. He handed it to Master Vaksana, who strode off to the rani's vehicle with the instrument on his shoulder.

The rani opened her compartment's small door, and her driver unfolded a step on the side of the ratha, but the step was still so high off the ground he offered his thigh to help her descend. She and Master Vaksana proceeded toward a cluster of tall boulders on the edge of the clearing where Master Tilan waited with two more soldiers.

Suddenly, it seemed that one of the boulders moved. Like the other boys, Sid's jaw dropped when he realized that another giant waited there. Her hair was light in color and tamer than Red's, and her long gray tunic was much like the color of her flesh and the rocks. The sight of manacles binding her wrists and ankles struck another pang of fear in him.

Fitting the tool's cloven head around one of the spikes that pinned the manacles to the stone, the soldiers put their weight onto it and pried the spike out. The rani herself produced a heavy ring of keys and unlocked the cuffs. Moaning softly, the giantess stretched her limbs and unfolded to her full height, making the astounded boys around Sid suck in their breath. Two soldiers picked up one set of her chains together. The giantess picked up the other, and they returned them to the wagon.

Was it his imagination or was the giantess staring at him? The boys shifted nervously as she deposited the manacles in the wagon bed. A head taller than the wagonmaster sitting upon his bench, she looked directly at Sid.

In a voice that grated like gravel, she said, "He has returned to stone."

Her words undid the comforting little assurances with which he had tried to wrap himself.

The giantess's proximity was too much for one of the other recruits, a slight boy who stumbled backward. Tripping over the wagon side, he fell to the ground on his hind end, causing the soldiers to laugh outright.

Though relieved to no longer be the center of attention, Sid knew there was no mistaking to whom the giantess's message had been directed.

After their supper Sid was glad to be hidden under the supply wagon as he watched the giantess bring a drink to the rani, then stand back behind her liege's chair and wait motionless on the edge of the firelight. She seemed a devoted servant, even answering to the Ascaryan name Greta and giving no sign of resentment about being chained, but he didn't intend to get too close. If Red's cry had already curdled his gut, the giantess's words doubled his pain.

She wasn't there. How could she possibly know? But that niggling voice in Sid's head would not let it go. *Giants never lie.*

Fighting down these uneasy thoughts, he was intent on holding tight to the possibility that all was well with those he left behind. He kept his focus on those members of the party the rani invited to entertain her.

Her defenders pretended great humility as they presented stories and songs, but a subtle competition animated them. Each time their rani gasped or laughed or raised a brow in disbelief she claimed a heart or dashed an ego. This exchange reassured the new boys—Sid not the least. When she asked a few recruits their names, and whether they had ever been beyond the woods, it reminded him of their first meeting, but since she had thrust him into the arms of the wagonmaster, she had not so much as looked in his direction.

The possibility that he had offended her troubled Sid greatly, mainly because he didn't know exactly what his offense had been, making it impossible to amend. It had to do with Red and Li. When he bid the giant to let him go and told him he would be fine, the rani's anger had ignited without warning, and when he tried to prevent the noble from shooting Li, she had boxed his ears!

Gradually the merriment subsided. The archers bedded down by the ratha, and the rest stretched out around the fire. Greta remained behind her liege's chair like a sheltering tree.

Lying on his stomach with his chin on his fists, Sid studied the rani. Her hair curled past her shoulders in glossy dark waves that flowed from under her kufi, much like her skirt flowed out from under her coat. She made no move to her vehicle but drew a piece of cloth from a bag in her lap and threaded a needle with long slender fingers.

What would happen if I got up and walked right over to her? Apologized for whatever it was I did? But Sid worried that he could not afford another mistake. *They're watching you already. If you take the wrong step you cannot take it back, so try not to look more stupid than you are.* The critical voice in his head sounded much like Li, and hearing it only made him more cross.

He argued with himself that it was them—Red and Lingli—who had acted recklessly. He nursed an old indignation about how the giant ignored his best ideas, and brooded on how Li, for all her problems, never hesitated to find ways to make him look bad. But these habits of thought were losing their potency and drifting far too close to questions of what had happened after he left. He stayed where he was, grateful for the comforting hiss of the fire that had almost lulled him to sleep before a growl startled him awake again.

A pair of boots and four huge paws stopped next to the wagon. Remembering how the wolf had been poised to spring upon Li, Sid's heart began to pound as the wolf bounded toward the rani, and he rose so suddenly he smacked his head on the wagon's axle. But his fear was misplaced, for the wolf thrust its muzzle into the rani's lap, and she stroked its shaggy head and talked softly to the beast. With a small whimper, it lay down at her feet like a tired pup.

Accompanied by the small man wrapped in white cloth, Master Vaksana approached and started to speak, but the rani pointed at the wolf and made a shushing sign, much as a mother might warn a father not to wake their child. When both the noble and the scout disappeared into the dark again, she resumed her embroidery.

After a long while, Sid finally put his head down and fell asleep, only to be haunted by a vision of Li standing in the meadow and wearing her blue outfit from last New Cycle Day.

In his dream, dark shapes hovered in the mist around her. She seemed unaware of them, though he all but yelled aloud to warn her. Sometimes he thought she heard him, but when she faced him, her eyes were milky white and the vein in her temple bulged grotesquely. She had never frightened him in life, but the Li in his dreams set loose a terror that woke him and nearly made him retch.

The faint light of dawn showed the rani's chair empty, the wolf gone.

Stop it. Li's fine, Red's fine, and there's no going back anyway, so why think of it?

After their midday meal, while the soldiers checked their horses' hooves and re-cinched their saddles, Sid and the boys cleaned cooking vessels near the back of the ratha. Crowseye passed them by and tapped on the side of the rani's vehicle. A small window slid open. Sid watched her fingers curl over the edge as she leaned close to the opening.

"We'll meet the new road soon, which means we should reach Muktastan in a few hours," Crowseye said. "Enough time to recruit a few strong ones before dark."

"We have not found the numbers I hoped for," the rani said. "Let us take time to make a reasonably attractive proposition."

"Only small hamlets remain, and I do not think we'll gather many from them. This area lost many to fever in the last cycle."

"Then let us remind them what a bright cycle winter can mean and that we can ease them of the burden of orphans, at least those old enough to be of some use."

Though this was delivered without menace, Sid didn't like the sound of it. More recruits only meant that he was going to become more forgettable, nothing more than another pack animal to abuse. He would have to put his pains in his pocket, as Red used to say, and work hard to regain her favor.

"How many days until we reach the Rock?" the rani asked Crowseye.

"Eight. The new road should cut at least two days off the journey."

"All the better. The novelty of this forest has quite disappeared, and the realm's business rushes on like a river in flood."

Sid's attention snapped back to his immediate surroundings as the wagonmaster threatened to horsewhip him and the others if they didn't pack up quickly. While they stored the vessels away, two soldiers retrieved the manacles from the supply wagon and attached them to a short chain on the back of the ratha. Her Majesty descended from her compartment and came around to lock the manacles about the giantess's wrists again. After she retreated inside, her driver planted the flag of Saatkulom amid a flock of blue and gold pennants on top of her vehicle, and the party moved on.

Shortly after they rolled onto a proper stone road, the herald began to strike a drumbeat. From houses, barns, and compounds, somber people emerged to line the road and stare at them, especially the bound giant, until they entered a broad central yard.

While the soldiers took their horses to drink, Sid and the other boys jumped down from the wagon and Sid began wrestling the camp table loose from where it was stored.

"I'll help you set up the table for Cr...for Master Tilan, sir!"

The wagonmaster looked at him with narrowed eyes, then shrugged. After hauling the table across the square, Sid spotted a soldier bringing the rani's chair down from the top of the ratha, and he hurried back, doing his best to avoid looking at Greta, who remained chained to the vehicle.

As he carried the chair to the table, he hoped the rani would see him dusting it and arranging the other stools, but everything was in place and she had not yet appeared. He tarried long enough for Crowseye to complete his discussion with the village headman and see that he was the nearest empty-handed boy available. As Sid had hoped, the noble ordered him to bring his records from his saddle pack.

Fetching a roll of parchment, Sid stood at Crowseye's elbow while he sorted sheets that had been stitched together. When the noble paused on a piece titled "Havpur," the village nearest Red's cabin, Sid saw the names of the two other boys recruited from there.

"Sir," he said, "why isn't my name in there?"

"Keep your nose to yourself," the noble growled at him, then stopped. "How...? Boy, do you know how to read?"

Sid nodded.

Staring at him with equal parts suspicion and surprise, the noble handed a piece of parchment to him. "Read this."

Sid put his finger to the words and read slowly. "'Day six of the eleventh moons. The party departed the border near Daza Tumuli in late morning. We shall visit the...Zahatara.... There the main company will...commence...its mission. The rani's party will continue to Baum, Havpur, and Muktastan to recruit youth for the works in...Nilampur.'"

The noble's sharp eyes burrowed into him, but he said nothing. Sid wished he had practiced his reading as often as the red giant had suggested.

"Works" in Nilampur?

Just then the herald blew a short phrase on his horn.

The headman ordered people to clear the way, though that was hardly necessary with everyone maintaining a good distance between themselves and the ratha with the giant chained to it. Crowseye called the soldiers to attention. The drummers again struck up a beat as the rani emerged wearing a bloodred sari with a thick border of gold on the hem and the pallu. Down a gauntlet of soldiers, Master Vaksana escorted her to the table.

The headman bowed and presented her with a garland of flowers. When she was seated, Crowseye beckoned to Sid, who had sidled back some distance from the table.

"Can you write as well?" he whispered.

"Yes…simple words," Sid said. He had the feeling that the rani was listening, but he did not dare look in her direction.

"Take down these boys' names."

Crowseye ordered one of the soldiers to bring another stool, and he set a piece of parchment on the table in front of Sid, then added an inkpot, a cloth, and a reed pen. Taking his seat, Sid kept his eyes focused on the parchment, lest someone notice how pleased he was.

The witch said I would do something important one day.

The headman nervously bowed to the rani again and said, "On behalf of our town, I welcome you, Your Majesty. While we stand in poor comparison with your great capital, we are honored to host your esteemed party." The headman stopped talking, swallowed, and looked at Crowseye. "Once again, welcome."

Crowseye nodded curtly, then addressed the crowd. "People of Muktastan, the Maharani of Saatkulom, Her Majesty Valena Sandhyatara of the House of Duran, greets you on this good day. Recognizing your status as a free town, we assure you that this company bears arms meant only for the maharani's protection. We bear no ill will but seek your friendship and appreciate your efforts to safeguard our shared borders.

"Hear now our news of Saatkulom's greatest work: At the boundary of our southernmost villages and the lands held by the House of Hudulfah, Saatkulom is building a new lake and a new city. The lake will be larger than any in our realm. When it is full, our villages and neighbors in Avakstan will find it a life-giving resource blessed by the ancestors. And the city there… Oh, it will be a mighty city. It will be called Nilampur and open to trade from Safed Qila to the orchards of Kirdun to the villages of Vasantrastra, including your town.

"Muktastan has no obligation of fealty to the Seven, yet we are here because this enterprise requires hundreds of masons, carpenters, and laborers. If there be youth here looking for an opportunity in our new city, we invite them to speak to us and answer our questions so that we may determine whether they are suited. Family compensation of two silver coins will be given in advance, paid in the rani's coin as token of her faith in the recruit's success."

Ha, I got five gold coins!

Whispers rose from the crowd, yet Sid saw that only a few lined up to approach the table. When Crowseye sat, he nodded to one of the soldiers who stood guard at the head of the line. The soldier let pass the first boy and an old man. The crowd was utterly silent.

"Your family name?" Crowseye asked the old man.

"Sanjhila. Zarin Sanjhila," the old man said. He kept one hand on the boy's shoulder. "My grandson here, also named Zarin, is a strong boy. A good worker."

Crowseye raised his brows at Sid, reminding him that he was supposed to be writing the boys' names.

"What skills would you offer Saatkulom?"

The boy was uncertain. "I know woodcutting, mortaring stone. I can hunt."

"Are there others to provide for your family?"

"Fever took my son and his wife in the third moon," the grandfather said. "This boy has an older sister, and a brother just a cycle younger. We can do well enough."

"Are you willing to leave your home?" Crowseye asked the boy.

The boy's eyes slid toward the bag of coins the noble had set on the table. "I don't want to leave them, sir. I want them to eat."

The boy's grandfather wiped his eyes with the back of his hand, and Sid felt his own eyes grow warm. He looked back down at the parchment and began sketching a row of stars.

"The terms of this labor are thus: Anyone who seeks service does so of his own free will. Our maharani will not accept those who are infirm, or less than thirteen cycles nor more than twenty. We will not accept those who have dishonored their ancestors through violent crime. Those who complete two cycles of service and are commended by a citizen of Saatku-lom shall be allowed residence in the new city if they choose."

Fixing the boy with his beady stare, Crowseye added, "You understand that you are bound to serve if you leave this town with our party, and you are not free to leave unless the maharani should choose to dismiss you."

The boy nodded, but his grandfather asked, "If this boy...if any of them do not serve you well, what will happen to them?"

Before Crowseye could answer, the rani tapped the table, leaned forward, and said, "We are not Mephistani traders, Grandfather. The Seven have never taken slaves. The coin I pay in advance serves as my promise."

The old man and his grandson looked at their feet while she spoke.

"You may go," Crowseye said. "We will call your name if you are selected."

More boys came forward with their fathers, grandfathers, uncles, or brothers. They were all thin, nervous, with nothing between them and desperation but their much-mended clothes. Crowseye repeated his explanation to each one, and Sid dutifully wrote their names.

When the last boy departed, the headman said, "I am sure any of our youth would serve you well, Maharani, though we can scarcely afford to lose even one." The rani simply stared at him until he laughed nervously and added, "We have minded ourselves since Akroyat went dark, but last cycle was so dry.... We buried more than we welcomed."

"My party is not greatly supplied," the rani told him, "but I will leave a gift of flour before we leave. For your vigilance concerning events in this region, I will send you a wagon of grain by the fourth moon."

Surprise and gratitude shone in the headman's face. "Thank you. Our harvest will barely carry us through the winter. Grain by the fourth moon will be a tremendous gift." The man wiped his eyes. "Pardon me, but I never expected such generosity."

"My generosity is as dependent on the seasons and the ancestors as your need," the rani said. "This is only the second in the last five cycles where our granaries have been full enough to allow me to share something with our friends."

The headman took his leave, and Crowseye picked up the parchment before Sid, scanned it, and passed it to the rani.

"This one can write," he said.

"How extraordinary," the rani said as she examined his script.

"I could use a scribe to draft contracts with the southern houses," Crowseye said.

The rani didn't answer, but passed the list back to Crowseye, who then handed it back to him. As Sid grasped the parchment, he managed to tip over the inkpot.

"Bah, what!" Crowseye snatched his records up beyond the spreading pool of ink. "Idiot!"

Sid quickly righted the pot and dropped the cleaning cloth onto the spilled ink. His fingers blackened. He considered sopping up the mess with his kurta.

The rani sighed and rose to her feet. The soldiers came to attention.

"Choose as many as you feel will serve us well, brother. Nilampur's manors and the market must be done before the new cycle, or my consort will force a renegotiation."

After Master Vaksana escorted the rani back to her compartment, Crowseye glared at him so hard, Sid marveled that steam didn't leave his ears. Dismissed, he returned to the supply wagon with his face still burning and sat with his back to the other recruits. The village boys waited with their families against the trading house's wall, and Sid remembered what the witch had told him when she taught him how to make tributes.

"Li says I can't make a tribute to my ancestors if I don't know them," he had complained to the witch.

"She is wrong," the witch said. "Your ancestors see you and hear you whether you know them or not."

"Do they see everything?"

"Everything."

This concerned him.

"Do not worry," the witch said. "You, dear boy, are adored by your ancestors."

"What if I...disappoint them?" Sid said softly.

The witch grew serious. "You won't. Offer your respect with an open heart and, one day, you will find them, and they will not forsake you. But you must not shrink from your destiny. Great deeds often have great costs. That is the way of the world."

"But I'm afraid," he admitted. "What if I don't understand what they want me to do?"

"Listen and you will know what you must do when it matters. The only question is whether you have the courage to do it."

Sid hoped that he had already met his destiny, that he had found it the day he met the rani, and he hoped that leaving home was itself proof of courage, but he wasn't sure.

As Crowseye called boys' names, Sid packed things away in the wagon and told himself, *I'm luckier than them. I'm already chosen, already on my way.* But if good fortune grew tired of him, what did he have to go back to? Each of those boys had a hand on his shoulder, a family around them—their *real* family. He didn't remember his mother's face, and the very idea of his father was as insubstantial as morning mist. *The only way forward is forward.*

CHAPTER 4

On the edge of a steep hillside, Lingli looked for smoke rising above the treetops, but there was nothing in the sky except the promise of a bright new day. Halfway down the hill an outcrop of boulders stood out among the trees. Waiting out the day would put her just that much farther behind Sid and his captors, but the rocks were the best cover she had seen in miles.

She was bone tired, too tired to be as scared as she had been when she first fled into the woods. After running until she was breathless and listening so hard for pursuers that she thought her ears would bleed, Lingli gradually remembered that the dark had never done her any harm. If she had to be afraid, she would save that for other Ascaryans. She breathed deep and considered the boulders below her.

What would Red do?

She crouched and slid down the hill's broken face. Missing a hold near the closest boulders, she passed the whole outcrop by the time she stopped herself. Nothing seemed to take notice of her lack of grace. A little stream running along the bottom of the hill beckoned to her with its sweet music, and she slid the rest of the way down.

At the creek, she drank deeply and washed her face. The cool water rushing over her hands felt good as she filled her waterskin. Upstream, an owl called out. Lingli stoppered the skin. A crow cawed as though it answered the owl. The hairs on her neck rose. Owls and crows were not friends. She scanned the woods. Nothing. Not even the sound of other birds. In her mind—as clearly as if he stood next to her—she heard Red say, *Downwind and uphill.*

In another wood, long before, the red giant knelt next to her behind some brush. She was very young, and this outing was during the rutting moon when stags left young trees scarred from their efforts to soothe the itch in their antlers. The giant held his sling and wore his skins, not the

Ascaryan clothes he wore to the village. He had rubbed dirt on her face and kurta to hide her smell, and she was cross.

"I'm cold," the small Lingli had said. "I want to go home."

"Hmmm," Red answered in his giantish way that was sometimes an answer and sometimes not. He leaned forward and peered over the bushes.

"We won't catch the deers. They're fast."

"And you are loud," he said. "Where is the wind?"

Small Lingli lifted her face to feel the air. She turned this way and that, then pointed in the direction the wind blew from.

The giant nodded toward the opposite direction. "We go this way."

"Why?"

"It is the way of deer. When you are hunted, to escape, go downwind and uphill."

Crossing a stretch of half-drowned scrub and debris, Lingli scrambled back up the hillside as quietly as possible. No sounds of pursuit followed as the dawn brightened. In her long black cloak, she was as exposed as a fly on a pie. She had barely reached the first outcrop when there was a sudden crashing noise in the brush below. She dodged behind a low limestone ledge and flung herself down onto her stomach.

Peering over the lip of rock before her, she followed the sound. A deer plunged through the brush and darted toward the stream. As it paused to leap, she heard an arrow *zfft*. The deer sprang and seemed to hang in the air over the water, then it fell onto the opposite bank. Its legs scrabbled, and it tried to rise but failed. Someone let out a great whoop. Lingli closed her eyes and hoped the deer was their only target.

When she looked again, two bearded men dragged the dead animal from the creek bank to a tree. One of the men drew a knife from his belt. The other produced a rope. A wave of nausea overcame her. She pressed her cheek into the gravel.

The sight of the men teased vicious fears she had barely kept down since leaving home—a reminder of those who had come for her in the cabin and of another time when men had put a rope around her waist. They had been bearded like these men. They had cursed her. They had pulled her behind them as if she were an animal.

Not now.

She couldn't afford to think of that day, not if she wanted to survive this one. She bit down on the inside of her cheek hard enough to taste blood and clear her head.

By the time she dared look again, the men had strung the deer up and were elbow-deep in its cavity. Soon they lowered the carcass to the ground, and one coiled the rope while the other washed the knives. They hadn't skinned the creature yet, only lightened their load. She took that as a sign that their home or camp must be some ways off.

Tying the deer's legs to a long branch, the men hoisted the branch and the carcass so it hung between them. After they tromped upstream and disappeared the sounds of the forest gradually returned.

Her right hand and the side of her face had begun to tingle. The vein in her temple pulsed. This was the way it had always been. If she was exposed to the sun for too long, the tingling would be followed by a headache. Soon her skin would blister and burn.

Jerking her hood forward, Lingli crept along the ledge. A little farther ahead another cluster of broken boulders emerged from the hillside. She felt her way along and finally found a fissure she could wedge herself into. Though she couldn't sit up straight inside, the space was deep enough for her to stretch out on her side.

Her heart was still beating too fast. Trying to breathe slowly, she patted the ugly vein in her temple. She could do nothing about the color of her hair, her eyes, or her skin, but she had been deeply tempted on more than one occasion to take a blade and bleed dry that cursed vein. Anything to stop the fear and anger aimed at her by everyone except Red, Sid, and the witch.

And Arnaz. Her friend.

Some time ago, she had made a friend. A girl had arrived in their yard with her hunger-ridden family, including a father desperate enough to ask a giant whether he had any work for food. Lingli and Sid had been sitting outside in the cabin's shade practicing writing when the family arrived, and, after the father followed Red to the hay meadow, his wife climbed down from the wagon and approached them. When Lingli put down her parchment and stood, the woman stopped and rocked back on her heels. Being used to this, Lingli dropped her eyes to the ground and pulled up her hood.

The woman asked Sid, "Do you know letters?"

Sid nodded, and the woman turned and quickly strode back to her wagon. In seconds she delivered two of her daughters to Sid.

"Teach them."

Sighing silently, Lingli went to the garden. She busied herself with plucking herbs and vegetables for their supper until she looked up to find one of the woman's daughters hanging about the end of a row of beans. The girl introduced herself as Arnaz and, to Lingli's surprise, accepted a handful of pudina she offered without any sign of fear. A minute later the girl was bobbing along the garden path next to her, chewing on a leaf. She asked the names of plants and wondered aloud how they kept the rabbits off.

"See this," Lingli said, uncovering a long, ridged cucumber from under a canopy of leaves. She twisted the cucumber from the vine and gave it to the girl.

"Let's eat it now," Arnaz whispered.

Lingli remembered it so clearly. The warm evening. The smell of the garden. The girl's mischievous smile framing a face brighter than the tattered clothing she wore. But most of all, she remembered how the girl had spoken to her as if she were like any other girl.

In two days, the father's work was done, and the family packed up their things.

When their wagon disappeared, Lingli was overcome by an aching loneliness that she tried to sing away and work away, but it held her tight. When Red announced that he was going to the village for supplies the next day, she hadn't been able to hide her excitement.

Delaying his trip until late in the afternoon after Lingli rose from her sleep, Red helped her find the family's rough hut at the edge of the village before he continued his errands. No one answered her knock at first, though she heard voices within. When Arnaz's father finally appeared, she presented him with an apple for each of his children. Pushing past her father, Arnaz took Lingli by the hand and stood with her until her father grudgingly invited her inside.

Once a moon, for almost a cycle, Lingli visited her friend, bringing their inkpot and reed pens to practice letters and make her invitation inside easier. Then, one day Arnaz's mother met her at the door, disheveled and red-eyed.

"Arnaz is gone," she said bitterly. "Gone with the ancestors, so there's no need for you to come here."

Arnaz's father appeared in the doorway and gently moved his wife behind him. When Lingli asked what had happened, he shook his head and muttered, "Fly fever."

"We were fine," her mother argued. "Fine! Until we came to this place."

The door closed.

Staring at the thin line of light that marked the world outside the fissure, Lingli considered Arnaz's death. Yes, that seemed to be when the villagers' wariness began to turn into hatred. Curled on her side, memories of what followed half a cycle after her Arnaz perished marched through her mind, unbidden and unstoppable.

The first day of winter and the apex of the frost moon was also New Cycle Day, which was celebrated with a large festival in the village. It was an auspicious day for all, and it should have been doubly so for Lingli—being the day Red had declared was her birthday—but the last New Cycle Day was one she wished she could forget.

In the excitement of imagining the food and interesting things they would see at the festival, she had somehow allowed Sid and Red to talk her into bringing her embroidered scarves, vests, and caps to sell. She'd even made herself a pretty blue tunic to wear for the occasion, though no one could see it under her cloak and coat. Yet as soon as she and Sid pulled their small cart into the maidan, she panicked at the sight of the crowd, especially the thought of asking anyone for coin, and she begged Sid to help her. With the promise of half the sales, he agreed. Tying one of her scarves around his neck, he stepped onto the cart and began hawking at the top of his lungs.

While he handled transactions, Lingli shyly showed the pieces the villagers asked to see. By the late morning, Sid patted the coins in his pocket and looked longingly at the hand pies.

"Just one pie," he pleaded. "I'll share it."

The pies did indeed smell wonderful, so she agreed, and he trotted off.

Soon after, three women asked to see her vests, and she spread some out for their inspection.

"I'll give you two paise for this one," one woman said.

To this absurdly low offer, Lingli pressed her lips together and said nothing.

"You've offended her, dear," another woman said.

The third woman was nearly as broad as she was tall, and her face was lined with cares—Arnaz's mother. She recognized Lingli at the same time Lingli recognized her.

"You don't want this," Arnaz's mother told her friend. "She's touched it."

Lingli's stomach tightened. She turned her face from the women and refolded a scarf.

"What do you mean?" the first woman asked.

"That's the creature that caused my girl's death. Cursed her with sickness." Arnaz's mother's voice grew angrier with each word. "She was such a good child. Smarter than the rest. Taken by the ancestors too early by this asura's design!"

Lingli didn't hear their words anymore but looked at the bottoms of the women's long tunics and their dirty boots turning this way and that as they tried to calm their friend. There was no point in arguing that she was the last Ascaryan who would have wished for Arnaz's death. No one but Red and Sid ever listened to her. To the world, she was a witch or demon, but in truth she was nothing but cursed, and only the stars knew why.

Growing very loud, Arnaz's mother threw the vests into the mud before the others moved her away. Lingli picked up the ruined pieces, put them into the cart, and searched the crowd for Sid, but he was nowhere to be seen, and Red had not yet arrived.

While the distraught mother continued to curse her with a string of foul words, Arnaz's father and his friends arrived, already flushed with drink and eager for any excitement the day might produce. Some of the men laughed at Arnaz's mother's fury and asked Arnaz's father why he didn't have better control of his wife, whereupon he vehemently backed his wife's accusations, pointed at Lingli, and made a protective sign.

Breaking free from her friends, Arnaz's mother came at her scratching, and Lingli's hood fell back in the melee, exposing her raked and bleeding cheek, but that was nothing next to the reaction the others had to her bone-pale color and the vein in her temple.

"You see! You see! She's unnatural. She's otherworld!"

"Take that thing away from here!" Arnaz's father yelled as he struggled with his wife.

The other men pressed around Lingli, and one had a rope attached to his belt. In seconds it was around her waist.

"We'll hitch her to a trough, Madam. She'll not trouble you anymore today."

The men seemed to take pleasure in cinching the rope as tight as possible and jerking her behind them through the crowd. More villagers pressed close; some sneered, and a few spat on her.

The musicians sat near the water troughs and played a merry tune on a bansari and a sarod until the men's raucous behavior interrupted them. Sid was there, still holding a hand pie. He pushed through the crowd when he saw her.

"Stay back, boy," the man holding the rope said.

"Get Red," Lingli whispered. Sid nodded and disappeared into the crowd.

While the man tied the loose end of the rope to one of the rings set in the horse trough, his friend said, "You've got some balls. That giant shows up and sees you've got his little witch, there will be a price paid."

The man with the rope said, "I'm not afraid of that fucking giant!"

"That's firewine courage."

Another man said, "Only two choices. Leave her here to be found, or...make her disappear for good. Only the ancestors know how many she's cursed already."

Lingli didn't remember much else about their talk, but she remembered their beards, their stinking breaths, and the rope holding her. She remembered, very well, one holding a shiny blade close to her face.

"You see this?" the man said. "A nick here and there, and your mouth will be bigger, but you won't be talking."

She felt her spirit escaping with her breath.

"You hear me, creature?" The man used the point of the blade to raise her face to his. "You won't be talking, will you?"

She shook her head.

"This is an ancestor-fearing village," he said. "It don't matter what kind of coin that giant carries, we don't need you skulking about and cursing us in our sleep." The man stopped talking when a commotion on the other side of the market got his attention.

"Time to go, boys!" one of his friends yelled.

Lingli closed her eyes and concentrated on the sound of Red stomping toward her. There was a scuffle, then a couple of fear-filled shrieks and crashing noises, and she opened her eyes.

Nearby, Red stood with his fists curled at his sides. Two of those who had tormented her lay on the ground and the leg of the one howling was bent at an impossible angle. At the edge of the crowd, Sid stood with his mouth open. She felt dizzy.

Then Red and Sid were at her side untying her, and she was free and in Red's arms. As they left the village behind, she tried to calm herself, but fear nestled within her. The brittle tolerance the villagers had accorded them was gone. They hated her, and now, because of her, they hated Red, too.

Events lined up in her mind: Arnaz's death, then the New Cycle Day Festival. The first four moons of this cycle had passed with her so terribly numb, she had secretly used her needle to prick the inside of her arms just to feel something. Now, when she had begun to think her spirit was healing, Red sat vigilant in his chair, and she had burned a villager in their cabin.

And Sid had left them.

Lingli touched the braided bracelet in her pocket. Red had made her Sid's protector and asked her to help him. *Have courage,* she heard Red say, but what if the curse she carried was stronger than she was?

After rummaging through her pack, she ate an apple and a stale piece of roti. The sun slid farther past its zenith, and she slept for a brief time, but memories of Sid turned in her mind. There was the pudgy toddler who laughed at whatever she said or did, and the boy who had entertained her and the giant even when he didn't mean to. It was true she trimmed the wick of his ego whenever possible, but didn't he know she also cared for him? Her friend and rival. The only part of her made-up family who remained.

He might not be here, she reminded herself, but he was just beyond. Just ahead. She had to stop thinking and start honoring Red's word.

After crawling out of her hiding place, she fished the map from her cloak. The mountain in the center had been drawn in more detail than the rest of the map. It was girded by a winding wall that contained a fort city called Safed Qila, and above the fort was a cluster of white buildings and towers—the palace Chandrabhavan.

Her main concern, however, spanned the left side of the map where the Mephistan Road ran a southerly course through the Western Woods to Akroyat, the fallen capital of Vasantrastra, before continuing toward the slave city it was named for. Next to Akroyat's sprawling fort the Rajpath met the Mephistan Road and passed through another forest before it crossed a plain and ended at the foot of Saatkulom's monolith.

Lingli sighed. Unless she caught up to them soon and Sid was able and willing to listen to her, it was going to be a long journey. Putting the map back into her cloak's hem, she slung on her pack and waterskin and climbed back up the hillside to the road.

Late that evening, a wagon rut turning off the road led Lingli to a clearing where she reckoned more than a score of horses had been tethered. *What could they be about? Trade? Scouting? War?* It seemed too large a group to think that their only purpose had been to steal Sid away. Before she could explore any further, something moved through the underbrush nearby, and she quickly shrank back into the deeper darkness under the trees.

A massive sun bear followed his nose into the campsite. The beast grunted and shook his shaggy golden head as he ambled. As long as she didn't challenge him, he probably would not be interested in her, but she was glad to be downwind. She watched the bear dig at a patch of ground, crunching on something he found there. When he finished and rose up on his hind legs, Lingli could see he was every bit as tall as her giant. The bear sniffed all around again, then dropped back to all fours and shuffled off toward the road.

After a few breaths, Lingli went to where the bear had scraped the ground. Shards of bone and scraps of fur littered the spot. Someone had cleaned rabbits there and not buried the remains deeply enough.

Though the moons were waning, their light was enough to catch on something else on the ground by her feet—a small metal disc. Turning the decoration over in her hand, she tried to remember what the noble with the bow had been wearing, but it didn't seem suited for his clothes. It reminded her of the woods witch's gown.

The witch never failed to appear at their cabin a few times each cycle. Once she and Sid had found her resting under a tree deep in the forest. Another time Lingli met her in the cabbage patch while weeding the garden at night. Usually, however, she was simply there, at their door, with her ancient satchel stuffed with mushrooms, roots, leaves, and her awful-smelling potions in tiny jugs.

Straight as an arrow with deep creases at the corners of her mouth, the witch could express caustic disapproval from a distance. Her most cautioning feature, however, was a scar and indentation running from the center of her forehead to just above her temple. This disfigurement, almost the inverse of the vein that vexed Lingli, must have been the result of a severe wound, yet somehow the skin had closed over it. As fearsome as the witch looked, it also reminded folk of her renowned powers to heal, and that was a precious gift—one the villagers could not forgo even if they resented having to wear protective amulets in her presence.

Once, when the witch had arrived on a winter evening, Lingli had taken her wet cloak and helped her remove a filthy shawl, then a thin coat, then a sweater, until the old woman was left in a threadbare gown that might have been gray or blue. The gown's only remaining decoration was a row of small metal discs along the neckline and each cuff, and even several of those were missing.

After Sid and the giant went to sleep, the witch surprised Lingli by pulling a delicate scarf from her sleeve. It was embroidered with colorful flowers, leaves, and geometric shapes. She pulled skeins of bright-colored thread from her pocket and patiently demonstrated stitches for Lingli to copy. They sat shoulder to shoulder in a warm silence, broken only when the witch had to explain a stitch or correct her. With the witch's help, patterns began to emerge under Lingli's fingertips that became more beautiful and complex as the moons passed. Sewing made her happy, and happiness, she found, helped keep her curse at bay. But happiness, like the witch's visits, never lasted.

Red never questioned the witch's demands, and there were plenty, whether she stayed a few hours or a few days. Yet no matter how dutifully he served her, the old woman would become restless. She would move things around the cabin, wring her hands and mutter to herself—at times staring at her and Sid as though she suspected them of great crimes, at other times acting like they were not there. Eventually she would accuse Red of trying to harm her or of harboring unseen others who would, though the giant did nothing to be so accused. In the end, the witch would gather her things and flee into the woods as if wolves were on her heels. She never said goodbye.

Strange or not, Lingli looked up at the moons above the trees and wished the old woman was with her.

Dropping the little disc on the ground, she started toward the road but decided that meeting the bear again was not a good idea. Staying downwind, she cut through the woods until she was reasonably certain she had passed the bear. By the time she made her way back to the road, Lingli had missed the junction with the new road to Muktastan, a road that did not appear on Red's map. After sleeping a few hours in the broad fork of an apinian tree, she hiked for another night with no signs of Sid or those he traveled with.

At dawn on the third day, after crossing hills that petered out like knobby bones at the end of a spine, Lingli passed through the remains of a gateway that marked the border with the realm of Vasantrastra and found herself on the edge of a broad plain. She hoped she would see signs of a crossroads, but there was no road other than the one she stood on.

Red had said three days on the Mephistan Road, but were those three days at an Ascaryan's pace, three days at a giant's pace, three days on horseback? The plain was speckled with scrub, and a dark line in the distance seemed to mark more forest. Lingli realized, suddenly, she could see that distance because the sky had lightened. She would need shelter soon.

Tugging her hood forward, she entered the plain. No birds twittered. No insects hummed. The silence around her grew heavy, as if her presence was not only noted but resented. The sound of her heels striking the road's stones seemed unduly loud. Of all the places under the moons and stars that Lingli had no intention of visiting, Akroyat was first and Mephistan was second. But if finding Sid meant passing close, she would force herself onward.

Only the eldest in their village claimed to remember when Akroyat had been a thriving fort, and Lingli hardly knew anything about the place other than the witch's tale of how it fell. Two stars had fallen in the western lands during an earlier bright cycle. The first had been a burning rock that terrified everyone as it roared through the northern end of the woods, igniting fires. It had burned for a moon, and the woods people prayed to the ancestors for forgiveness and guidance until the remains went dark in a place called Zahatara.

Weeks later people fleeing Akroyat spread news of a second star. This one, it was said, was smooth and shaped like a flattened egg. It took a hundred Ascaryans to encircle it where it had fallen in the gardens near the fort. When the noble advisors reported that it was made of some material unlike anything they had seen before, the raja proclaimed it a gift from the ancestors. The people brought offerings and paid homage.

But when the advisors began to sicken with a strange illness that caused their hair to fall out and sores to appear around their mouths and noses, the tributes ended. The sickness spread, and it was said that the pain was so terrible the afflicted begged for death. When the raja fell ill, he locked the fort's gates. Within weeks there were no more signs of life within the walls.

No one had dared go into Akroyat since then. Survivors in the surrounding villages declared themselves free Ascaryans, though they occasionally had to fight Mephistanis who abducted woods people and sold them in the great and terrible city on the edge of the sea. Alert to all these lurking threats, Lingli moved quickly and silently down the road.

Beyond a grassy berm cutting across the road, she passed densely packed rushes twice her height. The upright leaves were sharp as blades, and each shaft was crowned with clusters of tiny purple-black florets, nodding inflorescences that shaded the plant below. After she passed a second berm, the rushes thinned. The florets drooped and faded to a rusty brown.

Soon there was nothing but dead brown stalks on both sides of the road.

A strange smell caught in Lingli's throat. Holding the edge of her hood over her nose, she discovered a canal running through the middle of the next berm. The liquid within moved slowly—gray and thick as buttermilk and frothing with bubbles. She picked up a handful of gravel and dropped it in. The pieces hissed the instant they touched the surface. Ahead was a stretch of barren ground, followed by another berm with a band of vegetation beyond it.

This place is ferocious, but it is not wild. Canals and berms are built things. She hid her hands in her sleeves as her skin began to tingle. Her thoughts tightened like her empty stomach. *There is a gardener here, and I do not want to meet him.*

After crossing the second channel of milky fluid, Lingli was again surrounded by plant life that grew thicker and thicker until she found herself in an explosion of flora—small trees with strange fruit, thickly corded vines, palms with bristly stumps and saw-toothed fronds, clumps of colorful grasses, and flowers of all shapes and sizes. The jungle pushed up to the edges of the road, and creepers streamed over the stones seeking purchase.

Golden pollen furred her cloak and hands. She could taste it in the back of her throat. She stopped by a huge mound of grass and cut away the outer blades, hoping to hide inside until the sun descended, but as soon as she entered the shaded center, a web of delicate vines climbed her cloak and encased her arms. They were beautiful, fascinating, and the air was so heavy she felt sleepy despite the threat.

Then she heard Red say, *You have two good legs, two good hands, a mind, and a heart. Never be useless.*

Lingli wrestled her arms free, and tendrils burst everywhere. The wounded vines hissed like cats as she tumbled back onto the road. With her rabbit knife, she slashed until the flora fell back and kicked awkwardly at a few slithering vines, then rushed on. When one hand began to blister, she carried the knife in the other. The vein in her temple pulsed with a panic that she refused to acknowledge.

Akroyat's towers finally appeared ahead beneath clouds that churned the sky and flickered with lightning. Squalls of rain soon soaked her, but the drama of rain and wind was preferable to the sly rustling all around.

As she came closer to the doomed fort, flashes, bolts, and whole trees of light crisscrossed the sky above, casting everything in a greenish hue. Patches of mist that looked like wraiths curled in window wells and dissolved whenever she tried to get a good look at them.

Cold to her core, Lingli kept her eyes on her feet until she met the crossroads. Ahead and behind was the Mephistan Road. The westbound arm of the Rajpath ran straight to the fort's gates. The eastbound Rajpath, the course she was destined to follow, was in worse repair than the Mephistan Road—full of broken pavers barely visible in the surrounding plant riot.

If she had known her ancestors, if they had been honorable, Lingli would have pressed her forehead to the road and made a tribute to them right there. But she knew no such thing, so she tucked her wet hair behind her ears, closed her eyes, and called upon Red. She heard what he had told her and Sid more than once. *The world is not as strange as you. Trust that and find courage.*

She began hacking her way east.

The rain ended, darkness fell, and lightning only occasionally belched from the bank of clouds behind. One of Lingli's hands burned with blisters and her other arm ached from slashing in every direction. Thorns punctured her clothing, and grasses snapped like whips and occasionally cut her hands and face. The only good sign was her sense that the road had begun to rise just the tiniest bit. She crossed more berms that contained foul and frothy little channels.

If this is a bowl, I must find the rim.

The sharp-bladed rushes reappeared—still overrun by the half-sentient flora she had been fighting, but it was thinning. Contemplating what the garden's design might mean, she nearly walked into a sludgy pool where ill-formed vegetation emerged from the muck, stretched upward, and collapsed back upon itself. The pool stunk of rot, and the unnaturalness of life hatched and strangled so quickly made her shiver. She looked for a way around, but the water covered the road for some distance and stretched into the jungle on both sides. Having no intention of wandering into that mess, Lingli pulled up a loose stone from the roadway. When she tossed it into the center of the pool, the dull thwack marked the water as shallow.

Grabbing the shaft of a fallen rush, Lingli tested its strength. She stabbed it down into the pool and stepped lightly into the muck. With both feet in and mud sucking at her heels, she focused on crossing quickly. Halfway across the water reached only a little above her ankles, but two steps farther, it deepened. As she was about to take another step, a huge pale salamander rolled to the surface and fixed on her with its four eyes before disappearing again. When she put her foot down, the water poured in over the top of her boot. Wanting to scream, Lingli bit down on the inside of her cheek instead and waded on.

At last, teetering on the pool's far side, she took off her boots and emptied them. A fleshy leech the length of her palm clung tight to one calf. When she pulled the slimy creature off blood ran down her leg. Two more had to be removed from her other leg. She considered walking barefoot the rest of the night, but the danger of cutting her feet overcame her disgust.

With her boots back on, she hitched up her pack and trudged toward the dark line marking another forest edge. Daylight confirmed what she already knew; there were no signs of Sid or his captors. Sick with hunger and exhaustion, with blood pooling in the bottom of her boots, she remembered a day when she had made the world as she wanted it to be.

They were young, perhaps six and four cycles. Sid had grown cross with her because she had been trying to make him wear a coat and put his boots on the right feet. He had screamed at her, "You are not my mother!"

"No, but I am your sister," she had answered, unperturbed.

"You are not! You are an ugly old bone and I hate you."

Having already learned that the best way of getting Sid's cooperation often involved distraction, she had given him a piece of pie and considered his accusation quietly. Later she asked the giant, "Can I make Sid my brother?"

Red pretended not to hear her. She asked again, and he hummed deep in his throat and told her that there was a word for children who had no parents taking care of them. The word was "orphan," and Sid was an orphan, like her. That word troubled her. Its meaning had always been there, circling the edge of her thoughts, but knowing the word for it opened a hole that threatened to make everything she knew disappear.

Any other time, whenever she felt scared, she would have climbed into the crook of Red's arm where she would stay until the feeling went away. But there was Red, saying that word, and she didn't know what to do.

Her dismay must have been plain, for the giant, usually oblivious of the flurry of their Ascaryan emotions, knelt down and told her, "I will not say that word anymore. It is a useless word. You and Sid are of great worth, like silver and gold."

She remembered hugging his thick neck. "We will be your children, no one else's," she insisted. "Sid will be my brother, and I will be his sister."

"Hmmm," Red said.

But now she was no longer a child.

Her wishes and the world's truths were two different things. Somehow, at home, she had been able to refuse to acknowledge this, but home was gone, and if she didn't find Sid she would lose the last piece of the family she had made for herself. That she might never find him terrified her, but worse was the thought that he had wanted to leave and did not want to be found. Maybe she had been a fool for pretending he was her brother and trying to keep her notion of family stitched together this long. She should have known Sid would eventually rip her fantasy to pieces even if he hadn't meant to.

Lingli walked on, looking for a place to hide herself from the day.

CHAPTER 5

Sid cut three fine slices of ginger for tea. One for the rani, one for Crowseye, and one for Master Vaksana. The wagonmaster had finally allowed him to assist in preparing their cups after he trailed him relentlessly the day before.

The clink-clank of the kettle awakened the camp. Soldiers cleaned their teeth with twigs. The archers braided their hair in tight plaits. A cluster of sleepy-looking boys hoisted the bathing tubs and shuffled off to fill them for the rani and the nobles who bathed every morning. Soldiers and archers bathed as often as they wanted to fetch their own water. The recruits bathed whenever Crowseye declared he could not stand their stink.

Lining up the nobles' cups, the old man added a few drops of honey to each and gave Sid a curt nod.

Sid raced the rani's cup through the camp first, balancing it in his palm once he reached the ratha so the giantess could take it without touching him. Red had been bad enough—always knowing when he had done something wrong. Greta's gaze was like that, too, but more so, as if she could tell he was thinking of doing something wrong.

Greta rapped on the side of the ratha, and Sid waited until he saw the rani's tapered fingers curled around the cup before he dashed back to the camp table. Relieved to see the nobles' cups still steaming there, he race-walked the cups to them, wondering how to embellish this activity. Drop to one knee? Announce himself somehow? He might only be a tea boy, but it seemed a good idea to be the best tea boy in camp until he could find a way to be more than that. As the nobles sipped, he squatted on his haunches and waited.

Master Vaksana was nearly finished, but Crowseye was horribly slow. *Just sips at it like I've got all day. Yes, here we go. No? Stop grinning! They'll think you're a fool.*

He consoled himself that this was progress. Crowseye hadn't insulted him since the accident at Muktastan, and Master Vaksana, who spoke more to the wolf and the horses than he did to the rest of them, had even thanked him once. There was only one who still hadn't recognized him in the least.

As soon as the party resumed the journey, the recruits settled into their spots, dumb with the stupor caused by days of rolling along in dappled light under forest boughs. Sid dreaded this in-between state where there were no tasks to keep him busy, and it was still too early to claim a nap. When time ran loose and plentiful, memories threatened.

The sight of a swallow reminded him of the nest in their barn, which then made him wonder if Lingli had taken up his chores. Each time one of the wheels crossed a thick root, the wagon's thud bruised his tailbone and made him wish for his old cot and the cup of hot milk Li would bring him on winter mornings. A long habit of nurturing indignation made him imagine she was sorry about her past treatment of him, but his righteousness gave little pleasure. Despite their differences, he hoped that she did indeed still clean thalis and walk in the meadow.

Worse were memories of Red. All the giant had said that final morning was his name, but Sid could not unhear the betrayal that soaked it. Then there was that terrible sound that had shaken the forest. He could not abide the thought of that cry, so he forced himself to sink it like a stone thrown in a lake. He would not waste his days fighting memories of things that somehow went wrong even though they seemed to go right. If he had to think at all, he would make sure his thoughts were the kind he preferred—thoughts of the future and how he would meet it.

When the party stopped for their midday meal, Sid stared down a couple of recruits who began edging toward the table as soon as the wagonmaster set out the cups. His self-made role of serving the nobles was in jeopardy. Three cups were too much to manage at once. He called to Zarin, the solemn boy from Muktastan.

"Here, you," Sid said as though he had authority to tell anyone to do anything. "Take this cup to Master Vaksana, and this one to Crowseye." Zarin stared and held tight to a sack of vegetables he was hauling from the wagon until Sid barked, "C'mon now, let's go, you mindless worm!" in a fair imitation of the wagonmaster. Some of the boys laughed at this as Sid pushed the cups into Zarin's hands before he ran the rani's cup to her.

When he returned, two junior soldiers leaned against the wagon.

"See, here's one of the eager ones. Thinks no one's noticed," one of the soldiers said. "You'd like to earn an extra coin, wouldn't you, boy?"

"What do you mean?" Sid asked carefully.

"I mean, I've got a proposition."

The young soldier looked not a day older than him, but he was barrel-chested and his hair was cut so short Sid could see his scalp shining. He wore a purplish-red sash fastened to his left shoulder by a brooch in the shape of a tree. *House of Vaksana.*

"You bring me a cup of water whenever we break journey, and I'll give you a silver when we reach the Rock."

"Crowseye is not going to like this," his companion told him.

The first soldier ignored him. "Think on it. A silver coin for a few cups of water. You'll do a lot more work in Nilampur to earn that."

Sid *had* begun to worry about how he'd be paid in future after hearing snatches of conversation from the soldiers, where some pity and ridicule was aimed at those going to work in the new lake town. He wished he hadn't left the whole pouch of coins back in the cabin.

"Alright," he said, holding out his hand.

The soldier turned his head and spat.

"We're of the Seven, idiot," the rude soldier's friend said. They laughed as they walked off to retrieve their horses.

Zarin moved next to Sid's spot in the wagon. With his new ally serving Crowseye and Master Vaksana, things worked smoothly again that evening, but Sid was alert to their arrangement's precarious balance.

More opportunities must be out there, but where? As Sid surveyed those sitting around the fire, the ratha driver caught his attention.

The driver was a terrifically muscled man, as one would expect for someone who could manage a six-in-hand all day and keep the ratha repaired and moving. Small tiles woven into the man's long hair clicked when he moved, and he wore a thick bronze collar around his neck. He didn't speak much, and there was a vigilance about him that Sid thought marked him as foreign to those of Saatkulom.

When the driver put his thali aside and picked up a piece of harness to oil, Sid got up and approached him. He was a little afraid, but the only way forward was forward. "Sir, uh…I could do that for you, sir," he stuttered as he squatted before the driver.

Flint-eyed, the driver paused and handed Sid the oiling cloth. He gestured toward one of the harness pieces, which Sid pulled into his lap and began rubbing it with the cloth.

"Pass the whole length," the driver said. "The oil should be even."

Telling Sid to put the harness near the team when he was done, the driver soon went to make his bed by the ratha.

Sid oiled the tack thoroughly, trying on an attitude of quiet confidence that he hoped would impress the rani, but his hopes were dashed when the rani, who had been very quiet that evening, wrapped herself in a shawl and left the fire.

A little later, with tack draped over his shoulder, Sid headed toward the line where the horses were tied. Having no love for horses in general, especially not ones whose kicks could send him to the other side of the camp, he began speaking softly as he approached them. He was about to drop the tack and make his retreat when a voice made him jump.

"If Jeevan trusts you near our mounts, I suppose I will also," the rani said, stepping around one of the horses with a brush in her hands.

"Oh, my! I mean, my Maharani!" Sid pressed his palms together.

The rani nodded to him, turned back to the horse, and resumed brushing. "How have you found life with us so far, Sid Sol?"

"I…I am well, thank you. I am trying… That is, I want to be of service."

"You are making efforts, by all accounts, yet you do not strike me as a boy who sees service as his calling. Tell me, why do you wish to serve?"

Sid searched for an answer. He was fairly certain that *because you are the rani, and I want to win your praise* was not the right thing to say and proclaiming that a witch had told him he would do great things would lead to too many questions.

"Someone like me has to make the most of every opportunity," he said.

"Ambition?" In the light of the stars and moons, Sid could see her cock a brow at him.

"Uh…yes, but ambition isn't always bad, is it? Can't you want things for good reasons?"

"Perhaps. What are your reasons?"

He offered what he thought was a safe answer. "I want to be very rich."

The rani put her free hand to her mouth to stifle laughter, making the horse sidestep nervously. Sid wished he could take the words back. He sounded like a stupid child.

"If I were rich," he said, trying to keep his voice even, "I could provide for people. I could help them."

The rani regained her composure, though amusement still played over her face. "*Who* do you want to help, Sid Sol?"

"Well, Red and Li, I guess."

"Are you speaking of your guardian?"

Sid nodded. "I thought if I had more coin, I could be of some use. Red always told us to be useful."

"You do understand that the giant probably stole you from your real parents."

Sid's mouth hung open. He had never imagined Red capable of such a crime, yet he knew better than to contradict her.

"You mentioned someone else," the rani continued. "Who is Li?"

"Lingli. She is a bit older than me, and she's an orphan, too. She was calling me when…. Anyway, she was already living with the red giant when my mother brought me there. I was very small and—"

"Your mother? I thought you said you did not know her?"

"She died soon after Red took us in. He said Li and I were gifts he didn't expect."

"That seems quite strange. Did he force you to work?"

"Yes. No, just chores. But he was good to us. He never beat us, not even once."

"Tell me about her. Li." The rani began brushing the next horse in the line.

"Well, like I said, she's a little older than me. Strange looking. White skin, white hair, and her eyes are gray like rain. Bossy. And she has a—"

"You are describing an otherworld creature."

The vision that had tormented Sid since he left—Lingli standing alone in the eerie mist—immediately came to mind. He banished the image before she could turn and show him her milky eyes and the terrible vein in her temple.

"She scares people all the time, but she's just a girl."

"She has always lived with the giant?"

He nodded, and the rani pulled some knots from the horse's mane. Running her hand down the animal's back, she said, "It is natural that we grow attached to the people we see every day. But you must never believe that friends, no matter how dear, can replace your true family— the generations of ancestors whose spirits stretch from the oldest stars to you."

She tossed the brush toward the pile of tack and stepped away from the horses. With her palms pressed together high above her head, she searched the sky. "Only by honoring their sacrifice and making regular tributes can we receive their blessings and live fully."

Sid was quiet, ashamed that he had given up his nightly tributes and that the rani knew he was without ancestors.

"By accepting my invitation, you have become part of the fast-flowing river of life. One day you will find your ancestors and, thereafter, your destiny."

Gesturing for Sid to walk beside her, she said, "We're nearing the Naachmaidan, the great grasslands that mark the edge of our realm. In less than a week we will arrive at the Rock, the home of the Seven and soon your home, too." Her smile remained a little wistful, but her voice changed back to the measured tones she used most of the time. "I'm sure you will carry out your duties with honor."

Greta waited by the side of the ratha, and the driver was a dark shape lying near the hitch. This time when the rani paused, Sid understood that he should take his leave. He pressed his palms together and bowed his head. She continued to her vehicle, holding Greta's huge hand to steady herself as she climbed inside.

Crawling under the supply wagon to his usual spot, Sid tossed about and chastised himself for not doing more to make a good impression. He finally decided that her notice was far more important than his shortcomings. *At least she knows my name.*

The next day was humid and still. When they stopped in the late morning to rest the horses, Sid and Zarin hustled cups to the nobles as fast as they could, then Sid delivered to his new customers. The two dealmakers flashed him warning looks when he stopped near the front of the line holding the cups out in front of him. Realizing his mistake, Sid waited behind a tree at the side of the road until they came to him.

"Spilled half of it," the rude soldier said, looking down his nose into the cup. "If you make us wait until we're about to remount you'll get only half a silver from me."

"I've got to serve the maharani first," Sid said in a small voice.

The soldier shrugged. "You want full payment? Then bring us tea after dinner as well."

They stared him down, daring him to say something. He ran the cups back to the wagon and cursed himself for being tricked.

By late afternoon, their road ran along the edge of a hill of bare gray rock, chipped and split all down its bald face. Below them and as far as they could see to the south of the road was a different kind of forest. The trees were very tall, and their trunks were white and smooth. A breeze made their wispy, pale green leaves flutter, resulting in strange sounds and echoes.

"That's the Silver Woods," Crowseye told the boys as he rode to the back of the line. "Most of what people say is nonsense, but it's true enough that it is not a hospitable place. Do not wander out of camp tonight," he said over his shoulder. "I will not be sending out search parties for anyone who strays."

The recruits drew near the boys from Muktastan, expecting those with proximity would know the most.

"I heard that the trees move, and you can't find your way out if they don't want you to."

"I heard it's full of ghosts."

"My pa's pa saw a guardian spirit there."

"What kind?"

"Said it was an ancient, keeping watch in an old tower in there. Dressed in full armor and carrying a lance made of light."

"How'd your pa's pa get away?"

"Outran it 'til he crossed a stream, and it stopped chasing him."

"Aw, you're a liar."

"Am not. I swear it on my mother's heart."

"Why didn't the spirit strike him with that weapon then?"

"Don't know, but no one with sense goes in there."

The discussion drifted to a cataloging of the otherworld creatures, and there was a long argument as to whether a vetala possessing a live body was worse than one possessing a corpse, and how long pani asuras could survive out of water. Sid shivered as the wagon passed around the hillside and they lost sight of the strange woods. He did not like such talk, especially with night coming on. Dark thoughts bred bad dreams, the woods witch always said—and he already had enough of those haunting him.

There had been a time before when bad dreams visited him nearly every night. He grew used to waking in a sweat, his heart pounding from fleeing monsters. Once, during one of the witch's visits and while Red and Li were outside, Sid told the witch that his dreams bothered him. She immediately and rather forcefully pushed him down onto the stool near the hearth and began to feed herbs and leaves to the fire.

Soon a cloud of brown smoke rose, floated over Sid's stool, and just hung in the air over his head. He remembered not liking the sight of it. The cloud seemed aware somehow and looking at him as much as he looked at it.

The witch set about gathering things—a piece of roti, a cup of water, and a stone, which she put in an old brass thali she carried in her bag. Before he knew it, she had cut off a lock of his hair and put it with the other objects, then knelt in front of his stool.

The smoke over his head was thick and expanding when the witch began speaking strange names. Reciting her ancestors, no doubt, which was the way of beginning and ending of all tributes. The smoke roiled as if it intended to choke him. Just as he was about to jump off the stool and run to find Red, the old woman rose on her knees and leaned over the thali to hold his arms tight. Without pausing her tribute, she shook her head, telling him to be silent.

He closed his eyes and listened to her voice rising and falling, speaking fast then slow. When she went silent, he opened his eyes.

The smoke was gone. A circle of ash surrounded his stool and the witch. Putting her finger to her lips, she signaled to him to step over it carefully and follow her.

Outside the cabin, he whispered, "What was that smoke?"

"A shadow," she said, patting his head. "It has left you now, and you should not think of it. You are young and strong. Go play while the sun shines."

He had done as he was told and might not have remembered the incident if it were not for what followed. At dusk, while he threw stones out of the furrows in the field Red was plowing, Li came running toward them. Something was wrong with the witch, she said, and they hurried to the cabin to find her sitting on the floor, her mouth blackened with ash. Her eyes had rolled back in her head so only the whites showed.

After putting her in Sid's cot, Red gently wiped away the ash from her face. She took a breath and looked around her then grabbed at Sid and caught his sleeve.

"They come in great numbers," she whispered urgently. "Fly or fall!" She had looked frightened, which frightened him more. Then she lay back and closed her eyes.

Red pushed him and Lingli out of the cabin and told them to finish the chores. When they returned, Sid stayed far away from the witch. Lingli, however, was bolder in those days. She asked what she had meant, but the witch acted as if she remembered none of it. Giving no answer, she took her dinner with them, and that was that.

The party made camp that evening in a bare space where the road crossed an open plateau. Shallow dirt and scree barely covered the rock around them. Strange sounds carried from the Silver Woods, creating a watchfulness in the camp. The soldiers kept the fire low.

Working next to Zarin after dinner, Sid cleaned the thalis while keeping an eye on the wagonmaster as he began preparing the last round of tea. Even with Zarin taking care of Master Vaksana and Crowseye, he could not manage the rani and the soldiers at the same time.

"Hey, uh, would you be interested in earning some extra coin?" he whispered to Harno, the boy who had fallen out of the wagon on Sid's first evening.

"How?" Harno whispered back.

"See those two soldiers? There, the ones from Master Vaksana's house. I'm supposed to bring them tea, but I've got to deliver to the rani first, and Zarin's hands are full with the nobles."

"So why don't you take it to them later?"

"They won't pay me if it's cold," Sid said. "I could give you half if you take their tea."

The boy looked from Sid to the soldiers. "Just take the tea and fetch their cups back?"

"Ha, but don't let the old snake see you. Wait 'til he isn't looking."

When the tea was ready Sid made sure Harno got cups in the first round, then he took the rani's cup while Zarin served the nobles. When he returned to the camp table, Sid saw Harno waiting on the soldiers on the other side of the fire. One of the soldiers held his cup out, but just as the boy was about to take it, the soldier dropped it. When Harno bent to pick it up, the soldier's friend poured his tea on him. Harno jerked upright, putting a hand to his wet head.

The pair laughed a little too loudly, and Sid saw Crowseye turn his attention in their direction. Harno had nearly reached the camp table when the noble caught his elbow and marched him back to where the soldiers sat. Sid followed at a distance.

"Did you serve these soldiers, boy?"

"Yes, sir."

"Why would you be serving them?"

"Well...I...uh..." Harno stuttered.

Sid sighed. He didn't want to see what would happen if Harno lied. "It wasn't his idea, sir," he said as he came up to the group. "I made an arrangement with your men here to bring them tea, and I was afraid it would go cold by the time I got back from serving the rani, so I asked Harno to take their tea this evening."

Crowseye looked at him as if he was not surprised to hear he was involved. "What did they promise you for this service?"

"Well, sir, at first it was to be a silver for serving them water during breaks, but then I was late with their water so they told me I had to serve tea in the evenings, too, if I wanted a full silver. Of course, I would split it with Harno here because he agreed to help me keep the bargain."

The noble's voice was thick with ice as he addressed him and Harno. "You two have joined the Seven's service. Not theirs. The Seven will be feeding you, sheltering you, and paying for your service—not these two. The Seven have all rights to your time and labor. Understand?

"It might interest you to know," Crowseye continued, "that they have no silver to give you. They were playing you for fools. If I catch either of you trying to rent your services out again, that will be the day you are relieved of your obligation and duly punished according to our laws."

Sid and Harno bowed their heads, eager to back away but knowing better than to do so before they were dismissed.

"And you two," Crowseye said, turning on the soldiers. "What's the rightful punishment for those who would steal from the Seven?" The soldiers shuffled their feet. "Tell me!" he said, so sharply the others around the fire went silent and looked their way.

"Treasure from the ignorant thief, as dear as the object of theft," said the rude soldier's friend. "A finger or one cycle's imprisonment for the deliberate thief."

"Were you and your friend ignorant thieves or deliberate thieves of service due to the realm? Eh, Spartak? I ask you."

The soldier who had made the deal with Sid, answered quietly. "I do not know, Sir."

"I am not your grandmother—the one who should have taught you to honor the Seven as you would honor your own house," Crowseye answered. "But I will tell you that the dishonor you bring on yourself is far greater than any damage you bring to the realm. Complaints? Do I see complaints on your face, Spartak? Take it up with the head of your house, for I shall certainly inform my brother of this."

Spartak dropped his defiant gaze. For a moment, Sid thought Crowseye was done.

"Because it seems you have not grasped your mistake, you two shall serve my tea for the remainder of this venture and be reminded that even those born of the Seven serve their seniors."

The noble dismissed all of them. Sid and Harno hurried to the wagon without a word or backward glance.

Early in the morning, Sid curled on his side and contracted every muscle he had, fighting the need to relieve himself. It wasn't that he was afraid of the dark, it was being alone in it that he didn't like. But in his mind he saw Li rolling her eyes, and at last he crept out from under the wagon. Stumbling into a small wedge of forest hardly a stone's throw from the camp, he unknotted the drawstring of his pants and peed.

A twig snapped in the dark.

Fighting off thoughts of wraiths and vetalas that might have wandered beyond the edge of the Silver Wood, Sid finished as quickly as he could, but before he got his pants knotted, someone rushed him from behind and pushed him to the ground. Kicks slammed into his back, groin, ribs. He wanted to yell for help, but he was gasping for air. A weight fell upon him. He didn't see the fist that punched him before he blacked out.

When he came to the sky had begun to lighten. His eye hurt, and his side and backside were on fire. At the sound of someone approaching, he struggled to his feet, wincing all the while and quite unable to run away.

Greta lumbered among the trees as if she were out for a walk in the middle of the day. She stopped short some distance away and uncovered a lantern. "You are injured."

"Tripped on a root," he mumbled.

"Root punched your eye." She reached out to steady him as he hobbled forward, but he waved her away.

"Go on," he said. "I'm fine. Go away."

"Hmmm," Greta said. She took a few steps behind him and picked up something from the ground. It was his kufi. He snatched it back and limped away.

The boys parted around Sid as he staggered into camp. Even the wagonmaster stopped muttering breakfast instructions. Sid leaned against the wagon, holding his burning ribs, and the whispers spread until Crowseye appeared and peered closely at him. He directed a pair of boys to help him into the back.

"Your eye will be fine, and your legs work," Crowseye pronounced. "You'll heal."

Greta passed by, dropping a handful of bark on the camp table and proceeded to chop it up. After the noble left, she leaned over the side of the wagon and gestured at Sid's midsection with her chin.

"Kurta up."

With great effort he obliged. The giantess produced a jug filled with a dark mud, to which she added the bark, mixed it up, and smeared it over his injured ribs. While she worked strips of cloth under his back and around his chest, Sid almost stopped gritting his teeth, but then she gave a couple of tugs that made the pain roar back. Despite his gasping, the giantess continued to wrap his ribs with nothing more than the dull attention giants applied to every act.

"You should not have left him," she said, while tying a knot in the bandages. "Or her."

Surely the surprise could have been read on his face, but he thought it better to keep quiet. *Of course she knows Red. How many giants are there still in this world? Maybe she's related to him. But Li? How could she know about her?*

Greta left, and Sid stared into the sky above. Her words ripped loose whatever peace he had made with his decision to seek his destiny. She might have treated his injuries, but she also meant to wound him.

CHAPTER 6

Bearing east since she left Akroyat, the familiar ranks of oak, walnut, apinian, and fir trees had dwindled, and those remaining stood in contrast to a magnificently tall species of tree with pale bark and canopies of silvery green leaves. It was a beautiful forest, but the height of the new trees discombobulated Lingli, and they creaked and popped as if talking to each other. There were other oddities as well, but mainly it was the proportions of everything in the new forest that had changed, and she felt much shrunk down.

Becoming ever more anxious that she was falling farther behind Sid and the others, Lingli hurried along the Rajpath from dusk until the sun was tree-high, pausing only to look for food. The bounty of the fish and frog she had caught the previous evening would not last forever, and she could ill afford to miss whatever the forest might give, so when she discovered clusters of blue nightberries, she plucked them immediately.

They looked like those she had known in the Western Wood, only larger; but she heard Red clearly. *Strange fruit, leaves, roots shock bodies. Only one bite of new food a day.* Her mouth watered as she considered the plump berries rolling in her palm, but she gently dropped them into her pack.

Later, in a crease of damp ground between hills, she found a willow and scraped off long strips of bark, which could be boiled and used to clean wounds. Almost as uneasy about eating here as she had been near Akroyat, she even dug up some slickroot, the slimy base of a woodland plant that provided energy to anyone who could stand to chew it.

While adding the malodorous root to her pack, Lingli realized there was a pale gray stoat standing on its hind legs not more than a few skips away. It was shoulder-high—many times the size of any ordinary stoat. It drew back its lips to show its sharp teeth, and Lingli tightened her grip on her small knife.

The stoat's teeth were, however, clamped onto a vole the size of a cat, and the stoat was not so foolish as to drop its catch just to snarl at a startled girl. After a moment, it dropped to all fours and loped across the road, and Lingli hurried on, her heart racing. Red reminded her, *The world is not as strange as you. Trust that and find courage.*

She remembered an evening, cycles ago, when she and Sid and Red heard a large animal crashing through the brush. Red had plucked them up and carried them to a thicket, where they discovered an odd-looking deer in a tangle of briars. The poor beast lay on its side and panted as though it had run leagues. It was terribly thin, just skin over bone, with long sweeping antlers, one broken, and oddly shaped hooves. Its coat was darker and thicker than those of common deer, but most surprising were the small tusks that curled at the corners of its mouth. One eye, bloodred around the pupil, turned up toward them. Lingli was frightened, but she couldn't look away.

"What's wrong with it?" Sid asked. He clung tight to her hand.

"It has run a long time, and it is far from home," Red said.

"But no deer has tusks."

"You call this creature strange because you have never seen its kind before, but it is not strange to itself."

"It's very ugly," Sid insisted.

The red giant had answered, "We don't choose our life. We live it. This creature is no different."

"Can we feed it?" Lingli asked.

Red said. "Give it water."

Lingli went to the creek and carried back a leaf cup of water as best she could. As she dribbled water into the animal's mouth, Red held its head. The deer-thing blinked and swallowed, and Red let it rest. Sid was more than eager to leave, but she knelt by the creature and tentatively put her hand on its neck where she could feel its beating heart.

She remembered that Red seemed concerned by the animal's presence and sniffed the air for a long moment before hurrying them back home. The next day she accompanied Red to the thicket with an armful of hay, but the creature was gone.

Exhausted after a night of watching for giant stoats, Lingli cut her morning walk short when she spied a fallen silver tree not far from the road. The tree had crushed a fir when it fell, resulting in a jumble of broken branches that would cover her. She crawled under the branches and pulled some briars over the opening.

Her sleep was rarely deep, but she had hardly closed her eyes when she was jerked back to wakefulness. Something moved outside her hiding place. A shadow passed, followed by a soft clicking noise, then all was quiet. Eventually she stopped holding her breath and lay back, but when a howling cry rent the air, she bolted upright again.

Clicking sounds came from the direction of the road. Leaving her bower with her knife in one hand and fish spear in the other, Lingli crept toward the noise.

A dozen or more creatures clustered together in the middle of the Rajpath and slowly flicked their wings. Not birds. Winged insects. Butterflies. Their bodies were the length of her arm and covered with short, stiff hairs protruding from shiny carapaces. Their forewings, as big as bedsheets, featured beautiful arrays of orange and pink and creamy white. Each hindwing flashed a large brown and pink eye. When one of the creatures flicked its wings and rose, its antennae made the clicking noise she had heard earlier.

It settled down again near the shifting mass of the others, and Lingli prepared to back away until a hand rose out of the leaves and mud where the butterflies gathered. Someone feebly struggled underneath them, whimpering pitifully.

She hesitated, looking around for a trap, but she saw no one. Being attacked while helping a stranger was not her natural inclination, but it was plain that Ascaryans would be wise to help one another in this forest.

She charged into the road, yelling loudly.

The creatures rose into the air, their compound eyes swirling with iridescent colors as they faced her, hovering just beyond her reach. Only one remained intent on the body under it. Its long proboscis extended into a man's mouth, and its body pulsed obscenely as it fed.

The instant she threw her fishing spear at the flutter, they rose higher and separated. With her knife she stabbed wildly about the wings of the remaining creature as it pulled away from the Ascaryan beneath. Unsure whether she had struck any substantial part, Lingli was relieved to hear the crunch of its thin armor, followed by oily fluid spattering her cloak. The butterfly pitched forward and flapped a few beats before falling to the ground, its legs scrabbling.

The air around her continued to click, and she feared this would be a short retreat. Grabbing a handful of pebbles from the road, she spun around and threw them at the others, and they swarmed into the canopy of a silver tree. She stayed beyond the man's reach as he retched, gasped, and sat up.

"Are you whole?" she asked.

"Do I hear an ancestor?" the man replied in a hoarse voice. A dirty scrap of cloth still covered his nose and ears. He opened an eye that scarcely lit its cadaverous socket. "Not an ancestor. A ghost. My luck, my luck...all sucked away."

"I am not a ghost."

"Not a ghost, she says. Not a ghost. Not a ghost."

Mumbling to himself as if she was not there, the man rolled onto his side and pulled the face cloth down to his neck. Smears of mud, dry and fresh, striped his face and pasted down his long hair. With a weary sigh, he splayed his bony hands and pushed himself up.

Lingli took a step back and held tight to her knife.

He didn't move toward her but whispered as though he were telling her a secret. "They're learning. Oh, they're learning!" He winced and put a hand to his throat.

"Who are you?" she asked.

"No one," he said, eyeing her suspiciously. "Just a traveler. Yes, a traveler. Like yourself. And travel is what I must do. Must go. My son's waiting. He's in... Where was it? Time is passing too fast and too slow. Do you have any berries?"

"Berries?"

"Yes, those delicious blue ones, you know. Sazainga? Nightberries? So sweet sweet. I'm hungry. Always hungry. Always. They purge me quite often, you know."

Lingli took another step back and shook her head.

"Does the ghost think I'll harm her? That's not a ghostly thought. Not at all." The man weaved on his feet, looking as though he would fall in a strong wind. "Don't worry, ghost. The good deed shall be rewarded. I'll tell you what is obvious. If you eat the berries, they will come for you. You may fight them with your little knife. I had a bigger one once. Yes, I did, but they'll not leave off. Always hungry. See." He pushed up a sleeve to show his thin arm.

"You're just a big flower. And they love your juice. Ha!" The man adjusted the cloth over his nose and mouth again. "And if you don't eat, you'll die of hunger. Unless you're clever enough to catch something else. Oh, I have, I have. What day is it?"

"Twenty-third day of the eleventh moon," she answered.

"Eleventh *moon*? Eleventh *moons*, ghost! It's a bright cycle you know." The man looked upward as if the sky might give him a sign needed to resolve some dilemma.

"Mud's good," he said, gesturing to his face. "Slickroot—eat it. They'll ignore you if they can't smell you. I must go. My son's waiting. I'll pay his bond. Must go." And he commenced walking backward along the road the way Lingli had come. "Goodbye, ghost. Eat and die. Or don't eat and die. Of course, you're already dead so it doesn't matter." He giggled and turned away.

As soon as the man disappeared up the path, Lingli sprinted back to her hiding place. She poured out a little of her water into the leaf matter and made a thick mud, which she rubbed into her hair and over her face and arms. She took her pack to the road and dumped the nightberries out. From behind some brush, she watched the butterflies sweep down to taste the berries, then drift away again.

Keeping both her fishing spear and knife close, she walked through the afternoon with her hood up and her hands hidden in her cloak. Imagining a feathery rush of air behind her, she spun around more than once, but the butterflies remained in furled clumps high in the trees and ignored her.

On her third evening in the Silver Wood, the last bite of frog leg was gone. Nothing but slickroot remained, and she gagged when she put it to her lips. After forcing down two bites, with the dried mud in her hair cracking and sloughing off when she moved, she crept out of a patch of massive ferns to check her snare.

Like the previous days, the snare was empty. Though this disappointment seemed smaller than others, a sob leaked out, and she angrily rubbed her eyes. She heard the woods witch's accusation: *Self-pity will make you waste every step you've taken. For the sun's sake, move!*

Grabbing her pack, Lingli returned to the road and recalled the witch's last visit in the spring. In the early evening Lingli had found the old woman sitting in Red's huge chair knitting a scarf. For a moment Lingli was so happy she almost escaped the fog that she had wandered in since New Cycle Day. She fetched a kufi she had been embroidering for Sid, and the witch admired her work, praised it even and gave her some instruction, but as the old woman handed it back, she grabbed Lingli by the chin and forced her to look her straight in the eyes.

"Why are you hiding?"

Lingli was too shocked to do more than blink.

"Yes, I know, most of the villagers are vicious bastards without honor. They hurt you. Do you think they dwell on their cruelty and talk about it every day? Do you think they even remember you?" The witch clucked as tears welled up in Lingli's eyes.

"Stop crying! You have survived worse than this." The witch pulled her out of the cabin and turned her toward the west where the sun still sat on the horizon. "Look at it. Yes. Look!" Lingli squinted and shrank even as she tried to do as the witch commanded.

"There is your enemy. Not a day passes without the spirit of the First Father trying to kill you. And he has come much closer to succeeding than those stupid villagers. You don't remember it, but I have seen you so burned your head swelled. Your face was a sea of blisters and your small hands curled up into claws. We had to tie you down so you didn't scratch yourself to death."

The witch turned her around again to face her. "Are you a ghost? No. They did not kill you. You survived, girl. Why? To cut yourself up? To kill yourself? Do not give them the satisfaction. You must fight them. Always fight."

The witch loosened her grip. Almost gently, she touched the dark blue vein in Lingli's temple. "You are stronger than you know. Do not shame your ancestors."

But Lingli's emotions were shifting as fast as the witch's. How fear could turn into anger so quickly was quite beyond her understanding, but it took all her effort to not shove the old woman away. She wanted to scream, *What ancestors? Are they the ones who cursed me?*

Sid's mother had long, pretty hair and liked to make parathas, but what of hers? All Red would say about her beginning was that he had found her in a tree wrapped in a blanket, and that she was so small he had to trade for mare's milk to feed her. That was all. No mother. No father. No anyone. There was no past for her, never had been, never would be.

Forcing down a wave of bitterness, Lingli had wrenched free of the witch and returned to the cabin to make dinner. Images of clean, sharp knives and perfect lines of blood teased her all night, but the witch never let her out of her sight.

The next morning, as she climbed up into the loft to go to sleep, she remembered hearing the witch arguing with Red outside.

"It won't be long! Are you blind as well as stupid? Oh, give a giant a job, the simplest thing, and watch the oaf obstruct you." Red's answer was so low Lingli could not hear what he said. The witch was incensed. "Bright cycle or not, if you lose them now, after all this time, I will curse you until the last stone turns to sand. Do you understand? You are still bound, giant!"

As she trudged along, Lingli pondered once again whether "them" was Sid and her, and how Red could have possibly lost them, though they certainly had lost him in the end.

By the middle of that night, she was so tired she nodded on her feet. The Rajpath had dwindled to little more than a footpath as it looped around the side of a long hill, and after a couple of stumbles, she stopped to drink. Something in the woods caught her eye, and she lowered the waterskin to stare. All was dark for so long she almost gave up looking, then a bluish light brightened and faded at a spot among the trees. If the moons had been brighter, she likely would have missed it altogether. After a moment, the light shone again.

Whoever else might be in these woods was most likely a danger, but her stomach persuasively argued that they would also likely carry some supplies. Perhaps the bearer of this light was careless enough to miss a shadow pilfering food.

The blue light continued to brighten and dim as she stealthily moved toward it. Wondering if the display was some kind of signal, she stopped and looked behind, but everything in the shadow of the hill remained dark. Between her and the light was a scattering of boulders. Lingli tip-toed into thick brush behind one of them.

She counted to fifty. A sphere of light appeared in an open space ahead. Two tall figures were captured within it, facing the woods off to one side, their feet floating well above the ground.

Spirits?

The figures sharpened and faded, but when the light steadied, they saluted someone. Lingli peered in that direction but saw no one.

Both figures wore strange armor. The smaller one held a helmet of some kind under her arm, and she had short hair and pale skin. The other figure seemed male, given the breadth of his shoulders, but she wasn't certain. His helmet covered his whole head. The woman spoke first, and her words were direct and forceful, though in an unknown language. A moment later the other figure gestured in various directions while he spoke. When the woman spoke again, their images and the sphere flickered. There was a low, hissing noise. Their voices faded, and both figures suddenly leaned to one side as if they had lost their balance. The woman began to urgently repeat the same words she had used before; then the light and figures abruptly disappeared, and the woods were silent.

Lingli held her breath. This was otherworld magic unlike anything she had ever seen. After another interval, the light returned, and the figures repeated the same sequence. She watched the scene repeat itself three more times. This pair seemed to suffer a curse of some kind, and being one familiar with curses, she instinctively felt sorry for them.

All went quiet and dark again. She moved quickly to the next boulder to look at these beings from another angle, but when the sounds resumed, she could no longer see them or the sphere. All she saw was a point of blue light, as bright as a flame, that seemed to come from under a fallen log. The hairs on her arms stood on end.

She backed away, putting her hand on one of the boulders, but the boulder wasn't stone. It and the others, she realized, were made of metal. Tremendous power and skill would have been needed to make such things, and who knew for what purpose. Her curiosity shrank as her fear grew.

Flitting back to the road, Lingli put as much distance between herself and the spirits as she could. Her thoughts congealed on one thing—these woods were a trap. Startling at every noise, she limped along until dawn and paused only to gnaw at the nub of slickroot and drink the last of her water. Abandoning the idea of finding shelter, she pulled her hood forward as far as it would go, kept her hands hidden in her sleeves, and staggered on.

Late the following day, or maybe the next, long-tailed swallows blew across the path in front of her. Despondent and weak, Lingli stopped to watch them chase each other up into the sky, and when she looked ahead again, she found that the silver trees had thinned while she stumbled along. Near the edge of the road stood a grove of normal-sized chikoo trees heavy with fruit.

Pulling a rusty brown fruit from a branch, Lingli sniffed it. She meant to take only one bite, but then realized she had eaten the whole thing. Shrugging off her pack, she plucked and ate. She threw up, then ate some more before she lay down in the shade.

Sleep must have come, for the next thing she knew a boot was crushing her throat, and she was gasping for air.

"Get back!" someone shouted.

"By the First Mother, did you see its eyes, and what's that on the side of its head?!" said someone else.

She was summarily flipped over with her arms twisted behind her back. *Always fight!* the witch told her, but the instant a rope slithered around her wrists while someone's knee ground away at her spine, panic compressed her lungs and she could hardly breathe, much less fight.

Once bound, she was hauled to her feet, and a gag was forced into her mouth, bunching up under her hood so that only by tilting her chin could she see under the edge. Three faces. A bearded young man, a boy a little younger than herself, and a girl with braids. They wore vests over their kurtas and the tight pants worn by horse people. In fact, they stank of horses, but judging from their faces, she smelled worse.

Though the oldest one sheathed his long hunting knife, the fierceness of his expression told her he would not hesitate to put it through her. When the girl stepped around him, he put a restraining hand on her shoulder.

"You cannot escape," her captor told her slowly in the common tongue, his accent heavy. "It would be wise for you to tell us what we want to know. What is your name?"

Do they have Sid nearby? Should I tell them my name?

Lingli calculated. This sharp-eyed youth had younger ones to protect. *Cousins, or two brothers and their sister.* She nodded, and her captor signaled to the other boy to pull her gag down.

"Ling—" she said, choking on her own voice. "Lingli Tabaan."

"What kind of name is that?" asked the girl.

The young man's eyes never left her. "Who are your people, and where are they?"

"My people? I have no people. My…brother was taken away by…others."

She had no choice but to call Sid her brother. Whatever their relationship was, it was too complicated to explain. Besides, who would believe someone had wandered through the Silver Woods for a friend?

The boys discussed what they should do, and the girl pushed her way into their conversation uninvited. After putting Lingli's gag back in, the older one told the girl, "Watch her. We'll scout around. If any of her kin are close, they will be looking for her before it gets dark."

"But I don't want—" the girl began, until the young man raised his hand. The girl glared at him and fell quiet.

When they were gone, the girl circled her. "Don't think about running, you filthy witch," she hissed. "If I cry out, my brothers will run you through like this!" She made a stabbing motion and then climbed into the low branches of one of the chikoo trees to watch her.

In less than an hour, the brothers returned and made Lingli walk between them. Though it wasn't quite dark, the younger boy lit a torch and held it close to her. She flinched.

"What? Afraid of fire?" the younger boy sneered. He asked his brother, "You think it might be of the otherworld?"

"Be quiet. Pa and the others will say."

The girl ran ahead, and not long after her captor grabbed Lingli's shoulder and turned her around to face the way they had come, but she had already smelled the wood smoke and seen horses tethered not far ahead.

Soon three older men appeared, and Lingli knew they were wanderers—the loud, nomadic people who, on occasion, appeared in the Western Woods in painted wagons to trade horses and goods. The value of their talents barely kept pace with the general opinion that they were born charlatans.

The oldest man was gray-headed and simply dressed, but the others behaved as though he was their chief. The second man had thick brows, and a waxed mustache that curled upward at the ends. Though he would have drawn attention in most places, he was almost nondescript compared to the third man, who wore half a dozen golden chains, earrings and finger rings, and a large brass clip fashioned in the shape of the sun on his turban.

The mustached man spoke to her captors. "There were no signs of others?"

The older one shook his head. "No one nearby."

"Take her gag out."

Lingli took a breath and tried to swallow. Her lips had cracked again, and she tasted blood. The oldest man flicked her hood back, and all of their faces tensed.

The mustached man growled at her, "What are you doing in the Silver Woods?"

"I'm looking for my brother."

The old man's eyebrows shot up. "So there are others with you?"

"No, he…was taken, and I am trying to find him."

"Taken by whom?"

"The Seven."

The old man snorted. "Put the gag back in."

"No, please. I'll—" But the gag was back in her mouth before she could finish.

"Keep her out here, away from the horses," the mustached man said.

As her captor tied her to a small tree, Lingli counted her breaths and chewed on the inside of her cheek. *Survive first, then fight.*

It wasn't long before the girl reappeared with an old woman carrying a bowl of soup. Bone bracelets clicked and clacked from the old woman's wrists to her elbows as she planted herself in front of Lingli and stirred the bowl with a spoon.

Obediently opening and closing her mouth for each spoonful the old woman offered (and more grateful than the wanderers would ever know), Lingli ignored the girl making faces at her. No one spoke. The old woman seemed to be measuring her before she took the bowl away and ordered the girl to return to camp with her.

She knew she needed to be vigilant, but she was so tired. With the rope loose enough to allow her to sit on the ground, she leaned against the tree trunk and watched the flames of the wanderers' campfire through the trees until her half-full stomach betrayed her and her eyes closed of their own accord.

A sharp poke, and Lingli jolted awake again. It was deep night. A lantern illuminated the faces of several people around her, and every muscle she had tensed.

She was fairly certain the closest woman was the one who had brought the soup, but she now wore a long robe and a half mask with dangling charms. The men she had seen earlier stood on either side of the woman. Behind them several youths, including the elder one who had captured her, darted looks at each other. Fear bubbled in her gut.

"What are we to make of you?" the old man said. "Should we believe you are a girl alone, wandering the Silver Woods? Or do we stand guard for an attack by who knows what?"

The man decorated with shining chains and jewelry said, "It reeks of slickroot and that poisoned trap around Akroyat. Maybe it's possessed by a spirit from that vile place—come to steal our breath while we sleep."

"You're full of poetic notions, Anil," the old man said, "but let's deal with what is plain. Whatever else it may be, it is also certainly a spy trailing us. That won't do. Common sense tells me it would be best to dispose of it as quickly as possible."

Lingli tried to speak, but the gag muffled her voice.

The old man shook his head. While he, the other older men, and the woman spoke in hushed voices, one of the younger men elbowed the fellow next to him and said, "I wouldn't touch that for a bag of silver. It's unnatural. Probably cast out of its clan."

Another said, "It's so…weak looking. Disappointing for a bright cycle demon."

"Ha!" said the first one. "That's what it wants you to think."

When the elders turned their attention back to her, Lingli saw that two of the men wore long daggers at their sides.

The old man said, "Our healer has persuaded us that she can remove any disguise you may be using. If you are Ascaryan, we will know. If you are something else, we will know."

The man with the mustache stepped behind her and hauled her to her feet. She was certain that his blade would cut her throat, but he did nothing. Instead, everyone watched the masked woman. She produced a small clay cup.

Catching a horrid, rancid smell, Lingli shook her head and clamped her jaws shut.

Then the mustached man pulled down her gag and slapped her so hard she saw stars falling before her eyes. Grabbing her by the chin, he squeezed until her lips parted. The woman poured the drink into her mouth steadily though she struggled and gagged.

Starting in her stomach, all feeling in her body seemed to vanish. She fell to her knees then on her side. She was awake as they laid her out flat on her back with her bound hands above her head, but she could no longer feel the rope or her hands or her legs.

Drawing a blade from her sleeve, the woman straddled Lingli's thighs and Lingli waited for the panic to stop her heart. The woman pushed Lingli's kurta up and placed her hand on the center of her belly just above her navel, making the skin taut. Lingli's eyes crossed as she watched the woman lower the blade until its tip touched her skin. She could make no more sound than a muted grunt.

Leaning close, the woman whispered, "I have a steady hand, but this will be messy. Watch the stars, nothing else."

The woman began cutting. Lingli fainted.

CHAPTER 7

Something was happening. Boys chattered excitedly all around Sid, who pretended to sleep in the back of the wagon.

"Welcome to Saatkulom!" he heard Crowseye proclaim.

The team came to a stop, and he listened to the small thuds of the recruits as they jumped from the wagon to the ground. Opening his good eye just a little, Sid stared into a clear blue sky. Once he was alone in the wagon, he rolled onto his good side and cautiously raised his head high enough to look out.

No grand palace. No mighty walls or armored soldiers. Only the vast sky covering a plain that stretched as far as he could see, the panorama punctuated by a few trees and bushes in the tall, dry grass. When Sid's gaze fell back to the staggered edge of the forest behind, he saw the wagon-master and both nobles standing over the driver, Jeevan. They examined a wheel on the ratha, and Jeevan shook his head. Nearby, Spartak and his friend lay in the grass and laughed with other soldiers. They had not forgotten about him, he knew, but more worrisome was the giantess trudging his way. He slid back down into the wagon bed.

If Greta knew he was awake, she didn't say anything before she opened the bandages and applied more mud to his ribs. After she left, he stayed still while the midday meal was served. Eventually Harno remembered to bring him a bowl of beans, but the other boys did not return to the wagon. It seemed they would go no farther that day.

The afternoon sunlight was so bright, it gave Sid a headache even with his eyes closed. *How do people live in this place?* Jealous of the boys stretched out in the shade of the forest, he snatched someone's forgotten scarf and covered his face, but sleep evaded him. When he heard the rani call out to Master Vaksana, Sid again raised himself high enough to see.

One of the young archers from the House of Satya looked on miserably as Master Vaksana struggled to hold her horse. The rani, dressed in a riding kurta and pants, approached.

"Give me the reins, brother," she told him. "He's caught the wolf scent on you."

Master Vaksana seemed loath to leave, but the rani waved him off. Though the top of her head didn't reach the horse's withers, she planted her legs wide and gradually shortened the distance between them. Finally, she placed her hands lightly on the horse's muzzle and whispered to it. Sid could see the horse's ears flick nervously, but it stood still. The rani ran her hands along its side then swung up onto the creature's back in one fluid movement.

As soon as her heels touched its sides, the animal burst eastward with Her Majesty bent close against its neck, her long dark hair flying behind. Everyone watched as she and her mount disappeared into a draw, then emerged from the sea of grass and raced up the next rise. In seconds, she and the horse became a singular speck atop a distant ridge.

Suddenly, a cutting board was thrust in front of Sid's face. The wagon master's eyes shone with glee at having caught him out, and he slammed half a dozen potatoes down on the board. Sid peeled and chopped slowly as the forest's shadows lengthened. The others' voices were lost in the wind, and the big sky pricked at his conscience, setting loose memories of Red's cry, the wolf bounding toward Lingli, Greta's words. His heart wavered, but he fought its mutiny to defend his choices.

The witch said I had to seek my destiny, not wait for it. I'd never make it back anyway. And if I did, how could I face them?

Like a storm, the rani galloped back into the camp with her mount frothing with sweat. A smile lit her face as she jumped down and handed the reins to the anxious archer. Her happy attitude reminded Sid of the day he met her. He watched her untie a scarf holding red, round fruits that she set on the camp table.

"Anars," she said excitedly to those helping to prepare dinner. "Out here in the beyond. Can you believe that? Tonight we will all eat well thanks to the ancestors!"

She turned and tossed one of the fruits to Sid with a joyous laugh. He grinned and did his best to give no sign of the pain that erupted when he reached out to catch the fruit. She knew him. That was all that mattered.

The sky above had become a violet wash of starlight from the Doodhnadi. His thoughts of returning to the cabin faded as quickly as the blazing day.

That evening the proximity of the Rock seemed to have enthused the party as much as it had the rani, for they sang boisterous songs and jokes almost too colorful to speak in front of their ruler. After a few rounds, the rani beckoned the wagonmaster, telling him to give them pieces of the anars she had collected.

With a piece of the ruby red fruit in the palm of her hand, the rani asked all those around the fire, "Do you know why we say that the anar is a good fortune fruit?" No one volunteered an answer. She shook her head. "The recruits are excused, but the rest of you should know. It seems I need to speak to Master Avani about the extent of your history lessons. I will tell you the story of the anar while you eat the ones I plucked for you, but keep one of the seeds.

"You all know of Starfall, yes? It was a time when Ascarya Erde suffered ferocious storms. The sea rose. Mountains broke. And stars fell from the sky and scorched whole settlements, killing countless Ascaryans and other living things. We know of this from our chronicles, and this story particularly is one from the House of Vaksana." The rani paused and touched the arm of Master Vaksana who sat beside her. "This is your story, Brother Jordak. I am pleased to share the meaning of the anar, unless you would like to tell it?"

The wolfmaster shook his head. "No, m-my rani. You do my h-house an honor by telling our story. P-please tell it. These... They should know."

"Then I shall tell you how the ancestors of the House of Vaksana wandered the forests and plains far to the northwest—farther than the Western Woods, and farther than any of you or I have ever journeyed."

Her audience was snared quickly. Everyone, including Sid, listened intently as she described the travails of that age.

"The ancestors of the House of Vaksana wandered for cycles seeking a new home, and among the members of this clan was a young girl. She had spent her whole life running from storms, bandits, and wild people, and even creatures of the otherworld who were more common then. Her name was Padmini—a common name for girls who brought some beauty to their parents' hard lives.

"In those times, once each cycle, this clan had weddings for all the youth old enough to marry and for those who had lost their spouse but might still have children. To marry was a duty. It didn't matter if you wanted to marry. It didn't matter if you had to marry a cousin or an older aunt or uncle. Only one thing mattered, and that was bringing forth children to guarantee that the family would go on. Padmini would marry a young man called Jordak."

Several in the crowd chuckled at the mention of the name, which was also Master Vaksana's name, and Sid sensed some joke was at play from the way the rani raised her brows at the blushing noble.

"There was great excitement as the day of the weddings drew near. Despite their suffering, the clan made tributes and they feasted. But their happiness was short-lived. When they raised their voices in song to bless the newly married couples, they were attacked without warning. The House of Vaksana tells us that demons came from the sky that day, wielding white fire that struck people like flaming arrows. The elders stood shoulder to shoulder before their descendants, but they were no match for such otherworldly powers."

Sid huddled against a bag of lentils in the back of the wagon—both glad the others couldn't see how uncomfortable these kinds of tales made him, and wishing he was closer to the fire. As he scanned the others' faces, Spartak caught his eye and the delight in his expression ensured that Sid would not leave the wagon again that night.

"With nothing but their wedding clothes, Padmini and Jordak fled. The couple ran for days, hiding and watching for asuras in the sky. With no supplies, no tools, no medicines, they had to survive by their wits alone. And they grieved deeply, for they knew they might be the last members of their families.

"For three moons they wandered. The evil ones disappeared, but Jordak became ill. Burning with a fever that would not break, he no longer knew his wife. Padmini hid him and hunted for food and medicinal plants alone until one day, just before the sun's light disappeared, she found a small tree with red, round fruits. She had never seen such fruit before."

Whispers of "anar" circled the fire.

"Padmini was relieved but also afraid, for she did not know whether they could eat of this tree. She plucked a fruit and brought it to her lips, but she could not find the courage to eat. Seeking the wisdom of her family, she made a small fire and presented the only decoration that remained from her wedding day, a necklace woven from her mother's hair. Calling upon her ancestors, she asked for a sign as to whether to eat this new fruit or not."

The rani paused. There was not a sound in the camp but the snapping of the fire. "An ancestor appeared to her," she said quietly.

Many of the listeners shifted uneasily, including Sid. The woods witch had warned of such matters. Calling the ancestors was dangerous and not a thing to be done lightly.

"The House of Vaksana says that the ancestor's clothing shone like the sun, and he could fly, so naturally Padmini trembled in his presence, but the ancestor told her to fear not. When she asked the ancestor to heal her husband, he told her that Jordak's fever had already broken. He took the anar she had plucked and rubbed a powder on it before cutting the fruit in half to show Padmini that the seeds of the fruit were like jewels in their beauty and worth. Seeds that were not bitten but swallowed whole would make them strong, the ancestor said, but for every fruit they ate, they should plant one seed, and water it with a drop of blood so that the anar would thrive and feed those who would come after them. Then the ancestor disappeared in a shimmering light.

"At their camp, Padmini and Jordak ate the anar, and they were careful to keep one seed to plant. As the ancestor had foretold, Jordak grew strong again, and they continued on their star course. A few months later, at the old camp near Daza Tumuli, Padmini gave birth to a healthy girl who was named Asha, and from that time the eldest girl child of each generation has been given that same name in the House of Vaksana, just as the eldest boy child is given the name Jordak."

Sid shook his head to free himself from the story's spell. Everyone was quiet.

"Now," the rani said, "the tale is done but not the duty. Each of you give me the seed you saved."

Master Vaksana rose and collected the seeds from everyone. As the noble came close to the wagon, Sid realized he had eaten every seed in his piece. He felt about the wagon bed where the anars had been stored to see if a piece had been left behind. Nothing. Sid showed Master Vaksana his empty hands. Giving him a scolding look, the wolfmaster pulled a seed from his own pocket and dropped it onto the tray before he returned to the rani.

Using a small dagger on her belt, the rani pricked one finger and held it over the seeds in the tray, letting the blood drip down.

"We will plant these, in memory of Padmini, Jordak, and their daughter—their hope. In appreciation for nature's bounty, the wisdom of the ancestors, and the gifts they have granted." The rani raised the tray above her head. "May each of you have many descendants healthy and whole—for the strength of the realm!"

All repeated, "For the strength of the realm!" and saluted their rani.

Two days later, all excitement over the open land and sky had evaporated. The recruits pitched back and forth in the wagon as if it were a ship on a sea of grass, and each boy tried to suppress the unease common among those used to leafy shade and shorter vistas.

The sound of a horn could barely be heard over the wind, but Zarin pointed eastward to where Crowseye and the herald waited on a hilltop. When the party reached them, they stopped, and Crowseye called the boys to join him. He pointed toward a singular mountain that was hardly more than a dark smudge far to the east and south.

"Behold the Rock," he said. "For forty-two generations the home of Saatkulom, anchor of Safed Qila, and foundation of Chandrabhavan. Most of you will continue with me to Nilampur, but whether you stay on the Rock or at the lake, you will be trained in the ways of our realm, how to live with others, and how to serve. Try to appreciate the chance you've been given to serve honorably and try not to disgrace your house or ours while you are with us."

This last remark had been delivered with his gaze resting on Sid and Harno, but Sid was untroubled. The sight of the far mountain made his heart swell with the conviction that this way promised the destiny he had wished for.

After a long ride and a short night in the fields, Sid and the boys awoke to find that the Rock now dominated their vision. Arguing among themselves about whether the Rock had emerged from the ground or the ground had worn away from the Rock, they gradually discerned ledges, folds, and projections as well as changes in color that marked different mineral veins. Objects made by Ascaryan hands became visible—particularly the immense gate set in a wall that wound its way up the southeast side.

The party passed along the base of the Rock among boulders that seemed like pebbles in comparison with the monolith. When they stopped between two boulders as tall as trees in the Silver Woods, Sid was disappointed, but it was obvious the horses were too winded to make the climb ahead. Crowseye rode alone to the whitewashed gate that was hung with bright banners and disappeared inside.

While the rest of the recruits restlessly explored the gate and the scattered boulders, Sid took care to stay within sight of Master Vaksana just in case Spartak and his friends got any ideas.

By the middle of the day Crowseye returned, accompanied by eight men bearing a palanquin on their shoulders. The bearers were of similar stature, and all wore blue pants and kurtas with white vests and turbans. With their foreheads touching the ground, they waited until the rani came down from her vehicle.

She wore a dark blue lehenga studded with tiny starbursts of silver thread. Her anklets tinkled as she arranged herself in the palanquin, then the bearers rose to their feet as one and hoisted her high.

Sitting in the shade of the ratha, Sid watched the rani signal Crowseye to come close.

"At sunset I will meet you at the second gate and receive your advice," he heard her say, "but one night is all we can afford you, brother. You must reach Nilampur as soon as possible. We have little more than two moons to complete the construction before New Cycle Day."

Crowseye drew in his breath, as if he would speak, but then bowed his head and stepped back. The rani's slim hand darted through the curtains and grasped his arm.

"I know you don't approve," she said, "but I need your support in this more than any other endeavor. Nilampur is as critical to our future as rain and rubies."

Crowseye nodded. "It will be as you command, my sister."

The bearers loped off at the rani's command, followed by Greta and Master Vaksana and the wolf wearing its brass-plated harness. Then the remainder of the party prepared for the climb ahead. With the teams harnessed and the soldiers remounted, they lined up behind Crowseye and approached the gate.

As soon as the noble gave the password, the winches groaned as the portcullis rose and the huge wooden inner doors opened. Once the rear guards passed through, soldiers closed the doors again, pulling down a thick bar to secure them.

The high, whitewashed wall edging the path prevented them from falling off the mountainside, but it also obscured the view, and the boys took turns jumping out of the wagon to peer through archers' slits and report on the heights. Laboring upward for almost an hour, the horses' heads hung low by the time they reached the second gate—one equal in size to the first and far more decorated. Above the man-high foundation, a pattern of stars and the houses' insignias were depicted in colorful inlaid stones on the gate towers.

Zarin sat next to Sid in the wagon and pointed out, "A wheel, a bear, a blade, a tree, a swan," he said. "What's the sixth one?

"A chinkara," Harno answered, squinting at a symbol high above. "And the seventh is…"

"An owl," Sid said. He had studied the soldiers' brooches and learned all the house insignias.

In the center of the arch that connected the gate towers was a great sun of bright metal encircled by seven shining stars—the emblem of Saatku-lom. Blue and gold pennants flapped on poles atop the gate and along the walls on either side.

The guards opened the portcullis only enough to clear the top of the ratha. Awed, Sid held his breath as they passed through the gate tower, which was four wagon lengths thick. The other recruits also fell quiet when they reached the other side and realized they were surrounded by archers poised on high ledges like birds of prey. With the weary joy of those returning home, the young women who had accompanied them peeled away from the party and climbed steep staircases to join their comrades. Jeevan drove the ratha's team onward, but Crowseye directed the soldiers and the supply wagon into an enclosed yard to one side of the main path.

While the soldiers watered their horses, the recruits got down from the wagon and followed Crowseye through a hedge of gnarled thorn trees. They entered the mouth of a broad fissure cracking the rock face, and Sid saw that the stone on both sides was riddled with cave openings.

Before one of these caves, Crowseye stopped and pressed his hands together. Soon half a dozen children-that-were-not-children emerged. They were short and thin beings, and they walked stiffly. Their arms were longer than they should have been, and their foreheads slanted back from their brows.

Crowseye spoke quietly to the one who seemed to be the leader simply by virtue of his willingness to draw closest to the noble. He listened to Crowseye, who gestured toward the boys and the soldiers behind, then this small being and the others like him disappeared into the fissure.

Four more of the strange beings emerged from a cave carrying a string of pots on limber poles, which they set at the boys' feet.

"These are the zhoukoo," Crowseye said. "They lived here when the Seven arrived."

"Are they demons?" one of the boys asked, looking suspiciously at the small beings who stirred the pots.

"They are not," Crowseye said, "and watch your tongue. They can hear you, and they are not stupid. The zhoukoo share the Rock with us and have helped build everything you see."

Silently, the zhoukoo filled bowls with stew and passed them out. When the recruits saw Crowseye eat, they did as well. More zhoukoo emerged from the fissure with grain and fresh hay for the horses.

After eating, the boys claimed scraps of shade and whispered to each other about the zhoukoo and what they imagined lay within the fort until the sun fell below the wall and more mounted soldiers and a noble rode into the yard ahead of the rani's palanquin bearers. The soldiers came to attention, and Sid and the other recruits got to their feet.

The newly arrived noble was a lithe Ascaryan who wore a bear brooch on his shoulder. *Master Duvanya, commander of their defenses. He's the one I want to serve.*

"I've already chosen two dozen from Brother Jalil's latest collection," Master Duvanya said to Crowseye and the rani. "That's as many as we can start training until those from the House of Hudulfah move up." He told Crowseye, "You should take all these to Nilampur."

"*After* I make my selection," the rani said, giving both nobles a flat look.

"I need more soldiers to serve in this moon and the next," Crowseye said.

The rani's face flashed. "I will not see our soldiers turned into ditch diggers."

"I would not have them assigned to such work," Crowseye said. "With the number of southerners Prince Hassan has reportedly invited to oversee work on the market, I will be pressed to safeguard the camps, much less the other properties."

Master Duvanya answered lightly. "We can lend Nilampur most of this company and a few more from barracks."

Sid thought the rani looked little like the woman who had raced across the fields only days earlier. Her lips were pressed thin, and she seemed tired.

Crowseye called them to attention and spoke to all the recruits.

"Three days' ride from here, at the southern border of our realm, we are building the city of Nilampur on the shores of the new lake. One day Nilampur will become the greatest trading city and the finest oasis south of the Rock. As foretold by our late ruler, Raja Basheer, the people of Saatkulom and our southern allies will live there in friendship under a common treaty.

"A few of you will be required to begin service in the palace, by the maharani's word. The rest will accompany me to complete the market-place and compounds promised to the Seven and the Avakstan houses that have pledged allegiance. You will be fed and housed there. Now form a line."

Tugging at one of the fine chains around her neck, the rani still looked quite annoyed as she began her selection. Just before she reached Sid, she paused, but he saw it was Harno she was considering.

Of course, he's the smallest after all. How's he going to build a city? Why couldn't I be smaller?

The rani nodded at Crowseye.

"Fetch your bag, boy, and wait over there," Crowseye said.

The rani moved in front of Sid but remained unsmiling, implacable as the Rock itself.

Just breathe. Try to look useful. Red said one should always be useful.

To Sid's utter disbelief, she moved down the line and chose another boy.

"All of you reload supplies as instructed," Crowseye called out. "We rest here tonight and leave for Nilampur at dawn."

The other boys began moving, but Sid simply stood and blinked. He didn't want to dig ditches. He had to remain on the Rock if he was to make something of himself. Nothing else made sense.

Stunned, Sid watched the rani settle herself inside the palanquin once again. Through the sheer curtains, he thought she turned her face toward him, but the wagonmaster pushed him into a line where the zhoukoo passed supplies to the recruits. The old man was yelling, but Sid heard nothing until a hand fell on his shoulder.

"I suppose finding a scribe was too much to hope for," Crowseye said with a sigh. "Get your things," He tilted his head toward where Master Duvanya and his men waited near the archway. Harno and the two other boys the rani had chosen were already astride soldiers' horses there.

"Wh-what? She didn't…"

"She did. Shut up and go. If you have any sense, you'll keep your eyes open and your mouth closed."

After grabbing his bag and nodding to Zarin, who looked more glum than usual when he realized he would be continuing without his friends, Sid approached one of Master Duvanya's soldiers. The man pulled him up behind the saddle as easily as if he were a small child. As they moved out of the yard, he saw Spartak among those bound for Nilampur. The anger in the soldier's face was unmistakable, but Sid could not resist making a very tiny gesture of farewell before they passed under the archway and entered Safed Qila.

Brilliant daylight shot directly through a narrow window and hit Sid in the face. It took him a moment to remember where he was. Stone walls, floor, ceiling. His hand rested on a proper blanket. He was in a narrow bed, not on the ground, and the bed was in the palace—Chandrabhavan.

Burying his face in the pillow to inhale the scent of his good fortune, Sid heard the clattering sounds of a busy yard and remembered what high and bright sunlight meant. He jerked upright and pulled on his kurta and boots. Hadn't someone last night said something about training in the morning? It was still so confusing. He hadn't been picked and then he had, and no one told him why.

Outside his room dust motes floated through the hallway. Locks hung from all the doors except his. The hallway ended in a round gallery at the center of a tower where inlaid stones depicted a massive sun covering the floor, and the ceiling, several floors above, was painted like a starfield. A broad staircase before him was tempting, but a small door on the far side of the gallery looked familiar. Sid recalled that Master Duvanya's soldier had left him at the feasting hall the night before. The others had left with a steward, but Greta told him to follow her, and she had led him to a door in the tower that she barely fit through.

Behind the small door, Sid found a short flight of stairs that led outside. To his right, a covered walkway passed over a gate that connected the tower to the hall ahead. To the left, a garden smelling of thyme was tucked between a hedge and a high bluff that crowded the back of the tower.

At the corner of the hall, he passed through an archway and entered a much larger yard. The rock face at the back made the hall and even the tower he had exited seem puny in comparison. Another hall with an open veranda perched on a shelf of rock at the base of the bluff, and grooms led horses from stables nearby. On the opposite side of the yard two more smaller buildings huddled near a well where laundresses drew water and slapped clothing against knobs of rock.

Sid turned in a circle, taking in everything. The magnificence of these constructions, all finer and larger than any he had seen in his entire life, was overwhelming.

Climbing the steps of a stone platform, he entered the back of the closest hall. A few boys washed vessels in long sinks, and another stood at a table cutting the tops off onions. *The kitchens.*

"I, um, I was looking for the training yard," Sid said.

"You're nearly there." The boy cutting onions gestured with his head at another doorway on the far end of the room.

Sid's nose told him food was close, but he couldn't afford to be any later for duty. The next gate outside was ajar, and he slipped through to find himself in another large yard with two broad-crowned trees shading a hall hung with blue and yellow banners.

A group of boys and young men sat under the trees, and a noble whose beard was streaked with gray paced around a table where a scribe was writing. Owl brooches glinted on both the noble's and the scribe's shoulders. *House of Avani.* Sid stopped, unsure. When the old noble noticed, he waved him over.

"There's the missing one," he said to his scribe. "Take down his details when I dismiss the first group." Turning back to the others, he continued, "As I was saying, we will observe your skills and talents in several occupations over the next two moons. By the next cycle, you will be assigned to the post where we believe you will serve best. Come to the table as I call your name and take your supplies. Those in defense training should make a group here. Miners there. Those on stable duty there. Kitchen duty over there."

Sid waited while names were called, and recruits joined one group or the other. His face reddened when he stood alone, groupless.

"We will find a place for you, don't worry," the noble said. "Wait here with Parth while I deliver our new tunnelers to Roshan Sir." He clapped at the mining group and told them to follow.

The scribe, Parth, tapped on the parchment in front of him and asked, "Are you Sid Sol? Do you want to send your first cycle's wages home?"

Send them? She gave me my full wages. Sid nodded warily.

Parth made a tic on the parchment. "Fine. We'll tell the paymaster. Father's name?"

"Uh, my guardian?"

"Real father."

"I don't know."

"Well, you're not the first. You'll keep your own accounts then."

"No, I...I want to send some coin home."

"Very well. Your guardian's name?"

"The Red Giant."

Parth stopped writing. "I don't know what you're playing at, but I am not stupid."

"I guess I don't know his real giant name." Sid said.

"Sit over there. Tell your story to Master Avani."

Sid sat near those chosen for defense training. His friend from the journey, Harno, was in the middle of the group, huddled like a chick fallen into a nest of crows. *How could it be that the smallest recruit of all has been picked for defense training?* Sid considered going over to talk to Harno and quietly joining his group, but before he could work up the courage to try such a stunt, Master Avani returned.

"That one, Sid Sol, thinks he's amusing." Parth read from the parchment. "Says his guardian is a red giant."

The noble looked quickly at Sid then turned his attention back to the list. "We'll correct that later," he said. "Put him on kitchen duty to start."

Parth sneered as he handed Sid a folded apron.

Soon Sid was back in the room he had passed through earlier with a few more boys. A rotund man in a crisp white kurta met them.

"Your new bearers, Korvar Sir," Master Avani said.

"How wonderful. This kitchen can use as many young ones as you provide," the chef said. "One cycle ago, seventy-seven Ascaryans in the palace. Today, one hundred and four. Tomorrow, who knows? And all must eat every day." Korvar stared closely at each of the recruits. "There is no rest for my staff until late at night, and we are the first to work in the morning. Truly life is unfair. But ours is glorious work. Without the kitchens, the palace would be an empty, lonely place."

Master Avani told the boys, "What you do here will affect the opportunities that come afterward. Do not disappoint me or Korvar Sir."

When the noble departed, Korvar rubbed his fat hands together. "We will start with cleaning—your hands, the vegetables, and the stations. We do not poison people here. Not even the people who are rude and unworthy of our food. Put on your aprons and come with me."

CHAPTER 8

When Lingli woke her stomach throbbed and her bound arms were numb, but someone had bandaged her middle and thrown a blanket over her. She pretended to be unconscious when the mustached man and his son brought a litter to where she lay and did not make a sound when they placed her on it, though her middle burned. Wanderers whispered as they carried her past them.

"If it comes near my children, I'll kill it," a woman's voice hissed.

A man answered, "Quiet. Tiadona has seen the blood."

They deposited her into the back of one of the wagons. Someone put a hand to her head, but she didn't move. After they left, she opened her eyes. Her pack was gone, and everything had been removed from her cloak's hem and her pockets, even Sid's bracelet and the hawk brooch that she had kept pinned inside her kurta's collar.

As the wagon jerked forward, the skin on her stomach pulled taut, making her eyes tear. Her bound hands made it impossible to brace herself until she rolled onto her side and huddled against the wagon's side, gasping with pain whenever the wheels bumped.

Trying hard to focus on anything besides her stomach, Lingli eavesdropped on the girl's chatter from the bench. She could hear a woman answering the girl and felt sure she was the same one who had cut her the night before. Tiadona. The girl's name was Rekha. The mustached man was Rekha's father and called Rahman. Her brothers were Samir and Sachin.

When the caravan stopped for the evening, Tiadona poked her head through the canvas behind the driver's bench and climbed into the wagon bed. She knelt and untied Lingli.

Run. I must run.

After two bounding steps toward the back of the wagon, Lingli stumbled. Pain blossomed in her stomach. Leaning against the side of the

93

wagon, she covered her midsection with her arms and bit down on the inside of her cheek.

"I can treat you now or not," Tiadona said. "Of course, if you choose not, you will have fever by tonight."

The old woman didn't look as frightening as she had in the night, but the moons knew what they would do with her. And they had her things. And she didn't know where she was anymore. Reluctantly, Lingli uncrossed her arms.

When the old woman removed the bandages, Lingli could see that a thin layer of skin nearly as big as her fist had been removed from above her navel. The wound still wept thin, bloody fluid. Tiadona pulled out a small jug from her pocket, and Lingli winced, every muscle tense.

"Don't do drama," the old woman said. "I barely scratched you."

The salve was instantly numbing, and Tiadona's touch was light.

"Lucky for you, your blood ran clean, and they trust me. But that doesn't mean we won't get rid of you if you give us half a reason."

After the old woman rebandaged her stomach and left, Lingli shuffled back to the pallet and lay still for a long time. No matter where she might go in the whole wide world, her fate was plain. Everyone she met would see her and think "demon," "asura," "witch," and try to do away with her. She doubted anyone, including herself, would ever understand the cunning nature of the curse that had been leveled against her from birth.

For now, the only useful thing she could imagine doing was to eat the wanderers' food until she didn't hurt so much, then she would figure out how to escape. Hearing no one on the bench or near the wagon, Lingli gritted her teeth and slowly scooted up to the canvas between the bed and the bench, pulling it back as far as she dared.

Eight painted wagons and about fifty horses, she guessed. Men and women—she couldn't be sure how many—completed their chores and prepared supper. Children chased each other, shouting and laughing. *All one clan. The White Horse Clan,* she thought, judging from the rearing horse painted on every wagon. Seeing Rekha and Tiadona coming her way, Lingli dropped the canvas and pushed herself back to her spot.

"Why do I have to?" she heard Rekha say as they drew near.

"Because we all have chores, and this is now one of yours."

"What if it bites me?"

"The blood does not lie. She is a girl."

"And a spy! That's what Farid Uncle said."

"Imagine your father sent you to spy on someone," Lingli heard Tiadona say. "Suppose those people captured you. Should they kill you? A child?"

"Yes, if I was a spy, but I'm not a spy."

"Argh, you're hard, girl! Understand this, the White Horse Clan does not kill children even if they are spies, especially ones that might be of value."

"But it's...she's...not normal," Rekha said in a low voice.

"And that is her burden, not yours. Take these lentils before they go cold."

Rekha's head popped up at the end of the wagon. Balancing a bowl in one hand, the girl climbed in and came forward until she was within arm's reach, then she set the bowl on the wagon bed. Lingli raised it to her lips. She rolled the first bite of food around in her mouth then ate greedily.

"What's your name?" Rekha asked.

Lingli paused chewing long enough to mutter, "I already told you and your brothers."

"You said 'Lingli,' but that's not a name."

"It is a name. You've just never heard it before. Now I've told you, so you should tell me your name." She licked the remains from the bowl and wondered if the girl would lie.

"My name's Rekha," the girl said. "Rekha Mirajkar."

Lingli lowered the empty bowl. "Thank you, Rekha."

Disgust and curiosity battled over Rekha's face. "You're as white as snow," she said finally, before snatching the bowl and scrambling away. "I'm going to call you Snow."

Why not? You're just like the others.

As Rekha fled, someone in the camp began to softly thump drums. Lingli crept back up to the bench and listened as the wanderers' music struck a happy, quick beat. Peering out, she saw an arc of men and women clapping and dancing practiced steps around the campfire. Someone called out for Anil, and the decorated man she had seen before joined in.

The clan's leader, called Farid, was propped up on cushions between two crones whose thin braids curled around their sides. He cheered the dancers and pounded his cane to the beat.

When the dance ended, Lingli saw one of the women pat the feet of the young woman sitting next to her. A lute player plucked out a simple melody, and the young woman rose and began to sing a ballad. Never had Lingli heard such a beautiful voice; it rose, dove, and soared like a bird in flight.

A small movement between Tiadona's wagon and the one ahead caught her eye. Her captor, Samir, knelt at a small shrine set at the back. Pausing his tribute to listen to the singer, the tender feeling she saw on his face surprised Lingli. As if he sensed her gaze, he turned, and his eyes locked on hers. She immediately leaned back out of sight.

The next afternoon, judging by the position of the sun shining through the wagon's canvas, it seemed they were moving due south. She fretted about falling off course for Saatkulom. The longer she and Sid were apart, the more difficult it was to imagine their reunion. Would he be whole? Would he welcome her? Or would her arrival matter at all? It shamed her to admit it, but she feared he would forget her. Or maybe she would forget him. Whichever it was, time was against her as much as distance.

When they stopped, she asked Rekha where they were going.

"The next village," Rekha said as if any fool would know that. "We need more trades before winter."

Whatever thin familiarity had budded between them, Lingli knew the girl did not want to touch her, and she could take advantage of it. Spotting Farid drinking his tea at a small table, she ignored her wound and Rekha's command to stop and climbed down from the wagon. Clan members watched as she crossed the camp, holding a hand over her stomach. All were silent when she stood before Farid and the men around him.

"Sir," she began, "I thank you for feeding and sheltering me."

Farid snorted. "Well, I'll be! That's the first time I've been formally thanked by a captive." The men glared at her with such disgust Lingli nearly forgot her question.

"Sir, where is this caravan going? Will you be passing near Safed Qila?"

"What makes you think you can speak to us, strange one?" Anil interjected, putting down his thali and stepping between her and Farid. "Save your appreciation for the Mephisto who buys you."

Rekha's father joined Anil. "Get back to the wagon," he growled.

Lingli cringed, but she would not throw away her best chance. "My brother has gone to Saatkulom. I need to find him."

"Oh, I'm sure their rani will welcome your demon brother and you with open arms," Anil said. He turned to Rekha's father. "I'm not one to lose coin handed to me, Rahmanji, but we may be better off without this gamble."

She said, "I want to come with you—"

Before she could continue, Rahman had one arm twisted behind her back, which stretched the skin around her wound. She stifled a cry.

"Have you ever heard such from an otherworldly creature?" Farid muttered with an amused air at odds with the wariness of the others. Rahman propelled her back toward the wagon. "She doesn't know the treat she's in for."

The women stared with narrowed eyes. Young boys made a scene of squealing and running away as she drew close. Rahman waited for her to climb into the wagon, and she found Tiadona there, rummaging around in her trunks.

"Saatkulom's a powerful realm," the old woman said. "Your brother's either committed some crime, or he has impressed one of the Seven."

She said nothing.

"Good. Keep your mouth closed," the woman said. "It will be difficult for you to avoid drawing attention, but try. Especially avoid Farid's attention. I have barely persuaded him not to leave you staked in the woods to feed the crows. And Anil changes moods like the wind in the sixth moon. He'll do whatever he must to impress Farid."

"I have to find my brother," Lingli said.

"We will pass the Rock in the next moon. If you are quiet, if Farid doesn't believe you bring the ill will of the ancestors, we will leave you there."

"Why are you helping me?"

Tiadona took a pot from her trunk and climbed down from the wagon.

"How do you know I'm helping you?"

The question circled in Lingli's mind throughout the evening. She considered it when Tiadona and Rekha made their beds behind the bench. She was still thinking about it when the campfire dwindled, and she looked out the back of the wagon to watch the stars. Were Tiadona's words a warning or a trick? Every sense told her it was likely both, but there would be no escape until she healed a little more and got her map back.

When they stopped to rest the horses and make tea the next day, Lingli leaned out of the back of the wagon and noticed how little-traveled the path seemed. This was not the Rajpath. A group of riders drove their small herd of horses ahead of the wagons. Rekha rode over to her as the caravan began to move again.

Rekha asked, "Does everyone in your clan look like you?"

Despite Rekha's easy rudeness, Lingli enjoyed the girl's company. *She's just a child. She's only saying what her elders are thinking.*

"No one looks like me."

"Not even your ma?"

Lingli didn't answer.

"Pa says I look like my ma. I don't remember her much, but I remember she used to brush my hair so nicely. Never pulled it. Not like Tiadona."

"What happened to your ma?"

"She got sick. Died when I was five cycles."

The girl sounded at ease, but Lingli knew a little about disguising feelings. It was more difficult when you felt others were listening too closely.

"Could I help you with your mare tonight?" Lingli asked quickly.

"Yes, you... I should ask Pa," Rekha said. "If Pa allows, you may." She kicked her horse and rode ahead.

At the campsite that evening, Lingli got down and waited near Rahman's wagon while he tended one of the other's horses. Rahman Mirajkar, she had learned, was the clan's horse trainer. She watched Rekha make her request, and her father glared at her from under his thick brows, but Rekha persisted with the doggedness of a child who was rarely denied. Finally, he shrugged and returned to working on the horse's hooves.

Rekha led her mare to the high line and beckoned Lingli to follow.

"Don't comb her legs," Rekha told her. "Use the soft brush."

"Is she going to kick me?" Lingli said.

"Maybe."

Rekha chattered on about her mare's bad habits and how one day she wanted to ride the fastest horses in Ascarya Erde, a breed known as govadhi, which were used in the great races held in the north.

"Govadhi are very rare," Lingli said.

"Ha, they are, but our clan knows where to find them."

"Do you?"

"Of course—"

"Rekha!" Sachin yelled from where he groomed his horse farther down the line. "You don't go telling strangers our business!"

Rekha's face burned.

"Your brother's right. You shouldn't tell some things to people you don't know."

"I know that! I wasn't going to tell you *where* we find them!"

"Yes, you were," Sachin yelled. "You talk too much!"

"Well, she didn't tell me, so no harm done," Lingli said.

After Sachin left, Rekha said, "I was going to tell you *how* you will know a true govadhi. It's not just their funny ears, you know."

"Isn't it their long legs that gives them their great speed?"

"Yes, but that's not proof of a pureblood." Rekha looked around and then whispered, "It's their spurs."

"Spurs?"

"At the back of their fetlocks. Most of the time, you can't see them, but they're there—sharp as a rooster's!" Rekha picked up her mare's leg to show Lingli the spot.

"Most horses they call govadhis are not really govadhis, and they don't have spurs. Don't tell Sachin I told you."

"I won't," Lingli promised. "But don't put yourself in trouble, alright?"

As Matachand waned, she and Rekha became a team for feeding and grooming Rekha's mare. The wanderer girl even invited Lingli to take a turn at making a running mount—the latest stunt the girl was determined to master—but Lingli refused, certain that swinging herself up on a moving horse would rip her stomach wide open. Rekha still insisted that the least she could do was ride her mare to the end of the clearing where they camped and send the horse back so she could practice her trick.

Lingli sat on the saddle gingerly without thinking about anything but the tender spot on her belly. She took the mare only a short way into the field when she heard Rahman shout. Looking behind, she saw him grab his daughter by the arm and point toward the mare. She knew immediately that she had exceeded the limits of his tolerance.

She could have galloped off. She thought about it, but they would have caught her, and she would have given them the excuse they needed to get rid of her. While Rahman continued his vehement scolding, Lingli rode slowly back to the caravan, slid off the mare and dropped the reins on the ground. Half the clan looked upon their drama, and she wished she could save Rekha from further humiliation, but anything she said would make it worse.

Fully expecting she would be turned out in the woods, if not worse, Lingli sat at the back of Tiadona's wagon for a long while. When no one came she returned to her pallet and pretended to sleep. Eventually Rekha climbed in and sat sniffling at the back. The girl probably would not speak to her again, but why should she care? She would be leaving soon anyway.

Their caravan had hardly begun to move the next day when Tiadona suddenly stopped the team. Scooting to the front, Lingli lifted a corner of the canvas and peeked out.

Several high-sided wagons had stopped on the side of the path ahead. On each bench sat a driver and a companion with a crossbow—thick men with shaved heads, metal collars and bands on their arms. Thirty or more armed riders wearing half-mail rode with them.

In the middle of the path Anil and a few others had piled horse blankets and leather goods. It looked like a regular trade, but Lingli was not the only one counting the others' blades. Anil suddenly pointed at Tiadona's wagon, and Lingli drew back. She heard someone approach.

"They need treatment for a sick man," Anil's son Moraten said.

"What's wrong with him?" Tiadona asked.

"The ancestors know. His head is swollen. And Pa says bring the asura."

Tiadona climbed into the back of the wagon and went to her locked trunk. As the old woman took out supplies, Lingli caught a glimpse of her pack before the lid closed.

Muddling together herbs, honey and bits of apinian resin, Tiadona quickly shaped the mixture into six small balls and stuffed them into a pouch with pieces of willow bark. She put the pouch in her pocket, then ran her hand along the bottom of a cooking pot and showed Lingli her blackened fingers.

"When they examine you, be still," the old woman said as she dabbed at the skin below Lingli's eyes. "If they ask you anything, pretend you do not understand."

She pushed Lingli to the back of the wagon and told her to keep her hood up. Shaking, Lingli followed Tiadona to the group in the road.

"Where is the sick man?" Tiadona asked a big man who seemed to be the other group's leader.

Two men came forward carrying a third man between them. Lingli winced when she saw his face. One side was so hugely swollen his eyes were uneven, and his mouth was stretched. Tiadona observed him closely. She asked the ones with him some questions. Finally, she touched the man's neck lightly. He moaned and she pulled the pouch from her pocket.

One of the man's companions asked her how long to give the medicine. Tiadona showed him three fingers and held out her palm. The leader spat, fished coins from a pocket, and dropped them into her hand.

As the sick man was hauled back to his wagon, Anil ordered Lingli to come forward. Seeing no possibility of outrunning them, she complied and kept her eyes on the ground.

"An orphan," Tiadona told the leader. "No encumbrances."

The leader's eyes slid over her. "Is she sick?"

"Nothing a few days of decent food won't take care of," Anil answered.

The leader flicked back her hood. One of the other men made a sound of disgust. Lingli couldn't help putting her hand up to cover the vein that colored her temple.

Their leader shook his head and turned to Anil. "No," he said. "We'll take these only." He pointed to the goods on the ground.

"She's young——" Anil began, but the man's laugh cut him off.

"My men don't care to see their members fall off, understand. We don't need your trash."

Tiadona shrugged and shooed Lingli back to the wagon. Inside, the old woman handed her a cloth for her face, got back on the bench, and clucked to the team. As the caravan moved out, Lingli lay down on her pallet and wondered how long it would be before the wanderers found an agreeable trade.

CHAPTER 9

A week after Sid arrived at the palace, he sat on a bench in the kitchens nursing his morning tea and wondering how he was going to get into the defenses. *You did not cross the world to serve tea. Think. Maybe if I serve Master Duvanya, I can learn what he's seeking in his recruits.*

"Two mutton chops per person!" Korvar shouted as Sid and others got in line to pick up the thalis. "If someone asks for more, then serve your spare. Where are the oranges? Who is eating all these oranges? If we do not receive a delivery today, it will be dried apples tomorrow. Each of you seniors, give me a star-blessed count when you return!"

Though the regular staff were adept at carrying loaded trays, Sid and the other recruits wore boards braced against their stomachs to help them manage. As soon as Sid received the last items—pots of tea and a hot puri for each thali—he and the rest of his group hurried to keep up with Filant, the senior kitchen steward.

Serving Master Duvanya would have to wait. Sid's group was assigned the southern nobles' rooms in the new tower, and Filant was on hand to taste the food and ensure no debacles ensued, which was fortunate for Sid because Princess Mafala's quarters was his first delivery. He had been flattered to be assigned such a highly placed noble—until he learned that no one else wanted the duty. The sister of the rani's consort was known to be demanding, and woe to those who did not satisfy her wishes.

As soon as Sid reached the princess's quarters, he set his board down in the passage and waited for Filant's approval, then took up a thali in one hand and a teapot capped with a small cup in the other. The guard on duty rapped on the door and opened it.

The princess Mafala sat on her divan where a maid fixed tiny braids in her hair, a style favored by the women of the House of Hudulfah. Another servant mixed scents at a table and dabbed them on the princess's wrists.

"Stop," the princess said. "I told you citrine and torba root, not citrine and hyssop! Wash this off and make it again."

Sid took her breakfast to the balcony.

"Did I say I was eating outside, boy?"

"No, Madam—I mean, no, Princess."

"Don't presume. Bring it here."

He glanced at Mafala from the corner of his eye as he set the thali on a tiny side table. Skin the color of honey, light eyes, full lips. No one could deny that she was beautiful, but her cutting tongue soured the sweet.

"May I bring you anything else?" he asked.

Mafala sniffed at the food. "Every day chops, and what kind of chops! See the size? Rat chops. Bring me black buck steak tomorrow or you'll wear this thali on your head."

"Yes, Princess." Sid bowed low and shuffled backward a couple of steps before bolting for the door.

The next room was the easiest of his assignments. The rani's and Prince Hassan's son, baby Prince Aseem, had even better quarters than Princess Mafala, though the infant was too young to appreciate the décor. He was also too young to eat anything harder than mashed rice and vegetables, but his nurse had to eat well for his sake.

In a padded chair near the balcony the nurse basked in the dawn with her sleeping charge at her breast. She looked up when Sid entered and rearranged her scarf to cover herself as he placed the thali on the table next to her.

"It's a lovely morning," Sid said and immediately regretted it. *Lovely morning?* "I mean, I hope you like the greens." And he wished he hadn't said that either.

She's indispensable, he thought, *like being a guard. At least until the prince is weaned.* The nurse smiled shyly. He left wishing he could remember whether she was called Tareka or Tameka.

At the end of his shift, two thalis remained on his board. These were for Tal Daman, a cousin of Prince Hassan, who had no family with him, but each time Sid served him there had been someone else in his rooms, so he brought the spare thali just in case.

That morning a boy with dark skin and a shaved head sat on the floor near the bed, his face hidden against his knees. Tal Daman was nowhere to be seen. Sid was about to leave, hoping one thali was acceptable, when the southerner emerged from the bathing room, fully oiled and dressed in Hudulfah's traditional white toga.

As Sid placed a cup on the table, Tal Daman's hand brushed his. There was something deliberate about it that Sid did not dare acknowledge. Remembering Korvar's admonishments to the recruits to keep their thoughts to themselves, he delivered the second thali, poured the tea, and bowed too many times as he left, glad that Filant waited nearby.

The grounds were beginning to lighten when Sid began his return to the kitchens. Setting down his trays on the parapet in the central palace's main gallery, he recalled how all the edifices of the fort—the markets, trading houses, and homes—had awed him on his first evening, but even they could not compare with the splendor of the palace. The feasting hall and its colonnades before him were made of glowing moonstone, as was the central palace where he stood and its two towers. Moonstone shone white at a distance, but it contained facets of gold, blue, and pink that could be seen when the light struck at the right angle. Even this morning, Chandrabhavan's magnificence made his chest tighten.

Yet more than the difference between lime-and-salt plaster and moonstone separated the fort and the palace. When he entered Chandrabhavan, riding behind one of Duvanya's soldiers, Sid's heart had nearly stopped as they crossed the black abyss that cracked apart a third of the Rock. The single bridge spanning from the fort's third gate to the palace gate was slim and paved smooth, and it offered little reassurance that those crossing were safe from the darkness below. The palace wall blocked Sid's view of it that morning, but there was no ignoring the crack's presence. Its updraft constantly swirled through the palace grounds and blew his unruly hair back from his face even then.

Sid preferred not looking at it. He turned his attention back to the Ascaryans on the grounds below.

Guards changed shifts, staff took up their work, and the first merchants of the day began to arrive. This was the aspect of the realm that excited him most of all—the feeling that the Ascaryans here, even the common ones, were smart and quick. Everyone seemed full of purpose, and it made Sid hopeful that he would find his purpose, too.

The sound of claws tapping on polished stone interrupted his survey.

Master Vaksana and a dark-haired man approached with the rani's wolves on their leads. *Wolves!* Not one, but four slobbering beasts the size of ponies—Akela, Trechur, Titok, and Danior. All were harnessed and muzzled, though that gave Sid little comfort. The black one, Akela, paused as he crossed Sid's shadow. Ignoring a command from the handler assisting Master Vaksana, the wolf took a step toward him.

Sid met the wolf's green-eyed gaze and froze like a rabbit. White teeth gleamed through gaps in Akela's muzzle.

"C'mon, beast. You've had your feed," the handler said.

Sid held his breath as the dark wolf sniffed at him. When the man impatiently jerked the wolf's chain, Master Vaksana put a restraining hand on his arm.

"You wa-waste your strength m-making useless movements, useless commands. Respect Akela and he will obey."

Shrugging off Master Vaksana's hand, the handler answered mockingly, "Until he d-d-doesn't."

Master Vaksana's face darkened, but he said nothing.

The other wolves began to growl, and Sid found he was having difficulty swallowing, but when Akela abruptly padded on, the rest followed.

Trying to breathe normally, Sid watched the day captain, Jantan Gaddar, enter the front grounds with a cadre of his men. All day guards wore golden yellow turbans and cloaks, but Sid thought no one was as well-suited for the uniform as the captain. His mustache and brows were blacker than pitch, and his chestplate flashed in the sun.

Because Gaddar was not noble-born, his insignia was the sun and stars, but it shone as bright as any of the Seven's. And because he was not noble-born, his name was ever on the lips of the common people. He was pride and ambition bound together by talent, or the favor of the ancestors, depending on who you asked.

Sid shook his head as if to clear it of crumbs. *How the witch would cackle if she saw me hauling trays and thalis. I've got to convince Master Avani to move me to the defenses.* Despite his resolution, he worried that his last encounter with Master Avani might have left the old noble with a less-than-favorable opinion of him.

At the end of his first day in the palace, Korvar's son, Shankar, the boy he'd spoken to when he was looking for the training yard, stuck an elbow in Sid's rib as he washed pots. Sid immediately straightened when he saw Master Avani watching them from the doorway and looking even more like an owl than the insignia on his shoulder.

"How do you find the work?" the old noble asked, coming to Sid's side.

Sid saw Shankar shake his head as he moved away—a warning to answer carefully.

"It's good, sir. I will do my best."

"I do not know if you understand why my apprentice didn't believe you," Master Avani said softly, "but in case you have not noticed, there are no giants rambling about, except for the maharani's servant. Most will tell you that the rest were vanquished two generations ago."

Sid chewed his lip, unsure that insisting his guardian really was a giant was what Master Avani wanted to hear.

"But I once knew another giant with reddish hair. Am I to believe that he was your guardian in the Western Woods?"

Sid nodded.

"Does the rani know of this giant?"

"She told him to let me go when I joined her caravan."

Master Avani tugged at his beard. "Did the whole party see him?"

"Well, Master Vaksana did, and the scout who carried the rani's torch."

Master Avani looked troubled, and Sid decided not to say anything about Red's cry that shook the trees. He wondered if Master Avani knew he had already been given a full cycle's wages. Nothing gained if he didn't try.

"I didn't mean to cause your apprentice trouble," he said, "but if the paymaster doesn't know my guardian's name, how can I send my earnings?"

"Do you really think the giant needs your earnings?"

"I guess he won't," Sid said slowly, "but my friend might need it."

"Friend?" Master Avani snorted. "Delivering wages to all corners of the realm is an expensive proposition reserved only for recruits' immediate families once a cycle."

A commotion in the kitchens' inner room made them both look up. Staff began hurrying about, and Korvar's voice rose above it all.

"What a pleasure to have you visit us, Your Majesty! Pardon the conditions, please. We have taken in a new batch of recruits today."

The moment the rani emerged in the doorway of the backroom, followed by Korvar and Greta, Master Avani was at her side. Sid stood as tall as he could, still clutching the pot he had been scrubbing.

"There's no more important service in the palace than our kitchen service," the rani said in her musical voice. "Did you know that when I was a girl, before you joined us, Korvarji, I spent a whole summer working in the kitchens? Everyone should learn how to feed themselves, heal themselves, and defend themselves."

Her gaze had barely paused on Sid before she accompanied the chef and the noble out to the kitchen gardens. He hadn't seen the rani or Master Avani since.

Sid ran his hand through his hair, wondering if reminding the old noble about his wages was worth the risk. *Surely Red and Li can manage with the coin I left? Next cycle I'll send more.*

With no more time for daydreaming, he raced around the back of the feasting hall and met a cluster of bearers loading a cart with foodstuff. He was about to ask where they were going when he spied a group ascending the path up the rock face behind the stables. Guards led the way followed by several riders, a team pulling a wagon full of Ascaryans, the giantess, and far behind them all, Master Vaksana, the other handler, and the wolves.

"Where have you been!" Korvar shouted at him. "Don't answer that, just come along. We must get the food up there in the next hour or my head will be on a thali. And I am sure you young ones would not want to see such a thing, any more than you would like to see your own heads served for dessert!"

When everything was loaded, two zhoukoo pulled their cart along the top of the broad wall that separated the gardens from the stable yard. Sid and the bearers followed on foot. Beyond the mining hall the path to the top of the Rock grew steep despite the switchbacks. Sweat dripped from the zhoukoos' noses as they strained forward, and everyone huffed for breath by the time they reached the summit.

The sun beat down on a bare plateau of rock that stretched along the edge of the summit in both directions and ended at dry woods that covered most of the rest of the Rock's top. The view was even grander than the one from the palace. Not only was the entire fort laid out below, but Sid could see the Naachmaidan stretching to the horizon. Drawing his gaze back to his feet, he tottered—overcome with the feeling that he was being pulled over the edge. He sat down hard and those who saw it snickered.

Korvar and the rest moved across the plateau, past a garden of ancient chhatris that stood like odd stone crops, and into the shade of the dusty trees at the edge of the woods. A fountain bubbled in a stone basin there, and the earlier party's team and wagon were parked nearby. Clearing space for a gathering, the boys built a fire, tied bright cloths in the tree branches and set up the tables, charpois, and pallets.

When the sun passed its zenith, Master Avani and a few elder members of the Seven came along a path that skirted the forest. They washed their faces in the fountain, settled onto the pallets, and drank nimbu pani until the heat put them to sleep. A few bearers were assigned to fan them and keep the flies away, and the rest reposed in patches of shade while Korvar and his senior staff cut, patted, pounded, fried, baked, and stirred supper into its proper form.

While staring out at the memorials scattered over the plateau, a blade of loneliness poked at Sid. He got up and took over fanning from one of the other recruits. After some time, an old lady of the House of Duvanya, roused, repinned her hair, and asked, "Are you a southerner, boy?"

Sid shook his head.

"Where is your home?"

"Western Woods."

"Is that so? You don't smell like it."

"My mother died when I was very young," he said. "Her name was Afsana."

"East side?" the woman said. "Your father was a rascal, then." She turned away from him and called loudly for tea.

East side? East side of the realm?

The shade spread as the elders sipped their tea and nibbled snacks. After checking his bubbling pots, Korvar told Sid and two other boys to find the rani's hunting party and tell them supper was ready.

They followed a path into the woods for several minutes, making Sid wonder how the top of the Rock could stretch any farther, until a crashing noise nearby brought them to a standstill. The hissing *zfft* of several unseen arrows made the boys duck into the brush, but when a victorious ululation went up, they regained their nerve. Hardly a stone's throw away, the rani's party gathered around a fallen stag with two arrows in its heart and a spear jutting from its side.

"By the First Mother!" the boy next to Sid whispered.

At the center of the party Princess Mafala retrieved her spear from the deer. She wore a short toga covered by a vest with straps that crossed under her breasts and tied in the back. With the grace of a sand cat, she stood over the stag in her high-laced sandals and detached a small bowl from her belt, which she handed to her brother, Prince Hassan.

Tal Daman pulled the deer's head up to expose its neck, and Sid could see that the creature's eyes already stared into the otherworld. Drawing her kukri, Mafala looked to the sky and shouted words in her native tongue. In one fluid movement, she cut open the stag's neck and continued her tribute while Prince Hassan caught the blood in the bowl until it ran over the edge and dripped down his fingers.

Feeling ill and lightheaded, Sid squeezed his eyes shut when Prince Hassan put the bowl to his lips. When he opened them again, Tal Daman was laying the deer's head to the ground. Prince Hassan returned the bowl to Mafala, who sipped at the blood, then wiped her mouth with the back of her hand and passed the bowl on to the other southerners accompanying them.

Sid and the other recruits stood transfixed. Even the Seven's lesser nobles and guards seemed stunned, but the rani was undisturbed. While the blood-drinking went on, she had turned her attention to the wolves, kneeling by each one and speaking quietly to distract them.

Akela rested his massive head on his paws, and nothing more than the twitch of his ears indicated his interest. The other three, however, were not so relaxed. Ropes of saliva dripped from the jaws of the largest one, Trechur, who had accompanied the rani's party from the Western Woods. His eyes were locked onto the deer's open throat. The other two could not contain themselves even that much. Titok whined and the smallest, Danior, crept forward almost imperceptibly. When Master Vaksana issued a command and blew upon an instrument he kept on a chain around his neck, they trembled and lay still again, but the air was so thick with the scent of blood and musk that Sid could not blame them for their indiscipline.

After the zhoukoo loaded the fallen deer onto their cart and disappeared into the woods, the hunting party followed the boys back to camp.

Sid and the bearers served drinks while the nobles washed and changed clothes. Master Avani regaled the guests with the history of the hunting park and its maintenance until Madam Hansa, recognizing the guests' flagging attention, revived the party by juggling oranges. At last, the rani and Princess Mafala rejoined the party, arriving arm in arm like sisters and wearing matching long chemises over loose pants cuffed at the ankle.

The rani pulled Mafala to where Master Vaksana sat, tall and grim-mouthed. "Brother, will you make some space for the princess?"

The wolfmaster looked at the rani as if she had asked him to cut off his arm, but Mafala demurely stepped forward and sat next to him, seeming so gentle that Sid could not reconcile her manner with all else he had seen of her.

"You are wel-welcome, Princess," Master Vaksana muttered, color climbing in his face.

Prince Hassan and the other southerners ignored this game, but some members of the Seven raised their brows and whispered to each other until they were distracted by Korvar's dishes. The merriment grew as food was served and cups were filled and refilled with sura and firewine under a quarter-full Matachand who joined her little brother high above them.

As he deposited his umpteenth stack of thalis and cups into their cart, Sid's hunger had reached such a level he was considering stealing a piece of buttered naan for himself when Captain Gaddar passed by carrying two torches. Always on the lookout for ways to impress those in the defenses, Sid trotted after the captain, who handed him one of the torches, and bid him wait next to him and Greta behind the rani's seat.

"It's grown quite late and I'm sure many of you would welcome your beds," the rani told her guests, "but before we leave, I must pay tribute to my father on his birth anniversary." Greta opened a large pouch from which the rani drew a necklace strung with pale objects that rattled as she hung it around her neck. "I invite you to accompany me for a short visit to his memorial. It may help our honored guests from Avakstan better understand our realm."

The party wrapped themselves in shawls to ward off the cool night air. Holding his torch high, Sid brought up the end of the group that followed the rani and the captain across the stretch of rock dotted with chhatris. He shivered as they wound their way among the memorials whose stone caps both reflected the moonlight above and guarded the dark below.

At one of the larger memorials, the captain fixed his torch to a slender pillar while the visitors gathered. Sid was heartened when the rani smiled and took his torch, using it to light diyas on the floor and ledges encircling the columns. Soon the platform was bright, but the staring eyes of numerous small dolls on a table set in the center, combined with the wall of night behind them, tempered Sid's good mood.

Taking up a beaten brass thali, the rani placed small tokens upon it and showed them to Mafala, who stood next to her brother. The rani explained, "Powdered blue lapis to represent boundless love, a piece of darkice stone for strength, this pale crystal for loyalty, and a piece of sweet to satiate the longing for this world. These we offer our ancestors on days of worship. A fifth item can be chosen to venerate a particular ancestor."

She handed Gaddar a tiny clay cup, which he filled from his own waterskin.

"Father loved the Nemaji," she said, raising the cup. "He understood that our lives, all life, must have a secure source of water like the one the Rock gives us even in this dry season."

To Prince Hassan she said, "All that blesses our union was born of his accomplishments. He was the first who negotiated peace with your father and Ameer Ali. Just as he was the first to proclaim we would build Nilampur together and make it a city to rival all others."

When the prince inclined his head as sign of his agreement, the rani took her offering and knelt before the little effigies of nobles long dead. Speaking strange-sounding names, she pinched each pale object strung on her neck chain. They clicked and clacked through her fingers, and Sid realized they were small bones.

Behind Sid one of the older women whispered urgently to the man next to her. "She should not call him!"

"Hush, Mother. It is only a veneration tribute."

After the rani prostrated herself and touched her head to the floor, she picked up the thali again and stood before a finely wrought effigy made of carved wood and painted in bright colors. The doll's kohl-lined eyes shone bright, and black yarn had been carefully cut and applied to make a man's hair, beard, and thin mustache.

"Beloved one, Basheer the Valorous, Master of the House of Duran and Forty-first Raja of Saatkulom, hear your daughter. We remember your birthday and honor your vision that brought this realm to great prosperity. We bear witness to all achieved by your grace and the deeds that enrich us still. Though your spirit roams the Doodhnadi, your daughter and your people will never forget you. On this auspicious day we make this offering, Ruler of My Heart, and we ask your continued blessings."

The rani broke off a piece of the sweet on the thali and placed it before the king's effigy. She bowed to the doll and seemed about to leave the platform when the group outside the chhatri stirred and parted.

A tall and painfully thin woman appeared on the edge of the torchlight. Her hair nearly reached the ground in its loose braid, and her long gown and dupatta could hardly be called more than rags. But what shocked Sid were her eyes—milky orbs in dark hollows that immediately reminded him of the visions of Lingli that had haunted his dreams.

"I told you! The otherworld has ears!" the woman next to Sid told her son.

During the rush of whispered exclamations, Sid looked to Greta, but the giantess remained still.

"Welcome, faithful Seer of Saatkulom," the rani said evenly. "We venerate Raja Basheer on his day of birth as is custom. We make no demand of you, Oracle. Be at peace."

For a moment, the woman inclined her head to one side as if she was listening to something else, then her dead eyes squared upon the rani.

"Traps of time test all—from the stones to the stars," she said. "The past and future approach, and the present is littered with old deceptions. The path must be chosen carefully." With that, the woman turned and disappeared into the dark.

The entire party, including the rani, stood frozen until Princess Mafala whispered, "Who was that?"

Forcing a smile, the rani shook her head and said, in a voice meant to be lighter than it was, "Her kind have lived with us since Starfall, advising and tending our memorials. Although oracles are blind to this world, they see things we do not, and they hear the ancestors more clearly."

The rani's discomfort was lost on no one.

"My apologies to the House of Hudulfah. You were surprised. I should have informed you that she might visit us."

Captain Gaddar pulled his torch from its brace and signaled Sid to follow, which he was more than eager to do as soon as the rani stepped down from the chhatri and steadied herself on Prince Hassan's arm. The dark felt alive to Sid—as if it could quench his torch at the slightest provocation—and he looked over his shoulder more than once as the rani led them back to the lip of the summit.

At the head of the path day guards assisted the elders into the wagon and held the others' horses as they mounted. Korvar's workers waited there until the party reached the first switchback, then they returned to camp and ate the feast's remains.

The sweet relief of finishing duty revived the recruits as they took down the tents and loaded the cart, but Sid could not dismiss those blind eyes that reminded him of the friend he had left behind. Awash with a dread he did not understand, he looked up into the slowly turning field of stars.

Mother, help me find courage.

Vowing that he would not allow fear to ruin all that his new life promised, Sid took a deep breath, put on a jovial air, and proceeded to annoy the other bearers by telling every joke he knew as they made their way down the rock face to the starlit palace below.

Part 2

CHAPTER 10

Three floors below the rani's quarters, in a room barely large enough for her to lie down, Greta stood giantstill with her eyes closed, her breath hardly perceptible. It was early morning of the observation day for the twelfth moon, and she had stood like this for hours, seeing a wood, a creek, and a long hillside of clover leading to a cabin and a small barn, but she could not sense the one she longed to see. She knew that he had gone to stone and would not answer, but she offered her giant-style tribute anyway.

Returning to herself, it took a few breaths to remember how to move in this place made for smaller beings. She picked up her apron and tied it over the plain gray tunic she always wore. The tunic, the apron—these clothes were things Ascaryans insisted upon to make her seem more like them, but everyone knew what she was. There was her height and girth, of course, but also telling was the difficulty she had with their language, even now, after thirty-one sun cycles in the palace. Her limited speech was interpreted as a sign of stupidity, and because she could be still for hours and moved slowly, they assumed she was old.

Deception did not come naturally, yet she had not corrected these perceptions, having learned to appreciate the benefit of others' incomplete understanding.

While she finger-combed her hair and wound it into a knot at the back of her head, Greta sensed that her charge, the Maharani of the Seven, was awake. It wasn't that she heard her; the stone walls of the palace were too thick for that, even for her ears. Greta felt the rani rise with the day's light as distinctly as she felt her own heartbeat because she had been bonded to Her Majesty shortly after her birth.

115

For cycles Ascaryans had demanded her to confirm whether this sense was like a smell or a sound. It was neither—nor was it a wish or a hope. It simply was. Ascaryans did not possess the ability and though they called it "giantsense," they didn't know its true name.

Greta didn't either. She had left her own kind too soon, and she had learned so little before the wars and before Red left, but she never doubted herself. If anything, her ability was growing stronger. Greta was as certain of Dear Child's state that morning as she had been of the red giant's when he turned to stone far away in the Western Woods.

An array of pots and bowls sat on the table before her. She sniffed at one that held a mess of dampened herbs and dropped a few stems into one of her pockets before she left her room and headed toward the rani's quarters. The guards parted to either side of the chamber door as soon as she drew near.

In the inner room, amid a pile of cushions, the rani lay on her rumpled bed with one bare leg thrown over the covers. She did not stir when the giantess entered nor when she wedged herself through a smaller doorway to the bathing room where she lit the fire for the bath. Hoisting a brass vessel half as tall as a man and full of water, the giantess carefully maneuvered it onto an iron frame over the fire.

"Bring me my son," the rani commanded in a sleep-heavy voice.

Descending the stairs again, Greta trudged past guards who opened the door to another quarters. She went straight to the bed where baby Prince Aseem slept. On a pallet next to the bed, a plump young woman sat up quickly, her eyes wide. Greta nodded to the door and turned on her heels as soon as the nurse wrapped the baby and took him in her arms.

In the rani's quarters, the nurse passed Aseem to his mother. Greta poured the bath, and Valena Sandhyatara, naked as the day she was born, entered the bathing room cooing sweet words to her son. She slipped into the warm water and propped the baby against her legs for washing, then returned the baby to the Hudulfah girl for oiling.

When the rani finished bathing, Greta wrapped her in a drying cloth and gently herded her to the dressing table to cinch her into a petticoat before presenting a vermilion sari, an auspicious color for the twelfth moon's apex. Then, humming a note too low for Ascaryans to hear, Greta brought the rani the two neck chains she always wore. One, a gold chain with a short band of squared amethysts. The second, a longer chain with a moonstone pendant. The rani tucked both into her blouse.

Waiting patiently while the rani nibbled at her breakfast and watched a flock of parrots fly over the palace, Greta was grateful for this peaceful hour. It would not last. A quiet day in the palace was rare and entirely out of the question on the fourteenth day of any moon, particularly during a bright cycle. Already, her charge was restless. As soon as she secured a small diadem on her head, the rani went to her sleeping son and kissed him all over, making the babe protest.

Greta would never understand why Ascaryans rushed about so, but it was not her business to understand. It was her business to serve the rani, and she did so earnestly. Their bond was as complete, as compulsory, as it would have been with Greta's own child—no matter Greta's wishes or judgment of the rani's choices.

By the time Greta opened the door to the quarters, the rani had hidden her motherly face away like her neck chains, and they were immediately immersed in the echoed conversations and footfalls that were the breath of the palace. Staff and subjects bowed with respect as their rani passed, but there was no ignoring the spark of moonstruck excitement marking their manners. Greta kept a wary eye on everyone within striking distance.

When she felt Dear Child's energy flagging later that morning, the giantess knew the meetings had lasted too long. Madam Satya had spoken at length to prepare for court, and Krux had shared a detailed list of the accounts that needed attention.

Ignorant of the rani's darkening aura, Master Avani insisted that she join the Avani elders for a star reading. The rani had abruptly refused. Realizing his miscalculation, Master Avani begged her forgiveness, which the rani granted immediately, for the master of history stood high in her affections. After he and his apprentice left, Madam Hansa was the only one remaining at the table.

"Sister, I bring you some good and brief news."

"Please! These days the news either alarms or is unduly tedious."

Madam Hansa grinned. "The new looms are working. I have thirteen weavers in the fort spinning the remaining cotton from the House of Afreh. When they deliver the remainder, we will move looms to Aldea, which should keep them fully occupied through the wolf moon. They are developing a new technique for dying that I'm certain will impress you."

"Wonderful. Be ready to move more looms to Nilampur by the croaking moon," the rani said as she tugged at one of the chains around her neck.

Madam Hansa nodded and took a deep breath. "I also have news regarding the archers. Darius bid me to report on this unit, as I have had the pleasure of leading them. We have begun training the last cadre in mounted maneuvers, and they are learning quickly. I hope you will come with me to the upper field to observe."

"I would very much enjoy that," the rani said, "but after these recent travels, Krux will not allow me to leave the palace until the accounts are balanced, and that will take weeks. Bring your archers to the training yard as soon as you can."

"Yes, sister," Madam Hansa answered slowly, "but the presence of others complicates your proposal."

Greta immediately felt the rani's irritation climb again.

In a flat voice the rani answered, "Gayatri, if you advise me thus because of your discomfort with our guests from Avakstan, your concern is misplaced."

"It is not discomfort with outsiders that troubles me, Maharani. My students are only now mastering these skills. I want our unit to perform perfectly, and they are not yet ready."

"There is no better time than now for the southerners to witness our program. Afreh's youth are still uncomfortable with riding, and only a few from the other houses can manage any weapon on horseback. A basic demonstration will give them the confidence to join training with less fear of humiliation." The rani paused before adding, "But I believe the source of your hesitation is less practical. You do not trust our guests, as you have told me before. The question, sister, is do you trust me?"

The rani had not the least humility or inclination to seek others' opinions, Greta knew, but she somehow made others think that she did.

"Of course, but—" Madam Hansa stammered.

"If you trust me, then you know that everything I do is designed to enrich and secure our people. The southern youth are committed to serving Saatkulom for three cycles before returning to their lands in Avakstan. In that time, we will benefit far more than they. Do you not appreciate that?"

"Forgive me, sister. I am moonstruck, no doubt. I will arrange for the demonstration by the harvest moons. Performing sooner will encourage my archers to improve more quickly."

The rani reached out, and Madam Hansa gave her hand. "Let our fears not blind us to opportunities," she said. "We go forward boldly, sister, and together. Always together."

Dear Child needed to rest. As they left the council room and climbed the stairs to the rani's quarters, Greta kept the acolytes at bay. Once inside, the rani slapped Madam Satya's court list on her work table and rested her head in her hands. Greta was pouring her a cup of water when there was a knock on the door.

One of the guards announced, "The Prince Consort, Your Majesty."

Prince Hassan glided up to the edge of the table. His heavy eyelids gave him the air of a wise patrician, though he was a few cycles younger than the rani. Greta couldn't sense him fully, but his aura burned with a cold light.

"It seems Master Tilan will not be in court today," Prince Hassan said. "It is rumored that he will not have the market section nor my house's compound completed by the new cycle."

The rani sat back and coolly appraised him as if she had expected this visit all day, but Greta could almost see a coal of aggravation glowing within her.

"On my orders, Master Tilan remains at his post in Nilampur precisely for that reason—to complete the remaining work. I expect his report in four days, and I will gladly share it with you so we will all have the same information." The rani pressed her hands together as if the matter was resolved. "I do not think these rumors have substance, but if any delay is anticipated, you may offer suggestions for how to remedy it."

"Our agreement depends on Nilampur being ready for trade by the new cycle."

"Our agreement depends on a good many things."

"You could not have spoken truer words, Maharani."

Even after all these cycles Greta sometimes missed the true intent behind Ascaryans' words, but there was no mistaking the warning in these. The prince left without bowing or showing proper respect.

As soon as the door closed, the rani paced to her balcony and back. "This is the last time we hold court on an observation day."

Greta removed Dear Child's crown and watched her splash water onto her face and neck. Expressing concern would only further aggravate her, so she remained silent even though she sensed small pulses of pain building within her.

"It has been half a week," the rani said, more to herself than the giantess. "At least that. It is the humidity that troubles me today, of course."

Re-pinning the rani's pallu, Greta did not argue that the day was no more humid than usual.

With her arms outstretched before her, the rani's face creased with dismay as she examined her trembling hands.

Another knock landed on the door, but the guard did not even manage a foot inside before Greta gripped the edge and made it impossible to fully open.

"The maid can wait!" the rani shouted angrily. When the guard retreated, she caressed her hands and whispered, "They cannot see this." From her bodice she pulled out the chain with the moonstone pendant. "A drop only."

Opening a cleverly made cap on the end of the pendant, the rani touched it to her lips and tipped her head back. Greta watched her take more than a drop.

How many times had Greta heard Ascaryans declare that giants felt nothing, that their hearts were stonier than their limbs? But if that were true, her heart wouldn't have ached as she watched the rani convulse. Staring but not seeing, Her Majesty dug her nails into the table, threw her head back against Greta's chest, and gasped. The giantess held her tight until she finally slumped in her arms. After settling the rani on her divan, Greta brooded over the shadows under Dear Child's eyes and her shaky breaths.

Many cycles earlier she had seen the rani unwell like this, but her mother, Rani Shikra, had managed to hide her malady from most of those in the palace for several fraught moons. Unfortunately, her daughter's health never fully returned. Not for the first time, Greta wished the former rani was still a presence in the palace.

When color washed back into Her Majesty's face, Greta knew that she would not listen or even look at her for some time. There was nothing to do but follow her command and ready her for the evening's ceremony.

A maid was eventually allowed in to make the rani's lips match her sari's color, outline her eyes with kohl, and paint Matachand and Chotabhai upon her forehead.

When she left her rooms, the rani did not tremble. The line of her jaw was as firm as the lines of paint, her sari held its pleats, and her collar stood upright. She was the incarnate symbol of the Seven's authority—as constant as the stars.

Dodging wheels of flaming torches that had been lowered from the ceiling to illuminate the great hall, Greta took care to shuffle along the polished floor and not take loud, smacking steps that would make the Ascaryans laugh. The rani glided ahead like a gold- and ruby-colored fish, flashing bright where light touched her ornaments. At each bend in the river of observers, Greta sniffed to sense their mood. The room was full of cross currents both hot and cold.

The cavernous hall and its stone columns were a testament to generations of engineers who had made the space by carving away the Rock they lived upon. A huge shelf of stone made tiers of seats that could hold four score observers within sight of the throne. Though many more could be seated on the floor, only the tiers were open for court.

In the second tier, Greta noted the presence of the envoy of Dyuvasa who she knew reported the rani's every breath. On the other end sat the prince consort, his sister, and one of his cousins. A handful of young southerners who should have been training in the yards sat in the upper tier.

At a table between the observers and the throne stood the eldest of the Seven, Parama Azumirga of the House of Satya, who presided as judge. She was slim and her close-cropped silver hair made her seem more youthful than she was, but there was little of youth's softness in her expression. On either side of her sat Nartilya, who advised on business in the districts, and Krux, the master of coin.

As the rani sat on the throne, Greta took her place between the throne and the huge boulder behind where diyas and small venerated objects lined the ledges carved in the boulder's sides. High above the throne and the boulder, light from the room's single window glowed through a thin oilskin.

"In honor of the ancestors," Madam Satya announced, "on this fourteenth day of the twelfth moon, in the nine hundred and fourteenth cycle, we open deliberations to address the realm's business, according to the word of the maharani, Her Majesty Valena Sandhyatara of the House of Duran. Bring forth the first petitioner."

A guard signaled a man to step forward from the bench for petitioners and prisoners.

"Kamran Mandanavi, Chief of the Northeastern District," the man said, putting his palms together and bowing.

"State your issue concisely," Madam Satya said.

"Yes, Madam. On the ninth day of the ninth moon, a daughter of one of the farmers in the village of Bhadaka was reported missing. Another was reported missing on the seventeenth day of the last moons near Osiara. Then, on the third day of this moon in Adrista, several homesteads were burned to the ground, and all were—"

"Did these homesteads have girls of marriageable age?" Madam Satya asked.

"Yes. I know it sounds like raiders, but there was something else." The man rubbed his hands together. "In the last incident even girls were killed, and—"

"Perhaps the raiders were thwarted from abducting girls and frustrated passions overcame them?" Nartilya queried. "Such affairs, while tragic, should be addressed in the district."

"No, this is… They cut off their limbs."

Whispers spread throughout the hall.

"In all these instances the dead were missing arms and legs. Clean cuts. No parts found anywhere. This is nothing like raids we've seen." The chief wiped his face.

Greta rarely concerned herself with affairs that did not affect the rani, but this kind of brutality would panic the eastern villages and upset relations with Dyuvasa if it was not checked. She saw the eastern envoy rapidly writing notes. Several visitors in the tiers were making protective signs to ward off curses from the otherworld.

"An investigation will be necessary," the rani proclaimed, cutting the debate short. "Deliver your petition to Madam Satya and await summons to the council."

The chief bowed nervously and returned to the bench. When the crowd quieted, two requests to delay tithes due to drought were presented, and Krux required a complete accounting. The glow faded from the window, and the audience grew restive, as did the rani. When Krux issued judgment, Madam Satya ordered the prisoner remaining on the bench to step forward.

The accused was a young man wearing a filthy yellow kurta and pants common to apprentices in the day guards, but a bright owl was pinned to his shoulder. Greta felt the rani's consternation as well as Master Avani's great anxiety, and their emotions magnified when the accused raised his chin to reveal a badly bruised face.

"Ritin Amavasya of the House of Avani," Madam Satya began, "On the twenty-fifth day of the eleventh moon, you were arrested for the theft and smuggling of firewine from palace stores. We will hear the evidence against you and your testament. I remind you that this court is witnessed by the ancestors. Do not speak lies that will disgrace your house." She paused, then said, "Let the arresting officer come forward."

The whispering increased again as Captain Gaddar made his way to the floor. Though the day captain was widely admired, Greta measured him less favorably. That he had the rani's ear was true, but his opinions were the least of her interest in him.

"Captain Gaddar, you have accused this youth, an apprentice in the guard and a member of the Seven Houses, of a serious crime," Madam Satya said. "Why did you arrest this man?"

"I was informed that one of our apprentices had been caught trying to sell a cask of firewine to the ale house on the lower Rajpath. I went to investigate this myself, Madam, and found this youth," the captain gestured toward the prisoner, "being held by the ale house proprietor." The captain shook his head as if he was personally disappointed.

"The proprietor showed me a casket half full of drink and said that this one had offered it at a very cheap price. I for one was impressed by the proprietor's honesty. He could have easily profited by the offer, but he chose to tell us."

"What proof did you have that this youth was the one who offered the cask?" Madam Satya asked.

"I asked if he had tried to sell the cask and he said he did. I arrested him immediately. The cask's number did not match those we accounted for a day earlier, but when we checked the storehouse, we found one cask only half full. It seems the thief siphoned from it."

Greta's gaze slid past the captain to the accused, whose aura was a gray orb of fear and injury. The greatest agitation, however, was in the first tier where Master Avani glared at the back of the captain's head.

Leaping up from his seat, the noble said, "I'm sure you can see that there are any number of explanations—"

"You will be given a turn to speak for your house, Master Avani, but we are not yet done with this witness. Take your seat."

"Did this admission surprise you?" Nartilya asked the captain.

"Yes, sir," Captain Gaddar answered. "Ritin joined the day guard three moons earlier and served well. I was shocked that he would have done this. I informed Master Duvanya as required."

"How would he have carried even a small casket out of the storeroom unnoticed?"

Gaddar shrugged. "He must have kept it under his cloak."

"And the storehouse guard that night? Where was he?"

"He has sworn to the night captain that he did not witness any tampering or theft."

"Did the accused tell you why he had done this?" Madam Satya asked.

"He did not say."

"How was the accused injured?"

"I do not know, Madam."

The rani interjected, "I would like to hear the proprietor's description of events—and the storehouse guard's."

"The proprietor was called," Madam Satya said, "but we were notified today that he is ill. My steward could not locate the storehouse guard this morning. Are there more questions for this witness?"

Krux and Nartilya shook their heads. The rani said nothing, and Madam Satya dismissed the captain.

Greta sensed hesitation in Madam Satya, and the reason was clear even to her. Sentencing anyone noble-born on such serious charges was rare.

"Let the record show that additional information has been requested. However, according to the law, if the accused confirms his guilt, we will not delay in applying punishment." Madam Satya looked over a parchment on the table then spoke to the youth. "The captain has said that you confessed to stealing the firewine and attempting to sell it to the ale house proprietor. Do you agree that this is your confession, and that it is the truth?"

The young man looked from the noblewoman to the rani and hung his head.

Greta could feel Her Majesty's energy fading like the light from the hall's window.

"You have nothing to say?" Madam Satya asked. "Do you understand that we may come to a decision based solely on your confession as declared?"

Master Avani jumped to his feet, "My sister, the boy is afraid! An accused person may request another to counsel him before he answers the court."

"If you would but wait for the accused to ask for your guidance," Madam Satya answered, "I would welcome your participation."

The rani tapped her fingers against the arm of her chair. Master Avani clamped his mouth shut and wrung his hands.

The young man squeezed his eyes closed, and said, "I request the counsel of Master Jalil Komalratra of the House of Avani."

Madam Satya spoke over the groan echoing in the hall. "The accused has requested the counsel of his house. The court will conclude this matter after the proprietor of the ale house and the guard on duty offer testimony or the accused confirms his guilt, whichever comes first. The accused will remain jailed until then."

Court ended soon after, and Greta led the way, sweeping the crowd back so the rani could leave quickly with her guards.

"How much time?" the rani asked as they climbed the stairs of the palace's old tower.

"Hmmm. Less than two hours."

They entered quarters on the third floor. Except for an altar table and shrine in the inner room, cloths like mourning shrouds covered the furniture inside. These had been the rani's mother's quarters before she disappeared—Rani Shikra. Greta picked up one end of the altar table and pulled it from the wall. Raising a tapestry that hung on the wall behind the table, she felt along the stone near the ceiling and pushed a spot in the masonry. The wall receded almost soundlessly, and they faced a dark passage where it had been.

"I will go alone," the rani said. "Prepare the hall and return here."

"Eat first, Dear Child," Greta said, pulling an orange from her pocket. "You are tired."

The rani impatiently waved her away, lit a lantern, and disappeared into the passage.

When her footsteps faded, Greta dropped the tapestry into place and moved the table back. Telling the door guards that the rani should not be disturbed, she went downstairs and entered the feasting hall. Bearers scattered as she entered the kitchens and approached their chef, Korvar, who stirred a huge soup pot.

The chef set down his ladle when he saw her and went into the pantry, shutting the doors behind him. He soon re-emerged with a tray upon which sat seven small clay cups and a slim-necked surahi. He gave this to Greta, who took it to the great hall.

After listening to make sure no one hid in the hall's dark recesses, the giantess set the tray on a stone basin carved into the boulder. At the back of the boulder, higher than most could reach, she pried at a nearly invisible seam until a section of rock came loose. Underneath it, a dial sat upon a metal plate. Greta turned the dial a little then pressed the cover back into place. The basin filled with water that gently flowed over the lip and disappeared in a patch of gravel at the base. Satisfied, she returned to Rani Shikra's quarters.

After dragging the table away from the wall again, Greta sniffed the passage and went giantstill until Dear Child emerged from the darkness. Her eyes were too bright. Anise and something else floated on her breath. Greta hummed very quietly. This gift from the ancestors, one that should have healed her charge and given her courage, had become dangerous.

While Greta closed the passage and put everything back in place, the rani kicked away her clothing and took a black silk sari with a bloodred hem and pallu from an ancient wardrobe. The giantess draped the garment so the silk fell in rippling folds down the length of the rani's legs in the traditional style for the observation of the twelfth moon—the warrior's moon.

"After I marry," Dear Child said, picking at the collar of her jacket with annoyance, "I will not wear these old-fashioned costumes anymore. The elders can make their peace with me, as can my mother, wherever she may be!"

"Yes, Maharani."

"Don't try to placate me! I know you have lit countless more diyas for her than I. Are you lighting them still? Do you think I don't know that they call me callous? But I have not forgotten her! How could I? Especially on an observation day."

"No, Maharani."

"I won't be reproached by the likes of you, Less-Than-a-Servant." The rani's voice fell to a venomous whisper. "You are so very fortunate my son is whole."

"Hmmm," Greta answered as she placed the umbalvata, around the rani's neck.

The boy they had recently brought back from the Western Woods had not been bound to her companion, but he may as well have been, for the red giant could not refuse to take him in his care. The last time she had seen the red giant in the flesh, he had waited in the woods to meet them—the rani, the rani's first husband, herself, and a young nurse carrying the boy in her arms.

The nobles didn't have to use words to make the threat clear. She and the red giant understood they would be killed if anything happened to the babe they left with him.

"And you are the least of my concerns," the rani continued. "Many think their pretense is convincing, but they would enjoy nothing more than seeing me bend to fate's blows. I shall never give them that pleasure! Bright cycle or not—I will do whatever is required, everything, for the strength of the realm. And if any of them dream of stopping our ancestor-blessed progress, they will regret their poor judgment soon enough."

"Calm your mind. Breathe deep, Dear Child," Greta said, handing her the ceremonial neck chain.

The rani smoothed the umbalvata's small bones so they lay flat across her breast. Greta knelt and fastened her charge's padded slippers. By the time she rose again, the rani had already passed out of the room.

This time musicians heralded their ruler's arrival in the great hall with a blast of horns. Foreign guests, palace staff, guards, soldiers, and senior traders filled the tiers. Excitement swept the room. On long benches the leaders of the Seven Houses and their families faced the throne with more noble members clustered behind them.

Greta retreated to a corner where the stewards and kitchen staff stood ready. She did not like being so far from the rani, but observation ceremonies were sacred and, thankfully, brief. Among the new recruits eager to witness their first ceremony was the boy they had retrieved, Sid Sol, who pretended not to notice her and stayed just beyond her reach.

In the uncovered window, Matachand, the large, constant moon glowed with the color of new cream. The smaller orb, Chotabhai, had a reddish hue. Though most called Chotabhai a moon as well, his path was much more wayward, and his presence upset the seasons instead of steadying them.

The rani raised a hand and when the hall quieted, she went to the boulder and collected the surahi Greta had left there. She filled it at the basin, and Greta knew, though it was not visible to the crowd, that the rani also added a drop of elixir from her pendant into it.

Lifting the surahi above her head, Valena Sandhyatara stood before the crowd and began the tribute prescribed for the twelfth moon.

"We thank you, ancestors, for the light of Matachand and her brother in this bright cycle. In this season Raja Vijay defended the walls of Safed Qila after the ancestors ceased to walk among us. By this light and through the generations, our soldiers returned victorious from Osiara, from Hanani, from Mokantu and Jobat. Let no one doubt the strength of the warrior moon!"

As one, the heads of the Seven Houses stood and said, "Shine bright, Matachand and Chotabhai!"

"When the season turns, give us plenty."

"Shine bright, Matachand and Chotabhai!"

"When the storms rage, give us courage."

"Shine bright, Matachand and Chotabhai!"

"When the body weakens, give us peace."

"Shine bright, Matachand and Chotabhai!"

The rani poured the contents of the surahi into the seven cups and brought the tray to the nobles who gathered before the throne.

"Through all that has been visited upon us, through all that is to come, we remain your devoted children. On this, the twelfth apex, let us go forth and claim our destiny with honor. For the strength of the realm!"

The Seven raised their cups and shouted out, "Seven Houses, One Realm!"

After drinking, some of the nobles inhaled deeply and shuddered, others stretched their chins toward the ceiling with faces tensed as though a pain seared them. Greta watched the rani but was confident the contents of her cup would not overwhelm her. When the Seven leaned into their circle and grasped each other's hands in a sign of unity, the hall cheered.

Next to the giantess, Korvar ordered the bearers to line up, each with a tray holding tiny clay cups of firewine that they passed out to every-one in the hall. Refrains of "Seven Houses, One Realm!" echoed while the musicians played. There was bold talk and singing. Husbands and wives stood hand in hand. Youth sought their friends. Elders hugged one another.

When the celebration began to subside, Korvar collected the recruits. "Now you are true subjects of the realm and, for a time, you are subjects of mine. A bright cycle apex can cause the most sensible to act out, and you all are far from sensible. Follow me to the barracks, and Master Avani will explain how you can avoid making fools of yourselves."

Once the boy bobbed away with the rest of the recruits, Greta devoted all attention back to the rani. Her aura remained steady, but the effects of the elixir were not sustaining her as long as they used to. Wishing to move her charge out of the hall as soon as possible, Greta was grateful when Aseem's cries drew his mother's attention.

A nod from her gave Greta permission to approach Princess Mafala, who struggled with the aggravated little prince. The babe made great efforts to free himself of his clothing, causing Prince Hassan to walk away from the spectacle and leaving his sister the object of much amusement.

"The maharani requests her son," Greta said.

Princess Mafala laughed nervously and handed her the prince.

Before Greta took two steps, the rani met her with arms outstretched.

"He couldn't be bothered to bring our child to me, could he?" she muttered a little too loudly. "Let this union be worth the irritation!"

"You need to eat, Dear Child," Greta said. "In quarters you may feed him and have your supper."

"I am hungry," the rani said. "Best we leave now before I cry louder than my son."

Ignoring the knot of southerners who lingered, the rani led a jovial group of her house members into the gallery. She paused there to bid them good night and show Aseem the brilliant moons and the bonfire on the front grounds, but soon they proceeded to her rooms.

Inside, the rani pulled off her crown, the umbalvata, the padded slippers, and the princeling's offending clothes. Settling deep in the bed cushions, she curled around her son and put him to her dry breast to soothe him.

When their food was delivered, Greta brought it to the bedside. Taking the wilted herb that had remained in her pocket all day, the giantess tore it into pieces and mixed it into the lentils before eating a spoonful. Assured the food was clean, she urged the rani to eat.

Chewing the food down to a mash, the rani shared more with the baby than she ate herself. Soon Dear Child leaned back against the pillows and drifted to sleep along with the little prince.

As Greta covered them with a blanket there was a rap upon the door and the guard admitted Prince Hassan. His dark eyes shone as he looked upon the sleeping pair, but he did not smile.

"What is this? Sleeping after a moon ceremony? This is not done."

He flicked the blanket back and pulled the babe from his mother's arms. Greta remained still on the opposite side of the bed, taking care that he did not see her clench her fists.

"Take this child and be gone," he said, holding out the waking prince to her. "I have plans for your rani."

The disheveled rani tried to push her consort away.

"Ah, I see," Hassan said, straddling the rani on the bed and holding her arms down. "You want to play."

"Get off of me!"

"Come, try to fight me. I think the giant would enjoy watching that."

The rani stopped struggling and smiled at him, her eyes slitted like a well-fed cat's. "I think your sister would enjoy it more."

"Wha—? You have a filthy mind!"

"Is it my mind or my generosity that makes you hard?"

Hassan raised his hand to strike her. With the babe pressed to her chest, Greta grabbed his hand in one of hers and squeezed. The prince consort twisted around, pain scouring his face.

"Greta! No!" the rani shouted.

Releasing Hassan, Greta cupped the head of the fussing child. She did not move.

"I should kill you here and now," Hassan said, on his feet and facing her, his hand very close to the dagger on his belt.

Greta knew, as did the rani, that she could crush his windpipe with one hand before the dagger scratched her.

"You will go now," the rani said slowly. "Take my son and leave us. That is my word."

Greta took Aseem downstairs, hardly noticed by the revelers still milling about. After returning the young prince to his nurse, she retreated to her room and lay down on the platform that served as her bed, but she did not sleep. All night her giantsense was open, sifting the air, in case the rani should need her.

CHAPTER 11

Half a moon had passed since Rekha's scolding and the White Horse Clan had not thrown Lingli out, but the circuitous route they took from village to village made her doubt they would reach Saatkulom's capital before winter. That they had some plan for her eventual sale, kept her vigilant, but she found it difficult to count them strictly as enemies. She was well fed and free to her own pursuits in the nights while the clan slept, and she could have easily walked away into the dark—minus her things. As Matachand waned away and waxed again, and Chotabhai shone overhead like a bloodshot eye, Lingli pondered whether staying with them was prudence or cowardice on her part.

On the eve of the twelfth moon's apex, as the caravan rolled through fewer woods and more grasslands, Samir and another scout galloped back to Farid's wagon early to report a village ahead. Word passed from wagon to wagon, and the wanderers' excitement became palpable. They pushed the teams faster, stopping only long enough for the horses to drink, until, at the crest of a hill, they met a line of armed men. A village guard, it seemed—more of them carrying axes and mallets than proper blades.

Their headman dismounted, and Farid and his eldest son went out to meet them. The headman gestured toward a large field stubbled with the remains of harvest, and the wanderers pulled their wagons into the center to make camp.

Instead of their usual chores, clan members drew out poles and tarps from beneath the wagons. Lingli hung behind the Mirajkars as they drove posts in a large circle. Rahman and the cousin called Chatur fitted the end of a long pole into the hollowed-out end of a post and lashed it tight. The pole's free end had four ropes dangling from it. Rekha, Sachin, and Chatur's children took the ropes and ran toward a post on the opposite side of the circle, straining to bend the pole down. When the ends were fitted together, Lingli saw that a dome would be created.

"C'mon, Snow!" Rekha called. "Help us pull!"

Without thinking, she ran into the fray and grabbed a rope. The other children on that rope stayed as far from Lingli as they could, but no one dared let go. They pulled and slid back and pulled some more as the elders urged them on.

Once a few older ones added their weight to the effort, the pole bent to the post, and Rahman and Chatur secured it. The children cheered and broke away to reach for the rope ends of the second pole. She was going to join again, but one of the women stepped in front of her.

"Go away. We don't need your help."

Lingli returned to Tiadona's wagon, more hurt than she cared to admit.

The next afternoon, with her hood up despite the day's warmth, Lingli dawdled near the entrance to the big tent. She knew she should not draw attention to herself, but the excitement around the fair was too tempting. When a pair of village women wearing long dark tunics and dupattas passed, she followed them inside.

Several performances were underway. On one platform, boys from the caravan tumbled and bent themselves into impossible knots. On a second, women danced while balancing water jugs on their heads. A third platform held games of chance. Tables were full of goods for sale, and villagers gawked and haggled throughout.

A group gathered at the stand where Tiadona and Rekha sat surrounded by pouches of powders, bunches of roots, and medicines of all sorts. Reminded of the woods witch, Lingli watched as the clan's healer listened and occasionally put her hand to someone's forehead or asked them to cough. While Tiadona bundled assortments of remedies, Rekha took the coin and bartered items. She and Rekha were speaking again, but this time, as soon as she approached, Rekha asked to be allowed to go see the fair. After the girl happily skipped away, Lingli sat on Rekha's stool, keeping her face turned away from the villagers.

A small hut had been built in the center of the tent, and Moraten stood next to it, repeating a sing-song rhyme that promised answers to mysteries and comfort to those with troubled minds. Every few minutes he escorted a new villager to the hut's curtained doorway where Anil, with a magnificently painted face, ushered the customer inside.

"Anil is doing good business," Tiadona said. "If you had coin, what would you ask him?"

Lingli was tempted to say she had coins, and they were locked in Tiadona's trunk, but she answered, "I would ask him how I can find my brother."

"Then be glad you are poor. It has saved you from foolishness."

"Does he not speak to the ancestors?"

The old woman shrugged. "He may or he may not, but I know that, for all their designs, the ancestors are not the only ones shaping our lives." Tiadona continued, "Our lives are woven of our own choices, the choices of others, *and* the will of the ancestors. That is the weft and weave, and the pattern for each of us is never repeated," she said. "Your brother has already changed your course, has he not?"

When she did not answer, Tiadona said, "Not many are coming now. Go and see if Rahman has made any good trades."

Lingli left the tent and circled the crowd cheering a puppet show in one of the wanderer's wagons, then entered the corral where horse trading was being done. Ignoring the onlookers, Rahman leaned back on his heels and turned a chestnut gelding on a lunge line. Samir brought up a mare and tied her to a post near the villagers.

"She's not four yet," Samir said while the villagers checked the mare's teeth.

"There's something wrong with her," one of the villagers said. "Who sells a young mare if she is sound?"

"She's sound," Samir said, stroking the mare's neck. "We didn't breed her when she last came in heat. We wouldn't sell her if she was carrying a foal."

The villagers checked the mare's hooves and teeth, considering their offer. Finally, one said, "Why do I need an unbred mare? Let's look at the gelding."

Rahman led the gelding to the villagers for their examination. After some bartering with one villager, they seemed to reach agreement on a price, but Samir interrupted and said, "Before you spend your coin, sir, I must give you a chance to change your mind."

"What is this?" Rahman said. "This good man and I are making a fair trade."

The buyer's eyes slid from Rahman to Samir. "What do you mean?"

"Let's match that gelding to my mare," Samir said. "We'll race 'round that tree and back. Then you can decide which horse you'll take."

Lingli could see the man was suspicious there was a trick afoot, but he was also intrigued. He looked to Rahman, who shrugged and said, "I'll ride for you if that will bring peace to your mind. My gelding will win."

The villager agreed, and Rekha yelled, "I'll call it!" and ran into the field.

With arms outstretched, she faced her father and brother on their mounts. As soon as the horses quieted on the line, she shouted, "Go!" and the horses pounded forward, sending up broken stalks and clods of dirt in their wakes.

Rahman's gelding had the lead, but as the horses rounded a tree at the end of the field everyone could see that the mare had pulled forward on the inside. The gelding was only a half-length behind, but Samir was as close to the mare as her own skin. The mare won by a head.

A cry went up from the villagers, and they settled their bets.

"One race tells you nothing," Rahman said when he rode the gelding back to his would-be buyer, "Let us wager on two out of three."

"I won't be taken for a fool!" the man answered loudly. "I'm taking the mare."

Rahman bowed his head in respect and handed the gelding's reins to Sachin.

Samir said, "She's worth more, but I'll take the same coin you offered for the gelding."

The man's eyes lit up. Even Lingli could tell that he would not negotiate much more. Samir humbly acquiesced to the villager's counteroffer and a bag of fine goat hair.

As the villager led the mare away, she and Rekha accompanied Rahman back to the line to bring another horse to the lunge.

"He didn't know Samir is your son, did he?" Lingli asked shyly.

Rahman smiled. "No, but does that matter? The choice was his."

"He doesn't know the mare won't breed," Rekha said.

"Ahh, but Samir told him she didn't breed last cycle."

Rekha piped up, "But he didn't tell him about all the other times."

"Did the man ask?"

"No," Rekha said proudly. "He did not."

"That is how a three-coin mare fetches five."

The villagers ate their last sweets and played their last games, then hurried back to their homes at dusk. When the last one was gone all the tents, trunks, tables, and bags were packed, and the White Horse clan gathered to eat by the light of the moons.

"Grim bunch," one of the men said. "It pained them to smile."

"And hardly any carrying coin," Anil said.

"Ha, but they were generous with their goats. Were they not, Chatur?" Anil's wife said, and everyone laughed at the hapless Chatur, who had bartered his goods for several goats. His small son cradled a kid at his feet.

Lingli saw Rahman and Samir exchange looks, but neither spoke a word about their trades.

While she and Tiadona cleaned vessels, Rekha jumped from one foot to the other until her aunt took a pot from her hands. "Go, then. Take your dress to Dakshini Auntie and stay there until it's time."

Rekha scrambled into the wagon and jumped out again, carrying a folded dress on her head.

"They're preparing a dance," Tiadona explained. "The day's final tally is yet to come. No matter how poor or mean the place, we play for them, and music never fails us."

Clan members spread mats and cushions on the ground. Torches were set between the wagons, and a low wooden platform was hastily built next to Farid's wagon. While the musicians tuned their instruments, village men appeared in the field like wraiths called by the sound. Moraten ushered them into the camp as Anil stepped onto the platform wearing another fine suit and plenty of gold. He put his hands together in respect, then introduced Farid and the musicians.

Lingli recalled that the woods witch once said the ancestors preferred music to tributes. *Maybe they're listening now.* She stared into the sky, nodded to the full Matachand, and a plea for help trembled on her lips, but it would not come. To beg the venerated ones, knowing full well you would not be answered, was humiliating.

A group of boys, dressed in white with red sashes, emerged from the back of a wagon. Carrying carved sticks the length of their forearms, they faced each other in pairs and stepped high as they struck their sticks together in ever more complicated sequences. The villagers murmured their approval.

Next a bansari player floated notes that sounded like a bird call, and four girls took the floor. Rekha was among them, Lingli realized, looking much older than she was. Lines of kohl drawn out from the corners of the girls' eyes curled into intricate flower and leaf shapes on the sides of their faces. The girls hummed a melody as the music thickened, and Sonali appeared under a cluster of lanterns. Dressed in a yellow gown with a long dupatta covering her shoulders and her hair piled high upon her head, she shone so bright it made Lingli anxious, but her parents gave no sign of alarm or embarrassment.

While the girls stamped a tight beat with their heeled shoes, Sonali told a funny story in her song. Lines in the chorus had different meanings, which made Lingli smile when she understood it, and laughter rippled through the audience. This was followed by a drumming sequence and a dance by Moraten and a few of his cousins. After several jugs of fire-wine were purchased from Dakshini's wagon, the crowd settled again, and Sonali returned in a parrot-green costume ornamented with small pieces of polished metal sewn into the fabric. The dress twinkled in the lantern light, taking Lingli's breath away.

Sonali's ballad brought tears to more than one pair of eyes, and Lingli was mesmerized, feeling as if the night itself held its breath. When Sonali took her final bow, the crowd remained subdued through the tune Anil sang to bid them good night. After the villagers drifted away into the dark field, the clan moved to their wagons to sleep.

Still thinking about Sonali's beautiful voice and wishing she could inspect her gown, Lingli collected her sewing in the back of the wagon, climbed down, and sat on a log near the campfire's remaining embers. Recollecting the melodies of the evening's music, she suddenly realized how happy she felt and chided herself.

These Ascaryans don't care for me. They cut me open, for moons' sake. Yet she couldn't deny that Rekha felt like a friend. *That could be a pretense. She is a wanderer after all.* But wasn't she doing the same by pretending to like

Rekha? She certainly was pretending to be obedient until these wagons rolled her closer to Saatkulom. *Maybe I really do like her.*

Her reasoning was a tangle of knotted threads.

In her lap, upon an old scarf Tiadona had given her, Lingli had stitched a bare tree in black yarn. The tree had grown intricate branches over recent nights, and upon one branch she created a tiny blue bird from precious silk thread pulled from another scrap. She squinted at her work. It wasn't as fine as Sonali's dress, but it pleased her. The little bird sat boldly on its branch, like an open eye.

A scream—far away and quickly cut short—made her jump.

One of Farid's nephews who had been on watch entered the caravan's circle and glared at her as if she had been the one screaming. Lingli folded up her sewing and moved to the shadows between the wagons.

Several of the men, including Rahman, headed toward the village. The rest of the clan stayed quiet and watchful. When the men returned, Lingli hung behind those who gathered near the fire.

"Some moonstruck idiot went mad in the village," Anil said. "Killed his wife and attacked others before he was stopped."

"What has it got to do with us?"

"They say he was bewitched by our music."

"What? We entertain these cheap villagers, and they claim we made a man kill his wife?

"Others are behaving oddly, too."

"Moonsickness! It's not our fault they're weak!"

"Can't hold their firewine either!"

"You know that doesn't matter. It never changes."

"What do they want?" Tiadona asked.

"They want Sonali."

For a moment there was astonished silence. Sonali's parents crowded close to her.

"My daughter is no enchantress!"

"They want compensation."

"We will not give her up!"

Anil tried to quiet them. "Of course, we will not give up our songbird, but they outnumber us five to one. We have two choices. One, we negotiate a lesser price and run. Two, we fight and run."

"Will they attack?"

He shrugged. "At least a score of armed men wait at the edge of the village."

"They are simply trying to steal a woman on an apex night!"

"They are without honor! We will deny them."

Sonali had gone pale. Her mother encircled her in her arms. "Let this not come to blood on our side. We can negotiate."

"No, we should not give them anything. Not one coin!"

"We should give them the witch and be off!" This from Moraten, who had been pacing around the edge of the gathering. He cast a disgusted look at Lingli.

The idea hung in the air like smoke. Lingli felt her lungs constricting.

Rahman shook his head, but Dakshini said, "Yes, let us leave our bad luck behind!"

Farid raised a brow, then turned to his grandson and asked, "Why should they take bad luck upon themselves?"

"We will tell them she is a seer come from the east."

Rahman said, "Then we will have lost our opportunity to profit from her ransom."

"No one is going to want that star-cursed creature," Sonali's mother said.

"Her brother is in the Seven's company, and that sounds like coins rubbing together to me," Rahman said.

Lingli felt very light and far away, as if she had floated above them and what they said had nothing to do with her.

Dakshini snorted derisively. "Just offering her is risky. They may take greater offense."

"Our trades have not been what they were last cycle," Farid said. "We cannot afford to lose on any exchange between now and winter."

Rahman's words were measured, but his eyes flashed like distant lightning. "I don't intend to lose anything. I intend to keep her until we reach the Rock where she may be ransomed or sold, and the profit can be fairly shared among us."

Farid nodded slowly. "There's always a deal to be struck. The only question is how much profit or loss."

"If not her, what else could we offer?" Chatur asked.

"My brother," Rahman said, "I think we could relieve you of some goats!"

"What? You would take my poor trade and make me poorer!"

"I will pay you fair value for the goats. You know as well as I those are useless milkers."

"You will give coin to save the witch? You're the one bewitched, Mirajkar."

"I have a wager for any of you who dare make it," Rahman said. "If I don't match the value of my coin for her when we reach the Rock, I'll make it up with my next trade and a share of that profit goes to each one betting against me. If I do profit, and I intend to, I'll take a double share, and those of you bold enough to wager will still get a cut for your trouble."

"Ha, he's a confident one." Farid turned to his grandson. "Do you accept, Moraten?"

Moraten shrugged and spat in the dirt. "That thing is not worth one hair on our songbird's head. I say we're better off leaving her here, but if there's profit to be made, let us take Rahman Uncle's bet."

Some remained unconvinced, but no one decried the proposition. Farid nodded, and the deal was struck. Sonali's parents pushed her back to their wagon. Farid and Rahman went to speak to the villagers. Chatur's young son cried as his father led the goats away.

Lingli stared at the dirt and willed her spirit to come down from the sky so she could run away. Where her shoulder blades poked out, she imagined two great wings had grown. They beat slowly as she neared the ground.

"Do you not appreciate the price my brother has paid for your skin?" Tiadona said angrily, having planted herself in front of her. "Get in before I change his mind. We will drive as hard as we can to put a safe distance between us and them and hope they come to their senses by the morning."

Feeling like vermin, Lingli got in the wagon as the clan watched, though she despised herself for doing so. Rekha rolled over on her pallet and showed Lingli her back.

After the caravan moved out and all was quiet but for the horses' hoofbeats and the creak of the wagons, Lingli pulled a needle from her cloak's hem and pierced her arm on the inside of her elbow. A single, perfect dot of blood rose to the surface. As soon as she could take back her things, she promised herself she would find a way to escape, no matter the cost. How could Red have imagined she could protect Sid from anything when she couldn't protect herself?

Lingli napped fitfully until midday when the caravan came to a halt on open plains. Ignoring angry glares cast her way, she went into the field to relieve herself. The caravan began to roll out as she returned, and she made no effort to keep up. She half wished they would leave her behind, but there was no chance of that. Rahman's family could not afford more damage to their honor after last night's wager.

Walking suits me fine, she told herself, but that became less true as the sun approached its zenith. She boiled inside her cloak and hood and the wagons and riders were strung out far ahead. Never had she seen so much sky nor knew the sun could be so brilliant. When she dared squint out ahead of her feet, the world looked strange, as if the colors were draining away. Her throat began to tighten, and her heart was racing.

Stumbling into the broken shade cast by a few anar trees along the trail, she sat on the ground and tried to breathe deeply. The last wagon was a dark wavering blur climbing a rise ahead, and the last riders were only specks behind it.

She closed her eyes and rested her head on her knees, but when she looked up again, the world had become as white as the heart of a flame. All she could hear was the hollow roar of this unreal fire, and she was terrified. How long this panic lasted, she did not know, but her heart shifted from pounding to not beating at all, or at least that's what the pressure in her chest felt like. She dug a thumbnail into her palm to reassure herself that she was still alive.

Two dark objects streaked toward her in the whiteness.

"Come on, Snow!" she heard Sachin yell. "You're too far behind."

Lingli shakily got to her feet, blind and lost.

"What's wrong? What is it?" Rekha asked.

"Don't know," she croaked.

Rekha demanded Sachin help her. They pulled her to Rekha's mare and hoisted her up. When Rekha climbed onto the saddle in front of her, the girl was only a dark shape she clung to in a white field boiling with heat. The pressure grew inside and around her, and Lingli thought she would pass out. They had hardly started forward when the mare stopped suddenly. Then it came—a quiver in the earth itself. There was a deep swoop and more shuddering. The mare began to buck, and soon both girls were in the grass.

Lingli crawled over to Rekha, and they pressed themselves to the ground. Sachin, who had also been thrown, sat clutching his head nearby. The earth made another sickening shift. After another long roll and a few more shudders, the ground became still. The three of them slowly got to their feet.

"How can the ground move?" Sachin asked. His face was as pale as hers.

Lingli shook her head. Rekha held tight to her hand. When it seemed the ground would stay where it should, they began walking. Eventually Samir and Rahman appeared with the lost mounts. Rekha broke from her and ran to meet them. Envy pricked Lingli's heart as Rahman pulled his daughter onto his saddle, hugged her tight, and asked if she was whole.

"What happened, Pa?"

Rahman looked to the sky. There was a note of uncertainty Lingli had never heard in his voice before. "The ancestors have told us they are not pleased. We will make tributes tonight."

They rode to the caravan, each one as taut as a strung bow. The horses picked their way as if they were crossing ice. By the time her fear settled, Lingli realized her hands had been tingling for some time. Blisters already bubbled up under the skin. Bunching up her cloak so it covered her hands was all she could do. When they reached the camp, her hands were so swollen she couldn't hold the saddle.

Anxious families gathered each other close or knelt at shrines that had been hastily set up behind their wagons. Holding her swollen hands out before her, Lingli tried not to touch anything. Rekha loudly called to her aunt and demanded she come immediately.

"What under the stars!" Tiadona hissed.

Pain pulsed up her arms. The blisters were packed so tight the backs of her hands looked like jackfruit skin. "Too much sun."

Throwing back Lingli's hood, Tiadona put a hand to her forehead. "Well, you told us true, didn't you? The fever's already taken hold." The old woman peered into her eyes, "Open to light like a room without walls. Cannot reflect it, but she absorbs *all* of it." She drew back. "This isn't your first burn. How do you treat yourself?"

"I…I don't know. Red… They used to put poultices on my skin."

"What was in the poultice? Think! What did it smell like?"

"Like…madhumakhi bushes. I had some salve in my cloak."

Tiadona climbed into the back of the wagon and soon brought out Lingli's tiny pot of salve. Running a finger over it and sniffing, she said, "Good for later when the new skin comes, not now. I need treatments to help you bear the pain."

On Tiadona's orders Rahman and Chatur lifted Lingli into the wagon by her elbows.

"Still sure she's worth the trouble?" Chatur said flatly.

"Sachin! Fetch the firewine!" Tiadona barked, then she left the wagon muttering, "Barley and oats to take out the itch, but she must go *under* the fire, no other way."

Lingli could not look at her blisters, which had wrapped around the sides of her hands and onto the edges of her palms. Instead, she listened to White Horse Clan members invoking the ancestors on the other side of the wagon's canvas. Sonali began to sing a tribute.

"Shouldn't you join them?" Lingli asked Rekha, who had remained looking out the back of the wagon as if she were her guard.

Rekha shook her head and brought her water to drink. "I make a tribute to my ma every night, and I will tonight, too. She'll tell the others what I want."

Lingli had always ignored talk of mothers, but anything was better than thinking about her hands. Trying to keep her voice steady, she asked, "Does she answer you?"

Rekha wrinkled her brow and thought for a second. "Sometimes. But you know I'm a child. I ask for a lot of silly things that aren't important."

Tiadona returned with a cup full of herbs stirred into curd. "The pain will get worse. You need this in your stomach before I give you the potion. Then you must sleep as much as you can until the fire burns itself out."

When the curd was gone, Rekha fed her small pieces of roti. She swallowed a few bites, then Tiadona held a cup of firewine to her lips. The first cup went down quickly, the second slower, the third took time. Although the pain remained, it seemed to matter less, and she fell into an oblivion heavier than sleep.

Night reigned when Lingli woke the first time. Burning intensely on the inside, she was surprised her skin did not glow, but equally alarming was the sense of pressure building in her chest. The ground under them swayed slowly, then there was a short shake, and Lingli thought she would choke. Muffled cries erupted from other wagons. When the movement ended, her breathing grew easier.

Bringing her a cup of sour-smelling potion, Tiadona said, "You felt it coming, didn't you?"

She said nothing and drank without argument, the question of whether to trust Tiadona being the least of her concerns. While the healer dripped water on her head, she fell asleep again.

The next time Lingli woke it was day. The wagon lurched through a rut, and she touched the pallet to avoid rolling over, causing pain to stab up her arms. Her hands were as swollen as goats' udders, and fear tickled behind her ribs.

She had been burned before, of course. Playing outside with Sid too early in the evening or too late in the morning had made her ill, but not like this. On the few occasions she had blistered her hands or her face, "Madam," as Red called the witch, had treated her tender skin and scolded her, but Lingli's worst burn occurred before she had more than a few memories.

Lingli remembered Red patting her head and telling her and a very young Sid, "Many nights I sat in this doorway, half-asleep, while this girl played and talked to the stars. Then you came. You cried in the day like this—'Wah!' And she cried in the night like this—'Hey!' I was tired, but this girl liked to roam. I had a little string, and I tied one end to her leg and the other end to my finger. I thought, when she tries to go out the string will become tight and wake me. But one night this too-smart girl escaped! After I fell asleep, she slipped the string off and out the door she went!

"I slept until this baby"—and here Red would pat Sid's head—"started crying for milk. I heated the milk. I looked at my finger. I wondered why there was a string on my finger. Then I remembered! There was supposed to be a small girl on the other end of the string, but there was no small girl." At this point in the story, Red always smacked his own head with a force that would have knocked a man down, and this struck the children as extremely funny every time.

"I went outside. The sun had risen to the top of the trees, and what did I see in the garden? This fingerling dancing and looking straight at the sun! I snatched her up. Smoke rose from her hair. It was very bad. She almost went to stone before Madam came. I didn't sleep for many days."

Red ended the story by poking them in their stomachs. "You," he said to Lingli, "learned to mind better. And you, little one, knew no better but you saved her life!"

Tiadona put a cup of water to her lips.

"Sleep is easier," she said, "but you must try to stay in your body a little longer each day."

"My hands?" Lingli managed to ask.

The healer shook her head, "It is too soon. In three days we'll reach the home of a powerful spirit. Green magic, not otherworld. We'll make a tribute."

When the caravan stopped, Lingli trembled with cold as Rekha plied her with potions and firewine, and Tiadona slowly ladled a thick mixture of herbs over her hands. It took all her strength not to scream as the healer wound strips of cloth around her burned hands. When Rekha asked her aunt if she would live, Lingli tried to listen to Tiadona's answer, but she was already falling backward, away from them and down a dark, twisting tunnel, and then there was nothing.

Days later Lingli lay at the back of the wagon and groggily looked up at towering bluffs pocked with ledges and small caves. *Good hiding places.* She regretted the condition of her bandaged hands and sat up, hoping to shake off the fever that lurked behind her eyes.

The caravan followed a creek into a glade edged with blackened stone walls. Traces of several old buildings—most jumbles of rotted timbers that sagged under the weight of vines and saplings. When Tiadona stopped the team, they were on the water's edge, ringed in by the bluffs.

"What is this place?" Lingli asked.

"Mokantu," Rahman answered as he unhitched his team. He nodded toward a shoulder-high mound of rocks. A scrap of blue flag was tied to a post on top. "Built by the Seven. There was a battle here twenty cycles back. Saatkulom drove the southerners off, but the fort was ruined."

Mention of Saatkulom lifted Lingli's heart. *Are we close?*

Rekha found a trail leading upstream and demanded Lingli come with her. After days of inactivity, Lingli staggered after her, pushing away vines and brush with her shoulders until they came to the edge of a turquoise-colored pool. Its surface churned near the bluff where a spring erupted, but gentler water flowed downstream.

"We camped here last cycle," Rekha said. "No place is more beautiful than this, except our winter camp, Korongal. Do you know how to swim?"

"I can float," Lingli answered, recalling how Red had sat in the creek near their cabin with the water barely covering his chest. It had seemed so deep as she and Sid had balanced on his fingertips.

The pool whispered to Lingli, but the peace it promised eluded her. While Rekha dug into the sand with a stick, a heat rose within her and she didn't know if it was because of her burns or a portent of another ground shaking. Her hands and head throbbed. She was about to return to the wagon when Tiadona emerged on the trail, carrying blankets and clothes.

Tiadona told Rekha, "Help her undress. We wash everything."

Shaking out a blanket, the healer held it between her and the trail. Rekha helped her balance while she reluctantly removed her clothes. Her skin was so white it was an affront even to her. Though Rekha tried to keep her face empty, Lingli saw her glance at her chest and her sex. She felt like something found underneath a log. A creature grown crooked. A mushroom. A mold.

She stepped into a skirt Rekha held open, and they slid a kurta over her head and arms. Moments later Rahman and Sachin appeared with armfuls of wood and set about building a fire at the water's edge. Tiadona shook a sprig of sage above her head and chanted. Taking a shaky step away from the heat, Lingli saw Farid, Anil, and others watching from the bank. Fright climbed within her.

When Rekha wound an arm around her waist, Lingli meant to move away, but her head hurt so. Bees of light crowded the edges of her sight. She was afraid the world would begin to pitch again.

"Don't worry," Rekha said, "I won't touch your hands."

She could make no sense of this and took stuttering steps as Rekha guided her toward the pool. When Tiadona paused her incantation long enough to pull a small blade from her pocket, fear nearly strangled Lingli before she understood that the healer only intended to cut away the dirty bandages on her hands. Blotchy white and red claws greeted her. Patches of shredded skin hung where blisters had broken and drained.

Tiadona sniffed the skin. "No scent of rot. Can you move your fingers?"

She tried. The pain was not as bad as she imagined. She moved her index fingers and her thumbs. Rekha clapped.

Tiadona nodded. "Now we wash you properly in pure water."

Rekha and Tiadona walked her into the pool. The water moved fast below the surface.

"The spirit of this place is near."

"Spirit?" Lingli's voice was shrill to her own ears. "Can't I just put my hands in?"

Tiadona shook her head. "You must immerse yourself, or the fire will hide within and bring illness later. Do as I say and do not show disrespect to Mokantu Apsara."

Rekha tugged her forward. Resuming her chant, Tiadona's voice became urgent. Ahead, the water roiled above the spring. Lingli's skin grew goose pimples.

"It's freezing!" Rekha cried.

"Deeper," her aunt answered. "Go slowly."

Something in the faces of those on the banks told Lingli that if she resisted, she would not be long with this clan. With Rekha acting as her anchor, she shuffled forward until they were both hip-deep. Tiadona told them to stop and looked around at the others.

"Samir, help them." Seeing Samir's scowl, Tiadona added, "The current is very strong. Are you stronger?"

Removing his belt, Samir waded in and took hold of one of Lingli's arms above the elbow. When she gingerly touched her palms to the surface of the water, they tingled. She jerked her hands up.

"Do you want to know greater suffering?" Tiadona growled. "Find your nerve or come out."

Lingli slowly lowered her arms again. After the initial shock, the water felt like a living thing trembling under her ruined hands. The three of them moved to the middle of the pool, leaning against the current and slipping occasionally on the stones below.

Suddenly the bottom of the pool tipped toward the center. Rekha and Samir floundered for a few steps and all three braced with legs apart in the shoulder-deep water.

"It's not so bad now," Rekha said brightly, though her chin trembled.

"Stay there until I call you," Tiadona told them.

Rekha and Samir turned Lingli between them. Samir held her shoulders from behind and blocked the current a bit. Fighting for balance, Rekha stood in front of Lingli and grasped her elbows.

Heat from the fire behind Tiadona made the air quiver. The healer put a flower on the surface of the water, watching it spin circles in the pool before being swept away.

"Old one who is ever young, hear me!" Tiadona called out. "Guardian of these waters hear me! Sundari Apsara, hear me!" The healer held her hands up in supplication. "The wounds of this girl are deep. She pays tribute and seeks your healing."

Over the rush of water, Tiadona told Lingli, "You must submit completely. When I tell you to take a breath, it should be a big breath, understand? You will go under for a count of twenty."

Lingli nodded. The heat inside had fled, and she was numb with cold.

"Hold her steady," Tiadona told Rekha and Samir. "Now, take your breath."

As Samir pushed her shoulders down, the muscles in Lingli's legs bunched, and she wanted to fight her way upright but stopped herself. The water closed over her head, and the green- and teal-colored world around her became weightless and nearly silent, but for the beating of her heart. Clouds of sand whirled where Rekha's heels bounced off the bottom of the pool. Small fish darted by, glittering silver. Her hands with their ragged edges of old skin did not hurt, and the cold no longer mattered. But her sense of peace was disturbed by a flash in the corner of her eye.

She peered toward the darker, deeper waters. Something long and golden swam alongside her. It came very close, but she had only the briefest impression of wide-set eyes, watery tresses, and whiskers before it disappeared. Then Samir was squeezing her shoulders, and she was above the surface again. With water flying off the end of her nose, she looked around for signs of the visitor, but Samir and Rekha behaved as though they had seen nothing.

"Witness her tribute, Sundari Apsara," Tiadona intoned from the bank. "Heal her and let her live whole until the ancestors call her!"

"We did it," Rekha whispered through chattering teeth. "Now be well, because I'm not getting in this water again!"

When they reached the shallows, Samir grabbed his things and stalked off. Rahman wrapped Rekha in a blanket and set another blanket on Lingli's shoulders. The others left, but Tiadona stood at the water's edge staring into the pool as if she saw something there until Rahman kicked the fire out and called his sister. Lingli and Rekha climbed the bank, and they returned to camp.

CHAPTER 12

After the observation ceremony Korvar hustled the recruits up to the feasting hall's terrace outside the barracks, where they met Master Avani and a steward guarding a table set with butter cakes, breads, fruit, and jugs of thin firewine. Sid followed the steward's every movement as he poured cups of firewine and set them on the table.

"During the bright cycles' full moons we must take care," Master Avani began. "The moons' pulls affect us all—from noble to nit—and you are new here and without your families' protection." Holding his palms upward as if the First Mother would descend from the sky at any moment, he continued, "Controlling our emotions and desires is always challenging, and there is honor for those who manage it well. It is your responsibility to discover your true nature and how vulnerable you may be. If you're tempted to act less than honorably, we can help you, but you must let us know."

I'm going to act less than honorably if I don't get a cup of firewine soon.

"I remember very clearly my first observation ceremony after being named head of my house," Master Avani said. "It was... Well, the simplest way I can say it is that the world seemed to triple in size that night. I felt both lost and found, as some of you might feel right now."

The old noble could see that the boys craned their necks to look past him and get a good view of the cakes.

"Perhaps you have heard all you can hear tonight," he conceded. "Very well, let it be. Enjoy the food and drink and stay up as long as you wish, but you are not to leave this terrace unless you are returning to your rooms."

The old noble had hardly retreated to the barracks when they fell on the food like wolves on a goat. Only when they were scraping the platters and sucking their fingers did the recruits relax and admire the glow of countless tribute fires lit on the palace grounds and Safed Qila's rooftops.

151

The steward finally carted off the platters and jugs, and a few boys hoisted Harno onto the hall's roof and pulled each other up, one after another. Rud produced a skin of full-strength firewine and won everyone's praise as they passed it around. In short order, they ceased caring when they were teased, and the jokes told were the funniest they had ever heard. Individually their alliances might be as fickle as a laundry girl's favor, but together, it seemed to Sid that all understood that maintaining a united front against the rest served them well.

When most of the boys had left or fallen asleep where they lay around the rooftop, Sid got to his feet and looked into the starscape above. His past seemed far away. The future barely a breath beyond the present. *Chandrabhavan is my home now, Mother. I'll claim no other for as long as I live.*

In the front grounds below, a procession of people marched from the new tower. Senior soldiers from the House of Duvanya, wearing bearskin cloaks. Sid had heard that each house had its own ceremonies on observation nights, all of which were rather mysterious and kept secret from others. He watched the soldiers pass around the hall and continue to the palace gate where they made two lines facing one another. The soldiers drew their talwars and crossed blades with the one opposite. Someone spoke in deep tones. *A vow*, Sid thought. Then one by one, the men passed under the arch of blades and through the gate.

Annoyed with himself, Sid shook his head. *What am I doing? If I can't get off my lazy arse and grab my true destiny now, who's to blame?* As he began to climb down from the roof, he had an idea. *Maybe Shankar can help?* Korvar's son knew more about the nobles and their habits than most. *Maybe he could help me get Master Duvanya's attention.*

He could not waste another day wondering. Instead of going back to his room to sleep, Sid made his way down to the kitchens with the bakers who kept otherworld hours for the sake of bread. He did whatever they asked until Shankar arrived with his father for first shift—both of them shocked to see Sid rolling piecrusts.

As soon as the chef was out of earshot, Sid confided his wish to serve the defenses hall. "It's not that I mind being a bearer," he told Shankar as he floured a ball of dough, "but I've got to try defenses. If I serve Master Duvanya, I'll have a chance to make a good impression before the next rotation."

"You better," Shankar said, staring pointedly at Sid's round stomach. "You're eating too much pie."

"Can you help me?"

Shankar considered the request. "I'll try. Filant owes me a favor."

Trying hard not to appear too eager, Sid handed off the bottom crusts from baking and only slid sidelong glances at Filant when Shankar drew him aside. He almost mastered looking surprised when Filant passed his table and told him to take up trays for the defenses hall and the armory.

"Now you owe me," Shankar said.

"With pleasure," Sid answered with a bow.

A short time later, bearing a tray of puris and the tea service, Sid followed his new group to the defenses hall. On their way they met a contingent of three score young men clad in red tunics. The newcomers were lean, muscular, and lighter-skinned than many southerners. They ran into the training yard in formation, their feet pounding the ground in a unified beat. A boy in the front carried a banner with a long-toothed sand cat on it.

"Who are they?" Sid asked the steward with his group.

"House of Kirdun."

"But they look like us," Sid said.

"Us? *You* are not one of *us*, Woods Boy," the steward answered haughtily. "Their lands border Saatkulom to the southeast. Try to have some manners and stop gawking. All their presence means for you is more potatoes to peel and more thalis to wash."

In the large room above the armory, Master Duvanya sat at the head of a long, polished table, flanked on either side by Prince Hassan and Ameer Khush of the House of Afreh. Sid had observed that the head of Saatkulom's defenses had a habit of staring closely at whomever he addressed in a manner that could be intimidating, but Sid had never witnessed him speak harshly or rudely to anyone. The same could not be said for his guests.

The boys bearing thalis served the three nobles, and Sid followed, careful not to short or overfill the nobles' cups. He drew back to a sideboard with the other bearers to await Master Duvanya's signal for further service. *Stop fidgeting. You are exactly where you're supposed to be. Great destinies must be sought out.*

"The next exercises will be related to rescue," Master Duvanya said to the southern nobles. "We find it helps instill loyalty to their comrades even in difficult circumstances."

Prince Hassan translated this for Ameer Khush, who gave him a quizzical look, then the prince said, "Our youth have proven their loyalty already."

"To their own house, yes, but all our youth train together, even those who are not of the Seven," Master Duvanya explained. "We find that this practice helps them work together with greater trust as their assignments become more complex."

"We find that training among their house members helps them avoid natural jealousies," Prince Hassan said.

"By mixing the groups, that is exactly what we seek to overcome. If your youth train only by house, how do they learn to cooperate with one another in the field?"

Prince Hassan's lips stretched taut. His eyes narrowed. This was the prince smiling, Sid realized. Hassan turned to Ameer Khush and spoke to him in one of the languages of the south. The rotund ameer snorted when he understood Master Duvanya's question.

"He said," the prince translated, "his house follows the Te-dakah Covenant—our 'rules,' as you call them. Respect for authority is critical to all our interactions, and that discipline is easier to maintain if our houses remain independent. Joint missions have been rare."

"Our alliance will be a new experience, then. Have you prepared them for disagreements among commanders?"

Hassan shrugged. "The authority of the senior-most commander must be respected. Disputes within houses are rare but costly. Challenges often result in the loser's death."

"Who will be the senior commander under the alliance?"

"That is yet undecided," Prince Hassan said, taking a sip of tea. Sid noticed that he did not translate the last question for Ameer Khush.

The conversation hung heavy in the room.

Prince Hassan said, "Our practices may seem unduly strict to others, but we value each warrior and wish to avoid losses among those who protect us, a concern I am certain you share. Are you familiar with our practice of choosing these youth?"

"The rani has told me of the endurance test that your youth undergo when they are—what age? Fourteen sun cycles?"

"Fifteen," Hassan said. "The Hudulfah and Afreh youth here have all survived the Sabirgazi. They are considered avatars for their ancestors because they have proven their strength and defeated fear."

"But it is not required of everyone?"

"Half our young attempt it. Of those, one in ten will complete it. Only those who complete the Sabirgazi achieve warrior status."

Sid served puris to Master Duvanya and Ameer Khush, but Prince Hassan waved him away.

"I commend your youth for the discipline and aptitude they have shown in several exercises," Master Duvanya said. "There is, however, one aspect of training that the House of Afreh has not performed as well as expected."

Hassan looked surprised. He translated the defense master's statement for Ameer Khush.

Master Duvanya said flatly, "The unit assigned to archery training has refused to follow directions."

"Only that unit? No other?"

"No other has been assigned to archery training as yet. Please explain to the ameer that because he made it clear that he wanted his youth to learn all the skills we could offer, I felt it necessary to bring this to his attention."

After Hassan's translation was shared, Ameer Khush pushed back from the table and went to one of the stone lattice screens that overlooked the training yard. He called out to a group of fighters who were still eating. The youth from his house rose and stood at attention. Upon his command, a dozen or more boys came forward and climbed up to the meeting room. The ameer directed them to stand in a line and face the yard. As if the sun had passed behind a cloud, Sid sensed a sudden tension among them.

Ameer Khush asked the first boy a question. The boy answered, and another boy stepped forward in the line.

"This one leads this unit," Hassan told Master Duvanya.

The ameer spoke to the leader. Immediately the boy answered him and knelt with one leg forward.

Hassan said, "The honorable ameer told the boy that there has been a complaint about his unit's performance in archery training. The boy says that it is true, his unit did not follow the commands given."

"For what reason?" Master Duvanya asked.

"That does not matter. He failed to follow orders."

The ameer then pulled out a knife with a squat blade barely as long as a finger joint. He gave it to the first boy in line. The boy walked forward slowly until he faced the kneeling youth. He touched his fingers to his head in a sign of respect, then he quickly stabbed the youth's exposed thigh.

Sid couldn't help it. He gasped audibly and snapped his mouth shut when Prince Hassan looked his way. Master Duvanya said nothing and did not look away from the kneeling boy, who did not cry out or move, but said a few words through gritted teeth.

The boy who stabbed him handed the knife to the next in line, who also quickly stabbed the boy and passed the knife.

"He must ask forgiveness from each member of his unit," Hassan said.

Sid watched the red seep through the boy's thin pant leg, the stain growing with each strike. He began to feel lightheaded. *Nine more. Don't look at him. Look at the floor.*

Then the boy being stabbed made a small noise, and Sid looked. Not at the boy's face, just his feet, and one foot was red with blood. Blood soaked the end of his pant leg. Blood pooled on the floor. So much blood.

Sid put out one hand to steady himself and upset the tray of puris.

That's all he remembered until he looked up at a healer wiping his face with a wet cloth. The steward behind the healer glared at him. He struggled to sit up. The nobles, the wounded boy, and everyone else were gone.

"Can you get up?" the steward asked sourly.

"What?"

"You fainted, Woods Boy."

The healer helped him stand. "You'll be fine," he said.

But he knew he wouldn't.

Shame flushed Sid through and through as he made his way back to the feasting hall. Trudging toward the merciless teasing he was sure to receive in the kitchens, he heard a low sound he had never heard before and stopped, wondering what caused it. It deepened and spread. It seemed the Rock itself was groaning.

Pots and pans hanging in the kitchen's back room swung wildly. Thalis rattled in their stacks. Kitchen staff and recruits crouched and or leaned against the walls until Korvar began bellowing and they all made their way outside. Sid forgot his troubles as he and the other bearers huddled together on the platform. The feasting hall trembled, and they watched rocks begin to break loose from the rock face and strike the mining hall. Other palace staff and day guards sat on the ground or stumbled across the yard. Horses in the stables squealed in panic.

Soon it was over and so quiet it seemed the world itself held its breath. The kitchen staff and recruits had hardly begun to straighten and move apart when day guards ordered everyone to the front grounds. Korvar herded his workers up to the front of the central hall. On the way there, the ground shuddered again, throwing everyone into another panic.

Once the world stilled, staff, guests, and a few members of the noble families clustered in small knots at the base of the central hall. Some looked ill, and all looked shocked, but they braced themselves for more. The bright autumnal sun bore down on them as if nothing had happened, and their restlessness grew. Day guards stood at the gates.

At last, the rani came to the edge of the central hall's gallery. Greta and the great black wolf, Akela, stood on one side. Master Avani and Prince Hassan stood on the other. The rani raised her hand, and all eyes were upon her.

"The world shook," she said in a steady voice, "but we did not fall. We are standing. We are strong Ascaryans. We know fear, but we must put fear aside and show courage. Every section head, speak now and tell me if your people are accounted for."

There was a moment of silence, then Captain Gaddar called out, "Day guard! All present!"

"Housekeeping!" Madam Bren yelled. "All present!"

"Kitchens!" Korvar shouted. "All present!"

"Mines!" Sir Roshan yelled. "Eleven are in the belly! We will retrieve them with permission, Your Majesty!"

"Assemble at your hall and await my word," the rani answered.

The miners departed quickly, and the babble of voices rose even while other groups reported. Sid watched Master Avani lean close and whisper to Her Majesty. She grabbed the edge of the parapet and leaned forward.

"We do not know, yet, why this happened. It was unforeseen, but not unknown. Similar events have been described and faithfully recorded in our books in cycles long past. We will pay tribute and seek the wisdom of the ancestors. If the shaking returns, you will join me here under the protection of the sun and stars and the spirits of those who preceded us." She paused. "Take comfort in the strength of the realm. We will learn how to protect ourselves. For now, return to your duties. That is my word."

But even her word was barely enough to move them.

Staff held each other's hands and walked softly, as if their footsteps might cause the shaking to resume. The southerners erupted into loud talk and arguments. Captain Gaddar and the night captain, Master Duvanya's eldest son, chose people to assist in the rescue of the miners. A few recruits volunteered, but Sid was more relieved than disappointed when Korvar ordered his bearers into the kitchen.

Everything inside was in shambles. The boys encircled the cook as he turned in circles with his mouth open. Stacks of thalis had tipped over, and pieces of pots, clay cups, and jugs littered the floor. After a few breaths, the chef collected himself enough to issue orders and put all hands to work cleaning the mess and preparing supper while he tallied the damages.

Sid and the other boys hardly had time to sweep up the litter before a procession of elders gathered on the front grounds. To make the old ones more comfortable, the bearers hauled benches and tables outside, for they refused to sit inside the hall. Opinions on the cause of the shaking ranged from flooding rivers to the frightful possibility of a visit from the otherworld, and Sid admired how the rani soothed them with a demonstration of polite respect no matter how farfetched or emotional the argument presented.

Having winded themselves after a few hours, the elders returned to their homes seemingly reassured, or at least accepting the rani's request that they use their authority to calm rather than inflame the fears of their house members while more was learned about the event.

At supper they cheered the miners who were freed from considerable rubble, but there was no denying that the shaking had unsettled everyone.

Being forced to accept that a basic tenet of their lives had changed—that the stone they stood on could shift under their feet—created doubts and fears that did not go away. Everyone slept outdoors for several nights, and some hoarded food. Some were quiet, others angry. Most sought the wisdom of the ancestors, resulting in such a thick haze of smoke from repeated homages at shrines all over the Rock that Sid and many others coughed for a week.

Eventually, however, the inhabitants of the Rock stopped making long and repeated tributes, repairs were made, and everyday life returned. Sid's own small tributes became less concerned with the shaking and more focused on his earlier embarrassment in the defenses hall and the vexing question of his purpose.

She said I'd do great things. What? How? The only way I can come close to defenses is to let Master Duvanya's memory of me die away. Maybe serving Captain Gaddar in the day guards is a better idea than soldiering. Good clothes, respect, and I'd be in the palace, not more than an arm's length from the kitchens. But I still have to complete training.

Such thoughts circled through Sid's mind day and night. The cycle was wearing on, and where was he? Opportunities to improve his situation evaded him until one morning when he spotted Master Avani bumbling in the gallery alongside the rani and Prince Hassan. Hoisting his empty tray up on his shoulder, Sid slowed as he drew close to the nobles.

"Ah, you," Master Avani called out, his hands full of scrolls. "Pardon me, Your Majesty. Yes, you, Sid Sol. Come here. Take some of these, boy." He stuffed scrolls under Sid's free arm. "Don't crush them!"

"As I was saying," Master Avani continued, "I revisited the earliest sections of the Book of Avani, and there are a few passages, within our descriptions of Starfall, that include events like the shaking we experienced."

"Shhh, brother," the rani said. "Do not fan such fears. I would like to believe there is a less-otherworldly cause. Let us not draw conclusions from one house's description of history."

"One house or seven," Prince Hassan said, "it does not bode well if your elders fail to understand the message the ancestors are sending."

The rani said icily, "Do your elders know the reason? Should we expect word from Avakstan next week? What a relief that would be for everyone."

Prince Hassan drew back and smiled at the rani's aggravation, and Sid had the impression that he and she had had this kind of exchange before. He looked to the far end of the gallery and wished they would start walking again.

Master Avani said, "Well, certainly more interpretations would be welcome. That is why I must request our other houses to share descriptions of similar events from their books."

"I am not convinced the other houses will be inclined to share their chronicles," the rani said, "but I agree we must learn all we can about this, and the other matters we discussed this morning."

"Yes, yes, I'll speak to them soon," the old noble said, before turning to Prince Hassan. "Do your elders record the messages they receive from the ancestors in writing?"

"We keep no books," the prince answered. "The ancestors speak to us through the elders when they choose."

"Ah, this sounds very similar to what we practiced in the early generations," Master Avani said. "Our oracle still provides this more direct communication. Unfortunately, she says the ancestors have not yet conveyed any message on the shaking."

The rani said, "We will discuss this after we hear her word, dear brother, but I must leave you now. Much awaits my attention today."

"Oh, yes, of course, Maharani." Master Avani bowed as well as he could without dropping his scrolls.

The rani and her consort departed, and Master Avani asked Sid, "Have you ever seen a library, boy?"

Sid shook his head and followed Master Avani up the stairs of the old tower. As they climbed, the noise of the palace fell away. A guard unlocked one of the doors on the third floor and preceded them with a lantern that illuminated a room lined with shelves from floor to ceiling that held sheaves of parchment, scrolls, and bound books. Though he and Lingli had learned how to read the common tongue as children, Sid had never seen more than a few scrolls, much less read a book.

"This is where we keep all our shared documents—the reports of all our envoys and trade agreements, discoveries in the natural world, engineering methods, even the shared chronicles of the Seven."

"I thought each house had its own book?" Sid said.

"They do. Each house recorded their journey to the Rock. Each marked how they came, who made the journey, their customs and practices, their leaders and lineages. The original books were in each house's native tongue, but we took up the common tongue by the eighth generation, and that is also when the houses agreed they would share some information with the others."

For a moment it seemed that Master Avani was so inspired by their collected history that he had forgotten Sid was there, but then he turned to him and said, "Master Tilan says that you can read, but I cannot fathom how you would have learned how to read from a giant."

"I didn't. A woman taught me."

"A literate woman in the Western Woods? Was she from Akroyat?"

"I don't know where she was from." Sid ran a hand through his hair. He suspected this conversation was not going to move him closer to joining defenses.

Unrolling one of the parchments Sid had just deposited on the table, the old noble asked, "Can you read this?"

The script was freshly written, but Sid could only make out a few words.

"It's something about Matachand and Chotabhai."

"Yes, yes," Master Avani said. "This"—he tapped the parchment—"is a translation from the House of Avani's first book. The passage is transcribed from a section recorded more than forty generations ago—during the bright cycle at the end of Starfall."

"When the ancestors walked the world?"

Master Avani nodded. "When I first read it, I thought it was an exaggeration, perhaps the writer's dream, but given recent events, perhaps not." He leaned close and traced a line of script with his finger. "The translation was terribly difficult—."

There was a rap on the door and the guard let in Rud, one of the other bearers. Red-faced and breathing hard, the boy bowed to Master Avani and blurted out, "Pardon me, Masterji. Sorry to disturb you. Korvar Sir sent me to find Sid. All hands are required in the kitchen."

Master Avani closed his eyes for a moment. "All right," he told Sid. "I am not one to hamper the efforts of our good cook. Perhaps we'll speak more of this after rotations next week."

"About that, sir. I'd, uh… I'd like to join defenses next rotation."

"Would you? You and every other apprentice."

"I think I'd serve well as a guard."

"I see." Sid thought the old noble looked disappointed. "I will take your request seriously, but I make no promises."

As Rud pulled Sid from the room, he squeezed his arm so hard, Sid was about to shove him off.

"Come on," Rud said. "Korvar's lost his mind. He's ready to hand us bearers over to the jailer."

"What's happened?"

"Somebody's nicked something this morning," Rud said. "I don't know what, but it must have been precious, from the way he's going on. He's asking each and all about it and says the thief will be tossed over the first gate as soon as he finds him."

Sid shrugged. "I didn't steal anything."

"Where did you come from?" Rud said. "You didn't and I didn't, but the one who did will put it on us new boys. I'll vouch for you if you vouch for me. Is it a deal?"

"Where were you this morning?"

"I had the late shift and was washing my ass in a tub. Where were you?"

"New tower."

When the boys reached the feasting hall, it was nearly midday and the tables were crowded with more defenders and palace staff than usual. The service roster was forgotten, the bakers were cursing the rush, and Korvar bellowed at everyone who drew near. Sid and Rud slunk into the kitchens, and Sid sent a silent thank you to the ancestors when it became clear that the cook had no time to interrogate anyone.

While he delivered thalis, Sid saw that the day guards had formed a loose gauntlet stretching from the colonnade to the palace gates. New arrivals from the south began to flow along it. Still round-eyed by the palace sights and coated with the dust of travel, nobles, headmen, servants, and all their wives and children jumbled together in the hall, making small mountains of trunks and bags.

The recruits served for hours before the musicians began playing and heads turned toward the archway on the central palace's side of the hall. Prince Hassan and his sister had entered one end of the colonnade. Southerners prostrated themselves and pressed their foreheads to the ground as they passed.

With his tray propped against his stomach, Sid offered the prince and princess tea. Evidently this was not the proper thing to do, for the prince's glare could have seared skin, and Mafala said something in her language that certainly sounded like an insult.

Trumpets signaled the rani's arrival, and Prince Hassan immediately moved to meet her. The southern women began to whisper and poke one another as he escorted the rani into the hall. The rani and Princess Mafala wore almost identical skirts of the palest pink, but the smile on the rani's lips seemed to Sid to be more for her guests' pleasure than her own.

Among the southern nobles waiting to present gifts in the front of the hall, the ameer of Kirdun, stood out in his crimson coat and his loud, merry manner—seeming to befriend all he met. As the rani approached, he bowed and then prostrated himself before her, raising more chatter in the hall, but she received this impudence warmly and bid him stand next to her.

When he went to fetch more drinks from the kitchen, Sid found Korvar pacing in circles.

"What to do? A guest is a guest is a guest. Filant? Filant, where are you? Take some of these recruits and go to the butchery. Tell them nothing less than ten goats. I don't care if they have to collect from the zhoukoo."

"Some wanderers just arrived," Filant said. "They say they've got fresh venison."

"Venison? Oh, that's helpful. Yes, yes. Go." Korvar waved at Sid and a couple of others. "Help him bring it in, then off to the butchery."

A commotion erupted outside as the boys left the kitchens. A big bay horse hitched to a wagon danced in its harness next to the platform. Some of the boys tried to grab the deer carcasses in the back but drew back as the frightened animal slammed the corner of the wagon against the platform's edge.

The reason for the horse's growing panic was plain enough: Trechur and Titok were in the yard, unmuzzled and unchained. Feeling as though his feet had been nailed to the platform, Sid was dimly aware of Korvar ordering someone to find Master Vaksana.

The wolves sniffed the air and stalked toward the horse slowly, lips twitching.

The horse began to rear and plunge. A girl with two thick braids held tight to the reins and was being jerked off the bench for her efforts. Another person in a hooded cloak was at the horse's side pulling uselessly on its breast strap.

"Get a sack!" the girl yelled. "Cover his eyes!"

One of the boys threw a drying cloth to the cloaked person, who slapped it across the horse's eyes, but the distraught creature had the scent of the wolves just as they had his, and it knew better than to wait for an attack. With a sharp toss of its head, the cloth went flying, and the horse bolted. Sid watched the one who had clung to the horse's side fall in the yard, and the girl jumped from the bench just before the wagon tipped over.

Master Vaksana ran into the yard as the other wolfhandler came from the mining hall, toting harnesses. The wolves growled, seeming to dare the men to stop them. As he had after the hunt on the Rock's summit, Master Vaksana blew into the small metal object and ordered the beasts down.

"Get the venison!" Korvar shouted as he pushed Sid and other boys from the platform.

Scrambling for balance, Sid got to his feet and, with the others, ran toward the spilled goods with a speed inspired less by the urgency of the order and more by the proximity of the two seething wolves behind.

CHAPTER 13

An immense rock monolith before the wanderers' caravan rose so high it made Lingli's neck hurt to look at the top. This lone mountain, completely foreign to the plains around it, was marked by a white wall winding up its side that looked like a great snake from a distance. And now that they were close, she imagined the gate at its base was its head—its open jaws waiting to swallow her whole.

Are you here, Sid?

This was her best chance of ever finding him and keeping her promise to Red. This was also where Rahman and Tiadona's gamble would play itself out if she didn't escape them. They must have had the same thought, for as soon as the wanderers circled their wagons, Tiadona took her by the arm as she started to climb out.

"There will be no running," the old woman told her.

Rahman was behind his sister with a length of rope. Lingli instantly went cold inside as he tied one end of the rope to her ankle, and the other to her wrist.

Rekha came over to her father, and Lingli closed her eyes.

"Why, Pa?"

"There's a debt to be paid."

"But Snow is going to find her brother here."

"Best hope she does."

Lingli tried to calm herself. She hated the confusion on Rekha's face. She hated the rope and the touch of Rahman's rough hands. Most of all she hated herself for being so weak.

The object of the clan children's whispers for the rest of the evening, she leaned against the wagon wheel where they had tied her and watched Samir set up the family's shrine behind Rahman's wagon. When he finished his tribute, he walked back to where she sat and said, "I asked my mother to help you find your brother tomorrow." He walked away before her surprise allowed her to say anything.

At dawn, Rahman drove a wagon close, and he and Samir lifted her into the back, then loaded their supplies. Keeping one end of the rope around her ankle, Rahman tied the other end to the back of the bench. Before they rolled out, Tiadona leaned over the side of the wagon.

"I hope my brother makes a deal worthy of the aggravation of carrying you along," she said, her voice gentler than her words. She put Lingli's pack next to her. "Check it for your things if you want. We are not thieves. You can tell your brother that if you find him."

Unsure whether she had ever been more to them than the coin they hoped for, Lingli just looked away. *If I find him. Oh stars, how?*

They were not the first ones to approach the gate. A throng of southerners gathered there, and Rahman kept a good distance away from them as the sun passed over the Rock and lit the fields. Huddling next to a pile of fancy tack and four deer carcasses, Lingli sweated in her cloak and kept her still-tender hands drawn up in her sleeves.

Impassive as usual, Rahman sat quietly on the bench, but she knew he was sniffing the crowd for possible trouble or deals. Next to him, having worn down her father's resistance to bringing her along, Rekha chattered away. Samir rode his own horse and led two hooded colts that Rahman proposed to sell to the rani.

Everyone's attention snapped onto the guard who finally emerged from the gate tower and approached the first vehicle in line. It was a large, open ratha pulled by four pairs and covered by an elaborate umbrella that streamed with ribbons, obscuring the nobles inside. At least fifty Ascaryans followed on foot, all dressed in red like their flag, which featured a sand cat.

"House of Kirdun," Rahman said, in answer to Rekha's questions. "The only part of the Avakstan territories worth holding. Not much water, but enough. Orange trees, olives, and figs. Shrewd bargainers. You'll not win much coin from them."

Following the House of Kirdun were two smaller rathas hung with yellow banners. The Ascaryans behind them wore simple brown tunics, but their faces were brightly painted, and their ornaments were made of polished horn, copper, and brass.

"House of Afreh," Rahman said. "Unless you want buffaloes, wire grass, or metal, there's no reason to go there."

The gates opened and eventually Rahman presented his token, a brass disc marked with Saatkulom's sun and stars. With hardly a glance at Lingli, the guards let them pass and they followed the crowd winding up the Rajpath. The southerners ahead sang or called out to one another in loud, excited voices, but this didn't mask their nervousness. After they passed an eyrie of archers who looked down from their ledges with bows drawn, the visitors became quieter, both aware of entering foreign territory and awestruck by the unfolding splendor of the fort.

Despite Rekha's exclamations over the sights—paved streets, whitewashed homes and shops, well-dressed people flowing around them like water—Lingli hardly noticed any of it.

What if he doesn't want to see me? What if he is happy, and his memories of our life are half-remembered dreams? They seem so now to me.

When they reached the fort's stables, Samir and Rekha went to fetch water for the horses. Rahman leaned over the side of the wagon and untied her from the bench.

"If the rani's grooms are interested," he said. "We'll spend the night in the palace stables. I'll take you in and leave you free to look for your brother, but whether you find him or not, I'll strike a deal before we leave, understand?"

Lingli met his eyes. It was hard to tell what Rahman was thinking, but she'd never seen him break his word. She nodded and got down from the wagon as Samir and Rekha returned, the rope still hanging from her ankle. *I must escape them somehow.*

Rahman told her and Rekha to wash one of the colts he had brought along—the sickly, black-and-white spotted one with a habit of biting and whose jaw and ears were wrapped with a dirty cloth. Members of the clan had tried to persuade him to take a different colt that morning, but Rahman ignored them, and Lingli could not imagine why he thought the rani would ever consider such a creature.

While Rekha wiped away the mucus caked around its eyes, Lingli began washing the colt's shoulders and the white hair in one patch disappeared with the dirt. They re-wet their cloths and scrubbed at other white patches until they too completely disappeared. When Lingli began to wash the colt's wrapped legs, Rahman moved her aside.

"Careful," he said. "Don't give him reason to kick you down the Rock."

Picking up one of the colt's hooves, Rahman opened the bandages wrapping its pasterns. Behind the fetlock, a talon the length of Lingli's little finger emerged from the longish hair.

Rekha clapped a hand over her mouth and looked at her father wide-eyed. "Govadhi?" she whispered.

"It wasn't much of a trick when we went south but hiding him these last two moons has not been easy," Rahman said. He readjusted the dirt-spattered wrappings to make the colt look his worst. "We'll go to the palace as soon as they're rested, and before anyone here becomes too interested."

"He'll fetch good coin, won't he, Pa?" Rekha asked.

"I'll not tempt the ancestors to say."

Lingli understood now the assurance that had made Rahman and Tiadona willing to gamble on her. The rest of the clan didn't know about the colt. Whatever the outcome for her, Rahman could pretend some amount of the colt's sale came from negotiations for her ransom. Not that he would waste an opportunity to cut the best deal he could to rid himself of her.

They arrived at the third gate just as the portcullis began to creak upward and the inner doors were unbarred. The crowd of southerners ahead of them pressed forward, but the team pulling the Kirdun ratha stalled on the other side of the gate tower. Guards surrounded the vehicle as the driver fought to stop the horses from backing into the crowd. After they calmed the horses and got the ratha through, most of the southerners followed but a few stopped just as the horses had until the guards shouted at them.

A hundred nervous questions poured from Rekha, and she stood on the bench, straining to see what was happening until her father ordered her to sit. Samir checked the colts' hoods and put blinders on all the horses.

With a cursory glance at Rahman's token, the guard waved them on. Samir went first, pulling the colts behind. As they rolled beyond the gate tower, all but a thin bridge span simply dropped away.

A crack as wide as twenty wagons separated the fort from the palace grounds. The stone bridge was as pale and smooth as a bone, without visible mortar, joints, or walls. Hardly wide enough for a single rider to pass a team, Lingli knew instantly that it was no place for nervous horses or Ascaryans. They did not speak, and Rahman allowed no slack in the reins.

On the opposite side stood the palace gate. Its magnificent tower was made of slabs of pure moonstone with brass plating and decorated with indigo, green, and yellow tiles, but the visitors were in no mood to appreciate it. They could see southerners entering the grounds, but before the wanderers were halfway across, those ahead had bunched up under the tower and everyone came to a stop. The southerners still on the bridge cried out, imploring the others to move.

Lingli had to close her eyes as the dark swam up while the light plunged down and a wave of dizziness struck. Rushing air from below pushed at them. The horses snorted, and some of the southerners lost their nerve and sat down on the bridge. Guards at the palace gate urged the crowd to come forward. The guards behind stood on the edge of the span, talwars drawn.

At last, the line advanced, and Lingli knew she wasn't the only one holding her breath until they reached the other side.

Inside the palace grounds, Rahman presented a guard with his token again and explained his proposition to sell the colts. Sighing with the weariness of someone used to traders promising goods of dubious value, the guard looked skeptical as Rahman unwound the colt's bandages. Lingli guessed the change in the guard's expression was due to the curled ears he discovered.

"If you still doubt," Rahman said, "take my token to the rani. She knows horses, and she knows us."

In short order a groom arrived to escort them to the stables.

Lingli scanned every face they passed, growing more disheartened by the minute. *Anything could have happened. He might not have even made it here.*

At the stable yard Rahman gave Rekha the reins. "Go to the kitchens and let them unload the venison," he said, pointing to the hall they had just passed. Then, turning to Lingli, he added, "You'd best get looking before dark. We'll be here."

Calling Lingli to sit with her, Rekha climbed onto the bench, overjoyed to have the chance to drive. Lingli smiled at the girl's enthusiasm, but her attention was on the hall and the Ascaryans passing in and out the back entrances.

So many Ascaryans. She sighed as she untied the knot of rope on her ankle. *There's nothing to do but try.*

Rekha pulled the wagon alongside the platform behind the hall, and Lingli surveyed the young bearers and palace staff milling about. Her heart raced. Dry-mouthed, she climbed down from the bench, settled her pack on her back, and told Rekha, "I've got to go look for my brother."

"I know," Rekha said. "Are you going to live here with him?"

Wish I knew, Lingli thought, as the horse suddenly sidestepped and cracked the corner of the wagon on the platform's stone edge.

"Stupid horse," Rekha said. "Pa should have left those blinders on."

The horse began to throw his head and pull while Rekha struggled to hold him. Lingli attempted to calm the animal, but it only became more agitated.

"Get a sack!" Rekha yelled to a crowd of boys gathering nearby. "Cover his eyes!"

One of them threw a cloth to Lingli, and she tried to hold it over the horse's eyes, but he tossed it off. The boys yelled and pointed, and she turned in time to see two huge wolves jump down from a wall on the edge of the yard. There was no Red nearby this time, and no noble held their chains. The beasts raised their muzzles in the air, sniffed, and stalked toward them.

Despite their best efforts, the horse bolted, pulling Lingli along. Afraid of the flying hooves, she quickly gave up and let go of the harness. When she stopped rolling, she saw Rekha jump from the bench an instant before the wagon tipped over, throwing the horse on his side.

Dazed, it took Lingli a moment to raise herself and look behind. The wolves had sunk onto their bellies in the middle of the yard. A dark-haired man chained one of them to his belt, and the noble she had last seen in the meadow near her home stood over the other with a drawn talwar. Before she could make sense of all this, she saw one of the kitchen boys pick up her pack and fishing spear from where they had fallen as he trotted over to her.

He reached out, saying, "Don't worry, they've caught them." Then he stopped short. "Li?"

She struggled to her feet, unable to believe it was Sid. Such good fortune could only have been Red's doing.

They stared at each other, and her relief weakened her more than the accident. She wanted to pull him into a tight hug, but his eyes darted around her, and she realized he would be embarrassed. Moons of imagining how their meeting would be, and now she wasn't sure what to say. It seemed Sid felt something similar. Though he laughed, she saw his eyes shift from surprise to something more complicated.

"You best cover yourself," he said quietly, looking over his shoulder. "How did you come here?"

"Wanderers," Lingli said as she pulled her hood up.

Rekha brushed dirt from her clothes as she limped to Lingli's side. "It wasn't my fault, but Pa's going to beat me!" Then she looked at Sid and said, "*He's* your brother?"

"Brother?" Sid said.

Rekha yelled across the yard, "Pa, I've found Snow's brother!"

Rahman and Samir were running across the yard toward them, their faces tense.

"See that wanderer with the dark turban?" Lingli said quickly. "He's going to ask you for a ransom."

"What? Ransom?"

"I told them I was looking for my brother on the Rock! Oh, I can't explain everything now. I needed them to bring me here."

"I've got no coin!"

"Sorry, I didn't know what to do."

When Rahman reached them, he put his hands on either side of Rekha's face and looked her over. "Check the damage," he told Samir with a nod toward the wagon.

"I'm okay, Pa. There was no holding Jadu once those wolves showed up."

Rahman hugged Rekha and looked over at Samir unharnessing the cart horse. "You're lucky you didn't get killed, and even luckier if he hasn't gone lame." Then he addressed Sid. "Are you her brother?"

Sid glanced at Lingli and said, "I... Yes."

"Found her on the edge of the Silver Woods. Near starved." Rahman said, smoothing his mustache. He put his hands in his vest pockets, looking as if he was the most humble of traders. "She's eaten our food for a moon, but we carried her along. Said she wanted to find her brother."

"I'm grateful," Sid said. "No doubt you've been generous, sir."

Rahman fixed his eyes on him and waited.

"What do you want for your troubles?" Sid asked.

"Would you ask *me* the price of your sister's life?"

"I'm only a bearer. I've got nothing to...show my appreciation."

"That's disappointing, young sir, and more for your sister than for me," Rahman said, "what with the terrible effort she's made to find you. But there's a debt to pay."

"Wait, I didn't say I wouldn't... I just don't have coin, nor even goods to trade."

Rahman looked at the ground as if the circumstances pained him. "Alright then, she'll have to find another way to pay off the debt. We'll camp at the stables tonight, maybe a day longer considering the damage to my wagon and my horse, but I'm sure we'll find someone who can take her on."

Lingli had no doubt Rahman would do just as he said no matter how much coin he made from the colt.

"Are you coming back next cycle?" Sid asked. "I'll have coin then."

"Your best offer is next cycle? What do I feed my children this winter?"

"Leave her here, and I promise you I'll have two silver coins in the next twelfth moon."

Gratitude eased Lingli's heart. *He has not forgotten me.*

"Three golds are more like it, but I don't deal in promises. We have a trade today or we have no trade."

"What about your daughter?" Sid waved at Rekha. "What if I find her a position in the palace where she'll be sheltered, fed? Want for nothing?"

Rekha moved closer to her father's side as Sid spoke. Rahman shook his head. "Do you think that we would be parted from our children on a stranger's word? That we would put them under someone's rule for a stack of rotis?"

Sid beckoned Lingli to step away. He whispered a little testily, "What do you want me to do? I'm not made of coin."

A fair question. Lingli knelt to riffle through her pack, hoping Tiadona was true to her word.

"I'll pay my own debt," she said, fishing out the pouch of coins.

Rahman and Sid looked at her in surprise.

She drew out three coins and handed them to Rahman. "For your food and hospitality—and the wagon's repairs."

After weighing the coins, Rahman pocketed them and smiled. "It's a good trade when both parties are satisfied." He nodded and started to leave, then paused to wait for Rekha.

"Aw, Snow, I wish you could have seen Korongal," Rekha said as she reached out to hug her. "Next cycle, when we come, I'll tell you about it, and you will tell me about the rani."

Lingli patted Rekha's back, feeling her eyes grow warm. When Rekha returned to Rahman's side, she was glad Sid pulled her away.

"Good thing I left that coin," he said as they entered a colonnade on the side of the hall, "but he would have probably settled for two. Didn't you leave any with Red?"

Lingli shook her head and stopped. Her chest grew tight. "Sid, Red's gone."

"Gone?"

"Gone to stone."

The color drained from Sid's face.

"He told me to find you."

Sid leaned on one of the colonnade's thick columns. He turned away from her, looking westward. She thought of reaching for his hand, but a knot of confused feelings about the day of Red's death prevented her. Neither of them spoke.

Finally Sid rubbed his eyes and said, "Look, I cannot just give you quarters. The palace is full to bursting. Stay here. I'll be back."

"Wait!" She reached for him, but he disappeared into the crowd.

Peering around the column, she saw a broad staircase and a back wall separating what she guessed were the kitchens from the rest of the hall. Ascaryans of all sorts, including southerners she recognized from earlier in the day, filled the tables. Pulling her hands up into her sleeves, Lingli waited in the column's shadow. So much time passed, she began to wonder if Sid had abandoned her. Peeking into the hall again, she noticed there were guards everywhere, but it was the noble who she had seen twice now—the one who kept the wolves—who saw her, too, and now came straight toward her.

"Who are you and w-w-what are you doing here?" the noble asked her gruffly. The harnessed wolf at his side growled deep in its throat.

"Lingli Tabaan," she said, adjusting her hood. "I'm waiting for my friend."

"No," he said. "No waiting here. W-which house do you work for?"

"I…I don't have a house."

The noble suddenly pointed his finger at her. "Aren't you the g-giant's friend? F-from the Western Woods?"

Lingli nodded slowly just as Sid returned in the company of another noble with an owl insignia pinned to his shoulder.

After bowing to the wolfmaster, Sid made exaggerated eyes at her and said, "Master Avani, Master Vaksana, this is my *friend*, Lingli Tabaan."

At least he still counts me as friend. She pressed her hands together and bowed.

"S-she was in the W-Western Woods," Master Vaksana told Master Avani, "with the red giant."

"Is that so?" Master Avani said, staring at her.

Lingli swallowed hard, uncomfortable with the nobles' interest.

"Can she join service, sir?" Sid asked.

"You've hardly been here long enough to ask for such favors," Master Avani said, "but I suspect you have some compelling reason for this request?"

Sid nodded vigorously.

"I'll handle this, brother," Master Avani told Master Vaksana. Then he beckoned her and Sid to follow. "Come with me. We will speak in my quarters."

Lingli kept her eyes on the floor as they crossed the busy hall and climbed a staircase. At the end of the second-floor landing, the noble ushered them into a room crowded with tables and shelves, all covered with scrolls and piles of parchment.

Bidding them to sit on a low divan, Master Avani told Sid to blow on the brazier's coals, and said, "I understand, Miss Tabaan, that you would like to find employment in the palace."

"She's a good worker," Sid said quickly, but the noble held his hand up.

"This may seem indelicate, given our brief introduction, but if I am to help you, I must see to whom I am speaking."

Lingli glanced at Sid and lowered her hood. The old noble raised his brows, then asked, "Why did you come here?"

"Sir," Lingli said, "I don't have anywhere else to go."

"You started somewhere else. Did something happen to your home?"

He had a kind face, one Lingli was inclined to trust, but what did she know of life in the palace? She wasn't ready for this, and she looked to Sid, who nodded.

She took a deep breath. "The day Sid left, our guardian was killed."

The old noble looked back and forth between them and muttered, "Your guardian? Killed, you said?"

Sid ran his hand through his hair.

She thought she ought to comfort him. She should have done so when she first told him, but everything that had transpired since the day Red died filled her from head to toe. She was so tired. She would sink under the weight of her grief if she tried to carry it alone for one more minute.

"Just a few weeks ago I told young Sid here that I knew a red giant," Master Avani said. "If your guardian was the giant I knew—strong as a mountain? Able to take on several Ascaryans at once? Well, this is astounding news, and I am very sorry to hear it."

The old noble seemed to be truly moved by her news. He sighed deeply and added, "No doubt this will be difficult, and I wish it were otherwise, Miss Tabaan, but will you tell us what happened?"

Lingli shifted on the divan. Her words felt flat in her mouth. The event had played out countless times in her head, but she hadn't said it out loud before.

"That morning, when I saw that Sid was gone," she began, "I told Red, and he ran after him."

Lingli turned her attention to Sid. "We didn't know why you left, who you were with, or even if you left by your own will." A part of her was glad he squirmed and looked away.

"I followed Red and heard him call out on the hillside. Before I knew it, a wolf nearly had me in his jaws. The noble we just met downstairs held a crossbow on us. I wanted to look for Sid, but Red said we were too late and turned back. Then a villager jumped out of the mist. He must have been one of those who was angry with Red."

"Why," Master Avani interrupted, "would villagers be angry with him?"

Lingli stammered, "There was an incident last winter. Red—"

"Red broke the legs of a couple of men who were tormenting her," Sid said.

It was her turn to be shamed.

"I see," Master Avani said. "Go on."

"The villager blew a dart that hit Red in the palm."

"He knew how to kill a giant?" Master Avani muttered.

Lingli nodded. "Red let out a roar that shook the trees."

"I heard it," Sid said. "The sound put the fear of the First Father in everyone."

"He told me he was fine, but he was not. We barely reached the cabin before his legs turned to stone, and I…couldn't…do…anything." Lingli had to stop and breathe deeply to keep her throat from closing.

She looked at Sid and fought to keep her voice even. "He told me to find you. He said we should protect each other."

"That you made it here at all is a wonder," Master Avani said before he turned to Sid. "Can you remember anything else? What did Greta do when you heard Red's cry?"

Looking miserable, Sid said, "I don't know. She wasn't with us."

"Who is Greta?" Lingli asked.

"A giant in the service of our maharani," Master Avani said. "She was the red giant's companion long ago."

Another giant? She thought all the giants had been killed in the giant wars. She had avoided hurting Red with prodding questions on this subject for many cycles, but to think that Red had a companion and then lost her made her wonder what else he had never told them.

"Where under the stars was she?" Master Avani asked Sid.

"We met her the next day. She had been chained at a campsite, near the road."

Lingli drew back a little, shocked that anyone would do such a thing and shocked that Sid said this so casually.

"Oh, this is… Well." Master Avani rose and paced around the sitting area. "I'm sure we don't have all the facts and flavors of exactly what happened. Best not repeat this outside of this room. No, *definitely* do not repeat this! Do you understand?"

Lingli watched Sid, who frowned before he nodded his assent. Still unsure, she slowly nodded as well.

Then Sid got to his feet and blurted out, "Sir, I beg your pardon, but Korvar Sir has not dismissed me, and there will be consequences."

Master Avani looked annoyed. "Tell our cook that I've requested my supper here and you should bring food for your friend as well."

So, Sid wasn't a guard or a soldier as he always said he would be. He was a bearer. She felt a little sorry for him, but something unforgiving stirred within her as he hurried to the door. *How can he leave me here?*

"You, too, were an orphan in the red giant's care?" Master Avani asked her after Sid left.

"Yes."

"And you are how many cycles old?"

"Sixteen. Almost seventeen."

"Bright-cycle born?"

"We celebrated the day of my birth on New Cycle Day, but I don't know the truth of that. I think Red just wanted me to believe I could have some New Cycle Day luck in this life."

A strange look crossed Master Avani's face, and he excused himself. She remained on the divan, glad for the brazier's warmth. She watched the old noble consult a large leather- and brass-bound book on his work table. It reminded her of the one in Red's trunk.

Sid soon returned, bearing thalis. His mouth was set in a tight line that might have seemed like concentration, but she knew better. He did not want to be there. Whether it was because he was embarrassed that she had found out he was a bearer or because he was thinking about Red's death, she couldn't tell, and she didn't blame him for either. Yet a part of her wanted to grab him by the neck and shake him until he apologized for running off and leaving her alone when Red went to stone. But she couldn't very well do that in front of this noble.

Sid sat on the floor near her feet while they ate, taking only one of the pieces of warm naan off her thali.

When the old noble finished his food, he said, "I am sorry to hear this sore news about your guardian, but we will put it aside for now and discuss the most pressing matter—an accommodation for Miss Tabaan."

Requesting shelter in the palace was too large a favor to ask of a noble she had just met. "Perhaps I could find service in the fort, sir?" she said.

Master Avani dismissed this idea. "I think your safety will be best guaranteed here in the palace, at least until the spring. Wouldn't you agree, Sid?"

Sid nodded but said nothing. Fingering the bracelet in her pocket, Lingli decided she would not give it to him just yet.

"Whether you stay a moon or a cycle," Master Avani said, "the maharani must permit you to join the staff. What can you do?"

"I…I can cook. I can clean." She was growing more uneasy about the whole proposition.

"She sews!" Sid said with an enthusiasm Lingli did not expect. "Li sews beautifully. When I was clearing the terrace, Madam Sayed said the dancers need dresses for the maharani's wedding."

"Now there is a promising idea," Master Avani said.

The old noble returned to the divan with a piece of parchment on a thin board, a fine brush, and an inkpot. He dipped the brush in the ink and wrote a note, then sealed it.

"Take this to the guards outside the maharani's quarters," he told Sid. "We will see if she will address your petition tomorrow."

Managing a few hours of sleep on the divan after Sid left and Master Avani went to his inner room, Lingli woke before dawn and spent a few more hours worrying about what she would do if the rani did not give her permission to stay. Finally, she got up, carefully felt out the edge of the brazier, and blew softly until a live coal allowed her to light a diya.

Shuffling through the room, she made her way to a large tapestry that hung on the wall behind the noble's table. The colors were faded, and the menace of insects plain, but it was incredibly detailed. She traced circuitous routes where clusters of Ascaryans and animals faced a mountain in the center—the Rock, of course. She half expected to find herself stitched onto one of the paths.

"Beautiful, isn't it?" Master Avani came out from his inner room carrying a lantern.

"Is it the beginning of Saatkulom?" she asked.

"The beginning of the Seven, but not the beginning of life here." The old noble pointed to a cave whose darkness made a background for several small characters with long arms. "The zhoukoo were already here, and the ancestors."

"Whose ancestors?"

Master Avani smiled. "Generations have argued about that very question. Each house claims theirs were here first, but we all came from elsewhere."

A knock on the door made her instinctively pull her hood forward. A bearer entered with a thali, and Master Avani bid him fetch a second.

While they were eating, the noble asked directly, "Have you always looked this way?"

She resisted the urge to touch the vein in her temple. "Red said so. He thought I would die at first."

"Remarkable," Master Avani said. "I presume you cannot tolerate the sun."

"I burn."

"Are there other symptoms of your condition? Discomfort, extraordinary qualities of the body or senses?"

Discomfort? The truth was too large to speak of. She would not name the sadness that had crushed her since last winter, and the added weight of Red's death. And she couldn't even begin to describe the terror she felt or the vision she had the day the ground shook.

Another knock landed on the door, and Sid entered wearing his good kurta. "Sir, we must go if we are to be among the petitioners heard today."

Master Avani called Lingli to his bathing room and showed her a basin of water. Cleaning her face was a relief, and she did the best she could to smooth her hair, but when she emerged the noble handed her a sash.

"Wear this," he told her, gesturing at her head. "You must do everything possible to earn the maharani's favor."

Hurrying along passages with Sid and Master Avani, she repeatedly touched her head wrap. She had covered the offending vein, but nothing would hide her pale skin or her bloodless lips. Clutching the edge of her hood as they flowed into a hall filled with people, she kept her eyes on the feet of those who pressed too close.

When Sid took her hand and whispered, "Don't think about it, Li. I'll do the talking," she regretted how irritated she had been with him the evening before.

Sid went to a long bench on the floor, and Master Avani settled her on a hewn row of stone seats as the maharani arrived.

At first Lingli saw only the giantess who lumbered behind the rani. Her thin gray hair, combed neatly into a small bun, was nothing like Red's wiry mess, but the planes of her face and her heavy stride were familiar. *Did she know of his life in the woods? Does she mourn his death?*

When the giantess took her place behind the throne, Lingli turned her attention to the Maharani of the Seven, who sat very straight and commanded everyone's attention without saying a word. Her eyes were bright and beautifully painted under brows that arched like birds' wings. In a breath, Lingli better understood why Sid had left.

Petitioners were called one after another, and the morning withered away before Sid rose from the bench.

"Your Majesty," he said nervously, "I wish to introduce you to a seamstress who can assist with the preparations for your wedding." He motioned to her to stand. "This is Lingli Tabaan of the Western Woods. She was a childhood friend of mine."

The word "was" pinched Lingli, and the eyes of the crowd fell upon her like a heavy blanket as she made a small bow.

The rani beckoned them. When they stood before her, she said, "This must be the girl you mentioned while we were traveling."

Lingli found she could not quite meet the rani's gaze.

"Why are you wearing your hood inside, girl? Is my palace cold?"

"No, Your Majesty."

"Take it off."

Lingli desperately hoped the head wrap was sufficient to keep the rani's and everyone else's curiosity at bay.

"Lingli is very good with a needle," Sid said loudly. "Give her a piece of cloth, and she'll make the most beautiful dress. She can knit and stitch, and all such."

"Do you know how to embroider?" the rani asked.

"Yes, Your Majesty," Lingli said, "but my friend may speak too highly of my skill."

"There are not even two moons until the wedding. I have spinners, weavers, and tailors at my disposal, but all are occupied. Madam Sayed's hands are full with my dresses alone, and she insists we need another seamstress to prepare the dancers' costumes. Do you have a piece of your work?"

Lingli shook her head, certain she was about to fall off the thin limb she had ventured out upon.

"I do," Sid said.

From within his vest Sid drew out the kufi she had made for his birthday. He presented it to the rani who slowly turned it in her hands. To Lingli's dismay, she pointed to a spot inside the cap's lining.

"What is this?" the rani asked. "This tree inside a moon?"

"My sign," Lingli said, her voice hardly more than a whisper.

"Your sign? Do you sew it on everything you create?" Lingli nodded. "And how did you come upon this practice?"

"My teacher told me that artisans should choose a sign to mark their work."

"Your teacher told you that? Why did you choose the tree?"

"She asked me to name my greatest strength, and I couldn't think of any. She said my strength was like that of a young tree that survives storms by bending instead of breaking."

The rani was very still. She looked long at the kufi, then held it out to Sid. Picking at one of the chains around her neck, she said, "On the first day of the new cycle, which will also be the day of my marriage, our children will perform special dances, and they require twenty-eight costumes. You will complete them."

"Your Majesty," Lingli said, swallowing hard. "I don't think I can sew that quickly."

"If you want the shelter of these walls and our food in your stomach, you will sew that quickly," the rani said coolly. She told Sid, "Take her to Madam Sayed. She will serve according to her direction."

Following Sid's lead, Lingli bowed again, and they backed away from the throne together. Sid took her hand, and they hurried from the hall.

CHAPTER 14

On the mining hall's veranda, Engineer Roshan Balinbitta described the properties of the Rock's minerals to his new apprentices, and Sid sat on the floor among them wishing he wasn't there. Making eye contact with no one, he hugged his knees and shivered in the morning chill, convinced his promised destiny had slipped beyond his grasp.

When he fled the great hall with Li the day before, he had dared to believe that the ancestors were smiling upon him. The rani had not only allowed his petition, she had granted his request, and how many of his stature could claim this? His luck continued to hold when they met the dance teacher, Madam Sayed, and he had convinced that tart lady to take on Li. He was so proud of helping her—just as Red would have wanted him to—that he had almost shaken off the disappointment that had smothered him since embarrassing himself in front of Master Duvanya. He felt confident that Master Avani would put him into defenses training when the new rotation started the next day.

Then his luck ran out.

After the evening service, Sid had returned to the kitchens and plopped himself on a bench in the back room to eat his supper with Rud and Shankar when a housekeeper approached him.

"Gather your belongings," she said. "We've given your room to new guests."

"What is this? Where am I supposed to sleep?"

"Where you end up is not my worry, boy. Ask Master Avani."

Returning to his room in the old tower to find his meager possessions in a pile outside the door, Sid tied them up in his old pants and went back to Master Avani's quarters where he rapped on the door.

"Yes, yes, you're seeking a new room, I know," Master Avani said when he opened the door. "I've found a place in the barracks that will put you much closer to the other recruits."

Beckoning Sid to follow him, Master Avani led him down the landing to a small door in the wall before the regular barracks' rooms began. Inside was a closet deep enough to hold a pallet and a tiny table with a basin. There was no window and barely room to stand between the pallet and the door.

"Here, sir?" Sid said. "I'll suffocate!"

"Nonsense. You'll be snug from drafts and ready for a fresh start tomorrow. It's a fine place if you ask me, but even if you don't, this is your room for now."

Sid grumbled to himself after Master Avani left, but he fell asleep quickly and slept without dreams. Being used to working the early shift, he woke before dawn and stumbled down to the kitchens in the dark, but Korvar blocked his way at the kitchens' entrance. The chef pointed to one of the long tables.

"New rotation, Sid Sol. You're a miner now."

And so Sid found himself sitting on the mining hall's veranda in the still-chilly morning, ignoring Roshan Sir's lecture.

A miner. A mole. A dirt eater. Marked for death in a cave-in. As far from being a soldier swinging a fine blade on a sunny field as I could possibly be.

How should he understand his fate? Either he was entirely responsible for this debacle, which was Red's way of thinking (and Li's), or it was the doing of the ancestors. The witch might have agreed with this second possibility, he thought, but what could he do to remedy the situation? He had tried to show the ancestors he was worthy of them. He had offered tributes. He had been a fine bearer and served the realm honorably, if obscurely. He had even gained the rani's ear, at least for a moment. But the ancestors had denied him.

When he thought harder about all the foolish things he had done, the only crime that came close to being worthy of such a setback was failing to help Red when he heard that cry. Li's declaration of the giant's death had stabbed him in the heart. But now, as he poked at this pain, Sid began to wonder, *Has someone cursed me?*

Though he didn't think Li could or would curse him, no matter what others believed, she was angry. She blamed him for Red's death, of that he was certain, and he could not deny that his bad luck coincided with her arrival. Her sad, otherworldly face reminded him of all he had tried to leave behind, but here she was. Maybe her curse had spread to him?

Sid suddenly realized the buzzing noise around him had stopped. Boys were getting to their feet. Roshan had stopped talking and seemed to be waiting for them to do something.

"Move along," the mines master said as he gathered lanterns. "It will take some time to reach the slate excavation."

In ragged groups the new apprentices climbed the path that wound up the rock face. In front of the yawning darkness of a cavern's mouth, Roshan Sir handed a lantern to a boy at the back and carried another with him. They followed the engineer's bobbing light, uncertain of their steps until they realized the path was straight and mostly smooth. After a few minutes, a large, nearly round space that their instructor called the wheel room opened around them. The stone walls were interrupted by a few gates and boarded-over passages braced with mortared stone and wooden columns.

Picking up a rock from the floor while he waited for all the boys to catch up, their teacher asked the recruits to identify its type and uses. They tried to avoid his gaze.

"No one remembers the varieties of stone I described? Perhaps you can recall the gems crucial to our realm's wealth? No?" Roshan Sir paced back and forth in front of them. "The fine masters of the Seven may have a soft spot for you all, but not me. And it's not personal, you understand. I have absolutely no interest in you personally. My duties would hollow out three men. I have no time to waste on those who do not care to listen. You have this week to prove your worth or it's out you go. The ancestors know we can find other young ones willing to take up mining if it's not to your liking."

As this denunciation was underway, Roshan Sir pulled a smooth gray stick from his pocket. He struck it on the wall, and one end instantly began to blaze with a cold, bluish flame.

"This is a firestick," he said. "It is one of the gifts the ancestors gave to the Seven Houses when they arrived, and it is not to be toyed with or even touched by the likes of you. I am telling you this for your own good. Only the House of Tilan knows its full properties."

Looking around at the other boys, Sid realized that they had never seen one before. He had. In the red giant's cabin in the Western Woods.

"When we reach the excavation site perhaps you will begin to understand why listening to instructions is important and why failure to do so could have serious consequences. Mind your step as we go. If you are going to fall, especially if you choose to fall into the belly or any open shaft, please do not take down the Ascaryan next to you."

With that the mining master led the way into a broad passage, holding the firestick aloft. A large wagon could have moved through the passage without hitting the walls, but a bit farther the walls and ceiling around them completely retreated, and the firestick only lit the floor they stood on. They huddled together, listening to a rhythmic creaking noise nearby.

"This is the throat," Roshan Sir said, his voice echoing off stone unseen. "The ore comes up here from the belly." He swung his firestick around to illuminate two fat, greased ropes moving on pulleys that were bolted to a lip of rock. Two zhoukoo hunkered next to the ropes and caught baskets of ore as they arrived.

"Our Rock had some hollow spaces, but most of this was stone once. Taken out bit by bit over the generations. We're going down into the belly to show you the active mines. The current sites are not gem veins so most of the rough tonnage is darkice and moonstone. You will learn about gem work later if you stick on. Here we go. Hold to the ropes."

The recruits made their way down a short flight of steps carved into the rock at the end of the promontory. The stairs ended at a steep zigzagging path. At each turn there was a flat area where Roshan Sir waited for the last boys to catch up. Twice they crossed narrow stone bridges with nothing to grasp but the ropes at shoulder height. Sid did not slip nor fall, but he had the disturbing sensation of being pulled toward the pit that plunged away beneath them, a sensation that did not seem to afflict the others. He wanted to stop, but he was afraid the boys behind would push into one another and fall if he did, so he shuffled on.

When it seemed that they had reached the bottom, Roshan Sir told them to sit. A zhoukoo emerged from the dark bent nearly double and holding two straps attached to a basketful of stone on his back. Thin and dirty, with only a rag tied about his loins, he said nothing but stared with small, shining eyes until their instructor pointed to a spot on the floor. Hoisting the basket over his head, the zhoukoo poured it out and silently returned the way he had come.

Choosing two rocks from the pile, the mining master showed them to the boys by the light of the firestick. "This one is darkice," he said, "and this one is slate. Can anyone tell me where darkice is used in Chandrabhavan?"

One of the boys said, "It's the floor of the great hall, isn't it?"

"That is correct. The floor of the great hall is polished darkice. Completed in the fifth generation. Scores of workers mined and polished pieces over twenty sun cycles before the final section was fit into the floor."

Roshan Sir set the rocks at his feet and straightened. "Today, if you have any brains, you will learn something about how to free rock from rock. Of all the work in the realm, mining pays best, but it costs you, too. Most of you won't become miners. Those who do will be so dead tired, you'll forget why you came here. This work will break your back and your knees. It's going to make you cough for hours. But remember this, miners make this realm what it is. Without us, Saatkulom would be just a cleaner version of Daza Tumuli."

The boys looked at one another uncertainly. Roshan Sir clapped his hands. "Alright, then! Half Giant, hand me those," he said to a heavy-set boy, who carried two loaded packs on his back as if he were going for a picnic. The mining master opened the packs and began handing out gloves.

"Where's the...?" He pushed items around inside one of the packs and then sighed. "Which one of you idiots was assigned to pack belts this morning? Who didn't pick up the belts and put them in the bag?"

Sid suddenly remembered what he had been told to do when he had arrived at the mining hall. With a small sigh, he raised his hand.

"Why couldn't you follow instructions?"

"I forgot, sir."

"Forgot?" The engineer pushed the pack he carried into Sid's chest. "Take this and a lantern and go fetch the belts while your friends here take a nap, because there is nothing they can do without belts."

At the top of the throat, Sid nodded to the zhoukoo unloading baskets then stumbled away from the edge of the pit and sat down to catch his breath. *Why should I take all the blame? Any true master would have checked the bags before going down there in the first place.* He swung the pack onto his back again and picked up the lantern.

In the wheel room he counted nine passages, and metal gates stood in two of these. Two other passages were boarded over. Five passages were open. Sid entered the tunnel directly opposite the one from which he had emerged. *Is this the one?*

After walking for a few minutes he stopped and doubled back. He tried the next passage to his right. The way was even, but he walked for ten minutes and found nothing but darkness. By the time he returned to the wheel room, a small panic had begun to spread within him. The next passage soon descended and the walls were narrow, so he returned and tried again.

He was fairly sure he was wrong about the fourth one as soon as he discovered a fork to the left. Judging by the rubble on the floor, it was unused, so he stayed to the right. *The ancestors of the Seven must have had mole blood*, he thought glumly.

Soon, the floor tilted upward. He didn't remember walking downhill when they entered, and he was about to turn around again when his lantern's light glinted off the brass work of a door ahead.

Definitely not the way out.

But he hesitated. His lantern's wick was guttering. A breath of air came from beneath the door, carrying muffled sounds with it. The fear of being left alone in the heart of the Rock was far stronger than fear of what was on the other side. He put his shoulder to it and pushed but the door must have been barred on the inside. When he knocked, all went quiet on the other side. As he was about to knock again, he heard the bar being raised.

The door opened a crack, and someone said, "What business brings you here?"

"Uh, no business, as such," Sid said. "I've been a bit turned around in these passages."

The door opened, and the Ascaryan behind it growled, "Lost, eh? Get in here, Recruit."

Chairs scraped, and there was some cursing. The passage on the other side of the door broadened, making a room of sorts. In the poor lantern light, Sid could barely make out a handful of Ascaryans around a table. Hit with the stench of urine and unwashed bodies mixed with firewine, he already regretted being there.

Hands pressed together in a polite greeting, Sid shuffled forward and gave what he hoped was a charming smile. "P-pardon me, good sirs. Could anyone tell me the way to the mining hall?"

A boy burst out laughing. "Ha, did you hear that? Don't think I've ever been called a 'good sir'!"

"Shut up, Krill." This came from the long-haired man who had opened the door. Sid had seen him handling the wolves with Master Vaksana. With cards in one hand and a talwar in the other, the man asked, "Who are you and who sent you?"

"Sid Sol, sir. No one sent me. We were in the belly, and Roshan Sir told me to go back up and fetch the belts from the hall," he elaborated, trying to read faces he could hardly see. He unhappily noted a second man also had a blade in his hands.

That man growled, "Another foreigner, I'd wager." With his sooty head wrap and grimy clothes, he looked as if he'd just crawled out of the belly himself.

No sooner had this pronouncement been made than Sid noticed that the youth at the rear was shirtless, filthy, and barefooted. A short chain trailed a manacle on his ankle. Beyond those facing him, doors lined one side of the passage, and each door had a small grilled window. It dawned on him that he was in the realm's jail.

The long-haired man sized him up. "You came in with that last lot Brother Jordak collected, didn't you?"

Sid nodded.

"You may call me Vidkun Sir," the card player said, mocking Sid's high language. "Join us for a hand of Five Stars before you return to duty." He waved toward the table.

"I...uh...I don't know that game, and I should go. They're...waiting for me."

"No, no, not yet," Vidkun said. "Sit down. We'll get you out in a bit."

Sid saw a look pass between Vidkun and miner with the blade, and he knew he shouldn't argue.

"Who are your friends, boy?"

"Um, this is my first day with the miners, but I know Shankar and some boys in the kitchens."

Sid's answer seemed to satisfy Vidkun, whose crooked smile stretched across his face. He said, "Krill, pour him a drink. Watch this hand and learn."

Sometime later, Sid sipped his third cup of firewine and played his second losing hand of Five Stars. The others seemed more at ease, but he still had the feeling that leaving would be difficult. The one called Avinash also wore the chinkara insignia of the House of Satya, but the other boy, Krill, wore no brooch. The miner's name was Kadam, and the others were careful around him, but the prisoner's flat expression pricked Sid's fears the most.

"There you go," Vidkun muttered, a dark bidi clamped between his teeth. "Three stars and a pair of day guards! Pay up, bastards." He laughed loudly while the others sourly pushed over their coins. Sid put his second boot on the table.

"I don't want your stinking boots," Vidkun said. "What else have you got?"

"I told you I don't have coin," Sid said. He had not intended to make this sound like a challenge, but it came out a bit too loud. The table and the faces of his fellow card players swam in and out of focus a few times. He rubbed his eyes.

"Do you think it's right to play and not pay like the other fellows?" Vidkun asked. Avinash spat on the floor.

"Argh, what's wrong with you now?" Vidkun barked. "Soil our nest?"

"I was agreeing with you," Avinash said.

"You're of the Seven. Try not to be so crude."

"He needs to pay," Krill said, nodding toward Sid.

Kadam leaned back in his chair, seemingly bored with the game. Sid didn't like the way he cleaned his fingernails with the blade of his knife.

"You break into our festivities. We show you courtesy. We give you drink, and you lose not one but two games," Vidkun said. "How are you going to make this up to us?"

"Give him another wager," Krill said, getting to his feet. "A chance on the Nobles' Walk. If he does it, we'll forgive his debt this time. If not…."

"Yes," Avinash agreed, slapping Krill on the shoulder. "Let's see him hop!"

Vidkun smiled. "Kadam, are you agreed?"

The miner shrugged. "What's the coddling for? No more chances, I say."

"What's the Nobles' Walk?" Sid asked, acting as though he hadn't heard Kadam.

Vidkun's words were clipped and light. "Come along, foreigner. We'll show you." He handed one of the lanterns to the prisoner. "See, I trust you, Rit," he said, leaning close to the youth and patting him on the head like a child. "You can't play cards worth shit, but you're going to lead the way."

They passed the cells, and the passage floor pitched upward again. The walls' mortar had crumbled in several places. Broken crossbeams had been pushed aside. Sid shook his head, willing it to clear.

"Listen," Vidkun said.

They were almost silent, except for Krill's snickering, which ended when Kadam shoved him. Around his feet, Sid felt a stronger draft, and he heard a low moaning sound, sad as death.

"Here starts the Nobles' Walk proper," Vidkun explained, as if Sid was his own green recruit. "Built in the fourth generation after Bargast betrayed his house and the realm."

Sid's tongue felt swollen in his mouth. He wished he had some water, but he knew he would probably throw it up if he did.

"The walk is the last stretch, see," Vidkun continued. "When one of the Seven or a noble from another realm committed a serious crime, the penalty was death, same as for anyone, but they had a choice. They could lose their head by the raja's blade or they could take the walk. Most of them walked, it's said. Kept their dignity that way."

"Yeah, you ever seen a head roll around on the ground?" Avinash said. "That ain't no way to go."

They continued forward, and the moaning grew louder, as if someone's ancestor was declaring great unhappiness. A line of light marked the bottom of another door ahead. Vidkun pulled up the latch, then slid the rod back and gave it a hard push. The door flew open, making Sid jump. The moaning stopped, but the air outside roared. Though it was late afternoon, light flooded the passage.

Krill pushed up to the edge of the opening. "Come take a good look, Sid Sir," he said, with a bow and a grin.

Sid didn't move. His heart hammered.

"Aww, I don't think he's going to like the hop," Avinash said. He and Krill giggled.

Vidkun grabbed his arm and pushed him toward the opening.

"No, please," Sid begged. "I'm sorry. I'll pay you."

"Yes, you will," Vidkun said. "But we're not trying to kill you, not yet. Have a look, that's all."

With Avinash on his other arm, he had little choice. They tugged him up to the edge, and his head swam with light and dark and the rush of the air. The walls, the floor, everything dropped away on the other side of the doorway. They stood in a small rectangular opening in the sheared face of the Rock somewhere below the summit and above the palace and the depths of the crevasse that separated Chandrabhavan from the fort.

Sid sank to his knees, glad Vidkun and Avinash still had a grip on each arm. The edge of the training yard was to the right below, and the rooftops of Safed Qila beyond the crack.

"Impressive, isn't it!" Vidkun yelled in his ear.

"Let's see if he hops," Avinash insisted. He let go of Sid long enough to collect a long staff from the passage floor and thrust it at the door, which had blown back against a knob of stone jutting from the rock face. A piece of rope hung from the door's latch and Avinash snagged it with the staff and pulled it back.

"See there's the ledge on the other side," Krill explained. "That's the hop. You hold tight to the door and swing out. Then you hop onto the ledge."

"Why would anyone do that?" Sid said.

"Usually there's a reward involved," Vidkun said, "but in your case, you just owe me coin. Think of it as a way to pay your debt."

"Yeah, you drink our wine, you'll pay the fine," Avinash said. "Hey, a couplet!"

"Ritin, give Sid some advice."

Ritin had shrunk back against the wall of the passage. Kadam shoved him forward and leaned close over his shoulder to taunt him. "Tell him what happens to those who don't want to jump, Ritin. Tell him the other way he can pay his debt."

Ritin shook his head and said nothing.

A faraway horn sounded one long, dipping note and a second short note.

"Shit! Shift change already?" Avinash said.

Vidkun pulled Sid back from the edge. "You're lucky today, but you still owe me." Running his finger over the hilt of a dagger at his waist, he added, "We might keep you around and see if you prove useful, but you're either in with us or you're out. There's no telling others about our card parties. Understand?"

Sid nodded vigorously and Vidkun pushed him ahead into the dark passage. "Prisoner, get up here with that lantern."

They hurried back to the jail, where Kadam swept the table clear and deposited everything into a cell Vidkun opened.

"Here you go, Ritin. That's it, step right in. You've been a good prisoner today," he said, mussing the boy's hair as he entered the cell. "I think we should leave his chain off today, don't you?" he said to the others.

"Yeah, leave him," Avinash said. "They get dull if you chain them down all the time."

"Better move, or they'll notice," Krill said. He held open the door to the passage.

Vidkun pushed everyone out, and Kadam locked the jail's door behind them.

"Keep that key here," Vidkun told Kadam. "The last thing I need is someone asking me how you got a key."

Forcing Krill to kneel by the door, Kadam stood on the boy's thigh and put his key on top of the frame. Then they all hurried to the wheel room where Vidkun took one of the passages Sid had tried earlier, reaching the light steps beyond where he had turned back.

When they reached the mining hall, Vidkun pulled Sid aside. "Remember, no talking."

Sid peeled off from the others and prepared to meet his punishment, the threat of which was nothing compared to his relief to be free of the Rock and Vidkun and his cronies. Finding the hall empty, he trudged on to the feasting hall and climbed up to the barracks to report to Master Avani. He tried not to think of Ritin and whoever else might be in the cells back there in the dark.

CHAPTER 15

After the rani dismissed them, Lingli had followed Sid to the terrace of the central palace to meet Madam Sayed. In the shade of a canvas stretched between pillars, a group of girls practiced dance steps under the watch of a woman whose stern expression was at odds with the grace of the movement she demonstrated. When her students were finished, Sid approached her and bowed with a flourish.

"Madam Sayed, I would like to present to you a new seamstress recently approved by the rani. She's to assist you with the dancers' costumes."

Lingli stifled an urge to step back as Madam looked at her. From the serpentine-smooth, braided knot at the back of her neck, to the sharpness of her cheekbones and chin, everything about this woman made her nervous.

"Praise to our maharani!" Madam Sayed said before sniffing suspiciously at Lingli's headscarf. "What do you know of our celebrations, girl? Very little, I suspect."

"Nothing, Madam."

The dance teacher fixed her aggravation on Sid. "Were you the one inspired to create this elaborate mockery or was it someone else?"

"No, Madam, it… No, see here." Sid thrust Master Avani's parchment into her hands.

Madam Sayed quickly read the request inside and focused again on Sid. "If there has been any attempt to deceive Master Avani, the consequences will be severe."

"Of course," Sid said. "I would never attempt to mislead you or Master Avani. This girl is an excellent seamstress."

Lingli was both in awe of Sid's ability to turn the course of the conversation and troubled by his manner of speaking as though he didn't know her.

"Truly?" Madam put her hands on her hips and leaned over Sid. "One misstep, one theft or lie, and I will deposit her, and you, over the wall."

195

Sid nodded, and Madam flicked her hand at him. "Return to your duties." To Lingli she said, "By the stars, you best not disappoint. Follow me!"

Giving Sid a wan smile, Lingli followed the dance teacher across the terrace and into the old tower. Inside, lanterns burned next to two of the doors on the landing, but only one door was guarded. Madam continued up to the next floor and let herself in one of the rooms, telling Lingli to wait. When she returned, the dance teacher handed her a folded blanket and a lantern.

The next floor was empty, and the air was heavy with dust and quiet. There were only two doors on the floor, both wearing heavy, rusted locks, and the painted ceiling was much less impressive than it looked from the lower floors. From below, the ceiling depicted the Doodhnadi star field in a dark blue night sky, but now that she was close, Lingli saw that it was simply dark plaster dabbed with white paint and chips of moonstone. The stairs on that floor seemed to end at the ceiling, but Madam climbed them and pushed up a small trapdoor until it tipped back on its hinges.

Beyond the ceiling that became the floor, thin iron bars surrounded the trapdoor in a space scarcely larger than the length and width of a large bed. Madam fit a long iron key into a lock hanging on a gate and bid Lingli to precede her into the room beyond.

The space was all one room—floored, braced, and roofed with ancient timbers bound with rough mortar and stone between them, the unfinished top of the tower. Two open archways revealed small balconies on opposite sides. Afternoon sun blazed through one of them, lighting pieces of broken furniture, moth-eaten tapestries, and rusted trunks. A narrow cot, a table, and a chair stood next to one of the archways.

After wiping away the dust and grit from the cot, Madam Sayed showed Lingli the drain for washing and the chamber pot, then returned to the gate. "Food will be delivered," she said. "Tomorrow you will learn your assignments, and you can demonstrate whether I have been played for a fool or not."

As Madam stepped through the gate and locked it again, Lingli hurried over and grabbed the thin bars. "I've committed no crime, Madam."

"If you were staying in the female staff's barracks, I shouldn't worry, but Master Avani asked me to keep you in the palace. I don't know you, and it is a bright cycle—and we suffer from an excess of green recruits this moon. You'll be quite free to complete your tasks during the day, but for now this is the best way to protect you from unwanted visitors."

After the trapdoor closed behind Madam with a soft whump, Lingli let out her breath, disappointed but unsurprised. She was a captive again, of sorts, but what had she expected? Ignoring the bile in her throat, she promised herself she would not be locked in here for long.

All around the room, lost and broken things were heaped in piles. Wood-boring beetles, spiders, and a few mice scuttled ahead of her. Splintered pieces of wood turned out to be the frames of forgotten tapestries and paintings. Old timbers, scratched table legs, and cracked jugs and basins filled the far edges of the room. The curtains on either side of the balconies were made from moth-eaten chinkara hides. Behind one pile of boards, she found a tall staff with a dented brass head. She poked the staff through the thin bars surrounding the hatch and tapped four small swings that hung there, finally comprehending that the entry to this floor was an enormous bird cage.

In the dim center of the room, a frayed tapestry lay stretched over a trunk. As she was about to look more closely at the fabric, it slid from her grasp and slithered onto the floor, revealing the trunk's hammered metal lid and rusty lock. Almost before she knew what she was going to do, she struck it with the end of the staff, and the lock fell to pieces.

A child's time-ravaged clothing lay inside. The small, thin cotton kurta— a boy's shirt delicately embroidered at the cuffs and neckline—shredded in her hands. Beneath it was a small blue coat. Chilled from the feeling that someone watched her, Lingli knew the sudden wave of grief that overwhelmed her was not her own. Closing the trunk softly, she pressed her palms together and recited the tribute for the dead's safe passage.

Retreating to the cot, Lingli listened and watched for more signs from the otherworld, but none appeared. From the closest balcony, she watched guards pace the terrace of the feasting hall. The long-haired wolfmaster, with three wolves on chains, walked the top of the wall that ran to a large hall at the foot of the bluff. Crossing to the west-facing balcony, she squinted out at the central palace's terrace and the new tower, the rooftops of Safed Qila, and the wide arc of the world beyond.

A noise in the room behind startled her.

Please, spirit, I will not trouble you. We can share this space in peace.

Though unseen, the visitor was not otherworldly. A thali and a cup of water sat on the floor near the trapdoor. After peering into all the shadowy corners of the room, Lingli pulled the thali under the bars and returned to the balcony, bringing the little chair out as well. The Doodhnadi brightened while she ate, and Chotabhai glowed like an ember, but Matachand had not yet appeared when she set her food down and returned to the cot. She fought the exhaustion that suddenly possessed her but soon fell asleep.

Madam's keys were rattling in the lock the next morning when Lingli sat up with a start. She hadn't slept so much at night even when she was with the wanderers, and it was very unlike her to sleep so soundly at any time. Swinging her feet to the floor, she discovered her outer clothes had been removed. Her boots, minus her rabbit knife, stood next to the cot, but her pack and cloak were gone as well.

Confusion and fear seized her. How could she have slept through such a thorough robbery? Wrapping herself tight in the thin blanket, Lingli tried to smooth her hair—realizing too late that the headscarf Master Avani had given her was crumpled upon the pillow.

Her face stiff with distaste, Madam approached in a crisply pleated sari, the braids at the nape of her neck knotted tight and sleek. Lingli cringed at the comparison with her own state. Dropping slippers on the floor, Madam handed her a long gray tunic that all the low-level female staff wore.

Lingli asked in a small voice, "Where are my clothes?"

"The laundresses are cleaning them, if they can," Madam said.

"And my pack, too?"

"All in safekeeping." Madam said curtly. "I do not know who cursed you, Seamstress, but you cannot go about the palace looking like this. You will frighten my dancers and divert their attention, and I will not have it."

Understanding how powerless she was, Lingli swallowed her pride, deciding to pretend she hadn't lost everything as long as Madam pretended it was all housekeeping. She watched Madam set her basket on the small table next to the cot and make a row of tiny pots, boxes, and brushes.

"You have no idea how to use these, do you?" Madam said, as though she couldn't fathom such an extreme degree of ignorance.

Lingli smelled the lotion in the first tiny pot and dabbed some on her hand.

"Not that one. Begin with this." Madam handed her a brush. "Apply it with short, sweeping strokes," Madam said. "It will make you look more… It will improve your color."

Lingli awkwardly attempted to pat paint onto her cheek.

"Better, but you've missed a spot," Madam said. "No, the other side. Oh, no! Sit!"

Commandeering the chair and leaning close, Madam flexed her long fingers. Seeing her hesitate, Lingli expected she would retreat, but, with the look of someone determined to dive into cold water, Madam pulled the skin of Lingli's cheek tight with one hand as she rubbed a cream in with the other.

"New Cycle Day is traditionally our time to celebrate the harvest and a cycle well-lived," Madam said. "As usual the palace ensemble will make three appearances during the program, but this performance is special." She stopped her story abruptly. "What is this?" she said, peering at Lingli's left temple.

Lingli raised a cautious hand and touched the prominent vein. She imagined she could feel it swelling. "It's always been there," she said.

"Mother of us all!" Madam dabbed more cream on the spot, followed by more powder. Then she pushed Lingli's face to one side and began powdering her other cheek.

"On this occasion, the rani will enter into the sacred contract of marriage. Her vision for the program is to celebrate the future as well as the past. Accordingly, I must incorporate new and unique performances, in which the rani has asked for not only our dancers' participation, but the participation of the youngest members of the Seven. All of them."

While carefully applying kohl around her eyes, Madam said, "There will be a welcome dance before the rani's entrance. When she and her consort sit, the troupe will perform the dance of remembrance and blessing, as always. A third piece, completely new, will follow the proclamation of marriage. It has been choreographed to honor the southern houses entering the alliance."

Her eyes were closed but Lingli could hear the dance teacher shuffling through her paints. Flicking strokes along her eyebrows tickled. When the pulling and rubbing paused, Lingli opened one eye.

Madam turned her face from side to side. "Well, you're less frightening, if not pleasing. Stand up. There is one more powder I can apply to your hair," she said, opening her last box and pushing Lingli onto the balcony where the bright light made her wince.

Turning her around so her face was shaded, Madam said, "Look at the floor," and Lingli bowed her head as the dance teacher sprinkled brown powder onto her hair.

"My responsibility is to communicate nothing less than the story of the Seven, the majesty of the realm, the power of the ancestors, and the promise of a fruitful alliance! And all that with fourteen dancers of nominal talent, a horde of unruly children, and a seamstress who could easily be mistaken for a wraith or lesser demon!"

She waved her hand at Lingli's head. "There." Madam added more powder in a few places. "Do not touch it or make it wet or you will have a mess. As I was saying, with the new piece added to the program, twenty-nine dresses will be required."

"Excuse me," Lingli said, "but the rani said twenty-eight dresses, and even that—"

Madam snorted. "Oh, you're too smart by far. Factor this: At least fourteen costumes from last cycle's harvest dance can be repurposed with no one the wiser. Those will only need minor altering. However, we need fourteen new costumes for the welcome and the new dance, and there is the rani's dress. The total comes to twenty-nine." She put her hand over her heart. "Of course, I will design Her Majesty's wedding dress and the dresses for the new choreography, which leaves only the donkey work for you."

"Madam! I...I don't think I can—"

"Are you going to start braying before you've even begun? Are you so ungrateful for our rani's food and shelter? Yes, the assignment is challenging, but be assured I will put no additional distractions in your way. In the morning you will come to the terrace and sew. After the midday meal, you will sew. In the evening you will sew. Any cut-and-stitch fool-of-a-villager could do this."

Madam turned away as she said the last, and Lingli understood she was unable to bear her own audacity. The dance teacher packed her things, herded her to the gate, and pulled the trapdoor up, ushering her downstairs.

The first two days went well enough, though the tender skin on Lingli's fingers ached after hours of sewing and she was still very much worried that she would not be able to complete the work on time. The dancers ignored her for the most part, occasionally whispering behind their hands and glancing at her in ways they pretended were subtle. Still, she was somewhat reassured that their rudeness did not exceed the interest one would expect any stranger to elicit.

The third day, however, was very warm and bright, and Lingli kept shifting the pallet she sat on to remain in a thin band of shade at the back of the terrace. She had draped Master Avani's scarf loosely over her new brown hair and kept her hands in the shade but still felt terribly exposed. Too many days like this and her skin would betray her.

That afternoon only the older girls resumed practice after their break. Floating effortlessly among them, Madam positioned limbs, tipped chins, and clapped out the beat with sharper precision than the overheated drummer accompanying them. But all her energy could not defeat the afternoon doldrums, and their practice slowed.

The door to the old tower creaked open, and Master Avani appeared with a bag of scrolls and a wooden stand balanced on his shoulder. Telling the girls to continue practicing their steps, Madam hurried to meet him. The old noble trudged to the front of the terrace where he steadied the stand, and Madam looked over a scroll he opened.

Lingli observed a patience she had not seen before in the dance teacher. With one arm crossing her chest and her other hand lightly touching her neck, Madam listened to Master Avani with a great attentiveness. Her focus was broken only when one of the dancers plopped down on the terrace floor. In a blink, Madam straightened and clapped her hands.

"Girls!" she scolded. "Why are you looking at me like buffaloes in a pond when you could be stretching and practicing? Assemble! Let us perform for Master Avani before we end our work for today."

When the troupe concluded their dance, largely ignored by Master Avani, Madam sent them to Lingli to be fitted. It took time to collect all the measurements she needed, and the girls grew restless. Lingli suspected their giggles had something to do with their measurement of her, but at least no one feared to approach her.

After the last girl skipped off with her friends, she wound up her measuring strings and set her chalk and slate to one side while Madam Sayed and Master Avani conversed over a cylindrical object he had attached to his stand. Bundling together a small mountain of skirt pieces, Lingli approached them in hopes that Madam would dismiss her.

"Hello, sir," she said with a bow for Master Avani.

"Miss Tabaan!" he said, recognition blooming in his face. "Stars, but Madam has made you over!"

Madam looked skeptical. "Painting our dancers has given me a fair hand, but no one should inspect her too closely."

"You've done a masterful job. I am certain this girl's work with needle and thread will speak for itself. She comes highly recommended, you know."

"Have you finished the measurements?" Madam abruptly asked her. When Lingli nodded, Madam added, "Well then, take your supper and refresh yourself. Forty-four days now, isn't it?"

As soon as she entered her room, Lingli discovered her old clothes and cloak neatly folded on the cot. Her small pack, with her fishing spear peeking out of it, rested on the floor next to her boots. Dropping her bundle of skirts, Lingli examined each item and was surprised to find that even the bag of coins was in the pack and her rabbit knife was in her boot's holster. The only thing missing was the bone brooch she had worn inside the neck of her kurta.

She sighed. *Whichever laundress stole it will make sure I never see it again.*

Two dancers' vests had been repaired when Lingli heard footsteps and someone's huffing breath on the stairs below. To her delight, Sid popped up through the trapdoor.

He made a face at her and asked, "What under the stars happened to you?"

"Madam's paints," Lingli said, gingerly touching her hair. "What are you doing here?"

"Master Avani sent me to fetch you for some stitching, and Madam agreed," he said, pulling a key from his pocket.

"You don't need that. She's not locked me in yet," Lingli said. Frowning, she added, "What are you? Master Avani's new steward?"

"His new scribe," Sid said as he surveyed the room's broken furniture and checked the views from the balconies.

"I thought you meant to join defenses?"

"Not yet," he mumbled. "What is this place anyway?"

"My jail, I suppose."

Sid shook his head and said, "I've seen the jail, and believe me, this is better."

Quickly pushing her things under the cot, Lingli put on her cloak again and followed Sid downstairs. On their way to the feasting hall, he proceeded to tell her about his day as a miner, getting lost in the Rock, and the strange characters he had met there.

"You should be more careful," she said when they reached the barrack's landing. "They could have put you in one of those cells."

"They're alright," Sid said. "Funny fellows, actually."

"Well, I suppose it's for the best. You'd have fallen into one of those pits sooner or later." Realizing how cutting her words sounded, Lingli reminded herself to be kinder to him. "Anyway," she added, "if you do well with Master Avani, surely you'll have a better chance of impressing Master Duvanya."

Sid shrugged. "Maybe, but I can't let Avaniji think I'm too good to let go."

When they entered the quarters, Master Avani sat at his table pondering the same thick book that had rested on his table the last time she had been there. He bid Lingli to sit, then went to his inner room and brought her a kurta with holes in each elbow.

As she drew out a length of thread, Master Avani told Sid, "Just today Madam Satya gave me an interesting new transcription from their early chronicles. Tonight you will begin copying the passages I've marked in that material."

Sid looked less than excited as Master Avani put his finger on the open page and read aloud.

"'In the seventh moon, the ground became the sea and pitched us upon the waves. Ripples large and small persisted for two moons. We feared the calamity, and the ancestor and his brethren made tribute to little brother moon.'"

Moving to another sheaf of parchments, the old noble bent so close to it that Lingli worried the diya next to him might catch his beard on fire.

"And there is this: 'We crossed fields that moved like the sea in the seventh moon. Waves persisted for two moons, and everyone was afraid. The ancestor witnessed the small moon's path and made his tribute, calling his brethren each night.'"

"Both passages are from the House of Satya. The first piece was included in our shared chronicles. The second is the new transcription from the original house record. And see the differences!"

"Different writers," Lingli said softly, "different expressions."

She felt Master Avani's gaze and looked up from her sewing.

He asked, "Do you also know how to read and write? You have no idea how rare those skills are, do you? That Sid is star-blessed with this skill is the only reason he has evaded greater penalties for his recent antics. Perhaps you would be interested in helping him with the transcription?"

"I'll not refuse you, sir," she answered slowly, "but I fear Madam Sayed and the rani will turn me out if I don't make progress on the dancers' costumes."

"Quite right," Master Avani agreed. "Perhaps after the wedding we'll discuss this again." He noticed Sid playing with his pen. "Concentrate, boy! You'll fall far behind if I convince any of the other houses to share translations."

"Won't it be a waste of time if there are no more shakings, sir?" Sid asked.

"Make your tributes, but I have seen too many bright cycles to take that chance. Knowledge must be pursued. The question is, as always, whether the knowledge we can accrue will surpass our natural ignorance before the next crisis."

They were quiet for a time. Lingli completed the kurta's repairs while Sid played with his pen as much as he copied from the transcription. The noble seemed lost in thought as he paced around his quarters, occasionally returning to his table to compare the book's entries with those in the parchments. What the old noble thought these records would reveal she could not guess, but she was flattered he would consider taking her as an apprentice.

When she delivered the repaired kurta to the old noble, he noticed her massaging her sore fingers and asked what had happened.

"I burned my hands during the shaking," she said. "It was very bad, but the wanderers treated me."

"The same wanderers who lightened me of my wages?" Sid scoffed.

"The same," she answered. "Do you remember that *I* paid them?" Sid's ability to put himself in the middle of every story never failed to astound her.

"With my coin," he shot back.

Like the bracelet, she decided to keep the coin pouch a bit longer.

"Without the wanderers," she told Master Avani, "I might have never made my way here. I was lost in the Silver Woods and—"

"Those noisy trees gave me chills," Sid said.

She was about to say that things worse than noisy trees abided there when Master Avani suddenly realized the hour.

"Oh my, you must go. Sid, please ensure Miss Tabaan reaches her room. It won't do to ignore Madam's conditions."

Sid escorted her back across the catwalk that connected the feasting hall to the old tower, but she stopped him at the tower entrance.

"Give me the key," she said.

"Are you mad?" Sid said. "Madam will never trust me again."

She considered this a moment. "You will tell her you fell asleep before you could return it. I'll give it to you at first light and you can deliver it to her."

"What are you doing?"

"I'm going to see if Rahmanji can make a copy."

Sid shook his head. "If you're caught, they'll blame me."

"Sid! You have to help me."

"I think I have been helping you quite a bit."

"Please! I'll do as I promised, but I can't be locked in there."

Sid sighed and handed her the key.

"Go to bed," she said. "If you don't know anything about this, they can't blame you."

"That almost makes me want to come." His grin reminded Lingli of when he was a small boy up to mischief. "Mind the guards. They'll ask questions if they catch you out this late." He pointed toward one of the night guards on the wall nearby.

"What should I do?"

"He'll go around the edge of the hall. Follow me."

Sid led her inside the old tower and downstairs to the small door on the ground floor. From there they scuttled through the archway and hugged the wall that stretched to the stables and the mining hall.

"I don't know if there's another guard at the stables," he whispered, "but you and your wanderer friends will have to deal with that."

She gratefully squeezed Sid's hand before hurrying along the wall's shadows with the key tight in her fist. Pausing at the fence around the stables and seeing no sign of the guards, she ran to the stable gate and quietly let herself in.

Two grooms snored on cots in the stable's entrance. As she edged around them, a small movement caught her attention, nearly freezing her blood, until she realized she knew the bearded young man watching her under the roof's eaves.

Samir said nothing when she drew near but walked ahead around the corner of the building. She followed and discovered a small campfire burning in the yard where the horses were exercised. Rahman sat on a pallet. Next to him, Rekha was bundled under blankets.

"Who is this?" Rahman asked, but she knew he recognized her.

"It's just some paint," she whispered, patting her hair. "I'm...I'm sorry to bother you, Rahmanji, but I have to ask you something." She showed him the key. "Can you make a copy of this with the shoe metal?"

Rahman glanced at her, then took the key and examined it.

"If the smith allows me near the forge, I could," he finally said. "For a price."

She had expected this. From her cloak, she drew out one of the coins that had remained in Sid's pouch.

"That will more than do," Rahman said with a chuckle. "Don't show your coin so easily."

Behind him Rekha stirred and rubbed her eyes. "Snow!" she called out, getting up and hugging her. "What happened to your hair? Are you wearing lip paint? I saw the rani. Have you seen her?"

She held Rekha's hand and said softly, "Yes, I've seen her. She is beautiful, just as they say. She has a different dress for every day, and Sid says she has a tall golden crown."

"She came here, you know," Rekha said. "She asked Pa to put the colt through his paces. Paid Pa a lot of gold."

"Hush, child," Rahman said.

"Would you trace the key now?" Lingli asked Rahman. "I have to return it before it's missed."

Cocking an eyebrow, Rahman went to the wagon to retrieve a piece of slate and chalk. After tracing the key and measuring the thickness he gave it back to her.

"I'll send Sid to fetch the copy," she said.

"Tell him to come before midday. The wagon's repairs will be done, and we'll be leaving."

Rekha took her hand and led her into the back of the stables to visit the colt.

"These grooms don't know what to do with him," Rekha whispered, patting the black colt's cheek. He looked little like the wretched creature they had washed. He was sleek and fit, though his legs remained wrapped.

"They're keeping him away from the other horses because he bit one of those fat geldings. You're going to miss us, aren't you, Bad Colt?"

"I'm sure he'll remember you," Lingli whispered back. The colt sniffed her hair, and she thought it funny that they both knew what it was to be painted.

"Pa told the rani that Govadhi Sir has to trust her before she tries to ride him, and she better keep those grooms away. Pa says a govadhi will either accept you, kill you, or kill himself trying to get away."

"You're learning a lot," Lingli told Rekha. "Maybe you will become a trainer like your pa."

Rekha whispered, "I *will* be the next great horse trainer of the White Horse Clan!"

After hugging Rekha goodbye, Lingli followed Samir back to the gate. When a guard passed the feasting hall again, Samir told her to hurry and waved her through. As she returned to the palace, she wondered how one who had considered killing her just a moon or so ago now seemed, if not friendly, at least no longer an enemy.

Inside the old tower she took a breath. She would not be able to avoid the guards any longer. *Settle yourself. You've done nothing wrong. Well, almost nothing. Just act like you belong here.* She pulled her hood forward and wiped the brown powder from her hands.

On the main floor, the guard patrolling the gallery said nothing when she bowed and continued upstairs. The second-floor guards barely looked her way, and on the third floor she was surprised to find no guards, though lanterns burned outside two of the doors. Before she stepped upon the next flight of stairs, she heard a door open below.

Leaning out over the landing's railing, Lingli could see two pairs of legs. One pair belonged to one of the guards. The second pair of legs were clad in white pajamas that ended in juttis with pointed toes.

"Ah, guard, would you come with me?" asked the man wearing juttis. When he moved closer to the railing, she saw the hem of a dark robe. "I'm afraid my request may inconvenience you, and perhaps it is nothing, but I fear there may be a gap in the palace defenses. I will show you so that you may inform your captain and Master Duvanya."

The man and the guard disappeared from Lingli's view though she moved around the landing and leaned out as far as she dared to see more. Another door below creaked open, and a young woman in a pale gown appeared at the railing below, clutching her dupatta to her chest. Before Lingli could step back from the railing, the young woman looked up and her eyes grew large.

"Wraith!" she cried and fled beyond Lingli's sight.

The sound of pounding feet echoed from below. She couldn't run to her room without meeting Madam's guard on the floor above, and locks hung from the doors around her. The only option was the dusty curtains hanging at the back of the landing. Pushing these aside, she found, to her surprise, no alcove or door behind them, but a dark passage into the rock wall, blocked only by two timbers that she could squeeze between. The instant the curtains closed around her, she was in complete darkness.

Hearing guards on the floor, she eased back, brushing a wall with one hand and holding the other out to avoid hitting anything. Someone approached the curtains. She pressed herself behind a thick brace and held her breath as a light brightened the passage.

"Think it went in there?" a voice asked.

"Where else would a wraith go?" answered another. "But I'm not going in unless the captain's on my heels."

The light disappeared.

With muffled voices still coming from the landing, Lingli pressed deeper into the passage until, after some distance, she met a pile of rubble filling the passage. She passed the night at the base of the debris, returning to the opening only when distant horns signaled the morning shift change. At the edge of the curtains, she watched two night guards descending the stairs to the floor below. As soon as they were gone, Lingli cat-footed across the landing and up the stairs.

Closing the trapdoor as quietly as she could, Lingli found the gate to her room unlocked. While she stood there, debating whether it made sense to lock the gate behind her and pretend she had been there the whole night, a voice from a shadowy part of the room said, "By the ancestors, I've been told wraiths walked here, but you're the first I've ever met."

Lingli's heart stopped. She couldn't see who had spoken, but it was not Madam.

A man wearing a dark turban and cloak stepped out of the gloom, and she flew to the cot to retrieve the knife in her boot.

"I am not going to hurt you."

He raised his hands, but the light was bright enough to show her the blade strapped to his side.

She held the rabbit knife before her. "I am not a wraith."

"Then who are you?"

"A seamstress. I'm assisting Madam Sayed."

"Why are you sneaking around and frightening people?"

"I…I wasn't sneaking. Who are you?"

"Very well, because you told me your occupation, I will tell you mine. I'm captain of the night guard. Are you stealing from the guests, Seamstress?"

"No, sir. I only surprised that girl." Lingli put her hand to her temple and tried to gather her wits. She picked up one of the dresses she had been fixing to show him. "I am helping Madam with the dancers' costumes. Please don't tell her I was downstairs."

"Why shouldn't I tell her?"

She had no good answer that wouldn't lead to consequences for both her and Sid.

"Listen," the captain said, "no one wants to tell the rani that they've been chasing wraiths in the palace. Those kinds of reports do not please her."

"I won't do it again, sir."

"Consider this your only warning."

More was revealed as he edged toward the gate—dark brows and a sharp jaw, a bear brooch on his shoulder. *House of Duvanya.*

"Don't stab me. I wish to remain here even less than you want me to."

She watched him warily as he let himself through the gate and raised the trapdoor.

Pausing halfway down the stairs, he said, "If the night guards are asked to chase down any more wraiths or if I learn of anything out of place, I will be back."

She held her breath for a few seconds after he left, then went to the gate and locked herself in.

CHAPTER 16

Where to sit in the feasting hall had become an issue. Between fainting in the defenses hall and his ejection from Roshan Sir's service, Sid had become a joke among the recruits. Pretending he couldn't see their smirking faces, he weaved through the long tables, seeking a spot to eat his breakfast. The sight of his old friend Harno sitting alone was a relief.

Is he trying not to look at me?

Girding himself with a forced optimism, Sid sat down beside the slight boy who ought to have some mercy, he thought, considering he had once fallen out of a wagon in front of the rani and everyone.

"Where did they put you this round?"

"With the musicians," Harno answered, "and I hope to never leave them."

"May the ancestors grant your wish," Sid said, "but we've still got two more rotations before it's settled."

Harno shook his head. "A few apprentices have already been spoken for. A master can reserve you in his service any time."

"How do you know that?"

"They told us the first day," Harno said. "You were late, remember? Master Duvanya's already spoken for two boys from our group."

Sid thought to himself, *You have zero chance, Sid, none, of joining defenses now,* but he told Harno, "Well, no doubt there are many good duties to choose from, but I'd still like to learn how to swing a blade, you know."

"Right," Harno said.

They ate in silence for a moment, then Harno added, "A lot of recruits try to show off. Do the most exercises, take the worst tasks. But the ones he picked weren't any better than the rest of us. Masterji says the best defenders use their heads to solve problems before they use their strength, and they put their brothers and sisters before themselves."

211

Nodding in agreement, Sid kept his face pointed at his thali as Master Duvanya crossed the hall. From the corner of his eye, he saw the commander speaking to Master Avani and Madam Sayed a few tables away.

The sight of the dance teacher reminded him—*The key! I have to get it back from Li.*

"They say he's leaving soon to review defenders at the outposts," Harno said. "There's two others who may be choosing recruits for the next rotation."

"Who's that?" Sid hoped he didn't sound as desperate as he felt.

"His son Eshan, the night captain, and Captain Gaddar."

Maybe I still have a chance. Sid excused himself, slipped out of the hall and climbed to the old tower's top floor.

When he pushed up the trapdoor, Li got up from her cot, hurried over, and reached through the bars to put the key in his palm.

"They'll have a copy ready before they leave at midday," she said. "Would you bring it to me?"

"If you just showed Madam she can trust you, she would leave it unlocked."

"She might or she might not."

"This is not a bad place, Li. Mind you don't spoil your chance—or my good name."

"I won't."

Still slightly worried that her curse might be catching, Sid felt guilty about having these thoughts at the same time. He made a silent call to Afsana and asked her to keep him safe.

"I'm sure Madam will keep you on through the winter."

"You better go before she comes to paint me up."

Madam didn't spare Sid a scolding when he returned the key, but his reception at the stables was even more uncomfortable. The wanderer girl stared the entire time he was there, and her father looked him over as if he were a horse of questionable soundness. As soon as the wanderer handed him the still-warm key, he hurried to the library.

"Late again, Sid Sol?" Master Avani said with some exasperation. "You must truly enjoy my company since you just earned yourself another evening of extra duty."

Sid didn't answer but bowed and sat at one of the long tables, fighting to keep his face filled with earnest interest while the old noble lectured him on the privilege of scribing and the necessity of practice. All the while Harno's news fluttered in his head, giving him just a tiny bit of hope that his dream was not dead.

Adopting what he hoped was a posture of studiousness, Sid practiced drawing letters, though there seemed to be more than he remembered learning in the Western Woods. He also drew flowers and many-rayed suns and stars, until a fit of yawning made him cough, which caught the old noble's attention once more. Master Avani picked up a thick sheaf of parchments on his table and brought them to him.

"I acquired these this morning. Can you read this?" The noble showed him the title page.

Sid squinted at the strange writing style on the cover and read, "'Duran.' The rani's house."

"Yes. To have received this material is the highest privilege. Handle these very carefully."

After wading through a long list of descendants, Sid followed a story from the ninth generation about an ancestor visiting from the otherworld in what Sid understood to be some kind of ship that floated in the air. He was so deeply engrossed in descriptions of weapons that shot fire that he forgot that he had no interest in history.

Late in the afternoon, Master Avani's apprentice Parth entered carrying a tray of fresh reed pens and newly filled inkpots.

The old noble told Sid, "Parth will be your teacher as well as I. He's one of the best apprentices I have had, and I do not say this solely to elevate the House of Avani."

Parth deposited his tray onto Master Avani's table, bowed his head at his teacher's praise, and took a seat on the bench opposite Sid.

"I know you are eager to continue transcribing the Book of Avani for the shared chronicles," Master Avani told Parth, "but I have received more transcriptions from the houses of Satya and Duran, and Sid will not be able to keep up with them by himself. Aside from urgent council business, you and young Sid will make this work your priority."

"Do you believe it will happen again, Sir?" Parth asked.

"I do—sooner or later—and I am becoming more convinced that the shaking, and perhaps other unusual events, are not unique in our history."

After an exercise in transcribing oral dictation, the old noble's attention returned to the parchments piled on his table. Parth kicked Sid under the table. When he looked up, Parth held a finger to his lips.

"Sir," Parth said loudly. "I forgot to tell you that I met Master Duvanya, and he requested my assistance today."

"He did?" Master Avani said, without looking away from the manuscript before him.

"Yes, sir," Parth said. "He needs a scribe to record the names and ages of the southern youth who arrived with Ameer Ali."

"Very well, very well," the noble said. "You may go."

Parth said, "Sir, if I took our new apprentice with me, he could learn something about a scribe's work."

"You want Sid to accompany you? I suppose it couldn't harm him to see your example."

The boys scrambled off their benches and left. Parth blew out his breath as soon as they reached the second floor.

"What?" Sid said.

"You don't think that Master Duvanya really asked for my help, do you?"

"You made that up?"

Parth shrugged. "I've put in my time with the old man. You will, too."

The boys hurried out of the tower and proceeded to the training yard, passing a group of recruits and junior soldiers exercising under the watch of two soldiers whose capes were pinned with bright swans—Madam Hansa's twin brothers, Ilo and Lalzam.

"Where are we going?"

"Where we can see everything."

They approached the small window in the door of the guardroom at the base of the palace gate. Sid could see only the nose of the guard who asked them their business.

"Senior Apprentice Parth Lalpati and Recruit Sid Sol," Parth said. "We've come to deliver a message to Captain Gaddar."

At the mention of Gaddar's name, Sid stared at Parth incredulously.

He needed to take Parth's connections in the palace more seriously.

The door swung open and Captain Gaddar emerged, holding his thick belt in one hand and a polishing cloth in the other. Sid glanced at Parth, who barely dipped his chin. Sid offered a better bow to the day captain.

"Hello, Parth. What news?"

Parth's grin twisted. "Saikhanger is sending a senior soldier to attend the wedding. And the rani's giantess delivered a small cask to the kitchens today."

"Is that so?" Gaddar refitted his belt and rubbed a smudge from the buckle.

"Sir, with your permission we would like to visit the terrace. Young Sid here needs to familiarize himself with the Rock."

Sid tried to stand tall and hold his stomach in as Gaddar considered this request.

"Mind you get down from there before sunset," the captain said as he left the guard room.

"You're friends with the captain?" Sid asked.

"'Friends' might be too much to claim," Parth said over his shoulder as they climbed the steep and narrow stairs to the terrace, "but he knows me."

"Do you think… What I mean is, I want to join defenses. Could you put in a good word for me?"

"Maybe I could." Parth stopped at an archer's slit, and they caught their breath. "But it won't help if you faint at his feet."

Everyone knows. Sid tried to pretend Parth's taunt did not bother him.

Soon they reached the door at the top of the gate tower and stepped out onto the terrace. Behind them the palace nestled against the upper reaches of the Rock. Ahead lay the bridge over the crevasse that separated the palace from Safed Qila. The fort showed itself as so many rooftops on the other side. Cool air from the crack flowed over them like the currents of a river.

Leading him around the terrace, Parth showed him the gutters in the floor where hot pitch could be poured on intruders trying to attack the gates. He pointed out the narrow road that began on the far side of the front grounds and wound along the western face of the Rock to where he said another watchtower stood on the north end. They could see junior soldiers making neat columns as they pushed themselves up on fingertips and toes before the Hansa brothers. In the far corner of the yard, Master Duvanya and the ameer of Kirdun, unmistakable in his bright red coat, walked among rows of red-shirted youth.

"See there?" Parth said. "Ameer Ali is reviewing his fighters. They'll mix them in with ours. Over there, those from House of Afreh are teaching spears to the junior soldiers. That's Stefina at the well, and that fat cow Bimla's with the laundresses."

"I still can't believe I'm here," Sid declared.

"We can't believe it either, Woods Boy," Parth said with a sneer. "Enjoy your fine dreams for now. You'll learn that if you aren't the head of your house, you might as well be a zhoukoo."

Sid was not sure if Parth was joking. "I'll take what the ancestors send, but why are you complaining? You're House of Avani."

"Oh, yes, I'm at the end of that tree's branches," Parth said. "It doesn't mean much." Seeing Sid's questioning look, he explained, "Used to be that if you belonged to one of the Seven Houses, you were a lord. All the families lived in Chandrabhavan. The only people in Safed Qila were the peasants that got permission to trade here. But the families grew so there was no room for all the Seven, and bit by bit the noble families were pushed into the fort. Now all the houses, except Duran and Master Avani himself, live out there just beyond the span on High Marg. Soon we'll be pushed down the hill with all the common people."

Hearing the bitterness in Parth's voice, Sid said nothing.

"These days your name doesn't matter so much as birth order," Parth continued. "Only the eldest of each generation becomes a master. Only one person in each generation, no matter how many there may be."

"You're still of the Seven, and working in the palace every day doesn't seem so bad."

"Wouldn't seem so bad when you come from nothing, eh, Woods Boy? Well, when you've known better and then see it sliding away, you may feel differently."

"You're right," Sid said, trying to soften Parth's prickliness. "I don't know anything about life here. I'm just grateful for a chance to do something. I want to join defenses, but I'll do anything except be a woodcutter my whole life, and that was my fate until the rani called me."

"Called you?" Parth laughed. "You hold a high opinion of your fine self, don't you? Oh, the maharani's very generous. She picks up recruits from far and wide when those right across the span demand a little too much coin and too much respect."

Suddenly there was a deep rumbling below their feet. For a moment Sid's panic swelled with the thought that the shaking had returned. Then he realized it was the portcullis. They looked over the side of the terrace and saw a granary wagon on the bridge span headed toward the fort.

"The prince consort has kept his folk here for the last two moons like he has the right," Parth grumbled. "He's living better than the rani, and now the other southerners are pouring in, everyone from babes to grannies. We're feeding them too well."

"Surely they're only here until the wedding."

"Yes, surely. Like you all are here just for a cycle and then you'll be going back to the woods, right?"

"Not if I can help it!"

"That's what I thought."

Sid didn't like the way Parth looked at him as if he knew everything. It reminded him of Li. "The rani said she needed more people to build Nilampur," he said. "Aren't some moving down there?"

"Not me!" Parth said. "Father says it's a bad proposition. She's promised a manor and trading licenses to each house that sends kin there, but neither the manors nor the markets are finished. There's no security that far south and little trade. Avinash was going to go but news came back that spares were laying the roads, same as the common boys. Half of them can hardly walk because they've caught some mud sickness, and rations are poor."

Parth started walking to the end of the terrace closest to the palace. Sid came up alongside as he pointed at the central hall's terrace.

"We should have gone over there," Parth said, snapping his fingers. "The dancers are practicing for the wedding, and it's always fun to torment those girls a bit."

Sid snickered, glad to see his friend's mood was turning again.

Parth threw back his shoulders and tugged his collar up. "Wherever there are a few roses that need to be plucked, I'm the gardener for the job."

Sid squinted at the terrace. Was that Li in her black cloak next to the tent? He suddenly remembered that he had never given her the key he had collected from the wanderers, but his concern was fleeting. She wouldn't need it until later anyway.

Parth hooted and waved toward the feasting hall. "Look at the fools gathered up there already. Even Avaniji is going to notice that."

He followed Parth's gaze and saw a handful of youth sitting atop the feasting hall roof just as he and other recruits had the night of the last observation ceremony. One of the boys waved a firewine skin over his head.

In the training yard horns blasted. Captain Gaddar and two deputies in their bright yellow capes walked to the center of the yard to meet night guards in blue capes.

"We better go down," Parth said. "Night guard's about to take their posts, and we don't want Eshan's boys on our backs."

Sid followed Parth out of the tower, trying to think of ways he might make himself useful to the day captain. They parted at the gate, where Parth slapped him on the back and headed across the span toward his home in the fort.

The loneliness of the deepening dusk settled on Sid's shoulders. He hurried toward the feasting hall but hung back in the colonnade after seeing that the jailer Vidkun sat at the nearest table with one of the other boys he had met inside the Rock. Sid liked to believe he could befriend anyone, but he had no intention of reminding them of the debt they said he owed.

Taking care to avoid the night guards assembling for their watches, Sid snuck into the baths below the central palace. Only the noble families and the rani's guests could use the pools, but he had visited the baths once before just to breathe the warm, moist air.

Except for a pair of old women tending the fire at the other end of the cavernous space, there was no one around. He slipped along the shadowed alcoves lining the main pool until he came to a stack of drying cloths by the robe room. As soon as the old women turned their backs, he crept to the edge of the pool and dipped a cloth in it before drawing back onto a bench to wash his face.

The warm water felt wonderful.

Sid was about to venture out to the pool again when he heard voices near the entrance. Three men arrived. The rani's consort, Prince Hassan, and Ameer Ali unceremoniously dropped their robes on the pool's edge and stepped into the water. Another southern noble reluctantly followed.

"Do you know when Duvanya will leave?" Ameer Ali said.

Prince Hassan shook his head. "He must secure the agreement of the other houses."

"Duvanya's new campaign is poorly timed," the new southerner said in a voice clearly unused to the common tongue. Though he waded in water that only reached his hips, he held on to the pool's edge as if he feared being swept away.

"Is it?" Prince Hassan asked as he sat on the pool's bottom, brushing the top of the water with his outstretched arms.

"I believe we should join him," Ameer Ali said, wading near Hassan. "It may provide our houses an advantage."

"Advantage?" the new man said, "to bleed in some barbarian's frozen field and help them claw back stolen land? What advantage? Will you send your youth, Ba Hassan?"

Sid grimaced. *Politics.*

Hassan said, "How many nights have we talked of what, exactly, is the difference between the Ascaryans of this realm and our own houses? How have they achieved tremendous wealth while our people perish from the elements and lack of food and water?" He counted on his fingers. "The difference is not the amount of rain, poor ground, or because ancestors have cursed us. It is one thing only—confidence that we can act together for a common purpose."

"Your vision of an alliance is inspiring," the new man said, "but the elders of my house are not convinced."

"The elders do not act in haste," Ameer Ali interjected. "They must see the promise made real. I think Duvanya's campaign will demonstrate that. Our youth are already learning skills here that the elders only imagined. Saatkulom will certainly win this skirmish. This rani and Duvanya would not risk a loss so close to the completion of the alliance contract."

Hassan said, "By helping them achieve this victory, we will give our youth confidence that they are capable on a foreign field, and they will have the skills we need to strengthen *our* houses. Not to take from one another and make each other poorer, but to bring greater wealth and glory to all of Avakstan."

They were quiet, then the new man said to Ameer Ali, "Answer me, Honorable Ameer. What do you gain from this adventure?"

Sid saw the ameer's face bloom into a broad smile.

"The rani is generous to her friends, and we have been friends for cycles, but I would not risk the lives of two hundred of my house's youth for friendship. I expect to be quite well-rewarded in trade."

"Saatkulom needs this alliance," Hassan said. "Duvanya does not have fighters to spare, and the expansion to Nilampur has depleted them."

Sid frowned. *Saatkulom has the best defenses I've ever seen. Not that I've seen any other great realms.*

"Our houses have already agreed on many terms," Hassan said, "but it is not too late to join with us. The House of Afreh has just provided its demands, and it seems most of them can be accommodated."

The newcomer said, "The House of Idris has never put its fate into another realm's hands, and this realm has simply taken what it wanted, as have your houses."

Ameer Ali raised his hand as if to calm the man's concern. "Yes, we carry the past with us, but will we allow the past to kill the future? We are taking a risk, but you know as well as I that none of us, not any single house, could confront Saatkulom by itself. This time we can, with this good prince's support, force them to negotiate honestly if we stand together."

"Take a few days to consider," Hassan said as he moved to the other end of the pool. "If you choose not, you will still enjoy these festivities as my guest, but should you wish to hear the rani's word directly, I will arrange a private audience for you."

Ali and Hassan cajoled the Idrisi until he followed them to the deeper water, and Sid found opportunity to escape.

As he jogged back to the feasting hall, Sid thought, *If Master Duvanya's taking defenders on a campaign, maybe I'll be needed in the guard after all.*

CHAPTER 17

Half a moon had passed since Lingli had taken up residence at the top of the old tower. She had made progress on the dance costumes, and though Madam still locked her in, or at least thought she did, Lingli hoped they were coming to an understanding. Once Madam learned that she worked at night, she began delaying her application of the face paints until midday, allowing her a little more time to sleep. Still, Lingli moved carefully around the edge of Madam's pride and kept secret the copied key she used for small explorations about the palace when she was too restless to sew.

One day, as Madam filled in Li's brows with a light brown powder, the dance teacher asked abruptly, "Does your family suffer from the same... malady?" She waved at Lingli's temple.

"I never knew my family."

Madam said nothing for a moment, then resumed her careful work and said, "I was about your age when I lost my parents."

Lingli ventured a question. "What happened to them?"

"Nine moons of coughing sickness. After a rainy summer, folk here developed hacking coughs that went on and on. My parents had been so afraid I would catch it, they forbade me from leaving our quarters while those in the fort and palace fell ill one after another.

"Rani Shikra herself came to our door and apologized for the hardships," Madam said, looking into the space ahead and no longer marking Lingli's brows. "She praised us, saying that we must have made powerful tributes to the ancestors, for few families were left untouched. Only a moon earlier, her own son—our rani's elder brother—had joined the stars."

Madam Sayed sprinkled color over Lingli's head and brushed her hair until it was a sturdy nut brown.

"The noble families decided to call upon the ancestors together to plead for an end to the illness. Mother was of the House of Hansa so we were expected to attend. My father, however, was the first northern envoy invited here. He did not want us to go, but in the end, we went.

"There were bodies piled in the corridors." Madam's voice caught. "Mother tried to cover my eyes, but I saw them. So many shrouds."

"What happened?" Lingli whispered.

"Despite the tribute," Madam said, "the sickness continued. Father became ill and promised to return as soon as he felt better. He did not come back. A few days later, my mother began to cough. She would not allow me to come near her, but she didn't leave me. I tried to make sure she ate, but…" Madam closed her eyes for a moment before she said quietly, "Then I was alone."

She finished packing her paints into her basket and smoothed her already tidy hair. "But I survived, and the ancestors know I am grateful. Chalo! We are late for practice."

Madam had moved her sessions from the terrace to the great hall where the performance would be presented, and Lingli no longer worried about burning as she worked next to their platform on a pallet covered with costumes. The music was bright, the steps intricate and exacting, and she had to admit that some of the girls, despite their moods, were skilled.

She wondered at the perverse sense of pride growing within her. *How am I so persuadable? These girls have never spoken a word to me, and there is not a singer on this rock who could touch the hem of Sonali's gown. But here they are, trying their best, and I am sympathetic. Even if I am here at no one's pleasure, I must admit all of us together are making something beautiful.*

A mob of young ones had been called to practice the welcome dance that day, swelling the troupe to three times its usual size. With older sisters, brothers, and mothers accompanying the children, the hall echoed with their noise. Madam had become shrill from the effort to be heard. Indeed, her exasperation was getting the better of her, and she had banished three little dancers to a bench near the hall's doors to consider their behavior.

These chatty ones raised the alarm near the end of practice. "Rani! Rani! She's come! Shhh!"

Lingli looked up from her sewing in time to see Valena Sandhyatara glide past, swathed in heavy brinjal-colored skirts and a golden brown coat. Greta followed close behind, her head swinging from side to side as she scanned the room. Lingli so wanted to speak to the giantess about Red, but she was always in the rani's company.

"What a delight!" the rani said. "There is no greater joy than seeing our children perform so beautifully."

"It is an honor to have you visit us, Your Majesty." Madam Sayed's nose nearly touched the floor. "The children have been working very hard, but excellence never comes without effort, does it? In any case, one and all are excited about performing for you."

"I would like to see the third dance."

Madam Sayed swallowed. "Yes, Maharani, of course, but the girls are not yet prepared to demonstrate what will be a completely unique performance. May I suggest, if you please, that I arrange a special viewing for you next week?"

"I do not wish to inconvenience you. Perhaps you could show me the opening movements?"

To Lingli's knowledge, the older girls had not practiced the final dance since she had begun assisting Madam, and she suspected they did not know the steps, but she had begun to work on their costumes. She pulled one of them from her pile and went to Madam's side.

Bowing to the rani, Lingli said, "The lead dancer's dress is here, Madam, should you require it."

Madam Sayed looked around and quickly tried to mask her surprise. "Ah, yes...let me explain the concept for their costumes."

"This is lovely work," the rani said, looking directly at her. "Did you create this?"

Lingli nodded and dropped her eyes. Though the rani spoke politely, being so near her felt like facing a thundercloud that sparked with lightning. Lingli looked to Madam, who glared back at her.

"Well, this is a beginning," the rani said, "but I expected more by this time, Amina."

Madam Sayed's mouth opened and closed. She pressed her hands together. "Oh, Your Majesty, forgive me for misunderstanding you. We can begin the opening measure this instant. Nyla, come here and take position center stage. Music!" she shouted. "The new music, play it!"

The rani's smile stretched thin. "Be at ease. We must ready the hall for this evening's program. All are dismissed."

"Oh, yes, Your Majesty." Madam waved at the musicians who were already plucking at their instruments. "We are dismissed. Take all your things, children. Leave nothing behind."

The rani serenely watched Madam dash around and herd the children and their minders to the entrance. Gathering up the costumes and pieces of cloth, Lingli followed Madam out with the bundle on her head. When they reached the top floor of the old tower, Madam slammed the gate closed and locked it after Lingli entered.

"Has the moon addled you? Never speak so impudently in front of our rani!"

She departed quickly, leaving Lingli standing with her arms full of costumes, biting down on the inside of her cheek, and wondering why she had tried to help.

It was still dark when a flash of lantern light and the sound of the lock rattling woke Lingli, scarcely an hour after she had set her sewing aside and lay down. Lingli knew instantly that Madam was in no better mood than she had been the evening before.

The dance teacher hugged herself against the chill. "Well, get up! Hurry!"

Lingli pulled her tunic over her head and put on her slippers while Madam spread her paints out on the small table. Balancing Lingli's chin in one hand, Madam roughly rubbed the paint in with the other. Not even bothering with her other powders, Madam covered the offending vein at her temple and quickly added the hair powder.

"Keep your hood up," Madam told her.

"Yes, where—?"

"The rani's quarters. I wondered how long it would take for her to decide what kind of wedding dress she required, and now, with less than two moons left, she calls." Madam closed her eyes as if to seek strength. "You are coming to assist me. You are not to speak. You are not to offer brilliant ideas. Remain absolutely silent unless I tell you otherwise."

The palace was still quiet as she followed Madam down the gallery. The front grounds were empty, and the night guards had not yet been relieved of duty. In the new tower, she and Madam stopped before a pair of guards and ornately carved and gilded doors that marked the rani's quarters.

A guard knocked, and Greta poked her large head out the door, then allowed them inside. At the dressing table in her inner room, Her Majesty faced a long piece of polished metal that glowed in the lantern light. The rani's face was reflected there, as if the metal was a window to another, backward world. Lingli saw not only the rani, but herself, and Madam and Greta, too. She tried to discover any differences between the actual Ascaryans and their reflections until she realized that the rani was staring back at her. She stepped behind Madam.

"Good morning, Maharani," Madam said brightly, signaling Lingli to sit on the floor. "How may I serve you this morning?"

"How may you? In so many ways I can imagine, but I've called you for one particular task." The rani rose from her stool and went to her bed where a gown was spread.

Picking up a midnight-blue sari with a bright gold hem and pallu, the rani said, "This is the dress I wore for my first wedding." She sighed and laid it down again. "This time my gown will be more diplomatic. It must combine the symbols of my house with those of the House of Hudulfah. Their colors are white and gold, and the gold we share, so I will wear white and gold. And because both our houses venerate the sun, my dress should be decorated with it in some way."

The rani's instructions were offered with little enthusiasm. When Madam approached to look at the gown more closely, Her Majesty took her hand. "Will these details suffice?"

"Yes, Your Majesty. White and gold, purity and confidence. It is a good message. The richness of both houses' symbols will inform my design."

"Wonderful," the rani said, leaning forward to kiss Madam lightly on the cheek. "I look forward to seeing your drawings and a demonstration of the new dance. Please come and dine with me tomorrow evening."

Looking stricken, Madam bowed again and moved to leave. Lingli got to her feet. She tried to catch Greta's eye but could not.

"Leave your seamstress."

Lingli froze, and Madam gave the rani a questioning look.

"The princess Mafala also must have a gown for the wedding, and I assured her I would send a seamstress, but I have no intention of wasting your time. Your assistant will suffice for this assignment."

"Of course, Your Majesty."

A quick glance at Greta as Madam left the room told Lingli nothing. At the same time, she sensed the rani's close examination of her, and she was finding it hard to breathe.

"Take off your hood, Seamstress," the rani said. "I like to see the person to whom I am speaking."

Lingli complied and resisted the urge to grab a strand of her hair to check its color.

A small frown creased the rani's forehead. "Do you never see the sun? You're as pale as an eastern…" She did not finish her thought but shook her head and began toying with one of the chains around her neck.

"The princess of the House of Hudulfah will soon be my sister by law. Naturally, she wishes to impress and often seeks to flatter me by copying my dress. I charge you with the responsibility of making sure that doesn't happen on my wedding day. Do you understand?"

"You don't want the princess's dress to look like yours?" Lingli said.

"You will go to her now, and you will listen to all she says. You will make her a dress, a beautiful dress, but it may not be gold, or white, or of a style similar to the dress Madam makes for me."

Lingli bowed, hoping this was the end of the rani's instructions.

"Sid Sol told me you and he lived with a giant."

Lingli nodded.

"How old are you?"

"Sixteen cycles."

"Hmmm." Greta interrupted in her deep voice. "Council awaits."

The rani was quiet then waved Lingli to the door. "Go now. That is all."

Though relieved the rani had kept her no longer, Lingli's thoughts continued to circle Greta as she left. *She would have known Red when he lived here. She knows that I knew him. I've got to find a way to speak to her.*

Pulling her hood back up, Lingli descended the stairs and approached the princess's quarters on the floor below.

The young woman who answered the southern guard's knock on the door wore a rough-woven shift that came only to her knees, but her hair was elaborately braided in the Hudulfah style. She looked Lingli up and down, then held the door open.

The instant the southern princess entered from the balcony, Lingli realized she was the same young woman she had frightened in the old tower. Shrinking in her cloak, she hoped the princess would not recognize her.

"The rani has requested me to assist you with your dress for her wedding."

"What gown will the rani wear?" Mafala fixed her catlike eyes upon her.

"Her Majesty…has not yet chosen," Lingli stammered, wondering how she had so neatly fallen into a trap between two jealous nobles.

Proceeding to her inner room, Mafala held her arms up so her maid could remove her dress. It was tight across her chest and shoulders, and the maid struggled.

"You must open all the hooks, idiot!" the princess shouted into the girl's face as she stepped out of her clothes and stood in her blouse and underskirts.

To Lingli, she said, "Will you take my measurements or guess at them?"

Lingli pulled a long piece of string from her tunic's pocket and began her work.

"Find out what the rani is wearing, and I will have a dress the same color," the princess said.

"She favors the dark blue color of her house," Lingli said, marking measurements on her slate and blushing at her own nerve.

There was a rap on the door and the servant answered it. Lingli looked up from measuring the princess's hips to see that Prince Hassan had joined them.

"How many?" he asked.

"Good morning to you, too, brother," Mafala answered primly. "I am so glad to see you well this day." Prince Hassan said nothing, and the princess clapped her hands. "You have no sense of humor! Will this news do? Four hundred more Idrisis are coming."

"There's hardly that many in all their territory."

"Unless our scouts have forgotten how to count, that is the number."

"How soon will they arrive?"

"By the next moon. Nearly two thousand will camp at Nilampur by then."

Prince Hassan turned back toward the door.

"Wait," Mafala said, grabbing her brother's arm.

Lingli remained balanced on her haunches and kept her head down.

"You might like to know that the wife of that dog Penurika mentioned they have left half their party camped in the new city for fear the House of Afreh would encroach on their compound. There could be trouble between them before the wedding."

"More reason for me to go as soon as possible. We cannot allow them to jeopardize this alliance for such foolishness."

"You have become adept at making others think your efforts benefit them more than yourself."

"What else does a leader do after their people's bellies are full?"

"Ha, you can be amusing."

"Our house," Hassan said, resuming his customary seriousness, "is leading the south toward a prosperity none of us have ever known. It is a bold course, and not an easy one. We cannot afford to be distracted."

"Do you think I am distracted? I use the tools I have and keep the ancestors' favor."

Lingli could feel the prince's gaze on the top of her head. She didn't dare look up.

He finally said, "I need you to continue to build trust with our friend while I am gone."

Mafala shrugged. "That is not difficult. You waste my talents, brother."

After the prince left, Lingli took a few more measurements and promised to return when she learned more about the rani's wedding dress. Lying to the princess was surprisingly easy, and she found she didn't mind thwarting her ambitions.

Afternoon practice with Madam was not as tumultuous as Lingli feared, but the session was long. After the young ones were dismissed, the dance teacher continued to put her older students through their routines mercilessly. She introduced them to a new series of movements—Lingli guessed it was the third dance—and she performed the steps with them countless times, daring them to fall behind the count or make a mistake.

The day's light had faded from the great hall's single window by the time they left. Madam didn't offer to help her haul the costumes and material to the old tower as she usually did, but she sniffed a lot, maintaining an air of injury in Lingli's presence. When the dance teacher dawdled with the keys to her room, Lingli guessed that she wanted to know what had transpired after she left the rani's quarters.

"The rani commanded me to make Princess Mafala's gown for the wedding," Lingli said, "but she insists it must not look like her dress."

"Ha! You have stepped into it, haven't you."

"I have." Lingli said. *And so have you.* "What would you advise me?"

Madam seemed almost appeased by her question. "Use the most expensive material. What the Hudulfah princess lacks in taste, she makes up for in vanity."

When Madam departed, Lingli noticed that she left the gate unlocked.

Through the evening, as she worked on the costumes, Lingli asked herself how she could keep Madam's trust. It was not her wish to live in the palace forever—too many Ascaryans—but here she had food and shelter, and Sid close by. *It will be impossible to convince him to leave in winter. If he joins the defenses, moving him will be even harder, but better to make the argument in springtime.*

The thought of possibly living without Sid was like a dark bank of clouds on her horizon, but one task at a time. If she wished to stay longer, her work would have to impress Madam, and Madam had to impress the rani. *Be useful.*

Setting aside her stitching, Lingli picked up her slate, and checked a strand of hair. It was still brown, but she was grateful for her cloak and hood when she crept down to the main floor. She nodded at the guards while clutching her slate to her chest like a shield. *Act as if you belong here.*

Matachand and Chotabhai's light was weakened by clouds, and the gallery was dark save for the lanterns hung outside the council room and the doors of the great hall. She had hardly started down the dim passage when she nearly collided with someone bent over and looking at the floor.

"Oh, my dear child," a man said as he straightened, "you startled me. For a moment I thought you were a ghost. Rather late, isn't it?"

It was the eastern envoy, Kanaka. He was barely taller than her but much thicker. She quickly offered a small bow.

"I was quite certain I would sleep well tonight," he said, "but I have discovered that I have lost a very dear ring, which I wore only yesterday.

Following my mother's wise advice, I began retracing my steps, and that brought me here because I most definitely remember I wore it when I visited the new tower. Would you, my girl, be so kind as to help me look for it?"

Refusing him was impossible. "What does your ring look like, sir?"

"Ah, yes, that would be helpful information, though I doubt we will be confused by multiple rings lying about. It is a large, square-cut amethyst set in a silver band. Rather old-fashioned, and that is why it is so important to me. My father's mother presented it to me on the day of my induction as a Dyuvasan envoy. She said she had acquired it from a Saatkulom artisan many cycles ago, so I brought it with me when I was assigned here. I thought it quite a fitting piece to wear, and not only because of its origin, but because Maharani Sandhyatara favors amethyst, you know."

He assigned her to look on one side of the passage while he looked on the other, but neither of them had found the ring when they reached the end of the gallery.

"Well, this has been disappointing," the envoy said, "but my faith is great. I will see that ring again. Yes, you may go. It is terribly late, isn't it? Let us see if my search for sleep will be more successful."

Knowing the guards outside the rani's quarters would not tolerate her sitting at their feet, Lingli continued halfway up the next flight of stairs and sat where she could still see the decorated doorframe through the balusters. She drew the seven-pointed sun on her slate and added Matachand, Chotabhai and the stars in the constellation where the House of Duran's earlier generations were said to dwell. A theme for the wedding dress began to play in her mind.

When the doors to the rani's quarters slammed open, Lingli jumped and nearly lost her chalk.

Prince Hassan burst past the guards, carrying Prince Aseem, and the rani was on his heels. Lingli shrank back into the shadows on the staircase.

"It would be touching," the rani said, "to think that concern about your contribution, which was due moons ago, has made you eager to leave at this hour, but we both know better. When we hear the report in the morning—"

"When we hear that, half the day will be lost, and you will be that much closer to failing to honor your bargain."

"You question my word?" The rani was livid. "Not one of your people has been denied their due, nor even the excess they have demanded! Not one agreement has been broken! The date for this union was New Cycle Day and is still New Cycle Day, and all obligations shall be met the moment our contract is complete!"

The night guards at her door moved to either side of the rani, but she signaled for them to stay back.

"I would never question your word, dear one," Hassan said smoothly, "and I observe your actions even more closely."

There was a silent moment between them, then the rani said, "If you would go to Nilampur now and waste your time instead of completing the terms of our contract, then go. Please go and be reassured. And while you are there, perhaps you can find the four tons of cotton you have promised, but you will not take my son."

The rani spoke more quietly than before, but Lingli held her breath, having heard the blade's edge in Her Majesty's voice.

"You shall have both the cotton and the son, at least until he is weaned," Hassan said as he handed Aseem to her. "Then we will see with which house he aligns."

"He will align with both our houses and make us stronger for it."

"This compact will slide into the mud with the ruins of your lake town unless it has rulers Ascaryans will follow unto the world's edge, not weaklings tamed by palace entertainments and ruled by their moods. If this boy is to hold our bargain, he must be very strong, and I mean to guarantee that. Count his curls now. In time you may not recognize him, nor he you."

The rani forced a small, bitter laugh. "Sons and surprises, is it? Let us see who is more surprised."

Her Majesty returned to her room with the little prince, and Hassan charged downstairs. Lingli heard him call out to someone on the floor below, but soon the noise faded, and the easy breath of the dark hours returned. She waited until the guards settled back in their positions, then proceeded past them as if she was entirely unaware of the outburst she had just witnessed.

The moons had set when she reached her room, and she had to light a diya to examine her drawings. Copying her sketches onto the floor with her chalk, she discarded some and improved others until she refined a design that captured something she thought Madam would like. The question was how to convey this vision to the dance teacher.

I cannot simply tell her this is the wedding dress. She will reject the idea unless it is her own.

She embroidered a small portion of the design on a discarded skirt piece and kept it on the floor next to her cot, then rubbed out her drawings and tucked her slate away.

When Madam arrived near to midday, Lingli made sure the skirt piece was next to her while her daily transformation was completed.

"What is this?" Madam asked as she paused in powdering Lingli's face.

Opening one eye, Lingli saw that Madam had noticed her embroidery.

"It is a design I saw in a dream, Madam," she said. "A dream of a beautiful gown came to me in my sleep. When I woke, I stitched this bit very quickly before I could forget it."

"A dream?"

"I wanted to tell you about it, but I feared you would find it silly."

Madam peered closely at the cloth. "Is this our sun and stars?"

"Yes. In the dream I saw a woman wearing these symbols on her dress. I think she must have been of the Seven."

"Impertinence doesn't serve you well," Madam said sharply. "The ancestors occasionally speak to us in dreams, but your ancestors are not of the Seven."

"Of course, Madam. The woman wearing the gown didn't speak to me," Lingli scrambled to save her story, "but I did hear a voice. Yes. The voice was very distant. I thought it came from the originator of the gown. Another seamstress, I suppose."

"What did she say?"

"She said… She said, 'Mark this design if you are able. It shall be worn only once on a day remembered forevermore. Find the one whose talent will make this vision come true.'"

With Madam's permission, Lingli brought out her slate.

Part 3

CHAPTER 18

The rani dismissed Greta after she took her supper, but the giantess was loath to leave and had gone still outside the rani's quarters for nearly two hours. The apex of the thirteenth moon approached, and she sensed an unusual vibration growing stronger. Oblivious of the disturbance her towering figure caused for those forced to edge past her on the landing, Greta waited until her giantsense told her Dear Child was resting before resuming her climb upstairs to a short passage that opened onto the central terrace.

Six of the Seven clustered at the terrace parapet, speaking quietly to one another. The sky was bright with stars and the brilliant moons, but the night air was chill, and the nobles pulled their wraps tight about them. Master Avani had called for a late meeting, but the rani had declined the invitation, permitting him to proceed and saying she would take his report the next day. Uninvited and unnoticed, Greta waited in the shadows of the tower entrance and watched the rest gather where Master Avani had set an object mounted on a three-legged stand and covered with a cloth.

"I promise this will not take long, as I am certain you have preparations to make for the upcoming observation," Master Avani said. "The harvest moon has always been my favorite apex, though no doubt it will pale in comparison to the grand celebration we will witness in the next moon.

"As you know, Chotabhai peeks 'round his sister's skirts every seventeen cycles and remains for three. This has been recorded in our history since Saatkulom began, and those bright cycles have been consistent except for some change in the number of days the little moon is visible to us. When Chotabhai disappears, we return to the regular pattern of twenty-eight-day cycles with Matachand alone—marking the beginning of a new generation."

233

"My father always said, 'Two moons, three plantings, four storms,'" Madam Satya said. "In those days, we did not step out our doors during a bright cycle without a tribute."

"My grandmother fasted so often during bright cycles, we feared for her health," Master Avani said.

In the shadow of the archway Greta thought how proud these Ascaryans were of the knowledge they gathered in their short lives. Her own kind lived three times more cycles and would not have boasted of it.

"Please, brother," Crowseye said with some exasperation, "tell us why you have called us here."

"Yes, so I shall. Like my ancestors, I have viewed Matachand and Chotabhai every night they have been visible since I became master of my house." Master Avani gestured to the object next to him. "We use this stargazer, a blessed gift given to the House of Avani, to see distant objects and celestial bodies in more detail."

Master Avani removed the cover to reveal a long cylindrical object made of a dark silver metal. At one end was a black sleeve, which protected a hard, transparent material like the clearest moonstone. At the other end, a much smaller cylinder of the same material was fitted. A metal collar surrounded the small end.

"Tonight, I invite each of you to join me in viewing Chotabhai."

The others looked at him with surprise.

"Are you certain?" Crowseye asked.

"Yes, I invite you. I have long argued we should share more of our knowledge with one another, and it now seems important that we begin. Gayatri?" He beckoned to Madam Hansa. "Will you be the first?"

Madam Hansa tentatively came forward. She put her eye to the small end of the stargazer as he directed. Master Avani adjusted the metal collar. She suddenly gasped and stood back quickly.

"Is it the otherworld?" she asked.

Master Avani shook his head. "Members of my house have asked this question about our celestial bodies for generations, and we still do not have the answer."

The rest took their turns looking through the stargazer, and afterward they encircled Master Avani in awestruck silence.

"I am glad you have witnessed the beauty of our wayward moon in more detail than our eyes can see," Master Avani said, and he took a deep breath before he continued. "But what you cannot appreciate from your brief observation is that, if you viewed Chotabhai again, as I do each night, you would see that our small moon is making a mockery of his name. He seems to be experiencing a spurt of growth."

There were quizzical looks among the nobles. In the archway's shadows, Greta listened closely. Perhaps this had something to do with the different vibration, almost a sound, that she felt. Her clan would have had a name for this, she thought, and Red might have known what it meant, but she was as ignorant as the Ascaryans.

"According to our house's records, and what your eyes would tell you, Chotabha's diameter and circumference expands from the first night he appears to us as a moon up to the ninth moon of the first bright cycle. From that moon until the third moon of the third bright cycle, Chotabhai measures the same, and after that he shrinks until he is only visible as a point of light like any other star." Master Avani tugged at his beard. "Chotabhai's size should have stabilized by the ninth moon this cycle, but he has not. Our small moon is still growing. A very small amount but growing just the same."

Greta felt a chill, not from the night air, but emanating from the five other nobles, and she squinted up at the small moon where it sailed next to the larger one. Was the lingering ache in her bones due to its change?

"Perhaps there has been some miscalculation?" Master Duvanya said.

"I've repeated the measurements multiple times."

"And Matachand?"

"There has been no change that I can measure."

"Why didn't you tell us after the tenth moon?" Master Duvanya asked. "You knew then, didn't you?"

Master Avani rubbed his nose. "I informed the elders of my house and our sister, but the elders forbade me to share it in council unless the rani ordered it. I risk their displeasure even now, but I felt I must tell you."

"Which is why you have summoned us to this cold terrace tonight," Master Duvanya said. "You have brought us here because this is not a council meeting."

"Yes, and because I am concerned that the shaking is somehow connected to this. I was ill at ease keeping this from you any longer, and Valena knows I am informing you now."

"Two unusual events may not be more than coincidence," Crowseye said.

"True," Master Avani said, "but I cannot dismiss the timing yet. Also, I would remind you that, though we don't rely on the Mephistanis for honesty and fair dealing, their knowledge of the sea is unsurpassed. They learned long ago that Matachand and Chotabhai affect the tides, drawing the water up, particularly during an apex in a bright cycle."

"The last delegation of Mephistani traders reported unusual tides and sea storms occurring both before and after the shaking," Madam Satya said.

Master Avani nodded. "I am trying to learn whether Chotabhai's growth could disturb the land in a similar fashion."

Master Duvanya looked up to the moons with a grim expression. Alarm echoed in the others, also.

"Does anyone else know about this change in Chotabhai?" Madam Hansa asked.

"My scribes know I am looking for anything in our history related to the shaking, but I have not burdened them with knowledge of my celestial observations. There is only one other who I believe has the same concerns—the eastern envoy. Be assured though; I have shared no details with him as yet."

"Kanaka has been persistent in communicating Tajazan's requests to address banditry at our border, not a matter of moons," Master Duvanya said.

"He recently received word from Dyuvasa regarding the shaking," Master Avani said, "and he seeks a meeting with the rani. It is my recommendation that we present our shared knowledge to Valena before we counsel her to listen to others. I revisited my house's moon lore soon after I confirmed these changes, and a thread of useful information is there, but not the garment. I need the oldest records related to bright cycles, the moons, and shakings. This is why I've called you. I am requesting each of you to share such information—anything that is not already in our shared chronicles."

Greta remembered watching stars twinkle in the sky when she was very young. Her mothers and fathers had told stories of how the world suffered shakings and storms of great destruction when the small moon swelled. It had happened, not once—as the Ascaryans believed—but three times. Three ages. Every giant learned this, but it seemed that Ascaryans did not.

"Even during the cycles of sickness," Madam Hansa said, "no one has asked this of us."

"My father and aunts will resist," Crowseye said. "If you pose your request in more particular terms, perhaps seeking a transcription of a few specific bright cycles, their response may be better."

"I realize this is an extraordinary request, but we will have a much larger problem if another disturbance visits us while we are without answers. All I ask," Master Avani said, "is that each of you consider what I've told you. According to the law of the Seven, no one will be forced to share their books. But I will beseech my ancestors to convince you to help me, help all of us, explain this."

"After New Cycle Day," Crowseye said, "when the alliance with the southern houses is set, I will speak to our elders on this matter."

"We should support Jalil," Madam Satya said quietly. "There is no honor gained by hiding anything that could affect the realm. I have already shared a few passages from our earliest chronicles, and our brother has been most reverent with the material. Even if we do not all agree, I will continue to give him information from our books to study."

Greta sensed that Madam Satya's words stirred the others, but they remained unsure. Master Duvanya pressed his palms together in a gesture of respect for Madam Satya and Master Avani. The others did as well and soon all departed. Greta approached when Master Avani was alone with his parchments and stargazer.

"Good evening, Master," she said, bowing low.

"Oh, Greta, I'm glad you're here. Your help would be welcome."

She considered telling him what the giants knew about the small moon, but Ascaryans did not believe giants' stories, and he might not be pleased that she had listened to their meeting. Her words would not stop the new age from coming. No. She would tell Dear Child and let her decide.

She bundled scrolls into her apron, and the old noble carefully wrapped the stargazer. When he had balanced the stand on his shoulder, she followed him to his quarters. At the door, Master Avani took his parchments, and she stood and stared, making no effort to leave. There was something her words could change.

"Is something wrong?" Master Avani asked her.

"I am bound to serve the maharani."

"Yes."

"First, Rani Shikra. Now, Rani Valena."

"What are you trying to tell me?"

From a pocket of her skirt, she drew out a brooch made of bone. On it was a very fine miniature painting of a hawk, talons outstretched to grab some unseen prey, its wings breaking its descent.

Master Avani's brows rose high. "Where did you acquire this?"

"Madam Sayed's seamstress."

Having known Master Avani from the day she had arrived on this rock, Greta could sense him better than most, if not as clearly as she sensed the rani. She felt a storm of conflicting emotions pass through him, and she counted the heartbeats it took for his thoughts to calm. She had tried to ignore what the girl's breath and scent told her, but if he accepted her understanding, there was some hope they might act together. The simple fact of this girl would demand much from them.

After walking around his table with several tugs on his beard and holding the brooch up to examine in the moonlight, the old noble returned to the door and said, "She could have acquired this by accident."

"Hmmm."

"May I keep it for now?"

"Hmmm."

"This is, well… We must be certain."

"Hmmm."

"Good night, Greta."

"Good night, sir."

Early the next morning Greta watched the rani turn the colt on the end of the lunge line in the stable yard. She was struck by the idea that the two were very alike. As long as they were put through their paces, they were their true selves—creatures of grace and beauty. It was standing still that made them bad-tempered.

A groom came to the yard and took the colt while another brought the rani's saddled mare. The giantess left them then and began climbing the summit path, but a moment later the sound of hooves striking stone grew loud. Valena Sandhyatara flashed by on her horse and continued up the path. A metal tang in the air made Greta watchful, but she had not yet told her charge that a new age was beginning, and she had made no argument against going to the summit. She hoped that leaving the palace would give Dear Child some peace.

When she stepped over the lip of the summit, the rani was already lighting diyas in her house's chhatri and singing a morning tribute. Greta did not join her but continued along the bare rock shelf to two tall stone pillars. On spikes driven deep into the stone, iron rings hung from each pillar. The wolves were chained there at night or when they needed to be disciplined, but the rings were empty that morning, and the ground was littered with bone shards picked clean.

Greta stared at the rings for several minutes. Long before the wolves arrived, two young giants had been chained at this site for moons while Raja Sadul, Dear Child's grandfather, decided what to do with his war spoils. A male giant with wild, red hair. A female still and gray.

For nearly a cycle she had sat there, worn down to little more than a spark of rage after having borne witness to the deaths of her clan and hundreds more giants. Not deaths where they returned to stone whole and in peace at the natural end of their lives, but violent deaths that were the result of the war the Ascaryans brought upon them. The red giant had seen it, too, but he was stronger. He learned how to please the conquerors and speak their difficult language quickly enough to keep them both alive.

Being chained there had been intended as a humiliation, a mocking gesture for all to see, but the ordeal probably saved her life. Day and night chained to those pillars had allowed her to grow new skin over her wounds. The seasons turned, and the young giants, who were already old according to Ascaryan lifespans, survived.

Eventually Red proved himself useful and was released to serve the raja's son, who had become the new raja. The young rani of that generation, Rani Shikra, told her husband that she wanted to see if a giant could be taught housekeeping duties, and called for her.

"Live!" Red whispered in their giant language when armed guards took her down to the palace. "Live if you can, and I will, too. We will honor our mothers' sacrifices."

Answering his plea, she had committed herself to doing whatever she must to go on, but Red's death had scraped the dust from her promise. The sight of the iron rings before her made clear a choice she had pondered for weeks.

She was alone now, utterly alone but for the bond with Dear Child and complicated by her descendants. Would the remainder of her cycles see her committed to serving a realm that had brought the end of the giants? Or would she choose her own will and likely be put to death or chained there again?

Greta watched the rani leave her chhatri and follow the trail that ended at the bluff marking the Rock's highest point. Dear Child walked slowly, her manner as resigned as a prisoner approaching the executioner, and Greta soon caught up. Though many Ascaryans feared the oracle, the rani would never admit how much the oracle's visions disturbed her.

In the shade of the bluff, they entered a gate in a crumbling wall and reached a rough-made table and two chairs that looked like the remnants of a deserted homestead, but for a pitcher and two cups greeting them. The rani sat on one of the chairs and Greta stood behind. As the sun slowly rose over the Rock, Dear Child shifted in her seat, unused to petitioning others or waiting for them.

Stone scraped stone. Greta heard footsteps, and then the oracle was there, tall in her threadbare gown, with her blind, white eyes unveiled. She moved gracefully and sat opposite the rani, extending her hand across the table palm up.

The rani gave her hand slowly.

"Welcome, Daughter of Duran," the oracle said.

"Honorable Oracle," the rani began, "I have paid tribute to the ancestors. I have sought my own mind. Yet questions remain. I seek your wisdom."

"Your trust honors me. Ask your questions, and I will tell you what the ancestors have shown me."

The rani took a breath and asked, "Can I trust Prince Hassan to honor his agreement?"

The oracle considered the question and said, "Burning sands have measured his will. This son of Hudulfah has fed on his shadow and believes himself greater for it. Others will follow his word. Listen and you will know his true intention."

The oracle leaned forward and cradled the rani's hand in both of hers as if to warm her. Greta could sense Dear Child's heart pounding like a rabbit bolting from a fox. "You wish to ask me another question."

The rani swallowed and said, "Is my heir safe?"

"Sister, you pose a splintered question." The oracle smoothed the rani's palm and traced a line there. "Your word and your deeds shape paths, but every spirit has its own journey. Not even the ancestors dictate every outcome. Nor does blood and bone, or even the greatest force—love." Then, suddenly straightening in her chair, the oracle spoke in the rani's voice. "The one hidden could be found. The one found could be lost. The one lost could be hidden."

The rani, more frightened than before, drew back her hand and repeated the ritual acknowledgement. "By your word, Oracle. May the ancestors continue to give you true sight and serenity."

As they passed through the chhatris, Greta sensed that the rani's worries had only been magnified by the oracle's pronouncement, but she could not offer her any comfort or distraction for her own alarm was growing. Deep vibrations hummed in the giantess's bones. Walking ahead to the summit's edge, Greta sniffed at the heavy air while the rani caught her mare and led her to the path. A flock of green parrots circled above the palace. They fell silent all at once and darted toward the summit's dry forest.

Greta met the rani in a few long strides and grabbed Dear Child's arm. Surprised, the rani started to protest at the same time that her mare pulled free. The horse bolted for the woods, then the shaking began.

Pressing the rani down, Greta folded herself over her charge. The shaking started and stopped as if the world was taking racking breaths. The

Rock swayed, and there was a rumble of sliding rock. A cloud of dust and dirt rose on the northwest side, and the grinding noise deep in the ground gave Greta a pain in her chest.

The movement stopped momentarily, but more vigorous shaking soon followed. After it diminished, Greta raised the rani to her feet. A few more shivers passed through the Rock, then the cooling breeze from the crevasse and the normal sounds of morning returned. The rani staggered back from the edge of the summit and hurried to the oracle's garden.

The Seven's seer stood by her gate and looked directly at them as if she had normal sight.

"What is happening?" the rani called out, stopping some distance from the oracle.

The oracle spread her arms wide as if to embrace the sky. "The path has shifted. The ancestors are watching." She turned and walked back to her shelter.

CHAPTER 19

Slumped over the library's long table that morning, Sid almost wished he hadn't drunk quite so much firewine the night before. His head pounded, and Master Avani piled parchments before him with a nervous urgency that made Sid try to copy the texts faster, but the faster he worked, the worse his script looked.

When Parth arrived, the old noble provided another stack of parchments, and he was still giving instructions when they heard a deep groan, and the floor beneath them moved.

Sid scrambled from his bench and ran to the door, but when he looked back Master Avani remained at his table, clutching a book to his chest and trying to take up more parchments. Sid grabbed the scrolls away from him, and Parth took the book. They pushed the old noble out the door and joined the others running downstairs.

Outside the central palace, Ascaryans shoved onto the front grounds from every direction. They stopped moving when the shaking grew rough, then pressed on when it abated, but the shaking grew in frequency and strength, and soon everyone was cowering on the ground. Each movement seemed attached to something in Sid's aching head, and the longer it went on, the more afraid he grew.

With the crowd around them growing so tight they could barely move, Master Avani insisted they give him everything they carried. He wrapped all of it in his sash and told the boys to wait there for him before he struck off through the crowd.

Another tremor erupted and a long crack appeared in the wall separating the front grounds from the abyss. Parth held Sid tight by the arm, and the pain in Sid's head had grown so bad he thought he would be sick.

A column in the colonnade cracked, and everyone near it scrambled away.

"We should go to the middle of the grounds," Parth yelled.

As they struggled through the crowd, Sid saw Madam Sayed not far away, kneeling on the ground in a crush of palace staff. She leaned over someone—a girl with nut-brown hair and a black cloak who clutched Madam's skirt with a bone-pale hand.

Sid sighed and, for one moment, thought of pretending he hadn't seen them; then he pushed toward them. *Stars, Li!*

Seeing Madam's fearful expression, Sid knelt next to Lingli, about to ask her if she was hurt, but when she looked up at him, he drew back. Her pupils were constricted so small her eyes seemed nearly as white as they had been in his bad dreams, and the vein in her temple looked larger and darker than usual.

"Everything's on fire. I can't see," Lingli said, her voice cracking.

"Wait," he whispered. "It will end soon." *She's only a girl. Just a cursed girl.* Painfully aware of Parth behind him, Sid hoped that he and Madam blocked his and everyone else's sight of her.

"You'll be alright," he said, but he had no idea if that was true. Even when she had been at her worst after the attack in the village, her eyes had never looked like this.

Madam looked frightened, but she cleared her throat and told Lingli, "Breathe deep and slow."

The ground seemed to drop beneath them again, and cries filled the air. When the ground stilled, a woman with an owl brooch pushed her way to them and demanded Parth come with her and join others from his house.

Relieved, Sid helped Madam raise Lingli to her feet and drew up her hood. They half-carried, half-dragged her toward the middle of the grounds, but she soon straightened and walked on her own.

"I think it's over," she said. "I was frightened. I'm sorry." She shook her head and her eyes looked as close to normal as they ever did. Sid's head pain was easing, too.

The Seven gathered their clans. The southerners surrounded their nobles as well, but there was no sign of the rani in the gallery or on the grounds. Whispers began to swirl through the yard that she had been injured or worse.

When soldiers began ordering all recruits and apprentices to report to the armory, Madam told Sid to go. "I'll stay with her."

He squeezed Li's arm in farewell, still wondering whether any others were affected by the shake like her or him.

As Sid entered the stable yard with the other recruits, he saw a guard ahead point to the summit. There, leading her horse down the path, was the rani with Greta behind. A relieved cry of "Rani, Maharani!" spread over the palace grounds, and Sid remembered to make a silent tribute to Afsana and his invisible ancestors to thank them for his survival as well as the rani's.

At the armory, he was sorted into one of the groups that would be assigned to check damage and clean up sites once Master Duvanya reviewed the reports that had begun to flow in. Not only the recruits gathered there, but miners, junior soldiers, guards, and even stewards. Sid stayed at the back of the crowd, watching everything the defenses master did.

Please, Mother, I'll build you another shrine, but make me invisible to him or at least let him not recognize me today.

Master Duvanya called Madam Hansa, his son Eshan, and Captain Gaddar to lead the groups. When Eshan, their night captain, called his name, Sid wished he could have been in Gaddar's group, but this was better than being assigned to accompany Master Duvanya himself.

Their group hiked the path to the northern watchtower, a path that wound past the end of the crevasse and followed a ledge on the Rock's western face far above the fields. The vista was beautiful, but even a glimpse over the edge made Sid dizzy. Halfway to the watchtower, they were blocked by a slab of rock nearly as thick as the end of the feasting hall was wide. It had sheared off the monolith and slid onto the path, breaking the laid stone and completely gouging it away in a few places.

While the captain ordered the recruits to clear the way, the miners accompanying them drove spikes and hooks and tied off ropes that allowed them to bounce over the sheared rock and dangle like spiders while testing the remaining rock face's stability.

Hours later, their kurtas wet with sweat, some boys had begun slacking whenever the captain's back was turned, but not Sid. Moving rock might be as tedious as cutting wood, but he knew better than to let churlishness mark him. Even if Captain Duvanya was not his favorite captain, he couldn't waste an opportunity when his options were so few.

Confronting a boulder that was too large to budge even with a group of them on it, Sid asked the captain if he and the others could try to dislodge it with one of the miners' pry bars. The captain agreed and watched as Sid organized a group of boys to tip up a corner of the boulder while he fit the bar underneath.

Once it was in place, Sid stood up and saw that not only the captain, but all the others were watching. He swallowed. *By the stars, Mother, this has to work or I'm going to be their fool forever.*

He wiped his hands on his pants and grabbed the end of the bar, calling two other boys to join him. They pressed the bar together and the boulder resisted. One of the soldiers came to Sid's side and joined them. With sweat pouring down their faces, the boulder began to rise, but Sid could see they were nowhere near the tipping point. He had to have better leverage.

"Can you hold it?" he asked the others. They hardly glanced his way, the strain was so great, and Sid yelled for another recruit to join in. As soon as the boy took his place, Sid dove to the ground and wedged a piece of rock in with the pry bar. Then he moved to the other side and dug down into the rubble.

"Heave!" Sid yelled, and the boulder tipped a bit. The group cheered, even the miners whistled.

When the bar was reset a new group of boys took the next turn, then another after them. It took a long while to move the boulder to the edge, but when they got it there, the captain called for Sid and the others who had helped in the beginning to give it the final push. Everyone cheered as the boulder crashed down to the plains below, and the captain told them they could stop work for the day.

On the hike back to the palace, there was little talk among the exhausted group until one of the recruits elbowed Sid and asked if he would like a drink from his skin. Sid said no, he was fine.

"Ha, and this water is fine, too…as fine as fire," the boy hinted, his eyes bright.

Sid took the skin and smelled it. Firewine. He felt better just holding it.

Seeing that the captain was far ahead with a few of his guards, Sid took a swig from the skin and passed it on, but it came back around and around, and soon everything seemed more jolly.

Captain Duvanya waited at the small gate on the edge of the palace grounds as they entered. Glowing with good cheer as he approached, Sid wiped his sweaty face on his sleeve and smiled broadly.

"Sir, Captain Sir," Sid said, "my name's Sid Sol and it has been an honor, sir, to serve you. There's nothing I'd like so much as joining the night guards, sir, and I would not complain even if you made me move rocks every day."

The captain looked at Sid wearily, and Sid thought it best to stop talking. He pressed his hands together and bowed so low he had to put a hand out to keep from falling on his face. The recruits piling up behind him howled with laughter.

A pair of boys were kind enough to pull him into the front grounds before he made a greater fool of himself. Another made him drink water and poured some more over his head. Sid then bowed to his rescuers, which made them laugh some more. Then he threw up the bile in his stomach, and the day became more clear, though less wonderful.

By the time Parth found him and pushed him to one of the tables in the feasting hall, Sid was almost too despondent to eat.

The captain must have thought I was mocking him. It was not fair how fate twisted his every effort, but the voice in his head, which sounded a lot like Li, told him it wasn't fate but his own stupidity.

"Who are you looking for?" Parth teased, waving a hand in front of Sid's face. "Your girlfriend?"

"What? No."

"I saw her this morning, so stop pretending. But she isn't much, is she? I would have wagered you would go for...I don't know...maybe livelier girls—ones who would give you a bit of a challenge. Am I right?"

"I guess... I mean, no. She's not my girlfriend."

The hall grew noticeably quieter. Sid and Parth turned to see a dozen boys from Avakstan file in silently—new Idrisis just arrived. Their knees were thicker than their legs, and their collar bones looked sharp enough to cut wood.

As soon as the newcomers sat, bearers brought baskets of naan and thalis, but junior soldiers at a nearby table waylaid them and took the food for themselves. Sid could hear the rude remarks they made, but the Idrisis sat straight and kept their eyes on the table in front of them. Another table of Kirdun youth began to protest.

When Korvar entered the hall and glared at the soldiers, everyone quieted. The bearers replenished the southerners' thalis, but the Idrisis did not eat. Their leader made a sign, and they rose as one and left the hall. The soldiers laughed and clapped.

"They're not like us," Parth said. "I hear they eat once a moon."

"I get weak if I miss tea," Sid said, just before a hand landed on his shoulder.

"Where have you been, Woods Boy?" Avinash grinned at him.

"I'm...I'm scribing now," Sid said.

"He's Master Avani's new pet," Parth said.

"Isn't that wonderful. Been looking for you. Here's your chance to make up for your losses last round. Meet us here tonight when the kitchen's closed."

"What losses?" Parth asked with a smirk.

Avinash was gone before Sid could make an excuse.

Late that evening, Sid sat on the stable yard wall and watched the brilliant moons dim as smoke from countless tribute fires in the fort thickened. Tomorrow would mark the thirteenth moon's observation ceremony, but it was strangely quiet around the palace. Staff and soldiers had been dismissed early, as they had after the first shaking, and the southern youth were confined to their barracks after supper. No one was in a mood to celebrate, least of all Sid.

Still mortified by his earlier behavior in front of Captain Duvanya, Sid questioned whether the witch had lied to him about his destiny and whether he had lied to himself. *Maybe I was never truly meant to do great things, and she just told me that to make me feel better. Maybe serving as Master Avani's apprentice is the best I can hope for.*

But the woods witch had also said it wouldn't be easy. Was he giving up too soon? He might have destroyed all chances of impressing the House of Duvanya, but there was still Captain Gaddar to consider. The niggling thought that his setbacks might yet prove to have been due to someone's ill will or his exposure to a certain cursed Ascaryan would not be quelled. Recalling how Li's eyes had looked that morning gave him a chill.

Jumping down from the wall, Sid quietly entered the feasting hall. He didn't have a good feeling about meeting Avinash and the others, but he couldn't avoid them forever. *Run around the world*, he remembered Red saying, *and you end where you started.*

Seeing no one in the empty hall, Sid climbed the staircase to the barracks, prepared to argue that he had found no one before he went to bed should anyone ask, but as he reached the top of the stairs, someone in the shadows near the terrace door called his name. He froze.

"Thought you weren't going to show," Krill whispered as he and Avinash beckoned to him. "C'mon, you can help us with a little task."

"What is it?"

"You'll see."

Can't be worse than hopping.

He followed them downstairs again. Krill waved toward the far end of the hall where another figure detached itself from the dark.

"Let's get on with it," the miner Kadam said. He carried a small cask under one arm.

A faint glow came from inside the kitchens, and Sid guessed that Korvar and Shankar were still finishing their supper.

"We need to get into Korvar's pantry, see," Avinash whispered. "You're friendly with him, so you do the distracting while we go in and out with none the wiser."

"What do you want in the pantry?" Sid's mind whirled through all possible ways he might get himself out of this.

"What's that to you? Just keep him busy in the back. As soon as we're clear of the kitchen, I'll make a noise to draw old Korvar and let you know we're out. Meet us behind the mining hall and we'll show you the prize."

"I don't know. What am I going to tell him?"

"That's your problem."

"He'll kill you if he catches you."

"That's where you're wrong," Kadam said. "Any killing would go the other way." He patted a dagger at his side. "Be a shame, though. The man can cook fair."

"We've got to go," Krill said. "He's going to lock up everything any second."

Avinash pushed Sid toward the kitchens. "Get going! And don't let him back in too quick."

Sid stopped and looked back.

"Now," Kadam said.

Grimacing, Sid walked into the kitchens.

"Hello?" he called out. "Korvar Sir?"

Shankar and Korvar were at the table, wiping their thalis clean.

Making up what he hoped was a convincing lie, Sid said, "I'm sorry to bother you, sir, but a guard outside Tal Karil's quarters accosted me and said he wants another jug of firewine."

"What? By the ancestors, that southerner can put it away," Korvar blustered. "And on a day like today! You might think he would have better sense than to drink himself senseless in case the shaking returns, but no!"

"I'm sorry, sir. I thought I should tell you even though I'm no longer a bearer."

"Shankar, fill a jug for Sid to take up."

"What? Oh, I'm sorry, but I can't take it to him right now. Master Avani asked me to deliver a message for him."

"Is that right?" Korvar looked suspicious, but he turned to Shankar. "You run it up there."

Alright then, one down, one to go. He realized too late that Shankar would likely meet Kadam and the others on his way through the kitchens.

"Sir, before he goes, would you both come with me for half a moment," Sid said. "I want to show you something strange I saw. Just out behind. Please, take a look."

"What are you talking about?"

"No, really, before it disappears. Please, come with me."

Sid saw a look pass between Korvar and Shankar, but they followed him out onto the platform in the back. All three took a breath and admired the gold-hued clouds of stars behind the smoke.

"What is it?" Korvar asked.

"I…uh…I really don't know," Sid said, frantically searching for his excuse. "There was a white light just moving across the top of the Rock from there to there." He was glad it was too dark for them to see how his face was burning.

"Near the edge?"

"I think so."

"Must have been Master Vaksana chaining up the wolves."

"No, not him," Sid said. "It wasn't lantern light. It was very strange, like a bright cloud floating along."

"Perhaps it was the oracle."

"Oh, the one we saw the night of the rani's hunting party?"

"That's the one," Korvar rubbed his hands together. "Well, come then. We all need some sleep. Today left us with a mess and tomorrow's the harvest moon observation." He turned to go back into the kitchens.

"Wait. What…does she see?"

"You're acting very strange, my boy," Korvar said. "Shankar, be on your way. Take that drink to Tal High-and-Mighty."

Sid wanted to stop him, but Korvar was already suspicious. The boy returned to the kitchens, and Sid hoped the others would leave him alone.

"Is the oracle of the Seven?"

"No, but her people were known to the Seven from the first days. She comes from somewhere in the east. Take all your questions to Master Avani," Korvar said. "I am only a cook, and a very tired cook after a very long day."

"I've never met a seer before," Sid said. "Can she really tell the future?"

Korvar was already walking toward the back entrance. "The Seven say so."

There was a crash in the kitchen. Bursting past the cook, Sid ran through the back room to the main kitchen, where he found Shankar on the floor by the open pantry door. A cloaked figure knelt next to him.

"What happened?" Sid yelled.

Lingli scowled at him from under her hood. "Don't pretend—"

"Get away from him!" Korvar shouted, fists raised as he bore down on Lingli.

"Sir, sir!" Lingli protested, raising her hand to shield herself.

The chef careened to a stop. "Who are you?"

"I...I am Madam Sayed's seamstress. I was looking for Sid."

"Is that so?" Korvar seethed with anger. He leaned over his son and shook him lightly. "Shankar?" Pointing to the nearest table bench, he told them, "Sit there, and do not move."

Sid glanced into the pantry. Nothing seemed out of place. He looked at Lingli and made a sign for her to stay quiet.

"This is what happens when too many have too little to do," Korvar muttered. "Shankar, do you hear me?"

Shankar shifted a little. The skin around one eye was beginning to swell.

"What happened?"

"I...I picked up a jug," Shankar said. "There was a sound. I started to open the pantry and someone hit me from behind. Another hit me from the front."

"Who was it?"

"Don't know."

The chef looked hard at Sid and Lingli as he helped Shankar up. "If you had anything to do with this, you will regret the day, boy!"

"No, sir, I didn't—"

"Do not touch him—either of you," Korvar threatened as he settled his son on another bench and hurried out the back room shouting for the guards. Shankar winced and rested his head on his arms.

Lingli pulled Sid aside. "I saw you talking to those others," she whispered angrily. "I saw you betray him. For what? Some firewine?"

"You have no idea what they will do," Sid whispered back.

"Oh, I think I do! I saw that knife. You don't want any part of that!"

"I had no choice!"

"Why do you always involve yourself in such stupid things! You're not up to their games."

A curtain of anger descended over him. She was right about them, but she was wrong about him.

"You're a fine one to talk. You wouldn't be here if it wasn't for me. You do not get to tell me what to do anymore!"

"If I don't tell you what to do, who would?" she shot back, standing as well. "You have never been able to figure out who is honorable and who will eat your honor for supper."

He stepped close to her and realized, for the first time, that he was a little taller. "I don't have to listen to you, and I'm not doing one more thing to help you."

"Don't worry, I'll never ask you for help again!"

He heard the twinge in Lingli's voice and knew he had wounded her, but he could not stop himself. "You like making me and everyone around you miserable because *you* are cursed. All you know how to do is blame me for everything. Since you came here, it's more of the same. I know you're trying to make me suffer because Red went to stone, and I am sorry he's gone, but I didn't cause his death. You did!"

She seemed to grow smaller before his eyes. Seeing no point in being questioned by the guards or watching her cry, Sid ran from the kitchens and up the stairs to the barracks.

By the time he reached the landing he regretted what he had said, a little, but he couldn't worry about it just then. At the terrace door, he listened to the whistles relaying among the guards. Rapid footsteps passed by outside. Cracking open the door, Sid looked out.

"You are damned slow!" Krill hissed, his flat face filling the opening. "Chalo! Korvar's woken the ancestors with his yelling."

Sid followed Krill to the catwalk where they dropped over the side of the stable yard wall and ran toward the mining hall. Discovering no one there, Krill started up the path to the summit, but Sid hung back.

"They'll leave nothing for us if we don't catch up," Krill said.

"You go ahead," Sid said. "I'm tired. Think I'll go to bed."

Krill came too close to him. "Vidkun said to bring you. You're coming or I tell him you ran away. Then what? He comes after you himself? Or maybe he sends Kadam."

Sid couldn't argue with that.

Krill knocked once on the door to the jail and waited for a knock from the other side, then knocked four more times more. Vidkun let them in. When they entered, the others were playing cards much as before. In the middle of their table sat the small cask.

Half a cup of firewine, then I'll go.

"Ho, here he is," Avinash said. "The pretty bait that was nearly swallowed."

"A fisherman's gamble," Kadam said.

Vidkun remained in the doorway listening as if he expected someone else, and all were silent for a long minute. Finally he returned to the table. "Fill their cups, Ritin."

The Avani boy limped over to a small box where a tall jug and clay cups sat on top. Sid drew in his breath very quietly. Naked to the waist, Ritin's chest was marked with angry welts on his chest and shoulders. A woman's dupatta had been twisted tight around his neck. He kept his eyes downcast and poured firewine into cups he gave to Sid and Krill.

Sid sat between Krill and Avinash—staying as far from Kadam as possible.

The cards were dealt, and Sid tried to calculate how long it would be before he could leave. Before the first hand was finished, there was a single knock on the passage door. Sid, Krill, and Avinash jumped to their feet. Vidkun and Kadam rose more slowly, Vidkun went to the door and knocked back. After four more knocks from the passage, Vidkun opened the door.

The man who entered was dressed in a plain kurta and loose pants, like any commoner, but Sid recognized Captain Gaddar at once.

Gaddar froze when he saw Sid.

"Who is this?"

"This is Sid," Vidkun said. "He's alright, helped out with the lift tonight."

"You didn't need to bring him here," Gaddar said.

Sid couldn't tell if the captain recognized him from the day he and Parth visited the gate tower or not.

"Truth be told," Vidkun replied, "he came upon us last moon, and I thought, 'Why stick him right away? Maybe the boy can be useful?' Not to mention that we don't need the challenge of explaining a missing recruit."

"What would be better would be for you to not jeopardize our arrangement," Gaddar said, and Sid wondered how he dared speak so boldly to a member of the Seven. "How much does he know?"

"Only what you tell him, because I've said nothing," Vidkun said testily.

Gaddar made a small gesture, and Vidkun followed him into the passage. The others returned to their seats, but each kept an eye on the door and played out the round half-heartedly.

When Vidkun and the captain returned, Gaddar plucked up the cask on their table and inspected the cork and its seal. Dropping a pouch of coins on the table, he said, "This was the easy round. I doubt she'll leave it with Korvar again, and even if she does, he'll be watching. We need to find the source."

Vidkun grinned. "People have been seeking this gift for the last three generations."

"Perhaps they weren't properly motivated," Gaddar said in a way that indicated that Vidkun didn't have that excuse. He hoisted the cask onto his shoulder and left.

Pulling a bidi from his pocket, Vidkun rubbed it between his fingers and paced back and forth. After a moment, he went to the door of the passage and looked out.

"Damn you, Kadam!" Vidkun said, after he closed the door again. "You better have more grand schemes in your dark heart, because this one is finished."

Kadam chuckled. "Fetch it," he told Ritin.

Ritin disappeared inside his cell and returned with another cup full of drink. Kadam took the cup while Vidkun poured Gaddar's coins out upon the table, dividing them into four piles.

"These aren't for you," Vidkun told Sid. "If you want a coin on the next job, you'll do as you're told. If you don't want, you'll do the same because you've seen what we're up to. Understand? Gaddar would love to see me to march you out the end of the Nobles' Walk right now, but lucky for you I don't take orders from him."

Demanding all their cups, Vidkun put his eye close to the full cup Kadam passed to him. He took off his house brooch and used the pointed end of the pin to carry a drop from Kadam's cup into each of theirs. He topped off each cup with firewine.

"He better not come back to me on this," Vidkun said to Kadam.

"He checked the wax," Kadam sniffed. "He's got no idea he was cheated."

Vidkun held his palms over the cups and bowed his head as if he was offering a tribute. "All our lives we've seen our elders take the ancestors' elixir. They've grown stronger, unafraid. Avatars of each generation. Not because of any star-blessed natural talent, no. Only the great gift of being firstborn. But you and me? We've been kept thirsty. Spares who are barely seen but never heard. Isn't that so?"

There was a chorus of ayes.

Vidkun continued, "Well, no more. We'll share a drink, and don't think I'm grudging you this by the meager drop in your cups. This is more powerful than anything you've ever tasted. They say one sip lets the light in. Two will take you up to the stars to visit your eldest ancestor, and the third will push your spirit into the abyss out there with no way back."

"You've drunk it before?" Avinash asked.

Vidkun nodded. "The first time I was sneaking drinks after an observation ceremony. Saw a cup with some dregs and didn't think a thing about finishing it up. They say I passed out cold on the floor, but my spirit was…freed. I flew above the Rock and saw everything so puny below me. The ancestors finally told me who I was."

They contemplated the cups before them. Sid made a silent tribute, again asking Afsana for protection.

"Seasons change, and our spring is coming," Vidkun said. They all raised their cups. "To the Brothers of the New Order!" The jailer drank quickly, then slammed his cup down.

Avinash, Krill, and Kadam threw their drinks back. Sid hesitated until he caught Kadam's eye. He drank and waited.

Nothing's happening.

Then Kadam stood up, stretched, and smiled in a most unpleasant way.

Vidkun pressed his clenched fist to his chest. "That's it," he said. "That's our true rani, right there. Fair as the moon, strong as the sun. Oh! She hits hard."

Sid's breath caught. He felt as if his heart had stopped. Somehow, the dark retreated and everything around him grew brighter. Avinash was giggling. He was being pulled down the dark passage leading to the Nobles' Walk. The door at the end burst open and slammed against the wall with such force his head rang. For an instant there was a whirl of light that seemed lined with blades before it disappeared. There was a scuffle going on near him, then he realized it was himself crying out. Vidkun was laughing and crushing Sid's hands around the door's latch. They pushed him out. He heard air rushing and desperately clung to the door. Someone grabbed him roughly and he was scrambling on a narrow ledge. Time passed in fits and starts.

"You don't want another ride?" one of them said. "You'll roll off here before dawn."

They sent him back across. His upper half fell onto the passage floor, scratching desperately at the rock to pull his legs inside. Something slammed against the back of his head.

And then nothing.

CHAPTER 20

The night guard in front of her was becoming angrier, and Lingli knew she should try to answer him, but the sting of Sid's words made it hard to concentrate on what he was saying. It was only when Master Vaksana arrived with Trechur that her head began to clear. While the noble tethered the wolf, the guard began relating his concocted description of events. Trechur sniffed in her direction and lay down with his head on his paws, as if she was spoiled prey not worth his notice.

After bidding the guard to be quiet, Master Vaksana asked her, "Wh-wh-what were you doing in the hall s-so late?"

"I was visiting my friend," she answered, hoping that she wouldn't have to explain that her friend was a horse and she had gone to check him for injuries from the shaking. "I was returning to my room when I heard two boys on the catwalk talking about stealing something."

The night guard scoffed at this.

"Wh-who are these boys?" Master Vaksana asked.

She told the noble towering over her that she didn't know, and that was true, but she shared only general and vague details of the conversation she had overheard before the debacle in the kitchens.

After the shaking ended that morning, Lingli had tried to assure Madam she was fine, but she wasn't. Dizziness plagued her, and she even imagined she could see cracks in the walls and floors anywhere she looked. From her balconies, she thought she saw cracks in the Rock itself. With daily life in the palace completely upended, Madam left her to sleep until the evening. After she woke Lingli felt a little better and went to the stables to be sure the colt was unharmed. On her way back to her room, she overheard two boys on the catwalk.

One boy said to the other, "They say she makes it herself."

"It's the giant who always brings it," said the other.

"Giants aren't that clever. She does as she's told."

"You know it's our necks if we get caught."

"Then we don't get caught."

"We could put it on the woods boy if they catch us."

"*If* he shows up."

Afraid that she knew exactly who the "woods boy" was, Lingli had waited in the shadows until the plotters proceeded to the barracks on the feasting hall's upper level, then she entered the hall through the colonnade. Before long two boys came downstairs with Sid, confirming her fears. She hid under the staircase and listened as the scheme to rob the kitchens unfolded.

"Do you know these b-boys?" the wolfmaster repeated with some exasperation.

Lingli shook her head and said, "One of them wore clothes and a turban that looked like a miner's."

"Were they c-carrying anything when they left?"

She thought and said, "The miner carried something under his arm."

Korvar returned from the other room as she answered, and he bid Master Vaksana and the guard to accompany him into the pantry. She could not hear what the cook said but the tone of his voice made it clear he was upset.

When the men returned, Master Vaksana sat on the bench in front of her, sighed and said, "Y-you left one out of your s-st-story. Wh-what did the scribe, Sid S-Sol, tell you before he left?"

What indeed. She heard Sid clearly. In fact, the words echoed in her head: *You are cursed. I didn't cause his death. You did!* But telling the wolfmaster that the worst part of all this was that Sid had told her what was truly in his heart did not seem helpful.

"He said that he had nothing to do with the others," she answered.

At this, Korvar threw his hands in the air and turned away.

"She's protecting him," the guard said. "This theft may be related to the others, but you'll not get the truth out of this one. Sir, I am happy to continue the interrogation, if you permit me."

"I will t-tell you when your h-help is required."

"Why not give her just a moment with the wolf?" the guard said. "It could make the truth come quicker."

A look of distaste flashed across Master Vaksana's face. "We all have r-rules. Rules of b-beasts. Rules of Ascaryans. You must know wh-which you follow. Report to your captain. You sh-shall lead the search for the others, on my word."

After the guard left, fear climbed Lingli's throat as Master Vaksana untied the wolf and wound its chain around his fist. He made a sign with one hand and the wolf lay down at his side.

"Is it t-true?" the noble asked her. "Is the red giant dead?"

Surprised, Lingli nodded.

"D-did you know the v-villager who k-killed him?"

"No." *Is he going to accuse me?*

"M-master Avani s-said a dart was used. D-did it look like this?" The wolfmaster drew a dart from inside his achkan. The same size as the dart that had pierced Red's palm. The same silver metal. The same red and black striped fletching.

Lingli felt as if all her blood had fallen to her feet. "Did you have him killed?" she rasped.

Trechur growled at her.

"No." The noble sounded surprised. "He...he was m-my friend." The wolfmaster's eyes shone with what seemed to be honest sadness as he tucked the dart away.

What reason would this noble have to lie to me?

"He was like my father," she said.

Master Vaksana nodded and drew the wolf's chains tighter. "I should s-send you to j-jail," he said, rubbing his eyes, and Lingli remembered how terribly long the last day had been and how it was bleeding its way into this one—the harvest moon's apex. "Do you h-have anyone who will s-speak for you?"

She looked at the floor and whispered, "Master Avani?"

"Go then," Master Vaksana said, pointing to the kitchen's entrance.

Lingli climbed the stairs of the old tower on shaking legs. The wolfmaster's mercy did not compare with the sting of Sid's anger—everything he had said struck a blow against Red's admonition that they should protect each other. What kind of life could she make without Sid? Fears and promises weighed upon her.

From her balcony she could see the feasting hall's roof. Only three boys wrapped in shawls sat there and Sid was not among them. Unable to sew nor sleep, she watched the moons set and the stars wheel by, distant and cold. Hearing a heavy tread on the stairs leading to her room, Lingli fully expected a guard would appear and arrest her, but it was Greta who emerged through the trapdoor.

"Come," the giantess said, seeing that the gate was unlocked. "The boy is not well."

Greta led Lingli down to the third floor, stopping outside a door not far from the curtain-covered passage where she had hidden after scaring Princess Mafala. The door had never been attended before, but this night a guard stepped aside and allowed them to enter.

In the inner room Master Avani stood at the side of a curtained bed.

"He's found his breath again, thanks be to the ancestors, and Greta," he told Lingli, "but he's had quite a night."

Sid lay on top of the blankets, still as death. His face was bruised and swollen, and she was not much relieved by the sight of the rest of him—a torn sleeve and an arm already bandaged. Muddy pant legs.

"What happened?" Lingli whispered, suspecting that the thieves had turned on him.

"A beating and poison it seems," Master Avani said, "though we don't know who nor how. Answers will be found, trust that, but we need to wake him as soon as possible. It may be easier done if he hears a familiar voice."

She reached out and gently touched his arm. "Sid? It's me, Li. Sid, do you hear me?" Master Avani moved aside so she could come closer. "Sid, it's past breakfast. Wake up!"

There was no sign he heard anything.

"Keep talking to him," Master Avani said. "Tell him a story. Sing."

On the opposite side of the bed Greta leaned over Sid and gently wiped away dirt on his face. Humming deep in her throat, she said, "Dear Child will wake soon. I must tell her."

Master Avani said, "Very well, but she shouldn't find our seamstress here. Go slowly."

Greta left, and Lingli knelt at the bedside, keeping her hand on Sid's arm and struggling with what to say.

"It's ridiculous that you became a scribe," she said, finally. "Do you remember learning to read? Do you remember how you told Red you didn't need to know reading because you were going to be a goldsmith?" She smoothed Sid's hair back from his face. "You said that all you needed was one golden bracelet, and the witch could keep all her cursed vowels and consonants and the words, too. Yet here you are—a scribe in Chandrabhavan."

Sid didn't respond. She couldn't tell if he was even breathing.

"You must leave now, before the rani arrives," Master Avani said.

"You left me once," she told Sid, stroking his arm, "but I won't leave you for long."

She thought she saw Sid's eyelids flutter and her hopes rose, then his chest went taut in a spasm. Master Avani pushed past her, turned Sid onto his side, and wiped away the watery vomit that spilled from his mouth.

"This is a good sign," the old noble insisted, but she saw worry in his eyes. He spread the blanket over Sid and told her, "Go now, quickly. I will tell you how he fares."

On the landing, within earshot of the night guard, Master Avani said, "Thank you for your assistance. I'm sure the patient will rest easier now."

Lingli bowed and retreated to the stairway, aware the guard was watching. She climbed past the fourth floor and on to the fifth. Very soon, she heard Greta's heavy step below. A door opened and closed. Kneeling on the deserted landing, she lowered her head to the dusty floor and silently entreated Sid's ancestors to wake him even if she could not.

When Madam Sayed entered her room the next morning, Lingli fully expected that she would see her marched out the palace gate.

"Did you attack Korvarji's son or steal from the kitchens last night?" Madam nearly shouted.

"No, Madam."

"Are you in league with those who did?"

"No, Madam."

"No? You deny everything? What about making a fool of me?" Madam held out her keys in the palm of her hand. "I knew that you, somehow, managed to leave your room, but I said nothing. I thought, let me see if she can be trusted. Then Master Vaksana comes to my door in the night, and I have my answer."

Lingli stared at Madam's slippers as she crossed the room from one balcony to the other.

"If they come for you," Madam said bitterly, "I can do nothing. Do you understand? Be very glad that Master Vaksana has not ordered your arrest—yet."

Lingli began to apologize, but Madam interrupted, "I do not want to hear a word! Sit down so I may prepare you. The rani has called us both this morning."

Madam took her seat on the chair and set out her paints, and Lingli sat on the floor at her feet. *The rani will have me arrested. Today. Before the observation ceremony.*

"She knows, of course. Master Vaksana will have given his report," Madam said as she applied a heavy cream to the vein in her temple. When she sprinkled on the hair powder, Madam added in a calmer voice, "Perhaps this summons is a good sign. Why should she call you if she considers you guilty?"

There was no chance the rani's request was auspicious, but Lingli was grateful to hear something gentler in Madam's voice. That she had not dismissed her was the most luck she could hope for, and here it was—a kindness from someone whose nature roiled at imperfections, mistakes, and mishaps—all conditions she found clinging to herself.

Carrying the wedding dress pieces and Mafala's gown, she and Madam proceeded to the rani's quarters. Lingli resolved to continue to leave Sid out of her story about the night's events as much as possible. She only wished she had an idea of how to clear her own name.

Inside the rani's quarters Her Majesty met them wrapped in a bright robe of padded silk, but she looked tired and uninterested in exchanging small pleasantries. Lingli slid into Greta's shadow and attempted to match her stillness. The dress pieces Madam laid out upon the bed were not impressive. All the material was unadorned except two panels that Lingli had begun to embroider with long chains of golden suns and stars.

"The ensemble will be completed after this fitting," Madam said.

"I should hope so," the rani said dully. "This is more suited for a funeral than a wedding." Picking up one of the skirt pieces and lightly tracing the decoration, she said, "This is not your work." She turned to Lingli. "Is it yours?"

Hope of going unnoticed evaporated. "Yes, Maharani."

"My apologies. The girl gets above herself," Madam interjected. "I packed the wrong pieces this morning—"

"Shut up." The rani raised her hand. Her eyes never left Lingli. "Who taught you to embroider?"

"An old woman in the Western Woods," Lingli answered softly.

"The same one who taught you to mark your work as you did on Sid Sol's kufi?"

She nodded. When the rani said Sid's name, Lingli felt her heart pound. *Has she spoken to him already? What has he told her?* If she faltered, would she punish them both?

She heard Greta humming low in her throat.

"I find that story quite incredible," the rani said. "Almost as incredible as the word of a person found where a serious crime occurred, immediately after the crime was committed, and who still insists that she knows nothing about the crime. Wouldn't you agree?"

Lingli looked to Madam Sayed, but the dance teacher seemed too stricken to speak.

"Surely if such a person possessed even a small amount of intelligence, she would realize that naming the perpetrators would be of utmost importance. Unless, of course, she was cooperating with them."

"I am not a thief," Lingli said.

"What then are you? Amina, what do you know about this girl?"

Lingli knew Madam would not mention Master Avani's recommendation, and she couldn't blame her. She would not speak Sid's name if she could help it. What a pair she and Madam made!

"Your Majesty, I admit I know very little about her," Madam said. "Almost nothing. I am ashamed to say I accommodated her because of my need, and your permission of course. Surely you will agree there is skill here?"

The rani leaned against a bed post and looked at the skirt piece in her hands. "Skill does not equal virtue, Amina, nor does it excuse deceit, and deceit is thick in the palace these days."

"Of course, Your Majesty. I would not name virtues where none exist. The nature of the deceit you mentioned will hopefully be discovered soon, but what remains absolutely certain is that you require a glorious dress. Should we suffer the loss of this girl's nimble fingers? You could allow her to continue this work until evidence calls her to court."

Madam took the parcel containing pieces of Mafala's dress from Lingli's hands. "And…do you recall that you asked her to sew for the Hudulfah princess? See this." Unfolding the bodice of the deep blue dress, Madam held it up to display the difference in its cut and color.

Suddenly, the rani giggled, a sound completely at odds with her earlier attitude and it made Lingli more afraid. *Is she moonstruck?*

Greta's hum deepened.

"Ha! Beautiful. Mafala is going to be furious when I enter the hall," the rani said. "That may be the most delightful moment of the entire day. And this shade will not suit her either."

In another breath Her Majesty's mirth dissipated. She came very close to Madam. "I grant that much responsibility for the wedding program rests with you, and you need assistance, but is there some other reason you are protecting this girl? Are you bewitched?"

Turning to glare at Lingli, the rani added, "Her strange appearance draws the eye, but it is more than appearance. A curse accompanies her."

Lingli stared at the floor, struggling to breathe. Hearing the rani speak so plainly of her malady felt like a blade cutting to the bone. The silence continued too long and when she finally dared to look up, the rani patted the chains around her neck as she turned her attention back to Madam.

"You have had a respected career in the palace for so long, Amina. You've been trusted. Protecting this creature is neither worthy of you nor wise. Should you take such risks at this season in your cycles?"

Madam pressed her palms together in supplication. Her voice shook. "I am not protecting her, Maharani. Only considering your immediate requirements."

Going to the heavy curtains that blocked the chill from the balcony, the rani parted them and looked out for a long moment. "I require a wedding dress, and I trust you have the sense to see it through. Keep her for now. It seems I shall make one more bargain that likely favors demons."

She told Lingli directly, "Thank the otherworld for your talents, Seamstress, but do not imagine that I have judged you blameless of the crime against my palace. As long as your work pleases, your arrest will be postponed—until the day after New Cycle Day. Take your dress to the lovely viper. If you can convince her to wear it, I may even spare your life."

The rani raised her arms over her head. "Let us complete this morning's business, Amina. Come fit the sleeves."

Shaking, Lingli folded the pieces of the princess's dress and left. She had to get off the Rock, but how? Where? And how could she go before Sid was well again? She needed to think, but first she had to see Princess Mafala, never doubting the rani would hurry her prosecution if the scheme to humiliate the southern princess unraveled.

When Prince Aseem's nurse admitted her to Mafala's quarters, Lingli was alarmed to see the girl was disheveled, and her face was streaked with salty tracks. She walked stiffly and clutched her shift to her chest as she led Lingli to the inner room.

Mafala sat at her dressing table and allowed a maid to paint her face, but the rest of the room warned of the influence of the apex moons in a bright cycle. Twisted bedcovers had fallen to the floor, and thalis of half-eaten food remained on the tables. A jug of firewine had tipped over, leaving a dark pool on the stone.

"At last! Show me my gown," Mafala said. She dismissed the maid and issued a curt order in their language to the nurse. The girl staggered to a bed-roll that lay in the far corner of the room and lay down with her back to them.

Holding out the skirt portion for the princess's examination, Lingli hoped the richness of the heavy satin would distract her from the color. She barely breathed as Mafala circled her to view the material. When the princess unceremoniously dropped her robe to the floor, Lingli knelt and opened the skirt so Mafala could step into it.

A knock sounded on the door, and a booming voice called out in a southern tongue. Mafala laughed loudly and answered back, then retrieved her robe and covered the new skirt. She told Lingli to wait and went to the outer room.

As soon as the princess was gone, Lingli stood and tiptoed to the mattress. She whispered in the common tongue, "Are you whole?" but the nurse did not respond.

Nearby stood an open trunk with two fine chains stretched out on top—one was strung with emeralds, the other featured a rudely cut topaz. Below these was a heap of golden chains, arm cuffs, and thick bone and horn bracelets. Next to the trunk, a dozen or more small, lacquered boxes were lined up. Inside one of the open boxes was a ring—a ring featuring a large amethyst mounted on a thick silver band. It fit the eastern envoy's description of his missing ring perfectly.

Lingli tried to tell herself that she was moonstruck, made reckless by the fat harvest moons, but she couldn't deny the anger glowing within her, a small flame of indignant righteousness that lit at the sight of the stolen ornament. She plucked up the ring, dropped it into the hem of her cloak, and closed the box it had rested in. The nurse never moved or made a sound.

As the guest and Mafala exchanged farewells in the other room, Lingli fought to empty her face of all expression. The princess returned, and Lingli pinned the dress's final adjustments with sweaty, fumbling hands so that it took much longer than it should have. She could not remember any of Mafala's instructions, though she answered yes to each one.

When she was well out of those quarters and nearly halfway across the gallery, it dawned on Lingli that she had proven the rani's suspicions. She searched her conscience, but the pleasure of taking the ring still overwhelmed the niggling worry that there was precious little difference between her and those who had stolen from Korvar.

Is a thief's thief truly a thief?

CHAPTER 21

Sid took in such a breath of air it felt as if his chest would burst. He tasted vomit and coughed. Pain possessed him, but he could make out Greta, a great shadow at his bedside. She held a cup to his lips, and he refused, convinced that she was going to harm him. Pulling his head back, the giantess forced him to swallow.

And then nothing until a line of light coming from the bottom of a curtained window caught his attention. He was under a blanket in a large bed in a strange room, naked but for a loin cloth pulled up between his legs like a baby's diaper. Except for the bed and an altar on the opposite end of the room, the furniture was shrouded. Nothing moved but the flames of diyas lining the altar table. He was terribly thirsty. Fear and pain kept him still until he simply could not stand it. He shifted to one side and bit his lip.

My right hip—by the First Mother! And my head feels funny. The ribs again? But they're not so bad as my hip, and I can't see out of this eye. Oh, what's this? Someone's bandaged this arm so tight it's gone numb.

As time passed, he began to care less about his injuries and more that he could not recall how he had collected them. It must have been in the jail. Sid's memories were a jumble. Gaddar with a cask on his shoulder. Avinash passing him a cup. Three drops would destroy the drinker, Vidkun had said. A rush of air against his face.

We hopped.

The memory of scrabbling on the stone lip of the precipice returned with his heart pounding in panic. Someone had shoved him against a wall. A punch in the face. One of the others held Ritin in a choke hold while someone else…. He remembered someone screaming and decided he didn't need to remember more.

A door in another room opened. When Greta appeared at his bedside, Sid panicked. *If I am dreaming, I must wake up! Where are my clothes?*

269

But both better and worse was the sight of the rani behind her—her hair loose and curling around her head like a thunder cloud as she hurried to the side of the bed.

"I am glad to find you awake at last," she said. "How do you feel?"

"I'm…better." He wondered why she was there—and how injured he would have to be to stop saying what he thought would please her.

Sitting on a stool at the bedside, the rani put the back of her hand to his forehead. Her scent was like new grass and jasmine, but fear still clutched his heart.

Does she mean to put me in jail? Those fellows are hers after all. But that couldn't be right, could it? They stole from the palace.

"You must be terribly hungry. Greta has some warm food for you."

"I'm thirsty."

The rani poured water into a small clay cup and held it to his lips. He would have preferred firewine, but he dutifully sipped. Just raising his head made him dizzy.

"Poor child, you've been badly treated. Tell me what happened."

The ragged memories of his second visit to the jail surged forward. His heart raced, and he closed his eyes.

"Night guards found you unconscious in the mining hall," she prompted. "What were you doing there?"

Her voice was soft but there was something urgent in it. Suspicion took its seat next to his fears, and he shrank back in the pillows as much as his sore body would allow. *She wants me to confess.*

"Bruises? Ripped clothes?" the rani said. "You did not sustain these injuries by yourself. Someone abused you, isn't that right?"

Her words were reducing him to some green boy of no standing. He had no strength, and anything he said would invite trouble, but he wanted to improve the image of himself that he heard in her voice.

"I am not here to chastise you for taking too much drink or keeping poor company," she continued, "but do you realize that you were poisoned? And that means, Sid Sol, that someone did the poisoning. Moon madness or not, I cannot let that happen in the palace unchallenged. Do you understand me?"

He remembered the drops of drink Vidkun had added to their cups. *Poison is not the word for what they gave me.* He felt it, a deep tug in his gut and a sensation of expanding beyond himself, becoming all-seeing in a way that no mortal could. Like an ancestor.

He teetered with indecision—to tell her all or nothing? He desperately wanted to earn her confidence, but the circumstances would not favor him.

"I can't remember what happened."

The rani closed her eyes, then said, "I am asking you too much, too soon. There will be time to discover the culprits when you have regained your strength." She swirled a spoon in a bowl of soup Greta had given her and held it out to him, but he did not want it.

"You must take some nourishment," she said. "Are you afraid because I spoke of poison? Be reassured." He watched her drink from the bowl herself, which checked his panic but did not extinguish it. The rani turned to Greta who waited next to the altar table at the other end of the room. "Bring me the blue one."

Greta fetched a slim-necked surahi, beautifully decorated with lapis lazuli embedded in the handle. The giantess hesitated before setting it on the table, and a sharp look crossed the rani's face. She poured a small amount of the surahi's contents into the soup.

"See here," she said, offering the bowl. "A sweet delight and a medicine to heal you."

He sipped the tiniest sip possible. All he could taste was honey. He drank more and lay back. The rani put the bowl down and gently lifted his bandaged arm.

"Make a fist. Good. I will remove the wrapping and treat you. Perhaps then you will be ready to tell me more."

He fell asleep while she was talking.

When he next woke, the pain was less, but he still ached, and he had lost his sense of time. The room's window was dark. Master Avani, not the rani, waited at the side of the bed.

"Well, here he is," the noble said. "We were worried, boy."

Sid clutched the bedcovers in his hands. Li stood next to Master Avani. A chill passed through him. *What do they want? Li was there in the kitchens. Has she told him?*

"How are you feeling?" Master Avani asked.

"Thirsty."

"See, he's doing much better," Master Avani said brightly to Lingli as she poured him a cup of water. "You lived more in the otherworld than here on our first visit."

The lantern light disturbed him, as did the room's shrouded furniture, but his thoughts were worse. *They aren't what they seem. I am being tricked somehow, but at least I have clothes.* This he realized upon noticing his kurta's sleeve on top of the bedcover. Someone had washed and dressed him while he slept.

Li offered him the cup.

"Not that," he croaked and waved at the altar table. Li started toward it, but Master Avani stopped her.

"Water is best," he said. "Let some thin firewine be his reward for getting out of bed and fetching it himself." He abruptly told him, "Now, let's start with what happened in the kitchens."

Sid shot a look at Li, who shook her head almost imperceptibly.

"I don't remember much. I was…talking to Korvar, Sir, and there was a commotion in the kitchen. Someone attacked Shankar, I think, and maybe they took something? I…I left to look for my friends. We were going to play cards—"

"Stop," Master Avani said. "A boy is struck down and a theft takes place, and you choose to play cards?"

"I thought Shankar was alright. Isn't he?"

"Shankar is fine, praise the ancestors, but this is a serious matter."

"What was taken?"

"The rani's property," Master Avani said. "No one has been arrested. Only a few know that an attack on you happened the same night." The old noble paused and shook his head. "When this matter reaches the court, and it will, your involvement will be discussed in detail—as will the seamstress's. You should understand that it would be far better for everyone if you told us what you know before the thieves accuse you."

"I don't remember," he protested.

"Alright, don't upset yourself. What *do* you remember?"

Li's face gave him no clue as to what to say.

"I was talking to Korvar Sir behind the kitchens—"

"What brought you to the kitchens?"

"I...I had been in the new tower. One of the southern nobles thought I was still a bearer, and he asked me to bring some drink, so I didn't argue." He paused, frantically calculating how much he would have to say. He could feel the sweat beading on his face. "I went to the kitchens to tell Korvar Sir. We were talking outside..."

Li interrupted and put a hand to his forehead, "He's not well, sir. Let him rest for a moment."

Sid saw Master Avani's brows raise, but he stayed quiet when Li pulled an object from her pocket.

"I've brought something for you," she said. "I should have given it to you weeks ago." She handed him a small bracelet made of braided grasses.

"What is this?"

"It was in Red's trunk. He asked me to deliver it, but I think your mother left it for you."

He stared at the bracelet, both astounded to hold a gift from Afsana—something he had wished for so often in cycles gone by—and also ill at ease. Given all that had happened from the moment Li had arrived at the palace, he was more convinced than ever that whatever otherworld curse plagued her was spreading to him.

"If you like," Li said, "I could help you make a shrine to ask for healing."

He looked at her incredulously, recalling how little respect she had given his shrine in the cabin. *What does she want?* He wished both she and Master Avani would leave.

"Let me put it on for you." Li leaned forward to fit the bracelet, and he winced as she pushed his sleeve up. *Stop touching me, Li.*

They saw the wounds on his forearm smeared with fly balm. A rough circle of dark indentations—a bite.

Sid quickly tugged his sleeve down, but Master Avani said, "Who are these demons! This will not stand! Put it on his other arm, Miss Tabaan. You, my boy, need all the protections the ancestors can muster."

While she tied the bracelet loosely around his other wrist, her expression told him what he already knew: don't say too much.

"We will let you rest," Master Avani said, "but I implore you to try to remember the events that not only threatened Shankar but resulted in a crime against the realm—and may be related to your own injuries. A full, honest account will put you in better light, Sid Sol."

As time passed Sid was awake longer and his fears were leashed, but he also still had spells where his thoughts darkened and no one seemed trustworthy. Though he was glad that the rani and Master Avani were treating him gently, he wondered more and more *why*. It felt like a trap. They were cajoling him into telling on the others, no doubt, but what could they offer that was more convincing than Kadam's knife in his ribs when he wasn't looking?

On the third day of his recovery, the rani's mood took a turn. During earlier visits, she had given him a sip from either the red-handled surahi, which cleared his head, or the blue-handled surahi, which helped him sleep. But not this time. She hadn't been in the room two minutes before she told him he could go clean himself in the bathing room or she would instruct Greta to do it.

He did as he was told, and though none of his injuries appeared threatening anymore, he marveled at the range of colors the bruises painted upon his body. Washing quickly, he tried to look presentable when he re-entered the room.

"Do you think you are well enough to resume your duties?" the rani asked as she arranged objects on the shrine's altar and replaced offerings. He stood a little behind her and watched how she made her tribute.

"I will do my best, Maharani."

He had made a small shrine on the bedside table to honor Afsana—just a thali with a piece of orange, a cup of water, a pinch of dust, and the bracelet Lingli had given him. Compared to the rani's shrine, his display looked more like leftovers from his breakfast.

"I have never doubted your intent," the rani answered, "but your capacity is another matter. Have you seen those?"

She pointed to the wall over the bed. Above the canopy hung two short talwars with golden hilts decorated with gemstones—a noble youth's set. The blades were mounted over a leather- and brass-banded belt with two scabbards. Of course he had seen them. To pass the time he had examined everything in the room and had admired the blades often.

On the rani's command, Greta brought the display down. Her Majesty sat on one of the shrouded chairs and took them onto her lap, removing the bands that held one of the blades to the mount.

"These were my great-grandfather's gift to my grandfather on his thirteenth birthday—the cycle when he began his formal training in arms," she said. "See the design on the pommel? Not the sun and seven stars of the realm, but the upright blade, the symbol of our house."

Sid wished, as he often did, that he had a blade of his own. His desire to learn the defensive arts had never seemed so urgent, but he did not like the way the rani slowly raised the talwar—her gaze distant, the sharp tip of the blade seeming to pull her arm upward as if it had its own mind.

He shook his head, determined to rid himself of the silly, panicky thoughts that chased him. When he looked again, she had laid the blade down. Sid avoided her eyes, certain she could read the fear that possessed him.

"Are you still feeling ill?"

"I am mostly healed, Your Majesty, but I am…very thirsty. Could I have something to drink?"

The rani nodded at Greta, who went to the altar table to fill a cup.

"Your restlessness is to be expected," she said as she reattached the blade to the mount. "I once spent a moon in this room and thought I would go mad."

"Were you injured?"

"No. An illness swept over the Rock when I was still very young, and it took my elder brother. My parents were taking no chances on my life, and so I was kept here until the danger passed."

"You had a brother?"

"Faran. Six cycles elder to me. I remember very little about him except his laugh and the way he fed me. He would have been raja had he lived, and the stars know what my fate would have been." The rani paused her reverie and looked at something he could not see. "His death was the first hard winter in my life."

Greta handed him a cup. He was disappointed to find it was tea.

"While I was confined here, my father tried to pacify me by showing me the blades and telling me of my grandfather's exploits. His as well. Even at that age, I understood that if I was to follow them to the throne, I would have to learn the blades. I practiced with these as soon as I was strong enough to hoist them."

"I've always wanted to learn blades."

"And you shall!" The rani looked at him with an openness that Sid had not seen since the day they had met in the Western Woods, but the expression was fleeting, and she turned away, adding, "Attacks like the one you have suffered should make clear why all recruits must be trained in basic defense skills. Perhaps you will join Master Duvanya in the next rotation."

Sid hoped she couldn't tell how little hope he had of that happening.

She passed the blades back to Greta. "I think you will soon be able to leave here, perhaps by tomorrow. But do not think I have lost interest in the question I've put to you twice already, and to which twice you have claimed you have no answer. To spare us both embarrassment I ask you this instead: Do you trust me, Sid Sol?"

He felt like some poor goat on a spit, being turned slowly over the coals.

"Do not spit out some hasty answer. Consider our exchanges. Consider the treatment you have received since the day you joined my service. Consider also that I promise you, whatever your involvement in this matter in the kitchens, you will not suffer for it."

Why this boon? She wants something.

She stepped close to him and repeated, "Do you trust your maharani? That is the question of greatest importance, and the next time I ask what happened in the kitchens and who you were with, your answer will suffice for both questions. Whatever your answer, I will ask you no more."

With that the rani left. Sid wrapped a blanket around his shoulders. He went to the altar to check the surahis for anything that might counter the chill that had overtaken him, but they were empty.

All afternoon and evening he considered the rani's question. There was only one possible answer, and she had promised he would not be prosecuted. But whatever motivated her promise, there remained five more, not counting the prisoner Ritin, who would mark his absence on the bench if they were arrested. And they had allies—friends and blood kin. He would be looking over his shoulder for the rest of his life.

And no fool would accuse Vidkun or Captain Gaddar. Her Majesty will not believe it, and no one else will either. He wasn't even sure how to explain what had been stolen. A drink more potent than firewine? Vidkun's double-cross further confounded the mess. *I must keep this story simple and make sure Li does the same.*

Resigned to constructing the vaguest possible story of his involvement with descriptions only of the boys closest to his own rank if necessary, Sid spent the evening pleading for Afsana's protection at the rude shrine he had constructed. He was almost relieved when Master Avani arrived early in the morning.

"The rani tells me you are ready to return to scribing duties," the noble said brightly.

"Yes, sir." This was not as brightly offered.

"Come now, attending the council meeting will improve your spirit and perhaps your memory."

"I don't know, sir. I'm not feeling well—"

"Sid Sol, that is enough! The stars wait for no one, and you've got so much to learn." Master Avani rubbed his nose and moved toward the outer room. "What I mean is we've got cycles of records to compare, and it will not be achieved without your effort and Parth's."

A short time later, Sid found himself in the gallery outside the council room with a stack of clean parchments under one arm and a reed pen in his hand. *Beautiful*, he thought, examining the pen's point, *and sharp enough to use as a weapon. If I needed a weapon.* Small reassurances like this helped keep down the tension that swam in his stomach.

Parth had joined them, and Madam Hansa approached from the other end of the passage with one of the archery apprentices.

"Did you hear me, Sid?" Master Avani asked, poking him in the shoulder.

"'He hears beauty passing on kittens' paws,'" Parth teased, quoting palace poetry.

Sid stared, not at the girl with Madam Hansa, but at the two boys behind. Krill and Avinash. They stopped in the passage when they saw him. Sid's lungs constricted.

Gently pushing Sid through the council room doors, Master Avani repeated, "You will draft the comments from those speaking for the houses of Hansa, Vaksana, and Avani. Yes," he said sternly, "I will know what you miss from my own comments, so pay attention."

Inside, the other members of the Seven already stood behind their chairs. The sight of Master Duvanya nearly paralyzed Sid, though the defenses master showed no sign of recognizing him. Then he noticed Master Vaksana staring with a wrinkle creasing his forehead as Master Avani whispered to him. On the verge of telling Master Avani he was too ill to continue, Sid's chance to leave disappeared as one of the stewards proclaimed, "Hail Her Majesty, Maharani Sandhyatara!"

As the rani took her seat, Greta stepped behind the throne, and her head swiveled toward him. *Even the giantess knows I am accused!*

"It has been moons since all of us were here together," the rani began, "and there is much to address. Our first and main business will be led by Brother Darius. The question before us is whether or not we will take back our hold at Zahatara."

Sid watched Parth writing rapidly in a neat flowing hand. His own pen was inked, but his hand shook so badly he could hardly date his parchment. It was all he could do to resist jumping up from his stool and leaving the room.

"When Xirs's forces took Zahatara in the eight hundredth and seventy-third cycle," Master Duvanya said, "we could not think of recapturing it while the northern realm fully supported Daza Tumuli. Our pride burned, but Raja Sadul, then his son and then his granddaughter, wisely chose to not squander more blood and fortune than the territory warranted. Now, however, a new opportunity has presented itself.

"A few moons ago our envoy at Daza Tumuli provided information about Zahatara's defenses, and I and a contingent of defenders surveyed the hold and surrounding territory. I believe we could mount a successful campaign to take it back."

"What has changed, brother?" Madam Satya asked. "Have they mined the last of the dark star? And if they have, is Zahatara of any practical use to us?"

"It appears they have exhausted most of the unique metal," Master Duvanya answered, "and in the process of doing so, they have reinforced their defenses."

"That does not sound promising," Madam Hansa said.

Parth nudged Sid, who hastily made note of her comment.

I will not flee. I will not choke or faint. I will sit here and scribe as duty demands.

"To the question of Zahatara's practical use," the rani responded, "let us remember its value before it was stolen. That territory was not only the source of a unique metal. It has been important since Starfall because it borders the passage to the northwest—lands where my house and the House of Vaksana came from. There was not much trade from there for scores of cycles, but this is changing." She pointed to Madam Satya. "Your gown, Parama, was acquired from the north, was it not?"

Madam Satya nodded.

"We have studied the material and tried to recreate it," the rani said, "but we have not been successful because this silk is not made by our worms or the north's worms. This silk arrived in Avkorum from the northwest. It is strong, has a beautiful sheen, and takes dye well, and they are selling it for a very high price. We could take the advantage of redirecting these goods before they reach Saikhanger, or making them even better, if we held Zahatara again."

Several of the nobles spoke at once.

Parth told Sid, "She despises everything about Saikhanger, you know. One of the khan's spies killed her father right here."

"*Here*, here?" Sid asked, trying to sound normal.

"On the terrace," Parth whispered. "An attack in the night, not a battle. Ameer Ali came to the raja's defense, but too late."

Master Duvanya quieted the others and continued. "I told you Zahatara has been reinforced. That is a negative factor for laying siege, I grant, but it is a positive factor for holding. I propose that we will never have a better chance to take the stronghold. Varj Xirs has been seduced by the khan's attention. It's said he spends more moons in Avkorum than Daza Tumuli. His son Arzisi commands Zahatara, and he has no practical experience with warcraft."

"Even a weak leader can outlast a siege where defenses are strong," Master Avani said.

"Our envoy, Madam Tilan, reports that Xirs has been called to attend the New Cycle festivities at the khan's court. Next week he is to take an entourage with him, including Arzisi." Master Duvanya paused to look around the table, "She also reports that, for all its strengths, there were two breaches in Zahatara's walls after the first shaking. Evidently it was more severe there than what we experienced and damaged a wide span of outer wall."

"You be-believe we could breach the wall?" Master Vaksana asked. "Have they not re-re-repaired it already?"

Sid was glad for the few comments made by him so far.

"They are in the process of doing so," Master Duvanya answered, "but I'm sure the second shaking did not improve the situation and mortar cures slow in the winter—even slower if the masons have no ruler hurrying them along. Xirs will depart the khan's palace to return on the third day of the new cycle. This means if we strike and gain entry on this schedule, we will have about a moon to secure Zahatara before Daza Tumuli's forces could be gathered."

"A moment, please!" Master Avani said. "You strike with who? How many? What of the resources such a force would need through the winter?"

"I think we can assume they have planned for their own winter stores," the rani said.

"If we breach the walls, they may torch their stores," Madam Satya said.

"I do not make this proposal lightly," Master Duvanya said, "No less than six hundred soldiers are required—that being twice the number currently holding Zahatara. We will need five hundred more to hold it, and provisions for all."

"Eleven hundred soldiers?" Madam Hansa said. "Brother, I count no more than five hundred ready for deployment, unless you are planning to move defenders from other posts or from Nilampur."

Sid hurried to note Madam Hansa's comment. Crowseye shifted uncomfortably at mention of Nilampur.

"I recommend we take three hundred of ours and three hundred southerners who have completed training." Master Duvanya turned to the rani. "Once you receive my word, Sister Gayatri and Brother Jordak can make ready reinforcements and provisions. The second contingent of southerners will have finished training by the new cycle, and two hundred fifty of them can join our defenders from Jobat and Aldea."

"By that calculation, you are leaving only two hundred soldiers on the Rock after the wedding?" Master Avani said.

Master Duvanya looked directly at Master Avani. "This is our requirement in order to succeed. I will admit that having the privilege of regaining stolen territory appeals greatly, but we must all agree, or I will not pursue this plan."

"We may never have this opportunity again," the rani said. "We should also calculate our defenders as a whole. In addition to the remaining soldiers, we will have day guards and night guards who are fully trained in defensive skills, and I see no reason why we cannot bring three or four score defenders from Talomeer to the Rock as well."

"Will the southerners allow us to deploy so many of their youth before the contract is signed?" Madam Hansa asked. "Some remain suspicious of the proposed arrangement."

Sid wrote as fast as he could, but it was an ugly parchment. His lines rose up at the end, and the words were getting larger.

"They will need encouragement," the rani agreed, "but it can be done. I believe Ameer Ali will support it."

"How much 'encouragement,' Valena, and what exactly?" Madam Satya asked. "Our woven cloth is already promised through the fifth moon. Our gems trade is bearing the weight of the wedding gifts and Nilampur's construction, and we truly cannot spare any more foodstuff with the voracious population living here. Is this the time to send our defenders out?"

Not daring to look up when such open questioning of the rani's position was leveled, Sid concentrated on his parchment with his ears wide open. *Was this what those southerners were arguing about in the bath?*

"We can agree that our guests are not refined, and some border on savage, but if we were so much less fortunate than our neighbors, would we not reveal our envious selves?" the rani said. "I am encouraged by that envy. By sharing generously for this brief time, we will not only create the trust necessary to pursue our shared interests, but we will create forevermore a taste for our goods and resources. Southern envy will greatly profit us."

"I share your vision, sister," Madam Satya said, "but I question the timing."

"Hesitation will devour opportunity. Darius needs two days to assemble this campaign and eight days to reach the hold. We must give him as much time as possible to take it, secure it, and stock supplies before Xirs returns. After our allies sign the contract and partake of the breakfast on the second day of the new cycle, we will send a mounted escort with them for the first day's ride, then we will send Darius his reinforcements."

Sid saw doubt in Madam Hansa's face, and Master Vaksana seemed restless. Crowseye was unreadable.

"I would be more assured of this course if we had more defenders at our disposal in the next moons," Master Avani said.

Master Duvanya said. "I agree, but if we are successful, I will be satisfied that I have given the best wedding gift of all, even if I am a little late to the celebration."

"Will you return from Nilampur for the wedding?" Madam Hansa asked Crowseye.

The rani extended her hand to Crowseye and answered, "If Brother Ketan is not present to bear witness to the completion of Nilampur's facilities, there is no contract, and if there is no contract, there is no wedding. So you see, his presence at the wedding is in truth more important than mine."

Crowseye actually chuckled. "I'm sure you will defend us well, Gayatri, but I should be able to bring a company back with me for the wedding."

The council approved Master Duvanya's plan and spoke of other business. Sid captured most of it, with Parth's sharp elbow reminding him when he faltered. Then Master Vaksana spoke of the theft in the kitchens, and his fears awakened again.

"I have q-questioned two who were p-present," the wolfmaster said, glancing at Sid and looking away again. "But we be-believe others are involved."

Sweat ran down Sid's back. His part in the crime would be called out at any moment.

"What was taken?" Madam Hansa asked. "Perhaps the goods will name the thieves."

"Firewine," the rani said quickly. "Another cask. The item itself is not the concern, but this follows earlier small thefts. If a coterie is forming, it must be addressed. Disloyalty, betrayal—these wounds never fully heal. Advise both captains that I offer a reward."

Master Vaksana nodded and said, "We-we will find them."

To Sid's amazement, neither the rani, Master Avani, nor Master Vaksana added any other comment about his or Li's involvement or the attack he had suffered. The rani said something about the state of the treasury, and the council meeting was concluded. Though he was as relieved as if he had dodged a blade, he pondered why the rani had lied about what was stolen. If his answer to the rani's promised question failed to please, were both he and Li bound for jail?

CHAPTER 22

In the stables' deep shadows Lingli fed the young govadhi half an apple she had saved from her supper. A visit to the colt usually brightened her mood, but in these dark hours she felt stonebound, and seeing how he pawed at the ground and obsessively chewed the edge of the manger, she imagined the colt felt the same way. He and she were never going to be fit for this place. Yet here they were—in their fine cages.

She scolded herself. Soon she'd have more freedom than she would know what to do with. In twenty-three days it would be New Cycle Day, and she'd have to put down her needle and thread and find a way off the Rock before the rani's promise to arrest her came to fruition. She would be free to wander the Naachmaidan throughout the winter, seeking a new home she couldn't see even in her dreams. She'd be free to leave the one person she had crossed the world for, one who was injured and not himself. The one who acted as if he didn't know her, or didn't want to know her, and it broke her heart.

In the first days after the attack on Sid, she simply wanted him to recover, and he was too weak to do anything but cooperate. Each night she had waited on the old tower's deserted fifth floor until she heard Master Avani greet the guard outside the library. That was her signal to hurry downstairs, and together they would cross the landing to the quarters where Sid had been ensconced. Once at her friend's bedside, their familiarity with each other's expressions helped them evade most of Master Avani's questions, and she had excused Sid's unpredictable moods as simply part of his injuries.

She had been confident that he was improving and, because he had resumed his scribing duties the day before, she had expected to find him even better last night—well enough, she hoped, that she could apologize for berating him in the kitchens. His magnanimous acceptance of her apology would mean they could move on and work together to clear their names. That's all she wanted.

The moment she and Master Avani entered the quarter's inner room, however, Sid had pressed himself back against the headboard as if they were the rani's wolves. For a breath it seemed he did not recognize them. Making no remark about this, Master Avani greeted him with the usual familiarity, as did she. Gradually, he unclenched his fists, but she saw there was little trust within him.

"I know yesterday's council meeting was challenging," Master Avani said, "but have you been napping all day?"

"Master Vaksana had a lot of questions when he visited," Sid said grumpily.

"Did he? Well, I'm certain you were helpful in answering them. Have you had your supper? Why don't we get some hot food in your stomach to make the evening brighter and your sleep more sound? You'll need your strength for the transcriptions awaiting you tomorrow."

While the old noble returned to the quarters' door to request that food be delivered, Sid rubbed his head as if it pained him, and Lingli added that to her list of concerns along with the dark circles under his eyes, and his poor color. But none of these compared to her dismay that he refused to look at her.

Sid toyed with things in a little shrine he had made on the bedside table, and the silence between them grew. In the middle of his offerings sat the grass bracelet she had given him a few nights earlier. Still chiding herself for not giving it to him sooner, she was glad to see him kiss the ornament before he tucked it under his pillow.

"Why aren't you wearing it?" she asked innocently.

Sid leveled her with an angry look and said softly enough that Master Avani would not hear, "Why did you tell Master Vaksana I was friends with those in the kitchens?"

"I didn't tell him that."

"You're lying! I see Master Vaksana thinking it. The rani, too. They're going to arrest me."

Lingli's better judgment told her not to react to his accusation, but her tongue had a will of its own. "Well, that makes two of us," she said. "And the rani's not 'thinking' anything. She's plainly told me I'll be arrested after the wedding. Maybe we should leave before then."

"I'm not going anywhere with you."

"If you would tell them who did it and how they forced you, it would save us both grief."

"You know nothing about it!"

"Calm yourself."

"Shut up! If you want to go, go and leave me alone!"

She drew back, shocked. They had argued plenty, but this kind of sudden, seething anger had never been part of Sid's nature. Something was wrong with him.

Master Avani returned to the bedside, oblivious and full of instructions about diet and rest. Stinging with hurt, Lingli retreated to the far end of the room. In the small pools of light cast by the diyas, she pretended to admire the shrine's strange little effigy with its yarn mustache perched upon a tiny throne inside a bronze chhatri. Next to the raja doll, a braid of hair sat coiled on a similar chair. A wave of longing for her old home and her old life overcame her.

The thali arrived, and Master Avani described some new transcriptions he had received while Sid ate, but the visit was short. When the old noble bid Sid good night, Lingli followed him out to the door without another word to Sid. Master Avani blithely invited her to visit the library with him, but perhaps he had noticed her distress, for when she complained of not feeling well he dismissed her and she fled to her room.

Her eyes began to tear as the colt nuzzled her cheek, and Lingli pressed her face into his mane. If she didn't forgive Sid and help him, she was betraying her promise to Red. And if she didn't find a way for both of them to prove their innocence, she would definitely suffer, and he might, too. The rani showed Sid favor now, but for how long? She feared the rani only waited for him to name the others before the arrests would begin.

Red's voice came to her—comforting her as he had many times when she had floundered through despair, especially after her ordeal on the last New Cycle Day. *You have spirit, mind, two hands. Mind your words and deeds, and be useful.* She somehow had to make sure the true culprits came to the guards' attention.

Suddenly, Lingli heard the grooms stirring. She fell back into a shadowed corner near the colt's manger and watched as the grooms entered the next row of stalls, toting saddles and other tack. As soon as they began to ready Master Duvanya's and Master Vaksana's horses, Lingli hurried out the back of the stables and darted along the wall leading to the feasting hall. It was not yet dawn, but the kitchens were already in service, and she found herself in a crowd of bleary-eyed southern youth being given provisions and hustled by Saatkulom soldiers through the small gate to the front grounds.

She peeled away from the southern youth at the old tower door, but instead of going straight to her room, Lingli went to the first floor and peeked out the edge of the gallery. Scores of mounted soldiers and southerners on foot massed in the front grounds, and lanterns lit Master Duvanya and Master Vaksana as they spoke to the senior soldiers just below the gallery before mounting the horses the grooms brought.

Matachand had set, but Chotabhai could still be seen as the sun's first light passed over the Rock, and she could see the backs of the southern ameers and the rani who stood wrapped in shawls on the stairs that passed from the central palace to the yard.

Master Duvanya and Master Vaksana rode up to the other nobles, then Master Duvanya addressed the yard. "We begin our first joint campaign in the spirit of a fruitful alliance among great houses. Our soldiers have served the realm honorably before and will do so again. All new defenders here are ready to meet the field's tests. Southerners, hear the word of your ameers, and know that under my command, we will support you and defend you like our own. We will be brothers in the fight."

Prince Hassan stepped forward and spoke to the southerners in his tongue, then ameers Ali and Khush did the same. The rani stepped forward last, and shouted, "May the ancestors guard you and grant you victory! For the strength of the realm, and the strength of our alliance!"

Defenders in the yard drew their weapons and held them aloft as Master Duvanya rode to the palace gate. Master Vaksana brought up the rear holding two of the rani's harnessed wolves.

It was light enough now for Lingli to see a few palace staff in the colonnade waving the defenders farewell, and she looked for Sid there, imagining that he would wish he was among those leaving, but she didn't see him. Then the flash of a lantern on the feasting hall roof caught her attention. Several boys stood on the edge watching events, and one of them looked like Sid. When he climbed down to the barrack's terrace, she was certain it was him.

A pair of boys, followed by a miner, approached him. *It's those who robbed the kitchens.* Lingli left the gallery and jogged to the feasting hall.

When Lingli reached the top of the stairs on the barracks' landing, several boys preparing for duty gave her strange looks, but she could not concern herself with them. Farther down the landing Sid stood surrounded by the miner and two other boys.

Be useful.

"Sid. Sid Sol," she called out.

Sid and those around him looked her way as she walked toward them. One of the younger ones had reddish-brown hair and wore a chinkara brooch on his shoulder. The other boy's face made her think of a fish.

"Master Avani is looking for you." She hoped her voice didn't shake too much.

The thieves moved away from Sid and left through the terrace door next to Master Avani's quarters.

Sid looked almost as pale as her.

"So, they are not really your friends," she said softly.

Sid did not answer, but his eyes darted from one end of the landing to the other.

"Come," she said. "Let's tell Master Avani who they are."

"No," he said, grabbing her arm. "I can't tell him, and you can't either."

"Why not?"

"Because they'll arrest me. A couple of them are of the Seven—spares, I guess. And who am I? No one. Who's going to believe me?"

His answer frustrated her, but she was glad he was talking and glad there was none of the strange rage she'd heard in his voice the night before.

"Master Avani will believe you."

"Please, Li, don't say anything. I'll stay away from them, but if nothing happens, they'll forget about it."

"The rani won't. Do you remember I told you she promised to arrest me after New Cycle Day?"

Sid's brows drew together. "She's just trying to see if you know anything. You didn't tell her anything about me, did you?"

"No." Her heart sank. *Don't argue. He's still recovering.*

After opening the latch to his tiny room, Sid squeezed her arm and said, "Thank the stars you came up here, but better to stay out of sight for a bit. Lucky I've got an hour until I have to report to Avaniji." He ran his hand through his knotted hair, and she saw his eyes were bloodshot. Pulling the door almost closed so he was speaking to her through the crack, he added, "I think you better go and not let them catch you out either."

After he closed the door, Lingli thought, *He's wrong. Those fellows are not going to forget. Master Vaksana is not going to forget. Korvar Sir is not going to forget, and the rani isn't either.*

At the end of the landing she saw that a lock hung from the door to Master Avani's quarters. She returned to the old tower and checked a strand of her hair to make sure it was still brown before squeezing past a group of southern nobles, including Prince Hassan, conversing on the second floor. She understood nothing of what they said in their own languages, but it seemed they were bickering. They fell silent until she passed and reached the next floor.

On the third floor, she had to face the library guard.

"Please tell Master Avani that I've come to collect his sewing," she said, offering the only excuse she thought the guard would act on.

The guard grudgingly knocked on the door, and to her relief, the old noble came to the door and invited her inside.

"Sir, I need to speak to you about something important."

She wanted to trust him. She needed to trust him. But she would deal with her troubles one at a time to be sure. Digging into the hem of her cloak, Lingli produced the amethyst ring she had taken from Mafala's trunk.

"Where did you find this?"

"I'd rather not say, sir. I know my presence after the kitchen theft does not inspire trust, but I hope you will believe me when I tell you my only wish is to return this to its rightful owner."

"Do you know to whom this ring belongs?"

"Envoy Kanaka. He asked me to help him look for it some time ago."

Master Avani took the ring and held it in his open palm. "Should I tell him that you delivered it to me?"

"I'd rather you didn't. It doesn't matter, does it?"

"I suppose not, but why so modest? It's a fine ornament. The envoy might very well wish to reward you."

Remembering the hawk brooch Red had given her, Lingli wondered if she should have dug a little deeper in the Hudulfah princess's trunk.

"I did nothing but find it and deliver it. I need no reward."

Master Avani looked doubtful and the silence between them stretched. Lingli bit down on the inside of her cheek. *Twenty-three days left.* She had to do what Sid would not. *Be useful. Be useful.* Yet she was not entirely convinced she was being useful so much as completely betraying Sid's trust.

"I saw Sid in the barracks," she said.

"Did you? Good. We've finally coaxed him back to service, and high time."

"Sir, he's being followed."

"What?"

"A man and two others accosted Sid after the defenders left—just half an hour ago. I think they were the ones in Korvar Sir's kitchens, and the ones who beat Sid."

"Do you know them?"

"No, but the older one is a miner, I think. I told Master Vaksana that when he questioned me, but tonight I saw the other two younger ones. One has a house insignia—Satya. I wasn't certain I should—"

"And you're certain now?" Master Avani said sharply.

When she nodded, the old noble tapped the table and took a deep breath. "What does Sid have to do with them?"

"I don't know, but he's afraid of them. I believe they forced him to distract Korvar Sir that night."

Running a hand over his face, Master Avani said, "If you are correct, Sid has not helped himself or you with his thin tale. He will need protection until they're found." He turned to her quickly and added, "What about you? Do they know you saw them in the kitchens?"

"I don't think so."

"We must convince the rani that you were not part of all this."

"You know that she suspects me?"

"Of course I know. My sister has not kept her suspicions secret."

"Does she blame Sid, too?"

"Sid? Ah, likely yes." Master Avani looked away and began to pace around his work table. "This crime has stirred her passions, but Madam has kept you on, has she not?"

"Yes. The rani said I should continue with my work until the wedding, but I…I don't think I'll be able to stay after that."

Master Avani stopped and tried to sound reassuring. "This bright cycle drama will not ruin your name or Sid's if we act now. Our next task is clear. We must give the culprits' details to the investigators, and because Master Duvanya and Master Vaksana are away, that would be the night captain."

Lingli had begun to feel better about talking to Master Avani until he said "night captain." She did not want to speak to the one who had already warned her to stay out of trouble.

"Please, Sir," she said, "could you tell the captain?"

"The words of a witness are weightier than those of a messenger."

Lingli looked away.

"Your reticence makes you appear suspect, Miss Tabaan."

"I've told the truth, sir, but whatever I say will appear self-serving."

Master Avani considered this and said, "Perhaps it is best, for now, for you to avoid any more attention. I will convey what you have told me, but you should trust in truth's power. Speaking it feeds courage, and sometimes it befuddles enemies. Even powerful ones."

Unless those arrests came soon, Lingli doubted that the truth would prove as robust a defense as Master Avani believed it to be.

CHAPTER 23

During the first fear-laced days after the attack, Sid had paid Afsana regular tributes and remained unharmed. *The power of devotion*, he told himself, *and the rani's good medicines*. Yet the fear that had nestled in his gut since he took that drink in the jail still overwhelmed him now and again. He went about his days as tightly strung as a vina, desperately trying to deny the power these episodes had over him. Unable to banish the memories completely, he began to hunt for ways to protect himself.

Even before the run-in with his "friends," the previous morning, Sid had known in his bones that Master Avani's insistence that he move back into the barracks was a bad idea. Pushing his pallet against the door before he slept seemed a necessary precaution, as did the broken banner pole that he carried for added assurance when he emerged from his closet. There was no doubt he had narrowly escaped a beating or being forced into another crime only because of Li's intervention.

Ugh. I hate owing her, but better her than them.

Seeing no one menacing on the landing, Sid left his pole behind and made his way downstairs to the tables where people were eating. He held his breath and scanned the hall for Vidkun and the other card players. There was no sign of them, but his nerves had soured his stomach so thoroughly he turned away from breakfast and left the hall. He would be safer sitting in Master Avani's shadow in the council room.

As he crossed the front grounds, Sid recalled the previous day's early send-off for Master Duvanya, Master Vaksana, and a host of defenders and southern fighters. He should have been with them, off to win back the realm's lands, but he was on the feasting hall roof, a little drunk, only to be accosted by Kadam and the boys who acted as if the beating they'd given him was a joke.

Sid shook his head and banished the little demons that played on his mind. Today was a new day, and he intended to make something of it.

Outside the council chambers, he bowed to the steward, then entered quietly and slid onto his stool, ignoring Master Avani's and Parth's looks of surprise to see him reporting so early. He readied his pens when the rani and Greta arrived, wishing he had eaten a piece of naan beforehand, but with no sign of the other members of the Seven attending, the session should be short. Then the steward admitted Envoy Kanaka.

Sid looked pleadingly at Parth, who rolled his eyes and whispered, "You'll never keep up with this one. I'll take down on his words. You follow Avaniji and the rani."

"Your Majesty," the envoy began, bowing low, "I am honored to meet you this morn when there must be countless matters to address related to the celebration of your wedding. To have this opportunity to share with you, at last, a summary of the learnings we have compiled in Garzekhara related to the terrestrial and heavenly disturbances plaguing our realms, is one of my greatest rewards since arriving at your beautiful palace."

"Let us set aside the flourishes, Envoy Kanaka," the rani answered. "Share with me, briefly and immediately, your report."

"Yes, of course. Well, then, to begin, the first shaking Dyuvasa suffered this cycle came during the ninth moons. Though that event was mild, we considered it important enough to inspire my assignment here as envoy. Our realm didn't fare so well in the twelfth moons. Our capital and the major fortresses proved resilient, despite significant damage to more than a score of buildings. Worse, the last messenger I received conveyed that more than one hundred subjects in the villages died during that shaking."

"May the ancestors guide their spirits," the rani said. "What of the last shaking?"

"I have no news yet regarding the effects of the last one."

The envoy squeezed his eyes shut for a moment and took a deep breath. "I am certain you are aware, Your Majesty, that this has happened before. It is my noble duty—by the word of Raja Tajazan, who counts Saatkulom as a trusted neighbor—to inform you of what we know of those past episodes in order that we may better prepare for the future.

"According to our chronicles, Ascaryans witnessed very similar shakings during Starfall and briefly again during the bright cycles you count as the fifteenth episode after Starfall. We have recorded other disturbances associated with the past shakings—falling stars, eruptions of the fire mountains, and whole seasons that were never brighter than twilight."

"Has Dyuvasa witnessed any of these during *this* cycle?" the rani asked.

"Not according to the last report, yet there are signs that a fire mountain may be on the verge of erupting."

While Parth wrote quickly, Sid drew a series of moons and suns on the scrap of parchment he used to blot his pen. He tried to imagine what a fire mountain would look like.

The rani said softly, "Are you telling me that your raja believes we are experiencing something like Starfall?"

"Be assured that Raja Tajazan has not issued judgment. His advisors continue to collect information, much like you and the esteemed nobles of Saatkulom. What cannot be denied in Dyuvasa is that these events pose a threat we must address. Given our concerns, I was grateful for the opportunity to meet with you today, Your Majesty. With all due respect, I submit once again my invitation to join our raja—"

"Envoy Kanaka," Master Avani interjected, "would you tell the maharani about the celestial changes observed in your realm?"

Sid saw a fleeting look of consternation on Kanaka's face at Master Avani's interruption.

"There is one particular development our raja's celestial advisors have recorded that is certainly novel, though it may or may not be connected to these events. It is a small, very small mind you, and unexpected increase in the size of Skordawa, or, as you call it, Chotabhai. Dyuvasa's last communication confirmed that its expansion continued at least into the twelfth moon."

"I received news of this same phenomenon very recently," the rani said, looking at Master Avani.

A growing moon? Sid and Parth looked at each other, and Sid re-inked his pen, sensing that the old noble had been waiting for the conversation to take this turn.

"My measurements also show that Chotabhai has enlarged over the last four moons—a phenomena not found in any of our shared chronicles," Master Avani said. Leaning forward on the council table, he pushed a slim set of transcriptions to the rani. "I have shared this cycle's measurements here and included the records regarding Chotabhai in the last ten sets of bright cycles. Even in our oldest records, I have found no mention of fattening moons except for the usual bright cycle waxing and waning."

Kanaka said. "That is why a conference might serve to—"

"What do your seers say?" the rani asked the envoy.

"The seers? Yes, they have been engaged," Kanaka said. "They are... using all their means of communicating with the ancestors and will report to our raja by New Cycle Day. As you no doubt appreciate, understanding the ancestors' will is never a simple endeavor."

The rani shook her head dismissively. "Whether we understand the ancestors' will or not, I must address our folk. One event could be managed, the second has left many uneasy about the prospect of protecting ourselves. And now we must consider these changes in Chotabhai as well? No one can be faulted for smelling the otherworld in this." She paused, then said, "I agree that we need to gather our knowledge, but what shall I tell our people now? I cannot simply say that Starfall has returned and let fears blossom into rash actions."

For a moment all was quiet but for the soft scratching of Sid's pen. He had become so used to copying entries about Starfall from the Seven's books that he paid little attention to the details anymore, but the rani's words tickled fears he had been trying to keep down.

Before the envoy could try again to deliver his raja's invitation to a conference, Master Avani said, "Rather than simply trying to soothe the people, Maharani, why not nudge their thoughts into a productive channel? Ask them to help us find the answers we need."

"What do you mean?"

"We could employ the elders of each house," Master Avani said. "You could tell them that we seek greater understanding of the ancestors' intent. Giving no voice to otherworld fears, ask them to read the words of their mothers and fathers and present relevant passages and interpretations, so that we may find the answers."

"Yes, that would keep them busy, and it will please them," the rani agreed. "But what of the common Ascaryan? Those with the least knowledge use rumors to build great halls."

"What does the common Ascaryan value most? The safety of their own," Master Avani said. "Traders and artisans are always occupied with how to secure their enterprises. Encourage them to think broadly and recognize those whose ideas benefit the realm."

The rani smiled and pushed back her chair. Greta went to the door to await her.

"But, Your Majesty, what about our invitation to meet on this matter? I must inform Raja Tajazan."

"Thank you, Envoy Kanaka. Convey to your raja that I agree these events must be discussed. Conferring with him will be more fruitful after I have received the wisdom of my own. I will communicate with His Majesty in the first moon."

Sid almost felt sorry for the much-deflated envoy as he tried to appear gracious.

"Our raja will welcome your message," the envoy said. "I shall send a messenger immediately."

"It would be wiser to wait until I deliver my letter for him to your quarters."

The rani departed, and Sid turned to Parth as they gathered their things. "A fattening moon? That's new."

"Maybe it's nothing, and they're just trying to force the rani's cooperation." Parth shrugged and added, "I hope you caught all that. For each bit you missed, our master will add twice the words."

"Even so, he'll never catch up to the envoy," Sid said, grinning as he followed Parth and Master Avani into the crowded gallery where they were waylaid by the anxious easterner.

"Oh dear, oh dear," the envoy said, wringing his hands. "If Garzekhara is severely shaken one more time without her commitment to a proper conference, the value of an envoy here will be questioned. Do you think I should suggest dates before she composes her letter?"

"Not now," Master Avani said. "Even if a storm blew down the palace, she would not leave the Rock until her alliance with the Avakstan houses is secured. But if you would indulge me, sir, I have some ideas about how we can increase the likelihood of this meeting."

The old noble and the envoy began to move down the gallery with Parth and Sid close behind, but a steward approached Master Avani, and he stopped again.

"The maharani requests your scribe's assistance," the steward said.

"Very well," Master Avani said. "Sid, take Parth's materials."

"Not him," the steward said. "The other one."

Sid's stomach cramped into a knot while Parth grumbled and took his supplies from him.

Following the steward back to the rani, Sid bowed deeply even though the proper etiquette felt odd after the chats they had had while he was ill. Greta loomed over her charge and stared at him with baleful eyes, but he had learned to ignore her most of the time. What he could not ignore was Captain Gaddar, waiting with two other day guards just a short way down the gallery, and the captain's expression told him exactly what he feared.

Speak of what you saw in the jail, and you die.

"You look much improved, Sid Sol," the rani said.

"I am, Your Majesty." *For now.*

"You once told me you wanted to be a guard. Is that still your ambition?"

By the First Mother, she's going to give me over to her captain! Sid felt his throat closing. *She is, or she is not? How can she make her face such a mask?*

"Yes, Your Majesty."

The rani waved toward the parapet, and Sid followed her there. While she looked out over the front grounds, Sid glanced down the gallery to see if Gaddar was still there. He was.

"Do you know what a steward's duties are?" the rani asked. "They are not only tasked with attending meetings and programs. They are trained as guards in addition to maintaining protocols. Perhaps, until you have an opportunity to join defenses, you would like to take up a steward's training?" She did not seem interested in his answer for she immediately signaled the steward at the council chamber door.

"Aznaro, let this young man try your coat." The steward took off his long coat and held it out. It was a splendid blue silk. Sid put it on.

"It doesn't quite fit," the rani decided, "but it can be altered."

He shrugged out of the coat, and Greta took it from him. Was this the opportunity for which he had prayed to Afsana and every unknown ancestor? If he was trained in at least some of the defensive arts, perhaps he could repair his reputation and show himself worthy of joining the guards.

If my tributes are being answered, Mother, I also request you to see Captain Gaddar sent off to Zahatara with the reinforcements.

Sid's excitement, however, was pinched when he realized the rani continued to stare at him, the cloudy sky giving her face an amber tint.

She said, "I told you I would ask you my question one final time, and it is now. What happened in the kitchens the night after the second shaking?"

There was nowhere to run or avoid this. She would know if he lied.

"Some fellows told me to distract Korvar Sir," Sid said slowly, trying to breathe. "I didn't know what they planned."

"Were they the same ones who beat you? Why?"

"Because…" His mind whirled. It was not as if he had not practiced the answer to this question, but he had doubts about how well it would satisfy. "Because I didn't want to help them anymore, and they were afraid I would tell someone."

"You should have. Their names?"

"Avinash, Krill, and a miner, Kadam." In his mind, a voice insisted, *And Vidkun, the jailer and wolfhandler! And Gaddar! Tell her. Her favorite captain is a thief, too.* But he could not bring himself to say it.

The rani said, "I know you drank from the cask they stole, so do not deny it." When he nodded, she asked, "Was anyone else involved? The seamstress, perhaps?"

"No, she came later. She didn't know."

The rani pressed her lips together and scanned his face closely. "And what did they do with the cask?"

"I don't know." *These lies will cost me.* "The…the drink hit me hard."

"If you had told me this days ago, I could have had them arrested and you wouldn't have been vulnerable to them. Don't be such a fool again!" She slapped her hand down on the parapet.

Was he dismissed? He wasn't sure, but her eyes were not as stern as her last words.

"Go now," she told him. "Tomorrow you will begin to learn the blades."

Sid's heart sang, and not even being told to transcribe fearsome passages from the Book of Satya for the rest of the afternoon was enough to squash his mood. Of course, being a steward was probably the dullest service he could imagine, but he had to trust that this diversion would bring him a step closer to finding his promising destiny. A destiny that he felt swirling around him like the breeze from the crack beyond the palace grounds.

The rani was the key to it all. *She has done so much for me. But why?*

That question poked at Sid's thoughts all afternoon and evening, and even that night after he made his tribute. He settled himself on his short pallet in his tiny room and thought about each time the rani had spoken to him, every favor she had granted. Despite his involvement in the kitchen theft, he hadn't been arrested. She had put him in her mother's room when he was hurt. She had granted his petition to allow Li to stay in the palace. On the journey to the Rock, she had encouraged him. And deep in the Western Woods, she had approached him in the first place.

Is this how destiny works? Mother, if you've had a hand in this, thank you. While falling asleep he promised himself he would tell the rani about the others soon.

A little before dawn, a recruit pounded on his door, and Sid jumped up already dressed. As soon as the boy told him he was to go to the central palace's terrace for training, he rushed there with hope renewed, remembering the woods witch telling him that one's destiny wasn't at the end of any journey but discovered somewhere along the way.

A mist held sway when he opened the old tower door leading to the terrace, and Sid paused there, trying to make out a table near the front wall, and the cloaked figure walking around it. *One of the captains, but which one? One thinks I'm a fool. The other would be very happy if I disappeared.* He decided the cloak was darker than the lightening sky. The night captain. His luck seemed to be holding.

Crossing the terrace, Sid pressed his palms together and bowed, hoping that Captain Duvanya didn't remember how he had embarrassed himself after the second shaking.

The captain showed him three blades lying on the table—a long, decorated talwar, a khanda, and a short talwar that reminded Sid of the set in the room where he had recuperated.

"Pick one," the captain said.

Sid picked up the khanda.

"Good choice. Not the longest and not the shortest. A khanda will serve you well in most situations."

Quiet and observant, Captain Duvanya was the opposite of Captain Gaddar, and, to Sid's mind, very un-noble-like. He wore his house insignia but had no other ornaments and spoke no more than necessary. Sid had heard day guards make comments that gave him the impression the night captain was rather dull.

Sid held the khanda out to his side at shoulder height as instructed. The captain watched him calmly while cleaning the talwar until Sid dropped his arm.

"I did not tell you to lower it," he said.

There was no reproach in the captain's words, but Sid felt thoroughly and uncomfortably seen. Raising the blade again, he held it straight out from his side, but after a few seconds his hand and arm began to shake. The captain put his hands on his hips and walked around him in a large circle. Sweat beaded on Sid's face, and he had to lower his arm.

"Use your other hand," the captain said.

Sid counted out the seconds this time. It was the arm still sore from his last visit to the jail, and he didn't last long.

The captain nodded as if he had expected this. "There is much to learn and unlearn when you take up blades," he said, "but there is little benefit from skill if you have no strength."

He told Sid to run around the terrace. This was followed by instructions for various stretches. While the captain cleaned the short talwar, he instructed Sid to bring the end of the table up to his chest as many times as he could. Ignoring his burning muscles, Sid tried different stances and grips each time he lifted the table. He trembled all over when the captain told him to stop.

"Let's see what your balance is like."

Sid took a breath and raised his arms above his head, balancing on one foot.

"No, hold the blade as you balance, but don't drop it on your head."

By this time, Sid almost wished Captain Gaddar was his instructor. If death was coming for him one way or the other, he'd choose the quicker route. Taking a breath, he held the khanda as long as he could in his good hand while fighting to keep his ankle and leg from trembling. His balance lasted for an embarrassingly brief number of seconds. He did the same on the other foot.

"You are learning the most important truth about being a defender," Captain Duvanya said, taking the blade from him. "You will need every bit of strength you can muster, then you will need to borrow your ancestors' strength. In the field or at the gates, you must keep going. If the ancestors haven't marked you, the only difference between those who survive an encounter and those who don't is your will and your skill."

Sid nodded slowly, beginning to appreciate how fortunate it was that he hadn't ridden off the Rock with the captain's father.

"Good. We will continue practice tomorrow."

"Sir, aren't there other recruits in this rotation?"

"Rotation? You're not on a rotation. The rani has commanded that I train you."

"Why?" Sid asked in a voice that was almost a whisper.

The captain shook his head. "I do not question the rani's commands, I follow them. As should you."

Part 4

CHAPTER 24

Greta knew that Master Avani would eventually present the hawk brooch to the rani. She knew that the rani would admire the ornament and tell him that it was not hers. This was the truth and not the truth at the same time, and knowing that her actions had set this conundrum into motion concerned the giantess. A word changed here or there, and the common language could make a starscape of the consequences. She was fascinated by this, but she also worried that she might upset Dear Child when she was so terribly fragile. Perhaps she was becoming less giant and more Ascaryan, which was exactly what she had accused Red of before he was exiled.

The morning Master Avani presented the rani with the brooch she had taken from the girl's clothes, it was the fourth day a blanket of yellowish clouds covered the Rock. If there was a note of concern in people's voices as they regarded it, Greta hardly noticed, because she had smelled sulfur and ash since the second shaking. It reminded her of the land where she had been born, where mountains opened and closed according to the degree of fire in their veins.

"A mountain burns in the east," she told the rani when she awakened.

The rani rose immediately, took the winter robe she offered, and wrapped herself in it as she went to the balcony. She frowned at the sky then told her guards to request Master Avani to come to her at once.

Sensing the rani's mood, Master Avani answered her questions about burning mountains and the possibility of fire in the grasslands in a reassuring manner. Only when she was appeased did he attempt to convince her, as the eastern envoy had suggested, that this was simply one more sign that they would benefit from a conference with the raja of Dyuvasa. Then he pulled the brooch from his pocket and presented it to her in his open palm.

304 | L.A. BARNITZ

"I've discovered a small decoration I think might belong to you, sister," he said. "I suspect it is of significant value."

Though no one would have seen any sign of it, and Greta remained perfectly still against the wall of the rani's outer room, she opened her giant-sense fully. She wasn't nervous. Giants didn't possess that strange Ascaryan state, but she was certain that everything rested on Dear Child's response.

The rani plucked up the brooch from Master Avani's palm and examined it. "This is very precious. It is a sacred object for the easterners."

Her voice was even but her surprise echoed in Greta's senses, and the giantess could not have missed it if a herd of horses had galloped through the room.

"Does it belong to you?" Master Avani asked.

She shook her head and looked away. "It was offered to me once, and I refused it. Where did you find it?"

Greta's focus shifted to the noble, who was most definitely nervous. He was the only Ascaryan she had trusted with her discovery because he was the only one besides the envoy who might possibly understand its importance.

"It was in the possession of one of the youth recently recruited," Master Avani answered. "How the urchin acquired it, I do not know, but the child did not know its value and easily gave it up."

"Was it with Sid Sol?"

"No, not him. One of the others."

The rani shook her head. "It must be returned to Tajazan as soon as possible." She put the brooch back into Master Avani's hand and closed his fist around it. "It belongs to him until his son is of age. Give it to Envoy Kanaka and tell him how you received it. He must understand that I was unaware of it until now, and it was not discovered here. I will inform Tajazan in my letter, but you must also communicate this to the envoy."

Later that morning, after the council meeting ended, Ascaryans outside the council room flowed around Greta like a school of minnows around a trout. The boy had answered Dear Child's questions well enough and had been dismissed. While the rani and her guards ascended the new tower staircase, the giantess remained in the gallery, assuring herself that Dear Child's breathing was steady.

Forcing her senses in the opposite direction, Greta still felt the boy's excitement proclaim itself like a beam of light in a smoke-filled room, though he had moved well beyond her sight; but Master Avani was the one she had to find. She listened until she found the rhythm of the old noble's heart, then lumbered toward the feasting hall.

Passing the door to Master Avani's chambers, Greta left through the door that opened to the narrow terrace around the barracks. She leaned against the wall next to a window and went giantstill. The occasional apprentice or junior guard who darted along the terrace hardly dared look at her, and she paid them no mind. She concentrated on the conversation taking place inside Master Avani's quarters.

"You have my deepest gratitude for returning this to me," Envoy Kanaka said, emotion thick in his voice. "This is not a ring of immense value, but I treasure it. I do not understand why you won't tell me how you found it."

Greta frowned. The brooch, not a ring, was the decoration Master Avani needed to show the envoy.

"I did not find it, good sir," the old noble answered. "All I can tell you is that the one who retrieved it has chosen to remain anonymous and requests no reward."

"How extraordinary! What humility! Or perhaps a guilty conscience?"

"I believe it was delivered in great sincerity."

"Whatever the motivation, I am glad for it," the envoy said. "It takes away the sting from my failures." He sighed. "Five moons have passed, and I still have not convinced Her Majesty of the importance of this conference!"

"Do not count failures yet," Master Avani said. "If it comforts you, know that I myself have been hard-pressed to engage our rani in a substantive discussion about recent events. I believe we should help one another where it does not contradict our leaders. It may prove fruitful to pause our efforts and listen to what is not said."

"What do you mean?"

"Wouldn't you agree that what truly matters and moves us to action is often invisible despite our formal practices?"

"Never a truer word, good master! I think sometimes we put far too much importance on protocol, though we cannot live without it either."

"I would like to ask you something that may help us identify the inspiration we need to convince the maharani of the urgency. Will you indulge me for a moment? I surmise that you were present in the court during our rani's short betrothal to Raja Tajazan. Isn't that right? You must have completed your training at that time."

I was there, too, Greta thought, recalling the moons spent in Dyuvasa when the rani was young.

"Yes, I was nervously awaiting my first assignment, but winter came in the eleventh moon that cycle with a howl and a bite. An unexpected storm was the reason your rani and her escorts were delayed for so long. Oh, I remember when our raja learned they had been blown off course. He sent trackers out as soon as he could, and his mother, Maharani Jalara, was mortified at the thought that your princess and Maharani Shikra might have met their deaths while lost in the mountains of our realm. Thankfully that was not the case, though it was a half-moon before we learned they were with the sor—with Lord Aiman. Thank goodness for the hawks. We were able to convey to Raja Basheer that they were safe and whole."

"Yes, yes, but when they reached to Garzekhara was there an obvious attraction between our princess and your raja?"

"Mind you, more than three moons passed before they arrived, so naturally their courtship was a bit awkward. Princess Sandhyatara conducted herself with decorum at all times, but to my eye, she wasn't immediately enthused about the betrothal. She missed programs created for her entertainment so often that the people began to talk and close their hearts against her. It was all a miscommunication of course, and slowly the raja drew her out.

"He spent hours with her in the gardens. She was so fond of his birds, all animals really. Did you know that black wolf bit me once? She used to carry it with her to all kinds of events."

"You were saying," Master Avani interjected, "that you thought our princess became receptive to your raja's attentions?"

"Yes, yes. After a moon, they seemed happy together. It was unfortunate that Raja Basheer's death obliged her to leave so abruptly. Some blamed the end of the engagement on her—young females consumed with jealousy, I daresay—but most understood the tragic circumstances. I never heard our raja express anything but the highest praise when he spoke of her. Ah well, the noble's life is always constrained by obligations, isn't it? For anyone versed in statecraft, it was obvious that she had to take up her father's mantle immediately and quash the villainy that had been unleashed."

"We had no idea how large a web the north had spun," Master Avani said. "War did not follow—thank the ancestors!—but her father's death was a severe test. Only now can we confidently write the story of how she held the realm together and increased our prosperity despite her tender age."

"She is a magnificent leader and blessed to have the loyalty of her brothers and sisters. I must tell you that, although I have been impressed with Maharani Sandhyatara from the day I first met her, my experience over these last moons has only compounded my deep respect for your traditions of governance."

Greta felt Master Avani's pleasure with the compliment, but he quickly took up his inquiry.

"Did you ever witness your raja presenting our maharani with any particular gifts during their engagement?"

"Nothing so unique that it stands in memory," Envoy Kanaka answered slowly. "At the public announcement there was the usual exchange of foods and small, symbolic gifts, and we partook of a delicious feast of roast changra, but I do not remember anything extraordinary. Our raja's feelings were clear to most of us then and afterward. You know that he didn't marry until many cycles after their betrothal ended. Why do you ask?"

Greta sensed Master Avani working a small object in his hand—the brooch she had given him.

"Have you ever seen this ornament before?"

The envoy's long pause would have informed anyone listening of his surprise. His voice dropped and took on the furtiveness of a conspirator.

"How do you have this? I hope you will not tell me that the same person who delivered my ring also gave this to you, because if that is the sequence of events, I will take back my words of gratitude and suggest that you have met a thief trying to gain your confidence!"

"That was not the circumstance," Master Avani said.

Greta wondered if the envoy could tell how the noble's answer slipped around the truth without embracing it.

"I believe this is an object of great value to your raja, one he would not have given away casually."

"Casually? Not only is the painting exquisite, a work of art by one of our masters, but this brooch is made of sacred bone. It is called Rupa Prajña. Our custom of venerating the ancestors is much like yours, but our rajas not only contribute a phalanx at death. They also name another bone they will sacrifice, and it is used to speak to their future generations. Only the raja or rani may hold these objects and never, to my knowledge, have they been passed to anyone outside the line of succession."

"Then you will appreciate our intention to return it to your raja."

"Are you saying you believe he gave it to Maharani Sandhyatara?"

"That is what I suspected," Master Avani said. "I showed it to the rani and asked her if it had been gifted to her. She said it had been offered but insisted that she had refused it. She agreed that I should send it to Tajazan as soon as possible."

"If that is so, Master, where has it been? Why all these questions?"

"I don't know where it was hidden, but it was not in the maharani's possession. I wished to consult with someone who had witnessed her short betrothal to better understand the circumstances when she left Dyuvasa."

"I want to trust your rani's word and yours, Master Avani, but this is…. Oh stars, this could be taken badly in court! How could I know every exchange she and our raja shared? You must tell me how this came into your possession. There will be an inquisition when this is presented!"

"Calm yourself. I cannot give you the details right now, but I will see that no blame falls upon you."

"What do you intend?"

"I intend to send your raja his ornament and my own letter explaining all the details that I have. I will also inform him that the rani will meet him at Osiara on the tenth day of the first moon. If your impressions and my impressions of their relationship are correct, we have the fuel necessary to achieve the goal we share—compelling our leaders to prepare for future disturbances."

Greta sensed Master Avani's excitement, yet he was still not speaking plainly of the interest they shared—the girl. She had to trust he had a reason.

"Oh my, she has agreed to the conference? Why didn't you tell me?" The envoy paused, then said. "One moment. You plan to send your own letter? Pardon me, but the raja may not accept it."

"I understand you can only present my unorthodox missive, and all depends on the raja's humor, but I assure you this is important. I'm asking you, Kanaka, to trust me."

"Won't the rani include the discovery of the Rupa Prajña and the invitation to Osiara in her missive?"

"I know you have observed that she is disturbed by a number of pressing issues. The truth is I have not yet convinced her of the necessity of agreeing to your raja's invitation to meet."

"What are you saying? You are promising a conference that she has not agreed to? Do you hold me in such poor esteem, good master? I cannot be party to such irregular activity!"

"If you are convinced that we may be facing a cataclysm as serious as Starfall, you and I cannot let this opportunity wither. You know as well as I that if Raja Tajazan doesn't leave Garzekhara by New Cycle Day, he will not leave it until at least the fourth moons. Are you comfortable with that? Four moons?"

There was a pause. Despite his confident words, everything Greta sensed from Master Avani was soaked in doubt.

"You are certain she wished the Rupa Prajña returned?" the envoy asked.

"She immediately recognized that it rightfully belongs to your raja and should be passed to his son."

"You, sir, are putting my career at great risk. How will you convince her to go to Osiara?"

"With honey. When she receives your raja's message expressing his appreciation for delivering this sacred object and the opportunity for a conference on expanding trade as well as discussing the shakings and celestial events, she will undertake the journey. If the rani's letter and mine are dispatched today, his response should reach here the day after the wedding as long as he sends a hawk."

"What expanded trade?"

"Hadn't you heard? Our sister, Madam Hansa, has developed new techniques in silk weaving and has material to gift to our dearest trading partner. Being eager to recoup the expenses of her wedding, the rani is keen to deliver those gifts as soon as possible."

"What? Why wasn't I informed?"

"Do not take offense. Madam Hansa won't present the silks to our rani until tomorrow."

"Master Avani, I am shocked! Such calculations! And your younger sister, too? My stars! I suppose I should thank you for revealing another aspect of your governance that I was blind to before."

"Would you have me forget it all? Will we wait four moons and try again?"

There was silence, then the envoy said, "I could be dismissed, or worse, if this plan collapses. If she does not go, how do you propose to save my reputation?"

"I am completely confident that she will go, but if not, Madam Hansa and I will be there, and we will vouch for your efforts to establish the meeting while we explain how disappointed the rani was to not be able to attend."

Greta heard the *tok* of a lacquered box being closed.

"All these details are fluff and stuff in comparison to the future of our realms, Kanaka. You and I must not fail."

Raising her face to the overcast sky, Greta drew her giantsense back. The rest of the exchange inside would be nothing but the polite Ascaryan chirping. She was satisfied the envoy would cooperate, at least for now, even if the rani would not. There was time to steer Dear Child toward a gentler mood, but the larger problems were waxing—both the moons and the girl—and even now it might be too late to change the consequences.

CHAPTER 25

The last moon of the cycle, the frost moon, had begun, and Lingli was sorely reminded that only ten days remained before her work had to be completed and she had to leave or face the rani's judgment. She was nearly done with the costumes, praise the stars, but she remained worried that the new tasks Madam had thrown to her were going to eat up any extra time she might have.

Another skirt panel of the wedding dress rested in her lap, its rich gold embroidery of tumbling stars nearly finished, though more panels remained, and the steward's coat Madam had asked her to refashion was already neatly folded on her cot. Why she had to worry about stewards was beyond her, but Lingli guessed that the coat must be for someone serving in the wedding after Madam told her it had to be decorated with far more detail. Her addition of rows of small silk squares outlined with tiny gold and silver beads on the collar and cuffs contrasted well with the blue jute silk, and she hoped it would please Madam as much as it did her.

For more than a week, brassy clouds had obscured the sky, but this night Matachand was a slim waxing crescent, and her light, combined with Chotabhai's, shone so brilliant Lingli could sew on the balcony without a lantern. The light did not cut the creeping cold, however, and every few minutes she pulled her cloak tighter and kneaded her stiff fingers.

While pacing around the room to warm herself, Lingli heard a small clang. From her balcony overlooking the central palace, she could just make out the night captain setting out the blades for Sid's practice on the terrace, which meant that dawn was close.

Watching Sid practice (and suffer) his exercises with the captain had been her best entertainment in the last week. Only the day before she had used the old staff in her room to imitate Sid's moves, which of course he would never acknowledge, though she knew he saw her.

She was chuckling to think of how annoyed he must have been when the captain turned back from where he had been waiting at the parapet and looked straight up at her. Embarrassed, Lingli dropped back into the shadows of her room.

A sudden notion of where Sid might be drove her to the other balcony where she could see a few bodies huddled in clumps on the feasting hall roof. *Oh, yes, he's that foolish.*

With little time before the palace awoke, Lingli pulled her hood up and hurried downstairs as fast as she could without drawing attention. Pausing outside the tower, she waited until the night guards passed around the corner of the feasting hall, then crossed the catwalk and made her way to the end of the terrace outside the barracks.

Using the short rope that hung from the roof's edge, she pulled herself up and crept over to where someone with dark curly hair was bunched up on his side, wrapped in a shawl.

They hadn't spoken since she had interrupted the thieves harassing him in the barracks. Afraid that he knew she had told Master Avani about them, she had avoided him as much as he had her, but whether he was mad about that or not, it was done, and she felt better even though no arrests had been made.

She bent down and shook Sid's shoulder.

"Leave me alone!" he growled and curled into a tighter ball.

When the other boys sleeping on the roof gave no sign of waking, she pushed Sid onto his back, tossed aside the crushed firewine skin he had made his pillow, and began dragging him across the roof by his feet. He kicked out at her.

"If I can see you from my room, how hard would it be for those thieves to find you?" she whispered.

"I haven't seen them for days," Sid said, sitting up and rubbing his face. "And I hate you, you know."

"I know."

"Inside of my mouth tastes like rotten eggs," he said.

"You need to drink some water."

"What I need is some firewine, or something…better."

"No time for that. Captain Duvanya is wondering where under the stars you could be."

She almost laughed as Sid lurched to his feet and made for the edge of the roof. It was a pleasure to see what a mess he was. She ran along with him back across the catwalk, both of them slowing down to a quick walk inside the old tower. When they reached the door to the terrace on the third floor, Sid waved farewell before jogging out to meet the captain.

Lingli returned to her room, happy that Sid seemed like his old self again. She put her elbows on the balcony rail and cupped her face in her hands, smiling at Sid's perpetual clumsiness as he began his exercises and admiring the palace walls' soft glow. A flock of green parrots flew overhead and plummeted toward the fort. Whatever her worries, she had to admit she would miss this beautiful place when she left. There was a squeak from the trapdoor behind her.

Thinking Madam had come early to collect the coat, Lingli went to the cot and held it up to check her work one more time. Such a pretty, pale blue. The coat reminded her of the tiny shoes in Red's trunk.

It was not Madam, but Greta who rose up through the trapdoor, entered her room, and stood next to the gate.

Still holding the coat up before her, Lingli suddenly had a thought that shook her. There were any number of reasons to doubt herself, but she had the feeling that she knew who would wear that coat, and the feeling grew stronger as she refolded it and took it to Greta.

"Who is this for?"

"Hmmm. A boy preparing to become a steward."

"He will be wearing it for a special occasion?"

"A small feast of nobles."

"But…" Lingli added slowly as she handed the coat to the giantess, "he won't be serving?"

Greta shook her head.

Like stones stacked up to make a wall, Lingli's thoughts fit together one upon the next. She finally understood who would wear this coat.

"Does he know who he is?" she asked softly.

"No."

"Have you always known?"

"From the day of his birth."

She considered this for a moment and nodded, barely able to sort the fountain of questions erupting within her. *Giants never lie.* "Then you knew he was given to Red? Why?"

Greta answered slowly. "To protect from enemies."

"And now the enemies are gone?"

"Enemies are more." With the coat tucked under one arm, Greta stepped back through the gate and pulled it closed behind her.

"The same enemies who killed Red?" Lingli half shouted this at the giantess in hopes of delaying her. Even in the dim light, she saw how Greta's eyes shone with hurt, but she would not let this pass. Questions pressed against her throat until she thought she would choke. Grasping the cage's bars, she couldn't decide what to ask first, there was so much, and the giantess could leave at any moment.

"I think you miss Red," she told Greta. "I miss him, too. All these days I wanted to ask you, but you would not speak to me. He was our... everything. If I had known what to do..."

Greta closed her eyes and started softly humming. Lingli felt her questions about Sid's fate, even Red's, peel away from the chaos within her, and she was left with the unyielding questions she had buried for so long.

She whispered, "Who left *me* there? Who am I?"

The giantess's eyes widened though the rest of her remained still as stone. The moment was not long, a breath or two, but Lingli would not forget it—the way Greta's throat moved when she swallowed, the heavy silence, the pulse ticking in her ugly temple, and the feeling of being watched, as if the room were crowded with spirits she could not see.

"You are the red giant's child. He was bonded to you," Greta said. "As true a father as you were a daughter."

And with that the giantess left. The trapdoor thudded into place, and Lingli pressed her head against the bars. Alone again.

Returning to her cot, Lingli's first thought was that Greta had been alarmed by her last question. Her second thought was that a drop of blood, just a quick needle prick, would help put her question back into that empty place within. She'd done that for as long as she could remember—driven the question away to hold down the hurt—but her heart fought her now.

She threaded a needle and examined the point.

Pulling whatever Greta knew about her past would no doubt take a great deal of time and effort, but Sid's past and his future were here now, and he would know it soon. *Will he ever speak to me again? He has no need of me anymore, if he ever had.*

Sitting atop a pile of costumes in the great hall later that day, Lingli did her best to focus on hems and buttons, but her thoughts were awash with plots for how she could collect sufficient provisions from the kitchens before she left the Rock. *I will not be made useless.*

As soon as the steward admitted the rani and Greta, Madam hurried to Lingli's pallet. "Leave your things and go," she whispered as the rani settled herself on her throne. "Master Avani has requested your assistance in the library."

Lingli tried to catch Greta's eye, but the giantess did not acknowledge her. Disappointed, she bowed quickly to the rani and Madam before hurrying from the hall. Master Avani met her at the door to the library.

"Welcome, Miss Tabaan. I am inviting you, on what promises to be a most auspicious day, to join service with me as a scribe. I know you have other duties for now, but Madam has allowed me some time to begin your training, and I hope you will find scribing more intriguing than arduous."

"Truly, sir?" Lingli's throat tightened. "What I mean is I'm grateful, sir…but there have still been no arrests and—"

"Rest assured," he said, "the true thieves will be discovered, and I am willing to risk the suspicions cast upon you in exchange for your help in the meantime."

Whatever his faith in the investigation, her plans to leave could not be abandoned, but it gratified Lingli to know that the old noble thought so highly of her.

Showing her to a bench at the long table in the center of the room, Master Avani brought with him a large book bound in leather with a brass clasp and set it before her.

"There is a section marked for you. Before you practice your handwriting, read what you can of this to yourself and note the unfamiliar words."

Lingli nodded and Master Avani returned to his table. On any other day she would have been excited to learn what stories waited within, but she could not stop thinking of what lay ahead for Sid. The words burned in the book's leather cover gave her further pause. *The Book of Duran.*

"Sir," she said, "Should I touch this book? I'm not of the Seven."

The old noble looked up from his table and frowned. "Not of the Seven?"

"These are the words of the ancestors, aren't they?"

"Hmmm, yes, they are," Master Avani said slowly. "I see your point, but these are also extraordinary times, dear girl. I am of the Seven and you have a vital skill. The rani gave me permission to read these records, and I give you my permission to read them, as I gave Sid permission, and that is all that is required. Set to it."

I must concentrate.

The first two pages listed names—who was whose son, daughter, father, mother, in the twelfth generation, but the third page was not composed of words but an illustration. Within it a group of Ascaryans were depicted cowering or running along the edge of a river under a sky filled with lightning. Balls of fire fell from the sky and trees and fields burned. In one corner, two tall figures wearing strange helmets observed the scene.

The entry underneath the drawing read, *The ground broke and the ancestors wept. Foreigners were boiled away in the River Vykan during the fourth moon. We received their bones. A host of demons caused the sky to scream.*

The drawing made her stomach hurt. She tried to quiet the anxiety building inside her. *I cannot change history. I cannot know the future. Today, I must simply read the words.*

As she turned to a section where a loose piece of parchment had been inserted between the pages, Sid entered the library.

"Yes, very good," Master Avani said, handing Sid a small stack of parchments. "We're all here together."

"Li's going to scribe for you, sir?" Sid asked, his brows scrunched together in a question as he sat on the bench across the table from her.

"I will be sorry to lose your talents, but you told me that you will be taking up other duties," Master Avani said. "Besides, Miss Tabaan will be in need of a new position very soon, and I am certain she will serve us very well."

"Are you joining defenses?" she asked Sid, fighting to keep her voice light. "Is that why you're learning blades?"

"Um, I'm training as a steward, for now," Sid answered, making a game effort to disguise his regret. "The rani recommended it so I can make myself ready for defenses training when Master Duvanya returns."

He doesn't know.

Certain that any self-doubt Sid possessed, however small, would wither under his pride once he knew what lay ahead, Lingli did not feel at all compelled to tell him.

Master Avani came to her side of the table and placed his hand on the book's open pages. "I think Sid can help us with the story I've chosen for your assignment. He's already learned it in an earlier exercise. Will you please tell the story of Saisenbhai, Sid? Hearing it may help Miss Tabaan glean the meaning of some difficult words she will read later."

With a small sigh, Sid got to his feet, ran his hand through his unruly hair and began narrating the story.

"Saisenbhai was a spare in the House of Duran—younger brother to Novaya, master of his house in the twelfth generation. Novaya fought in many campaigns, but Saisenbhai was small and walked with a limp. He preferred making tools and blades instead of fighting with them. His best work was a talwar he made for his brother—a beautiful blade with a jewel-encrusted hilt, and Novaya won many battles with it.

"One day, when they were battling vicious tribes from the north, Novaya lost his fight, and he was nearly killed. He managed to retrieve his blade, but his pride was hurt. In the camp that night Saisenbhai told him he should rest and let him fight in his place the next day, but Novaya sneered at him, and Saisenbhai was quiet."

As Sid warmed to his storytelling, Lingli thought of their falling out in the kitchens and tried to decide which of them was Novaya and which was Saisenbhai.

"The next morning," Sid said, "a scout reported that their enemies' chieftain had been killed in the night. This was good news, but no one knew who had vanquished him, and the chieftain's two sons vowed revenge. The battle resumed that day and again their forces lost ground. When Novaya returned to camp, Saisenbhai offered again to fight in his place, but Novaya cursed him, and Saisenbhai was quiet.

"One of the chieftain's sons was killed the next night," Sid said. "Duran's defenders whispered that a new champion had taken up their cause, which made Novaya even more angry and jealous of the attention this mysterious champion was receiving. Suspecting that this newcomer would try to slay the chieftain's remaining son, he crept into the son's tent that night and waited hidden until a cloaked figure entered and raised a talwar with a jeweled hilt over the son's bed. It was Novaya's own blade.

"As soon as the figure dealt the killing blow, Novaya took back his talwar and stabbed the assassin with it. When Novaya threw off the assassin's hood, he saw it was Saisenbhai.

"Saisenbhai said, 'When you needed rest, I took your burden, and it mattered not whether this blade was wielded by you or me. Tomorrow, when you face the field alone, you will know your heart was blinded, but do not grieve. I will send blessings from our starlit halls, for we remain brothers as we always were and will be forevermore.'

"Novaya fought for his brother's glory the next day and the battle was won, but his honor could never be restored. He broke his blade and fought no more."

Sid sat, and Master Avani said, "Well done, Sid. What is the meaning of this story?"

Sid shrugged. "Don't stab people if you don't know who they are?"

"Well, that is certainly one lesson," Master Avani said, but it was obviously not the answer he wanted.

When the old noble turned to Lingli, Sid called out, "Respect your brother!"

"Yes, that is it." Master Avani smiled wistfully. "We respect each other because the future of our houses depends on all our members' support, no matter what role we play. Do you understand?"

Master Avani turned to Lingli and added, "I think you would agree that Novaya had an excess of arrogance, but what did he lack?"

"Trust," Lingli said softly.

Master Avani nodded in approval. "Trust is vital. No matter our skills and talents, we accomplish very little alone in this world."

When the old noble returned to his table, Lingli began to read the marked section in the Book of Duran, which was the Saisenbhai story, and she copied the strange words she found there. Sid slowly transcribed the parchments given him until Master Avani's attention was deep into his pile of manuscripts. Then he kicked her under the table.

"Thank you," he whispered, "for, um, interrupting those fellows outside my room."

She gave a half nod and re-inked her pen.

"I told the rani. You don't have to worry about being arrested now."

"Have they been found?" Lingli whispered back, fixing him with her gray eyes. "Until they are, maybe you don't have to worry, but I do."

"What do you mean? They've already come after me. They don't even know who you are."

Lingli blotted her pen an excessive number of times. She took a breath and said, "I wish you the best on your next apprenticeship. I mean it."

She saw something within Sid relax and she knew he was glad she wasn't angry with him. That was some comfort. Enough to keep her promise to Red and stay true to Master Avani's lesson for the day. *Protect each other. Respect each other.*

Before long the library door opened again, and the guard informed Master Avani that the rani's servant had arrived.

"Already?" Master Avani asked, rising from his table as Greta entered.

The giantess looked briefly at her, then turned her baleful stare on Sid. Lingli felt her throat tighten.

"Come, Sid," the old noble said, beckoning him to his table. "I hope you will remember some of what you've learned here. Understanding our history is the closest we will ever be to our ancestors in this world. When the river of life carries you far from here, call upon these stories."

Master Avani's voice was full of emotion, making it sound as though he was bidding Sid farewell for a long journey, which in a way he was, Lingli thought. Sid looked confused.

"Go on, then. Greta will escort you to your next assignment."

Sid bowed quickly to the old noble, then raised his chin toward her in a hasty goodbye.

When the door closed behind Sid and Greta, Lingli put the Book of

Duran on Master Avani's table and mumbled some excuse about needing to return to her stitching. The old noble asked her what was the matter, and she blurted out, "Sid is the rani's son, isn't he?"

Master Avani closed his eyes for a moment and nodded. "The rani plans to make the announcement tonight."

She gave him a questioning, miserable look.

He said gently, "Young Sid doesn't always appreciate what you and, dare I say, what many others have done for him, but give him time. I am certain he will not forsake you."

Forsake me? Perhaps not, but he will forget me. How could it be otherwise? The rani and every Ascaryan he meets will have their demands. The life he's always imagined for himself will be as full as a river in flood.

Lingli left the library feeling very alone. Her presence in the palace was barely tolerated and, for all his kindness, she couldn't imagine that Master Avani would cross the rani's orders if she chose to prosecute or exile her. No one seemed to understand what she saw so clearly. Though Sid would no longer need her, she still needed him.

CHAPTER 26

Greta showed Sid into his former sick room, where a pale blue coat lay on the bedcovers next to a white silk kurta and pants. Running a finger over the beads lining the collar, Sid thought it was the most handsome coat he had ever seen.

"Am I to wear this?" he asked Greta.

"Hmmm, yes." She set a pair of pale leather juttis with curved toes on the floor at the end of the bed and took the coat away from him. "Bathe first."

In the bathing room Sid thanked Afsana for this new opportunity, ignoring a little twinge in his stomach. If good fortune had found him once again, should he worry about why? To do so would only release the fears that he had tried hard to banish. From the dull, constant worry of not knowing his ancestors, to the pain that had lanced him the day Red cried out, to the terror of the night he drank from the cask, and they beat him senseless at the Nobles' Walk, sometimes Sid felt half his life had gone to trying to overcome fear.

He left the bathing room better dressed than he had ever been before.

Greta looked him up and down and asked, "Where is your kufi?"

As soon as he retrieved his cap from the inner pocket of his old kurta, Greta plucked it from his hands and pinned it on his head.

Doubting this was how most stewards began their service, Sid frowned at her, but the kufi was one familiar thing and it pleased him.

"Are you taking me to training?" he asked.

"Hmmm. Taking you to a dinner."

Well, that didn't sound bad. Stewards were expected to learn how to direct the bearers and introduce guests at nobles' events.

The sun cast its last rays through the room's narrow window as Greta moved to the altar table to light the diyas and a lantern, then she shooed him ahead of her to the door.

Practically prancing across the terrace in the handsome coat and juttis, Sid was excited to see a tent covering a large swath of it, complete with carpets and countless lanterns hung about the outside. Musicians played softly, and Korvar and his staff assembled the food under a canopy nearby. Sid resolved to offer the chef the apology he had meant to deliver since the night of the theft, but he hesitated when he caught Shankar's eye. The boy looked almost frightened by the sight of him.

Greta clamped a huge hand on his shoulder and turned him toward the entrance of the tent.

Master Avani and Madam Hansa and her husband were approaching the tent also. Behind them were Captain Duvanya and his mother, and next came Madam Satya and an old man wearing the wheel of the House of Tilan. *Crowseye's father, I'll bet.* Behind the old man, and much to Sid's distress, Vidkun followed. He looked down his nose at Sid as he passed.

All of the Seven? Sid's throat went dry.

Greta prodded him inside and indicated he should sit near the center of the table at the back, flanked by long tables on each side.

"It will be fine, my boy," said Master Avani, as he joined him, "but don't speak to the guests until you are introduced."

"Introduced?" Sid rasped, unable to grasp why he was sitting and wrestling with a mounting wave of anxiety.

Southerners began to enter the tent—Ameer Ali and his wife, Ameer Khush and his two wives, and Ameer Temer of the House of Idris. Next came Princess Mafala and Prince Hassan with two elders who he guessed were their parents—Aza Mussan and Azi Kebedi. At the end of the procession was Envoy Kanaka.

Korvar's staff served drinks to all, but Sid could drink nothing with Vidkun staring at him through narrowed eyes.

"Masterji, what is happening?" he whispered to Master Avani. "Why am I here?"

"You will understand soon."

All rose and bowed to the rani when she arrived. Dressed in a plum-colored silk sari with a golden pallu and laden with ornaments and a golden tiara, the lantern light danced over her. After welcoming her guests, she suggested they eat dinner before she shared news of the festivities planned for New Cycle Day. To Sid's shock, she settled herself in the chair to his left and Greta took her post behind them.

The rani turned toward him, smiled gently, and whispered, "Do not worry. All of this is the will of the ancestors. I will explain everything."

Bowls of soup appeared before all the guests and were whisked away again as each one finished. When Filant approached him, his eyes asking permission to take his untouched bowl, Sid nodded and drained his second cup of firewine. Master Avani bumped his leg.

"For the sun's sake, eat a piece of naan at least!"

He tried. Then he pretended to eat the fried venison and chana served in the first small thalis so he could avoid the looks being cast his way. Mafala's eyes were like daggers, and, on the rani's other side, Prince Hassan's jaw pulsed so hard as he chewed that Sid felt sure he would break a tooth. Among the Seven, Madam Hansa worried him the most. She sat tall and stiff in her seat. When she wasn't staring at him, her eyes swept over the southern guests and kept returning to the tent entrance, as if she was plotting an escape. And then there was Vidkun, sitting far down one of the tables, hovering at the corner of Sid's sight like a dark cloud.

By the time the second thalis were served with koftas swimming in rich curry, bitter gourd and brinjal, and more hot naan, Sid couldn't decide if this was some elaborate joke being played at his expense, or if he was dreaming. Neither explanation seemed right, but the faint scent of opportunity, which he rarely missed, was also just too fantastic to trust.

The rani seemed happy, but she said nothing more to him and paid no mind to the confusion he was certain was painted on his face. Whatever was coming, she knew of it and held its reins.

Calm down. She has been the key to everything from the moment you saw her. Echoing this thought, he heard Red say, *There is nothing stranger in the world than you. Trust that and find courage.*

At last, the rani signaled Korvar. The musicians quieted and the bearers withdrew. When the rani rose to her feet, all followed.

"In less than half a moon," the rani announced, "the Seven and four noble houses of Avakstan will be joined in a historic agreement to open trade in both realms. This is a peaceful expansion of our existing cooperative arrangements that was my father's dream many cycles ago, and now it is mine to bring into being. There have been setbacks, yes, but Raja Basheer was right. Our realms are better served by sharing some resources and making fair trades for others. On New Cycle Day, we will celebrate this joint agreement, and I and Ba Hassan of the House of Hudulfah will formalize our union through marriage."

The rani extended her drink toward the prince consort. "Venerated for his foresight and wisdom, Ba Hassan is admired by not only by his people but other bold houses of the south. I am certain these are qualities he inherited from his esteemed parents and ancestors. Let us toast to the prince's good counsel and welcome him as the soon-to-be lord and regent of Nilampur!"

Like the rest of the guests, Sid raised his glass to the prince and drank. Because the rani remained standing, everyone else did the same.

"There have been so many fruitful endeavors between our houses, I sometimes lose count," the rani said. "But the most important product of all is maintaining our connection to the ancestors and the descendants—both ends of time shape our present lives. Ba Hassan has paid tribute to my ancestors on the summit, and I have paid tribute to his at his house's altar. In Nilampur, which I invite all of you to visit, you will see the beautiful temple we have built for the veneration of ancestors from both realms. As for the descendants, one small blessing is already here."

The nurse, dressed in a fine-spun Hudulfah gown and looking very pretty, entered the tent carrying Prince Aseem. The rani took the babe into her arms and kissed his cheek.

"See our son, Aseem! Proof our union will see the future and bring honor to both houses!" She raised her glass, and all joined the toast.

Sid darted looks at Mafala and Hassan. *All these nice words, and they're still angry?*

"If the weight of our mighty houses seems too much for such a small boy," the rani continued, "be assured that there is another who will share the burden." She turned to Sid and placed her hand on his shoulder. "My firstborn son, Siddharth—my heir and the heir of his father, Ba Zakir of the House of Hudulfah."

CHAPTER 27

Sid looked out at the faces focused upon him, not completely certain of what the rani said after the word 'son,' and it was clear that the guests' shock was nearly as great as his. Crowseye's father covered his mouth and puffed out his cheeks, Ameer Khush's eyebrows were raised near to the top of his head, and Vidkun's mouth hung open. Time slowed and stretched.

Either she is playing some elaborate joke, or it's true.

No one acknowledged the joke.

Sid was acutely aware that he was weaving on his feet, but another part of him became wary and kept himself upright.

Hassan and Mafala appeared to be moonstruck. Their father, Aza Mussan, showed no reaction Sid could determine, but their mother, Azi Kebedi leaned forward, waiting to be recognized. When the room settled, the rani nodded to her.

"You have honored our house with one new son, Maharani Daughter Valena Sandhyatara. How can it be that there are two? This boy is a stranger to us. If he is Zakir's son and heir, where has he been? Who was witness to his childhood?"

Feeling a little sick from the weight of Azi Kebedi's questions, which added to the many unspoken ones he felt bearing down upon him, Sid's eyes slid to the rani. *Yes, who knew I was Zakir's son? Who knew I was your son? Why didn't you tell me?*

"Your questions are wise, Azi Mother Kebedi," the rani answered. "As I know Zakir informed you, he and I put Siddharth in the custody of a guardian to avoid the threats that surrounded us when he was a young child. Unfortunately, Zakir is no more, nor is the guardian."

Red. Did he know? Sid's thoughts were as scattered as frightened birds.

"It is only in this cycle that I dared retrieve our son. And only tonight, in this good and safe company, that I dared make this revelation. I do not expect you to take my word alone. There should be no doubt in anyone's mind, least of all yours. I ask for demi-mukera."

The guests looked at one another, unsure. Sid could feel his stomach twisting into a knot.

"You won't need that kufi anymore," the rani told him. "Take it off."

Sid did so, reluctantly, and left Li's cap on his seat. Handing Aseem to Master Avani, the rani ushered him to the center of the tent where they met Azi Kebedi and Princess Mafala. Unsure what he should do, Sid chose graciousness. He bowed low to this southern elder who claimed to be his grandmother, then he bowed to Mafala. Azi Kebedi smiled. Mafala did not.

The Hudulfah elder's face was a web of fine lines in a warm brown face, and her long braids were woven with brass ornaments and charms similar to the rani's driver. From somewhere in her dress, she produced a small pot and opened it to reveal a powder sprinkled with dark mineral. Putting some of the mixture into one palm, she touched her fingertips to her forehead, plucked a few hairs from his head, and began to chant.

She closed her fist holding the powder and his hair. Rolling her wrist and opening her hand again, a green fire burned upon it. As she cupped both hands around the flames, those at the tables leaned forward to see.

Sid looked to the rani, and she nodded as if to reassure him—just as Azi Kebedi clamped her palms on either side of his face. He gasped, registering heat and the pain of burning flesh for an instant, then the sensation was gone. Pale smoke roiled from under the Hudulfah elder's hands as her chant continued. Sid's worries bloomed. This was much too similar to the long-ago day the woods witch had studied a cloud of smoke over his head.

The smoke grew and churned throughout the tent—a sight that greatly interested the Hudulfah women and the rani until it dissipated. Sid feared he might sneeze.

"This boy is of Zakir's blood," Azi Kebedi loudly announced. "Do you agree, Bi Daughter?"

Mafala nodded in miserable agreement, and most of those in the tent seemed relieved, though Sid felt more scorched by Prince Hassan's look of disgust than he had by the fire that had touched him.

There was another moment of silence—this one seemingly more calculating, less shocked. Sid noticed the rani and Madam Hansa watching their southern guests closely.

The tension in the tent was becoming uncomfortable, then Ameer Ali burst out cheerfully, "If there are no more surprises, dear Maharani Sandhyatara, may I offer a toast? I have known the leaders of both these venerable houses my entire life. From my uncle, the honorable Aza Mussan, I learned what it means to rule a house and protect people. From the honorable Raja Basheer, I learned how to ride and much of all the rest that I know. The joining of these houses, now doubly bound, brings joy to my heart. Congratulations to the bride and groom, and welcome to both of their sons. May our realms prosper!"

Everyone drank to that.

The guests said little afterward and soon dispersed. Master Avani was the last to leave him and the rani.

"Do not think that your title excuses you from a scribe's work, Prince Siddharth," the old noble said, smiling. "There will be much to learn from the books of your house, and I expect my sister will set you to transcribing bits for me very soon."

Siddharth? I think I like it.

The rani offered her arm when they were alone.

"I wish I could have told you before tonight," she said, "but it was safer for you this way."

Sid did not understand why, and he added this to the vast sea of ignorance he was floating in. By the time they reached the quarters where he had dressed earlier, he realized he was exhausted. He leaned against a bedpost, while Greta set about removing the shrouds from the furniture and the rani made a brief tribute at the shrine. She seemed pleased to have him once more ensconced under the watchful gaze of her father's effigy and her mother's spirit made manifest by the braid of hair. When she declared these would be his permanent rooms, Sid thanked her, but he was already contemplating turning the raja doll's face away from the bed.

"I wish you could have known Father," she said. "And Mother would have scolded you much as she did me, but she would have welcomed you, too."

"If the ancestors are always watching us," Sid said, reaching for his last reserves of energy. "I'm glad I now know to whom I should give a proper tribute."

"There is so much to share with you," she said, "but much must be accomplished in what remains of this cycle and even more in the next, and the river of life waits for no one. I would grant you one question before we begin our duties tomorrow. What shall it be?"

"One question?" Sid took a breath, unsure how to choose among the questions that had piled up in his mind. Finally he asked, "Who is Zakir?"

The rani laughed. "Clever! To ask a single question that requires half a moon to answer."

She set Aseem on the bed and put a finger to her lips, considering her answer. "Imagine a young man, two hands taller than me, who looks something like a younger Aza Mussan but with Azi Kebedi's coloring," she said. "He is muscular, with broad shoulders and a winsome smile, but his best quality is the respect he commands from his people."

She looked out the room's window, her gaze sunk in memory. "Imagine he is standing atop the palace gate tower, looking over the fort with Ameer Ali at his side. The sun is nearly gone, and his eyes are the brightest lights there. That is how I first saw him."

She seemed so unguarded, Sid felt embarrassed. He wondered if he should comfort her, but she resumed her story.

"Our relations with the south were not strong then. We had negotiated for peace and made some small exchanges with Kirdun only, until Zakir came. Father said he was the first to understand his vision for cooperation between our houses, and they spent weeks developing the first large trade agreement. I was timid and hardly dared speak to this prince from the south, though he made efforts to ask my opinions and include me when I intruded upon their discussions.

"After your father returned to the south, the palace seemed lonely. His absence pained me, but I had duties to fulfill." The rani sighed. "It was cycles before we met again. When he finally arrived on the front grounds, bringing wagons of cotton, trunks of rough sapphires, and other goods, my father was already among the stars, but I knew Father's mind and his plans for Saatkulom better than anyone. I saw that Zakir could help me achieve them. When the prince of Hudulfah asked for my hand, I gladly gave it."

Sid wished she would go on. Every word felt like a sip of water for a thirst that had been with him for his entire life, but Aseem was already drifting to sleep on the blanket next to him, and he noticed redness in the rani's eyes and how she hugged herself as if she was cold.

"Your father was my sun and moon, and you were his."

"He's...dead?"

She nodded. "You have no idea how much I wish he was with us to teach you all you should know, but my tutelage will have to serve. Rest now. There will be time to learn more about your father, but beginning tomorrow you will accompany me and others of the Seven so that you can learn all that is important to the realm." She squeezed his arm. "This is no apprenticeship and no dream. Destiny is one part fate, one part courage, and eight parts duty. This is yours, determined by the ancestors—your father and I among them."

The next morning Sid's great good fortune still spun in his head like a coin thrown on a bet. How many times had Red and Li hinted, or outright argued, that he was too sure of his destiny and too much a dreamer? How many times had he doubted himself? But here he was, awake, not dreaming. He was a prince now, and everything seemed possible.

After a sharp rap, Sid heard the door of the outer room open. Filant soon appeared, made a quick bob of a bow, and set a thali on the bedside table.

"May I bring you anything else, Prince Siddharth?"

"C'mon, Filant," Sid said. "You know me."

"Of course, Prince, but you know Korvarji's rules."

"I won't tell him."

"Thank you, Prince."

Sid said nothing else. He knew that tone. It was the one all the bearers used when they served nobles they didn't like. Filant had bullied him a bit, just as he did all the bearers, but now it felt as though a door between them had closed. Filant was on the side of the kitchens, a place bursting with noise and food—and friends—while he was here in grand quarters, alone.

Sid ate quickly and donned the silk kurta and pants and the wool ach-kan Greta had set out for him the night before. His old kufi was there as well, and Sid stuffed it under a pillow on his bed.

On his way to meet the rani, staff and guests in the corridors bowed their heads as he passed. *This is better.*

Soaking in the sunlight that streamed into the gallery, Sid tried to guess what the day would bring, and it made him giddy. Yet the voice in his head that always sounded like Li argued, *No resting on her name. You haven't earned any of this.*

When he was admitted to the rani's quarters, Greta stared down at him with the utter lack of expression giants usually wore. He felt judged all the same. The rani came to him, smiling broadly, her mango-colored lehenga shining like the sun.

"Good morning, Prince Siddharth. I was about to send a guard to find you. Did you eat? Come, join us."

The first thing he had planned to ask his mother was why she had left him in the woods for cycles, but Madam Satya, the eldest of the Seven, waited at the rani's work table. Trying to look intelligent, Sid understood that he would have to wear a prince's public face for now and pretend he had the right to be in the confidence of these two leaders of Saatkulom even if he didn't feel it. His stomach hurt.

"We are reviewing petitions that will be heard in court this week," the rani told him, her tone crisp. "A good first lesson in the business of the realm."

Though Madam Satya was more plainly dressed and silver-haired, there was nothing frail about her. Petitioners sometimes withered under her questioning in court, and Sid was quite certain he did not want to bring such scrutiny upon himself.

Tapping an open parchment on the table, Madam Satya told the rani, "We need to conclude these matters before the next cycle, particularly the amendment to taxation. This petition addresses the fort, but if we can settle the main question, it will support our position in the Nilampur contract."

"Very good," the rani said. "We should begin negotiating in earnest by the end of this week.

"Have you considered who will lead the negotiators?"

"You and I will address first principles. Brother Ketan should handle the property details and we will bring Krux into the taxation matters. There may also be a place for Prince Siddharth," the rani added brightly. "Perhaps as liaison between our realms?"

Liaison?

Madam Satya seemed less enthused. "He is well-placed to broker trust between us and the House of Hudulfah, if not the others, but he has not had instruction in first principles, much less this contract's intricacies."

"We have time to prepare him to convey our interests, if you will assist."

"Where better to begin than to have him learn what guides our decisions on these petitions?"

Seeing the pleased look on the rani's face, Sid decided to count this as an opportunity. He asked, "What are the first principles?"

Smiling for the first time, Madam Satya answered, "The first principle is respect the law."

"The second principle," the rani said, "is respect the law."

"And the third principle," Madam Satya said, "is respect the law."

After promising to tutor him, Madam Satya left, and the rani showed him to the divan. She sat next to him and asked him to read aloud from the petitions. Occasionally, she interrupted to explain laws and penalties as well as events that had shaped the Seven's decisions on important matters. Unfortunately, her lessons were mostly lost under the deluge of questions and inner conversation loudly racing around Sid's mind.

How could I not know she was my mother from that first day? She smells of jasmine, horses, and…something else. How did she find me? Why did she leave me with Red? Why didn't she tell me who I was when we met?

Hearing very little of what the rani said, Sid didn't dare ask anything, but he nodded along. At some point he realized she was speaking as though *he* was going to rule the realm one day, which of course he was, and this added a low drumbeat of terror to his thoughts. As she went on explaining details within the petitions, the idea of being prince began to look much more complicated than he had thought.

"All these laws and decisions," he said, clearing his throat. "How do you know what to do?"

"When the solution is not plain, seek and respect knowledge," the rani answered, seemingly pleased with the question. "Gather it from others, from the books, from experience. Examine the challenge from all sides and listen very carefully to what the Seven and the ancestors tell you."

"But I don't know anything. I mean, of course I can learn, but what if it's the wrong decision?"

"It may be," she said. "We are imperfect, but you cannot allow indecision to become your decision. The river of life runs one way. The only way forward is forward."

To hear his own maxim caught his attention. *That's what the woods witch always said.*

The door guard knocked and Greta allowed him in, accompanied by an elderly southerner who spoke the common tongue and informed the rani that the new prince was invited to share the next meal with the House of Hudulfah. When they departed, the rani closed her eyes for a moment and patted the neck chains that were tucked into her blouse.

"Very well," she muttered as she got to her feet. "Greta, fetch the gifts."

Looking him over from head to foot, the rani said, "They've acknowledged you already, but you must not give offense. When you enter, go to Aza Mussan first, bow, and do not rise until he tells you to."

"Aren't you coming?"

She shook her head and said with a wry smile, "My presence has not been requested. This is a meeting of those with shared blood." She fastened the topmost hook of his achkan. "Answer their questions truthfully and ignore any criticism leveled at you or me. Can you do that?"

Clear that he had no choice in the matter, Sid nodded, and Greta returned with four small gifts wrapped in blue cloth. The rani explained, "Moonstone bracelets for Azi Kebedi and Bi Mafala. Brooches with sapphire for Aza Mussan and Ba Hassan."

The giantess already had her hand upon the door, and the rani herded him toward it.

"Remember what they say and do," she told him. "You will tell me everything tonight."

And with that he was turned out onto the landing. He hurried to keep up with Greta stomping toward the stairs.

My first duty as prince—a combination of good guest and spy. Don't mess this up. I wonder what they eat?

When they reached Aza Mussan's guest quarters, the southern door guard hardly looked at him but tensed at the sight of Greta. Sid told the giantess to wait outside. But when he was announced and entered the quarters, he heard her following.

Stars! Stupid giants.

Azi Kebedi, Mafala, and Hassan flanked his stern-faced grandfather and silently stared as he entered. Awkwardly clutching the gifts to his chest, Sid bowed and was prone so long he was becoming dizzy from the blood running to his head before his grandfather said something that Sid took as permission to rise.

Prince Hassan said stiffly, "We are greatly pleased the ancestors guided you to us, Ba Siddharth Nephew."

The prince's face reflected no such great pleasure. Azi Kebedi smiled at him, but Aza Mussan's face remained as expressive as a piece of slate, and if Mafala had possessed a blade, he would have run away. Greta's presence no longer seemed an imposition.

Sid stammered, "Thank you for inviting me today. I have some… Please accept these gifts."

Mafala received the gifts, sniffed, and said, "What about Aseem? Surely he is just as worthy?"

This was followed by a rapid stream of words in their language by his grandmother and a stern look of disapproval. Color climbed in Mafala's cheeks as she lowered her gaze and took the gifts to another room.

Inviting Sid to sit next to her at a low table laden with dishes unfamiliar to him, Azi Kebedi asked straight away what he knew about his father.

"The rani told me he commanded the respect of his people," Sid answered slowly.

"Yes, Zakir was a strong leader, and the joy of my heart," Azi Kebedi said. "Did she tell you that he found his first oasis when he was twelve cycles old? That he killed his first raider at thirteen? That the contract he wrote for my esteemed husband—the first with Saatkulom—created trade that fed twelve hundred house members for a dry winter?"

Her pride in her departed son appeared sincere, and Sid hoped she would be pleased with him by extension, but even with this reassurance he could not bring himself to look at his uncle and aunt. Nor did he care for the way his grandfather tapped his yellowed nails on the tabletop while Azi Kebedi shared tales of his father's exploits.

Once served, they commenced eating in silence, which made Sid no more comfortable, but it was to be expected. Everyone knew that food was so precious in the south it was their custom to savor every bite, and speaking while eating was considered an affront to the ancestors. Sid chewed slowly and occasionally glanced at his grandmother's thali to make sure he did not outpace her.

When tea was served Aza Mussan at last muttered something in his language.

"He is asking what your birth date is," Azi Kebedi said.

"Um, the fourteenth day of the seventh moon. The solstice," Sid answered. "That is what the...what my guardian told me. The rani will know for certain."

Mafala emitted an amused laugh into her teacup.

"Yes, she will surely know," Azi Kebedi said, banishing the stunned look on her face before translating for Aza Mussan.

Aza Mussan then uttered something to Hassan in their language. The prince consort answered him, his hooded eyes grazing Sid as he spoke.

"You performed so well," Azi Kebedi told Hassan. "Perhaps you should be the one to train him."

"It would be my pleasure," Hassan answered, staring at Sid with all the warmth of a serpent sizing up a chick fallen from the nest. "A fitting tribute to my dear brother."

Whatever it was they meant, Sid sensed that Hassan did not share his mother's enthusiasm for Zakir.

"How far can you run?" Hassan asked. "A league?"

"Well, I don't know. I haven't measured it."

"What about water-tapping?"

Sid shook his head.

"Ah, I see. You have probably not learned how to treat wounds from our flora, or, ancestors forbid, a goyra bite? Have you ever traveled the desert?"

"I, uh. No."

"Of course he has not," Azi Kebedi interjected. "He has been in hiding for most of his cycles. How he performs the Sabirgazi will depend on your skills as a trainer, my son."

"We will begin on the second day of the coming cycle," Hassan told him. "You may wish to start petitioning the ancestors for strength from today."

Azi Kebedi told the servant to refill Sid's cup and said lightly, "This is a challenging time for the maharani, isn't it? So many obligations before New Cycle Day, including a campaign far away. Did you know we have more than two hundred youth pledged to your mother's fight in Zahatara?"

"I didn't know," Sid admitted.

"She has not informed you of the campaign?"

"Well...um, I know of it, generally, but this is my first day. As prince."

"Of course." His grandmother's eyes sparkled in a web of wrinkles.

Aza Mussan pushed his chair back from the table, and the others stood with him, so Sid did as well.

A servant appeared next to Mafala, her arms full of gifts. "Please accept these simple gifts from our noble house," Mafala said, her face cold with disdain. "Welcome to the House of Hudulfah, Ba Nephew."

Bowing deeply to each of them and not waiting for Aza Mussan's permission to rise, Sid eagerly followed Greta to the door, but his grandmother bid him to wait. She presented him with another gift, a golden sun brooch. As she pinned it to his shoulder, Sid reached up to pat the ornament, and Azi Kebedi made a sound of surprise. She took his hand and pushed his sleeve back, examining the bracelet Li had given him.

"Where did you get this?"

Sid stuttered, embarrassed that he had ever believed Afsana was his mother but not yet ready to stop seeking her protection. "I think my guardian kept it for me."

"This is besari grass," Azi Kebedi said, running a finger over the bracelet's weave. "I made it for Zakir when he was a child." She squeezed his arm then let him go. "Keep it with you always. It will guide Zakir's spirit and mine to you and protect you from the otherworld."

A gift from my father. Sid's heart lifted again.

The Hudulfah servant followed them back to the rani's quarters and set the gifts on the small mountain of others that had appeared over the course of the day.

After Sid related the meeting and subjects of conversation, the rani laughed.

"Perhaps now you understand why I asked for demi-mukera. My dear consort would love nothing more than to prove you are not Zakir's son."

"I...don't understand. Why?"

She looked at him with some surprise, then said, "You are my firstborn son, which makes you heir to the ruling house of Saatkulom, not Aseem."

He hadn't thought about what his naming would mean for the baby prince. Now Aseem was a spare. Recalling Parth's bitterness about the fate of the later-born and Mafala's question about the gifts, he wondered whether the rani had deliberately withheld giving him a gift for his half brother.

"And you are the son of Zakir, Aza Mussan's firstborn son," the rani prompted. "That makes you what?"

"Heir to the House of Hudulfah," Sid said slowly, feeling as if he had eaten something that didn't agree with him.

"Yes, and a great inconvenience to your uncle, who believes himself to be not only the leader of his house, but of an alliance of southern houses. An alliance that may fray if the other ameers believe him weakened."

"I didn't...know," Sid stammered. "I mean, I didn't intend to..."

The rani shook her head and touched his cheek gently. "Do not apologize. This is not your fault, but it is your destiny. Do you understand?"

He hadn't counted on enemies. However his destiny unfolded, it seemed he would need protection from his uncle far more than from the otherworld.

CHAPTER 28

Maybe someone had poked at Madam Sayed's pride that morning or maybe her anxiety about the pending wedding was simply getting the better of her, but whatever the reason, dance practice had begun poorly and gotten worse. Madam's expectation that the senior dancers would give their undivided attention to their performance was shattering into pieces. Observing the dance teacher's jaw clench harder each time she demanded the dancers repeat a sequence, Lingli decided to keep her eyes on her work. The dancers, however, had no sense of danger and continued to make mistakes with a regularity that seemed almost purposeful.

Then the pudgy Hansa girl suddenly forgot her steps and the other girls bunched up around her, completely throwing the dance into confusion. Madam shouted at all of them to get off the platform, and a few of the girls who imagined themselves better dancers whispered and laughed behind their hands as they slinked away from the crying girl like cats who drank the cream. A Hansa boy, enraged at the mocking of his cousin, shoved one of them, and that girl did not simply trip, but fell with a dramatic cry followed by much wincing and sniffling.

"Enough!" Madam shrieked. "Out. All of you, and don't show your faces here again unless you intend to take your meager skills seriously. Tomorrow we'll let the rani decide whether you should continue or be replaced by the zhoukoo."

An idle threat, Lingli was certain, but the dancers scattered, and she and the musicians were quiet. While Madam composed herself, Lingli finished the last stitches in Princess Mafala's heavy raw silk gown.

When Madam came to dismiss her, Lingli held the dress up by its shoulders and awaited her inspection. *She'll find no great flaws, but that won't stop her from complaining about something.*

Not that Lingli resented her. The good lady had helped her a great deal, but reworking sleeves or necklines for no good reason was not something she looked forward to—not when she had to give Master Avani any hours as she could spare, and she still had two panels of embroidery to finish on the rani's gown. *And supplies to collect, too.*

So far, she had packed a blanket fashioned from scraps of material. A short coat Madam had claimed no longer fit her. A discarded clay cup. Salt and a small cooking pot were the next items she was seeking. *I should trade something with Korvarji and ask him for some dried foods.*

Madam hardly looked at the dress before saying, "The princess won't be able to refuse it, even if it is the wrong color."

After refolding the dress, Lingli wrapped it in a clean cloth and left with it. As she walked along the gallery toward the new tower, she saw the rani and Sid, followed by Greta, coming her way. Having only seen him from afar in the days since he had been named prince, she hadn't yet offered her congratulations. Sid smiled as he approached, his face shining with happiness, and she stopped in the middle of the passage. But there was a glitch in his step as the rani leaned close and said something to him. When he looked forward again, he stared past her.

What's wrong with him? He's gotten everything he ever wanted.

The rani, however, did not look away. Feeling the heat of her stare, Lingli's gaze fell to her feet and she walked on.

At Princess Mafala's quarters, Lingli informed the guard that she had come to deliver a parcel. He told her to wait, and she practiced her denial of any knowledge of a missing ring, should the princess ask. After some time, Ameer Ali and Mafala emerged from her quarters.

"Thank you for the invitation," the ameer said. "I'm star-blessed to have your advice on these details. We all are."

"Please tell my brother that," Mafala said with a small laugh.

"Your leadership will also be critical in the days to come," the ameer said.

As he took his leave, Lingli stepped forward.

"What do you want?" Mafala said.

"I've completed your gown, Princess." Lingli bowed and presented her parcel.

"It took you long enough," Mafala said, snatching the cloth from her hands. Before Lingli could ask if she wanted a final fitting, the princess closed her door.

Relieved to be done with outfitting Mafala, Lingli climbed the stairs and took the passage leading to the terrace. At the parapet, she looked skyward at the round bottoms of hundreds of little clouds squashed together for as far as she could see.

She had always loved overcast days. Dull light gave her more time to live a day like everyone else, but there had been so many cloudy days recently. Except for the morning of the day Sid was named, she couldn't remember the last bright day that had visited them.

Unlike the view from the balconies in her room, she couldn't see the fields beyond the Rock, only a dark smudge of horizon beyond Safed Qila's rooftops. Remembering her journey to Saatkulom as she focused on that distant line, Lingli thought, *I must not forget how to live in the wide world. Master Avani means well, but I cannot risk that being named his scribe will protect me. I must find a way to one of the weaving villages.*

She intended to say goodbye to Sid and leave the morning of New Cycle Day while everyone was busy with final preparations for the wedding, and before the rani could have her arrested, but the cold air from the crevasse and the northern wind chipped at her courage. There was no use denying that she would have to go on alone. Without Red and without Sid. With no one.

Sobered, Lingli didn't hear the footsteps until they were close behind her. She pulled her hood forward, and hoped whoever it was would pass by quickly.

"Hello? Aren't you Madam Sayed's seamstress?" Captain Gaddar asked, coming to her side and bending down to better see under her hood. "I've been meaning to speak to you."

Making a hasty bow, she saw there was no one else on the terrace but a pair of Kirdun fighters proceeding toward the old tower.

"When I heard that you were involved in that incident in the kitchens," the captain said, "I asked myself, 'Why would a seamstress have anything to do with such a crime?' Since your arrest was not ordered, I thought perhaps you were a victim of circumstances."

He had a casual way of speaking, which was one of the things that endeared him to palace staff, and he smiled as he spoke, but she felt uneasy.

He leaned in closer. "Then I learned that someone saw more than what they first told Master Vaksana. Someone accused others of that theft with no evidence. I think it was someone who wanted to clear their own name, but who could it be?"

Lingli could barely breathe.

"There were only two others found in the kitchens that night. Yourself, and the new prince. I've heard you're friends. Is that right? Did either of you name names?" When she said nothing, Gaddar sighed.

"The common Ascaryan has their ups and downs, don't they? And fate can be so fickle. I'm sure you can appreciate how terrible it would be to suffer from someone's false allegations."

His breath was warm on her cheek.

"If you remember any more details and feel inclined to share that information, come to me first. Do you understand?"

She nodded, and the captain left her.

Shaking, Lingli tugged her hood forward and hurried to the old tower where she rapidly climbed the stairs and locked herself inside her room. Once her breathing calmed, she laid out the last pieces of the rani's wedding gown on her cot. Threading her needle, she resumed stitching her pattern of golden suns and stars. Accused or not; arrested or not; made a scribe or not—all that guaranteed her freedom for these last days in the palace was this gown.

CHAPTER 29

Frantically digging through the wardrobe in his inner room, Sid wondered how dressing had become so complicated. He used to put on his work kurta and vest or his good kurta and vest and get on about his day. Now, having been given a dozen kurtas, pants, vests, and coats since being named prince, he managed to be late for breakfast with the rani every day.

Add to that the problem with choosing shoes, but he did have a favorite pair he wore whenever possible. The House of Kirdun had given him a pair of soft leather juttis covered with golden embroidery and small rubies, making this pair even nicer than the ones he had worn that star-blessed night he discovered his true history and his destiny. He actually *wanted* to wash his feet before putting them on.

I've got to show these to Li, he thought. As he turned one shoe over something fell out and scuttled away.

A tiny, golden-colored scorpion.

Jumping back, Sid threw the juttis at it, but his aim was poor, and the scorpion ran under the altar table. He attempted to smash the creature with a brass surahi but missed, and it taunted him from behind one of the table legs. As he shoved the table aside, a thali crashed to the floor with a loud bang.

The door guard rushed into the room with his blade drawn, his face tight with alarm until Sid pointed out the little beast menacing him. When the scorpion made another feint that sent Sid scurrying backward, the guard ground it under the heel of his boot.

"Are you injured, Prince?" The guard frowned in exaggerated seriousness meant to hide his amusement.

"I'm fine," Sid answered testily, ashamed that he hadn't managed his own scorpion-killing.

"The rani requests you meet her at the stables this morning," the guard said.

Horses. Wonderful. Sid reluctantly put away his juttis and stepped into a pair of riding boots after ensuring there was nothing in them.

In the small exercise yard behind the stables, he found the rani turning a black colt on a lunge line.

"A fine day for riding," she proclaimed as she slowed the colt and led him over. "Do you notice anything unusual about this colt?"

Sid saw nothing but a horse that pawed the ground and tossed its head as if issuing a dare, but seeing the rani's exuberant mood, he tried to match her. "He looks like he'll be fast."

"He's a govadhi," she whispered before putting the colt in a stall. "I've told them to keep his fetlocks wrapped, but see his ears."

The colt's ears curved so the pointy tips almost touched. *Can't trust a common horse, and this one looks like a fox's cousin.*

"He's going to be a magnificent horse—fit for the leader of our house. Fit for the raja of Saatkulom," she said, her eyes shining with pride. "He'll be yours one day."

A wanderer with a big mustache carried a bucket of water into the stall. The same man who had negotiated the price of Lingli's passage and given him the counterfeit key.

Oh no. They're back?

"Ah, Rahmanji," the rani said happily. "This is my son, Prince Siddharth. And this is Rahman Mirajkar of the White Horse Clan—the best horseman in four realms!"

Rahman bowed and quirked a brow at him but said nothing of their acquaintance. Sid could practically hear the wanderer calculating his increasing leverage in the palace.

The rani moved to the next stall and patted a beautiful golden-colored horse inside. "Rahman's just delivered my wedding present for Prince Hassan. He'll serve as an excellent stud, even if Hassan never learns to ride him." Speaking to the wanderer, she added, "I will exercise the stallion when I return. I hope his gait is smooth?"

"As smooth as butter, Your Majesty," Rahman answered.

A groom brought the rani's mare and another horse for Sid. The rani was already out the stable gate when he failed at his first attempt to make it to the saddle. Waving away the groom who tried to help, Sid then launched himself from the ground so forcefully he nearly fell off the horse's other side.

As he caught up to the rani, she said brightly, "There are so many things I want you to see. Of course, there is no time for half of it before New Cycle Day, but these are a mother's worries! If your father were here, he would laugh and tell me to be patient. 'Treat each day as a gift from the ancestors and you will never feel cheated,' he used to say."

They had hardly crossed half the training yard before Captain Gaddar rode up. Squaring his shoulders, Sid made every effort to not allow his nervousness to show. *What's he going to say? You are the prince, remember?*

"Your news?" the rani said.

"We were short eight guards this morning," the day captain said. "I requested three from the night guard and five from Roshan Sir's mining company to fill the gap."

"Where are the missing defenders?"

Gaddar hesitated. "I believe they answered Prince Hassan's request for more men in Nilampur. He pays very well."

The rani's face became the mask Sid had seen before.

"Find Madam Hansa," she told Gaddar, "and tell her to meet me at the third gate."

The captain rode ahead, and the other guards escorted them out the palace gate and onto the bridge span. When his mount took a few mincing steps at the edge of the abyss, Sid clutched its mane in terror, grateful when one of the guards took his reins. The horses' hooves echoed loudly on the span, and the cold air rising from the dark below made Sid so dizzy he squinted his eyes nearly closed and concentrated on his mother's back until they reached the other side.

Madam Hansa met them under the fort's gate tower. Beyond earshot of the guards, the rani asked her, "Did you know that Hassan plucked more of our defenders before he departed for the lake?"

"Gaddar just informed me, but this problem has plagued us for five moons," Madam Hansa said, "and I have news from Nilampur that is more complicated." She glanced in Sid's direction.

"Speak freely before the prince," the rani said. "I have no time to waste, and he must learn everything that happens on the Rock in any case. But please do not tell me we are not going to complete the Hudulfah compound or the marketplace construction by New Cycle Day."

"Ketan reports the compound was completed five days ago, and the marketplace is almost finished."

"Why does good news leave you with such a troubled expression?"

"During the prince consort's last visit to Nilampur, Ketan says he brought new laborers inside the walls. They're raising constructions that are not part of the original design, including within the Vaksana compound."

The rani sighed and looked up to the sky as if to ask the ancestors for patience.

"Madam Vaksana denies any knowledge of a change in the contract but admitted that she has allowed the prince consort to extend his compound to the edge of hers. Not that she would know where one boundary touches the other, because she has never been to the lake."

The smiling horsewoman of a moment earlier was gone. Sid could almost feel the heat of the rani's rising temper.

"Another complication to factor into our contract," the rani said. "Trust that I will extract a price for every unplanned building and each inch encroached, or I will see the work entirely pulled down."

Madam Hansa decided to press all her concerns. "It seems Prince Hassan has also recruited some villagers to labor in Nilampur. I do not mean to cause alarm, but Ketan reports they are treated like chattel. If we raise concerns now, before the wedding, we might prevent some abuses and ensure they are released by the spring planting."

"We will determine the course this evening, sister. There will be two messages to deliver. One for our brother and one for my loving consort."

"I will send Ilo out tonight."

The crowds parted as he and the rani continued their ride down the Rajpath, and many Ascaryans pressed their hands together in respect or threw flowers in their path. The rani did not speak, but as Sid added the morning's issues to those he had witnessed in the previous days, all the adoration showered on his mother seemed well deserved. He sat a little taller in the saddle, proud, but also realizing that he didn't want to be simply another one of his mother's ornaments.

Soon I will have to do something to earn their respect as well.

Captain Gaddar met them at the first gate, and Sid feared his smugness was invisible to all but him. As the day captain led them into the fields, Sid itched at the thought of his complicity in keeping the man's secrets.

With the Rock behind and tall grass spreading to the horizon, Sid felt small. He'd almost forgotten the world outside. To the southwest, he could just make out some low hutments where smoke rose from cooking fires.

The rani pulled her mare back to ride next to him. She nodded toward the hutments and said, "Your uncle's servants and a few from Kirdun. They're preparing for the guests we cannot accommodate in the palace."

"Which comes first?" Sid asked as they took a smaller path that curved around the southern end of the monolith. "The alliance or the wedding?"

"I will first present Hassan with the contract, which he will give to his father and the other ameers. The contract lists our conditions and assurances for those houses that seek to share the governance of Nilampur. It stipulates that they will provide resources like cotton, rough-mined stone, and the ore we need at a fair price. Also, in return for training, they will pledge some of their youth to our defenses for two cycles so we may better defend our territory from Bakarn to Osiara."

"Bakarn is near the border with Mephistan and Osiara borders Dyuvasa," Sid said, happy to show off his recently gained knowledge whenever possible.

"Yes, very good. These trade and defense benefits are why we cannot walk away from this opportunity to ally with the south—as tempting as that might be."

"There's never been an alliance like this before?" Sid asked.

"No, though your grandfather laid these plans cycles ago. He thought we could convince the south to align with us by trading goods cheaply until they developed a taste for them. It was a risk. Krux will tell you it was too much risk, but I disagree. The only problem with offering honey is that you catch daubers as well as bees, and you must be able to tell the difference."

"And Nilampur is the honey?"

"You are learning."

She was quiet for a moment, then added. "Gayatri and Ketan think I've accommodated the prince consort too much, but our advantage is ultimately secure for two reasons. These are not secrets. Can you tell me what they are?"

Sid spoke slowly, his mind circling the possible answers. "Well, is it that our weapons are better made, if it came to that?" With an encouraging look from the rani, he continued, "As you have said, they distrust one another."

"Those are stars in our favor," she said, "but there are two larger facts. Come."

The rani kicked her mare into a full gallop, outstripping Gaddar and the other guards. Sid's horse followed without encouragement, pounding along the path and jumping over muddy ruts. Begging the ancestors to keep the saddle on tight, Sid bent low and held on despite losing all sensation in his tailbone.

At the crest of a small rise, he saw where the Nemaji river emerged from a fissure in the Rock's southern end. It flowed under a bridge ahead. The rani had already crossed it and turned her horse in a wide arc toward a stone building where an immense water wheel turned.

The guards pounded to a stop behind Sid as he reined in his horse near his mother's mare and the building's entrance. Gritting his teeth as he dismounted, Sid tried to walk normally.

The rani and he entered a large room echoing with the roar of the stream, which he could see through an opening in the floor that contained a smaller wheel set horizontally. Below the wheel's shaft, a series of wooden gears turned. An old man with a wheel brooch on his shoulder jumped up from a bench at the back of the room.

"Priya Maharani! They didn't tell me you were coming. Welcome! Such an honor! It's been a long time since you've visited."

The rani pressed her hands together in greeting. "Be at ease, Vodyarji. I am always pleased to see you, and I wanted to introduce you to someone who has need of your wisdom." She put her hand on Sid's shoulder. "This is my son, Prince Siddharth."

The old man's eyes widened. He looked him up and down with his mouth open.

"Zakir's son lives," the rani said.

Sid bowed to the elder.

"Mahir Vodyar is my father's cousin and master of our canals," the rani explained. "During my grandfather's reign his father began this work, and when Father ruled, Vodyarji sat with his father and drew the plans for the canal and the Talomeer reservoir. Even then, and the rains were more favorable at the time, Talomeer and nearby villages were in famine every other cycle."

"Ah, yes, well…long time ago, you know," the old man shuffled his feet. "What do you know about our water system, Prince Siddharth?"

"Nothing, sir."

"That makes it easier. Come with me, and we'll start at the beginning."

They climbed narrow stairs to a hatch in the ceiling that the canals master opened and climbed through, helping the rani and Sid up behind him.

On top of the lockhouse, the old master pointed Sid first toward the Rock. Like the previous several days, it was cloudy, but the sun broke through occasionally, and when it did, the monolith's veins of moonstone shone bright.

"At this natural curve, you see the Nemaji continues to the east-southeast." Vodyar yelled to be heard over the sound of the water. "It will eventually join the Vaihantay in Kirdun and flow to its end in the Kalamaidan." He pointed at a canal that bent away from the stream. "Raja Basheer built our canal to redirect water to our southmost villages."

"Father spent his life out here," the rani said. "There wasn't a day that he didn't visit the workers building the canal from here to Talomeer."

"And on many of those days," Vodyar chuckled, "there was a small girl on her bad-tempered pony pounding across the fields behind him or fetching food for the workers."

The rani smiled then turned her gaze onto the western fields. While the old master continued explaining, Sid saw her wipe her eyes with the tail of her house sash.

"When my father first presented the plans," Vodyar said, "the raja told us we were not bold enough in our thinking. I, being a brash boy in those days, said, 'Your Majesty, we've measured the volume of water needed by the villages and we've accounted for it.' And the raja said, 'There will be cycles of toil to make this canal. We're not digging it twice in my lifetime. The canal must carry three times the water you have planned. Make the reservoir at Talomeer large enough to hold water for every man, woman, and child there for a cycle.' We obliged him, and he was right."

Vodyar spread his arms. "Sixteen leagues of canal that's seven feet deep and six feet wide; dug out, rocked, and mortared. Four spans on the way. Then there's the guard towers between here and Nilampur, not to mention the reservoir, but the main work now is stabilizing the lakebed," he said. "That was your mother's contribution in the last ten cycles, and I don't think my father could imagine the scope—a hundred acres excavated, berms all around, and soon we'll fill that lake."

The master of canals took Sid to the edge of the lockhouse roof and pointed to the iron fittings in the canal below.

"My father designed the locks," the old man said. "You may think of this canal as a child of the Nemaji. The canal is nourished by the mother river, which we cannot risk depleting. We can close the locks to stop the flow any time the rains come south of here. I will show you how the mechanism works."

While Vodyar explained his winches and gears and other features, Sid suddenly realized the rani was no longer on the roof with them. Scanning the fields, he caught sight of her at the edge of the canal a little downstream. Gaddar strolled by her side.

I should have told her about him already.

Apologizing to the canals master as soon as he could interject a word, Sid took his leave and hurried downstairs. The rani and Gaddar walked back toward the lockhouse, and he saw the captain's hand brush hers. When they noticed him, they separated.

Blushing furiously, Sid continued walking toward them, knowing he couldn't tell her anything while in the captain's company.

"Vodyar has released you so soon?" the rani asked.

"Um…yes, well, I told him I didn't want to delay you because you have to complete messages for Master Tilan and Prince Hassan this afternoon."

When her expression flattened, Sid knew he had said more than she wanted Gaddar to hear. The captain smiled very slightly, gave the rani a small bow, and walked off toward where the other guards held the horses.

For a long moment, she looked westward to where a smudge of smoke hung above the southerners' camp. Sid girded himself for a scolding, but then she beckoned him to follow and abruptly returned to the lockhouse.

"Vodyarji," she said, meeting the old master at the entrance, "I must return to the palace, and I need you to do one thing as soon as I and my company are out of your sight. Shut the locks. Close the canal until I, and only I, order you otherwise." Vodyar looked startled. "For the strength of the realm," the rani said.

"For the strength of the realm," Vodyar answered.

They exited the lockhouse and remounted. When the rani rode ahead of the guards, Sid tried to keep up with her.

"Now can you tell me what indispensable advantages our realm has over the southern houses?" she asked him.

For once, Sid thought he had the right answer. "The Rock, of course. And water," he said. "We are more defensible."

She nodded, her smile bright again, then she kicked her horse hard and galloped away. Soon she was just a tiny, dark spot on the field, far, far ahead of him.

That evening Sid took his supper with her and read through chronicles of Saatkulom's laws again. The next day would be the last court session for the cycle, and he intended to be ready in case Madam Satya tested him. Eventually the rani told him to prepare his pen and parchment. He would serve as scribe for the message to her consort.

"'My dearest Prince,'" she dictated. "'Your eagerness to see the completion of Nilampur is matched only by mine. To ensure that all efforts are concentrated on the most important constructions, according to the plans we agreed upon, I have commanded Master Tilan to assign all laborers to completing the marketplace. I trust the realm's subjects who have accompanied you will also give their entire effort to this purpose alone.'"

The rani paced to the far end of her table and pressed her fist into the wood, as if she needed support to remain upright. Pen inked and ready, Sid waited for her to continue, but she pulled up a moonstone pendant on one of the chains around her neck, unscrewed the end of it, and sniffed at the contents, then closed it again.

Greta waited against the wall by the door, and Sid heard her humming deep in her throat, just as Red used to.

"'There is another matter of great urgency,'" she said, continuing her dictation. "'Reports of laborers suffering serious illness in Nilampur are quite troubling. The malady has been described as exhaustion and a weakening of limbs. This disease is no doubt from a foreign source. To protect my subjects, I have ordered the canal be closed until after the wedding so that it may be cleaned. The southern houses may take water from the tanks until we ensure the problem has been corrected.'"

The rani uttered a short sharp laugh, turned back to him, and said, "He will understand my meaning." Restlessly pacing about her outer room and rubbing her arms as if she felt a chill, she said, "As soon as Parama returns the alliance contract we've drafted, I want you to read it. I know it sounds terribly dull, but you must understand the terms to be negotiated...."

She didn't finish and seemed distracted by the pendant, which she pulled out again. Sid thought he saw her hands shake and was about to ask if she was ill when there was a knock on the door. By the time the guard announced Madam Hansa, the rani had returned the pendant inside her blouse and seemed composed.

"Ilo is ready to leave by your word," Madam Hansa said.

Taking the parchment from Sid, rolling it, and sealing it with wax, the rani said, "I have told my dear consort the canal will remain closed until the contract and our vows are concluded."

The corners of Madam Hansa's mouth turned up just a little as she took the message.

"Draft a message for Ketan before Ilo departs," the rani said. "Tell him what I've done and that I invited the heads of each southern house to the palace the evening before the wedding for the bonding feast. We will use that occasion to raise the issue of the treatment of our subjects who have joined the southerners' service."

Madam Hansa nodded. "I hear there has been good news from Zahatara."

"Yes, Darius reports that the hold has been taken. Jordak should be back soon to collect supplies and the additional defenders they will need."

What? When was she going to tell me this?

"I will request Ketan bring more of the Nilampur defenders when he comes."

The rani nodded. "Very well. He should have completed the work critical to the contract before he leaves."

Madam Hansa bowed and had started to leave when the rani added, "Gayatri, use my son as your scribe. He needs to practice his hand, and I would like him to learn from all members of the Seven."

Sid jumped up and went to join Madam Hansa, but the door guard poked his head into the room to announce Azi Kebedi and Prince Aseem had arrived. A questioning look passed between the two noblewomen before Madam Hansa slipped out without him.

His grandmother carried Aseem, who played with the objects woven into her hair, and Sid remembered to bow and show respect after a nudge from his mother.

The two noble women shared pleasantries, then Azi Kebedi made space on the divan for Sid and handed Aseem to him. "I don't want to impose so late in the evening, Maharani, but I learned that Prince Siddharth was with you, and there is so little time before the festivities, I thought it a good opportunity to bring these brothers together. The bond of brothers is very important, don't you agree?"

"Yes, of course. They are family already, but now is the time for them to become familiar."

Aseem poked a finger into Sid's ear, and the two noble women laughed at Sid's expression.

"Your noble mother has great expectations for you, as do I," Azi Kebedi said to Sid. "It will not be a simple matter for you to serve two realms, but hear me when I say that I will support you and see that your claim is honored in our lands."

"I am honored and look forward to your guidance," Sid said, approximating what he thought a formal response would sound like. His mother smiled, though there was a frost about her.

"Your protection will be important to Siddharth in the cycles to come," the rani said.

Protection. The word seemed to hang in the air around them.

"I could do no less for the son of my firstborn," Azi Kebedi said.

The rani was silent a moment, then said, "I will also ensure that Aseem's claim is honored here and that he has a worthy title in the administration of Nilampur."

"I thank you. Let us use our strength as mothers to make their paths a little easier." Azi Kebedi rose and pressed her hands together in respect. "I must leave you now, but seeing these two together fills my heart with joy. Our futures are truly shared now."

"May the journey enrich both houses," the rani said.

Sid escorted his grandmother to the door and when she left, he turned back to find Greta holding the rani's hand and pressing a finger to her wrist. His mother looked pale, and she patted her chest with her free hand.

"What's wrong?" Sid asked, balancing Aseem on one hip as he approached her.

"It is nothing." She drew her moonstone pendant from her blouse, her brows knitted together in concentration on something unseen. Greta took Aseem from him and hummed louder, and the rani glanced up at her.

"Be quiet," she said. "He must understand."

She leaned across her table to pull her cup close, then she showed him the pendant and said, "This contains a gift from the ancestors—the most powerful one of those our house was blessed with. It is the elixir we share during observation ceremonies, in a much-diluted form, and it is what has given our people strength in battle and on journeys since Starfall. It is sacred to the children of Duran." Her voice grew colder. "It is also what the kitchen thieves stole and what you tasted."

"I didn't know," Sid stammered. "I thought it was some kind of firewine." His memory of the elixir's taste and his desire for it began to coil in his stomach.

Removing the pendant's cap, the rani put two drops into her cup, which she handed to Greta to fill with firewine.

"The ancestors were with you that night," the rani said.

"Were they? I felt so…powerful. I thought I could do anything." Sid struggled to look away from the cup his mother clutched to her chest. Memories of the difficult days he had spent in convalescence seemed far away.

"Members of our house have gone mad from this," the rani said sternly. "A few have died." She motioned to Greta, who gently set Aseem on the floor and went to the inner room. "That is why you will not touch the elixir again until you are prepared, and that is why we must find what was stolen."

When Greta returned with another clay cup and a small wooden box, the rani opened the box and pinched a powder within. Adding the powder to the second cup, the rani waited for the giantess to pour a little firewine in it before pushing the drink across the table to him.

"We do not choose the gifts the ancestors give us, but we must control their use. Your first taste should have never happened the way it did, but now your training must begin. You will drink with me, as I once drank with my father. I will take the elixir. You will take the cure."

The rani raised her cup and waited for him to do the same. Greta hovered just behind the rani's shoulder. Sid peered into his cup, which barely held a mouthful of drink.

"I gave the remedy to you when they brought you to my mother's quarters that night, but you don't remember that, do you?"

Sid shook his head.

The rani sipped her drink. To Sid it seemed that nothing about her changed. In his mind's eye, he saw the silver-bright drop that had fallen from Vidkun's pin into the cup on the card table that night and something within him twisted with desire.

Nothing in his cup smelled strange when he sniffed it, so he drank all of it at once. *I cannot fail any of her tests.*

Taking a second sip, the rani raised her chin and stretched her neck. Suddenly she gasped, and Sid's memory of the power, the limitlessness he felt after his first taste of the elixir, bore through him like an arrow through butter. He thought he could smell the sweet, strange smell of it on his mother's breath, and he could barely restrain himself from reaching for her cup.

Once the shock passed, the rani moved away from the giantess and picked up Aseem. She seemed larger somehow, and her eyes glittered.

Suddenly, Sid began to feel warm. After another breath he jumped up from the chair and ran to the balcony where he vomited violently. Wiping his mouth with the back of his hand, he began to straighten when his stomach clenched and again he vomited.

So it went for half an hour. In the end, Sid slumped against the parapet of the balcony, shaking. Embarrassed and completely drained, he could not evade Greta as she lifted him and carried him to the divan. She brought him a cup of water and wiped his face.

"You said that was the cure," he rasped, reeling from the violence of the drink and the thought that his mother would subject him to such pain.

"It is the only method we have to bring back those who drink too much. If the antidote curbs your thirst for some time, thank the ancestors. The elixir is to be used for the strength of the realm, never for your own amusement."

"And your father gave it to you, just like that?"

"Yes, and I was upset about it, too, much like you. I forgave him after he showed me how to use the gift safely, but I...was a poor student during my instruction, and I paid a heavy price for it." The rani's lips thinned, as if the memory pained her. "The ancestors never let me forget."

She returned to her table, bouncing the baby on her hip as she looked through parchments while he recuperated. After a few minutes she said, "I still have work to finish this night. Can you walk?"

She wants to be rid of me. The realization was galling. Getting to his feet, Sid wished he understood the rules of her games.

"Of course," he said, his throat still burning. "I'm quite fine. I'll just finish my reading for Madam Satya and prepare myself for court."

The rani smiled wanly and returned to her parchments before Greta closed the door behind him.

Trying to show no signs of the weakness he still felt, Sid turned away from her door and ignored the guard that his mother had insisted should accompany him at all times. The cold night air on the terrace was welcome, and he paused to look up at the half-full Matachand, recalling the days of misery and fear after the first drink with greater clarity. *But she takes it. I must learn her method.*

Inside the old tower Sid grabbed the stair railing and pulled himself upward, going straight to his quarters and closing the door behind him. He knew better than to confide anything to a guard, but if he didn't talk to someone about what had been happening, at least some of it, he was not going to sleep.

After a few minutes Sid cracked the door open. Only the night guard remained outside.

"I would like a skin of firewine."

"Now, Prince?"

"Now."

When the guard left, Sid waited until he could not hear his footfalls, then he left his room. The guard at the library door across the landing looked at him questioningly.

"Where am I going to go?" Sid said, pointing upstairs. "Be at ease. I'll return soon."

On the fifth floor, where the stairs ended at the ceiling, Sid raised the trapdoor, stepped up into the huge bird cage, and seeing that the gate was unlocked, entered Li's room.

She looked pleased to see him. Besides his mother, Madam Satya, and his Hudulfah family, she was the first person he had spoken to since being named prince who didn't bow to him. She didn't even press her palms together in respect. He was glad for that.

"Sit," she said, moving a stack of costumes and offering her chair.

Sid crossed his arms over his achkan and realized that Li had no coat—nothing but the standard gray tunic and pants and her old cloak, which was dull with wear and struck above her ankles. He decided he would give her some of his coats that she could tailor for herself.

When he sat, she returned to the cot and continued sewing, peering closely at the seam of some small Ascaryan's vest. "Tell me, then. What's it like being a prince?"

"It's…" Sid thought for a moment. "It's a lot. So much depends on the rani and the Seven. Accounts. Other realms trying to take advantage.

Laws. You have no idea." He trailed off, then added, "But the food and clothes are excellent."

Li laughed. "It will suit you."

Sid got up and went out onto the balcony overlooking the feasting hall. "I hope so," he said softly. The palace grounds below were quiet. The waxing moon and her small brother hid behind heavy clouds.

The familiar silence between them calmed him. He hadn't known he missed it so much, but he still felt off-balance. He couldn't decide if this was due to the lingering effects of the elixir's antidote or because, as with his mother, he had not told Li the entire story about what had happened the night of the theft in Korvar's kitchens.

"How is it with old Avaniji?" he asked over his shoulder.

"Good. I'm copying from the parchments the houses are sharing," Li said. "I read nothing but the names of children by this ancestor or that one for hours, and then there's a story of a terrible drought, or an attack by demons, or goyras, or descriptions of other strange things. I still haven't read anything about shakings."

"Your master's looking for something else," Sid said, returning to Li's chair. "I probably shouldn't tell you, but he says that Chotabhai is growing larger than it ever has before."

Li put her sewing down in her lap. "That sounds serious."

"Bright cycle trouble, I reckon. It will pass."

"I hope so." She was quiet for a moment then said, "Do you ever think about all those who've come before? I wonder about the adventures that have never been written."

"Don't worry, I'll write you into the Book of Duran one day," he teased. "The Amazing Seamstress of Chandrabhavan!"

"That will be a short tale if those thieves aren't arrested." Li looked at him expectantly. "You must have told the rani. Do you think they'll be caught soon?"

"All the guards are looking for them." He couldn't face her.

"I have a bad feeling that they have some friends protecting them."

"Why do you say that?"

"Yesterday," Li said, "Captain Gaddar warned me not to cast blame on others. He mentioned you, too, but I doubt he'll trouble you now."

"Gaddar?" Sid felt his throat tighten.

"Why would a captain trouble himself over a stolen cask, unless…" Li paused her stitch and raised her chin. "They stole something more valuable than firewine, didn't they?"

Sid took a breath and held it for a moment. He knew he shouldn't tell her, but he was no good with secrets, and she kept them so well. Besides, who else could he tell?

"A gift from the ancestors," he said. "An elixir given to the House of Duran. It makes you feel…strong. I'm not explaining this very well, but it's dangerous."

"How is it dangerous?"

"It's like you are watching yourself," Sid said. "You have no fear, then nothing but fear. I think it opens a path to the otherworld."

Alarm was building in Li's eyes. "You drank it, didn't you? That's why you were so strange after the beating."

He pinched his fingers together. "That much only."

"Are you whole now?"

He shrugged. "I'm fine."

Li shook her head. "Is this why your mother hates me? She thinks I stole her gift? Where does she think I've hidden it? She must be very eager to get it back."

Mention of his mother gave Sid a sharp jab. *What am I doing? If the rani finds out I told anyone…* "I should go," he said. "I'm supposed to prepare for court tomorrow."

Following him to the gate, Li said, "I know you hate advice, but keep plain tea in your cup." She laughed a little, seeing that he dismissed this suggestion. "Alright then, but if you know how to return the rani's gift, I'm sure she would be impressed."

"And you wouldn't have to worry about Gaddar."

"Or her, I hope."

He shifted from one foot to the other, on the verge of telling her about Gaddar and Vidkun, but then he turned away. *The less she knows about it, the better.*

"You must have all kinds of duties for the wedding," Li said, "but could you… Would you meet me here the night before New Cycle Day?"

Sid shrugged. "Why? Do you have a secret?"

"I just need to tell you something, and I don't think the rani wants to see you talking to me."

"I'll come." As much as Sid knew he should leave, he also wished to stay. Talking to Li had somehow taken a weight off his shoulders.

As he edged toward the gate, she said, "You're walking funny."

"Uh, yeah. I rode with the rani all morning. I saw your wanderer friend, Mirajkar, at the stables."

"You did? When did they come back?"

"He's brought a horse for Prince Hassan. A wedding present, I guess." Stepping through the trapdoor, Sid said, "Say hello to Avaniji and Parth for me."

He heard her call after him, "Take care, Prince Sid."

CHAPTER 30

On the edge of the lantern light illuminating the dancers' platform, Lingli watched the older girls perform the final dance planned for the rani's wedding. The costumes—dresses adorned with rich white embroidery, blue sashes, and gold beading—were finally complete, and Madam had allowed the girls to wear them for practice to ensure their fit. They put aside their petty jealousies for once, and Lingli's heart swelled as she watched them move like stars on their unalterable paths in the Doodhnadi.

It saddened her to think that she wouldn't see their performance on New Cycle Day, but she couldn't lose her nerve. She had been trying to learn more about a fort town called Osiara—a town that had looms, according to Madam. It seemed like it might be a good place for her, and now, thanks to Sid's news, she had an idea of how to get there. She would go see the Mirajkars that night and find out if they would pass near Osiara on their way back to their winter camp. If they were, she hoped Rahman would carry her along for the single coin she had left.

When the dance ended, Madam dismissed the girls and approached her as she collected her things. "How goes your work on the maharani's gown?"

"Nearly finished," Lingli answered. "I will give it to you tomorrow."

Looking much relieved, Madam dismissed her, and Lingli took the musicians' coats with her for some small fixes.

It was a court day, the last of the cycle. Already a dozen or more Ascaryans gathered outside the great hall. Tugging her hood forward, she headed toward her room, planning to dispose of the coats before joining Master Avani in the library.

Talking to Sid the night before, barbs and all, had lightened her heart, but he didn't seem to have any more hope that the thieves would be arrested than she did. Leaving him behind would be the hardest thing she had ever done, but as long as he knew Osiara was her destination, she promised herself she would find the courage to go.

There was one other she needed to speak to before she left. Greta. She wanted to make amends for her outburst the day Sid was named, but she also wanted to tell her about Red and see if the giantess could be cajoled into answering some of the questions that still burned in her heart. As she climbed the stairs of the old tower with her arms full of mending, she thought it might be a long time before she had another chance.

Hearing a sudden small yelp, Lingli looked up to see Prince Aseem's nurse tottering at the edge of the landing a few steps above.

The nurse pitched forward and slammed against Lingli's side as she fell. Lingli sat down hard on the stairs, scattering the coats. When the nurse finally caught herself, Lingli held out a hand to the young woman.

"I hope you're not hurt too badly?"

Fright was written on the nurse's face, but she shook her head. Taking Lingli's hand, she pulled herself up very close and whispered, "I am sorry," in the common tongue before turning away and hurrying downstairs. Collecting her mending, Lingli continued upstairs, but when she reached the landing, Princess Mafala and two Hudulfah youth blocked her way.

"Here she is," Mafala said. "Search her."

One of the southerners knocked the coats from her hands again and pulled her arms behind her back while the other patted her cloak and reached into the pockets of her tunic. The day guard outside Madam's room watched but did not intervene. The second southern youth pulled something from her pocket and held it up for Princess Mafala to see—a bronze arm cuff.

"See here," Mafala called out loudly to the palace guard. "This cuff is my property. You have witnessed its discovery on this thief."

Before Lingli could think, Mafala's assistants shouted at her as if *they* were palace guards and marched her downstairs, hauling her back to the doors of the great hall, which had filled with Ascaryans attending court. The steward at the door hardly glanced at Lingli in her gray servants' tunic when he promised Princess Mafala he would present her complaint to the judges for further action, but the princess only became louder and louder in her demands for her petition to be taken up immediately. With the princess's accusations carved into his ears, the steward hurried inside to relay the message.

"You thought you were very clever, didn't you?" Mafala told her. "How long did you think it would take for me to figure out how that fat old man got his ring back?"

The steward returned to usher Mafala, her guards, and Lingli inside.

The platforms in the hall were full, and the floor was crowded. Like the night the wanderers had been forced to flee those angry villagers, Lingli's fear reached a point where she became numb. It felt as if this was happening to someone else. Memories of every bad thing that had ever happened to her and the weight of the conclusions that so many, so often had formed about her kept her tethered to the ground. She should have known her curse was never going to leave her.

Behind the judges' table, the rani was resplendent on her throne in a heavy, white cloak and wearing a painted mask of silver around her eyes to mark the approaching winter season. Sid sat in a smaller brass chair by her side, wearing the coat Lingli had stitched. His kufi had been replaced by a band of gold half hidden in his curly hair.

A guard shoved her down onto the bench, and Lingli caught Sid's eye for a moment. He seemed shocked but quickly looked away.

When the previous petition was concluded, Sir Krux set the arm cuff in the center of the judges' table and the hall began to buzz. Madam Satya drew herself up in her seat and announced, "Let the noble petitioner approach."

Princess Mafala glided over the floor to face the judges. She shone in a deep red lehenga, and her braids glittered with small amulets woven into them. Lingli didn't need to see the princess's face to know that she was perfectly composed. The lies unspooled smoothly from her lips.

"She was the only foreigner who entered my quarters before the cuff went missing, Your Majesty. I have been looking for her since then, and today, when she was discovered, I demanded my men search her in the presence of one of your defenders." Mafala gave a small laugh and shook her head in disbelief. "Such boldness! She carried my family's heirloom in her pocket in front of me. So practiced in deception, she did not even try to hide the object. Who knows what else she has stolen!"

How convenient. She knows Her Majesty suspects me of other thefts.

Whispers floated through the hall. The rani's gaze never wavered from the princess as she made her charges, but Sid shifted in his chair.

Mafala waited, her head bent in homage to humility. The guard on duty at the bench hoisted Lingli to her feet. She did not realize that Madam Satya had asked her a question until the guard shoved her.

"I said," Madam Satya repeated slowly, her eyes as sharp as a hawk's, "did you steal the cuff that sits on this table and was discovered in your pocket today?"

"No," Lingli said softly. "I did not steal her ornament."

Madam Satya raised her brows, looking as if she wished to warn Lingli against making ridiculous statements. Sirs Krux and Nartilya hardly bothered to look up from the parchments they shuffled. Greta remained giant-still, and Sid continued to stare at the floor, making Lingli want to scream.

Only the rani met her gaze, observing her with the coolness of someone who had never seen her before, never praised her handiwork, never asked her to conspire in stopping Mafala from copying her wedding dress. Lingli understood that this petition's outcome was already decided.

An ember of indignation within her glowed and ignited. *They will gladly let these lies strangle me for no more reason than they don't like my face. It's always the same. I've nothing to lose by spreading any truths I can.*

"What is surprising," Lingli blurted out before Madam Satya could speak again, "is that of all the precious pieces I have seen in the princess's quarters—golden belts, sapphire necklaces, pendants, and rings, especially a large amethyst ring I admired—one that looked exactly like the ring Envoy Kanaka was missing—of all those fabulous ornaments, that cuff is surely the ugliest bauble in her collection. No one would bother to steal it."

The hall erupted in laughter and jeers. Princess Mafala would not deign to look back at her, but Lingli felt her fury just the same.

Madam Satya put a hand to her brow and signaled the drummers for a beat to quiet the room. She said, "You imply that someone else stole this ornament and made you appear guilty. Who would do this?"

Lingli weighed her words. The truth would not serve here. Even if the judges had any inclination to believe her, which they did not, their prosecution would turn against the nurse, who had no choice but to do Mafala's bidding.

"I don't know, Madam," Lingli answered.

"We have heard your testimony. We will make our judgment."

Lingli's anger dissipated. The remains of her spirit fluttered weakly against her ribs, seeking a way out.

Their consultation lasted hardly a minute.

Madam Satya said, "We have determined that the seamstress, Lingli Tabaan, is guilty of the theft of a cuff belonging to Princess Mafala of the House of Hudulfah of Avakstan."

Master Avani's other apprentice, Parth, wrote rapidly as excited chatter broke out again. Madam Satya continued over it. "In accordance with the law of this realm and guided by the wisdom of the ancestors, the accused shall sacrifice a finger as a reminder of her crime, and so that she will find it difficult to steal in future."

"A finger?" Mafala cried out over the din. "She should pay with her life."

"Because the cuff is your property and you are not a subject of this realm, a more severe punishment is not prescribed."

Southerners in the hall booed with disappointment. The princess was livid, but the only reaction Lingli cared about was Sid's. All the color had fled his face. He swallowed and looked from Madam Satya to the rani and back again, but never at her.

A drummer tried to drown the noise with a rapid beat.

Madam Satya said, "The punishment will be exacted immediately, according to the law. May the ancestors protect and guide Saatkulom today, tomorrow, and for cycles yet to come." Madam Satya paused and looked to the rani, but when Her Majesty said nothing, she added, "Court is ended. This is my word."

As Lingli was propelled from the hall, she could hardly breathe, but the pain from a guard's grip on her arm helped her keep her balance.

I will not cry for them.

They came onto the front grounds under the burnished light of the evening. Already, the first-shift staff and apprentices were hanging about the feasting hall's colonnade, waiting for supper to be served.

The guard pushed her against the chest-high mounting stone that nobles used to enter and leave wagons and rathas. In the crowd encircling the stone the prince consort's mother, Azi Kebedi, stared at her with a grim expression, but next to her, Mafala's face flashed with glee and loathing in equal measure. Lingli hoped for the sensation of floating beyond her stonebound body as she had before, but her mind remained fixed where she was.

The crowd parted to allow Captain Gaddar through with Madam Satya, followed by the rani and Sid. The rani bent close to Sid so the dark curtain of her hair fell before his face as she whispered something to him. Sid shuffled toward the stone like a blind man.

In her mind, Lingli shouted, *Look at me! You know I didn't steal anything!*

The guard stretched her arm across the slab, palm down, and all fell quiet.

With a casual flex, as if he were performing a trick at a festival, Captain Gaddar drew his talwar. He held the hilt out to Sid, and the rani touched her son's shoulder. Sid looked at the captain's blade with alarm.

Madam Satya said in a low voice, "Maharani, the prince has not been prepared for these duties, and if this does not go well it may reflect poorly on him. If you will allow me to deliver the punishment, we will avoid that complication."

The rani stared at Lingli with her head tilted slightly, much as she had in the great hall the first time they met, and Lingli could not say which of them was more mesmerized. Despite the praise the rani had offered for her skills in the past, Lingli sensed a depth to her loathing that she couldn't understand. Rather than mercy, Her Majesty seemed to be calculating how to impose a greater punishment and save them all time and trouble.

"Your Majesty," Madam Satya urged, "it will be swift and done."

The rani nodded.

Waving the crowd back, Madam Satya adjusted Lingli's hand, splaying her fingers wide upon the stone. The guard held her tight by both arms. Then the eldest of the Seven drew a slender pata from her belt.

"Hear me, Lingli Tabaan!" Madam Satya ordered. "We exact this punishment as prescribed by the laws of Saatkulom, witnessed by Maharani Sandhyatara and the ancestors."

Lingli fixed her gaze on Sid, who seemed to hear nothing and see nothing but her hand on the stone.

"May the ancestors show you mercy!"

Quicker than she thought possible, so quick Lingli didn't actually see her strike, Madam Satya brought the blade down.

CHAPTER 31

Sid watched Li's little finger separate from her hand, and he felt sick.

"Sid?" she gasped.

He couldn't speak, couldn't breathe. Guilt was choking him.

The blood poured forth, making his legs tremble as the rani pulled him away from the stone.

The next thing he knew, Greta cleared the way, and his mother made it seem as if he escorted her back to the palace, but he could do little more than stay upright while the rani moved him up the stairs to the gallery.

I should have done something to stop them, but when? When Mafala made her charges? When the judgment was given? In the yard? The other, needling voice in his head replied, *But you did nothing. Nothing! You're a coward of the highest order.*

They had just entered the gallery, when, as if she heard his thoughts, the rani whispered to him, "I am sorry that you had to witness that at your first court appearance. I know she used to be a friend of yours…"

'Used' to be? Sid stopped. "I should have—"

"There was nothing you could have done," she told him firmly, her brows drawn together with concern. "The law is very clear, and the judges applied it as is their duty. As leaders, we must respect the consequences even when it is painful to us. Especially then."

The law. Respect the law. Yet the law and logic couldn't soothe his guilt.

"But what if Mafala was lying?"

The rani glanced over his head toward the guards, and Sid winced, prepared for another ear boxing. Her eyes were as cold as distant stars as she said in a low voice, "Whatever your suspicions, do not question the integrity of other nobility in public. Never. It is both demeaning and dangerous."

"She…she wouldn't have stolen that cuff."

365

"Do not speak like a petulant child. To make such a claim demands evidence, and if you had such information, you should have shared it."

He was not making himself understood, but this did not goad him any further. The humiliation the rani offered was exactly what he deserved—though for a different reason. Part of him, the shrill part that had dominated his arguments since Li had been hurt in the village skirmish almost a cycle ago, still argued that her fate was not his responsibility, but that part was drowning in the truth of their history together. She had fed him, dressed him, taken care of him when he was sick. Of course, she had bullied him, too, but like a sister. Malice had played no part.

And he had repaid her, even after she intervened with Vidkun's gang just half a moon ago, with pure cowardice.

From the other end of the gallery, Master Avani hurried toward them. Bowing to the rani, the old noble said, "My apologies for having missed court, sister. Unexpected business detained me."

"Your would-be apprentice revealed a darker nature," the rani answered, her gaze shifting between Sid and the old noble—as if she dared either of them to argue.

"Yes, I heard. Very disappointing." Master Avani looked pained.

She'll never become a scribe now. Another blade of guilt slid between Sid's ribs.

"We should consider ourselves fortunate she had not formally joined service," the old noble said, "but I doubt she will be the last apprentice to be moonstruck this bright cycle."

"Moonstruck? The chaos of the otherworld emanates from that one."

"What I meant to say, sister, is that we should not lose sight of pursuing the others involved in the earlier theft. If you wish, I will stress my concerns with the captains of the guard."

Gaddar will be so helpful.

"When the captains report to me," the rani answered testily, "I will repeat the concerns that I have already conveyed."

"If you can spare the prince," Master Avani said, "I would like him to deliver a new transcription I've composed from the Book of Satya. Entries from the second and fifteenth generations highlight events similar to the shakings, though I am still at a loss regarding Chotabhai. But let me not delay you with the details."

"Very well," she said, "but if we suffer no new maladies more serious than a sullen winter sky, I am not likely to study your transcript until after the wedding."

Though Sid was glad to avoid any more argument with his mother about Li's nature, there was no relief from the guilt and shame washing though him, and judging from Master Avani's expression, he could expect questions about what happened in court soon enough.

The halls were crowded, and he and Master Avani did not speak until they reached the second-floor landing where Ameer Ali met them.

"Ah, I have been looking for you, good master," the ameer said jovially, "and what luck to also find the prince who will help us guarantee the success of our new alliance."

Sid bowed stiffly, the praise scorching his unworthy heart.

"I know you've only discovered your southern family," the ameer told Sid, "but your reunion with Hudulfah encourages our houses, too. Don't you agree, Master Avani, that Prince Siddharth could serve as liaison when we introduce the contract? Perhaps inspiring greater confidence among all?"

'Liaison' again? He's been talking to my mother.

"He would no doubt make a fine ambassador."

Uncertain whether they were teasing him, Sid began to wonder if either noble understood how much his uncle loathed him.

"Would you be so good as to meet with me and Ba Hassan upon his return?" Ameer Ali asked Master Avani. "I have tried to explain the importance of your library to him, just as Raja Basheer tried to explain it to me many cycles ago, but I'm afraid I've not conveyed it well. Your recordkeeping, for example, is so thorough it must give you great confidence in understanding the will of the ancestors. I'm afraid the small efforts I have undertaken in my house to record activities do not compare. Even now the demi-nobles fight me."

"Our methods differ," Master Avani said, clearly flattered, "but I am certain the southern traditions of preserving knowledge are more than adequate to safeguard your history."

"Of course, of course, but if Ba Hassan could be convinced of the value of the written word, others would open their minds to adopting this practice to complement ours. I suggest a meeting with Aza Mussan and Ba Hassan. If you, and the prince, could share a few clear benefits the chronicles have provided, it could inspire our adaptation of written records." The ameer threw his hands up dismissively. "I know. My enthusiasm for new ideas often outruns what is practical."

"If Prince Hassan is amenable to the subject," Master Avani said, "I will gladly take part, and I will encourage the maharani to allow the prince as well."

"Good," the ameer said, pressing his hands together. "Let us discuss the details when I receive an answer from Ba Hassan."

Once Sid and Master Avani were alone in the library, Master Avani gave Sid the stern look he had expected. "I heard what happened in court. Tell me, was the law served?"

"The judges said so," Sid answered bitterly. "The rani, too."

"And you?"

"I don't know why Li had that cuff, but she's…she's not a thief. They've made her into something she isn't."

Master Avani rubbed the bridge of his nose and said softly, "I couldn't agree more. She needed an ally. Still does."

"I know I should have done something to stop it, but I didn't know what."

"I doubt you could have done anything in that instant. The question is what you do now. She is doubly marked as a thief, and that is going to be difficult to overcome."

"I told the rani about the boys in the kitchen that night."

"Well, that is something," Master Avani sounded greatly annoyed. "But have you told her that a member of the Seven Houses and a reputed defender are also involved?"

Sid blinked. "How did you know?"

"I was not in court today because I was at the jail helping my nephew prepare for his next appearance regarding the theft *he* has been accused of. He has been badly abused, but he finally named the culprits who have been involved in both matters, maybe more. They are practiced in pointing the blame at others."

Sid remembered how Vidkun had shoved Ritin into a cell the first time he visited the jail. He suddenly had a vision of Li crouched in the same kind of dark place.

"I'm sorry I didn't tell you before."

"Are you sorry you didn't tell me or sorry that I found out you chose not to tell me?"

"Both."

"Then clean your conscience and tell my noble sister the whole truth."

Sid bit his lip. The truth had often caused him trouble and becoming prince had not made those troubles go away.

"We need to know how far this betrayal goes," the old noble said. "Neither Captain Gaddar nor Vidkun are selling that stolen gift on the Rock."

Does everyone know about the elixir?

Master Avani continued. "Whoever is buying it will do whatever they can to keep it secret, and who better to accuse than someone like Miss Tabaan, whose reputation is already tainted."

"But she wasn't involved."

"Take comfort in that if you can. The rani wants an arrest soon."

On a blade's edge of criticizing the rani, Sid could see Master Avani was as uncomfortable as he was.

"I do not want to disappoint her. The rani, I mean," Sid said.

"Nor do I, but what is our duty?"

"Respect the law. Protect the realm."

Master Avani nodded at his answer, but that only aggravated Sid. Running a hand through his hair, Sid continued, "If that is my duty, then why are you scolding me about Li? I agree that she shouldn't have lost her finger, but how, sir, do I respect the law, protect the realm, and protect Li? And...somehow"—Sid tried to lower his voice—"in all of this, I am supposed to keep my mother's trust and avoid maddening my uncle even further."

"There," Master Avani said with a sigh. "You've learned that challenges breed like rabbits in the life of leaders. I hope that you will trust I am here, not only to scold, but to offer my advice, and perhaps a solution to part of it."

Sid swallowed hard, regretting his outburst.

Master Avani said, "My dearest hope is that, in time, my sister will look more favorably on Miss Tabaan, but for now we must help her stay out of the maharani's sight. I am my sister's devoted supporter in all decisions affecting the strength of the realm, but sometimes even a rani's vision may be clouded. I can make arrangements to find a safe place for Miss Tabaan if you agree."

A wave of relief surged through Sid. "That would help, I think."

"Perhaps an apprenticeship in a weaving village," the old noble mused. He picked up a few bound pieces of parchment, handed them to him, and said, "Take these to your mother. Too many dramas demand attention, and the larger ones, I fear, are being overlooked."

"Sir, don't misunderstand me," Sid said, "but why risk the rani's trust for a girl you hardly know?"

"Because, Prince, the ancestors blessed me, as they bless most of us, with the intelligence to sense right from wrong, and I hope I find the courage to choose right. What will you do?"

"I know I should have named Gaddar and Vidkun already."

"Will you do it?"

"I will. I'll go see Li first, then I'll tell the rani."

"It will do you no good to meet Miss Tabaan tonight," Master Avani said. "She's been given a potion to blunt the pain and put her to sleep. Let your first duty be to inform the maharani of this unsavory business."

The old noble's praise encouraged Sid but keeping his promise would not be easy. Outside the library he circled the third-floor landing twice, ignoring the looks the guards passed between them.

I must do it now, right now, but I won't mention Li. That will just annoy her, and nothing I can say will change her mind or fix Li's finger. No more delay. If I cannot tell my mother the truth, how can I call myself a prince? He shoved open the door to the terrace and marched to the new tower.

When Greta admitted him, Sid set Master Avani's transcription on his mother's table, drew up his courage, and said quickly, "I must tell you something else about the kitchen theft."

The rani did not seem particularly surprised as she set down the parchments she had been reading.

"Those fellows I told you about? The thieves? They took the cask to the jail and gave it to Vidkun. He kept some of the elixir, watered down the rest, and gave the cask to Captain Gaddar."

She said slowly, "You witnessed this?"

Sid nodded, fighting the urge to take a step back in case her anger ignited, but the rani showed him the chair before her table.

"A spoiled captain and a spare from a declining house who imagines himself a master," the rani said coolly. "Of course."

"I know I should have told you, but Vidkun is of the Seven," he said, "and I knew you favored the captain. Before you declared me your son, I didn't think you would believe me. Afterward...I was ashamed I hadn't told you the whole truth."

Sid glanced at Greta, who stood giantstill against the wall by the door to the quarters. He knew she heard what he said. *Just like Red. I won't blame her if she serves my weaknesses up to me one of these days.*

"Is this the extent of it?" the rani asked. "Was anyone else involved?"

Sid shook his head. *Let her not bring Li into this.*

"You said Vidkun diluted the elixir and gave the cask to Gaddar," she said. "What did he do with what he kept?"

"Except for what he shared with us, I do not know."

Tugging at the chains encircling her neck, the rani said, "He has either hidden it or sold it." Turning to him, she added, "This will not go unanswered, but we will not rush the accusation. Much of ruling well is learning when to act and when to wait. Let us discover who is buying, then we will find the solution to this problem together."

In the brief time he had been by his mother's side Sid had begun to recognize when her words were polite nothings, required business, or heartfelt, and this seemed earnest. Instead of berating him, she was treating him like a true heir, guiding him in a way he had craved his entire life.

"They will not want the others to name them," Sid reasoned out slowly. "Isn't that why Captain Gaddar hasn't made any arrests?"

"Once they were convinced that you had told no one, there was no reason to put their accomplices in jeopardy, but secrets like this are hard to keep in Chandrabhavan." The rani tipped her head to one side and tapped her fingers on the tabletop as if considering different courses of action. "Eshan hasn't made any arrests either."

Sid could not imagine that the night captain, Master Duvanya's own son, was involved, but he had not suspected Gaddar either.

"Perhaps a more attractive reward will spur some honest action," she said.

"I would like to help," Sid said. "I mean, if I am a prince, shouldn't I do something? Should I tell Madam Satya what truly happened?"

The rani took his arm and walked him to the door. Greta moved aside silently.

"That time will come, but not yet," she said. "This has been a difficult day for you, and I am tired, too. Take your ease and rest early. Tomorrow we will make our plan." Then, placing one hand on his cheek, she said softly, "I ask only one thing of you tonight, son. Wish me good night as you did when you were my baby boy."

"Good night, Mother."

"Good night, *Amma*."

Sid hesitated for an instant. Such tender words might suit his mother, but not his rani. He sometimes forgot to whom he was speaking.

"Good night, Amma."

As he returned to his quarters, Sid stopped on the terrace and looked up. The Doodhnadi shone bright—an amethyst river where countless stars sailed. No light shone from Li's room at the top of the old tower. *Will she forgive me for what happened, for what I did not do?*

Here was the greater destiny he had imagined all his cycles. If everything he might accomplish in this life would be in service to Saatkulom, he had to keep his mother's faith and trust. The question now was whether he could walk a careful course through everything galloping toward him. He had not only failed Li that day. He had failed himself. He had to find greater courage.

In the morning he would face Li's anger and explain what Master Avani proposed. Then he and the rani would ensure that Vidkun and Gaddar were arrested. The course seemed clear. He would make his mother, *Amma*, proud.

Part 5

CHAPTER 32

Hollow. That was the only way Greta could express what she felt in the common language.

Following the three of them, each on their separate path, was taxing her. When the boy left the rani's quarters earlier that evening, the giantess dulled her sense of him as she had for the girl after her mutilation. She still followed the rani, but because Dear Child was soaking nearby in her bath, Greta did not need giantsense to know her breath was steady and the hitch in her heartbeat had relaxed.

Too much elixir, the gift-that-was-not-a-gift, was tormenting Dear Child, but she would not listen to the giantess's counsel to stop. The worries and fears that consumed her were not long banished by the drink, but they steadily increased her reliance on it. Only a little earlier, while the boy visited Master Avani, the rani had taken her second sip for the day, and the strength Dear Child so desperately sought hardly rippled through her before she threw it all up.

An Ascaryan might have thanked their ancestors for ridding her of the drink so quickly, but Greta sensed these episodes were only signs that the rani had absorbed her limit. Her body had begun to fight back erratically and dangerously, like a trapped wolf. Despite taking every precaution to keep Dear Child away from the stressful encounters, every day delivered more, and Greta could only bear witness to her charge's decline in strength and judgment.

The boy was too much like her.

Greta had clearly sensed the boy's hunger for the elixir, and it produced a vision that surprised her. Imagination didn't come naturally to giants, but her time among Ascaryans must have strengthened her capacity, for Greta suddenly saw herself in this same room, with the same cloth, cleaning the boy's face like she did his mother's. She felt almost as ill-prepared to prevent him from falling prey to the elixir's demands as she had with the rani.

The girl's appearance in court was another failing on her part. She had been negligent, ignoring the poor child who still carried the red giant's scent and miscalculating that she would be safe enough until the wedding gown was completed. When the girl had been hauled before the judges it was impossible to intervene, nor could she offer any more solace afterward than to give Madam Sayed a salve to stanch the blood and a powder to help her sleep.

Dangers were growing around both children like shadows on a short autumn day. Greta's only consolation was that their heartstones, which the Ascaryans called spirits, were still pure, and the baby boy—whose nature was still more water than stone—didn't yet demand her attention.

Returning to the bathing room, Greta helped Dear Child dress for bed, then took her post near the door. The rani, however, did not prepare to sleep, but settled herself at her table, lit three lanterns, and perused the transcript the boy had delivered.

After some time, the rani pushed the parchment away. "The great flood of the Vaihantay and burning stars? The last visit of the ancestors?" she muttered. "Does Brother Jalil think I don't know our history? Bring me my book, and Father's."

In the inner room Greta took down a tapestry hanging at the head of the rani's bed. Behind it the stone wall looked no different from the rest, but the giantess ran her fingers along the mortar until she touched the spot that hummed with a power known only to the ancestors. While she pressed down with her thick finger, the stone retreated and slid to one side, revealing a cavity that held the two most recent chronicles of Duran.

The current book kept by the rani described events of the forty-second generation, and the other one was a hastily recopied record of Raja Basheer's rule during the forty-first. It was not unusual for the rani to refer to her house's chronicles when something troubled her, but as the hours wore away Dear Child showed no signs of retiring. Instead, Greta could feel her growing more agitated. When the rani suddenly rose from her table, fitted her slippers, and wrapped herself tight in her robe, Greta's hope that she would find peace in a good sleep was ripped away.

Grabbing a lantern on her way out of her quarters, Dear Child spoke not a word to her or the door guards. Greta followed her across the gallery and into the old tower in the darkest hours. On the forlorn fifth floor, the rani handed the lantern to Greta.

"Stop that humming," she commanded.

The giantess swallowed and climbed the last stairs, butting the trapdoor up with her head. As she unlocked the gate the rani squeezed past her and silently crossed the room to where the girl slept.

The child's bandaged hand rested upon the blanket, and her white hair spread around her head like a halo of moonlight, contrasting with the dark, prominent vein in her temple.

With her hand over her mouth, the rani stared down at the the girl and stayed silent for several breaths, then she whispered, "How? How can it be? Or am I going mad?" She looked up at the giantess. "Are you practicing mother's potions again? This cannot be." With her hand outstretched, nearly touching the girl, she said, "From that day to this, only Amina, you and I remain among those who knew she ever drew breath, and even my memory is not complete. I was glad for those potions that carried me into the otherworld, and all this time I thought I left my curse there."

The rani drew back and approached the small table nearby. Hesitantly, she touched the costumes and the spools of thread. "And now, in this fraught hour, I discover this changeling who walks and talks and sews and steals by an asura's will."

From the day the boy introduced the girl and showed the rani the fine white kufi she had stitched, Greta had felt doubts rise in Her Majesty, and the disturbance the girl produced had only grown since then. Not even the spectacle of the girl's mutilation or the boy's accusation of the true thieves lessened the rani's suspicions.

Taking the lantern from her, the rani backed away from the cot and went to a dusty trunk near the cage. She opened it and removed a small blue coat from within, then closed the trunk lid and sat on top, smelling the coat and watching the sleeping girl.

"Brother," the rani whispered, "protect me."

The girl stirred on her cot, and the rani went still until it seemed she would not move again. When Her Majesty drew her neck chains out from her robe, Greta said, "Dear Child, this girl has made a most beautiful dress."

"A trick." With the moonstone pendant in her fist, the rani returned to the girl's bedside. "The ancestors have brought me here. I must not fail them."

Of all the dangers the child had faced, Greta knew the greatest risk came from Dear Child herself. The rani knelt next to the girl, pinching the cap of the pendant. The giantess guessed she would force the girl to drink all the elixir she carried.

This was the darkness the giantess had discovered within her charge long ago. For moons, even cycles, it shrank and became nearly invisible, but here it was again. She would have to act very soon, and to do so would probably cost her life. She wished for Red's wisdom, but not as much as she wished that Rani Shikra was there to stop what had been stopped before and had to be stopped again.

But the rani did not act. The pendant swung in her shaking hand.

At last, she drew back. "I cannot. I cannot. Oh, why this torment? All these cycles my house and Saatkulom have been first in my heart, and I am weakened now? Father, my faith is true! Haven't I been tested enough?" She let go of the pendant and held her head in her hands.

"Dear Child, you say the ancestors are merciful."

"You know nothing!" the rani hissed bitterly, shaking as she remained poised over the cot. "You speak as my mother taught you—empty words and diversions. She led me away from the rightful action long ago, and now you would do the same."

"This girl defied the gift once," Greta said, "and now she is stronger."

The rani grimaced and stared at the girl. After several breaths, she shook her head and grudgingly returned to the stairs.

Greta locked the gate behind them, moved ahead of the rani, and held out a hand to steady her as she descended the steep stairs. The rani's aura still sparked erratically, but to Greta's relief, Dear Child returned to her quarters and went straight to bed.

The remainder of the night did not pass quietly. Greta watched her charge toss and turn and cry out in her dreams. When the rani woke and sat up before dawn, she demanded water and gulped it down as if she had been walking weeks in the Kalamaidan. After pacing about her rooms for some time, the rani waved the giantess aside, opened the door to her quarters, and informed the guards that the seamstress was banished from the palace. She ordered them to shackle her at Giants' Post immediately.

The command calmed Dear Child instantly. After the guard was dispatched, Greta lit a lantern for the rani as she settled herself at her work table and resumed her perusal of her house's chronicles. Until the sky began to lighten, the rani read quietly, then asked her to fetch the baby prince.

On her way to rouse the babe's nurse, Greta chose to descend one more floor and take a very few extra steps so that she would meet Master Avani and Madam Sayed in the gallery. Their faces were grave.

"We know," Master Avani told the giantess before she said anything. "Madam Sayed witnessed her arrest."

"The child cannot be left there," Madam said.

"No, but it is too dangerous to keep her in the palace," Master Avani said.

"Wanderers have brought Prince Hassan's horse," Greta said. "They will leave soon."

Master Avani raised his brows. "That might be our best choice. There are too many demands for my sister to pursue the child if she disappears. We will find a way to collect her when the time is right."

"She must be hidden until they leave," Madam Sayed said.

"Rock's heart will protect her," Greta said.

"Quickly then," Madam Sayed told Greta. "The Vaksana spare and the beasts have not yet returned from the fort."

Numerous passages had been hewn through the Rock over generations, but the tunnel behind the House of Satya's gate was one of the few that opened to the summit. The giantess who served Rani Shikra had been present when the secret to opening the gate had been given to the young Parama, and they had all thought Greta too stupid to understand. Choosing that route now, the giantess emerged on the summit at the back of the oracle's garden and trudged across the plateau toward the columns of rock that had held her and her companion long ago.

CHAPTER 33

Lingli shivered within her cloak at the base of the rock column where the guards had left her chained. The cold wind racing over the summit cut nearly as deep as her new, brutal understanding that the rani sought a penalty more severe than the one she had already suffered—and she would not wait for the judges' pronouncement to apply it.

She could level charges against herself just as easily. *Why did I think Mafala would ignore what I had done? I should have left when I returned the envoy's ring, but…Sid.* She didn't want to think about him, but her thoughts continued to circle the mounting stone, the blade that struck so fast, and worst of all, Sid's silence.

Nothing! He said nothing. You are forsaken.

She had to stop these shrieking thoughts.

How did she return to her room yesterday? She couldn't remember, but she recalled that Madam Sayed had cleaned her shortened finger and settled her on the cot, then held a cup to her lips. The drink was bitter.

"Stop coughing," Madam had demanded, but her usual curtness had gone soft on the edges. "The giantess said this would help you heal, and if you want that southerner to regret her lies, that's what you must do."

The last thing Lingli recalled was watching the tip of her bandaged finger slowly turn pink. "It's gone," she murmured, her eyelids growing heavy.

"You'll hardly notice it by tomorrow," Madam said. "Madam Satya did you a kindness. You should thank the stars that she's a master of short blades. Prince Siddharth likely would have taken off your whole hand."

Perhaps because of Madam's potion, she had dreamed of a little spirit that inhabited the shadowy space in her room. On the trunk's lid, a boy with dark, curly hair like Sid's sat hugging his knees in the room's wreckage. Waves of sorrow rippled from him, and Lingli wanted to speak to him, but her dream carried her away. The empty perches in the cage swung as if birds sat upon them. A wolf growled

379

under the trapdoor. She was afraid, but not of the wolf. The reason turned into mist and disappeared.

Then, in the faint beginning of dawn, she woke to the sound of raised voices and the trapdoor flew open. Madam emerged with the keys, and a day guard's head poked through the opening behind her.

"Have you no decency!" Madam said as she unlocked the gate. "Wait! I will help her dress and bring her out!"

The guard disappeared, and Madam stomped across the room to Lingli's bedside. She leaned close and whispered, "The maharani has ordered you out of the palace immediately. Take everything."

Cold to her core but unsurprised, Lingli tugged her pack out from underneath the cot with her good hand. The pack was full now with the small cache of supplies she had ferreted away. She pulled on the pants she had worn to the Rock moons earlier.

Madam nervously flitted around the room. "No time," she muttered, "and here we are at winter's gates."

Stepping into her old boots, Lingli reached inside, reassured to feel the haft of her rabbit knife.

Madam opened her paints and hastily covered her dark vein. "Don't argue with them," she said. "When they leave you across the span wait near the gate. I will speak to Jal—Master Avani. He'll send someone to meet you."

While Madam combed color into her lank hair, the guard banged on the trapdoor.

"Patience!" Madam shouted, putting the pack on Lingli's back and fastening her cloak.

Lingli tottered down the stairs, and the day guard waiting below wore his disgust openly, turning on his heels as soon as she touched the fifth floor. On the second floor another guard quietly fell in behind Madam. The first guard turned toward the door to the catwalk instead of the stairs descending to the front grounds.

"Where are you taking her?" Madam asked.

"The summit," the guard answered. "Giants' Post."

Lingli faintly remembered Master Avani mentioning that place, but she saw Madam's shock, and fear began to sour her throat.

"Oh," Madam said. "I did not think she..." The dance teacher stopped, then called out as they pushed her on. "I will send someone as soon as possible."

And here she was, sitting among bits of dried viscera and bone shards on the top of the Rock.

If she didn't get loose soon she would either freeze to death or become just one more piece of prey for the wolves. Blowing on her hands to keep warm, Lingli folded the fingers of her good hand into a tight bud, but the cuff was too tight. She worked the manacle on her ankle up and down her boot to see how far the iron would slide. Not much.

Under scudding clouds the color of a spoiled egg, she paced as far as the chains would allow until a small jingling noise caught her ear. If it was the wolves returned, she could only hope her end would come quickly, but to her great relief Greta approached, carrying her heavy ring of keys. Kneeling by her side, the giantess freed her from the manacles.

"How do I get off this rock?"

"Hmmm. Wanderers will leave soon. You will go with them, but stay hidden now." Greta tucked her keys into her pocket and walked back the way she had come. Lingli staggered after her. In the shadow of a bluff that marked the highest part of the Rock, they passed a stone table and chairs of woven grass and rushes.

"What is this place?" Lingli asked.

"Where ancestors gathered," Greta said, without pausing. Lingli followed her into a narrow cave opening. After lighting a lantern, the giantess continued a few paces farther inside until they faced what seemed to be a solid stone wall. To Lingli's amazement, Greta squeezed herself through an even narrower opening disguised by a fold of cleverly painted stone. In the broader passage ahead, Greta turned around, so the lantern light danced on figures that decorated a metal gate behind them.

"Upper Gate of Satya," Greta said. "Start with Satya, end with Satya. Follow the pattern."

Lingli watched the giantess press her palm to the chinkara, the symbol of the House of Satya. When a buzzing noise sounded, Lingli took a step back, but Greta continued, touching the House of Duran's upright sword, the House of Avani's owl, Tilan's wheel, Vaksana's tree,

Duvanya's bear, Hansa's swan, and finally she pressed the chinkara again, ignoring one other symbol carved upon the gate—an armored man. The gate slid closed.

This was otherworld magic. Lingli had so many questions, but Greta was already several strides ahead, forcing her to run to catch up. The floor pitched downward and tracked back and forth, but the passage itself was completely unremarkable. Only one small wooden door opened in the passage wall some distance below the gate, and they passed it by.

At the end of the passage a lantern burned before another gate like the one above. Greta drew out a package of food from her apron pocket, along with a small waterskin, and handed them to her.

"Safe here," the giantess told her. "Wait two days. Remember the pattern?"

Lingli pressed her good palm to the chinkara, and the metal stung, making her flinch.

"Heed not. It will pass."

Wincing with each sting, Lingli pressed the other symbols in the sequence Greta had used at the upper gate. The gate slid back, and a yawning black void opened ahead of them.

Greta stepped through. "Two days. Wait, and I will come. Now close it."

CHAPTER 34

Bleary-eyed, Sid sat on the edge of his bed and wondered if he had slept at all. Horrible half dreams of being trapped in a box of some kind had exhausted him. Then there had been what seemed like hours of Li staring at him accusingly with eyes that were nothing but pale orbs like the oracle's. The vein in her temple had etched the side of her face with spidery blue lines. He shivered.

But he must have slept at some point, for he didn't remember when the thali sitting on his bedside table had arrived and the tea was still warm. Cursing the day, the night, and his own cowardly behavior the day before, he began to dress. His resolve to apologize to Li had frayed, but it had to be done. He wrapped a roti from the thali inside one of his many gifted sashes and stuffed it inside his vest.

After tossing his golden juttis halfway across the room to be sure the scorpions had departed, Sid slipped them on and left his rooms without a plan. He nodded to the door guard and his ever-present escort, prepared to suffer their curiosity even if they reported his visit to the sixth floor to the rani.

As he reached the stairs and was about to start climbing, the door to the library opened. Parth emerged carrying an armful of parchments.

"How's your Book of Avani transcriptions going?" Sid asked in what he hoped was a casual manner. "Up to the second generation yet?"

"What? The prince deigns to speak to a mere spare?"

"Stop it," Sid said. "You know more than half the nobles at the council table."

"I've often wondered if they feed you nobles something to make you stupid."

"You should know. What we don't eat gets scraped back into Korvar's pots for you all."

Parth chuckled and asked him, "Heard from your girlfriend? You know, Madam Sayed's seamstress, the thief. Pale thing? Missing a finger?"

Sid tried not to wince outwardly. "She's not my girlfriend."

"Well, she's got spirit, I'll give her that," Parth said. When Sid stared at him blankly, he said, "Didn't you know? Our glorious rani had her banished to the summit, but when Vidkun took the wolves up this morning, she was gone."

"Gone?" Sid's thoughts stumbled over the sequence of events. *Banished?*

"Some say she's the one the day guard's been looking for since Shankar was walloped." Parth shifted the parchments under his other arm. "Considering that the rani already promised good coin for information on the kitchen thieves, I'd like to wager that the reward for helping them find this girl will be even higher. What do you think? Safe bet?"

"I…I suppose so."

Parth laughed. "I must attend to my never-ending duties, Prince Sir. Dismiss me, won't you?"

Sid forced a laugh and waited for Parth to pass downstairs before he took the door opening onto the terrace, eager for the chilly breeze to clear his head.

Banished after paying her penalty? That's not in the law. At least, I don't think it is.

Sid came to a sudden stop at the top of the stairs in the new tower. Halfway down the flight ahead one of the wolves strained to reach Rud, who cowered against the wall and held up his serving tray like a shield. A smirking Vidkun held Titok's chains.

"Just answer me and stop wetting yourself," Vidkun said. "Were you on the summit this morning?"

"I told you I wasn't."

"What are you doing?" Sid said.

Vidkun, Rud, and Titok looked up at him.

"Good morning, Prince. I'm doing my duty. Protecting the realm and its allies. A criminal has escaped—a girl I believe you know. We must find out if she has accomplices. I am simply questioning all those who were late for duty this morning."

"He told you he wasn't there."

"Did he? I didn't hear him."

"Call the wolf off."

"Of course, Prince." Vidkun ordered Titok down, and the wolf turned his head and snarled at Vidkun.

"I said down!" Vidkun shouted as he removed a blunt-headed shishpar from his belt.

Titok crouched, but not completely, and his lip rippled back to expose his teeth.

The end of the shishpar in Vidkun's hand suddenly glowed blue, and Titok went onto his belly, but Vidkun applied the weapon anyway. Sid could not see how the blunt head would have caused much pain, but the huge wolf cried and yelped like a pup.

"Stop it!" the rani shouted from the foot of the stairs.

Vidkun jerked upright and holstered the weapon, as the rani ascended the stairs with Akela at her side and Greta behind. She waved the trembling Rud away and knelt to feel Titok's ribs.

Now she'll have him arrested, Sid thought happily as he joined his mother.

Looking up from the wolf's side, the rani said angrily, "Do you think abuse will buy his loyalty?"

"I would not abuse them, Maharani," Vidkun groveled. "We are… adjusting to one another."

"If your authority relies on force alone," she said, "you will lose. Maybe not today, but eventually they will turn on you, and you will fall. Do you understand? Your brother would wield that weapon only as a last resort."

Vidkun looked through the mane of hair that fell over his eyes. "I beg your pardon, Your Majesty, but I am not my brother."

"That is all too apparent."

Vidkun twitched and lowered his eyes.

"Well? Aren't you mounting a search for the escaped thief?"

"Yes, Your Majesty."

"Go then, before she reaches Mephistan, and triple whatever rations you've been giving my pets. He's starving."

When Vidkun left them, the rani breathed deeply to compose herself.

"Where have you been?" she asked him. "I thought I told you we would review the accounts today."

"I am sorry," Sid said. "I didn't sleep well."

Already descending the stairs ahead of him, the rani said, "My sleep was not easy either. What is troubling you?"

"Bad dreams."

"What did you see in these dreams?"

Knowing her question was more an effort to exercise her frustrations than any real interest, Sid feared asking about Li's banishment, but if he did not ask her then, he would never find the courage later.

"I saw Li."

The rani's step hitched then she continued. Sid stayed by her side.

"Why did you banish her? Didn't she pay her penalty to the realm?"

They were only steps from her quarters, and the rani did not answer until Greta closed the door behind them. Sid tensed, waiting for his mother's mood to define the day.

"I needed to pacify Mafala," she said. "Hassan will take offense when the canal goes dry, but he will move his people here soon enough and take up more productive business. Mafala, however… She will hold on to the smallest slight until the last star falls."

Her answer flowed too smoothly. He knew it was not more than a small piece of the truth.

"You didn't tell me."

"I gave the order at dawn, and you were not there. If you heard of her banishment, I suppose you also heard of her escape, but why is this your concern? Why are we discussing this again?"

"She…she was with me when I had no one else," he said, surprising himself because he had never said that before.

"No one else? You were never abandoned. We, your true family, wished for your return to the Rock every day you were away from us."

"How would I know?" Sid said. His voice was sharper than he intended, but the wound that had shaped his early cycles still ached. "I grew up thinking my mother was buried in the cairn by the meadow, and you still haven't told me why you left me there."

"Shall I tell you now?" the rani said, trying to disguise her impatience. "Shall we let the day's business hang so you may hear the story." She curtly directed him to sit on her divan.

"You were born to me shortly after your father and I were married. I was new to the throne—battling drought and bandits and more, not that you should care—but understand it was a difficult time for me, and more so for Zakir." She had begun her story in a flat voice, but suddenly a passion began to color her voice. "Everything we did, everything, was to protect our rule and to protect you."

His pulse pounded so loud in his ears Sid worried he couldn't hear properly.

"On the day of your naming ceremony, your father presented you to his house's elders, and this is not done in the south. Some elders took offense, accusing your father of adopting foreign practices, and the threats began immediately. We had not realized how deep the jealousies in his house had grown. Your father did not want to send you away, and neither did I, but in the end we agreed it was necessary.

"Greta told me that the other giant who had served Saatkulom, the one my mother had exiled, lived in the Western Woods. As long as the giantess was in my service, we trusted that you would be as safe with him as you could possibly be."

Sid looked at Greta, who remained so giantstill by the door it was easy to forget she was there. He remembered the giantess's first words to him during the journey to the palace.

"We thought we would leave you there for three cycles," the rani said. "Maybe four. Only until Zakir was named head of his house. But then your father died."

Sid's throat closed. *I asked for this.*

His mother looked toward the ceiling as if her memories hung there. "It was quite sudden. He had gained assurances that the elders would recognize your right, and we decided to bring you back. We talked about what we thought you would look like and wondered if you would remember us, but before we could fetch you from the forest, Zakir was called back to his father's lands.

"Aza Mussan had received a message saying that traders had been way-laid by a gang of thieves. He was old even then and not fit for battle, yet he was preparing to rescue his people, and Zakir could not allow that. He left immediately, determined to take his father's place."

The rani toyed with a chain around her neck and laughed bitterly. "Your father was stupid that way. Stupidly proud, stupidly brave, and very soon after he left on this errand, stupidly dead. He walked into a trap that some say had been set for Aza Mussan, but I think it was set for him."

She paused, as if to measure his willingness to hear the rest of the story, and Sid did not look away.

"All that I know," she said. "All the rest that I am telling you, is what I learned from a scout who was a member of your father's party.

"When Zakir reached the high dry lands where the traders had supposedly been attacked, they came upon a trail. In the rocky overhangs and ledges that marked that place they found a torn cloak, such as the traders wore. Soon after they discovered a cave, so naturally they had to explore it to see if the bandits or missing traders were inside.

"After a short passage, the cave opened into a large chamber. Zakir told his men to look for passages, and they explored the cracks and corners but found nothing. As they prepared to leave, Zakir raised his torch, seeing only stones and shadows until he noticed, high at the back of the chamber, a ledge with something upon it that caught the light."

The hairs on Sid's arms rose.

"A huge serpent rested there. The scout called her Naga and said she might not have taken any notice of the men at all if her sleep had not been disturbed, but a few fools threw their spears, and in an instant, she was coiling on the ledge above them. When she raised her huge head to strike, the men panicked and began to rush the passage. Zakir, too, recognized her advantage and began his retreat, holding out his torch with a few others to keep her at bay.

"The first time she struck, the scout recalled, she knocked the torch from Zakir's hand. He and the remaining men drew their blades as she reared up and still hardly moved her great length. When she struck the second time, she rammed his legs with her head, causing him to stumble. He managed a shallow stab in her neck, but this only further angered Naga.

"The scout told me he understood her language plain enough. She said, 'You are mine, Ascaryan, because I am stronger and more patient. You are going to tire of striking me or you are going to run. Either way, you are mine.'

"I like to believe that Zakir delivered his own message when he dove for his fallen torch and tossed it onto the serpent's coils. Then he turned and ran with everyone else.

"The scout said that Zakir emerged from the cave. He had taken a step into the sunlight when they saw Naga's fangs flash as she lunged from behind. She struck him on the side of his neck and shoulder, delivering her venom almost like a caress. Zakir struggled to escape, but she twisted her loops about him. His blade lost, his arms stilled. He looked to the sky, no doubt pleading with the ancestors to end his torment. Naga pulled him back into the darkness, and that was the last anyone saw of your father."

Sid blinked. In all his cycles, he hadn't had an image of his father, just the idea. A few days earlier he had begun to see him more clearly with each word his mother and grandmother uttered about him. And now the vision he had of Zakir was much fuller, but the father was permanently and forever gone. The questions he would have liked to have asked had flown away—flushed like birds fleeing the arrows loosed in his mother's story.

"Now you understand why we did not collect you sooner," his mother said. "From that day to this, I never believed his death was an accident. Someone plotted to kill your father, and the plan was not laid by Naga. I had to reconsider my future and yours. The wisest course of action was to leave you where you were until I could be certain it was safe to bring you back."

Vacillating between a sense of relief that his father's final act was a noble one and an untethered grief for a parent that he had never met, Sid wished he had just one more story, one to help him see Zakir without a serpent on his neck. But his mother was already tucking her feelings away. Asking more about him felt like an unkindness while not asking felt disloyal, as if he were one of those in the party who had failed to save their commander.

He finally said, "Why didn't you tell me who you were when we met?"

"Would you have believed me?" the rani said. "I rather hoped you were too bright for that, and I didn't have time for your questions. More interesting to me was your desire to come. You were so eager I hardly needed to offer coin. You were ripe fruit, easily picked."

Sid clamped his mouth shut.

The rani unfolded a parchment on her table. "Come now. The business of the realm does not wait for anyone, Siddharth, and as my heir, you cannot waste your days wondering about things that might have been. Krux and his accounting will not allow it."

Reluctantly, Sid came to her table where she showed him a listing of the sale of gemstones, rough and finished, as well as the revenue from the sale of woven cloth. He wasn't completely stupid. He knew that the tale of Zakir's last encounter and the business of the morning—all of this—was meant to distract him from Li's banishment. Yet, as he brooded about how skillfully his mother parried that subject, he couldn't help but appreciate her suspicion that someone had gone to great lengths to cause his father's death. *They wouldn't need half that effort to bring about my end.*

He pretend to care when she pointed out that recent revenues were surpassed by the expenses for foodstuff, metals, timber, and other items required by both the Rock and Nilampur. Sid's thoughts, however, circled back to his mother's persecution of Lingli and her failure to arrest Vidkun or Gaddar despite their earlier conversation.

"All that we enjoy," the rani said, "requires a fine balance in finances." She must have seen that his thoughts were elsewhere. "Siddharth!"

He jumped. "Yes, finances." He racked his brain for a plausible suggestion. "Couldn't we sell more gems?"

The rani sighed. "There are more veins, but we cannot dig as carelessly as in the past without hollowing our Rock. Gems are treasure we can discover but not reproduce, and neither gems, nor ores or metals, can be farmed."

"So we must acquire them elsewhere," Sid said. "That's why we need to take back Zahatara."

"Very good. The ore from that fallen star has powerful qualities that can make stronger armor and metalwork. Even if little remains, we need it."

There was a knock on the door, and Greta opened it for the guard who said Madam Sayed sought a meeting. The dance teacher entered with a wrapped parcel.

"Your wedding gown, Maharani. Shall I do the fitting?"

Sid thought Madam looked nervous, as if she half expected a blow to land on her. *Because Li worked for her.* His mother's expression was impossible to read.

"Take it inside," the rani ordered, then she escorted him to the door of her quarters.

"We will return to the accounting work soon. In the meantime, I suggest you join Madam Satya for a review of the amendments to the trade agreement we will present to Mephistan in the spring."

"I'm glad you told me about my father," Sid said.

"You are much like him. Trusting, and loyal."

As Sid reached the door, the rani grasped his hand.

"I know you may not accept this, but as your mother, it is my duty to protect you at all costs, you must understand that there will be an endless number of Ascaryans pretending to be your friend. It is a sad tax imposed on all nobility. This…seamstress…is a thief, Siddharth. You cannot indulge her."

His chest tight, Sid muttered, "What you say is true about many, but not everyone, Amma. If it is so plain to you that Li's crimes are worthy of exile, what about the others I told you about? What about Vidkun? Or Captain Gaddar? Aren't they pretending to be *your* friends?"

The rani raised her brows. "I have tried to explain to you that I can act against those you named only when the time is right. Don't you understand that? If I only provide your word as evidence, the court may not be prepared to judge correctly."

How could he deny this logic? He couldn't hold her gaze for long.

The rani opened the door for him and said softly, "I think you would agree that I cannot allow any criminal to build a reputation upon my defenders' embarrassment. When the seamstress is captured, her penalty will be the most severe."

Sid understood her perfectly. He felt the blood freezing in his veins as he backed to the landing.

"For your sake," the rani said, just before she closed the door, "I will be most glad if she has managed to leave the Rock already."

CHAPTER 35

When Greta left her, Lingli sat near the lower Satya gate for a long time, reviewing her supplies and wondering how to acquire a few more practical things—namely more food, and wool pants. Whatever the perils in the beyond, focusing on these things was better than thinking about Sid. That hurt cut too deep, much deeper than the actual injury done to her, and thinking about it would only show her bones that shouldn't be seen, so she put it aside.

Eventually she dozed for a few hours, then got up, took the lantern and the waterskin, and began to explore the passage. She hiked back to the upper gate, returned to the lower one, and climbed up again, learning every step in between so that even without the lantern she could move quickly without tripping. Near what she guessed was dawn of the following day, she explored the rough-hewn side tunnel behind the small wooden door closer to the top of the passage. After following it downward almost the same distance as the main passage, she found no gate but a mound of broken rock and old timbers blocking the way.

Atop the rubble, Lingli moved along the edge of the rockslide where it slumped against a wall. When her lantern flickered in one spot, she began moving rocks aside with her good hand. Gradually, she uncovered the lintel of a doorway and a shallow opening beneath it. Once the space was large enough, she crawled into it, pushing the lantern ahead and keeping her injured hand tucked up under her chin. On the other side of the lintel the space opened to a ceiling little more than an arm's length above, and Lingli found herself on an identical rubble pile in a second passage, which ran perpendicular to the first one.

Is this the one I saw before? Before she could scoot down the rockpile to explore further, the stones around her began to grumble and hiss.

Grabbing the lantern, she quickly crawled back the way she'd come. Small rocks and dirt broke loose from the walls and ceiling. Stones she had moved aside shifted back against her hips and legs before she could clear the lintel, and her lantern was nearly buried. Eyes squeezed shut in fear that the ceiling would collapse, Lingli braced herself, but the rock around her went silent. She stayed still and waited. The silence held.

Not a shaking, just a settling.

Her wounded hand was pinned to her side. Her legs didn't hurt, but she couldn't move them. She focused her thoughts on breathing, remembering the first time she had been stuck in a dark, tight space.

Once, when she was very young, Red had set her in the branches of a tree and told her to practice counting birds while he cut wood. There was a dove, a thrush, so many crows, but counting was new to her, and she liked the sound of the numbers as she said them. She continued even after Red stopped his work and went giantstill to listen for something she couldn't hear. Then he fetched her down from the tree and quickly carried her back to the cabin.

Inside, he had pushed back his chair and surprised her by opening a door in the floor. It was the first time she had seen the large, brass-bound trunk resting below. The things inside looked terribly interesting, but the giant quickly wrapped everything he removed in a bear skin and pushed it all into the loft.

"We will play a counting game," he said, setting her in the trunk. "Can you count the birds again?"

She frowned, not understanding how she could count birds that were not there.

"You saw birds, yes?"

She nodded.

"Remember each bird and count it," Red said. "Close eyes and see them in the forest. Can you see them? Count slowly. I will open the trunk when you've counted all of them."

She had never been scared of the dark before, but she didn't like the sound of the lid closing above her, and she liked the small space even less. She did as Red asked. The first bird she had seen was a crow that had cawed at her from a neighboring tree. She counted him and went to the next. And the next. And the one after that.

The tears came when she counted the forty-first bird, another crow that had mocked her. She touched the trunk's lid and drew her hand back, afraid to push. Losing place in her count, she started over.

When Red finally opened the lid, she rose shakily. "Seventy-two birds," she said, tears of relief streaming down her face.

He had hugged her close and wiped her face. "We have guests," he said as he carried her to the cabin door.

On the far side of the yard, a woman stood holding a baby with dark curly hair.

"She's bringing you a friend," Red said.

She had been so happy and eager to play with the baby Sid, the memory of the trunk was nearly forgotten, but now she lay in the Rock's embrace. No "friend" was coming this time. Her tears stung.

As dear as a brother but he utters not a word in my defense and did not spare me before the blade came down.

For a long while she considered obliging the Rock and remaining there until she returned to stone, but Red's voice nagged at her. *Living things have purpose. Living things have choice. Never let anyone make you useless.*

Those were his words after the attack at the festival when she had become scared of everything. Yet he had somehow nursed her through that gray spring with her desperately clinging to his words until the colors of the world slowly reappeared around her. She had thought she was whole again. She wanted to believe it, but then Sid left.

It didn't matter. It would be even more useless, in Red's opinion, to die in a pile of rubble than to die from fear of what the villagers had threatened.

Her shoulders were nearly past the lintel. She turned and twisted until, bit by bit, the gravel shifted. With her good hand she slowly freed the other, then her hips, then her legs. When she finally pulled free, she found herself bruised but whole, suffering only from a soaked leg where the waterskin had leaked.

Unburying the lantern, she contemplated the space where she had been stuck. *Better to keep all passages open.* With one eye on the ceiling, she slowly cleared a wider passage and rolled larger rocks under the lintel to better support it.

Upon returning to the lower Satya gate, Lingli pinched the lantern's wick to save oil and ate the remains of the food Greta had given her. After trying to sleep for a short time, she hiked to the top gate and back again. The hours slogged by. She was certain two days had passed.

She's not coming.

Lingli re-lit her lantern, stood before the gate panel, and contemplated the symbols. *Chinkara, blade, owl, wheel, tree, bear, swan, chinkara. Ignore the armored man.*

She took off her cloak and draped it over the lantern. Holding her little rabbit knife in her good hand, Lingli hardly felt the stinging as she pressed the sequence. The gate slid open as if the rock around it was water.

Tensed and ready to spring back, she looked into the blackness and listened. Nothing. Once her cloak was refastened, she raised the lantern.

Before her was a large, nearly circular cavern room with several passages like the one she stood in. Only one other passage had a similar metal gate. The rest were barred with old timbers or stood open. Tiptoeing into the middle of the space, Lingli turned her face in one direction, then the other, until she sensed a draft between the two broadest passages. She took the one she hoped would lead her out.

After a short walk, she saw a patch of starlight ahead. Quenching her lantern, Lingli hugged the edge of the cavern opening and discovered she was in the mouth—the same cave opening she had passed with the guards on the way up to the summit. Outside, hazy stars cast the palace grounds in golden light, and she felt her exile as sharp as the point of a blade, but she would not allow herself to dwell on that. Whatever delayed Greta could not be good. If she meant to escape this place, she would have to find the wanderers herself.

Creeping across the summit path, Lingli leaned over the edge to look down into the stable yard. The horses were quiet. No fire was lit where the Mirajkars had camped before, and the wagon was gone.

Have they left without me?

On the verge of sneaking down to the stables to look for the wanderers, she heard a noise coming from further up the summit path. Someone rounded a switchback. Lantern light shone out, and Lingli scurried back into the mouth.

Two zhoukoo pulling a heavily laden handcart passed the cavern opening and continued downhill. Behind the cart, three figures followed. The last one—a tall, long-haired man—held a drawn talwar. She knew him. *Master Vaksana.*

After the group passed, Lingli moved back to the edge of the path and watched them descend to the mining hall. They had just reached it when two more figures detached themselves from the shadows of the hall's veranda. Swallowing hard, Lingli realized how close she had come to being caught.

Master Vaksana's group and the two newcomers seemed to know each other. There was some conversation among them, but she couldn't hear what was said. The newcomers joined the others, but they had barely resumed their walk along the path, when one of the figures, a turbaned man, fell behind Master Vaksana, raised a dagger, and stabbed him in the back.

The noble yelled out in anger and pain, and Lingli clamped her hand over her mouth to squash her surprise.

Spinning away from his assailant, the wolfmaster took a defensive stance. The one who had attacked him danced backward into a shadowed spot, and Master Vaksana and another in the party took the fight forward. She heard blades clash and muffled cries. Creeping out onto the path Lingli saw the noble emerge from the Rock's shadow, still holding his talwar at the ready. One of the others came to the wolfmaster's side as if to lend his help.

In utter disbelief, Lingli watched the man draw a blade. As Master Vaksana turned, the man plunged it into his chest. Teetering to one side, the wolfmaster collapsed.

The zhoukoo, who had waited motionless alongside the cart, now abandoned it and scaled the rock face like spiders. The others ran toward the cave, leaving Lingli no choice but to flee ahead of them. Certain they were gaining on her, she jumped behind a column of rock on the edge of the passage and crouched low. They ran past, their lantern bobbing, and she waited until she could no longer see any light or hear their footfalls. Still holding her knife in her good hand, she returned to the cavern's mouth.

The fallen wolfmaster lay on the path near the abandoned cart. She watched him rise on one elbow and pull himself toward the cart, but he soon fell back with a groan.

He said he was Red's friend.

Murderers were behind her. The palace ahead. There was no way off the Rock that she knew without passing the fallen noble. Seeing no one else and hearing no cry of alarm, Lingli drew her hood forward and hurried down the path to Master Vaksana.

"You too?" he grunted.

"No, not me," Lingli said, holstering her little knife and kneeling by his shoulder.

His breath was ragged. When she lightly touched his chest, the sticky dampness under her fingers smothered her hope.

He moved his hand at his side as if seeking something. Hanging from his belt was a chain with the odd metal instrument she had seen him use to control the wolves. Lingli put it in his hand.

"Call," he whispered.

She shook her head. "I can't."

"Tell them...traitors." The wolfmaster closed his eyes and stiffened as the last rattling breaths left him.

Leaving him there seemed wrong, but she knew she should run. Before she could gather herself, she heard the zing of someone drawing a blade behind her.

"Get away from him," a voice commanded.

Captain Duvanya stood on the path, talwar drawn, with two more night guards behind him. As she moved back, the guards kept their blades ready while the captain knelt and touched the wolfmaster's neck. Bending close, he repeated a tribute to protect the dead from the otherworld, and when he rose the moonlight illuminated the anger in his face. He stepped toward her suddenly, and she cringed, but he stopped beyond her reach. Lingli realized her hood had fallen back, and judging from the captain's expression, the powder Madam Sayed had applied to her hair must have worn off. She lowered her head and turned her swollen temple away.

"Here lies one who was true to the realm," Captain Duvanya said. "Stabbed to death. May the ancestors have mercy on you, seamstress, or whatever you are, because I will not. Not this time."

"I didn't do this. There were two men, more—"

"Shut up, and do not give me an excuse to commit the night's second murder. Take off your cloak and your boots."

He quickly checked her cloak's pockets, turning out several spools of thread and yarn and a wool scarf, but he evidently did not understand the usefulness of deep hems and did not find her needles, her flint and steel, her soup spoon, or Red's last firestick. The rest of her provisions waited in her pack at the lower Satya gate.

As soon as she stepped out of her boots, the night captain drew out her rabbit knife.

"Look closely," she said. "There is no blood on it."

He glared at her and tucked the little knife inside his vest before dispatching one of the guards back to the palace. Once more, the night captain circled the wolfmaster's body, his grief plain.

"You are witness to tonight's events," the captain told the remaining guard. "Witness this. On this eleventh day of the fourteenth moon, I arrested the seamstress Lingli Tabaan for the murder of Jordak Vaksana, master of his house. The body was discovered stabbed near the mining hall. That is my word."

"Take this," he said bitterly, tossing her cloak to her. "You'll need it in the jail."

She left her boots behind when the captain ordered her to go back up the path.

The guard carried a lantern and led the way and the captain followed behind. Occasionally feeling the tickle of his talwar's tip against her back, Lingli gritted her teeth. Her cursed fate had shown itself once more. Guilt or innocence didn't matter, and it required no great imagination to see that the Seven's judges would take more than a finger this time.

At the cavern mouth the guard hesitated, giving her an idea that she didn't have time to think about. She kicked the next small rock she stepped on. Its patter in the passage ahead of them caught the guard's attention. When he raised the lantern to look, she bolted forward and knocked it from his hand, plunging them into darkness.

Ignoring the stones scraping and bruising her bare feet, Lingli held out her arms wide and hurled herself forward. There could be no hiding along the way, and there was no time to grab the lantern she'd left there. She expected to feel a blade in her back at any moment, but she had to try.

When the sounds from her footsteps echoed differently, and Lingli guessed that she had entered the wheel room. She stopped and tried to touch the passage walls but found them gone. Grateful her pursuers had fallen behind, she began creeping across the open darkness, trying to judge which direction would bring her to the Satya gate.

When she touched stone again Lingli frantically swept the wall with both hands, searching for the opening. The sound of a flint being struck somewhere behind her made her bite down hard on the inside of her cheek. If they lit their lantern before she found the gate, her escape would be over.

At last she found the edge of the open gate and stumbled inside, shaking as she traced the shape of each symbol before pressing it. Before she pressed the chinkara for the final time, light glowed in the wheel room and footsteps pounded toward her. Then the gate closed with a tiny whoosh, and she leaned her head against the passage wall, trying to slow her racing heart.

Her relief hardly lasted a full breath. An arm encircled her neck, and a hand covered her mouth.

"Shouting won't help you," a voice hissed in her ear.

"Who is it?" another voice asked.

Another lantern was lit. Facing her were two boys with dirty faces and dirtier clothes. The one who held her pack had a chinkara brooch on his shoulder. The other—the fish-faced boy—chewed on her last piece of naan.

"Stars, you're ugly," the fish-faced boy declared.

"Bind her hands," the one holding her said.

The Satya boy pulled some rope from his belt and tossed it to the one holding her. "I think this is the seamstress they chopped," he said.

The site of the rope was enough to make Lingli sweat, but the rope was all but forgotten when the one binding her jerked the knot tight and turned her around to face him. The miner. The one who had threatened Korvar that night in the kitchens. He was much too close to her face.

"Star-cursed, aren't you?"

Then a fourth member of the group edged into the light. He had a thick belt studded with metal rings, and long dark hair hung over his face. She didn't need to see the anar tree on his shoulder, to recognize the jailer and wolfhandler, Vidkun, brother of the murdered Master Vaksana.

He regarded her surprise and said, "You bore witness to our last scuffle, I see."

His voice had an odd lilt, and he looked ill. "Where does this passage go?" he asked.

"The summit."

"We should go back up there," the Satya boy said.

"Forget that," Vidkun scoffed. "The nightguard will be all over up there looking for you."

The miner shoved her down on the floor, and all four moved away, conversing in low whispers. When they returned, the miner asked, "What are you to the prince? Servant? Whore?"

She didn't answer.

Vidkun smirked, shook his head, and said, "We're lucky there's a reward for your ugly face, but you're luckier." To the others, he said, "We're going out the way we came in."

"They'll be waiting," the Satya boy said.

"Maybe yes, maybe no. We'll put her out first and see what happens. If anyone's there, I'll tell them you helped me make the arrest. We're giving them what they want."

The miner sniffed, pulled her to her feet, and moved her directly in front of the gate, clamping a hand on her shoulder.

Vidkun ordered her to tell him the sequence.

She said nothing until the miner leaned close and whispered, "I'll carve you up into seven pieces and give your head to the rani for my reward."

"The chinkara," she said.

Vidkun jerked his hand back when the gate stung him. Cursing her, he wrapped his hand in the end of his coat and continued as she named the symbols.

She tried to free her mind, but she remained stubbornly tethered to her body—a body she fully expected to be hit with a volley of arrows or struck by a blade as soon as the gate slid open.

They were met with lantern light, and an immediate order not to move. The guard who had accompanied Captain Duvanya stepped forward with his blade drawn.

"Ah, good we met you," Vidkun said. "We caught the thief that escaped the summit."

"Thief?" the guard said, lowering his talwar. "She's accused of murder now, sir. I'm sorry to be the one to tell you, but your brother... Master Vaksana's been killed."

"What?" Vidkun said, feigning disbelief. "When?"

"We found him behind the mining hall only a little while ago. She was messing about his body, before she, uh, escaped us."

"Have the ancestors forsaken us?" Vidkun's voice dripped with sorrow. "My brother was a defender of great skill. How could this...this asura... have killed him? Take me to his body, now!"

Vidkun stepped toward the guard, and Lingli felt the miner's blade prick her back as he pushed her forward. The guard and Vidkun led them back toward the cave entrance, and Lingli found herself between them and the miner and the boys.

"Where is your captain?" Vidkun asked.

"He's gone back to help bear your brother's body to the palace. He left me on watch here in case she or any of the others showed up."

"Others?"

"Signs near the body look like more than one was there," the guard said. "And the zhoukoo told my captain with their hand language they were forced to do the bidding of some group on the summit."

"Is that so?" Vidkun said.

Vidkun looked back over his shoulder and raised his chin. Immediately the miner stepped behind the guard and drove his blade into his back at the base of his neck. The man made a garbled sound, his eyes bulging, before he dropped the lantern and fell to the floor.

Lingli's choked cry was cut off when the Satya boy clamped a hand over her mouth and pushed her into their huddle around the guard's body.

"What'd you do that for, Kadam?" the fish-faced boy whined, touching the body with his foot. "We were going to get our reward."

"One more stupid word from you, and you're next," the miner said, wiping his blade on his hip.

Vidkun said, "Did you not hear? They're looking for more than just her. You cannot go back to the palace."

"What do we do?" the Satya boy asked.

Hearing a small sound, Lingli looked behind. From the dark, three Hudulfah fighters emerged.

Vidkun straightened and waved toward Kadam and the two boys. "They had some trouble."

"Where are the supplies?" one of the four asked stiffly in the common tongue.

"Well, you see," Vidkun said, "after the noble was vanquished—"

The southerners talked among themselves, their expressions questioning.

"He means," Kadam interjected, "once he killed his brother, we had to run."

"What choice did I have!" Vidkun hissed. "You and your vaunted handiwork left me no choice."

Lingli couldn't believe it. *Vidkun struck the killing blow.*

The southerners looked skeptical. The fighter who had spoken before frowned at Lingli and asked, "Who is this one?"

"She is the one I'll turn over to the guard," Vidkun said. "Once I do, there will be no suspicion directed our way, and no obstacle to your prince's plan."

Despite his words, Lingli could see that Vidkun was nervous. The boys, too. Kadam remained quiet behind her.

The southerner said, "No. You will come with us. Ba Hassan will decide."

Hassan? What are southern fighters doing in the Rock?

"Do you not understand? I need to hand her to the rani quickly."

"Ba Hassan will decide."

The three southerners began to move their hands toward their weapons.

"I see you are loyal to the prince," Vidkun said. "As am I. We can share the reward for this creature if you like, but we must go before they send other defenders to dig deeper into the mines. We don't want more searches in the Rock right now, do we?"

The leader of the southerners remained watchful but directed the others to break a board barring one of the passages. As they dragged the guard's body to the opening, Kadam muttered to Vidkun, "If you plan on thinning our cut down to nothing, think again."

"I'm not cutting you out," Vidkun whispered angrily. "I'm trying to prevent you from being cut up. Hassan and his people must trust us if this is to work to our favor."

"*Our* favor is not the same as yours. They may think they'll gain something from humoring you since you're the new master of your house, but why do they need us?"

"Do as I say," Vidkun replied in a low voice. "You won't get out of this without my help."

"I'll take my chances."

Kadam clamped a hand on her shoulder and began backing away, pulling her with him.

"If we pass her to the snake eaters," Kadam told the two boys, "they'll drop us in the pit. You best decide who you're with."

The Satya boy and the fish-faced boy looked afraid, but they didn't move. Vidkun, too, remained where he was, his lips pressed into a thin line and hands flexing, ready to pull a blade.

Lingli noticed one of the southerners circling around them, approaching her and the miner with blade drawn. The other two pressed closer from the front. All it would take to end her was a quick stab.

She was holding her breath when Kadam sidestepped, his foot slipping a little on the uneven floor. Taking their chance, the southerners rushed them, one thrusting his blade at Kadam and entirely too close to her ribs. The blow was barely blocked by the miner, and the fight began in earnest while the other southerners challenged Vidkun and the boys.

Kadam managed to cut his opponent, who moved out of reach. Grinning as if he had waited for this encounter for a long time, he changed the blade to his other hand.

Lingli backed away from the melee. With her arms still bound, there was no way she could re-enter the Satya gate and close it quick enough, but the broad passage opposite the mouth lay behind her. Seeing that all of them were engaged in the fight, she stumbled toward the passage and away from the lantern light.

Banging into walls, tripping and bruising her feet, she focused on counting her steps. On her one hundredth and twenty-seventh step, she stopped to listen. All she heard was the occasional creaks that make up stone talk and drips of water, but even these small sounds echoed differently. Moving several steps to each side, Lingli realized the passage had opened into another large space.

There it was—the echo of a breath, a step. For a few minutes she listened so hard her ears hurt.

Then three quick flashes of lantern light broke the darkness. Lingli crouched down where she was, her heart hammering again. The brief light, which seemed to come from a distance away, had shown her that the floor she stood on ended not far ahead. The light had also revealed a row of four stalagmites to one side of her. Arms still bound, she shuffled over until she bumped into one jutting up from the floor about hip high. Moving behind it, she knelt down, listened, and waited.

Soon the signal repeated, illuminating the stone wall that rose high behind her. There was the rumbling sound of many feet, but more worrisome was a sudden burst of light from the passage she had come from. Lingli huddled in the stalagmite's shadow.

Two figures emerged from the passage with a covered lantern that barely cast light on their feet. When they reached the floor's edge ahead they raised the lantern and lifted the cover so their light flashed out three times.

One breath. Two. The signal repeated from farther away.

Light flowed around the spot where Lingli hid. Peering around the edge of the stalagmites, Lingli saw that two of the southerners they had met in the wheel room carried their lantern openly now, and more lanterns shone at a distance, but between them was nothing but darkness. They were near the edge of a huge void in the rock.

The two southerners took a path at the edge of the pit and disappeared, but the light from across the pit grew brighter. She could hear Ascaryans talking softly. Soon four fighters arrived on the ledge and took the passage to the wheel room. More voices and footsteps approached, and she held her breath. They seemed to be waiting for someone. Then Lingli heard two familiar voices.

"Yes, several delicate decisions remain," Ameer Ali said, "but this plan cannot be reversed now."

"Would you wish to?" Prince Hassan replied, his voice skeptical. "You were convinced this was the time only a moon ago."

"I have no doubts. All I am saying is that bold steps are not without cost, and this is nothing if not bold! I will share the consequences, whatever they may be."

"Your words relieve me, though I am aware I am asking much more of you and your fighters in the next few days. We have a star-blessed advantage, but we cannot underestimate the Seven, and the rani's moon-addled heir complicates my position."

Sid!

"I would think the boy's dual lineage is to your advantage," Ameer Ali said.

"I certainly hope so," the prince said, "but there cannot be a ray of light between you and me, and our purpose, if we are to succeed."

"You have achieved what no one else under the southern stars has: an alliance among four houses—four!—that could change everything," Ameer Ali said. "We cannot know the motivations of all parties, I grant, but now is the time. As long as Duvanya does not return, our fighters can smother any skirmish until all is ready."

"Duvanya will not interfere," Hassan said. "My cousin will ensure he does not arrive in time. Thus, I say to you as I do to the others, we must not be goaded. If we can maintain pretenses until New Cycle Day, the less we will have to raze."

"Patience has rewarded you for cycles. I see no reason to deviate from your plan."

Prince Hassan snorted. "Please, go flatter my betrothed while I stiffen the resolve of the Idrisis and clear the way for their pet."

"So be it. I much prefer my role to yours!"

With one eye looking out from behind the pillars of stone, Lingli could see fighters encircling the ameers, waiting for them to conclude.

Ameer Ali said, "If I may offer one other suggestion?"

"Go on."

"Once we act, the Seven will resist answering our questions, but many of their secrets are on parchment already. We should acquire their books."

"Planting records and battle stories? I am not convinced their much-vaunted books have any greater value than their parchment, but if you can achieve it without raising suspicions, proceed."

"I can. Avani is, if anything, more susceptible to flattery than the rani."

Prince Hassan chuckled, and the fighters shifted. Lingli drew back as Ameer Ali and his fighters took the passage to the wheel room. Prince Hassan and his fighters returned the way they had come. The ledge grew quiet, and the light retreated.

Whatever the details of the southerners' plans, Lingli's stomach twisted at the thought of the battle that was about to unfold. She owed this realm and the rani nothing, but she hated the idea of Hassan and Mafala sitting side by side in the great hall and tormenting Sid and Master Avani and Madam, among others. Or worse. Worse was possible.

Red's words echoed loudly in her head. *Whatever your path, walk it. Be useful.*

She had to warn them.

CHAPTER 36

As he climbed the stairs to his mother's quarters, Sid rehearsed how he would present himself to the rani henceforth. All uncertainties about his suitability would be banished in her presence. He would stand tall, know where his feet were at all times, and, if the ancestors allowed, learn how to mask himself even better than she did. No rebuke would ever pierce him again. But more importantly, he would waste no more time admiring clothes or food or any of the accoutrements of being prince until he demonstrated, somehow, that he was worthy of the respect due the title. Whatever else his mother presented to him, he vowed he would be more than her escort, and more than ripe fruit.

He also tried to convince himself that Li's disappearance two days before was the best thing that could have possibly happened. *Amma surely doesn't have time to chase her with New Cycle Day so close. Li must be leagues from here by now.*

Greta met him at the door to the rani's rooms before the guards could announce his visit. In the outer room, she grumbled as quietly as giants can speak, "Walk carefully."

The rani was at her dressing table in the inner room. She wore a shapeless wool gown and sat with her face tilted to the ceiling while a maid painted her. Both of them were reflected in the large piece of polished metal that hung on the wall there.

In a flat voice, the rani said, "Have you heard? My brother Jordak Vaksana has been killed."

Genuinely shocked, Sid asked how.

"He was murdered." Turning her head to look directly at him, the rani said, "Stabbed. Once in the back. Once in the chest."

"Who did this?"

"Captain Duvanya found the seamstress kneeling over the body behind the mining hall. He arrested her and was taking her to the jail when she somehow escaped, again."

"The seamstress?" Sid felt his chest tighten.

"Yes, the seamstress—your friend."

"But how? I don't think—"

"Yes, you don't think!" The rani's anger came boiling to the fore. "She has used you to find a way into the palace where she can feed off our fears at her leisure! Yet you continue to defend her, even with so many signs of unnatural powers."

"I'm…I'm not defending her," Sid said. "Wait. You said 'powers'?"

"*You* said you discovered her in the kitchens next to Korvar's son the night of the theft. The others named cannot be found, and the boy cannot remember who struck him. I am doubting anyone else was involved. It was her. She has bewitched you. She has bewitched us all."

"No, the others were there," Sid protested as the rani spoke over him.

"Do you expect me to believe your account when you hardly knew your own name that night? Think carefully before you contradict me, Siddharth."

Her eyes glittered like darkice. He wondered how much elixir she had already taken.

"She has deceived us both—meeting me, the envoy, my night captain, Madam Sayed, Master Avani, and who knows who else, and all the while she planned her next otherworld mischief." The rani pressed her hands together as if to ask the ancestors for forgiveness. "By mere chance we discovered her guilt in another crime, and the punishment was insufficient. Now my brother, Jordak, has fallen by her hand! Who knows how many she has cursed?"

The rani settled back on her stool, and the maid gingerly resumed her work but again drew back when Her Majesty abruptly rose and approached him.

The black kohl drawn around the rani's eyes contrasted with three thick, white lines streaking her cheeks and three more crossing her forehead. This paint, Sid knew, was prescribed to protect mourners from whatever might cross into their world when a spirit departed, but he could not help thinking that, in this moment, his mother appeared more like an asura than Li ever had.

To Sid's chagrin, the rani pulled him to her chair at the dressing table as if he were a small child. The maid positioned his face and began her work.

"I saw her on her balcony while you practiced blades," the rani said in a venomous voice. "She made every step you made. You raised your arm, she raised her arm. You turned, she turned. She has marked you."

"I am not cursed, Amma, and I promise you she has not harmed me."

"Curses do not always strike like bolts of lightning! They can rob you slowly—so slowly you may not even notice."

Shaking her head, Her Majesty paced the room while the maid painted over the shame in Sid's face. His resolution to earn the rani's respect was crumbling. When the maid finished, Greta handed him a plain-spun coat and pants, which he took with him into the bathing room.

When he re-emerged, his mother waited for him at the door to her quarters. She told him to take off his golden juttis and leave them there.

"Whatever our disagreements," she said, obviously choking down her anger, "they do not go beyond this room. We speak with one voice in council and in public."

Soon they were hurtling along the gallery with Greta following behind.

In the council room they met Madam Hansa, Master Avani, and Madam Satya in their bare feet, and wearing plain clothes, and similar paint. Sid shook his head at Parth, who glanced at the rani and dropped his eyes back to his parchments. All were silent until the stewards left.

"Our brother Jordak," the rani began, "was dear to all. May the ancestors welcome him, and may he watch over the descendants of the House of Vaksana forevermore. His murder will not go unanswered."

While Madam Satya summarized Captain Duvanya's report of the murder and Lingli's subsequent arrest and escape, Sid saw earnest tears in the rani's eyes. His throat grew tight and he didn't dare look at the others, wondering if they blamed him for Li's presence in the palace. Yet he still could not imagine her capable of such a crime.

"The cart loaded with weapons and other signs tell us that more were present," Madam Satya concluded. "The captains have been ordered to make this investigation their priority."

Stars. I must speak to Captain Duvanya.

"It hardly seems possible that the seamstress could have delivered such blows," Master Avani said. "She—"

"We are not dealing with a mere seamstress," the rani interrupted. "Signs of a conspiracy have been afoot within the palace for weeks, and we have been blind to it. She may not be acting alone, but she is, I fear, the inspiration and perhaps the leader."

What of Gaddar and Vidkun? Does she listen to anything I say?

"Perhaps we can identify members of this…conspiracy if we can discover who met Jordak yesterday," Master Avani said. "I, for one, had no idea that our brother had returned."

"I only received a message from him last evening," Madam Hansa said. "He requested that we meet early today."

"There's one more thing," Madam Satya said, unrolling a small scroll. "This note was delivered to me after it was discovered on our brother's body. It is from Darius."

She read, "'On the twenty-eighth day of the thirteenth moon, Saatkulom's forces took Zahatara and now serve as protectorate of it and the adjacent village. Losses were minimal—thirty-two southerners, nineteen of ours, and the wolf Danior.'"

Sid saw his mother close her eyes for a moment, then Madam Satya continued, "'The officer of rank is held alive and confirmed that the nobles of Daza Tumuli have been called to Avkorum for New Cycle festivities. Brother Jordak will brief the council on details and a shortfall in our supply of arms.'"

The rani looked to her kinsfolk and asked. "Does anyone know what he meant by 'shortfall'?"

"He and I discussed this briefly before the forces departed for the northern campaign," Madam Hansa said.

"Explain." The rani's voice was brittle, and one hand strayed to the chains tucked inside her dress. She saw him watching her and lowered her hand.

"Weapons are assigned to recruits as soon as they complete training," Madam Hansa said. "Three hundred forty-four southern youth have received a weapon, which might be a talwar, khanda, bow and quiver, or lance. Over the last two moons, many weapons were sent to the armory for repair as the southerners were unfamiliar with proper use. It seems that when the repaired weapons were returned, some were given to the wrong persons."

"What is this 'seems'? Do you not keep a tally?"

Though Sid knew it was a cowardly impulse unworthy of a prince, he felt a flush of relief for not being her temper's target this time.

"The tally is there," Madam Hansa answered, "but as the fighters prepared to leave several southerners could not produce the weapon they had been issued. Some pleaded ignorance. Some reported they shared the use of a weapon with another recruit. They were asked to deposit their arms, and we were missing fifty-seven pieces. Replacements were collected from the armory and packed for the campaign."

"Could these missing pieces be those found on the cart?" Master Avani said.

"There were only twenty-two pieces on the cart," Madam Hansa said. "We'll know soon if they are some of those we seek."

A steward approached and announced the arrival of members of the House of Vaksana. Sid watched his mother attempt to compose herself as everyone rose to meet the wolfmaster's family.

Madam Vaksana was a tiny woman with inky black hair and a face that Sid suspected was dour even in the happiest times. The bones of her umbalvata bristled around her neck like a wreath of claws. She accepted each person's condolences, and prepared to bow to the rani, but Her Majesty grasped her hands and shook her head.

Madam Vaksana took Jordak's seat and Vidkun stood behind, his expression empty as he stared at the tabletop. The other Vaksana children, two bone-thin girls and a boy with a shaved head, kept their eyes lowered and slouched on a bench along the wall.

"Dear Mother," the rani began, "we grieve the loss of our brother with all the members of your house. We will stand with you this afternoon."

"You honor our house," Madam Vaksana said. "We will hold last rites on the palace terrace, with your permission, Maharani. Vidkun's advice is sound on this matter because I am quite too disturbed and unsteady to climb to the summit."

"Of course."

"I humbly ask Your Majesty for four more guards at our home until the next moon when Jordak's spirit journey has been completed. I am without a husband, without my eldest son, and I still have children to protect. To see a greater complement of guards will reassure them."

"They will be available to you."

"It cannot be said that any house has offered more regular or sincere tribute, but the stars know our house has suffered," Madam Vaksana put a hand over her heart. "Our spirits have been blighted in these cycles since my husband's death, and now, without my son's support, I do not know how we will face the days to come."

"You are of the Seven, Mother. Neither you nor your children will ever want for any necessity as long as Chandrabhavan stands on this Rock."

"Thank you for your reassurance, but I will rest easier when Vidkun is recognized by the Seven as is his due." She took Vidkun's hand. "He is our guiding star now. If he can be recognized before the wedding—"

"It will be impossible to manage that quickly," the rani interjected, "but I promise you we will hold the naming ceremony the second day of the new cycle. Our first task will be administering the rites and finding the creature discovered next to Jordak's corpse before the trail is hidden."

Madam Vaksana spat out, "May the murderer's spirit shrivel and wander forever without passage to the stars."

Blanching at the curse, Sid wished for a drink.

The rani turned her head and gave him a brief, knowing look, as if to say, *Even this woman sees what your 'friend' is.* He felt ill and heard little else before the meeting ended. The Vaksana family and most of the nobles had departed when he realized his mother was waiting for him to offer his arm. With Greta behind, they swept into the gallery where Ameer Ali and Princess Mafala awaited them.

"On behalf of my house, please accept my condolences," the ameer said. "Your brother, Vaksana, was a true heart. Oh, I know many suspected he preferred animals to the Ascaryans around him, but I deeply appreciated the gentle essence of the man."

"He will be missed," Mafala said.

"Would that these young ones could have known him longer," Ameer Ali said. "Such a rarity; a man whose only ambition was his duty, but there is no thwarting the will of the ancestors, not even for the valorous."

The rani shook her head and said, "My brother's spirit heeded no ancestor's call, Aliji. His life was cut short by a murderer who has fooled us for too long, and my part in failing to stop this crime pains me more than you could know."

Murderer. Sid bit down on his tongue to prevent the weight of his mother's opinion from showing in his face.

"Rumors of the culprit have already reached me," Ameer Ali said. "That is why I sought you out. Two of my men reported seeing the seamstress in the fort early this morning. I had my doubts and wondered if this was the result of too much firewine, but they said she had one bandaged hand. They claim to have given pursuit but did not catch her."

"I will share your report with our captains," the rani said. "I have commanded every available defender to search for her. Good coin is offered, and the wolves will be loosed if need be."

While diligently trying to contain the alarm roiling through him, Sid realized the affront of Li's escape reflected poorly on the rani's authority as well.

"No doubt the ancestors will reveal her presence," the ameer answered. "Your brother's sweet spirit will not go unrewarded." He and Mafala took their leave.

The paltry lunch served by the House of Vaksana on the central palace's terrace was followed by sour firewine that warmed no one. Scores of plainly dressed, shoeless members of the Seven offered condolences and sniffled weeping as the musicians played a simple drumbeat. Atop a tall pyre, Jordak Vaksana, dressed in an indigo suit with his wild hair held in a braid, was laid to rest.

Only when Sid saw the body did this death seem real. The loss overcame him as he remembered Master Vaksana guarding their camp at night, his quiet control of the wolves, and how Mafala and the rani had teased him.

When his mother left him to meet with the Vaksana elders, Sid hugged the parapet and scanned the steep rock face rising behind them. *What happened, Li? Why were you there?* He wished he could ask the former wolfmaster who had caused his death.

Madam Vaksana and her children approached the pyre and stood around it on short stools. The fallen noble's youngest brother placed a wolf carved from stone at Jordak's feet. The girls set trays of sweets and anars on either side of the body. Vidkun fixed a skin of firewine in his brother's stiff hands.

Master Avani left a group of mourners from his house and came to Sid's side.

"Li didn't do this," Sid whispered. He was glad to see the old noble seemed to agree. "Do you know where she is?"

"Somewhere in the heart of the Rock," Master Avani whispered back just before the rani beckoned them both to join her.

Madam Vaksana stepped onto one of the stools and posed above her son's shoulder with her eyes closed while a musician played a somber tune. When the music ended, she handled each bone on her umbalvata and recited a stream of strange names and a tribute in their house's old tongue.

"She is asking the ancestors to recognize her son," Master Avani told him, falling into his role as teacher. "She shows them his bones."

When Madam Vaksana held up a set of three, cleaned phalanges, strung together and tied to the end of her umbalvata, Sid involuntarily rubbed his fingers. He better understood Li's penalty now—a symbolic death, meant to weaken her connection to her ancestors. Symbolism, however, wouldn't satisfy the rani any longer.

While the tribute continued, Master Avani said, "She asks the First Father and First Mother to allow Jordak's spirit to live with them among the stars. There he will know no fear, no hunger, no pain. She asks them to guard his spirit on its journey and protect it from demons and from becoming lost between this world and the otherworld."

The rani was the first of the Seven to be invited to the pyre. She placed a flower on Jordak's chest.

Sid whispered to Master Avani, "Li must stay hidden until after the wedding," His chest was so tight he could barely get the words out. "Then I'll ask the rani to pardon her. As a gift to me."

Master Avani shook his head. "We cannot depend on my sister's mercy. We must deliver Miss Tabaan to a safer place as soon as possible and for as long as necessary." The old noble then took his turn at the pyre.

When all the nobles had delivered their flowers Vidkun took a long torch and touched it to a brazier, then lit the pyre. A ring of blue-edged flames bloomed, and smoke soon obscured the body of Jordak Vaksana. Turning his face up to the bronze-colored sky, Sid murmured the farewell tribute with the others.

As the flames grew high and the air began to shimmer with heat, Sid watched Captain Gaddar join the line of mourners and bow low to Madam Vaksana and Vidkun.

One would think they didn't know each other very well.

The captain didn't even glance Sid's way when he approached the rani, and Sid knew Gaddar fully counted him as a coward.

"I have news, Maharani," Captain Gaddar said. "My defenders learned of a youth who we believe is part of the murdering cabal. He's been seen in the fort."

"Who is it?"

"A mining apprentice called Krill. My informants say he knows the seamstress and is one of those accused of involvement in the kitchen theft."

Krill? Have they turned on each other?

"Add five silver coins to the reward for the one who apprehends this Krill, and they should bring both him and the seamstress to me. Inform Duvanya."

When the captain left them, the rani said, "At last one of those you named has been discovered."

"Yes. And I named Vidkun and the captain, too," Sid said, searching his mother's face for some explanation.

"Whatever Vidkun's involvement, I cannot arrest him at his brother's funeral. As for the captain, don't you see that we must depend either on evidence that will make his arrest inevitable, or we need Vidkun to give him up? I would wager that the latter is more likely, wouldn't you?"

I would wager that these two will pay no price for what they've done. Only the common Ascaryans, the Krills and the Lis, pay for crimes.

As the light of day dwindled with the pyre's flames, the immediate family was left alone to attend their fallen member. The rani had given her last condolences and they were leaving when Vidkun caught up to them.

"Your Majesty," he said, "grant me permission to take up my brother's duties as wolfmaster and join Captain Gaddar's search for those accused."

The rani's expression was not warm. She stared at him so long Vidkun had to look away. Finally, she asked, "Can you hold them?"

"Two, not three."

"So be it. Akela will stay with me. Both captains are at your disposal."

Sid's stomach twisted at the thought of the wolves pursuing Li. It was a scenario far too close to his worst dreams. He touched his mother lightly on the arm and said, "I would like to serve as well."

She raised her brows at him, then her eyes softened. She told Vidkun, "Prince Siddharth will lead the search as my representative."

It was almost a pleasure to see the confusion on the jailer's face as they left him.

When they were beyond earshot, Sid asked, "How can we make Vidkun accuse the captain?"

The rani answered easily, as if she had been thinking the same thing. "We must let him know, subtly, that I suspect the captain and will handsomely reward the one who brings him to court."

"You mean to protect Vidkun?"

The rani sighed. "Pure good exists only in the halls of the ancestors, pure evil only in the unprotected lands of the otherworld. In this world we must manage the mix as best we can. With the loss of Jordak, we have no choice but to accept Vidkun as master of his house or forsake them all and diminish the Seven. Would such a course strengthen the realm? That is the question the ancestors put to me, and to you, today. How would you answer?"

"His brother or sisters couldn't serve in his place?"

"Unless Vidkun admitted guilt, accepted exile, and asked the council and the elders to name another, no. He has chafed as a spare his entire life. He would never accept the demotion our laws demand."

"But no one will trust him."

"Sometimes we must live with a snake. For the strength of the realm."

"Then we let him be," Sid said finally, resigned to losing the argument for the time being.

Respect the law. Strengthen the realm. The two rules he thought he could rely upon were no help at all.

That evening Sid's daily escort and two more guards accompanied him across the span and through the fort to the second gate where they met Vidkun and the wolves, Captain Gaddar and his men, and, to Sid's relief, Captain Duvanya and a contingent of night guards. Believing Li capable of murder was impossible, but he had to know why the captain had arrested her.

Addressing all of those gathered, Gaddar made an obsequious bow in Sid's direction and said, "We have an important task tonight. A prisoner and a suspect are loose, and this humiliation must not stand. All involved in their arrests will be commended, and our glorious maharani will give five silver coins to the one who discovers the mining apprentice, Krill. Ten for the seamstress, Lingli Tabaan."

"Is this reward good whether they be alive or dead?" one of the guards shouted.

"Alive," Gaddar answered, "so they can face the punishment they deserve." He grinned broadly. "Though you may be assured that if anyone kills either creature by accident or in self-defense, you would still receive some small reward even if I have to pay it myself."

"Which side do you want, captains?" Vidkun asked. "I can take the beasts either way."

Captain Duvanya said, "I'll take the northern side. If it pleases you, Prince, you are welcome to accompany me and the night guard."

Sid immediately agreed, but Gaddar's smug expression troubled him. Together, he and Vidkun could concoct any plan.

Initially Captain Duvanya's night guards stayed on the Rajpath, knocking on every door as they moved uphill. Each person they questioned claimed they had not seen anyone matching his descriptions, and some openly scoffed at the idea that a female could have laid Master Vaksana low, but most said as little as possible, clearly eager for the guards' departure from their doors.

"Are you sure she killed him?" Sid asked Captain Duvanya as they trudged along.

"I am sure she knelt over his body," the captain answered. "The rani and her judges will decide her guilt or innocence."

"Did she have a knife?"

"A small one in her boot."

"Big enough to kill him?"

The captain shrugged.

"She could have arrived after the murder."

"Much as she arrived after the theft in the kitchens?" Captain Duvanya queried, his opinion clear. "And did someone else put that bauble in her pocket? Perhaps Master Vaksana was killed because he believed her lies once too often. I was less than vigilant, and I lost her. I will not make that mistake again."

"Captain," Sid began, "I need to tell you something in confidence. Set aside what happened last night. I can promise you that Li, the seamstress, is not guilty of the earlier theft in the kitchens, nor does she have anything to do with the other suspects we seek."

"How can you be certain of this?"

"Because Krill and the others forced me to help them that night," Sid swallowed hard. "The seamstress arrived later and knew nothing about it."

The captain said nothing for a moment, and Sid's thoughts raced as he considered whether he should tell him about Vidkun and Gaddar. The rani had not forbidden him from doing so, but he was sure she would not be pleased—and he was not sure the captain would believe him.

"I have heard you knew her before she arrived here," the captain said.

"We lived in the Western Woods."

"What was her reputation?"

"Reputation? Some villagers didn't like her, but she never did anything to them." Sid sighed and added, "She cared for me when I was young."

The captain stopped and looked closely at him. "I do not mean to offend you, Prince Siddharth, but she is a strange creature, and the circumstances that swirl around her are stranger still. Do you doubt she could commit murder?"

"I do. I know you must arrest her, but I don't want her to be harmed." Sid raked a hand through his hair. "There's something else—"

A commotion arose ahead. Captain Duvanya put a hand on the hilt of his talwar and ran. Sid jogged after him to meet a small group gathered where a path branched off the Rajpath.

"A man, Captain," one of the men explained. "Came from over there." He pointed across the street. "Ran like demons were chasing him."

Sid took a deep breath. *Maybe Master Avani was right. Maybe Li's still hidden.*

Trechur and Titok appeared on the footpath the man had indicated. Their eyes glowed like green coals as they strained forward. Leaning back on his heels as a counterweight, Vidkun was plainly struggling.

"Which way did he go?" Vidkun bellowed at the crowd. One of the men nodded toward the path behind them. The new wolfmaster and the wolves plunged on, followed by a handful of day guards.

As Captain Duvanya and Sid followed, Gaddar jogged up behind them. "Did they see her?" he asked, breathing hard.

"No, a male it seems," Captain Duvanya said.

"In that case, perhaps we shouldn't all be chasing this one," Gaddar said, stopping in the path. "I'm going to run a few of mine up to the granary. Best catch up with Vaksana. I'm not sure he can hold those beasts much longer."

Unsure, Sid turned back as Gaddar charged across the Rajpath.

Captain Duvanya blocked his way. "You cannot go with him," he said, raising his chin in the direction Gaddar had taken.

"Why not?"

"Your mother forbade me to leave you with him or Vidkun alone."

Sid shook his head and wondered how long it would take for him to be able to guess his mother's next moves.

Following the night captain into the maze of paths that ran among shops and homes behind the Rajpath, they caught up to Vidkun and the wolves in an alley where the guards banged on every door. Trechur and Titok whined and trembled. A guard ahead called out and pointed farther down the path, and Vidkun and the wolves burst forward, each beast vying for the lead in the narrow space and everyone else following. After a sharp turn, Vidkun pulled them up. They had reached the alley's end.

Sid could just make out a shadowy figure atop a rubbish pile ahead. Leaping for a handhold on the top of the wall, the figure missed. He looked back only once, and when the lantern light caught the whites of his eyes, Sid knew that the fish-faced boy was terrified.

Poor Krill. They gave him up.

Despite Vidkun's and Captain Duvanya's commands to stop, Krill leapt again, got a grip, and began to scramble against the wall.

As Captain Duvanya ordered his men to take Krill down, Vidkun battled to hold the wolves, but the beasts felt no compulsion to wait for orders. Titok and Trechur sprang forward together, and Vidkun pitched onto his face. As if the chains were a mere nuisance, they sprang again, dragging Vidkun along behind.

Legs flailing, Krill pulled up and had an elbow on top of the wall when Trechur clamped down on the boy's leg.

The harrowing scream that followed terrified Sid, but worse was the sight of Krill losing his grip, fingertip by fingertip. He was pulled down between the wolves that clawed and lunged and snarled with blood fury.

Sid told himself he must shout, but he had no voice. He told himself to move, but his legs refused. It wasn't until he saw Captain Duvanya and his men kicking at the wolves' heads that he collected himself enough to join the fray. By the time he drew his useless ceremonial blade, Titok had knocked down one of the guards with a swipe of his paw and turned toward him.

Captain Duvanya drew Titok's attention, and other guards beat Trechur off the fallen boy. Shoving the captain aside, Vidkun wielded the shishpar, which buzzed like a dauber's nest. Titok cringed at the sound of it, but Vidkun struck the wolf on the nose and pressed the weapon to the wolf's side until Titok cried. When both wolves were beaten into submission, Vidkun straightened and heaved for breath as he drew their chains short.

Krill lay flattened on the rubble like just another piece of rubbish. The fish-faced boy's throat was ripped open, his body awash in dark blood. His wide-set eyes already stared into the otherworld.

While Sid vomited in the alley and fought off the urge to fall to the ground, the night captain spread his cape over the body and ordered the guards to find a strong plank.

"On this twelfth day of the fourteenth moon," the captain declared, "the apprentice Krill was killed in Tenan Alley. Fleeing the maharani's guard, he was brought down by her wolves. That is my word."

"The idiot had to run, didn't he," Vidkun grumbled.

He and Gaddar fixed this. Probably promised him a coin. A fury was building in Sid as he muttered, "He had nowhere *to* run, did he?"

"Let his mother do the mourning," Vidkun said, giving at Sid a mocking look. "We must join Gaddar and see if he's found the seamstress."

"First we return the boy's body to the palace, as the law requires," Captain Duvanya said.

"Do your duty then, Eshan," Vidkun mocked. "But it will not be said that I missed the chance to capture my brother's murderer and serve our rani's command.

Vidkun left with the wolves while guards lashed Krill's body to a board. Sid nervously shifted from one foot to the other. A vision of Li stuck in some dark place with the wolves approaching filled his thoughts.

"We should catch up to them," Sid said.

Ordering the guards to move out, the captain answered Sid in a low voice, "You are worried the seamstress could meet a similar end?"

Sid nodded. "I can give you no reason to believe me, but I hope you don't doubt me either. All I can tell you is that Captain Gaddar and Vidkun knew this boy before he was arrested. His death will not disturb them, and they will be happy if the seamstress pays for all of the crimes, whether she has done them or not."

The captain continued apace behind his men bearing Krill's body, but he looked sharply at Sid. Ready to gamble on the captain's trust, Sid said, "Ask the maharani if you don't believe me. She told you to protect me from them. She knows they cannot be trusted."

They had reached the edge of the Rajpath. The captain rubbed his chin and looked up the road. "Accompany the prisoner back to the palace and tell the rani exactly what happened. I will catch up to them."

She's got to be in the Rock, Sid tried to tell himself as he reluctantly followed the guards bearing Krill back to the central palace.

After they left the boy's body with the healers, though healing was out of the question, Sid had every intention of going straight to the rani's quarters just as Captain Duvanya had said, but he pivoted in the gallery and headed to his rooms instead. Doubts about where Li was along with images of Krill's terrible wounds played in Sid's mind, convincing him it would be better to steady himself with a cup of firewine before he met his mother.

At his door Sid met an exhausted steward who was relieved by the night guard escorting him. The guard entered the quarters to light the rooms, but multiple diyas were already lit on the altar table. As he shuffled to his bedside to grab the firewine surahi he kept there, the guard made a startled sound.

"What is it?" Sid asked.

Pointing toward the altar, the guard raised his lantern. A message was written on the wall in red wax that dripped like blood. Reading it, Sid left his cup and demanded the guard accompany him to the rani's quarters.

CHAPTER 37

Certain that every small sound she made or heard on her way back to the lower Satya gate would be followed by a blade in her back, Lingli breathed deeply only after she was able to use her elbows to close the gate behind her. Against the sharp edge of a column of rock in the passage, she rubbed away at her binding for hours until it frayed enough she could slip free. Her feet were scraped and bleeding, but she made her way to the side passage, descended again, and wriggled through the rockslide— never stopping until she reached the old tower.

Peeking through the curtains she had hidden behind more than a moon earlier, she saw that only the library guard and a steward at the door to Sid's quarters stood watch on the landing. She waited. When the steward stretched and went to talk to the other guard for a few minutes, she saw that Sid's door was unlocked.

He must be in there. But with no way of knowing for certain, she didn't dare to run out, pound on the door, and hope he answered before they drug her away. She had only one chance to deliver her warning. From her cloak's hem, she pulled out the last of Red's firesticks. With her knife, her fishing spear, and her brooch gone, it was the last of Red's gifts, and she hated to use it, but it had to be done.

She studied the distance between the curtains and the railing around the open shaft in the middle of the landing. The steward was half-asleep on his feet, but the library guard was the one who had to be distracted. More hours passed before her chance arrived.

The quiet that had suffused the entire tower was suddenly broken when a door slammed on one of the floors below, and a murmur of voices carried up to her. The steward opened his eyes and closed them again, but the library guard strolled up to the railing and looked down.

Immediately, Lingli struck the firestick against the floor. It did not ignite. Cold sweat made her good hand slippery, but when she tried again, the firestick sparked and hissed. Resisting the panicky desire to throw it instantly, she looked out.

The library guard seemed satisfied that nothing below needed his attention. As he turned away from her to return to his post, Lingli pushed the curtain aside and tossed the firestick, watching it turn end-over-end and fall in the open center of the tower. Drawing back, she counted to four before it exploded, making the curtains swing.

The steward was jolted awake, and the library guard spun around as shouts erupted below. When both of them rushed downstairs, she cat-footed to the door of Sid's quarters, pulled the bolt back, and slipped inside.

The door had barely closed behind her before she heard footsteps on the landing again. Huddling behind a divan, she held her breath. The door creaked open, and light shot into the room. Two breaths, then the door closed. The bolt slid into place. There would be no going out the way she came in.

The outer room's window was a slit in the wall about two hands wide. The starlit terrace was not far below and empty, though Lingli knew night guards would appear on their rounds soon enough. Getting down to the terrace was the easy part. Bootless, she would have to climb along the rock face pressed against the back of the palace and hope she could eventually find a way to the fields. If she wanted the cover of night, she couldn't afford to wait for Sid. She scoured the room for something to write with. No parchment. No reed pens.

In the inner room, faint light came from an identical window, and a single diya burned on the altar. Lingli searched through the tribute items left before the brass chhatri at the center of the shrine. The wilted offering of flowers wasn't helpful, but she was grateful for the orange she discovered. With her back to the raja doll and its baleful stare, she ate the orange as quickly as she could peel it. Wiping the juice from her chin, Lingli noticed the diya's flame gutter and she had an idea.

She took a twig from the kindling at the back of the shrine, lit it, and re-lit all the diyas and the two fat red candles on either side of the effigies. Tipping one of the candles over the thali, she let it drip, then poked the twig into the wax and wrote her message on the wall.

"Danger. Traitors in the Rock. Hassan, Ali."

The wax was too thin. Lingli retraced the letters and grimaced. Her script was crooked, and the letters dripped at the bottom. Anxious that time was running out, she added "Protect books" below the first message. Setting the stub of the wax-covered twig in the lap of the raja doll, she hurried to the window, but a muffled noise at the door meant her escape would have to wait.

She frantically looked for a place to hide. The wardrobe reminded her too much of the trunk she had been stuck in as a child. The chairs would not hide her, nor would the outer room's divan. Hearing the bolt slide back, she had no choice but to scoot under the bed. Its side boards hung lower than the woven coir holding the mattress, but it would take little effort for a guard to find her.

The door opened, and Lingli twisted onto her back and pulled her cloak close, tucking the ends in her pants. Grabbing the coir above her, she ignored the throbbing in her bandaged finger and pulled herself up off the floor.

A guard passed the bed, then another pair of feet in dirty boots entered the room and stopped at the bedside table. *Sid.*

"What is it?" he said as he moved toward the guard at the altar. Her message frightened him. She heard it in his voice as he ordered the guard to accompany him, and both left the room quickly.

Arms shaking, she dropped to the floor as the door closed.

Rolling out from under the bed, she got up and looked out the window. Not only were there two guards on the terrace, but they had lit lanterns all along the parapet. *Whether I stay or go they'll catch me.*

A strange calm descended over her. Warning Sid of trouble had been her purpose, and she had done it. What was the point of worrying anymore? Not that she wanted her head in a noose, but when they found her, she could take some comfort in knowing she had done her best.

She wished she could have spoken to Sid. Not the prince, but the one who used to pick berries with her, the one who bickered over supper. Whichever Sid he was now, it would end the same. He would remain in Chandrabhavan, and she would not. She went to Sid's bedside table to sniff at the jug there. After taking a big gulp of firewine, she returned to the window. A third night guard crossed the terrace. He led Greta, the rani, and Sid toward the old tower.

Returning to her spot under the bed, Lingli found her footholds and handholds, and pulled her cloak tight around her, but she remained on the floor. She would have to save her strength until they began looking.

First, Greta's huge feet lumbered by, leading the way to the altar. Next came the rani's delicate slippers, then Sid's boots, followed by another pair of boots. Lingli twisted her neck to watch their feet move around the room.

"See here," Sid said. "Do you think the ancestors have sent us a message?"

"By the First Mother!"

Madam Hansa.

"Not unless the ancestors have begun eating oranges," the rani said.

Oh, no. The peel!

"Could it simply be a joke meant to frighten the prince?" Madam Hansa said.

"But here, Gayatri? Siddharth's quarters? The joker would have to be one of us or someone unusually skilled."

"But if the southerners are planning something—"

"This message is suspect for many reasons, including the timing. We are on the eve of a historic agreement, and I will not falter because someone holds a grudge."

"Shall I fetch Jalil and Parama?"

"Bring them quickly."

While Sid paced back and forth at the end of the bed, the rani and Greta remained near the altar table.

"Did you write this?" the rani asked.

Sid stopped. "Me? No." He sounded shocked by her question.

"I must ask you because the guards insist that no one has entered your rooms. Someone is lying. If there's anything I should know, tell me now."

"But why would I...? I don't know who wrote this."

Lingli held her breath as the rani approached the window, standing exactly where she had earlier. If she reached out, she could almost touch the hem of Her Majesty's long skirts.

"You claim that Vidkun and Gaddar have betrayed their duty and stolen our house's gift," she said. "If this is true, I would not be surprised if this was meant as a diversion to make us look for trouble elsewhere."

"Their diversion was Krill—the boy who was killed," Sid said. "He was one who could have spoken against them...and getting rid of him gained them your reward."

Krill. That's what they called the fish-faced boy.

"Let us assume you are correct," the rani said. "How could either of them have written this message while they were in the fort with you?"

"They couldn't have," Sid said.

"So it follows that someone else sent this message. Someone who perhaps wanted to help those you accused, and certainly someone seeking to sow more discord."

"You think it was Li," Sid said accusingly.

Lingli's throat closed. She was afraid she would cough.

"Let us not repeat her crimes and virtues," the rani said. "But do you not find it curious that while both Vidkun and Gaddar proclaimed they were searching for her in the fort, they did not find her? At the same time someone enters your room and delivers this message? Perhaps they are allies."

Allies!

"What if...what if someone is truly trying to warn you?" Sid's voice wavered.

The rani stepped closer to Sid, and spoke more gently, "Whoever it was, whatever their intent, I will find it out, and you will help me, but our sacred responsibility to protect the realm is our first duty."

A sharp rap on the door, and Sid went to escort another pair of slippers and two pairs of boots into the inner room. *Madam Satya, Madam Hansa and...?*

"Jalil was not in his quarters or the library," Madam Hansa said, "so I brought another brother."

"I'm glad you're here, Ketan," the rani said softly. "I only wish our brother Jordak was here to greet you, too."

It's Master Tilan. The one they call Crowseye.

"Gayatri told me what happened, but I cannot believe he's gone,"

Crowseye said. "And his murderer has escaped? How?"

I did not kill him!

"She will be found," the rani said, "trust that. Jordak's murder is the greatest crime of this bright cycle, but I'm sorry to say it's not the only one. Someone, or some group, is intent on upsetting our alliance as well."

"Well, this makes Darius's note all the more concerning," Crowseye said.

"I did not find our brother's field report cause for alarm," the rani said.

"Field report? I received a personal message from him three days ago."

"Do you have it?"

They crowded the altar table, and Lingli heard the rustling of parchment.

Crowseye read aloud: "'Dear brother, we hold Zahatara but we are challenged from within. Tal Daman declares that he represents the southerners in our campaign and demands equal authority. I have denied him. My word holds, but he threatens to abandon the effort. I have sent Jordak back to inform our maharani and gather reinforcements. Return to the Rock as soon as you can. Take at least three units with you.'"

There was a pause, then Crowseye asked, "Jordak didn't report to you before he was killed?"

"No."

"Sister, I winded a perfectly good horse to return as quickly as I could because of Darius's note, and more. I know I have said more than once that our defenses are strained, and you believe me to be an alarmist, but please hear me.

"In the last week the southern encampments have completely surrounded our work at Nilampur, but for the side backing to the lakebed. After the canal ran dry, two hundred or more from the House of Idris assailed the gates. They threatened the guards and catapulted filth and stones before Prince Hassan intervened. By the ancestors' grace he and other nobles contained their members. I understood your message, but forgive me—I could not press the point with the prince at that moment. The clamor had hardly quieted when I received Darius's message. By then Hassan had departed, leading large numbers."

The rani's long skirts were still, but Lingli saw Madam Hansa and Sid shifting uneasily while Crowseye spoke.

"You say Hassan left before you?" the rani asked.

Listen to him! Prince Hassan is already in the Rock!

"A day and a half ahead," Crowseye answered, taking a deep breath. "We rode hard and passed many of those who left with him, but we didn't meet Hassan."

Madam Hansa said, "He could have arrived here before Jordak was killed."

"Gayatri!" the rani said sharply. "Do not allow grief to inflame your prejudices!"

"I am only adding the hours."

Madam Satya's slippered feet moved subtly between the rani and Madam Hansa. "There are many threads in this tapestry, too many to trace them all immediately," the eldest of the Seven said. "We must sort out which concerns should take precedence."

"I agree. We should take some rest while we can," the rani said. "Our defenders have already been put on alert. Let us collect Jalil and reconvene in the council room at dawn."

"By your word, dear Maharani," Crowseye said, "but when were the summit and the Rock's passages last surveyed?"

Madam Hansa answered quickly, "The night guard reports on the summit every dawn and has shared nothing out of the ordinary. As for the Rock, Gaddar's day guards have been checking passages and mining sites since the search began for some petty thieves weeks back. No disturbances or discoveries have been reported."

Lingli noticed that Sid had begun to tap his foot at the mention of Gaddar.

"Which is exactly why we must not overreact to a message that may have only meant to serve as a distraction," the rani said.

"The number of tents in the fields below this Rock is not a distraction," Crowseye said. "Only minutes ago, I prayed to the ancestors that my path to the gate would not become a gauntlet. Thousands are out there, and thousands more will arrive soon. I tell you they are coming with more in mind than enjoying a bountiful wedding feast.

"I propose we send defenders now, this hour, to check the summit and the eastern gate thoroughly."

The room was absolutely silent as they waited for the rani's response.

After two breaths, Crowseye said, "Sister, I mean no—"

"Say no more, Ketan," Madam Satya said. "Our maharani knows your judgment is sound."

Lingli felt the tide of opinion change in the room, and it seemed the rani felt it, too.

"I do not doubt you, any of you," she said, her voice small and rough. "We will act together, as always, for the strength of the realm. You, Ketan and Gayatri, shall direct the defenders in those tasks. In case there is the slightest possibility that this message is sincere, I will make use of the remaining night to prepare an antidote to any southern nonsense. If the threat appears as real at dawn as it does now, we will refine our plans to counter them.

"Parama, will you inform Jalil? We will not alert the House of Vaksana until we are certain. And Gayatri, would you keep Prince Siddharth at your manor for now?"

"Of course, my sister," Madam Hansa said, relief ringing in her voice.

Lingli watched Sid fall in next to Madam Hansa as the nobles left, knowing he would be grateful to be out of this haunted room.

When only the rani and Greta remained, the rani muttered, "A wraith I thought I sent to the otherworld mocks me while allies and traitors test our resolve."

Wraith.

The rani stopped pacing, and Greta said, "You must not take more of the gift. Two days, at least."

"You forget yourself." The rani's laughter was bitter. "Who will be the most happy to see me fail? The murdering asura? Hassan? Or you?"

Asura.

"Hmmm," Greta answered. "You will not fail, Dear Child, but you need all your strength."

"I will discover soon enough whether my good captain made the sale as ordered, but whether he did or not, it is also possible my consort plans some bold display for his advantage. We must check his arrogance while preserving the contract. Ancestors help us."

The rani passed close to the bed and stopped abruptly. Lingli held her breath.

"He has reanimated her somehow. Only he could have returned her to our world."

"She is a girl," Greta said.

"She has been otherworld from the beginning. I knew it. Mother knew it. And you knew it, too. Twice, when I had the chance to end this, I doubted and took half measures. Now I must fight on two fronts and with all means. Move this table!"

Certain the rani meant her, though she didn't understand who "he" was, Lingli felt just as she had in the village field when she traveled with the wanderers—as if she would float up and away from the world. The rani was no friend of hers, that was plain, but she spoke as if she knew her. Did she have answers to the questions she had kept buried so long?

As Greta pulled the table across the floor, Lingli turned onto her stomach. Edging forward on her elbows, she watched the rani raise one end of the tapestry that hung behind the altar table. Greta pressed a spot on the wall near the ceiling and Lingli heard a familiar buzzing sound. Behind the tapestry, stones separated and slid back, and a dark passage appeared. Chill air oozed into the room.

After the rani took a lantern and disappeared inside with Greta close behind her, Lingli crawled out from under the bed, unfolded herself, and rubbed her numb joints. Outside on the terrace, the guards remained at their posts.

Hovering before the open passage, Lingli's intuition was to follow the rani and see if she might find a way out of the Rock. The danger there, however, forced her to consider searching for Sid instead. She had used to imagine Sid and herself racing away over the fields to find a new home. *But I am the only one seeking. Sid is already home.*

Or, she could stay where she was, but what was the use in that?

Taking a diya from the altar, Lingli silently entered the passage and found a descending staircase only a short distance inside. Holding her breath, she listened for the slightest breath of sound but heard nothing. Slowly, she took one step after another down the steep spiral. The flame of her diya struggled against the darkness. The walls and steps became colder and damper. Descending felt like falling, very slowly, into a well.

At the bottom, she faced a door with a metal panel featuring the same symbols as the Satya gate. Although Lingli knew what to do, it took her a moment to work up the courage to touch the panel. If the rani was on the other side, Lingli could only imagine how happy she would be to dispense of this unnatural creature in such a hidden place.

Lingli set her diya on the floor and flexed the fingers of her good hand. *The only way forward is forward.*

Following a sequence that began and ended with the upright blade of the House of Duran, Lingli pressed the symbols, but the door did not open. She tried again with the House of Satya's chinkara. It did not work. She considered the panel carefully. Seven houses and eight sigils. She pressed the symbols again, this time starting and ending with the armored man. The door opened.

Darkness and the sound of flowing water met her. No cry was raised. No one approached. A lantern glowed in the distance.

Shielding her diya within her cloak, Lingli shuffled forward. What frail light escaped revealed stalactite and stalagmite teeth on either side of a stone path. The ceiling of rock above was not very high, enough for Greta to stand upright and not much more. She had no notion of the room's size, for the light did not reach any walls.

The rushing sound grew louder, and she found herself on a bridge not much above the water. On one side was a pool—its surface unbroken but for a thick iron column that rose from it and extended into the cavern's ceiling. On the other side of the bridge, the water poured away in a channel that passed into darkness. A small coracle bobbed in the channel, tied to an iron ring that was driven into a rock.

Beyond the bridge, Lingli's path toward the lantern light turned along a narrow shelf of rock on the channel's edge. Following distant voices, Lingli pinched the diya and carefully edged along the shelf until she reached a crevice in the rock wall.

She cautiously looked inside the opening. Greta and the rani stood in a long, narrow space with their backs to her. Along one side of this room was a workbench with cabinets and shelves above. A cold bluish light lit the bench and, at the far end, a bank of diyas and candles burned around another shrine inside a delicate chhatri painted blue and gold.

"Marpeela root," the rani said, waving at Greta.

The giantess reached into a jug and passed the rani a dried root. Lingli watched her add various ingredients to a mortar and pound away at them, occasionally wiping her face with the back of her hand.

"Oh, how I wished to see this alliance through without drama, but if Hassan demands a lesson on governing, I shall give it!" The rani paused and shook her head. "And our traitors? As soon as Hassan's recklessness is curbed, I will hunt down each and every one and hang them from the gate. The seamstress first. Let that be my answer to the demon who sent her."

Greta brought a metal box and a pot down from a high shelf. When the rani opened the box and struck a flint, a blue flame erupted around a metal ring in the center and burned steadily with no other fuel that Lingli could see.

Centering the pot on a rack within the box, the rani removed the lid and poured in some liquid and the contents of her mortar. She smelled the contents, then abruptly turned around.

Lingli jerked back. When she looked again, Her Majesty had opened a slim vial that she tipped into her mixture, counting aloud the drops that fell. A glow appeared above the pot like a cloud of golden dust, and the air became thick with the scent of mogra blossoms.

"Let them bring tens of thousands!" the rani said, giggling like a child.

The flame below the pot abruptly disappeared, and the rani poured a small amount of her potion into an empty cup. Carrying the cup to the shrine, the daughter of Duran knelt on a small stool and touched each of the objects inside the chhatri to begin her tribute.

"Hear me, O Fathers, O Mothers! Your daughter offers this humble tribute to all those who came before and who come after…"

While the rani murmured a litany of petitions for guidance and protection, Greta poured the contents of the pot into a small cask. As soon as the giantess refit the lid, the smell of night flowers disappeared.

When her tribute ended, the rani returned to the bench and opened the door of a high cabinet. The inside of the cabinet glowed with a blue light. She drew out another vial from several held upright in a metal tray. Lingli could hear Greta humming.

"Fetch another cask and stop that noise," the rani said as she carefully set the vial in a small container on the workbench. "If our enemies find some means to counteract the first move, we must have other options."

Greta shook her head. "Rani said the gift must be kept secret."

"*I* am the rani! Not her! Do not speak of her as if she still whispered in your ear, and do not presume to tell me what I can and cannot do!" The rani glared at Greta and pushed a strand of hair behind her ear. "I will secure the realm any way I can."

Taking a stoppered jug from another cabinet, Her Majesty opened it, smelled the contents, and said, "This is the last of it. We will have to go north this spring."

She dispensed the contents of the second vial into the jug, and there was no cloud, but Lingli detected an odd smell, something like anise. Using a long-handled spoon, the rani stirred the jug's contents gently. Then, taking a chain from around her neck, she opened the end of a moonstone pendant, dipped it into the jug, and tasted the contents.

"Fill the cask," the rani told Greta as she put the chain around her neck again, but she had hardly uttered the command before she gripped the edge of the bench and arched backward in a terrible spasm. Lingli feared the maharani would break in two until Greta hugged her close.

Lingli held her breath, remembering how Sid had behaved much the same after he was attacked. *This is the otherworld gift Sid spoke of!*

After briefly scratching at Greta with the madness of a cornered animal, the rani slumped in the giantess's arms. Cradling her charge, the giantess pulled a tiny, stoppered jug from her pocket, which she opened and held under the rani's nose. In a few breaths the rani was back on her feet and unfolding in a long, sensuous stretch.

Potions and poisons are kin, Lingli remembered the woods witch saying. *It's easy to mistake one for the other.*

The rani's strength returned and grew until it exceeded her. "Their plans will fall to ruin," she purred. "The House of Hudulfah will have to beg their ancestors for strength."

Though Greta did not seem disturbed, Lingli felt the air around the rani practically crackling with power, and she readied herself to run. This was otherworld magic—as strange and unnatural as a deer with tusks.

Splaying her fingers at her sides as if preparing for an unpleasant task, the rani returned to her shrine and said, "I should have done this the day we returned from the south. I would have, too, were it not for my mother."

Lingli could not see what the rani was doing, but she felt a sudden pain in her temple and pressed a hand to it.

"She was never named nor recognized by the elders. Let me sever, once and forever, this ill-starred thread of spider's silk joining our worlds."

Falling back from the opening, Lingli tried not to make a sound as she clutched her side, which suddenly burned as if she had been branded with a live coal. The pain spread along the side of her body and down one leg. She hobbled away along the water's edge as quickly as she could, knowing the rani and Greta would soon follow.

Among the boulders near the coracle, she set her unlit diya down and waded into the water, grateful for even a little relief from the burning sensation. Submerged up to her chest before she found the channel's bottom, Lingli resisted the current's pull by holding tight to the little boat's rope. The light from Greta's lantern had emerged behind her and drew closer.

Water lapped at her nose as she watched the rani and Greta, who carried both casks, cross the stone bridge and pass through the gate. In utter darkness, Lingli bobbed in the water with the coracle.

As soon as she pulled herself up among the rocks, the burning sensation re-intensified. Chewing on the inside of her cheek until her mouth was awash with blood and fumbling with her flint and steel for a long while before she could light the diya, Lingli made her way back to the rani's hidden chamber in agony.

At the chamber's entrance, Lingli surveyed the pots, jugs, boxes, and sacks of powders, dried leaves and seeds, bones and shells, and things for which she had no name. Perhaps the ancestors blessed the rani's use of otherworld magic, perhaps not. All that was certain was that the rani wished to destroy her, and she was the only one who could prevent that from happening. She had to act quickly. Pain was carving away the flesh in her leg, and she feared she soon might not be able to walk.

Staggering into the room, Lingli faced the cabinet that held the vials. The doors had no handles or knobs to grasp and could not be pried open. Raised symbols there seemed like the markings on Red's firesticks, but after pressing several combinations of those, she resorted to beating the cabinet with a pestle, which also failed to have any effect.

Be useful? Lingli sighed. For now all she could do was try to check the rani's powers.

She laid waste to everything she could. Sacks and crates were emptied, cups and jugs were broken. She scooped up as many small things as she could carry and dropped them in the rushing channel. Could this break the curse that had wrapped itself around her bones since birth? She didn't know, but if the stars allowed, Sid would never be poisoned by the rani's gift again.

After knocking a container off the workbench, Lingli paused when it fell open at her feet. Inside nine slender darts rested on a soft material that hugged their shape. Her hand shook as she tried to examine one more closely. Its sharp tip was hollow and the other end was marked by red and black fletching—the same as the one Master Vaksana had shown her—the same as the one that had killed Red.

She gave the villagers that dart.

Her leg was weakening, but an anger roared through her. Fitting one of the darts into the hem of her cloak, she hobbled over to the rani's shrine and swept many of the diyas to the ground, cursing every ancestor the rani ever had. She picked up the chhatri at the shrine's center, determined to throw it in the water, and paused only when she saw the venerated objects it had sheltered.

The small throne before her held no raja doll nor a braid of hair, but two cloth objects, egg-sized and egg-shaped. One was made of brown felt with two green stones for eyes and black yarn on top for hair. The second was wheat-colored with a blue coat. It had dark stone eyes, dark yarn hair, and threads stitched to make a smiling mouth. Below these, on a smoldering pile of incense and kindling, a third egg-shaped object lay on its side. That effigy was featureless and completely wound in white yarn like a shroud.

Lingli pushed the white effigy from its pyre, and the pain in her leg subsided. *What is this?* She poked it again, then limped to the water's edge with the faceless thing and doused it. Her relief was immediate.

Cupping the sodden white effigy gently in her hands, she returned to the wreckage of the shrine, plucked up the other crude dolls, and put all of them into her pockets. Then she returned the way she had come and paused on the bridge, considering the wisdom of riding a coracle downstream in the dark. *No. I will speak to Valena Sandhyatara before I leave this realm.*

Her side and leg still ached a little as she began her journey back to the palace above, but not as much as her dark, burned spirit.

CHAPTER 38

The cold air rising from the abyss was more than matched by a blade-sharp wind blowing straight into Sid's and Madam Hansa's faces as they left the palace gate. Sid stopped at the edge of the bridge span and took a deep breath.

"Don't look down," Madam Hansa said.

Why does everyone say that? Who would look down? I don't have to see the crack to know it's there.

This would make his third trip across it that day. He thought he should be used to it. Yet he was grateful when Madam Hansa took his hand in hers and more grateful still for the guard leading the way.

"I heard what happened in the fort last night," Madam Hansa said when they reached the fort gate. "That must have been difficult for you."

Sid grimaced, not wanting to think about Krill. "I didn't know they would… It was…"

"It was bad work," Madam Hansa said. "Jordak would have never let that happen. The wolves are for the rani's defense, not killing suspects."

"Being part of the Seven. It's an honor, of course, but…it's a lot, isn't it?"

She smiled. "Not one of us has asked for the role we were born to play, but whether an heir or a spare, we do our duty as best we can."

They turned onto High Marg, where the nobles' manors lined the way like defenders standing between the starblessed palace and the stonebound fort. The Hansa compound barely contained the sprawling residence where Madam Hansa led Sid through multiple, twisting hallways. She brought him to a small room with a tiny, screened window that seemed to suck in the cold air, but the furs blanketing the bed promised a good sleep.

"Try to rest," she said. "I don't think you'll find many more opportunities until after New Cycle Day."

"I'd rather come with you and Master Tilan," he said quickly, which wasn't totally true, but he wished it was.

Madam Hansa raised her brows. "Well, I'm sorry, but I'll not be flayed for taking you along, especially not when there's talk of treachery and the possible threat of a siege."

"Have you ever been in a siege?"

"No. The Rock hasn't been attacked in my lifetime, not even my father's and mother's lifetimes, and that's part of our problem."

"How is that a problem?" Sid asked.

"Can you win a race if you've never run? Can you win a fight without throwing a punch?"

"But Saatkulom has won many battles," Sid said. "Master Avani has made me memorize them already. There's the wars with Saikhanger in the thirteenth, sixteenth and twentieth generations, the battle for Jobat in the twenty-second generation, and the siege of Talomeer in the thirty-seventh—."

"All you name are battles in our distant forts and districts, and all are in the past," Madam Hansa said. "Our current defenders, including me, have not been challenged by any force greater than bands of northern raiders."

Sid had never thought of this.

"I shouldn't worry you with my concerns," she said. "We have an immediate threat to answer, and your mother is entirely correct. We must investigate as thoroughly and quickly as we can. The hardest task the ancestors can set for us is not confronting obvious enemies," Madam Hansa said pointedly. "It is confronting friends who have betrayed us."

He wasn't sure if, by 'friends,' she meant the southern houses or Li.

Sid hadn't expected to get much sleep, but after Madam Hansa left it felt like he had hardly sat on the bed before someone was pounding on the door and her brother Ilo was shaking him and telling him to get up.

When they left the manor, Matachand had set and a rusty-looking Chotabhai hung low in the southwest sky. Ilo, seemingly untouched by the cold in his cape trimmed with swan feathers, marched across the crack so quickly Sid hardly had time to think about the deep dark below. They went straight to the council room where Madam Satya, Crowseye, and Master Avani were already seated.

Ilo bowed to them and said, "My sister will arrive soon," before he left.

"Has no one called Vidkun?" Crowseye asked as Sid took his seat.

"No! And no one shall," Master Avani answered vehemently. "He is not a master, nor should he ever be!"

This encouraged Sid. *Surely Avaniji can convince them Vidkun is not to be trusted.*

Madam Satya put her hand upon Master Avani's arm. "We will need all our strengths."

"If you only knew what he has done, Parama! I don't mean what happened to that apprentice last night, though that in itself should tell you why he's not suited to take his brother's duties, but while you and the others were deciphering messages, I learned that he's abused his authority as jailer—"

A steward opened the door and the maharani entered with Greta and Madam Hansa. The rani's severe black achkan was girded with a golden belt and a ceremonial dagger, as if she were about to lead a hunting party.

As soon as she sat down, she said, "I realize more than one challenge faces us, but we must first determine the intent of the message in Prince Siddharth's quarters. Is the accusation against my consort and our longtime ally from Kirdun fair warning of a plan to betray us, or is it another attempt to deceive?"

Her voice was strong, and her eyes glittered, and Sid wondered how much time she had before she would need more elixir.

Crowseye looked around the table and spoke first. "The southern encampments have extended to the Rock's eastern side, and there were too few Nilampur defenders to examine the outside of the east gate safely. Instead, I sent three night guards down by the inner passage soon after we left the prince's quarters. They were told to return within two hours regardless of what they found.

"One has reported that they discovered a wanderer and a pair of zhoukoo badly beaten on a lower level of the mines. The wanderer swore that he and his son had been forced into the theft of weapons, as one might expect, but he also claimed, with no prompting, that southerners are inside the eastern gate."

All were quiet as a chill spread around the table. At last Master Avani cleared his throat and asked, "What of your other two defenders? What

"They have not returned."

The rani rubbed her forehead and asked Madam Hansa, "What of the summit?"

"Archers approached the park from the northern tower." Madam Hansa sounded hesitant. "They tell me that approximately fifty Ascaryans—southerners for the most part, a few zhoukoo, some miners, and nearly a dozen day guards—are camping at what seems to be a depot in the woods."

Feeling a little sick, Sid wished he had begun blades practice sooner.

"Are we to believe our own are working with the southerners?" Master Avani asked loudly. No one answered.

"Could it be that they are forced against their will?" Madam Satya asked.

"Possibly the zhoukoo, the miners," Crowseye said, "but not the guard. Not that many." He turned to Madam Hansa. "Did you find Gaddar?"

She shook her head.

The rani pressed her eyes closed for an instant, then leaned forward and said, "Disloyalty among our own pains me far more than the deceptions of foreigners, but we must dress the wounds caused by our kin *after* we have averted any threat to the realm. That is my word."

"Then," Madam Satya said quietly and firmly, "let us take advantage of the binding feast tonight. The ameers and nobles of all four southern houses will be in the palace and we can deliver our warning with less risk."

"We should lock down their fighters' barracks," Madam Hansa said.

"As soon as we do, they will know we are aware of their plans," Crowseye said.

"Hassan and the other nobles will enter for the feast tonight as planned," the rani said. "All any of them will see is that we are proceeding with the program in all innocence. We will quietly lock the gates behind them and take up our defense."

"My eyes tell me our defenders may be fewer in number than the southerners we have already allowed inside," Crowseye said.

"Then we use these precious hours to put the balance back in our favor." The rani turned to Master Avani. "How can we move as many southerners off the Rock as possible in this short time without raising suspicions?"

"Their field camps will be setting up the feasting tents for tonight and tomorrow," Master Avani said. "We can request the youth in training here to assist their houses."

"What of all their noble families?" Madam Satya asked.

"Let them stay exactly where they are, unarmed and unharmed," the rani said. "It seems I will be giving the first wedding gift at the feast tonight. We will make clear the foolishness of any attempt to use force against us."

Sid thought his mother's response made light of the dilemma. He looked to Crowseye and Madam Hansa, but they were practiced at keeping their faces empty.

"And those who may be inside the eastern gate and on the summit?" Madam Hansa asked.

"If they fail to stand down, we can starve them out."

"If there are as many in the fields as Ketan reports, they might be able to swarm the walls," Master Avani said.

The maharani waved that suggestion off. "Their people are not so coordinated. Without orders from their ameers, they are far more likely to attack each other than us. We will make sure the ameers are occupied."

Turning to Madam Satya and Master Avani, the rani said, "Represent us on the field. Lead the southern youth down, then accompany the nobles back here for tonight's feast. Your welcome will give the impression that we are unconcerned and showing them the greatest respect."

Madam Satya said, "Why bare both our necks? Jalil does not need to accompany me."

"I could go with Madam," Sid said.

"Send you to the field and serve you up to them like a tea snack?" his mother said. "No."

Sid could feel the heat rising in his face. Embarrassment certainly, but also a spark of resentment. *A prince must do more than read history and study laws.*

"I prefer you go together," the rani told Madam Satya and Master Avani. "I also need you to take Vidkun to the field, without my wolves, to ensure he is incapable of any more debacles."

"What do we tell him?"

"What do we tell him?"

"Nothing but what we tell the southerners—that tonight's and tomorrow's programs are unchanged. Though I am tempted to leave Vidkun out there, ensure he returns."

Madam Satya said, "You have described the first steps, but you have not explained the plan."

"It will be my responsibility to set the trap, and the fewer who know the details, the more certain our success. I will inform all of you when we gather in the evening." The rani nodded to Crowseye. "Take command of the day guard, and ensure we have good numbers in the feasting hall tonight. If Gaddar reappears, bring him to me. You and Gayatri must keep eyes on Eshan, too. Under no circumstances should either captain know our plan."

Madam Hansa said, "I cannot believe that Darius's son would—"

"We are all children of the Rock, yet it seems some of us have taken the wrong path! A treacherous path!" The rani's cool demeanor fell away.

Does she truly doubt Captain Duvanya, too? Or does she simply not want them to know she favors Gaddar?

The rani rose from her chair, and all joined her. "Defense of the Rock is our first and most noble purpose. With the blessings of the ancestors, trust that we will counter the south swiftly, and if they see reason, we may be able to preserve part of the alliance."

"One moment, my sister," Master Avani said. "I have no argument with putting our physical defense first, but we should not forget the last line of the message, which Gayatri tells me was, 'Protect the books.'"

"What could the southerners hope to gain from our books?" Madam Satya said. "Few are literate and fewer still understand the value of chronicles."

"I'm afraid," Master Avani said, rubbing his nose, "that I may have persuaded Ameer Ali of their value."

Sid watched his mother tighten her grip on the table's edge.

"Return my house's book to my quarters," she said.

"And mine," Madam Satya said.

After the council meeting ended, Sid and the rani returned to her quarters in silence. He continued to brood on his fear that his mother's ensconced in her quarters again, Sid said, "I can help defend the realm, if you would allow it. I'm not completely useless!"

He expected a sharp retort of some kind. He was ready for it, but she gave him a wan smile and turned away, going out onto her balcony.

"Do I disappoint you?" Sid said as he followed her outside.

"You've been here far too short a time for that."

"I've been here three moons!" Frustrations he had not admitted even to himself began to spill out. "I've read every parchment you've given me, most of the laws, but now this is happening"—he waved toward the fort—"and I don't know blades, I can barely ride, and you won't even allow me to go, *escorted,* to the field."

"What we face today is no exercise, Siddharth," she said, her voice oddly flat. Greta brought the rani a cup of tea, and Sid saw her hand shake as she grasped it.

The elixir is waning.

She sipped the tea and looked skyward, following the paths of some green parrots flying above. Sid held his breath. He didn't understand all her motives, and the small bit he had begun to grasp had proved to be more complex than he had imagined. He had not appreciated that the destiny he had so desired was like standing in the middle of a storm, and she was the lightning. Prepared or not, this destiny was his. If he didn't hold close to it, it would likely strike him down.

"They see our defenses are thin, and they are correct." The rani sighed. "They think that if they can cut off the palace from the fort, they will be able to take control. They won't be able to do either, but if Hassan gives them the signal, they will try, and that is what we must thwart."

There was a knock on the door. The guard delivered a note to Greta, who brought it to the rani. As she read, Sid saw her brows crease. When she finished, she waved the note at him.

"From Krux. A representative from Saikhanger has arrived. He wishes me a happy marriage on behalf of their khan," she said sarcastically. "*And* he requests that I pay his khan in full by the second day of the new cycle."

"For what?"

"Have you retained nothing from our discussions? The rani's voice was sharp. "For our debts from trades in the last cycle and this one."

"How much...?"

But the rani shook her head and ignored him. "I wonder if this 'wedding guest' knows we've taken Zahatara? He'll hear it before he leaves, of that you can be sure, because no one on this rock can keep their mouth closed."

Turning on her heels, she went inside to her table where two small casks sat next to a water jug. Greta's humming deepened as the rani patted one of them and said, "We'll have to invite the khan's representative for tea."

When she spoke to him, her voice was husky with emotion. "I was only a little older than you when my father told me his greatest wish. He wanted this alliance with the south so that we would prosper and become the northern realm's equal, if not surpass it.

"He believed that the only way we could rival them was to lean on one of our greatest strengths, the cooperation among our Seven Houses, and to expand our alliances with Dyuvasa and the south to form a mutual defense that could hold Saikhanger and the Mephistanis at bay."

The rani spoke softly but rapidly. She had hooked a finger around her neck chains and drew them up, then let them down again.

She's thirsty. Sid resisted a sudden impulse to lick his own lips.

"Before I left him, before he was killed by a northern assassin, I promised to see his dream manifest. I promised him, Siddharth!" She held her palms together before her and circled the table. "The cycles of my life have been devoted to this. Can you understand? I lost my father. I lost your father. But I will not lose the realm because of the desires of the sandblind, cruel Ascaryan who I call consort, or for a few debts paid late."

Sid's stomach twisted in knots. He looked to Greta, who was edging closer as his mother rifled through her table's drawer and pulled out a small box. Inside was a transparent cylindrical object. One end of it was covered with a bulb of some soft material, like skin, which the rani pinched between her fingers. She told Greta to fetch her a surahi.

"The ancestors were good to our house and left us more than one gift," she said, tapping the tip of the little cylinder against one of the casks. "I prepared this one to slow the southerners' ambitions. Its effects are temporary and harmless."

Tapping the other cask, she said, "You know what this one is. I have prepared it, as I have prepared earlier ones, to pay our debts."

Her words were painting an ugly picture in Sid's mind. *Has she allowed Gaddar to sell the elixir?*

Greta returned and set a surahi on the table. Then she put a large hand on the top of the cask with elixir. "You should not take more now."

The rani clucked at her. "Not me. I must make some ready for that cat-shit northern spy."

As Greta pulled the cask's top off, something in Sid's stomach awoke. The rani pinched the top of the small object in her hand and hovered over the open cask. She dipped the cylinder's pointed end into the elixir, then drew it out and examined the liquid within. Holding the cylinder over the surahi, the rani bent close.

Sid's mouth felt absolutely parched. He watched the drops fall from the end of the cylinder and counted, *One, two, three.*

She smirked and handed the surahi to Greta. "Fill this with firewine and put it in his room."

Sid pressed his lips together, shocked by the rani's intent and afraid to say so.

Greta took the surahi to the inner room, and the rani set the lid on the cask lightly. The tremor in her hands was plain to see.

Trying to think of something, anything, to distract her from her mood's path, he said, "Amma, tell me how I can help with your plan to stop Hassan."

Tearing her gaze away from the cask, she looked at him quizzically. "Plan? Yes, we will see the plan through together." Her voice trailed off as she drew the moonstone pendant from her blouse and glided out onto the balcony. Sid meant to follow her, but he found himself staring at the lid of the cask containing the elixir.

Then Greta was beside him, putting her heavy hand on top of his. When he pulled away, his mother returned to the room. She held her cup in one hand and smiled sweetly, her neck chains tucked out of sight.

"No, Dear Child," the giantess said, as the rani put the cup to her lips.

Faster than Sid thought possible, Greta pushed him aside and smacked the cup from his mother's hand.

The rani's face contorted with rage. "You defy me?"

"Hmmm," Greta said, "your own strength is enough. She always said so."

"By my word, Giant, you have courted your end!"

Bowing her head, Greta stretched her arms out before her, palms up.

The rani touched the small dagger at her side.

"Amma!" Sid cried out.

The guard beat on the door and began to open it as the rani glared at them both and lowered her hand. Greta went to the door and held it so the guard could only look in around the edge.

"Maharani?"

"All is well," she answered. "Only a broken cup."

Greta closed the door, then lurched toward her charge before Sid realized what was happening. His mother was falling to the floor, but the giantess caught her and moved her to the divan. He knelt at her side, hating the sight of the spittle at the corners of her mouth and the purple half-moons under her eyes.

Whatever the rani's mood, from the day they had met in the woods, Sid had imagined he would never tire of basking in the light of Valena Sandhyatara. But now he understood the elixir had taken residence in her spirit like a moon, sometimes waxing, sometimes waning. He feared it would do the same to him. The difference between his own will and the elixir's demands were becoming hard to tell apart, and he no longer had faith she could distinguish the difference either.

"Amma? Amma, can you hear me?"

Receiving no reply, Sid looked to Greta, who dabbed at some tiny pot of salve she had produced from her apron. She applied the salve under the rani's nose. Her Majesty stirred and drew in her breath, but her eyes remained closed.

Greta turned her baleful eyes upon him as she wiped his mother's face. "She cannot take more, but she cannot go without."

"What should I do?"

"Hmmm. Do you know your mother's true wish?"

"To protect the realm?"

Greta nodded. "If you would be prince, you must do your duty."

CHAPTER 39

fter the long climb to the top of the hidden passage, Lingli faced a flat metal panel without symbols. She examined the edges for a latch, or anything that might show her how to open it but found nothing. Her stomach tightened with hunger, but her bitter demand for answers drove her on. She *would* escape and she *would* confront the maharani about her pretty darts and her charming little effigies.

Above the panel, where the stone wall touched the ceiling, one stone stuck out farther than the others. Stretching as far as she could, Lingli's fingers only grazed the bottom of the stone, but when she jumped up to tap it, the panel slid into the rock wall, and she found herself facing the back of the tapestry and the altar table in Sid's quarters.

Shoving the table forward, she re-entered the room and tried to still the storm swirling around her heart. She knew what she had to do. The only question was how.

Taking the thali that sat before the raja doll on his tiny throne, Lingli returned to the passage and stepped inside, hardly out of sight. She slammed the thali against the open panel. *Tang, tang, tang.* She heard the door to the quarters open. A guard called out. As his footsteps approached, she held her breath.

He paused next to the end of the altar table, just beyond the opening. The light from his lantern battled with the passage's darkness. It was hardly three steps from the opening to the stairwell, and Lingli hoped his attention was fixed on that dark hole.

He took a step inside, then a second, one hand on the hilt of a khanda at his waist.

She slammed the brass thali into the side of his head with all her strength.

Staggering, he twisted toward her, blade in hand, but she hit him in the face. As he hit the floor, his blade skittered away into the dark. She kicked him, and he grunted. She brought the thali down again.

Satisfied that he would not soon get up, she pulled him feetfirst down a few stairs then climbed over him and returned to the quarters. Moving one of the chairs to the opening, she stood upon it and ran her good hand along the stones touching the ceiling, just as Greta had done. Next to one stone, there was a round button in the mortar. When she poked it, the panel closed snugly, all but invisible. All she had to do was drop the tapestry and move the altar table back, and no one would know an opening had ever existed.

Instead, she tied threads of one of the tapestry's tassels to a bolt holding it to the wall and opened the passage again. She got down from the chair and left it and the askew altar table where they were. Satisfied, she went to the quarter's door and cracked it open. No one waited there, but the guard at the library door remained at his post.

Closing the door, she banged the thali against it as hard as she could then ran to the bed in the inner room and knelt down along the far side. It wasn't long before the door opened, and the guard called out, coming inside when he got no answer.

She waited for what seemed like a full moon before she heard the second guard enter the inner room. All the while shouting for the first guard, the second guard moved toward the open passage. When he finally entered, she silently rushed to the chair next to the opening. Inside the passage, the guard made a noise of surprise, and she guessed he had found the other.

Climbing atop the chair, Lingli pushed the button in the mortar, and the passage began to close. The second guard rushed back to the opening but could only thrust his arm and shoulder through it.

"Get back!" she yelled. "You'll be crushed."

The guard cursed but drew his arm inside, and the panel closed. Jumping down from the chair, she lowered the tapestry and pushed the altar table back into place.

They might starve, she thought, but this inspired no particular urgency in her.

In the gallery, the palace staff and guests hurried back and forth, and the noise was so great, Lingli wanted to hold her hands over her ears; but she resisted this and glided along with her hood pulled forward as far as it would go. These Ascaryans still smiled and twittered with excitement about the New Cycle Day celebrations, unaware of the pending invasion.

She soon found herself outside the council room at the rear of a crowd eager to meet their noble patrons. Clutching the yarn dolls in her pocket, she waited for the rani.

If Sid was with her, before the rani had her dragged off to jail or killed, she would tell him that she was his sister, and even if he pretended not to believe her, he would know in his heart that it was true. At least, that's what she wanted to believe. It would be enough.

When the stewards opened the doors, Master Crowseye and Madam Hansa appeared first and hurried down the gallery, shaking off those who followed. Next Madam Satya and Master Avani emerged, and their acolytes swarmed them, leaving Lingli exposed.

The instant Master Avani saw her, his eyes widened. He detached himself from those seeking his attention and ushered her away to one side of the crowd.

"You should not be here!" he whispered.

"I should not be anywhere, yet here I am." With anger feeding her, she felt more certain of her purpose than she had since arriving at the palace. "I must speak to the rani."

"This is not the time."

Noticing her brother's distraction, Madam Satya broke from her followers and came to them. Her hand slid to the hilt of her short blade when she recognized Lingli, but Master Avani moved between them.

"No, Parama. A moment."

"She is accused of murder."

"Wrongly accused," Master Avani said, all the time moving her and his noble sister farther down the gallery and away from the council room. "There is more to learn about her and from her."

Madam Satya stared at her brother as if he were mad, but she finally took a deep breath. "I do not know what you mean, Jalil, but we need no more drama today. We have very little time to prepare for…what lies ahead."

"Yes, and I'll explain everything, but you must trust me. All is for the strength of the realm."

Lingli watched Madam Satya struggle with her decision and look toward the ceiling as if calling on the forbearance of her ancestors. It reminded her of herself, giving in to Sid.

"You will not let her loose again," she said. "Tonight you must explain in Valena's presence."

"By your word." He grabbed Lingli by the elbow, but she pulled loose.

"I have questions, and I will ask them!"

Madam Satya raised her brows and kept her hand near the hilt of her blade.

"Seamstress," Master Avani said in the coldest voice she had ever heard him use, "you have no authority here. Come with me now, and speak before the maharani later, or submit to arrest. I would prefer, for your sake, that you choose the first course of action."

They climbed up to the third floor in silence. The landing was bereft of guards, and Lingli saw that Master Avani noted the absence but neither of them said anything. He pulled a key from his pocket and unlocked the library door just as Madam Sayed arrived from the floor above.

"Thank the stars, you've found her," Madam said in a low voice.

Master Avani raised his brows. "Ah, yes, well she is here and whole. If you don't mind, Amina, would you be so good as to bring us some nourishment?"

Madam looked offended, but then she nodded and said, "Of course."

Master Avani added, "Perhaps something soothing. Perhaps some tea. Yes, I think a calming tea would be good. Miss Tabaan has passed some difficult days. She is no doubt weary and needs to rest."

Madam continued downstairs as Master Avani ushered Lingli into the library.

As soon as the door closed behind them, he said, "Today is not the day to bring attention to yourself! If you only knew what transpired overnight—"

"I know as much as you," Lingli said calmly. "Did you think an ancestor left that message for Sid?"

"That was clever! I do not discount your information. I would have you tell me more. Tell me exactly what you learned."

Lingli opened her mouth to reply then closed it again. Everyone else's problems always stepped in front of hers. Not this time.

"Sir," she said, unsure whether anger or sorrow guided her words, "you have helped me, I agree, and you have seemed to befriend me, but it is a kindness full of secrets. I may be simple, but I cannot abide more lies or excuses for telling me nothing at all." She looked at her feet, suddenly tired and deflated.

Master Avani rubbed his chin and looked away from her. "From your first day I have seen that you are a sensible girl, and I think you would agree, knowing that we are threatened, that this is a very inauspicious time…."

Lingli thought she saw it clear. He would leave her to her fate as easily as anyone else, and she could not bear to hear her suspicion made true. She turned to leave, sick at heart, but Master Avani stepped between her and the door and held his hands up.

"Please listen. I am certain you did not kill Master Vaksana, and I doubt you are responsible for the thefts attributed to you. I am only sorry I have not convinced my sister of the same."

Lingli shook her head and held up her dirty bandaged finger. "You did not convince her to leave me in one piece either. Where were you when your sister judged me?"

"I regret that deeply. The maharani sees only one thing plain, and that is that her enemies are emboldened and multiplying. I am grateful that you made the effort to warn us. Will you tell me what has happened since you left the Giants' Post?"

"No, sir." Lingli wiped viciously at her tearing eyes. "I will not. Not until *my* questions are answered."

There was a knock on the door. Master Avani admitted Madam Sayed bearing a tray of food and cups of tea.

"What a welcome sight," the old noble said with some relief as he took the tray. "If I had half this woman's wisdom, I would have served the realm much better."

Madam's cheeks colored at the flattery, but Master Avani took no notice.

"Time is bearing down on all of us, and I must explain recent events to Madam," he told Lingli. "If you will have but a cup of patience, we will have a common understanding and then we can address your questions. Is that acceptable?"

She hesitated, unwilling to be put off, but Madam served her, and the orange in Sid's quarters had done little to curb her hunger. While she inhaled the naans and fruit set before her, Master Avani told Madam about her message and what had transpired in the council meeting.

Madam's brow wrinkled into a deep frown throughout the retelling, and Lingli guessed that her innocence remained uncertain in the dance teacher's mind.

"Even if this…this fantastic explanation of the message satisfies you," Madam said to Master Avani, "what I still do not understand is why she was found next to Master Vaksana's body." She frowned at her. "All signs point to you as a murderer."

"I didn't kill him, but I saw those who did. They wanted to see me arrested to save themselves."

"Do you mean the killers are known to Captain Duvanya? And how did you escape from him?"

"No. Captain Duvanya arrested me before I met them," Lingli said, shaking her head. "Oh, it's a long tale. I'll tell you all of it, but first I will ask my question."

The embers of what she had vowed as she climbed up from the maharani's hidden room had burned low, but she dug down into her cloak, grasped the tail of the dart, then decided against starting with that crime. She produced the three felt figures instead and, as she set them on the table in a row, the elders' faces drained of color.

"I took these from the rani's altar in the Rock's heart. Tell me what they are."

Madam and Master Avani looked at one another. Madam said, "Effigies like these are made by many mothers in Saatkulom."

Mothers. The word hummed in Lingli's mind.

"They make them," Madam continued, "to seek the ancestors' blessings for their living children and to remember those who have died."

Master Avani reached out and patted Madam's hand. "We can avoid this no longer."

When Madam nodded, he said, "If you wish to know why the maharani keeps three effigies, I will tell you what I can, but it is not the whole story."

Lingli nodded.

"Cycles ago, when Rani Shikra and Princess Valena returned from the east after her father was killed, the realm grieved, and none more than his daughter," the old noble began. "After the final rites, I, with the other masters, were consumed with completing the agreement with the south that Raja Basheer had drafted before his murder. It had been very important to him, and Rani Shikra demanded that it be completed to secure the realm and give her daughter the confidence she needed to rule.

"As soon as we issued the contract, Valena was named maharani, and soon after Rani Shikra announced that her daughter's betrothal to Raja Tajazan was broken. The princess would marry Prince Zakir of the House of Hudulfah. Marriage outside the Seven was a rarity, but Raja Basheer's marriage had been to a northerner, and he had sought permission from the council for his daughter's first betrothal before his death, so there was little ground to argue against it, but the people were uneasy. We barely saw the new maharani, who was still in mourning and remained in her chambers most of the time."

Madam Sayed interrupted impatiently, "As you might have guessed, as any woman with eyes knew at the time, the young Maharani Sandhyatara was not merely mourning. She was with child."

"You do know how to move a story to its point, Amina."

"We have little time for looking back when so much lies ahead." Madam rested her hand on top of Lingli's for a moment. "Forgive me if this story pains you.

"Rani Shikra pressed me into her daughter's service soon after the proclamation that she would marry Zakir," Madam Sayed continued, "saying that grief had made her daughter ill. Though grief no doubt played its part, the balance of truth was that her illness was the result of using every potion and poison at her disposal to rid herself of the babe in her womb. Nothing worked. The babe clung fast and the damning effects wounded the young rani herself."

As Madam's words piled on her chest like stones, Lingli felt her spirit seeking a way to leave, to just float away. She fought to stay in the room with them and hear them out.

"Rani Shikra had aided her daughter in these attempts, but she finally accepted that the ancestors had put some protection on this babe. When she called upon me to serve her daughter, I was so foolish as to think that I had been asked to sit with her as a companion. I grew to dread those hours. The young maharani walked in both worlds. In her sleep, and sometimes in her waking hours, she spoke to unseen people. She tore out her hair and refused to eat, refused to bathe. My primary task, I discovered, was to prevent her from ending her own life."

"Valena was still quite young," Master Avani interjected. "Her father had just been killed by an assassin, and she had abruptly ended her betrothal to Raja Tajazan. She also had to demonstrate that she could rule, that she could negotiate a trade agreement with the House of Kirdun, and then she was betrothed again—all in a matter of three moons."

"I was there when the babe was born," Madam said softly. "It...*she* was small, weak, and sounding more like a mewling kitten than a noble proclaiming the next generation of her house. I had never seen a newborn so fresh. I couldn't help thinking that this little one, who was so unwanted, had somehow managed to draw breath in this world and should be given a chance to find her way. The maharani, however, would not look at her. She did not touch her or feed her."

Lingli could hardly breathe. She could not look away from the white felt effigy.

"Eager to see her daughter returned to health, Rani Shikra took the babe away and pretended she did not exist. She spoke as if our young maharani was recovering from fly fever or some accident. I was quite beside myself, for I had seen the babe passed into Rani Shikra's quarters, and I feared her spirit would be set loose before her bones could harden.

"I had no practice with babies, and I could not rescue the infant myself. All I could think to do was rely on Rani Shikra's respect for tradition, and so I feigned alignment with her intent and proposed to make the infant's death shroud, a beautiful gown, so that the weak thing could be sent to the arms of ancestors with all due care required…to ensure our maharani's next child and proper heir was favored."

Emotion had thickened Madam's voice. She turned her face from Lingli.

"The babe was fortunate to find such an ally," Master Avani continued. "In addition to our good lady here, there was one more. Rani Shikra handed the newborn to her personal guard, a creature she trusted as much as she trusted the Seven—the red giant. It was her mistake, for he bonded instantly with the babe, and giants will give their lives for those to whom they are bonded. Though I do not know how or who, the giant found some nurse for the babe—at least that is what I assume—for she did not die. When the poor thing began to strengthen and demand nourishment, Rani Shikra's heart softened enough that she pushed back her plans for infanticide to a more opportune time."

"And Master Avani," Madam said to Lingli, as she refilled her cup of tea, "played his part in that, too. I told him of the babe's existence and asked him to convey to Rani Shikra his condolences for the child's weak state."

"I believe I said I had implored the ancestors to safeguard the babe if it was their will," Master Avani said. "Never had I seen Rani Shikra so furious. She demanded to know who told me her daughter had given birth. She must have suspected Madam, but the blame finally fell on the red giant, for she had him banished shortly after that. In any case, she absolutely forbade me to tell anyone else of the child, saying it was a bad omen to acknowledge a weak spirit marked by the bright cycle."

"Still, Rani Shikra could not be sure that no others knew," Madam said. "She could not do away with the babe in perfect secrecy, and this meant my suggestion served her better. I sewed the gown as slowly as I could, but in less than a moon, Rani Shikra demanded it from me. Maharani Valena and her consort were preparing to leave for a visit to his people to ensure blessings of their union. I well knew the babe's end was near, but I had no choice but to deliver the gown. As expected, both ranis and Prince Zakir left for the south with a baby. They returned a moon later without one."

Madam looked at Master Avani, who said, "We never imagined the babe had survived."

Lingli did her best to stay present, but she was utterly exhausted. There was a strange taste in her mouth. Her eyes closed. The last thing she heard was Madam saying, "Perhaps we could secret her out by the northern tower...."

CHAPTER 40

Clean and dressed in one of his best new suits, Sid lit diyas for his grandfather's and grandmother's effigies and looked up at Li's warning that still marked the wall. *Now would be a good time to leave the Rock, Li. If you can.*

Stars know how tonight will end, he told Li in his head, *but I won't likely be invited for tea by the House of Hudulfah afterward.*

A much-needed bath had calmed him since he had left his mother's quarters earlier that afternoon, but Greta's warning still echoed.

While his mother had sweated and thrashed on her divan as if she were fighting demons in her dreams, he'd grown anxious, and his own thirst threatened to overcome him when Greta removed the moonstone pendant from around his mother's neck.

"She must be weaned," Greta told him. "She can take a drop at dusk and dawn only." The giantess poured out the remaining elixir and refilled the pendant with two drops and more firewine.

"What if she doesn't listen?"

"Hmmm. She will return to stone."

Sid went to the room's narrow window and looked upon the bustling front grounds below. He wished he had learned about her plans besides the use of the potion. Everything depended on his mother, his beautiful, angry, smart, deceptive, and powerful mother, who had a weak spot at her center. If she would trust him, he could help her, and he could do his part for the strength of the realm.

Returning to the bed, Sid climbed up and carefully brought down the twin blades mounted on the wall. Admiring their jeweled hilts as he buckled his great-grandfather's scabbard, Sid silently asked the ancestors to prevent any reason he might have to use them. Then, from under one of his pillows, he pulled out his Hudulfah grandmother's grass bracelet and hid it in his sleeve. Lingli's kufi came out from under another pillow, and he fit it into his coat pocket before he left his rooms.

Across the landing, he saw Parth pressed against the library door. When he called out, the scribe turned quickly.

"Do you know where he keeps the Seven's books?" Sid asked. "The maharani wants hers back."

"I'm not sure where he keeps them, but we won't be looking in the library. He's put on a new lock and didn't tell me. It's a shame how fast the old man is losing his memory."

"Eh, yeah." Sid looked around. All doors were locked, but no guards were on the floor except for the one waiting behind him. *Shift change already?*

As they walked downstairs, Parth asked, "Did you scribe for them this morning?" When Sid looked confused, he added, "That council meeting at dawn. Avaniji never called me. I thought they must have put you to work."

"No, just last-minute plans for the wedding," Sid said, unwilling to share the Seven's plans. "Not really worth the ink."

"I don't think you miss writing 'til your hand cramps."

"No, don't miss it at all," Sid said, "but I miss our firewine breaks."

Parth snorted. "You can always command me to bring you some. You can even command me to drink it with you."

Confronted by the gathering crowd in the front grounds, Parth waved and hurried off. It was nearly dusk. Sid weaved his way up the steps of the colonnade and into the feasting hall, which was crowded with excited staff and guests. Every sconce was lit, and the clean, green smell of fresh rushes perfumed the air. Great swags of indigo cloth covered in small crystals hung from the ceiling, making the hall look as if its guests stood under a twinkling night sky. Rows of long tables spanned the width of the room before the dais, and small thalis of beaten bronze waited upon them.

Despite the promise of a merry evening, Sid noticed that Trechur and Titok were already chained to the walls on either side of the dais, and there was an excessive number of night guards in position in both colonnades. After tallying up the archers watching from the landing above, Sid nervously rubbed the hilt of one of his great-grandfather's blades.

Where are the Seven? Did plans change? No one tells me anything.

He almost jumped when Madam Hansa tapped him on the shoulder and led him to where other members of the Seven's families waited in the front grounds. In the midst of them, his mother shone like the evening star itself. Her soft, amethyst-colored gown and fine filigree crown made her look terribly vulnerable, and Sid was glad for Greta's looming presence as well as the black wolf at her side.

The maharani's brows raised at the sight of the ceremonial blades on his waist, but she was amused. He was relieved to see nothing in her eyes of either the weakness or the mania that vexed her.

"They have all come," she said softly. "All the nobility of their four houses. See their faces. They understand that our strength exceeds any head count. Our relations will soon be rebalanced."

Sid whispered, "Is...the drink ready?"

The rani smiled and nodded at the southerners who had begun to enter the hall. "When I call for a toast, you must not drink what is given to you. Pretend, but spit the drink back into your cup."

"What if some of them don't drink?"

"My intent is that no one will be harmed, but if it should come to that, we will face them with courage, yes?"

Sid went cold at the thought of what she hinted. He nodded slowly.

Her eyes shone with resolve. "The House of Duran shows no fear, whatever the challenge."

After the maharani explained her plan to her noble brethren, minus the houses of Duvanya and Vaksana, Master Avani took Sid aside.

"Has Li left the Rock?" Sid asked quietly.

"No, but she's safe for now." Master Avani produced a small roll of parchment as he spoke. "This is a list of the most important Ascaryans in Saatkulom—the youngest of the Seven's descendants. Despite my raging about Vidkun this morning, I hope you understand that all our children are indispensable to the strength of the realm."

The musicians began playing, and Sid could see the rani was waiting for him to escort her. Master Avani sighed, pressed the roll into Sid's hand, and said, "If there is any doubt and fighting breaks out, I will seek your help in securing these young ones. I'll explain later."

He quickly tucked the parchment into his vest and hurried to his mother's side as the procession began to shuffle forward into the colonnade.

They paused in the archway while leaders among the fort's traders were ushered to the hall's back tables. Next, the eastern envoy and the newly arrived visitor from the north, still very much alive, were seated just before the southern nobles and their families entered.

Ameer Ali and his wife were resplendent in brilliant red robes. Ameer Khush of the House of Afreh wore a beaded achkan and a tall headdress of polished horn. His two wives sat on either side of him, completely covered in yellow shrouds. A huge claw of some creature hung from the sash worn by Ameer Temer of the House of Idris, and his face was painted with concentric black lines, making him look more a warrior than an honored guest. Next to him was a very small wife, no more than ten cycles, Sid thought, and with her kohl-lined eyes darting all around, she seemed as nervous as he was.

Last, the extended members of the Seven Houses entered the hall just as splendidly dressed as their guests, and the masters of Saatkulom's houses joined Sid's Hudulfah grandparents before the front benches.

In the opposite colonnade, Mafala took Aseem from his nurse's arms. The Hudulfah princess wore a pale lehenga scarcely visible under her ornaments. Her brother, wearing a heavy white toga with a gold belt, accompanied Mafala and Aseem onto the dais.

The rani muttered angrily, "A wealth of sand kept their house thin, yet they didn't value even the meager goods they had until Father and I introduced them to our traders. I have ceaselessly promoted their house, and for all this they repay me with treachery and deceit."

Watching his mother from the corner of his eye, Sid feared she was weakening already.

The prince consort escorted his sister to a small chair on the far end of the row on the dais then took the seat between Mafala and the throne. For a moment, Hassan stared at the rani and him with lightless eyes, and Sid's throat went dry.

The processional music ended, and a different drumbeat was struck. The rani urged him forward. Concentrating on not tripping, Sid left her standing before her throne and took his seat next to her, on the opposite side of Hassan. Akela, ears pricked, lay on the floor behind the rani near

Greta's huge feet. When the drumming ceased the crowd bowed in respect before they sat.

Prince Hassan issued greetings in the common tongue, then repeated them in the language of his house and the three languages of the other southern houses. Even his common tongue remarks were as dry as the wind in the ninth moon, and Sid found he was fighting to stifle a yawn. His small half brother seemed to feel the same. As the prince of Hudulfah enumerated the benefits of the arrangement he and the maharani proposed, Aseem began to fuss, his vocal displeasure ascending to such a pitch that Sid wondered if Mafala had pinched him.

Hassan paused and said something low to his sister who gave him the darkest of looks before she rose and carried Aseem from the hall. After a moment of quiet chuckling from the guests, the prince resumed his stultifying speech.

Anticipation and boredom warred in Sid's head. He studied the faces of everyone he could see who wore a dark cloak, but Li was not among them. With the shame of failing her still weighing on him, he made a small, silent tribute to Matachand, the spirit of the First Mother. *Watch over her. Guide her far from here.*

There was a shifting in the audience. Suddenly Sid realized Hassan had returned to his seat and the rani had risen. Everyone was standing. He scrambled to his feet. Bearers served the guests, and Korvar, sweating profusely, brought a tray to serve the rani, Hassan, and him.

The rani raised her cup and said, "Tonight's feast is not only a celebration of our impending marriage, but it is also a moment where our realms set aside doubts and boldly choose to take a shared path into the future. This union shall benefit all our people and descendants yet to be. Let us drink in honor of the ancestors and celebrate this alliance as brothers and sisters. All of us, the children of Ascarya Erde!"

She brought her cup to her lips and very convincingly appeared to drink from it. Everyone followed suit. Sid took a sip into his mouth. Whatever else it was, it tasted of sweet firewine and smelled of mogra blossoms. It promised happiness. He badly wanted to swallow, but the stern expression on Master Avani's face helped common sense win out, and he spat the stuff back into his cup.

The musicians began to play a joyful tune, and Madam Hansa rose to sing.

Sid pretended to watch her and the crowd indifferently, but he could hardly stop himself from staring at every gesture or movement for signs of the potion's effects. The rani belied no such concern. She and Hassan spoke quietly over Akela's head as though they were having a chat about wedding plans.

"Of course it's ready," she said lightly. "You will have it as soon as the feast is over, should you still feel like reviewing it tonight."

"Gentle words from the bitch who cut off water to Nilampur."

"What? The tanks hold two weeks' supply for all the laborers there. That should have been sufficient for your people for a few days."

"You knew it was not enough." Hassan blinked his eyes and shifted in his chair. "Not that it mattered.... It was better that we moved—" He stopped and leaned forward, squinting at Aza Mussan, who had slumped against his mother's shoulder. "What have you done?"

"Only my duty," the maharani said.

Hassan rubbed his eyes, but they closed soon after, and his head dropped to his chest.

With his stomach knotting, Sid looked out into the room. Madam Hansa sang the ballad's final chorus as Ameer Ali's wife rested her head on her arms, and Ali rose, pressing his fists into the tabletop. Ameer Khush suddenly toppled backward off his bench. His cloaked wives knelt by his side and cried out in alarm as the ameer of the House of Idris called for his fighters. They and a few others who had not drunk the firewine faced a room ringed with defenders.

Beside him, his mother stood and took the prince consort's hand in hers. The loathing on her face could have curdled milk, and Sid thought that she might strangle Hassan in that moment. Removing the half-drunk cup from her consort's hand, the rani made a small toast to Sid and threw the contents in Hassan's face. The son of Hudulfah did not react.

Among the tables, an Afreh spearman pushed past the guards and charged the dais. Akela sprang between him and the maharani, teeth snapping. To Sid's shock the man veered toward him. Night guards seized the southerner before he could use the small blade he carried.

Everyone not asleep was shouting, but the defenders held the room. The rani rested one hand on Akela's head and raised the other, waiting until the din subsided. She looked around the room and to the landing above where more recruits and staff huddled.

"Understand this," she yelled forcefully. "The southerners have broken their word and violated our agreement. There are ten thousand on the field with plans to storm the Rock. We will resist." The hall buzzed with raised voices, but she continued, "The realm has faced such trials before. We will show courage before our ancestors. Lend your hand according to the guidance of your house or duty master."

Madam Hansa and Master Avani ordered defenders to take the southern men to the yard and hold the women and children in the hall. The rani turned to Crowseye, who had joined them on the dais. She asked him if the gates were secure.

"Yes, and our defenders are in position, but we are stretched thin."

"Has anyone seen the day captain?"

Crowseye shook his head.

"How quickly can you make your gift ready?"

"I need two hours."

"Begin. When you hear my word, seal the eastern passage."

As Crowseye left the hall, an angry cry rose from the floor.

Azi Kebedi brandished a blade over her husband, who lay unconscious at her feet. While she swiped at one of the defenders, the rani left the dais. Taking a talwar from another defender's hands, she marched forward and drove it into Azi Kebedi's side.

Sid stared in horrified fascination at the dark blood spreading over his grandmother's dress. As she crumpled to the floor, she stared at him and said, "Heed the ancestors, Son of Zakir. Be brave. Soon, I will welcome you."

Greta pushed him into the colonnade, and the next Sid knew, he stood by his mother's side. She leaned into his face, forcing his eyes up to hers.

"When what is precious is threatened, when the way is clear, we never hesitate to act. Now come. The battle has only begun."

Despite his shock, Sid tried to match his mother's pace as she marched from the hall with Greta, Akela, and four defenders who carried the inert Prince Hassan by his arms and legs.

She was an old woman, What had she threatened, truly? Sid wished for a drink of firewine that seemed unlikely to appear.

Outside Mafala's quarters in the new tower they bunched on the landing while a guard pounded on the door. More defenders arrived behind them, prodding or toting southern women and children.

"Princess? Are you sleeping?" the rani said loudly. "I'm so sorry to wake you, but this really cannot wait until morning."

There was no answer.

"So be it, my dear."

Defenders took turns landing blows with heavy mauls until the door began to sag and split. The rani again pressed herself to the door and shouted, "We certainly shall continue if necessary, and you best hope they don't drop your brother on his head while we are delayed."

The bar inside was raised. Mafala, wrapped in a heavy shawl, stood in the doorway.

His mother pushed past her, and the defenders trudged to the inner room and swung Hassan onto the bed.

"He's unhurt," the maharani told Mafala.

"At last I know your true heart, and I cannot claim to be shocked." Patting a waterskin lying next to a large silk bag at the end of the bed, she continued, "But I am surprised you would leave on the eve of battle. You may lack originality, but you are a woman of courage—like your mother. Don't you know your house cannot stand without you?"

Mafala's eyes lingered on the talwar the rani still carried. His mother's smugness only served to harden the defiance in the princess's face.

The rani stepped very close to Mafala. "We could have shared so much, my never-to-be sister." Then she signaled the defenders still on the landing. "Bring them in."

The women and children who were awake were herded into one corner. Defenders laid the rest out on the floor until there was hardly space to move.

"Inform your brother that I will give you opportunity to reconsider your decision to attack us—a decision that has no chance of success, be assured. If no call to bear arms against the Rock is issued by dawn, we will parley. The contract will be revised, of course, and understand that if you continue to test me, I will detain you and all your remaining kin until you see reason."

"What have you done with the rest?" Mafala managed to ask through clenched teeth.

The rani simply smiled and swept from the room. Sid followed quickly. On the landing, she called for an extra guard on the door to Aseem's quarters before marching upstairs, talwar still in hand.

The quiet of his mother's quarters was a relief. She bid him follow her to the inner room where she had a small altar similar to the one in his quarters.

"We don't have much time, but we must make a tribute before it begins."

"Before what begins? You said they would negotiate once they understood they could not win."

"They will, but they have lost face, and some will fight to regain their dignity."

Pressing her palms together, the rani bowed to another small raja effigy, but the bronze chair next to him held a cloth with a parrot embroidered upon it instead of a braid of hair.

Lighting another diya, his mother placed it in the thali and knelt on the floor. Sid knelt beside her, keeping his palms together under his nose while she recited the names of the masters of the House of Duran from bygone generations. When she touched her forehead to the floor, he followed. When she held her hand over the diya's flame and washed her face with its smoke, he did, too. Sid's thoughts, however, continued to circle his grandmother's death and her last words.

Why did she say she would welcome me?

When his mother rose from the floor, he asked, "How can I ask some of my ancestors to vanquish some of my other ancestors?"

"Oh, Son of Zakir, you should not. Your request should be to understand your rightful path and to meet your destiny with courage."

"But how can I face Hassan?"

"You will not face him without me by your side, but you needn't fear that he will harm you today when all hangs in the balance. To do violence to a descendant would dishonor his house for generations. Leave the confrontations to me and the Seven."

Sid said no more but questioned whether murdering a nephew could possibly bring more dishonor than failing to avenge the murder of your mother.

The tribute was hardly finished when Greta, an anxious-looking maid, and a steward appeared at the threshold of her inner room. The rani invited the maid to place her paints on her dressing table as she waved the steward and Sid out.

The steward presented Sid with a stack of fresh clothes and proceeded to dress him. After putting on the pants, the kurta, and a light vest, Sid slid his arms into a cream-colored war coat lined with mail and panels that stretched from his ribs to his knees. The coat felt bulky and strange, as did the turban, which the steward explained was fitted with a metal plate to protect his head. That was not reassuring, and Sid was certain that he looked a fool, but at least he had kept his golden juttis.

After the steward departed, Sid put his great-grandfather's blades on again, hid the grass bracelet in his sleeve, and moved Lingli's kufi inside his mail. He collected Master Avani's list and wandered onto the balcony to read it.

Descendants' names were listed by house. Under Vaksana were the names of Jordak's three youngest siblings, and under Duvanya Sid recognized the names of the night captain's younger sister and brother. Skipping to the entries under the House of Duran, Aseem was at the top of the list, then the names of the healers' grandchildren—cousins Sid hadn't met. Next was his own name, which made him frown for he had no intention of going into hiding, but there was one more name below his: Lingli Tabaan.

Why is her name here? This handwriting is Master Avani's, but he must know that trying to hide Li among noble children will only enrage Amma. As Sid turned away from the front grounds, another explanation came to him. His chest tightened. He really needed a drink.

Seeing the maid skitter out of his mother's inner room and leave, Sid hastily rolled up the list and pushed it into a pocket.

In the middle of the room, the rani stood in a long, white gown certainly fit for a wedding. The many-rayed suns and golden stars that adorned it seemed to tumble down the skirt and collect in a mass at the hem, and a golden chain studded with precious stones had been woven into the rani's hair, but the ornamentation ended there.

Her face was painted indigo blue from her hairline to her cheekbones, a dark mask broken only by Duran's guiding star, shining bright white between her brows. Greta buckled the collar of the rani's mail around her throat and tightened the scabbard for her talwar.

"How long?" his mother asked, her eyes pressed closed. She didn't need to reach for her pendant for Sid to know what she wanted.

"When sunlight touches the palace gate, it will be time," Greta said.

The rani breathed deeply, and a part of Sid wanted more than ever to tell her he meant to do whatever she asked and more, but another part of him—the part that had just gone numb with fear that everything he thought he knew was crumbling away—kept still.

"Come, Siddharth," she said lightly. "We will face this New Cycle Day as the ancestors demand."

The moons had fled by the time they entered the stable yard. Defenders lined the walls and archers paced along roofs and terraces. More blew on their hands and huddled around small fires encircling the southern prisoners lumped together on the ground.

The rani gestured toward the summit path. "Run up to the mouth and find Master Tilan's defender-in-charge. Report back to me whether they are in position yet. I will give the signal if we must make use of Ketan's gift."

Despite the uncertainty racking Sid, he was grateful for something to do and hurried to the stairs, skirting around the mining hall then trotting up the summit path. All the way to the mouth he tried to sort out what was true.

The list is a lie meant to secure some protection for Li. Or the list is not a lie and Li is of some nobility undetermined. Or, Li is of the House of Duran and is my cousin. Or Li is my sister and heir...and I am a spare. How?

Inside the cavern, lanterns revealed a string of defenders in the passage, reminding Sid of the scope of the conflict they could face. He conveyed his mother's message to Ilo Hansa's twin brother, Lalzam, and a sentry was posted at the cavern opening to await the signal.

Returning down the summit path, Sid saw that defenders covered the palace grounds. A proper unit of defenders encircled the mining hall, and another waited at the training yard gate. Near the back of the feasting hall, he could see Master Avani directing apprentices with mail vests to join one unit or another. He intended to speak to the old noble as soon as he reported on his task. He had to know. *Am I heir or spare?*

By the time Sid reached the stable yard, some hostages had awakened. There were about thirty altogether, and the four ameers huddled in the middle of them, including his grandfather. Shame again crowded into Sid's anxiety. There was little enough to like about the ameer of Hudulfah, but if anything he had been told was true, he was his father's father.

"Our parley is about to begin," the rani said as Sid approached her. "We shall speak to the ameers one by one, explain the futility of their plans, and invite them to renounce all plans of violence. Depending on their choices, we may conclude this business by breakfast."

Sid searched his mother's face for any similarities with Lingli and found none. *What is Avani playing at?* There had to be some other explanation for including her in the list. Knowing full well that raising Li's name in this moment would not serve him well, Sid tried to focus on the immediate task.

"Will you bring out Prince Hassan?" he asked.

"Only if I must," the rani answered. "As long as he is kept separate, they will doubt their next steps."

The defenders had made a path through the cluster of hostages, and Madam Satya met the ameers. Ameer Temer was on his feet and propping up Ameer Khush, but Sid saw that his grandfather remained sitting on the ground with an arm around Ameer Ali, who still appeared unconscious.

One of the guards who attempted to move Aza Mussan and Ameer Ali, suddenly yelled out, "A disguise!"

Blades were drawn, and Madam Satya pulled away the scarf worn by the man slumped against Aza Mussan's shoulder. He also wore a crimson-colored coat, but he was not Ameer Ali. Aza Mussan laughed loudly and spat at Madam Satya. Then he saw Sid and stopped laughing.

Vidkun, who had been circling the hostages with all three harnessed wolves, rushed to the rani's side and declared, "By your word, Your Majesty, I shall interrogate this impostor so we will know who planned this madness."

The rani said sharply, "Did you bring Ameer Ali's body from the hall?"

"Did I bring the ameer? Uh, several of ours carried them out, but I held the wolves, of course," Vidkun answered. "Command me, and I will mount a search for him!"

Such pandering, Sid thought, would have been comical if the cause was not so alarming.

"You will remain in this yard and guard the hostages until Madam Satya tells you otherwise," his mother fumed. "Stake the wolves. I will need them to encourage the parley."

Turning on her heels, the rani hurried toward the feasting hall with Sid and Greta trailing in her wake. Before they reached the platform behind the kitchens, a steward intercepted them.

He swallowed hard and said, "Your Majesty, we cannot find Prince Aseem. One of his guards is missing. The other was beaten so badly he cannot speak, and prince is not in his quarters nor yours."

Even in the faint light of the fading stars, Sid could see fear flit across his mother's face. It fluttered in his chest, too, as he contemplated the possible consequences for his baby brother.

"His nurse?"

The steward shook his head.

"Have you looked among the female hostages?"

"Prince Aseem is not among them."

The rani looked back over the yard and said, "Both those missing may be together. Search Ameer Ali's quarters and await me there."

Sid looked around for Master Avani, but could not find him in the yard, and his mother was already moving away, pausing only long enough to tell the steward, "Tell Madam Satya that she must ensure that no messages reach their allies while I look for Ali."

Defenders snapped to attention as they entered the training yard. The rani turned toward the palace gate.

"Where are we going?" Sid asked.

"I know Ali. He has no imagination and plays others' games, but he plays well. I have lost a round. With your help I will not lose another."

Whatever his own worries, Sid knew he had to swallow them. Aseem's life could be in danger.

"If he..." Sid said. "If Ali took Aseem, wouldn't he be trying to escape?"

The rani shook her head. "Ali will use him to curry favor with Hassan and secure his own interests."

When they reached the gate tower the Rock still shaded the palace grounds, but the sky was lightening. A day guard opened the door to the room at the base of the tower, and they crowded inside.

"Where is your captain?" the rani asked."

The guard swallowed hard. "I do not know, Your Majesty."

"Is the night captain in charge, then?"

"He's on the terrace, Your Majesty. Shall I call him down?"

"No. Stand watch outside until I return. No one crosses."

When the door closed, Greta sniffed the air and said, "It is time, Dear Child. One sip."

The rani's hands shook as she leaned against the wall to unbuckle the collar of her mail and pull out her moonstone pendant.

Sid turned away the moment she put the open pendant to her lips, yet his stomach stirred as if some other thing lived there and would demand what it wanted no matter his plans.

When he looked again, the pendant had been hidden, and his mother bit down on her own hand to stifle a cry. Greta hugged her close. Not for long, but for too long, what little light the room's lantern offered was reflected in the whites of her eyes.

As Greta gently brought his mother down to the floor, an idea came to Sid that he wished he had thought of earlier. Asking Greta a question, *the* question, when his mother was weakened stank of disloyalty, but if he was to ever know the truth of Avani's list, this was his chance.

"Is Li my sister?"

The giantess had opened her salve and was about to dab some under his mother's nose. Her head swiveled toward him briefly. "Hmmm, yes."

Giants never lie.

Everything about Sid's imagined destiny fractured.

Within a few breaths after Greta's ministrations the rani tipped her chin to the ceiling and breathed deeply. The room seemed to almost vibrate with the power that rippled through her as she got to her feet. Her gaze pinned Sid like a small bird.

"Even if I am still, I can hear," she said crossly, but her next words were more carefully chosen. "Shared blood and bone matter little when a spirit is cursed. She is sick with it, Siddharth. Anyone can see that. Do not be fooled. She is otherworld."

"But she is your daughter?" He pushed the words out, wishing she would deny them.

"She was born from me, but she was marked before she drew her first breath. I would not disgrace the ancestors by allowing her to remain in the realm. Never."

"What did you do?"

The rani took a deep breath and said, "We left her in the desert."

Her answer made Sid's heart shrink. *An infant alone in the burning sands.* He felt he was balancing on the edge of a deep and abiding darkness within his mother—one he could easily fall into if he didn't learn how to sort lies from truth.

"Then how…" he stammered. "How can Li be that child?"

The rani looked at Greta as she said, "It seems I was betrayed." Her hands flexed as if she itched to draw her talwar. The giantess did not move. "That…star-cursed creature will be reckoned with, I promise you, but not until we have dealt with this morning's business. The realm and your brother need us. Now."

Us.

Stepping onto the first stone step leading to the top of the gate tower, his mother waited for him.

Sid hesitated. It all seemed so unlikely, but he tried to see through her eyes: a cursed child, the need to prove herself a worthy ruler, the elixir, another consort, another child. If she could carry all that for cycles, surely he could hold the questions that banged inside his head until they found Aseem.

He followed her up the steep spiraling stairs.

When they reached the top, the rani paused next to the terrace door and Sid leaned on his knees to catch his breath. No, he was wrong. He could not quell his questions.

"You should have told me."

"Would that have made it easier for you? To know you shared blood with an asura?"

Sid wished he could have seen his mother's face better, but, except for the star on her forehead and the whites of her eyes, she was shifting shades of gray in the stairwell's shadows.

"She's never done a thing but help me," he said, "in all those cycles you were not there."

Her voice was ice. "I will not waste another breath on this. There are southerners at the gates, and your brother is missing. For once, act like a prince."

With that, she pushed open the door to the gate tower terrace, and Sid nursed the stinging blow she had landed.

He spotted two archers who had journeyed with him from the Western Woods, a handful of apprentices he knew, and Parth, who waved from the opposite end, in the midst of a group of defenders. Captain Duvanya came to meet them.

"We have some complications," the rani said. "Ameer Ali is missing, and my youngest son may be with him. Have you seen either since the feast?"

"No," the captain answered, surprised. "But my attention has been elsewhere. I can take up the search if you so command."

"You will stay here, and I will take the guards downstairs for the hunt."

"By your word, Maharani."

"Quickly," she said. "What news from the field?"

"Banners fly for all four southern houses, but there has been no charge or call for parley."

"Are our defenses in place?"

"We have six hundred thirty-one defenders on the walls," the captain said. "All the commoners older than ten cycles, more than two thousand, will defend the fort as best they can, yet we are outnumbered."

"The walls have never failed, Captain," the rani said. "They will not fail today."

Turning to Sid, she said, "You will stay here and represent my word until we begin the parley."

Sid's hopes fell down into his juttis. There was no "us." *She only wants the night captain to mind me.*

As soon as the captain left them, the rani said, "I am not punishing you. I am guaranteeing you, too, don't go missing. After I secure Aseem, you will be at my side for the final moves in this game-that-is-not-a-game."

Disappointment and frustration made Sid reckless.

"From the day I met you," he said, "I thought of nothing but how I could serve you and the realm. You told me, only hours ago, there was no honor in murdering descendants, but you murdered your true heir, or tried to. You told me that the heirs of Duran fight for the realm, but you mean to hide me away. Why? Is it Aseem you want as heir? Will naming him save your alliance?"

He saw that he had surprised her.

"I would have helped you find him even so," he added. "I am not so jealous as to wish him ill."

The rani took him by the shoulders and waited for him to look at her. "Put your doubts aside and hear my word, Siddharth." Her eyes shone with tears. "As long as you walk in this world, you are my heir, and I will have no other."

These were words he had desperately wanted to hear, so why did they warm him so little?

The rani left quickly, and Sid stared out over the parapet at the parrots circling above the crack. He could not trust his mother or the promises she made, but he still craved her approval, and every accusation he leveled against her somehow pointed to his own shortcomings.

When brooding failed to bring answers or comfort, Sid squared his shoulders and sidled up to a group looking at a rough map of the Rock that someone had drawn on the floor of the terrace. Like several others there who seemed nervous about the day ahead, Sid listened carefully as Captain Duvanya patiently explained where the southerners would likely try to attack the walls, what defenses would be used, and how to understand the flagged signs on the fort gate.

Half an hour passed. Boredom was taking the upper hand among those on the terrace. Seeing that his mother and Greta had rejoined her defenders in the yard, Sid took this as a hopeful sign that Aseem had been recovered and the attack had been stemmed. A few others came to the same conclusion and asked the captain to be relieved of duty, but he refused, and the grumbling grew until a deep booming noise caught everyone's attention.

They crowded the parapet facing the palace grounds and silently watched a cloud of dust boil out of the cavern in the bluff. After a long moment, defenders emerged with the sun and stars banner, and a victorious cry went up. Those surrounding Sid breathed easier, and some slapped each other's backs as they watched the distant figures make their way down to the yard.

Soon a company led by Crowseye marched toward them. When they halted at the foot of the gate, Ilo Hansa came up to the terrace and immediately pulled Captain Duvanya aside. After a short conversation they approached Sid.

The captain's expression was more serious than Sid would like as he said, "Master Tilan and Madam Hansa request my presence at the first gate. Ilo will advise you now."

"Advise me? Wait, what?"

"Prince Siddharth," the captain said, "did I misunderstand the maharani's command? Did she not leave you here in charge?"

"Y-yes, she did."

A quick glance at Ilo made Sid think the defender had his doubts, but Captain Duvanya leaned in and said, "Signs are in our favor, but the southerners have not yet stood down." He waved toward the crack. "You and these defenders stand between the palace and the fort. The risk is not large, but this is a great responsibility—and yours by birthright. Until word comes from the Seven, you must hold this gate."

Doing his best to appear up to the task, Sid nodded.

The winch and gears groaned as the portcullis rose into the gate tower's bulkhead. Sid followed Ilo, Captain Duvanya, and a small cadre of night guards to the stairwell door.

The night captain saluted him. "For the strength of the realm!"

"For the strength of the realm," Sid repeated, glad that Ilo did not leave with the others.

Moments later the company below marched across the span and entered the fort. As the portcullis was lowered back in place and the gate closed, Sid and Ilo returned to the side of the terrace overlooking the palace grounds. He was wondering how long the parley would take, and what, exactly, a prince-who-was-really-a-spare should be doing in the meantime, when cries arose from the stable yard.

THE STONEBOUND HEIR | 475

Grabbing the edge of the parapet, Sid leaned out, trying to see. Half-way up the bluff more figures had emerged from the mouth. Southerners. But something else moved in the dark behind them. There was a fraught silence among those on the terrace as they squinted at the cavern.

Then Sid saw it—a huge reptilian creature lumbered out onto the path.

"A goyra?" Ilo said.

It couldn't be. Goyras were monsters from the desolate lands of the Kalamaidan in the far south. Sid gasped as the beast stretched out its full length. Fighters rode on its back and more fighters swarmed around the creature as they descended on the stable yard.

"We must help them!" Sid shouted, looking around and wishing that someone else would suggest something sensible.

"The rani gave her orders, and the captain gave his," Ilo argued. "We are charged with defense of this gate."

The goyra clamored down the bluff face headfirst then leapt upon the roof of the stables.

Raking his hand through his hair, Sid heard Captain Duvanya say, *Hold this gate.* Master Avani said, *What will you do?* The rani said, *You are my heir.* And all their voices became one voice—his. *The only way forward is forward.*

"If we don't do something to stop them now, this gate won't matter!"

Ilo rubbed his jaw, "Your command is to join the battle, Prince Siddharth?"

"Yes, my command." It felt good to say.

Ilo nodded, and they approached several day guards gathered at a corner of the terrace. Injecting himself into the center of the group, Sid found that the defenders' attention was fixed on the palace's front grounds. He pushed up to the edge next to Parth.

"What is it?" Sid asked, unable to imagine what could possibly demand his attention more than a huge goyra and fighters flooding the stable yard.

"See for yourself, Prince," Parth answered.

The front grounds were empty, but a few figures crowded one of the new tower's balconies. Sid recognized a slender woman in a pale gown—Mafala. Next to her, seemingly propped up by two southern matrons, Prince Hassan. The Hudulfah princess raised her fist to the sky. To Sid's astonishment, Parth and the day guards around him did the same.

"We must go…" Sid said hoarsely as he stepped back, but his voice died when he heard the zing of blades being drawn. Before he could move, a day guard reached around Ilo and pulled his chin up with one hand while cutting his throat with the other. The Hansa soldier's eyes widened, a crimson line appeared, then the blood poured forth and he fell, clutching at his neck.

Sid stumbled to him, fighting the lightheadedness that threatened to tip him over. He tried to stop the flow of blood with his hands, but worse than the sight of the blood, much worse, was the wild terror in Ilo's eyes until the light left them.

Cold with shock, Sid trembled. Though he knew his actions had been useless, he was confused as to why no one else had helped. A handful of guards and archers had drawn on those surrounding him. For a moment everyone seemed to be holding their breath, but that ended when one of the day guards with Parth threw his short blade, and it sank into the chest of one of the other guards. The traitors quickly advanced on the rest and subdued them.

Parth ordered a guard to bind him.

"The days of your mother's house are over," the scribe said. "If you're wise, you'll cooperate and serve your uncle—if he allows it."

Sid closed his eyes, trying not to faint, but nothing was as clear in his mind as the dark blood that dripped from Ilo's neck. *This is failure. Real failure. The faithful die, and they will make me a game piece. This cannot be how my story's written in the Book of Duran.*

Hands shoved him into the stairwell and down to the base of the tower.

CHAPTER 41

Someone called out to her. *A boy in a blue suit? Sid?*

Lingli woke disoriented and anxious, feeling wood above her head. For an instant the thought that she had been returned to Red's trunk terrified her, but then she felt the stone floor below and realized she was under a table. Throwing off the blanket wrapped around her, she crawled out and picked up a lit lantern left on the floor nearby. She was still in the library.

A dull thud from the door made Lingli hold her breath. When no one opened it, she cautiously went to listen, but the small noises coming from the outside stopped. After a long moment she quietly tried to open it but found it locked.

Alone once more. Locked in and locked out.

Her wounded finger had been rebandaged, but her feet were still bare—and cold! Rubbing her head to calm an ache, Lingli grimaced when she touched the vein. It felt enlarged. Was this the cause of her ill feeling, or was it the curse that had followed her throughout her whole life? More likely the potion Madam had given her should be blamed.

And they ask me to trust them!

The dolls sat in a row on Master Avani's table. Lingli sat in the old noble's chair and rested her chin on the table to examine them, her mind still circling around what Master Avani and Madam had told her.

If it's not true, why would they tell such an elaborate story? How could anyone know? Except Red, maybe. Then she remembered that Red would never be able to tell her either. *But if it is true, it changes everything.* Their story bound Sid and her together as she had always wished, but not like this.

She reached out and pulled the little blue-coated effigy forward from the line. *Somehow Sid was right. He had the courage to go and find his path.*

She slid the little white effigy next to the blue one, then moved it ahead and tried to imagine herself as heir to the realm. The events and crowds. The arranging and plotting and presiding. Impossible. She felt ill just thinking of it. To act as heir would suit her no more than it would suit the rani.

The rani. To address her in any other way was not something Lingli was prepared to do.

The anger that had surged through her in the rani's secret room had subsided, but it wasn't gone. She reached down into the hem of her cloak and felt the dart she had kept. No matter if the rani struck her down or had her jailed, Lingli promised herself that she would demand answers about Red's murder.

Putting the dolls back into her pocket, Lingli tried to push the pending clash with Her Majesty to the back of her mind. There were more urgent problems to address.

Was my message heeded? Is Sid safe?

She wished the library had even one small window where she could see what was happening, but it did not. She was confined to riffling through materials on the old master's table, looking for clues. There were notes in Master Avani's hand that referenced a flood recorded by the House of Satya in the eighteenth cycle. There was a collection of parchments detailing the weather in the last four series of bright cycles, and a stack of reports from the districts that described the shakings, but nothing that told her whether anyone had acted on her warning.

Suddenly Lingli felt the vein in her temple begin to throb painfully. With pressure also building in her chest, she grabbed the table edge and sank to the floor, panicked at the thought of another shaking. The pressure was so great Lingli thought her ears might bleed. Ripples of white light blinded her once again, then a tremendous boom shook the tower.

The next thing she knew, Madam Sayed was kneeling next to her, shaking her and calling her name.

"Thank the First Mother you're awake," Madam said.

The tension in Lingli's chest eased and her sight sharpened. A coat, a waterskin, and her boots sat on the floor next to her.

"I am sorry we had to leave you here, but everything is in such a tumult."

Lingli had never seen Madam so disheveled. The dance teacher's eyes were red-rimmed, and she repeatedly tucked loose strands of hair behind her ears after she helped Lingli to her feet.

"What happened? Have the southerners attacked?"

"The House of Tilan has a powerful gift that can break stone. They used it to protect us, and our maharani has put Hassan's cabal in some disarray, but the threat persists. Master Avani and I believe it prudent to move the descendants to safekeeping."

"Where is Sid?"

Madam shook her head. "I haven't seen him since last night, but stars protect him, he must be with the rani." Handing her the waterskin, Madam said, "Can you walk? We need to go."

"You gave me a potion," Lingli said flatly, remembering the trickery that had landed her in the library.

"Yes, we did. You wanted the truth, and we delivered it as best we could."

"And you locked me in here."

The library door cracked open. Five children, two wearing vests that Lingli had mended, peered in at her from the landing.

"Meeting the maharani yesterday would not have served you well," Madam said. "Now, please put on your boots. Retrieving them was not easy."

"I am not a thief, nor a murderer, but I am cursed," Lingli said, her voice husky. "I want to know why."

"Your inheritance is…complicated. I do not have to explain to you that gaining your mother's acceptance will not be easy. These children"— she waved at those on the landing—"may be able to go home in short order, but I hope you understand that you will not."

"So it's exile?" It was almost amusing that she and Red shared a similar path.

"Removing you from the palace, for a time, will allow us to encourage other nobility to acknowledge your identity and provide you some protection."

"What of Sid? If I am recognized as heir, what will happen to him?"

"He would still be prince, still allowed the privileges of nobility, but as a spare like his younger brother."

To be a spare, after all this…. He will never speak to me again.

"No one would wish me to be heir."

"We select our friends, not our descendants," Madam answered with an exasperated sigh. "If I had first met you in the marketplace, I would not have chosen you to be my seamstress, but I would have been wrong. I might have offended every ancestor we share if your grandmother's talents hadn't been so obvious."

"What do you mean?"

"Rani Shikra was the finest artist with a needle I have ever known. I noticed your stitches on the first dancer's vest you completed—small and even, polished work on inner seams—and I began to wonder if she had sent you to me, but I had not imagined you were her descendant. We are lucky that Jalil's sight is better than mine. He recognized you first."

Such a lucky descendant, Lingli thought indignantly. She was tempted to remind Madam that her so-called grandmother's first instinct had been to kill her in the womb.

"I will see the rani."

"By the moons and stars, child! We cannot allow you to throw away your future, and ours. Put on your boots!"

Lingli did not understand. She did not care. She barely heard what Madam was saying. Making an effort to keep the turmoil out of her expression, Lingli pulled on her boots—regretting that her rabbit knife was still missing—and followed Madam out.

The children were quiet, their eyes large, but it wasn't her that they feared, or at least no more than they seemed to fear everything. Acting with her usual purposeful manner, Madam herded the children to the head of the stairs, but Lingli noted the tension in the dance teacher's neck and how she repeatedly counted them.

"Can we go home now?" one of the smallest ones asked.

Forcing a smile, Madam said, "As soon as this trouble is over, I will gladly deliver you to your homes."

And I will have the pleasure of running for my life to try to find one.

On the second floor, the door to Ameer Ali's quarters had been hacked to splinters and furniture had been thrown onto the landing. Cries carried up from the gallery and the floor below, and the only guard remaining was a Dyuvasan outside the envoy's quarters. Looking down his nose at the children, he read the note Madam carried bearing Master Avani's seal and reluctantly let them enter.

Inside the quarters Envoy Kanaka stood in the middle of his outer room, hurriedly filling a trunk with the help of a servant and seemingly deaf to the roar coming from beyond the balcony. He pressed his hands to his head as they entered.

"Oh, no. No, Madam, no," he said, waving at Lingli and the children. "I cannot…"

"I'm not asking you to take all these children," Madam said. "I will manage them. Our request is only for Miss Tabaan."

What is this? Lingli frowned at Madam.

"You surely know that I hold Master Avani in the highest esteem," the envoy said, wringing his hands, "but must tell you that I have not committed to his request. There is no time—"

Suddenly the noise from the yard grew even louder, and the envoy's servant herded the children to the divans.

"What has happened?" Madam asked.

"I am afraid the southerners were not daunted by Saatkulom's opening gambit, and you haven't seen what they brought with them." He led Madam and Lingli to the balcony.

A shocking number of southerners steadily emerged from the cavern opening in the bluff behind the palace, flooding the stable yard. Palace defenders met them in a deafening clash, and Lingli nearly choked on the thought that Sid was likely out there, but even this violence had not prepared Lingli for the monster in the yard.

A huge reptilian beast stood on its hind legs and leaned over the roof of the mining hall with five fighters holding tight to chains that were somehow pegged to its back. Nearly as long as three teams and wagons from its nose to the tip of its tail, the beast had a thick, slate gray hide with a pale belly and spots of white and yellow on its neck and chest. A forked tongue flickered from its hideous mouth, and its unblinking eyes seemed to look everywhere at once.

This was a goyra, Lingli knew, having read accounts of them in the Book of Duran, but who had ever seen such a creature in these cycles? Her heart pounded. Her feet told her to run, but she couldn't look away.

From a corner of the mining hall roof, three archers moved closer to the goyra, steadily drawing and releasing arrows aimed at its head, but most glanced off its skin. When one arrow pierced its nostril, the beast pointed its snout at the sky. Two arrows found the goyra's softer throat, but the advantage was lost when it lunged forward with otherworldly speed. Its jaws snapped shut on one of the archers.

Making a strangled cry, Madam attempted to pull Lingli back from the balcony's edge, but she would not let go. The remaining archers continued to shoot madly until southern fighters speared them from behind. As the envoy joined Madam to force her back inside, Lingli watched the goyra's neck convulse as it tried to swallow its prey.

Noise from the yard leaked all around the curtain that hung between the balcony and the envoy's outer room. She and Madam leaned against each other, keeping their faces turned away from the children so they would not see their fear. The envoy had already hurried to the door to consult his guard.

Madam said, hoarsely, "We must leave as soon as possible."

"Sid's out there—" Lingli moved toward the balcony again, but Madam grabbed her arm and did not let go.

"Prince Siddharth has every defender at his disposal, but this is your last chance," she whispered furiously. "Whatever happens, you cannot stay here!"

Lingli clamped her mouth shut. She could not stay, and Sid would not leave, but what Madam didn't understand was that she had unfinished tasks. Whether or not she should believe Master Avani and Madam's story, Sid remained her brother in her heart, as he always had been, and she couldn't simply leave him in this fighting.

Ordering his servant to lock the trunks, Envoy Kanaka returned to them, his face flushed with worry. "As soon as the guards return," he said, "I will depart with my attendants. There are simply too many uncertainties for me to entertain this request any further."

Madam put her hand on Lingli's shoulder and told her, "Take off your hood."

Lingli pushed her hood back, pondering why Madam and Master Avani would imagine that Envoy Kanaka would help her, especially now, but her pale visage didn't seem to disturb him. It wasn't until he saw the side of her face where her vein's branches spread that he put a hand over his mouth.

"There is no uncertainty, sir," Madam insisted. "Her ancestry is plain. Your own test has revealed it."

Lingli looked sharply at Madam. *Test?*

"You do not understand," Envoy Kanaka said, distraught. "I am not a bone mage. I know only basic blood and bone signs. She would have to submit to the seers for a true reading."

"Then you must take her to them," Madam said. "How can you leave one of your own behind in these circumstances?" She waved toward the balcony.

"Do you mean that I have…relatives in the east?" Lingli asked. She felt lightheaded. For cycles she had expected nothing, asked nothing, and now things were happening too quickly.

The envoy took a deep breath. "It is possible. All I can tell you is that you have *some* eastern ancestry."

This news felt like a golden thread dangled before her, too delicate to offer her any assurances, but a way, perhaps, for her to escape the rani's persecution. She shook her head. First she had to find Sid—and the rani.

Madam was still arguing with Envoy Kanaka, and Lingli looked from one to the other as if watching a duel.

"If she does not accompany you, how will you explain a child of eastern descent being imprisoned in Saatkulom?"

"See reason, Madam! How would I inform my raja that I myself was imprisoned for kidnapping or extricating a murderer from Saatkulom?"

"I am not a murderer," Lingli said.

The envoy frowned. "Miss Tabaan, the most serious accusations have been leveled against you. Despite the good word of your champions, I know nothing about you, and there is no time to verify anything."

Madam Sayed pinched her brows together and said, "Ask her about the ornament you sent to Garzekhara."

The envoy took Madam aside. Lingli could hear them whisper-arguing until they returned and the envoy asked her, "Have you ever possessed a fine ornament?"

When Lingli nodded, he said, "Describe it."

"It was a brooch. Made of bone." She wondered why her brooch, of all things under the stars, mattered to the envoy. Madam stood between her and the balcony, arms crossed and biting her lower lip.

The envoy showed no reaction. "A plain bone?"

"No, a hawk in flight was painted upon it. The work was very fine. You could count the hawk's feathers, and its talons were outstretched as if it was about to snatch its prey."

Before the envoy could ask another question the door to the quarters was thrown open and the guard said urgently, "They've taken the yard. We must leave now, sir."

CHAPTER 42

S id's captors drove their hostages through the fighting like goats going to slaughter. Somewhere along the way to the stable yard, the traitors delivered them into the hands of southern fighters, but Sid could think of little else than the blood coursing from Ilo's neck and the bile in his throat. *Do not faint!* It was only when the fighters hauled them onto the platform behind the feasting hall and made them face the yard that he understood the breadth of the calamity surrounding him. There was so much blood everywhere that Sid couldn't focus on any of it, and his aversion shifted into a general sick feeling deep in his gut.

Southerners amassed at the stables. A long phalanx of defenders stretched from there to the training yard gate, holding the ground behind them for their rani and their southern hostages. He could see Greta snatching up fighters in both fists, breaking their necks, and throwing them back on the others, and he assumed his mother was nearby, but it was impossible to see her in the swift-moving carnage.

The embattled yard was sufficient to force him from his morass of self-incrimination, but the dark, hulking lizard being brought around from the mining hall inspired a terror that completely cleared Sid's head. Weirdly indifferent to the savagery around it, the goyra seemed as if it had come from the otherworld. Its stocky legs gave it a shifting gait that seemed slow until it wasn't, and on its back, Idrisi riders held on to chains attached to the creature's hide. How useful the chains were was in some doubt, for it also took a number of fighters on the ground to prod the goyra toward the phalanx.

Two riders shielded the others from the rain of arrows, but the occasional arrow that pierced the beast seemed to have no affect. Crushing friends as well as foes who failed to move from its path, the beast moved haltingly across the yard. When part of a leg fell from the goyra's jaws, Sid wanted to vomit.

The fighting grew more frantic, and Sid silently begged his ancestors to protect the defenders who deftly cut down southerners throwing themselves at the line. *There are too many of them.*

When shouting erupted behind him, Sid turned to see Korvar and Shankar stumble out of the kitchens' back entrance. The cook kept repeating that he was not a defender, as if the southerner shoving him understood or cared, and Shankar shook with fright. The southerners seemed to be weighing the father and son's worth as hostages, and Sid feared the calculation would find them wanting.

His hands were bound, and the blades he wore, but could not reach, were meant to be a child's ornaments.

As the fighters pushed the cook and his son to the wall, blades drawn, Korvar caught his eye, and Sid shrank from his pleading expression that so closely matched Ilo's dying gaze. Red's words about being useful echoed in Sid's head. *How likely is it for them to kill me after taking the trouble to bring me here? As far as they know, I am the prince. If today is all the time I have, I should enjoy that joke now.*

Headbutting the bound night guard standing next to him, Sid started a ripple of stumbling among the hostages, and he ground the heel of his jutti into the foot of the nearest southerner, then he pushed up to the edge of the platform.

Balancing above the yard's chaos, Sid felt the blood and spittle spray from blows struck in front of him. He could hardly stand to look at the defenders, whose faces were lit with the reckless ferocity of those losing their home, and he recalled the day Korvar had pushed him into the yard from the very same spot. It was the day he had found Li. He jumped.

His knees took the landing hard, but he managed not to fall. Dodging the hacking, swinging, and stabbing around him, Sid burst forward. There was nowhere to go, of course, and no way he would make it to his mother and the other nobles. His only goal was to distract Korvar and Shankar's killers and give them as long a chase as he could while avoiding the spears and blades around him.

Less than halfway across the yard the fighters had him again. He dove forward and tasted the slicked earth before they jerked him back up to his feet. They cursed him, and one of them punched him in the side of the head. Sid looked back. The other hostages were still held tight, but Korvar and Shankar were gone from the platform, and he simply had to hope they were in a better situation.

As the fighters began to drag him back through the yard, Sid made every step they took as difficult as he could. *Like a child having a tantrum*, he thought, but at least he had done something, and anything was better than being useless. He imagined he shared this notion with the small bunches of defenders that were slowly being overwhelmed. Soon there would be no one left to fight for Chandrabhavan but those in the phalanx protecting the rani.

Suddenly, his captors stopped, and Sid thought they had done so to avoid the swinging end of the goyra's long tail. Then he heard the southerners raise a chant.

"Aza Ali! Aza Ali!"

High above the yard, a team and wagon rolled down the summit path. Sid recognized the wanderer driving at once, but what made his heart burn was the figure standing behind the bench under a sand cat banner and wearing a brilliant crimson coat—one arm raised as if he were surveying his own grounds and blessing his own fighters.

An otherworldly shriek shredded the air around them. The goyra's riders and the fighters on the ground had forced it against the front line and the defenders fell upon it. Blood flowed from countless wounds as the creature threw its head and made jerking steps. With numerous spears in its sides and neck, the goyra made one more ear-piercing cry, then it collapsed, its riders jumping free as it fell. The fighting around the beast didn't slow, but Sid could see that the ends of the phalanx had shrunk. Fighters were beginning to encircle Saatkulom's forces.

Ameer Ali's wagon had rolled to a stop near the stable gate. As the ameer got down, he was mobbed by a group of Hudulfah fighters bearing a body in a blood-stained white toga. Even from a distance, Sid could tell it was Aza Mussan that they laid in the back of the wagon.

After bowing to Aza Mussan's body, Ali made his way toward the place near where Sid had last seen his mother that morning and where he guessed she remained, judging by Greta's proximity. The flag for parley, a white flag with a black ring, went up among Ali's company and was matched by a second one hoisted among the defenders. Gradually all stood down and took defensive positions, and Sid swallowed hard. Bodies from both sides littered the yard, but there was no doubt which side had the advantage.

A brilliant white light shone behind the defenders' line and the phalanx pushed out around it, creating a cascade of curses and feints that threatened the parley before it had begun. Sid had never seen anything like the beams that glowed in a grid pattern, nor had anyone else, it seemed, for the southerners stayed back and even the defenders made space around it.

His captors rushed him forward to where Ameer Ali stood with standard bearers from all four southern houses. The ameer of Kirdun smiled at Sid as warmly as he ever had.

"Thank you for helping us secure these grounds."

Before this day, before he found himself in a yard stinking of death, fighting had been but a fine and noble expression of valor in Sid's thinking. Actually harming someone himself hadn't been reckoned, but in that moment, he wished nothing so much as he wished to murder Ameer Ali.

Between the fighters and defenders, a path opened with Ali and himself on one end and Greta standing before the brilliant light on the other. Hearing that unnatural light crackle as it pulsed like a heartbeat, the fighters on the edge of the path made protective signs. Bars of light crisscrossed one another to form a dome that enclosed his mother, Akela and two ameers kneeling in the dirt with their arms tied. At the center Madam Satya stood with eyes closed and arms upraised, chanting under her breath. The light seemed to stream from her fingertips.

A gift of the House of Satya?

Two of Ameer Ali's fighters pushed Sid down the path toward Greta and the dome. They stopped when they were almost within arm's length of the giantess.

The battle had colored the rani's gown dark with dirt and blood, but Sid was relieved to see that she appeared unharmed as she paced around her captives, talwar drawn. She nodded to him, and Sid nodded back then looked at the ground.

I had one task, and look at me now.

From behind him, Ameer Ali said loudly, "Release our nobles and honor the parley, Maharani."

"You do not know 'honor,' but if we are taking steps in this dance," the rani said, pointing her chin to the feasting hall, "release the hostages and let them and these defenders enter the fort unmolested, then I will give you the ameer of your choice."

Sid winced, but he understood. She would be more vulnerable, as would he, but if she didn't save her remaining defenders, they would be cut down the instant the parley ended. *All for the strength of the realm.*

Ameer Khush began to protest her terms, and the rani kicked him in the back. A smattering of spears flew toward the dome of light, but they were turned as if the light was as solid as stone. Ali bellowed an order and the southerners quieted.

"A bold demand," Ameer Ali said, "You understand that both of these nobles must be freed. Promise me that."

"If my demands are met, they will be."

The two ameers at the rani's feet wore fearless expressions that Sid wished he could imitate, but he wondered if anyone else had noticed that Madam Satya's chin had dropped to her chest, and her arms trembled.

At Ali's word, the Kirdun fighters formed a cordon from the phalanx to the training yard gate while two of them ran to the feasting hall. The hostages who had accompanied Sid were cut free and pushed to the gate where they waited, still surrounded by Kirdun fighters.

The remaining defenders guarding the rani and Madam Satya's dome of light shifted and looked around them uncertainly.

"Hear my word," the rani shouted. "Your honor is not sullied, and this wicked day is not ended. I will see you released into the custody of the Seven in the fort. Go now, for the strength of the realm."

With their hands close to their weapons, the battered and humiliated defenders walked the gauntlet. When they were gone and Ali's messenger reported they had entered the fort, Ali nodded and the southerners closed the gap, surrounding them completely.

"Release Ameer Khush," Ali said.

The rani cut Khush's bindings and pushed him close to the pulsing bars of light while Akela snarled at Ameer Temer. After a quick glance at Madam Satya, the rani waited until the light dimmed, then pushed Khush through. The big Ascaryan shuddered and gasped for breath, leaning heavily on an Afreh fighter who led him to Ali.

"Now, free my son," the rani said.

Was it his imagination, Sid wondered, or was the length of time each pulse of light dimmed increasing? Sweat dripped from Madam Satya's face.

"It is your turn to go first," Ali said.

The rani shook her head, but Sid could see the tendons in Madam Satya's neck were taut, and he feared Ali saw it, too.

Suddenly a knife was launched from the crowd behind Sid as the light dimmed. Unlike the earlier spears, it passed the bars and struck Madam Satya full in the thigh. The light pulsed rapidly then disappeared altogether as the noble grabbed her leg and fell with a guttural cry. Sid looked over his shoulder and saw Afreh fighters praising the culprit. By the time he looked ahead again, the rani held the point of her talwar to the ameer of Idris's neck. The fighter holding him put a blade to his neck at the same time.

"Give me my son."

"I will guarantee the prince's safety while he's in my company," Ali said evenly, "but you must release Ameer Temer."

Sid felt the blade point turn and break the skin. *It's just a prick, just a prick*, he told himself, but he couldn't stop seeing the river of blood that had left Ilo. Sick with fear of what he thought was about to happen, he tightened the muscles in his gut and bowels.

Ali commanded the fighter to release him, and the blade slid away from his neck.

"By my word, Valena. He is yours."

As Ali stepped forward, holding Sid by the arm, his mother jerked Ameer Temer to his feet. Another step forward, and Greta shifted aside to allow him and Ali to pass. The rani pushed the ameer forward, and he staggered by to be greeted by the fighters.

When they stood before the rani, Madam Satya pulled the Afreh blade from her leg and pressed the wound. She looked as though she had aged a score of years but held her pata in her free hand.

His mother asked him, "Are you whole?"

He nodded.

Ali spoke softly. "I come to you as an emissary only, but if my youth perceive I am in danger, they will act. Give me your blades."

"We will not." The rani's eyes glittered with outrage.

"Do we need to count the bodies, Valena? The longer we stand here, the more likely Hassan will rejoin us, and your noble sister and your son will pay the price," Ali said. "To wait it out will not upset the day's course, but it would be such a loss for both your houses."

The palace is lost.

The muscle ticking in his mother's cheek told Sid that she knew this, too.

"What honor could be found in killing one more elder? I will give you my blade if you will see that Parama is escorted to safety."

Madam Satya began to protest, but the rani ignored her and sheathed her talwar.

"I will need you, sister," the rani told Madam Satya. "More later than now."

Ali spoke quickly to the other ameers. To Sid's eyes it seemed their concession was grudging, but it came, and fighters carrying a litter came to the fore.

Madam Satya dropped her pata, and Valena Sandhyatara slowly laid her talwar on the ground.

Ameer Khush bellowed a cheer that the fighters began to repeat like a taunt.

In this din, the rani said mockingly to Ali, "Ever so helpful in our times of need. Ready on every occasion to remark about your friendship with my father and flatter me. Truly, you have played the longest game."

"My game has changed so often, I hardly recognize it," Ali said, "and I have not earned your praises by myself. Our Idrisi cousins ultimately agreed to join us, and the goyra certainly helped after your attempt to close the passage, but the critical assistance came from your side."

Ignoring this remark, the rani helped Madam Satya onto the litter. At Ali's command, the fighters raised it up and carried her toward the old tower and the central palace.

The rani said, "I'm surprised that you joined in this, Ali. You know that you cannot hold the Rock, and do not quote me numbers. You cannot hold it because you cannot trust my consort or your cousins."

To Sid's surprise, the ameer nodded. "No glory without risk."

"Perhaps I could decrease your risk."

The ameer chuckled. "One moment, Valena! Hassan is being roused to witness our progress and learn that he is the new ameer of his house thanks to your quick blade. Indeed, he should reward you, but let us see."

Sid shivered at the mention of Hassan. Getting rid of an inconvenient nephew would be his uncle's first task, and he would do so even more easily than the rani had dispatched both his parents.

Seeming to share this concern, the rani said, "Then let us discuss a gentler topic—the safety of my sons. I must admit, abducting Aseem was a stroke of brilliance on your part. I need your word that he is safe."

Sid noticed that the ameer became still when she said his brother's name.

"Your baby is not with me."

"Do not pretend, Ali. You were the only one who was awake and free long enough to secure him." The rani, despite the anger that Sid knew brewed within her, spoke calmly, as though she and the ameer were on equal footing, as though she was not defeated. "Your part in this will not endear you to Hassan, but I have an idea."

Seeing that Ali was listening, she continued. "He will blame me for Aseem's disappearance, naturally. I will not disabuse him of this idea. In return, you will safeguard Siddharth."

Sid's head spun, and not because of the little blood trail on his neck. Would he ever have even half his mother's abilities to think quickly in such moments?

The ameer sighed and said, "I can keep Prince Siddharth on the summit for now, but I will not defy Hassan if he calls for him."

"No," Sid said to his mother, his mouth dry. "I will stay with you."

But the rani glared at him. "You will obey my word."

Ali called two fighters over to take the blades and accompany Sid to the wagon. "Be glad you have some value to me as well as in your father's and mother's houses," the ameer told him.

Sid squashed his fear down. His only value was tied to a title that wasn't truly his and made him more a target than a treasure.

A fighter was about to take him away when the rani called out, "Allow me a moment to speak to my son."

Ameer Ali told the fighter to let him go and went to speak to the other ameers.

When he drew near her, Sid said, "I'm sorry I didn't stop them.... Ilo fell."

"Do not apologize," his mother said. "I am the only one who bears fault." Squeezing his arm, she added, "Remember that Chandrabhavan is not the Rock. We will not despair."

Sid straightened like a soldier awaiting inspection and asked, "What should I do?"

"Ali will keep his word, for now," the rani said, "and I will pray for your protection until we meet again, but if the chance arises, escape. Go to the northern tower." She pressed her eyes closed for an instant.

"Amma, are you whole?"

"I am."

Quickly unbuckling the top of her mail vest, his mother drew out her moonstone pendant and placed the chain over Sid's head. Her smile was strained as she tucked the pendant inside the neck of his coat. "How can I ask you to face the day with courage, when I carry our house's gifts?"

"But you will need it," he whispered urgently.

She shook her head. "I must rely on my own courage for the remainder of the day." Smoothing his hair back from his face, she said, "Whether the ancestors favor us or not, I will bear the test and ask them to help you do so, too. Do not give in to fear, Siddharth, and do not give in to this." She patted his coat, her hand over the pendant. "There is only one honorable purpose for its use today. If all else fails and you must escape Hassan, at least one route is guaranteed. Do you understand?"

Three drops.

Ameer Ali approached them and said, "The prince must go now if we're to avoid your consort."

"You are a son of Duran," the rani told him as a fighter pulled him away. "All that we do is for the strength of the realm."

CHAPTER 43

Envoy Kanaka's questions for Lingli evaporated as soon as the guard made his announcement. When the envoy rushed to the door, Madam roused the children. Lingli went to the balcony.

The monster lay dead in the yard and fighting had paused, but there was little comfort in this because the only defenders she could see were passing down a cordon of southern fighters before they disappeared from her sight behind the feasting hall.

Finding Greta in the crowd was easy enough. Just behind the giantess, Lingli could see Akela pacing around the rani who helped someone off the ground. It was Madam Satya. Then fighters brought Sid, with his arms bound, to his mother.

Madam Sayed was at her elbow, her voice shrill. "Come. We must move."

Lingli held tight to the balcony wall despite Madam's grip on her arm. "I can't leave him."

"We cannot lose you, too."

Lingli hoped her tear-streaked cheeks were convincing. "I'm coming. Please, a moment."

"A short moment, child," Madam said before she retreated inside.

Squinting and shifting, trying to glimpse Sid through the fighters that encircled him and the others, Lingli saw that he was face-to-face with the rani. Not far away, Ameer Ali huddled with the ameers from Afreh and Idris, but there was no sign of the Hudulfah prince.

Then a fighter pulled Sid away from his mother and marched him to a nearby wagon. Immediately recognizing the driver and his son, who was leading the colt from the stables, Lingli felt a wave of shame for having ever trusted them.

Ameer Ali's fighters tossed Sid into the back, and the rani, Greta and Akela remained surrounded by fighters too numerous to count. Bearing

496 | L.A. BARNITZ

witness to Sid's abduction, Lingli ignored Envoy Kanaka's guard until he peeled her grip loose from the balcony wall.

"Listen to me!" Madam Sayed demanded, though Lingli's eyes remained locked on the wagon that Rahman drove toward the summit path. "The envoy has agreed. You are going to Dyuvasa with him."

She allowed herself to be herded from the envoy's quarters with the other children, but Madam's stream of instructions was no more than dull buzzing in her ears. On the landing, the envoy loaded his servant with all he could carry and issued orders to his guards. Cries and panicked shouts echoed through the old tower.

After tugging up Lingli's hood, Madam peered into her face and said, "Master Avani entrusted me with a letter regarding your history. It is vital we give it to the envoy to afford you some protection. Mind the children while I retrieve it. I'll meet you in the front grounds."

She nodded and Madam hurried down the stairs that led to the main floor. The envoy was still giving his men instructions.

Fleeing up the stairs, Lingli touched the third floor before the Dyuvasan guards realized she was gone. In the darkness behind the curtains at the back of the landing, she quickly reached the rockslide she had come to know so well. She paused to listen once she climbed the rubble. A distant voice called for a lantern.

Squirming under the lintel at the top of the slide, she rolled two large stones into the middle of the opening and swept in as much gravel as she could. Then she turned to the dark and began her trek up the passage.

You had to get caught, didn't you? she told Sid. *I don't even know if they're taking you to the summit. What if they hide you somewhere else?* She pressed a hand to the vein in her temple. *You better hope I've guessed right.*

When she reached the small door where the side passage joined the main one, Lingli stopped. She heard nothing. She saw nothing. But she was certain there was someone in the main passage. It wouldn't be the Dyuvasan guards who had let her slip away from Envoy Kanaka's and Madam's plans, but it could be southerners or any number of Saatkulom subjects who wished her ill. She reached for her rabbit knife in her boot before she remembered it was gone.

A voice called out, "Announce yourself. Friend or foe of Saatkulom?"

Master Avani. Relief flooded her. "Sir, it is me. Lingli Tabaan."

She heard him blow his breath out.

A lantern was uncovered, illuminating the old noble who was dressed like a southerner. Several defenders and the rani's ratha driver stood with him, all filthy and worn and carrying open blades.

Master Avani put his talwar back into its scabbard and said, "How are you here?"

"Sid was captured in the stable yard. I think they're taking him to the summit."

"I know about Siddharth," Master Avani said with some frustration, "but I had hoped, in vain it seems, that *you* would already be beyond reach of this incursion. Didn't you meet Madam Sayed and Envoy Kanaka?"

"I met them. The envoy told me a fanciful tale about relatives in the east."

Master Avani tugged at his beard and signaled the defenders to go ahead. "Come," he told her. "We will free Sid, ancestors willing, then we will get both of you and the other descendants to safety."

Though grateful for the old noble's company, Lingli hadn't forgotten who had kept the rani's secrets for so long and who probably knew more about her heritage than he had divulged. As they continued up the passage, she said pointedly, "The envoy said he couldn't risk taking me east, even though you had requested that of him."

"He denied you?"

"At first. How would it look for him to be abetting a murderer? But Madam argued that I had passed a test of some kind—a test that showed I have some eastern ancestry—and he questioned me about an ornament. I thought that was strange because the only ornament ever given to me was stolen soon after I arrived on the Rock."

Master Avani nodded and kept walking. "Your brooch. With the hawk painted on it."

"Did you take it?" she asked, trying hard to keep the anger out of her voice. "Or was it Madam?"

"It was Greta. She brought it to me."

"Why?"

"Because she knew who you were before we did. Because it became very clear, very quickly, that you were going to need protection."

"Oh, yes," she said. "That's gone very well."

"I understand, child. Everything we've told you must be difficult to believe or understand, let alone accept."

It was too late. She had lost control of both anger and a sorrow that she had no name for.

"Could *you* accept, sir, that your mother wanted you dead before you were even born?" Her voice rose. "Could you accept that her intention has not changed even seventeen cycles later?"

Two of the defenders ahead stopped and looked behind them. Master Avani told them to keep walking.

"I hear you, and your anger is righteous," he said in a low voice. "I only ask you to not let it make you reckless. I can disavow my sister no more than you can disavow your brother, and the faithful defenders need to know you are no threat to the realm, despite what they have been told."

"Does Sid know…about me?" Lingli asked, wiping furiously at her eyes.

"I gave him a list with the names of all the noble children. Your name was there, but I had no opportunity to explain. He may find it hard to believe, but in time he will accept the truth even though it checks his ambition."

"You don't understand," Lingli said, exasperated. "I don't want him to accept anything. To serve her and be her heir is all he has ever dreamed of. Even if it is truly my birthright, even if the rani did not strike me down the instant I stood before her, I would not take Sid's place."

"None of us know the will of the ancestors. We can only do our best to meet their example." Master Avani gestured toward the gate ahead where the others waited. "Go ahead and open it. You know the sequence."

When they emerged from the passage, the defenders led them through the ruins of the courtyard Lingli had seen when Greta freed her. There was no sign of Sid or southerners, but a single, gaunt woman sat at a table there. Master Avani bid the defenders to lower their blades and keep watch at the courtyard's broken gates.

Despite her apparent poverty, the woman had the bearing of a noble and rose gracefully as they approached.

"Pardon the intrusion, Oracle," Master Avani said. "A daughter of Duran accompanies me."

"Welcome," the oracle said without surprise.

When the woman turned her milky eyes on her, Lingli sucked in her breath and put a hand to her temple though she knew it was unnecessary. The oracle gestured to them to sit.

Seeing Lingli's hesitation, the old noble told her, "The oracle is a trusted ally. We are here to seek her guidance."

Master Avani sat and held his arms across the table, palms up. Lingli perched on the edge of her seat, uneasy with this strange woman.

The oracle took Master Avani's hands in hers and said, "Your question, son of Avani?"

The old noble spoke hesitantly, as if he was about to be chided by an elder. "How should I serve the descendants of the realm on this fraught day?"

Sitting very straight with her fingertips lightly touching the old noble's hands, the oracle seemed to listen to some voice Lingli could not hear.

"The small moon is deceptive, and a long winter approaches. The cold must be borne. Gather what seeds you can and pass them to friends. You shall tend their departure and their return."

Master Avani sat back. To Lingli's eye, he seemed more troubled than before.

The oracle nodded as if she had heard his thoughts aloud. "The boy is not far. Send him to me."

"And his sister?" Master Avani asked.

"Let her remain here to meet him."

Master Avani thanked the oracle and escorted Lingli to the edge of the courtyard.

"You say you are here for Siddharth," he said. "He did not save you from the court's judgment or your exile or your mother's mistreatment, yet you risk everything for him. Why?"

"Because…he is my brother."

"You honor your brother despite his flaws, yes? You see that one day, if the ancestors allow, he could achieve great things. We see that in him and in you, too. Just as I have seen it in my noble sister."

Lingli looked away, glad she had not told him how little regard she had for the rani.

"Siddharth and the maharani are not your only family." The old noble took a deep breath and spoke slowly, looking apologetic. "We gave Envoy Kanaka the finger bone you lost. His reading confirmed that you have eastern ancestry. The brooch, however, was as important. We believe at least one of those relatives is noble. One could be Raja Tajazan. I wrote to the raja and told him we will respect his judgment on this matter, but whatever is determined, I have requested him to keep you safe. This is why I asked the envoy to take you to Garzekhara."

"Oh." Lingli felt dizzy. She wished she could sit down and examine this news closely and from all sides, but she saw the defenders growing restless by the gate. *And Sid is waiting.*

Master Avani looked over the plateau as he spoke. "When Siddharth joins you go to the wheel room and wait for me inside my house's gate. You will know it by the owls. The path there will provide a far safer route to the northern tower. I will meet you at day's end or not at all. If you do not see me—"

"You will meet us," Lingli said. The old noble's tone reminded her of Red's last words, and the fears she thought she had left behind were resurrected.

"Yes, but if I cannot, you will bear right at the first fork and left from then on."

The old noble began to walk away, then came back to her. "Forgive me for leaving you with news that changes nothing and everything. Trust the oracle."

She nodded and he quickly squeezed her arm, as if he would impart some courage, then he led the defenders out of the courtyard and into the summit's dry forest.

Lingli looked over the summit and tried to make sense of what the old noble had said.

A family? A father?

She had made a small, somewhat tidy life once, when she had no one. Now, the idea that there were some who shared her blood threatened to completely unbalance her. Sid was her only constant.

When I see you I will tell you what I must, and you will believe it or not, but you will go on being prince, and I will…go on.

Taking a deep breath, she returned to the oracle.

The blind woman was elbow-deep inside a heavy-looking bag on the table. She pulled out what looked like a decrepit jewelry box, then closed the bag and passed the strap over her head and shoulder.

Putting the box into Lingli's hands, the oracle said, "Follow my footsteps. Pour the contents onto the ground in an unbroken line when I tell you to begin."

Lingli followed her along the broken wall to the point where it joined the bluff. When the blind woman began to retrace her steps, Lingli opened the box and poured out not jewels but a thin line of gritty powder until the oracle passed the gateway and stopped on the other side where the courtyard wall remained whole.

They returned to the gateway where the oracle took a dead torch out of her bag and lit it using some small metal object that behaved like a flint and steel. She handed the torch to Lingli, and they waited inside the broken gate. Searching the plateau until her eyes watered, Lingli silently called Sid. At last, the sounds of raised voices and the clang of metal reached them, and there was Sid, running among the chhatris.

The oracle moved gracefully and calmly, this time removing a knobby object the size of a jackfruit from her bag. Slipping two fingers through the ring on top, she said, "Tell me when the prince is within six wagon lengths of the gate. As soon as he is behind us, light the powder."

CHAPTER 44

When the southern fighters unceremoniously tossed Sid into the back of the wanderers' wagon he couldn't catch himself with his bound hands, and his head slammed against the bed, making him cry out in the most unprincelike way. The southerners surrounding him laughed, as did Parth and a pair of day guards who jumped on the back. Sid shifted against one side and focused on his knees, and breathing.

The driver did his best to maneuver the team around the fallen bodies in the yard, and soon they climbed the summit path. Sid's gaze never left the rani where she stood, surrounded and growing ever smaller. Whatever she had done or said, or not done and not said, mattered little. Sid recognized that the same recklessness and love of the gamble ran within them both.

What a destiny. It was embarrassing to think how certain he had been when he knew absolutely nothing about the world. *And what I know now could be counted on my toes.*

The moonstone pendant, filled with his mother's most treasured and most dangerous gift, tapped his chest each time they bounced over a rock, whispering how it could give him the strength and courage he badly needed. *It's too powerful. But if I just tasted the rim...* Shaking his head, he thought, *No. Not unless I need three drops.* He hoped he wouldn't.

If he leaned over the edge of the wagon, Sid could still see the figures in the yard below, but he could no longer tell who was who. Their stories became part of the tapestry of the greater vista below—a palace beset, a fort spawning numerous fires under a blanket of smoke, and the fields beyond crawling with Ascaryans seeking their fates and fortunes. Wishing he knew how the defense of the fort was going, Sid asked the ancestors, and Afsana, to protect the rani and all the loyal defenders. *And Li, wherever she might be.*

At the last and steepest part of the path, the wanderer stopped the team, and everyone, including Sid, got out of the wagon as they pulled the horses and the wagon over the final lip of rock. Inside a cluster of southern fighters, Parth marched Sid to the campsite where he had served the rani's guests moons before. The fighters' uncomfortably direct and close appraisal of his coat and the jeweled belt and blades made it clear that whatever protection his status as a valuable hostage had afforded him, it was unlikely to last for long.

"Not such a wonderful day to be prince, is it, Prince?" Parth said.

You're a son of Duran, his mother said. Sid squared his shoulders.

Vidkun sat on the edge of a cart in the campsite, grimacing as a southerner bandaged his arm. "Well, stars, look at what you caught," he said to Parth. "I take back most of the things I've ever said about the House of Avani."

"Ameer Ali wants him kept safe," Parth said.

"Of course." As he put his mail back on, Vidkun asked, "Did you see Hassan?"

"They say he plans to sleep through all this."

"Don't you wish. By the way, I haven't seen Gaddar since yesterday. Did your hero run away?"

Sid's ears pricked up, but the Avani scribe who was never at a loss for words said nothing.

"Ali paid him, you know. I hope he didn't make off with the coin he promised you," Vidkun said, "but never mind that. I need you to watch these jackals."

Sid began to sniff at a wedge between Vidkun and Parth. *So Ali is the buyer.*

Vidkun waved to the Hudulfah fighters as he said this, and Sid thought resentment simmered in their faces, but the wolfmaster was oblivious and ordered them and Parth to take the wanderers' team and wagon into the forest.

"What about him?" Parth asked, pointing his chin at Sid.

"Oh, I'll keep him whole alright—like a new bride—awaiting his uncle's pleasure! Load all the weapons that remain and wait for my word."

If Vidkun's in charge of this depot, he must be Hassan's man, and Parth serves Gaddar. And Gaddar serves Ali? Must be.

The wolfmaster led Sid to a nearby cluster of saplings.

Seeking any possible argument for his survival, Sid steadied his voice and said, "You know Hassan looks weak. Sleeping in his sister's quarters with the women and children while the battle rages, and his son's been kidnapped. You think the other houses, and his fighters, haven't noticed?"

Vidkun looped a rope around Sid's waist and tied him tight to a small tree. "And what? Do you think they're going to name *you* ameer?"

"I am also the rightful heir to the House of Hudulfah, you know."

Vidkun snorted.

"I am only saying Ali is leading them down there. I'd be careful in choosing who to swear fealty to."

"Like you know anything about it. I'll not serve these sand eaters for long, but I'll happily deliver you to Aza Hassan and be the most loyal of the loyal until I get my due."

"Will you be given a lordship, too?"

"What?"

"A lordship. That's what Parth said Ali has promised him."

Vidkun tested the knot, one brow cocked. "Don't waste your wits on me, Prince. You'll need them soon enough."

Sid's shrug made no impression on the wolfmaster as he returned to the campsite. *A poor ploy, but I've got to try something.*

From where he stood tied to the little tree, Sid could see beyond the chhatris to where, on one end, Trechur and Titok paced arcs under two tall stone columns. On the other end lay the head of the path to the palace. The few day guards and miners who hadn't left with Parth and the wanderers huddled among the remaining southerners. Sid reckoned the danger of their paltry number was becoming apparent to them, but they, like him, were trying not to show it.

He pulled against the ropes holding him. He tried every angle and rubbed his wrists raw to no effect.

The smoke above the fort dulled the sky, yet the sun slowly crept along, flattening shadows as midday approached. Parched and barely able to make spit, Sid closed his eyes for a moment and reminded himself that his best chance of escape was now, while his supposed title was still worth something. Remembering the witch's promise that he would do great things almost made him laugh. *Her vision latched on to the wrong child.*

Suddenly, the wolves broke out in furious howling. Sid watched them strain toward the summit's edge, sniffing the air. Southerners and traitors alike looked over the edge and seemed pleased by what they saw.

"Ba Hassan-Aza Hassan." The Hudulfah prince's new title was on everyone's lips.

Imagining Hassan leading hordes that looted and killed at will made Sid's head hurt. *How do I save my skin?* he wondered. Each time he moved, he felt his mother's pendant shift against his chest.

Three drops. An act of courage, or not?

Turning his head as far as he could, Sid caught sight of Vidkun speaking to the few day guards in the camp. These guards quietly took positions around the loot, and the new wolfmaster, accompanied by a pair of southern fighters, disappeared down the forest path.

A group of southerners hauled three long, highly polished pieces of metal over to the summit edge. While the young fighters jostled each other for the privilege of holding the giant-tall pieces, a Hudulfah man gave instructions, and, depending on the word he spoke, one pair of fighters or another tipped their metal piece back and then forward again, some quick and some slow. They paused and looked downward, then all of them talked at once. The instructor yelled out orders, and they tipped the metal pieces in the same sequence.

A message. They're using sunlight to send a message. It probably says, "We've got your stupid nephew. Can we kill him now?"

With sweat trickling down the back of his coat and into his fine shoes, Sid tried to twist his hands free of the rope for the hundredth time. He went still when he heard someone behind him.

"It's time for you to go, my boy," a familiar voice whispered. Master Avani was dressed like an old Idrisi swaddled in a homespun shawl. Sid felt him saw at the rope around his waist.

"When this is off," Master Avani said, "you will run to the oracle's garden. She will protect you until you join your sister."

"My *sister*," Sid whispered. The word warmed him, but he pretended annoyance. "You should have told me sooner."

"Yes, I should have," Master Avani said. "But here we are. Both of you must go to the northern tower as soon as possible. I've told Miss Tabaan how to go there."

Sid glanced toward the summit's edge where the southerners remained focused on sending their message. "Have you always known that I was a spare?"

Master Avani didn't pause in his efforts to free him. "No, but what under the sun and moons does that matter now? Did Ilo complain to you about being a spare when he was killed? Do you know how many have fallen today? We all bleed the same."

Sid hung his head. "I didn't mean that. It's just that I feel so...stupid. I didn't know."

The rope around Sid's middle fell away and Master Avani began to work on the knot binding his hands.

"How could you? Your mother named you heir. I only wish that had kept you safer. If Aseem is recovered, your value to Hassan is even less than it is now, but your value to us, whether heir or spare, does not change. By the First Mother, Siddharth, the risk to each of the faithful with me right now should be proof enough of your worth."

Looking beyond the old noble into the copse, Sid saw that defenders had replaced the traitors Vidkun had left behind. They had been silent, but the bodies at their feet could not be hidden. His hands were free.

"Thank you, sir," Sid said, rubbing his wrists. "But *how* is Li my sister?"

"That will be explained later." Master Avani pointed him eastward. "You have got to reach the northern tower, understand?"

"You're coming, sir?"

"If the ancestors are willing. Now go!"

With his arms tingling like a hundred ant bites, Sid ran. A commotion in the camp behind him erupted by the time he reached the third chhatri. Looking over his shoulder, he caught a glimpse of Master Avani and the defenders, talwars drawn, facing the southerners. As Sid slowed, a handful of traitors emerged from the woods with Vidkun. They approached the fray stealthily.

Sid stopped. *I've got to help them. A prince would help them.* The awful memory of Ilo's death burned in his heart.

"Behind you!" he yelled.

Master Avani turned on his heels to face Vidkun, and Vidkun saw Sid. The traitorous wolfmaster diverted from the fighting and sprinted toward the chained wolves with a pair of former day guards joining him.

Sid remembered to run again.

The highest point of the Rock, a short, pocked bluff, lay ahead. He hoped it was where he was supposed to be going, because the growls and yaps he heard behind meant the wolves were loose. At the base of the bluff, he could make out the gateway of some long-abandoned edifice. Two figures stood there, shoulder to shoulder. One wore a black cloak.

When Li made a chopping motion with her hand, he remembered games they had played in the Western Woods and ran harder. *Like crossing the great sea.* He jumped over brush and leapt over rocks, his lungs burning. In his earlier nightmares, it was Li being pursued by wolves. His destiny and hers seemed to have knotted up from tip to tail.

Still a few wagon lengths away, Sid saw the oracle raise an object in her hands. He couldn't hear what Li was yelling, but it didn't matter because the oracle threw the thing far and high. It passed over him and burst with a tremendous noise, making him stumble as a wave of pressure slammed against his back. The wolves yelped like frightened pups, and when he looked back one guard lay crumpled on the ground, but Vidkun and the other were already regaining their feet.

He ran straight toward Li and the oracle with all the speed he could muster. As he cleared the gateway and tripped to a stop, Li put a torch to the ground. A blue line of fire flared to life, running along the edifice's crumbling walls. He stood with her and the oracle as flames rose shoulder-high between them and his pursuers.

Vidkun cursed with frustration. Mindful of the wolves sniffing along the fire line, seeking gaps, Sid looked beyond the flames for Master Avani, but there was no sign of him.

The oracle chanted in a foreign language and pulled out another knobby object like the one she had thrown before. She nodded toward the bluff behind, and Li grabbed his sleeve.

The thin woman's chant reached a keening pitch so high and sharp that the wolves cringed and Vidkun took a step back. As the oracle lifted her weapon, Li pulled him toward the base of the bluff. They had nearly reached it when pressure from the second explosion struck. Scrambling forward, Li dragged him into a shaded crack in the rock where the path turned abruptly and plunged them into total darkness.

By the time they reached a lantern sitting on the passage floor, Sid's hearing had returned, but he was still dazed. It was only when Li began to frantically push symbols engraved on a large metal panel that he realized they had passed through a gate—an ancestor-blessed one that somehow closed of its own accord. He looked at Li with his mouth open.

"You do have otherworld powers."

Lingli rolled her eyes. "Greta showed me."

"So, you are my sister after all." He tried to say this lightly, but he knew he wasn't fooling her.

"That's what Master Avani and Madam say."

"And Greta," he said. "Greta said so."

They were both silent, then Lingli said, "But not the rani."

She had turned away from him, and he felt the yawning abyss behind her words.

"She did," he said. "She didn't want to, but she told me this morning." He hoped knowing this would help somehow, but he was not prepared to tell her what else their mother had admitted.

Both of them jumped at the sound of a ringing blow on the other side of the gate. Li waved toward the lantern, and he picked it up and hurried after her deeper into the Rock.

PART 6

CHAPTER 45

When the fighters hauled the boy to the wanderers' wagon, Greta sensed the rani's anxiety roiling the air around her, but she remained almost giantstill, only pivoting on her heels to keep the vantage should the ameer or any other southerner act against Dear Child. Her hands itched, but from the day of Valena Sandhyatara's birth, she had been bound to her for good or ill, and she would not shirk her duty for the satisfaction of grinding a few dozen more southerners to dust unless it benefited her charge.

The closest enemy, the ameer of Kirdun, was still deadly but less likely to act impetuously after relieving the rani of her weapon. He wanted something, and Greta judged that a bargain for Dear Child's safety could still be struck.

"Your children will not be harmed on *my* orders," he said.

"You'll pardon me if the sight of the dead in this yard has made me fairly deaf to your promises."

Ali bowed his head for an instant and spoke more softly, as if he wished to keep the other ameers from hearing. "I wish it were otherwise, dear Valena. I wish we could go to the summit and enjoy the panorama as we have in past, but all is in motion now. Much depends on your choices, and it would help both of us if you put your mind to these choices before the negotiations begin. Every decision will be discussed to death because all of this"—Ali gestured broadly at the fighters behind him—"is a combined effort."

"I see," the rani said. "You are the mind behind this betrayal, Hassan is the face, and both of you allow Afreh and Idris to think they have some role other than shielding your fighters with theirs."

"The revenue from Afreh's new gem mines, albeit reduced by your refusal to pay fair value, makes their house a delightful partner, and Idris has its uses. As for 'betrayal,' you would have done the same had you help from an equal number of disgruntled subjects, but let that be for now. I'm afraid our frank talk must wait."

A new cluster of southerners crossed the stable yard, most of them wearing Hudulfah's white and gold. Amid them, the rani's consort seemed still affected by the sleeping potion. He moved arm in arm with his sister, Mafala, who was dressed like her house's fighters. Their faces were painted with the constellation that guided their people, but the paint did not hide their anger. Greta made sure she was positioned to interrupt any move they might make toward Her Majesty.

When they arrived, Hassan shook himself loose from his sister, ignored his betrothed, and addressed the ameer of Kirdun as if he were his general.

"Is the route secured?"

"The meager guard at the eastern gate wisely joined our efforts," Ali reported. "As you were still incapacitated last night, I consulted your sister, and we concluded that we could proceed. There was no resistance until Master Crowseye destroyed the eastern passage, but once they left, the Idrisis' goyra swept it better than scores of miners could have done."

"What of the fort?"

"The last word was that all gates remain closed, but there has been a breach of the wall on the southmost end. Fighting has been heavy."

Hassan looked to the Rock's summit. "Have they signaled our status to the field?"

"We have just moved your nephew up there for safekeeping," Ameer Ali said. "As soon as Prince Siddharth is secured, they will message the field."

"You took it upon yourself to safeguard my nephew, honorable ameer? Have you shown equal concern for my son and heir?"

"I would have," Ali said, "if I had found him. He is missing."

Greta felt the threat lurking in Hassan's words, but Ali answered as if he had not. More games with words. She hoped she could understand their intent quickly enough to aid Dear Child.

Hassan's hooded gaze slid to the rani. "You will not keep him from me. Not if you want your elder son to survive the day."

"You speak of 'my son,' 'your son,' but the ancestors know they both share our blood. Both must survive the day." The rani's words were measured. "No matter how many ways we betray each other, Hassan, I would never harm our sons. Will you promise the same?"

Contempt soaked Hassan's answer. "If you had the same reverence for my mother and father, perhaps I could have made the promise you seek. But Aza Mussan and his wife now wander in the ether, and I cannot guide them, not with what lies ahead today. My only consolation is that their spirits' call for vengeance will bring the otherworld down upon you."

Hassan's aura was dark, and Greta readied herself to strangle him if he so much as shifted his weight forward, but it was Ameer Ali who came between the maharani and her consort.

"Pardon me, Aza Hassan, but I think we should press our advantage. Your esteemed father once told me that there is always time for vengeance, but rare moments for victories."

He and the other ameers gave orders to the fighters, and they soon moved out. Ignoring those who dared to prod her with their blades, Greta fell in behind the rani and Akela as they marched to the wide-open palace gate. In a band of shade at the base of the gate tower where the slain defenders were piled, they watched Idrisis carry long pieces of polished metal into the guard room while the fighters formed a column. Trembling with war courage that nearly made them deaf to direction, the fighters eyed the open span, but Ameer Khush managed to channel their excitement with a booming chant that they repeated back to him with much glee.

"Do you know what the honorable ameer is saying?" Hassan smugly asked the rani. "Four have defeated seven."

His taunt produced no noticeable change in the rani's demeanor, but Greta felt the fear, the waves of shame, and the itch caused as much by the absent pendant as the missing sons. Worse, the giantess sensed that Hassan had become calmer, resolved to his next actions, and she observed him all the more closely.

"You don't need us to tell you that the battle is over, Valena," Ali said. "The palace is lost, but not its people. Not the people of Safed Qila. By your word, we can end the fighting quickly. We can prevent the ransacking of the palace and lessen the ruination of the fort."

"I will never give up the Rock."

Ali sighed and shook his head. "I'm afraid the Rock gave you up days ago when we burrowed into it."

Looking out toward the slender bridge that spanned the abyss, Hassan said, "If we have ever agreed on anything, Rani, it has been the importance of the future of our realms. My people have been hungry more days than not. Like them, I saw the crumbs you offered, and I was grateful, but they want more. Should I ignore them?" He shrugged. "The ancestors showed the way, and I choose to act on it."

"Crumbs?" the rani said. "You have never appreciated the concessions I championed to make this alliance and provide you with trade, markets, a stake in the lake city. I took food from the mouths of my own people to help yours."

"That is not my concern. I serve Hudulfah, and a united Avakstan."

"Such a beautiful dream. Did the ancestors show you to be their avatar? Soon you will realize that you have made your greatest mistake."

Hassan drew a cylindrical object from his short cloak—the House of Avani's stargazer. Pleased by the rani's obvious surprise, he put the gift to his eye and looked through it toward the span, making a show of twisting the cylinder one way then the other.

Opening her giantsense, Greta searched for Master Avani and was relieved to sense his spirit near the summit. "He lives," she told Dear Child, hoping to tamp down her worry.

Hassan lowered the stargazer and said, "I had heard that this sacred gift could shift space, but it has shifted time as well." He handed the rani the Avani gift. "See the future for yourself."

The rani hesitated, then put the stargazer to her eye, but Greta did not need it to see the Ascaryans, mostly children and some mere babes in their mothers' arms, clustered on the third gate's terrace.

"I see a fort on fire and too few defenders," Hassan said. "Yet they look to you for relief. Will you not save them?"

Pain enveloped Dear Child.

"Cross the span and tell them to open the gate," Hassan said. "Each mother may choose one to spare and send them here before our forces renew the fight."

Even as the rani drew on the last reserves of her strength, Greta felt resignation begin to infect her heart.

"How can you ask this of any mother? Of me?" the rani shouted. "What is your word, Hassan! Give me your witnessed word that our sons will be kept whole and that all the Seven's youngest descendants will be allowed, unmolested, to freely leave the Rock. Then I will give you my answer."

Hassan shook his head. "Only the two who share my blood concern me, and there we have a stalemate, do we not?"

Before the rani could respond, Ameer Ali interjected, "Aza Hassan, they are children and very few at that. We will break the gate even without her cooperation."

"She has made her choice," Hassan said. "Let her lose on both counts."

The new ameer of Hudulfah looked back to the Rock's summit where bright lights flashed. Four short pulses, one long. The sequence repeated. Hassan walked away and called out to the fighters on top of the gate tower.

Ali said quietly, "I am sorry, Valena, but I will honor my promise as long as I can."

His sympathetic gesture bothered Greta, for she sensed he hid some other interest.

While the ameers issued orders to their fighters, the rani swayed on her feet and took Greta's arm.

"I cannot... Are they whole?" she asked, staring at the ground.

Though Dear Child was shamed by the pending fate of the children on the gate, Greta understood that she meant her two sons only, her concern made narrower than Hassan's by excluding one of her own blood. Opening her giantsense again, Greta was assured that the baby prince was uninjured though distant, but alarm was high in both the boy and the girl.

"They are whole," Greta said.

CHAPTER 46

Lingli fairly flew along the passage, but Sid stumbled and banged against every stone despite the lantern lighting his way. She stopped and waited for him to catch up.

"You're slow," she said.

"I've already run half a league."

The hammering at the upper gate continued to echo around them. Taking Sid's free hand in hers, she jogged on with him until they reached the small gate at the head of the passage connected to the old tower. Sid set the lantern on the passage floor, put his hands on his knees, and panted quietly.

"I'm sorry about that," he said, waving at her bandaged finger without looking at her.

She could not believe it. The effort those words must have cost him. If they hadn't been fleeing for their lives, she might have berated him a good deal more, but his guilty look was the admission she needed.

"I should have said something," he said.

She shrugged. "You couldn't have known Mafala's plan. I only hope you don't believe I killed Master Vaksana."

"Of course not." Sid ran a hand through his hair, "But I don't know how to convince Am...the rani."

She had been so sure that she would lay out all the items she had gathered from the rani's hidden room when she found Sid again. She would tell him about Her Majesty's crime against her and her crime against Red and dare him to deny it. But here he was, exhausted and apologizing for himself, and she hesitated to wound him further.

The muffled banging suddenly stopped. Lingli moved farther down the main passage. "We better go."

"Hold on." Sid gestured at the small passage. "Where does that one go?"

"Down to a cave-in where it joins another passage to the palace."

Sid shook his head. "And this one?"

"To the wheel room."

"Won't fighters be there, too?"

"Maybe, but we have to go this way. Master Avani wants us to wait for him behind his house's gate."

Sid unbuckled his belt and took his war coat off.

"What are you doing?"

"We need to slow them down, right?" He rubbed the coat against his cheek and trotted down the side passage. Lingli kept her ears tuned to the upper passage while nervously waiting for Sid to reappear. He returned without his coat, but the fancy belt and short blades still hung low on his hips.

"Maybe that will put the wolves off for a bit."

"You are smarter than you look."

Sid snorted at that, just as a loud boom sounded from the upper gate. Then they were rushing down the main passage again.

She was afraid, yes. Vidkun would not easily give up on recapturing Sid, but within the fear a small ribbon of joy was woven. All sorts of gauzy thoughts filled her head. *After we escape, we must live in some hidden place. It will be like living in Red's cabin again. Only Master Avani will visit. Perhaps Madam. Sid won't like it, but it will be only for a short time—until he can return to Chandrabhavan.*

The lower Satya gate was closed when they reached it, but there was a large bulge in the center that had not been there when she last passed through. She wasn't sure she should open it.

Sid slid down onto the floor with his legs splayed out. He patted his chest, a gesture that immediately reminded her of the rani.

"There's a lot of things I don't understand," he said, "like why she hates you, and why she put you with Red, same as me."

"I don't know the 'why' either," Lingli said, looking into the dark behind them, "but she meant to kill me when I was a baby, if Master Avani and Madam have it right."

Sid rubbed his face and looked away from her. "Oh. That's...that's harsh."

"I don't think she put me with Red. I don't think she knew I was there."

"But she knew Red was there," Sid said. "She definitely sent me there with a nurse."

Lingli shook her head. "We'll spend cycles trying to figure it out unless you can convince your mother to tell us the truth."

"*Our* mother."

"No," Lingli said, shaking her head. The very idea fanned her anger back to life. She dug into her cloak to find the dart. "*Your* mother is a liar." She handed the dart to him, and as he turned it over in his hand, she said, "She gave one of these to the villagers. She's got—"

A small sound, a low growl, echoed in the passage. The hair on her arms rose.

"Open it," Sid whispered, scrambling to his feet and thrusting the dart back into her hands.

Lingli pressed the panel's symbols with practiced speed, and the gate clicked but did not slide back. Sid picked up a piece of loose rock at his feet and banged at it, which raised a string of barks and growls from the wolves, but it was impossible to tell how far away they were.

"Give me one of your blades!" she hissed.

Sid drew one from his belt and handed it to her. Wedging it into the seam where the metal met stone, Lingli suddenly felt a force run up her arm like lightning, slamming her backward.

When her senses returned, she was lying on the floor, and Sid was shaking her shoulder.

"Get up, Li. You've got to get up!"

Her limbs tingled and she couldn't see well, but she stood. The gate had opened hardly more than the length of her foot, but Sid pushed her through. She heard running footsteps and claws clattering on the stone.

Sid tossed the lantern through and passed her his belt. Shaking off her dizziness, she took his arm and pulled while he twisted and turned and finally squeezed through.

She still wasn't thinking clearly, and the stink of goyra, mixed with blood, was overpowering. While Sid buckled his belt, she raised the lantern to look for the Avani gate, and her urge to gag became worse.

Broken and crumpled bodies, both defenders and southerners, were scattered throughout the room.

"Stars," Sid whispered, looking deathly pale in the lantern light. "You go first. I can't look at them."

Trying not to step on anyone, and conscious of Sid breathing loudly through his mouth, Lingli moved forward and looked for owls on the other gate frames. On the other side of the passage that led to the pit, she found the Avani gate, but it was boarded over and a number of bodies were piled against its timbers. As she and Sid contemplated which boards would be easiest to break, the wolves suddenly threw themselves against the Satya gate behind them, making her jump.

Thrusting their muzzles and paws through the narrow opening, the wolves snarled and snapped until Vidkun kicked them aside. Half of his face was visible in the gap—one eye glaring at them, one hand reaching out.

"Prince, it's all done but the crying," Vidkun said, pretending regret. "Your mother may have lost, but your uncle's brilliant. Conceived of all of this. I can present you as a noble with value—heir to both realms. Think! When the blades are sheathed, he'll need supporters. You will be so very important."

"Don't answer," Lingli whispered. She pinched the lantern's flame. "He's lying."

"I know!" Sid whispered back.

"Is that you, Slippery Seamstress?" Vidkun called out. "Love the dark, don't you? You may as well give up if you're dreaming of saving a prince and seeking mercy. No one's ever going to forgive you for killing my brother you know."

"*You* killed your brother," Lingli said.

"He did?" Sid said.

The new wolfmaster resumed battering his way out, and Lingli and Sid rolled one of the bodies out of the way, then heaved another to the side.

Suddenly Vidkun cried out and Lingli guessed that he felt the same shock she had, but he returned to his efforts quickly. The metal groaned as he pried at it and cursed even louder.

Sid whispered, "We don't have time for this," and she had to agree. "We should hide in the pit."

"No. Too easy to fall in the dark and full of who knows how many southerners and their beasts."

"If you know which passage is the mouth, I know of a safe spot."

"We cannot just walk out there."

"Trust me."

She and Sid shuffled across the wheel room. As soon as the draft told her which passage led to the palace grounds, she showed Sid and he felt his way along the wall to the next passage. Several steps inside, Lingli re-lit their lantern.

Sid said, "It's funny, actually."

"What?"

"No one knows that you're the true heir."

Lingli knew Sid didn't care about anyone's confusion. He wanted to know whether she would claim the title. Looking at his dirty, tired face, she remembered the boy who had made daily tributes at his shrine despite her teasing, so certain his destiny was a bright one.

"How could I ever be heir to the one who wishes me dead?" she said. "If you don't tell anyone and I don't, and Master Avani and Madam promise to be quiet—and Envoy Kanaka—no one else needs to know."

"You forgot Greta."

"Yes, Greta too. You will always be the rani's heir." When she saw Sid relax, she added. "Though I cannot imagine why you would want the title after today." She gave him the lantern.

"It's not the title, though that does bring one nice things," he said, pointing the toe of one of his golden juttis toward the lantern light. "I want to have a prince's courage."

"You have courage," she said.

"Ha," he said dismissively. "Not enough. Not for a day like today."

"Who does?" She grabbed his hand and squeezed it. "But the day's not over. Let's go."

Both of them huffed for breath by the time they reached a door blocking their way—an ordinary wooden door crossed with brass bands. It was locked. Lingli ground her teeth, trying not to shout at Sid for taking this route.

"Bend your knee!" Sid said.

"Really? This is not the time—"

"I know where there's a key!"

She knelt and he balanced on her thigh, feeling along the top of the door frame. Then he jumped down with a key in hand, fitted it in the lock, and opened the door.

He slipped through first. She was still on the threshold when she heard something in the passage. Green eyes glowed in the dark not far behind.

"They're coming!" she said, shoving the door closed, and Sid dropped the bar as the wolves hurled themselves against it.

She couldn't imagine anything could smell worse than the goyra stink in the wheel room, but Lingli nearly choked on the stench of sickness and filth.

"What is this place?" she asked as she followed Sid around an old table and chairs in the room that was barely more than a wide spot in the passage.

"The jail," Sid answered.

The continued up the passage, and Lingli paused opposite a row of doors with small, barred windows.

"Come on," Sid said. "We're nearly there."

"Nearly where?" A stitch in her side burned terribly, but she didn't want to admit it.

"Nobles' Walk," he said.

She tugged at Sid's sleeve and stopped. "Did you hear that?"

"He's trying to break down the door. How could I not?"

"Not that. Listen." The low moaning sound made her think the Rock itself cried in pain. She was glad she could not see the countless spirits she imagined were trapped in this place.

"It's the wind. Chalo!"

A line of light glowed along the floor at the bottom of the next door they met, and the moaning Lingli heard seemed to come from there. Setting the lantern down in the passage, Sid unbarred the door and shoved it open, holding tight to a piece of rope tied to the latch. The sunlight outside was blinding, and the roar of air deafened them.

Holding her hood forward to block the light, Lingli looked out. Below was rock and the black gash of the winding crack. Above, sky. They stood in the sheer rock face and the only sign that they were still near the palace was a stretch of the fort wall in the distance and a small sliver of the training yard visible below. She stepped back to escape the vertigo that threatened to pull her over the edge.

"Don't worry," Sid yelled. He set the lantern on the floor and wound the rope around his hand. Leaning back, he pulled until the air reversed its effect and slammed the door shut. With some effort, he pushed it open again to demonstrate. "You just hang on here. Clamp the door with your legs and swing across to that ledge."

"You're mad! Across that?" Lingli shook her head at the narrow ledge he pointed to. "It's barely wide enough for a goat!"

"It looks bad, but I've made it there. Anyone can. See that knob over there? When you land, grab it and scoot behind. There's a wider spot. See it?"

"Then how does this save us from Vidkun?"

"We'll keep the door on our side, of course."

She shook her head. Every sense she had told her no.

"All we have to do is stay beyond his reach long enough to be rescued," Sid continued enthusiastically. "Not even an archer will be able to hit us."

Lingli closed her eyes and stepped back.

"I've done it, Li," Sid insisted. "You'll see."

He pulled the door closed again, and she grabbed his arm and put her lips to his ear, "Do you hear them?"

They held their breaths long enough to know the pounding on the jail's door had subsided. She imagined she heard the faint clatter of nails far back in the passage.

"You go first," Sid said.

"No. No, I can't."

The thought of swinging across that drop completely unnerved her, and she looked around for any other way to escape. There were no other doors in the passage, and their lantern showed only dark, old brackets holding the stumps of torches unlit for countless cycles. But above them, just a few steps back, ancient beams crisscrossed the passage ceiling.

"Up there," she said, completely unconvinced. "If we're quiet, they might not notice us."

"Now who's mad?"

Lingli closed her eyes. "I cannot."

Blowing out his breath with exasperation, Sid said, "Climb fast."

This time Sid bent his knee so she could step on it, and she got a foot onto a torch bracket. Her fingertips and wrist of her good hand burned with the strain, but she managed to grasp a beam and pull herself on top.

Hanging down from the beam as far as she could, Lingli reached out to Sid. He pulled one of the blades from his belt and passed it to her, but that wasn't what she wanted. She set the blade on the beam and shook her hand at him again.

A low growl carried through the passage.

She could barely see him wave her off and pull out a pendant on a chain from inside his kurta. *The rani's potion?* She nearly called out to him, but the next growl was much closer.

Sid tucked the pendant away and backed toward the end of the passage.

Trechur and Titok emerged from the dark, their giant, shaggy heads thrust forward low to the ground. There was no sign of Vidkun.

"Finally!" Sid said, his voice playful. "I thought you were never going to get here."

The wolves' ears pricked forward and fell back again as they quivered like drawn bows beneath her.

She thought of falling upon the one closest and driving Sid's blade into its back, but Sid suddenly called out to them, "Come on, you flea-bitten beasts! Yes, I am talking to you. We're going to take a ride!" He ran for the door. The wolves leapt after him.

Sunlight washed the passage walls white as the door swung open, carrying Sid into the brightness. The two wolves, close on his heels, could not stop themselves fast enough. Titok loosed a frightful howl and disappeared. Trechur followed, then Sid yelled, but Lingli could barely hear him over the wind. The door opened fully on its hinges, and she could no longer see anything from her perch. She jumped down and ran to the threshold, leaning into the blasting air.

The door hung just short of the narrow landing on the cliff's edge. Sid clung to the latch, his knuckles white with strain.

"I would have made it," he cried, barely audible over the wind, "if it weren't for him."

Blood leaked from between Trechur's long teeth, which were clamped onto Sid's leg just above his ankle. The wolf scrabbled furiously, raking long dark trails into Sid's pant legs.

"Hang on!" Lingli yelled.

She spun around the passage seeking anything that might help her pull the door back. Grabbing an old torch stump, she leaned out as far as she dared and thrust it toward the loop of rope that dangled under Sid's arm. Try though she did, she could not capture it.

Flinging herself down on the floor of the passage, she gripped the bottom of the door with both hands, but the rushing air and the weight of those attached held it in place.

Pain and panic etched Sid's face as his fingers began to slip.

CHAPTER 47

reta and Akela pressed the rani against the gate tower to shield her from the rush of fighters that poured through the palace gate and onto the narrow span. Led by ameers Hassan, Temer and Khush, the mob soon passed, and Ali ordered a few remaining Kirdun fighters to watch them as he and Mafala entered the guard room. She and the rani witnessed the fighters mass at the fort gate and throw up grappling hooks and ladders—far too many for the defenders there to repel. The rout shamed Dear Child to such a point that she stared without seeing.

It was plain to Greta that the boy was in severe distress, but she was unwilling to add to the rani's pain by telling her so when there was nothing either of them could do. Instead, the giantess said, "If you send Akela to Prince Siddharth, he will be encouraged."

"Will he?" the rani answered in a small voice.

Watching for Ali and Mafala's return, Her Majesty crouched down next to Akela and took his head in both hands.

"Go to Siddharth and protect him. That is my word."

The black wolf whined softly and pushed his head against her. When she gestured to the summit, he bolted across the yard as if demons chased him. The uproar among their Kirdun guards was short-lived, for they were not carrying spears. As Akela disappeared through the training yard gate, Greta felt the rani breathe a little easier though the giantess knew her thirst for the elixir was growing.

Ameer Ali and Mafala returned, and Ali said, "Come, Valena. The palace will provide us better vantage and allow more security for the negotiations."

Mafala led the way and Ali walked at Dear Child's side as if she were not his prisoner, but the pretense died the instant they rounded the corner of the feasting hall. Bonfires fed on palace furniture. Southerners sang and quarreled over loot and barrels of firewine. Most pitiful were the cries of palace staff as their guards took delight in tormenting them.

When the crowd realized who accompanied the princess and Ameer Ali they closed in, cursing and spitting upon the rani. Though Greta sheltered Dear Child as best she could, someone threw a rock that struck the rani on the side of her face, and the giantess's roar did little more than give the crowd a moment's pause.

The rani touched her cheek in surprise, and Ameer Ali put his arm around her shoulders. After barking orders to his fighters to hold the crowd back, the ameer instructed Mafala, "Find the senior-most defenders on these grounds, take a few of mine and yours and at least one from Afreh and Idris, and demand order. If you do not, there will be anarchy."

Mafala looked doubtful of the assignment. "Or we could kill her now and satisfy them."

"We safeguard this maharani for *our* benefit," Ameer Ali said. "These Ascaryans look to their palace as we look to our elders. If there is order here, even if it is our order, control of the fort will come easier."

With a sharp nod, Mafala climbed the lower stairs that led to the central palace's gallery and began calling fighters' names. Ameer Ali's guards forced the crowd back, and the ameer hurried the rani into the palace with Greta behind her.

Once the doors of the great hall closed behind them, muting the rampant din of the palace, the ameer ordered a sweep of the room and told Greta to light the lanterns. As she lit the diyas on the boulder behind the throne a burst of shouting erupted from the hall's dark recesses. Ali drew his blade and Greta returned to the rani's side until one of the fighters led out a small group of children and Madam Sayed.

"Oh, Your Majesty, praise the First Mother!" Madam said when she saw the rani. "When their fighters stormed the palace, I was afraid to take the children out...."

Seeing the rani's expression, Madam fell quiet.

"Look, Maharani, you still have descendants to safeguard. Tend the children over there, good madam, until we've concluded our business," the ameer said, pointing to the platform built for the wedding program. His fighters barked at the children and Madam to sit, then returned to the hall's doors to stand guard.

The ameer tried to inspect the scrape on the rani's cheek, but she angrily batted his hand away. He was restless, his face animated with an eagerness the giantess could not interpret.

Pulling a scroll from his coat he said, "You will think me insincere, Valena, but we have little time so let me not waste it with useless apologies." He handed her the scroll. "I offer nothing less than a means to change the balance of the day."

The rani looked skeptical, but Greta could feel hope spark within her as she unrolled the parchment and pressed it to the judge's table. While reading it her expression turned incredulous.

"You have given yourself exactly what was Hudulfah's share. How do you know the details of the contract?"

"Hassan showed me a recent draft. He had to provide all the houses assurances about your terms in order to make his own incentives more attractive. There would have been no cooperation for this enterprise otherwise."

"This 'enterprise' being the invasion of our sovereign realm?"

"You surely understand that I was faced with a choice. Upon hearing Hassan's proposal, I could join and negotiate for my house, or declare I was not interested and be held in suspicion from that point forward."

"How can you imagine that you would take the lead now? What incentives does Kirdun promise that could exceed Hudulfah's?"

Ali seemed encouraged by her question, but Greta knew the rani was stalling, her thoughts darting about like a netted bird.

"We can offer significantly better grains and metalsmithing tools, and I have with me two chests of silverwork that should be helpful, but I will need your support."

"Even if I agreed to give you the Nilampur governorship, Hassan would still hold title here as my consort."

"Ah, yes, that would not work. Our houses would constantly chafe. That is why, instead of marrying a man who cares not a chikoo for your happiness or the interests of the Seven, you must marry me."

The rani was speechless. Placing his hand over hers, Ali said, "We can salvage Saatkulom if we act quickly."

Suddenly, Greta's giantsense burst open, freezing her in place. To have another spirit pry her mind open had never happened before, but she had no time to consider the reason before the girl's panic manifested as a blinding white light. Behind that beacon, the boy's fear and pain flooded her every nerve. The danger surrounding them declared itself so loudly she wondered how the Ascaryans could not hear it.

Struggling to dampen her connection to the young ones, Greta focused her thoughts on the rani and found herself still standing behind the throne. The ameer pointed to a line on the open scroll on the judges' table. The rani hugged herself and shook her head. Time had leapt forward.

"There, she's back," Ameer Ali said, looking at Greta. "I think I understand now how we won the giant wars."

"The maharani must rest," Greta said, lumbering behind her charge. Absorbing a wave of Dear Child's pain—the headache, the tightness in her chest, and her terrible thirst—the giantess resisted saying anything about the boy and girl.

"The maharani must sign this contract," the ameer answered testily. "Why do you refuse? Would marriage to me be so horrible?" He forced an amiable tone. "Surely you understand this alliance would be the most profitable of all. Without my protection, you will not live to see the spring. With it, we would control a mighty realm and gatekeep the south's trade, much as you have promised Hassan. He will be the only one to challenge this contract if you trust me."

As rage gathered in the maharani, Greta tried to put herself between her and the ameer, but Dear Child moved around her.

"You think you see it clear, but saving my own skin is not enough!" she protested.

"What about your sons' skins?"

As if water had been poured on a coal, the rani's spirit cooled. Greta slowly edged to a position where she could reach the ameer.

"You have provided no guarantee that my sons, heirs two times over, would be any safer with you as my consort."

"How could they not be! Aseem is already far from here and quite safe, I promise you, but even more importantly, he is the leverage to keep Hassan from rash action. And Siddharth? By your word, I would adopt him to solidify our realms."

"You would?" The rani was incredulous. "What a fantastic promise from one who already has an heir in Kirdun."

"Complicated, of course, but if Saatkulom and Kirdun were united…"

Greta tried to stay with Dear Child, but her giantsense broke open once again.

CHAPTER 48

Ripping a strip of cloth from the end of her tunic, Lingli tied Sid's blade to a torch stub and thrust it out, using the fancy hilt like a hook on the bottom of the door, but she could pull it only a little.

Sid panted and flexed his arms, trying to stop his slide off the latch.

Trechur rolled his eyes toward her. One flailing paw struck the blade and nearly drove it from her grasp. The door swung back to its earlier position.

"I'm going to push you to the ledge," she yelled over the wind.

On her belly, leaning out until her shoulders were beyond the floor of the passage, Lingli jabbed at the door with the blade's hilt, and the wind moved it to the far ledge.

"Get your foot on it!"

Sid pressed his forehead to the door's edge and tried to raise his free leg. The wolf also scratched at the cliff, but neither could find purchase on the lip of the ledge.

"Your heel!" she shouted. "Get your heel on it and pull yourself over."

He tried, his foot sliding off each time. He let his leg hang. She could see his chest heaving from the effort, and the ferocious wind whipped his hair around his face. "Stop, Li."

"No! You can do this."

"Li… I… Listen!" Sid said.

His knuckles on the latch were so white they were blue.

"Don't let go!" Lingli begged. She tried to swing the blade handle down on Trechur's head, but it barely tapped the wolf.

Sid moaned as the wolf's jaws tightened. His grip was failing.

"Not your fault," he said, mustering a smile. "Shame about my juttis."

"No, Sid!" Panic constricted her heart.

Sweat poured down Sid's face, every word an effort. "Amma is what you said, but she's more. Tell her I didn't drink it. I tried…for the strength of the realm."

"Don't!"

"I will miss you…sister."

Boy and wolf plunged downward. Lingli screamed. The wolf released Sid and fell away. For a moment, the sun shone bright on her brother. He fell with his arms outstretched, like a bird gliding toward its nest. Then he passed into the abyss's waiting dark, and she saw him no more.

The wind howled.

CHAPTER 49

The boy's fear overwhelmed Greta. Rushing air. Darkness and light flashed and spun, making the giantess dizzy. Then her sense of him broke like a thread snapped. He was gone. The girl howled.

Ali was still speaking when Greta came back to herself. Unbalanced by the boy's last moments, she tried to focus on the dangerous urgency pulsing through the ameer.

"Hassan and the others will return soon," Ali said, holding out a reed pen to the rani. "I can hold them at the palace gate. All we need is a bit of time to convince the other houses to agree."

The offer to spare a son's life was too great a temptation. Dear Child was exhausted and sick with thirst. She took the pen in hand.

"The boy has gone to stone," Greta said.

Ameer Ali frowned with confusion, but Dear Child understood. Despair washed through the rani. She bowed her head, and the pen fell to the floor.

Sensing that Dear Child's legs would not long hold her, Greta reached out to take her arm. That was the giantess's mistake.

On the other side of the rani, Ameer Ali slipped an arm around her throat and pulled her away. As she struggled, a blade in his free hand glinted in the lantern light. He stabbed her in the ribs, and she gasped and became still.

"Stand back, giant!" the ameer yelled. Greta moaned loudly but she had no choice but to comply even as Madam rushed to her side, begging for the rani's release. The ameer's first strike had been a warning, but the blade was too well-placed.

"My vanity will recover," he said, "but I cannot allow you to betray me now and inform Hassan who has taken his child. Nor can I afford for you to instigate a war among our houses. That would upset all my plans."

He pushed the rani to the throne and forced her to sit. Using her sash to bind her, the ameer stared at her for a breath, then opened the neck of her mail. Every muscle in the rani's body went taut when he plucked up her amethyst chain and pulled it from her gown. His laugh was short and cold, and his blade was still too close to Dear Child's neck for Greta to act.

"What? Where is your greatest gift? You do realize a cask of it fetches more gold than a trunk of gems," Ali said. "Even the watered-down casks your people have been selling to me." He opened his vest and brought out a metal tube strung on a leather cord. "Good thing I've kept my own sample."

"No, Ali. Please," the rani turned her head away. "Bring me Aseem."

"Shhh." The ameer pushed a strand of hair back from the rani's cheek. "Your youngest will outlive you. What greater blessing could you seek?" He uncorked the tube. "They say not to take more than a drop of this potion in a full cup, but what about someone like you? Someone used to its effects? You will need all the courage it can provide when Hassan returns."

The odd, sweet scent of the elixir filled the air, and the rani breathed deeply. She looked serene, though Greta knew this was only an expression of resignation—all paths closed to her.

He touched the tube to Dear Child's lips, and Greta rumbled like a mountain about to blow apart. Madam fell to her knees and began to recite a tribute for protection. Holding his blade between his teeth, Ali pinched the maharani's jaw until her lips parted. Then Valena Sandhyatara closed her eyes as he tipped the contents into her mouth.

When he took the tube away, the ameer ran his finger over its rim, tasted it, and tucked it and his contract back into his vest. "Are you pleased to have thwarted me? To have forced me to go on playing the stalwart ally today? Know this: In time I will know the secret of making this sweet poison, and a new balance will be struck between Kirdun, Hudulfah, and all the rest."

"You were honored here," the rani whispered, "treated like my father's brother, and this is how you repay him."

"This? You think this is a mark upon my honor? I paid out all the honor I have ever possessed when I killed your father in his own palace."

For an instant Greta, too, was made still by the rani's shock, but when Dear Child spasmed so hard it seemed she would break her binding, the giantess managed to prevent her head from slamming against the back of the throne.

Ali touched his fingertips to his forehead and strode off. The scent of smoke and sounds of raucous laughter carried into the hall until his remaining fighters barred the doors again.

Quickly untying the rani, Greta and Madam eased her onto the floor. The giantess took a clay cup from one of the boulder's altars and filled it with water, then rummaged in her apron pockets for her salve.

Holding the rani's hand, Madam prayed to the ancestors as Greta dabbed salve under her nose. She didn't stir. After a few breaths, Greta took a pinch of powder from another packet and put it on the rani's tongue. She turned her head away.

"Come back. Aseem calls you," Greta said, stroking the rani's head. She would not mention the girl whose spirit had become a dark void.

Dear Child's pulse raced thin and fast like a rabbit seeking cover.

CHAPTER 50

Lingli leaned against the wall and stared at the rectangle of sky at the end of the passage for so long, she couldn't fully close her eyes. Her face was scoured from the wind, and all strength and reason had fled. In her mind's eye blood oozed from between Trechur's jaws. She heard Sid sigh, saw his fingers sliding over the latch. He fell again and again.

There was a noise. Someone approached. Someone spoke. Someone kicked the blade and torch stump away from her. None of it mattered.

The traitor Vidkun paced back and forth in front of her. His face was flecked with dirt and ash, and he smelled of the oracle's burning powder. He gestured madly and struck her across the face.

"—led me all this way, and no prince. Nary a wolf!"

There was another with him, a ragged-looking youth in filthy clothes who wore an owl brooch on his shoulder. The boy took her poorly made tool and laid on the floor, but when he removed the torch stump and tried to fit the blade's point under the bottom of the door to draw it forward he found, as she had, that the angle and the wind made that impossible.

No one will ever know that Sid fell here. No one will remember him.

"—and all I've got to give him is you," Vidkun continued ranting, "an asura who should have been hung moons ago! My worth was measured in wolves, a few loyal thieves, and a seat in the council, but I've been made a pauper in a day. Will Hassan keep his end of our bargain now, Ritin? Will he? I have my doubts."

Taking a slim rope from Vidkun, Ritin made a loop at one end and tossed it toward the upper corner of the door. His aim was good, but the rope slipped free each time he tried to pull it taut.

"You tell me, Asura," Vidkun said, tapping her chest with the point of his talwar, "why I don't push you off here like that addled prince, eh?"

Lingli stared at him.

"Oh? Cared for him, did you?" Vidkun chuckled. "Wasted effort. That boy only had eyes for his mother. Didn't even understand he lined up with the wrong side of the family."

There was the smallest of noises in the passage. The rani's black wolf, Akela, emerged from the dark and fixed his green eyes on Vidkun. When the noble ordered him down, the wolf snarled at him.

While Vidkun cursed and fumbled for the shishpar on his belt, Ritin left his task and stepped behind him. Without haste, the Avani boy took the ends of the rope in both hands, slipped it over the noble's head, and pulled it tight against his throat.

Vidkun hurled himself backward, and they slammed into the opposite wall. Throwing his weight forward, Vidkun attempted to pull Ritin off his feet, but the Avani boy kicked the back of the noble's knees and never lost his hold. The noble's talwar fell from his grasp as he clawed at the rope. Flailing as though he was on ice, Vidkun's eyes rolled up into his head. Finally, he was still.

Breathing hard, Ritin watched the wolf cautiously as he recoiled the rope and took Vidkun's scabbard and blade. Then he pushed the traitor's body forward until it slid over the edge.

Sunlight glinted off Akela's brass harness as he slowly approached the precipice and sniffed at the floor, seemingly uninterested in either of them.

To avoid the wolf, the Avani boy pressed close to Lingli's side of the passage and dropped Sid's blade at her feet. "I'm sorry," he said softly before he walked away into the passage.

Lingli hugged her knees, barely aware of any of it.

When Akela crouched at the end of Nobles' Walk with his tail between his legs and howled, she felt it like her last scream. The wolf approached her stiff-legged, and Lingli counted the white hairs on the underside of his muzzle. He could have taken her whole head in his maw, but he did not. She breathed in his wild, blood-laced scent and realized she had no fear left.

Akela moved away and looked back over his shoulder, waiting. She staggered to her feet, stuck Sid's blade in the waist of her pants, and followed him down the passage.

The wheel room was lit by occasional showers of sparks spewing from the Satya gate's broken edges. The wolf stepped gingerly over the bodies in their path, and Lingli recalled the ghosts on the walls of Akroyat, convinced she could feel the spirits of the dead swirling around the cavern roof above them. *Maybe I have always been one of them and was just stuck accidentally in this body that goes on and on.*

She and Akela hiked up to the side passage and down again. After crawling through the rubble at the cave-in they continued through the curtains at the back of the old tower's third floor. Sounds of ransacking came from every direction, but Lingli didn't care.

Nothing can harm me now.

When she paused outside the locked door to Sid's quarters, Akela butted his head into her side until she moved toward the stairs. On the first floor, at the end of the gallery, a knot of southern fighters burst into surprised cries and fell back at the sight of Akela, but a few drew their blades.

Lingli reached inside her cloak's hem and drew out the oracle's powder box. Befuddled, the southerners chattered as she approached them with the box balanced on one hand while dribbling grit along the floor with the other.

Two of the fighters grinned in a toothy way and stepped to each side, as if they would encircle her. Unbothered, Lingli took a torch hanging on the wall and touched its burning end to the floor. Fire raced along the grit, separating them from the fighters by high flames and thick smoke. She followed Akela to the great hall.

The wolf scratched at the doors, and Lingli waited silently, confident that he would bring her to the rani. Her good hand strayed to the hilt of Sid's blade, then fell to her side. If she could resist the urge to think about what she meant to do, it would be better for all concerned.

Muffled thumps and crashes came from inside before Greta opened the doors. Kicking the crumpled bodies of two Kirdun fighters aside, the giantess rebarred the doors and led Lingli and the wolf along a path of lanterns until Akela leapt ahead. As Lingli glided over the dark ice floor, she passed a few of the Seven's children huddled at the edge of the dance platform. To see them there, clasping hands and comforting each other, made her chest hurt. Her howl remained close, but she fought it back and followed Greta to the throne.

Fat candles surrounded a prone figure on the floor where Greta knelt. Looking over the giantess's shoulder, Lingli realized it was the rani lying on her back and wearing her gown of tumbling stars. The rani's head rested in Madam Sayed's lap—the top half of her face painted dark with a star between her brows—and her eyes were all but closed. Lingli was unsure whether the rani lived until Akela nuzzled her cheek and she blinked.

A rustling noise from the far reaches of the hall drew their attention. The oracle emerged from the dark in scorched skirts smelling of smoke. Her face was streaked with ash and dirt, but she gracefully sat on the floor facing Greta and Madam with the rani between them. The giantess shifted and pulled Lingli down onto the floor next to her.

"Speak, child," the oracle said.

She had no idea what the oracle wanted her to say, Lingli looked at the giantess and the dance teacher dumbly.

"Soon she will join her ancestors," Greta said. "Speak."

Madam, her eyes red-rimmed from weeping, nodded to her also.

Lingli looked upon the rani's still face—plump lips, brows that rose like birds' wings, dark wavy hair. So many of Sid's features were hers, but she and Her Majesty had nothing in common. The longer she looked at this woman they said was her mother, the more angry Lingli became.

In a rasping voice, she managed to say, "Prince Siddharth is dead."

The rani's eyelids fluttered and cracked open.

"He is…was…sorry…." Her words trailed away. *His message. Deliver his message!* "He asked me to tell you that he didn't drink your poison, and all he did was for the strength of the realm."

With bile burning in the back of her throat, Lingli continued. "He was your son, but did you know him? Did you know that he would do anything for you and this palace that shines like the moons? Everything he did was for you."

Pulling the dolls from her pocket, Lingli leaned forward and waved the brown doll with green eyes in front of the rani's face. "This one is missing." She held out the doll with its blue coat and a stitched smile. "And this one is…gone." Then, shaking with anger, she raised the white, featureless one.

"But *I* am here! I am still here!"

The rani's eyes closed.

Part of Lingli wanted to flee somewhere, anywhere, and not have to look upon this woman who had tried to kill her. Part of her boiled with a darker purpose. Her hand strayed to Sid's blade, but Greta grasped it first and set it aside. Akela raised his head and growled.

"You must see," the oracle said.

Producing a small pouch of herbs from her skirts, the oracle softly chanted as she poured leaves and stems onto the floor and lit them. After washing herself in the smoke, the gaunt woman took out a small blade and raised one of the rani's hands, deftly cutting a shallow line diagonally across her palm. Though the rani made no sign she felt anything, the blood welled, and Akela whimpered.

Then the oracle cut her own palm and peeled back the skin to reveal a smooth, pale organ that Lingli had never seen before. After sprinkling the herb ash onto the cuts in each of their hands, the oracle gripped the rani's cut hand with her own. Their blood mingled and dripped upon the wedding dress.

Bent low to the rani's ear, the oracle whispered, "Stay a little longer, sister."

Lingli began to get up, but Greta pulled her back down and swiftly forced her face to the floor. She had no strength to resist the giantess who turned her head so that the horrible vein in her temple was exposed. As Greta held her tight, the oracle leaned across the maharani. Lingli felt the tip of the oracle's blade on her temple and closed her eyes.

This could be my end. Part of her wished that it was.

A small cut, not deep. She smelled the ash sprinkled on the side of her head.

The oracle's palm pressed her temple, and the pulse of the muscle she had seen felt like a living thing. Lingli's head began to thud like a drum. Blood ran across her face, but Greta did not allow her to move. The oracle then pressed the rani's bloody palm to her temple and held them tight together.

Visions burst into Lingli's mind, some bright and some dim, and many too fleeting for her to make sense of. Energy and light spun within her and around her. The hair on her shoulders was plaited in loose, messy braids, as if she had just woken, but they were dark, not white. She thought a stream was nearby, but it may have been the wind for snow blew about her.

Realizing she *was* the rani, or at least she saw from her eyes, Lingli smelled dirt and wet leaves in a winter wood. She sat on a broad chair covered with furs, and a black wolf pup slept in her lap. A man with pale hair stoked a fire. A sharp mountain peak was framed in a window, and she smelled blood.

Then she paced the paths of a small, walled garden. She was lost? The garden smelled of fir trees, and she disliked their cold shadows. A different man with sad eyes held a hawk on his fist. There was a grand hall, and people danced, but she felt trapped.

Excitement flooded her as a younger Master Avani took her hand and she stood before a crowd on the front grounds. Red was there, too, but the moment was quickly gone. A cup was given to her. Her stomach clenched with a pain greater than she thought possible. A small hawk beat its wings against the bars of a cage. Sorrow—or was it fury?—weighed on her as she rolled a tiny piece of parchment to attach to the hawk's anklet.

Then a southerner put his hand on her cheek and spoke softly. Hot wind blew, and the sun burned the top of her head. She screamed in anguish. No, some distance away a woman screamed. Lingli's vision split. She was both the suffering maharani and she *saw* her in a desert scape, bent double and wearing a white mourning sari. Another woman embraced her, and her long fingers seemed familiar, but Lingli could not see her face.

The smell of horses. Sid's kufi was in her hands, and she felt the embroidery under her fingertips. A tree was stitched in the lining, and the sight of it alarmed her.

Akela's whining broke the spell she was under.

Lingli's heart pounded as hard as if she had been running. Greta loosened her grip, and she pulled free to sit up and put a hand to her bloody temple. On the floor before her, Valena Sandhyatara's lips were gray. Her eyes remained closed.

"Dear Child has gone to stone," Greta said, her eyes fixed on her charge.

"She saw you," the oracle said, "and you saw her. The visions that came to you are shared memories."

Lingli felt empty. Even in death the rani had defeated her. Each image, smell, sound, and emotion she had experienced had been forcibly delivered. She feared they would lodge within her like a bone sickness.

Her face awash with tears, Madam tore off pieces of her underskirt to wrap the oracle's hand, then she made a bandage for Lingli's temple and a new one for her short finger. They sat in silence until the oracle stood, bowed deeply to the rani, and walked away into the dark recesses of the hall.

Lingli dully watched Madam fetch more diyas so the rani was soon enveloped in a bright ring of light broken only where Akela lay with his muzzle on her shoulder.

Pulling a few hairs from the rani's head, Greta put them atop kindling in a thali.

"Burn this," Greta told her. "Smoke will call her ancestors."

Lingli stared at Greta and Madam, confounded by their instructions and actions when everything was pointless.

"You are her descendant," Madam said. "*You* must do this."

Placing the thali on the floor above the maharani's head, Lingli lit it while Madam gathered the children.

"Call them," Madam told her, but Lingli had no idea of the names of the House of Duran's ancestors.

Greta carefully pronounced "Say-lee-ka."

When Lingli remained silent, Madam prompted the children to repeat, "Sayleeka."

"Ta-neez."

The children repeated, "Taneez."

Recitation of the masters of forty-two generations went on long after the hair had burned.

Let them take her if they will or banish her to roam the otherworld. She was nothing to me.

Basheer's and Shikra's names still echoed in the hall when they heard stone scraping stone. Madam drew the children close to her, and Greta rose to face the newcomers marked by bobbing lanterns shining in the dark.

Two exhausted-looking day guards from the House of Hansa appeared, and Master Avani came behind them.

Upon seeing the rani's body, grief laced their faces. They pressed their hands together in respect, knelt, and bowed their heads to the floor.

Madam took Master Avani's hand and said in a broken voice, "Prince Siddharth has also perished."

The old noble looked to Lingli in shock. She dropped her gaze to the floor, stabbed anew by Madam's declaration. After some brief whispers to Madam, Master Avani announced, "We must go now."

"Hmmm," Greta said, her head swiveling from the rani's body to Master Avani. "Rites must be completed."

"Breaking tradition for any reason is inauspicious, especially on such a day of loss," Master Avani answered slowly, "but I will not bear witness to our end. Not if I can move these children to safety." Putting his fist over his heart, he said, "By my authority as a noble son of the Seven and Master of the House of Avani, I grant you, Greta Gray Giant, the sacred duty of safeguarding our maharani's body until the Seven can usher her spirit into the starlit halls of her ancestors."

Greta bowed her head, and Master Avani turned to the children.

"The way out will be difficult, young ones," he said sternly. "You must do as you are told, be silent and be swift—for the strength of the realm. Do you agree?" The older children nodded solemnly. The younger ones just stared.

The guards began to lead the children and Madam to the back of the hall, but Lingli did not move. She did not intend to disobey, nor did she want to remain near the rani's corpse, but her limbs were heavy with grief and resentment, and their plans seemed to have nothing to do with her.

"Lingli," Master Avani said, placing his hand on her shoulder. "We must go."

She glanced up at him then resumed staring into the light of one of the diyas.

"No one bears a greater share of today's grief than you, but ask yourself, would Siddharth want you to stay here until they come for you? Or wish you to remain a wraith haunting the Rock forevermore?

"We will make him a fitting tribute, I promise you," Master Avani continued. "You and I and his friends will mourn because we held him dear, and many more will mourn because he was his mother's chosen heir, but he was not and is not our only path to the future. Dear girl, whether you want this responsibility or not, you are now the heir to the House of Duran and the next rani of Saatkulom."

How little the realm mattered to her must have been written on her face, for the old noble closed his eyes for a moment before adding, "I beseech you to come with us, but I will respect your decision. If you refuse, I will stay as well. When they come, I will defend you with my life because you are a daughter of Duran. This is my duty."

He began to bend so he could sit by her side, but Lingli stopped him and got to her feet, tucking Sid's short blade back into her waistband. Saatkulom could burn, but she would not be the cause of the old noble's death.

Speaking in the language of giants, which sounded more like rocks sliding down a hillside than words, Greta leaned down and addressed Akela. The wolf whined and nuzzled the rani's face, then reluctantly came to Lingli's side.

Making one last bow to Valena Sandhyatara, Master Avani led Lingli toward the defenders' lanterns shining in the recesses of the great hall. When she looked back, Greta stood with her head bowed, holding the rani in her arms like a sleeping child.

CHAPTER 51

They traveled a narrow passage that stretched from a hidden entrance in the floor of the great hall to the edge of the pit. There they joined a path leading them to a contingent of defenders, miners, and a few zhoukoo waiting at what remained of a passage entrance. Broken rock and rubble piled on both sides, but a broad opening remained.

After sending defenders into the passage to clear the way and secure support beams, Master Avani explained that the northern tower was surrounded, and they had a new plan for the descendants' escape. While the old noble conferred with the others about the way ahead, Lingli sat down on the path next to Akela some distance behind the rest.

Sid's gone. she put a hand over her aching heart, telling herself that she had delivered his message even if she had failed to carry out her darker intentions.

Watching Madam Sayed give each child a sip of water and a bit of naan, Lingli was reminded that it had been almost a day since she had eaten or drunk anything, but she wanted nothing. Nothing mattered.

At Master Avani's command, everyone filed into the passage. Keeping Akela company, Lingli remained at the back and followed a pair of nervous defenders who kept looking over their shoulders to be sure they kept up. Wrapped in her grief like a second cloak, she kept her mind empty and focused on the path under her feet.

They walked downward a long time, and the children nodded on their feet before Master Avani called a halt when they reached two wagons.

The first carried food stuff and supplies as well as the rani's driver, Korvar, Shankar, the baker, her daughter and infant granddaughter, and Ritin—the Avani boy who had killed Vidkun. He nodded to her quickly and looked away.

A worn-looking Rahman Mirajkar sat on the second wagon's bench. One of his eyes was swollen shut.

"Well, Snow has found us again," he said when she drew near. "If I'm destined to carry you off this rock just as I carried you to it, I hope you've still got coin."

Unsure whether Rahman had been forced to do the southerners' bidding earlier or was being forced to do theirs now, Lingli said nothing.

"Never mind," he said. "I'll collect on a more auspicious day."

At the back of his father's wagon, Samir gave a leaf of hay to the black colt tied at the back. The sight of the govadhi gladdened her a little, but Samir waved her away when the colt nearly pulled loose from his lead.

"He's caught the wolf's scent," Samir said.

Lingli backed away as he applied more dauber's wax to the colt's nose.

Master Avani ordered them to wait there while he led most of the defenders farther down the passage. The handful of exhausted guards who remained with them lay down around the wagons.

Ignoring Madam Sayed's request that she get in Rahman's wagon with the other children, Lingli sat next to the wolf and rested her head on her knees. Time dragged by slowly, until a night guard returned, roused the other defenders, and began giving instructions to the drivers. Lingli overheard him talking to Rahman.

"We are close to the eastern gate," the guard said. "Very soon Master Tilan's men will create a diversion on the field outside. We must be ready to push through at that time."

Madam Sayed leaned on the back of the bench. "How will we avoid the southerners?" she asked.

The soldier rubbed his nose. "It will be a fight."

"What about the field?" Madam said. "There could be thousands of the brutes out there."

"That we must leave to Master Tilan and his company from Nilampur."

"Oh, truly? How do you know they're still there?" Madam said. "No. This is not a plan! How can you imagine I would take these young ones into such a trap?"

Rahman said, "Death finds us when the ancestors call. If we take the children back, they will be the first they kill. If we take them forward, they might see us succeed and survive."

The dance teacher glared at him.

"If we don't reach the field," the guard said softly, "Master Avani and Master Tilan's efforts will have gone to waste."

Madam Sayed hissed, "Fools! All of us!" and fell back into her place in the wagon.

Soon they were on their way down the passage's last stretch. When Akela growled so low that Lingli felt it more than heard it, she tried making a calming gesture that she had observed Master Vaksana use. To her surprise, the wolf went quiet.

They stopped once more so the defenders could ready themselves. Lingli wished she had a blade. She watched Samir wipe all the horses' noses again and put blinders on the teams. After checking the colt's tether one more time, he turned to her and said calmly, "The wolf can defend us better if you ride in the wagon with the others."

She climbed into Rahman's wagon and didn't resist when Madam took her by the elbow and put her close behind the bench.

Half a dozen defenders surrounded Rahman's wagon. Five of them wore chinkara pins on their sashes, marking them as youth from the House of Satya. The sixth was a sharp-nosed member of the House of Tilan who drew back when he saw her in the lantern light, and she realized her hood had fallen back. She touched the bandage on her temple, and stared back until the guard dropped his gaze.

How can anyone still be alarmed by me on this terrible day?

"It is time," a Satya guard said. "We will protect you as best we can, but we must pass through quickly. Stay in the wagon."

Lingli sat next to the youngest of the Duvanya children, a boy of eight or nine cycles who wore one of the vests she had decorated. His blank expression was a mirror of her own, and his knuckles whitened with the strain of trying not to bump against her as they rolled out. She remembered that the boy's father had not returned from the north and his elder brother, Captain Duvanya, was probably in the thick of the fighting in the fort.

Battle cries ahead grew louder. Rahman urged his team into a trot, pulling the colt behind, and Samir rode alongside. Unrolling an oiled canvas, Madam spread it over all of them in the back, but Lingli and the

Duvanya boy poked their heads above the cover at the back of the bench and bore witness as they entered a room larger than the feasting hall.

A tremendous din filled the eastern hall. Blades swept and flashed. Blows rang against shields. All the southern houses were there—Hudulfah, Kirdun, Afreh, Idris—but she saw no Saatkulom traitors fighting with them. Flames from the braziers cast shadows that, combined with the smoke, obscured the true number of those who challenged them, but it was clear there were too many.

The defenders held open a path halfway to the huge gate on the opposite side of the room. Those surrounding Rahman's wagon kept the fighting back as best they could, but both wagons slowed, and the teams stamped and shifted from side to side to avoid clashes. When one of the Satya defenders near the wagon fell with a spear in his back, Lingli saw the colt kick out wildly, and she feared he would tear loose. A pair of zhoukoo pulled the panicked team forward as Rahman lashed them and they jumped forward again, the wagon tilting to one side or the other as the wheels climbed over the fallen and came back down with sickening thuds.

Looking ahead, Lingli saw that a score of defenders and zhoukoo had reached the gate's winch, but the southerners were all about them, and fighting there grew desperate. Before she could give them a fleeting thought, a pair of Idrisis landed in the back of the first wagon like birds of prey. Biting down on the inside of her cheek, Lingli watched Ritin try to defend the baker's daughter and her babe. He could barely keep his balance in the rocking wagon, and the fighters bore down upon him. Luckily, defenders on the floor cut them down, and she breathed again.

Despite the other driver's efforts, southerners were forcing his team to one side. She saw that they were trying to use his wagon to block their way as well. Defenders shielding those at the gate could not help the driver, and there were too few on the floor near the first wagon. Samir, too, must have seen what was happening, for suddenly he kicked his horse forward to help. Akela followed, and the southerners slowed when they saw the wolf break a Hudulfah fighter's neck in one bite and gut another in the second. It seemed Samir and the rani's driver might be able to put the first team back on course, but Lingli lost sight of it when Madam pulled her and the Duvanya boy down by their legs, and they slid under the canvas.

The children's terrified faces were fixed on the one Madam hovered over—the chubby Hansa girl who had been so tormented by the other dancers. A spear had pierced their cover and planted itself deep in the girl's shoulder. The dance teacher had pushed the canvas up the spear's length, making a tent over the girl and herself, but there was little that could be done about the stain that spread over the embroidered dress Lingli had stitched for her. Madam's eyes implored Lingli for help as she tried to soothe the girl with gentle words, but what help would another hand pressed to the wound be and what else could she do? Help, if help could be found, was somewhere else.

Lingli crawled out from under the canvas as the wagon stopped again. Rahman jumped from the bench and plunged toward his son, who was about to be pulled from his horse. Defenders around them blocked and hacked at their enemies, but it seemed they would be overwhelmed if they didn't escape the room soon.

A sliver of daylight shone through the cracked-open gate ahead.

Suddenly everyone fought harder or fell faster, but Rahman's wagon remained stalled in the middle of it all. The colt kicked at the back like a mad thing. On either side, their defenders battled, and still the distance between the wagons grew.

The Duvanya boy pulled on her cloak and pointed to southerners climbing onto a broad ledge on the opposite wall. Fighters from the House of Afreh readied their spears and aimed for the horses. Lingli heard Red say, *Never let others make you useless.*

Climbing quickly onto the bench, she flicked the reins. The horses threw their heads and took hesitant side steps until Akela whirled by like a fountain of death and brought down a fighter harrying a palace guard. With this motivation, the team jerked the wagon to one side and avoided the first volley of spears. Focused on the opening, Lingli grabbed Rahman's whip and lashed the team without mercy.

The rani's driver had his team pulling again, and Rahman and Samir were fighting their way back toward their wagon, which barely shuddered forward while the colt balked at the rear.

Dodging fighters, Rahman leapt onto the bench and took the reins. Samir whipped his horse past them, and Lingli looked over her shoulder in time to see him cut the legs out from under a southerner who had dared climb into the back.

When Rahman pushed her over the back of the bench, she tumbled over the Duvanya boy and looked up to see Madam slap a fighter leaning over the side of the wagon. The man laughed as he raised his blade. Lingli didn't think as she grabbed the hilt of Sid's blade, but a defender on the floor struck the fighter down. Rahman's team began to move faster, and she hurled herself to the end of the wagon.

We're not keeping you safe, she thought as she reached the colt, *we're holding you back.*

A spear grazed the colt's neck and he pulled back hard, making the knot in the lead rope impossible to untie, but Lingli cut through it with Sid's blade and wound the end of the rope around her fist. In the breath that passed between them, the colt twisted to one side and Lingli slipped a leg over his back. Her only thought was to reach the light streaming through the partially open gate. Burying her face in his mane, she hugged the colt's sides as he leapt forward.

Defenders at the gate were back-to-back in desperate battles, and she glimpsed Master Avani among them as the colt galloped into the gap.

A number of southerners seeking escape ran alongside the colt, but Crowseye's defenders waited outside. Blood flew and fighters cried out as they were cut down around her. Lingli cringed, expecting a blade to land at any moment, but the colt galloped on.

Squinting ahead, she saw three riders bunched in the path.

The colt didn't slow. He ran harder. All she could do was hold on. A few paces away from Crowseye's men, Lingli felt the colt's muscles tense for a mighty jump, and her heart lightened as they left the ground. For a glorious moment they were as weightless as birds.

Then they fell back to the hard ground.

When she turned to look, the eastern gate had already grown small. The daylight was blinding, and their flight made her eyes stream. The colt raced along a trail that ran between the Rock and a fen full of tall grasses and rough brush, then they plunged into a small wood where the path was overgrown.

A home in some deep woods. A quiet place. Those I meet will never know I am a murderer, a thief, a wraith, a sister, a rani's heir, perhaps a raja's heir—and whatever else they call me. None of that matters.

Lingli hoped the way might open so she and the colt could flee into the plains, but hoofbeats were coming up fast behind them. One of the colt's curly ears twisted around. She pressed his sides and stayed low, urging him on, but his pace slowed. Among the trees to one side another horse and rider passed them. A tall bay crossed their trail and blocked the way ahead.

Ignoring her attempts to kick him onward, the colt slowed to a trot, then a walk as they approached the other horse and rider.

It was Samir—battered and blood-spattered. He reached into a bag slung across his shoulder and held out a handful of grain. Her traitorous mount stretched his head forward to nibble at it.

"Will you go on alone?" he asked. "In winter?"

She looked away from his sharp eyes and pulled up her hood, quite aware of how foolish she appeared.

He said nothing else. After a moment, he attached another lead to the colt's halter and led them back the way they had come.

CHAPTER 52

Near a small spring at the base of the Rock, Lingli and Samir met a fence of drawn blades carried by battle-sore defenders. Samir raised his hands, and she did the same as Madam hurried to them, professing her gratitude for the ancestors' protection. When the senior soldier told his defenders to stand down, they did so grudgingly, still on alert for signs of ambush.

Lingli got down from the colt and allowed Madam to lead her to where the children rested. Passing Rahman's wagon, she saw that the dead Hansa girl remained covered in the back. Hansa soldiers, Ritin, and the rani's driver built a pyre nearby.

She accepted the cup of water Madam offered and sat in a shaded patch of grass. Pulling her hood forward, she drew her hands up into her sleeves and hugged her knees to her chest, thinking of nothing.

A long, low whistle sounded. Everyone's heads snapped back toward the trail. "Of the Seven!" someone sang out just before a small group of defenders and half a dozen zhoukoo appeared. Four of them carried Master Avani on a rough-made litter.

"Oh, Jalil!" Madam put a hand to her mouth.

"It is not serious," he said, grimacing as the zhoukoo set the litter down near Lingli and the children. "But walking has become more difficult than usual." One of his legs was wrapped tightly above the knee.

Korvar joined them and said, "Masterji, your wound must be cleaned properly!"

"Ha, and the wounds of every one of these loyal ones, too." Master Avani waved his hand at the ragged bunch who had accompanied him. He turned around to look at the children. "The battle is far from over, but our first business is to secure this victory."

"We lost one in the melee," Madam said sadly. She dabbed at her eyes before adding, "Another gave us a fright." She looking pointedly at Lingli. "But she is whole."

While Madam Sayed removed the bandages from Master Avani's leg and cleaned the wound, the old noble beckoned the rani's driver and Rahman to him. "You must leave as soon as the horses are ready and ride hard. I and every defender here will return to the fight, which, if we don't prevail by tomorrow, may last through the wolf moon or more.

"At the end of the Rock this trail will fade, but you will strike out north by northeast. Continue in the same direction tomorrow and you should catch up to Envoy Kanaka's party. I advise you to stay near the Rajpath, but keep good scouts ahead. If our messages have reached Dyuvasa, you should encounter Tajazan's party on the road by the tenth day."

"We are bound for Korangal," Rahman said dryly.

Master Avani nodded and opened a pack that lay on the litter next to him. He removed a small pouch and drew out ten gold coins from within.

"Your heading is the same. All I ask is that you carry on with the easterners to the crossing at Osiara. Their soldiers can accompany the children from there. I hope this will suffice for that inconvenience." He gave five coins to the rani's driver and put five coins in Rahman's palm and then enclosed the wanderer's hand in both of his. "Intentional or not, the White Horse Clan has served the Seven valiantly today. We will not forget."

"Does the eastern raja know the full value of *all* these children?" Rahman asked.

Master Avani paused before answering. "Our last message was that the Seven's children are precious and require his protection. Do not speak of this. The envoy will communicate the particulars when necessary."

The drivers departed, and Madam continued to tend Master Avani. Lingli watched Korvar pour oil on the pyre.

Her voice shaking, Madam told Master Avani. "I found your letter, but I could not retrieve the book after they entered the palace."

"Do not worry, Amina. I have the transcriptions we completed. They will suffice."

He tugged a sheaf of bound parchments from his pack and asked Madam to help him stand. "I think this may have saved my life today"—he showed Lingli where the goatskin binding the pages had been scarred by a blade—"but it is yours."

She did not reach out to take it.

The old noble sighed, and Madam took the transcription from him and put it back in the pack.

"The Seven have served you poorly," Master Avani said. "And I among them. I should have told you as soon as I realized who you were, but I convinced myself that it was better to wait until the ancestors looked upon you more charitably. With Siddharth's help, I believed we could find a way to soften the maharani's heart. There's no time to explain everything, and I know it seems your own ancestors have been merciless, but you are not forsaken. I will ask my ancestors for your protection."

Lingli stared at the funeral pyre, unmoved.

One of the defenders from the House of Hansa approached them and nodded toward the pyre. "It is ready," he said.

The defender gave Madam his cape. She went to Rahman's wagon, climbed into the back, and wrapped it around the Hansa girl. After the stewards brought the body down and placed it on the pyre, all the defenders from the House of Hansa gathered, and the capeless defender recited the farewell tribute and lit the wood.

The horses had begun to fret, and Lingli saw they were uneasy with Akela sitting on his haunches under some small trees a short distance away. She got up and went to the wolf, ignoring a pain that ached in her bandaged temple. The closer she got, the clearer one of the visions that the rani had passed to her became.

She sat on a chair covered with furs. A black pup rested in her lap, and a man stoked a fire. She smelled roasting meat and firewine. She was… happy? The oracle had said these were shared memories. *But where am I?* She tried to shake off the vision, confused.

Akela watched her, his eyes more gold than green in the sunlight.

As empty as she was, she could do one useful thing.

The wolf did not move when she extended her hand. He allowed her to unbuckle and remove his beautiful, bloody harness. For a long moment Akela looked at her, then he got up, trotted off into the fen, and disappeared.

Master Avani and Madam waited at the back of Rahman's wagon. The old noble said, "In Garzekhara, you will be afforded refuge, perhaps you will find family. Envoy Kanaka will advise you. We will fight for our home, and when this is over, it will be your home, too. I will send word as soon as I can."

Madam pressed the dead girl's swan brooch into her hands. "In case there are times when it's better if others don't know you're a daughter of Duran."

Master Avani hobbled back to his litter, and she and Madam stared at the burning pyre. The fire popped. The cloth covering the Hansa girl was a blackened shroud. *And Sid, my brother, lies broken on some dark rock.*

Just as vividly as her previous vision, Lingli suddenly saw herself running ahead of Red and opening the cabin door so he could stagger to his chair. With his last breath, again he told her to go.

Numb to everything, Lingli climbed into the wagon and settled herself behind the bench.

While Samir tied the colt to the back of the wagon, Madam handed Rahman the pack with the transcription inside. Then she leaned over the side next to her and said, "The Rock is my home, and he is…" She looked back to where Master Avani rested. "Forgive me, I cannot come with you."

Lingli nodded, and Madam drew back. Rahman flicked the reins, and the team began to pull.

After a while Lingli could no longer see Master Avani propped on his litter, nor Madam Sayed standing next to him. The smoke that rose from the dead girl's pyre faded into the brown haze that hung over the entire Rock. She turned her face forward and did not look back again.

Characters

Afsana: young woman who brought Sid to Red's cabin

Ali: ameer of the House of Kirdun

Amina Sayed: dance teacher and seamstress

Anil: member of White Horse Clan

Arnaz: friend of Lingli Tabaan

Arzisi: son of Varj Xirs, steward of Zahatara

Aseem: infant prince; son of Valena Sandhyatara and Prince Hassan

Avinash: spare from the House of Satya

Aza Mussan: ameer of the House of Hudulfah, father of Prince Hassan
and Princess Mafala

Azi Kebedi: mother of Prince Hassan and Princess Mafala

Basheer Sandhyatara: former raja of Saatkulom, father of
Valena Sandhyatara

Bren: head of housekeeping

Chatur: member of White Horse Clan

Dakshini: member of White Horse Clan

Darius Palika: leader of the House of Duvanya, master of defenses

Eshan Palika: son of Darius, night captain of Saatkulom's guards

Farid: leader of the White Horse Clan

Filant: senior kitchen steward

Gayatri Prabhugita: leader of the House of Hansa, mistress of textiles,
archery trainer

Greta: a giant and servant of Valena Sandhyatara

Harno: recruit

Hassan: prince of the House of Hudulfah and consort to
Valena Sandhyatara

Ilo: brother of Gayatri Hansa; twin to Lalzam

Jalil Komalratra: leader of the House of Avani

Jantan Gaddar: day captain of Saatkulom's guards

Jeevan: Valena Sandhyatara's driver

Jordak Dharmavyadha: leader of the House of Vaksana, wolfmaster

Kadam: miner

Kamran Mandanavi: chief of the Northeastern District

Kanaka: eastern envoy

Ketan Karmika: leader of the House of Tilan, master engineer,
    known as Crowseye

Khush: ameer of the House of Afreh

Korvar: chef

Krill: mining apprentice

Krux: master of coin

Lalzam: brother of Gayatri Hansa; twin to Ilo

Lingli Tabaan: an orphaned girl under the guardianship of the red giant

Mafala: princess of the House of Hudulfah

Mahir Vodyar: master of canals and cousin of Basheer Sandhyatara

Moraten: member of the White Horse Clan, son of Anil

Nartilya: advisor concerned with business in the districts

Parama Azumirga: leader of the House of Satya, chief judge

Parth Lalpati: scribe and member of the House of Avani

Rahman Mirajkar: member of the White Horse Clan, father of Samir,
    Sachin and Rekha

Red: the red giant, guardian of Sid Sol and Lingli Tabaan

Rekha Mirajkar: member of the White Horse Clan

Ritin Amavasya: member of the House of Avani

Roshan Balinbitta: member of the House of Tilan, senior engineer

Rud: kitchen bearer

Sachin Mirajkar: member of the White Horse Clan

Sadul: former raja, Valena Sandhyatara's grandfather

Samir Mirajkar: member of the White Horse Clan

Shankar: Korvar's son

Shikra Almansar: former rani, mother of Valena Sandhyatara

Sid Sol: an orphaned boy under the guardianship of the red giant

Sonali: member of the White Horse Clan, singer

Spartak: soldier

Tajazan: raja of Dyuvasa

Tal Daman: cousin of Prince Hassan

Temer: ameer of the House of Idris

Tiadona Mirajkar: member of the White Horse Clan, aunt of Samir, Sachin and Rekha

Varj Xirs: lord of Daza Tumuli

Valena Sandhyatara: maharani of Saatkulom, leader of the House of Duran

Vidkun Dharmavyadha: spare of the House of Vaksana

Woods Witch: healer in the Western Woods

Zarin Sanjhila: recruit

Place Names

Afreh: a territory in Avakstan bordering Mephistan

Akroyat: the fallen capital of Vasantrastra

Avakstan: the southern region, ruled by several competing houses

Avkorum: capital of the northern realm of Saikhanger

Bakarn: fort town in Saatkulom

Chandrabhavan: the palace of Saatkulom

Daza Tumuli: a stronghold within Saikhanger, near the border with Saatkulom

Dyuvasa: the mountainous eastern realm in Ascarya Erde

Garzekhara: the capital of Dyuvasa

Havpur: a village in the Western Woods

Hudulfah: a small realm and territory bordering Saatkulom in Avakstan

Idris: a desert territory in Avakstan

Jobat: fort town in Saatkulom

Kalamaidan: the desolate desert of the far south

Kirdun: a small realm and territory bordering Dyuvasa and aligned with other houses in Avakstan

Korongal: the wanderers' winter camp in Dyuvasa

Mephistan: a vast city-state on the coast of the western sea

Mokantu: a deserted stronghold in Saatkulom

Muktastan: a town in the Western Woods

Naachmaidan: the great grasslands of Saatkulom

Nilampur: a town and a lake being built on Saatkulom's border
  with Avakstan
Osiara: a fort town on the border separating Saatkulom and Dyuvasa
Saatkulom: a realm in the center of Ascarya Erde, also known as
  the Seven
Safed Qila: a fort serving as the capital of Saatkulom
Saikhanger: a powerful and ruthless realm in the north of Ascarya Erde
Silver Woods: a forest with unusual trees and strange creatures
Talomeer: a town and reservoir in southern Saatkulom
Vasantrastra: the fallen western realm
Western Woods: a vast forest, formerly part of Vasantrastra
Zahatara: a small fort and village in the Western Woods controlled
  by Saikhanger

Glossary

Achkan: a high-necked, knee length coat, slightly flared below the waist
Ameer: the title of a ruler in Avakstan
Apsara: a female spirit of the air or water
Ascarya Erde: the wonderous world
Ascaryans: the humans of Ascarya Erde
Asura: a demon
Aza: a title proceeding the name of a male ruler in the houses of Hudul-
  fah, Afreh and Kirdun
Azi: a title proceeding the name of a female ruler in the houses of
  Hudulfah, Afreh and Kirdun
Ba: a title proceeding the name of a young male noble in the houses of
  Hudulfah, Afreh and Kirdun
Bansari: a flute
Bi: a title proceeding the name of a young female noble in the houses of
  Hudulfah, Afreh and Kirdun
Bright Cycle: a cycle when Chotabhai is visible
Brinjal: eggplant
Chana: chickpeas

Changra: a mountain goat prized for its meat and its fleece

Chhatri: an elevated dome-shaped pavilion built as a memorial for someone who has died; usually for nobility

Chinkara: a gazelle known for its speed and gentle nature

Chotabhai: the smaller, secondary moon of Ascarya Erde, appearing every seventeen cycles and visible for three before disappearing again

Cycle: a year

Darkice: a type of rock found in Saatkulom

Dauber: a stinging insect whose wax is used to blunt the sense of smell

Dhol: a drum

Diya: a small oil lamp made of clay or metal

Doodhnadi: a dense starscape visible over most of Ascarya Erde

Dupatta: a long scarf or veil, common to women's clothing

Effigy: a sculpture or model of a person; a doll

Envoy: a messenger or representative of another realm

Firestick: a gift of the ancestors that can burn brightly or serve as an explosive

Firewine: an alcoholic drink made of fermented grapes and chiles in Saikhanger and western Saatkulom

Govadhi: the fastest breed of horses in Ascarya Erde

Goyra: a giant lizard from the Kalamaidan

Khan: the title of a ruler from Saikhanger

Khanda: a straight-bladed sword of medium length with a spike in the pommel

Kofta: a spiced meatball

Kufi: a round, brimless hat, close-fitting

Lehenga: a three-piece ensemble consisting of an ankle-length skirt, a will-fitted blouse and a dupatta

Lunge line: a long, single rein used with horses during training

Maharani: the title of a female ruler from Saatkulom, Dyuvasa or Vasantrastra

Maidan: a gathering place or a field

Marg: a road or street

Matachand: the primary moon of Ascarya Erde

Mogra: a type of jasmine

Moonstone: a type of rock combining the qualities of marble and opals

Naan: a type of leavened bread

Otherworld: where the ancestors and demons dwell; an unseen world in another dimension

Pallu: the end of a sari worn over one shoulder or the head

Paratha: a type of flatbread

Pata: a short, straight and slim blade used often by assassins

Priya: adjective meaning dear one

Pudina: mint

Raja: the title of a male ruler from Saatkulom, Dyuvasa or Vasantrastra

Rajpath: the ruler's road in Saatkulom

Rani: the short title for a female ruler from Saatkulom, Dyuvasa or Vasantrastra

Roti: a flat, round unleavened bread

Sabirgazi: a test of endurance for southern youth

Sari: a garment consisting of a long piece of material draped around the body and worn with a fitted blouse

Shishpar: a club or mace

Skordawa: the Dyuvasan name for Chotabhai

Starfall: a period of planetary and climatic upheaval throughout Ascarya Erde

Stargazer: a gift of the ancestors that magnifies objects at a great distance, bestowed on the House of Avani

Sura: a strong distilled alcoholic drink

Surahi: a slim-necked pitcher

Talwar: a sword with a slightly curved blade

Thali: a round, rimmed plate

Umbalvata: a necklace strung with the smallest finger phalanges of a family's ancestors, common to the noble houses of Saatkulom and Dyuvasa

Vetala: an evil spirit that can possess a corpse or even a weakened living person

Zhoukoo: small humanoid beings native to the Rock

Acknowledgments

Many people contributed expertise or offered support that made this story and the book bigger and better than what I originally imagined. To all my beta readers, especially Tasha Livingstone, Jean Levasseur and Kyle Gambrel, thank you for your time and encouragement when the story was nowhere near done (or coherent). I would also like to thank all my ARC readers for their feedback and thoughtful reviews. Thank you, Rachel Oestreich, for looking at the forest first, then the trees. Your editing taught me a lot. Thanks to artist Cristina Bencina for her beautiful cover art and patience. Graphic designer Loren Jabami not only brought the cover typography together but also created the insignias for the houses of Saatkulom. Sarah Waites drew the book's charming map with nothing but terrible sketches from me for input. Amie Norris's proofreading expertise saved my sanity, and Ross Feldner was there to put all the pieces together for print, laying out this whopper from the first page to the last. Also, lucky for me, I ran across a video where Associate Professor of Astrophysics Dr. Ann-Marie Madigan described the orbits of detached objects beyond Neptune, and she connected me to University of Colorado Boulder graduate students Tatsuya Akiba and Jane Bright, who helped me visualize Chotabhai's orbit and understand its potential effects on Ascarya Erde (See Book Two of The Cursed Cycles series for more of the story!). I'd also like to thank Florencio Paraon for taking such a nice photo of me for this book.

My sister Ellen Villeme has my deepest gratitude for reading not one, but two full drafts. Her enthusiasm and suggestions made it all seem possible. And finally, I thank my husband Abi and my daughters Ava and Diya from the bottom of my heart for reading bits, encouraging/tolerating me, making tea, and joining me to explore the parts of India that inspired the story in the first place.

About the Author

L.A. Barnitz has bachelors' degrees in journalism and humanities from the University of Missouri-Columbia and a master's degree in international affairs from American University in Washington, DC. After spending many good years working in communications, raising her children, and exploring the world, she has returned to her lifelong passion of writing fiction and tending living things—splitting her time between Maryland, Missouri and India. She founded Little Hawk Books LLC to help other independent writers bring their stories to readers. *The Stonebound Heir* is her first published novel.

What's Next?

In The Cursed Cycles Book 2, Lingli pays a price for home and hearth, and the subjects of Saatkulom fight for their survival as growing planetary disturbances unravel alliances and open the gates to the otherworld.

Keep up with L.A. Barnitz's books and stories and sign up for her occasional newsletter at https://laurabarnitz.com

Made in the USA
Middletown, DE
04 September 2024

59785865R00316